THE STORY OF HAN XIANGZI

韓湘子全傳

湘子像

Han Xiangzi

THE STORY of HAN XIANGZI

~ *The Alchemical Adventures of a Daoist Immortal*

YANG ERZENG

TRANSLATED AND INTRODUCED BY PHILIP CLART

A CHINA PROGRAM BOOK

UNIVERSITY OF WASHINGTON PRESS   *Seattle & London*

This book was supported in part by the China Studies Program, a division of the Henry M. Jackson School of International Studies at the University of Washington.

University of Washington Press

P.O. Box 50096, Seattle, WA 98145

www.washington.edu/uwpress

Library of Congress Cataloging-in-Publication Data

Yang, Erzeng, 17th cent.

    [Han Xiangzi quan zhuan. English]

    The story of Han Xiangzi : the alchemical adventures of a Daoist immortal / Yang Erzeng ; translated and introduced by Philip Clart.

      p. cm. — (A China program book)

    Includes bibliographical references and index.

    ISBN-13: 978-0-295-98690-6 (cloth : alk. paper)

    ISBN-10: 0-295-98690-5 (cloth : alk. paper)

    ISBN-13: 978-0-295-98725-5 (pbk : alk. paper)

    ISBN-10: 0-295-98725-1 (pbk : alk. paper)

    I. Clart, Philip, 1963– II. Title.

PL2698.Y26H313 2007

895.1'34—dc22   2006033318

The paper used in this publication is acid-free and 90 percent recycled from at least 50 percent post-consumer waste. It meets the minimum requirements of American National Standard for Information Sciences—Permanence of Paper for Printed Library Materials, ANSI Z39.48-1984.

FOR INGE, MY MOTHER,

FOR HER CONSTANT SUPPORT OF MY CHOICES

AND FOR MY WIFE, USCHI,

AND MY DAUGHTERS, ANNA, LAURA, AND SARAH,

FOR THEIR PRECIOUS GIFTS OF RESEARCH TIME

CONTENTS

PREFACE &

ACKNOWLEDGMENTS

The karmic seeds for this book were planted in two graduate seminars I attended at the University of British Columbia in 1992 as a student in the doctoral program in Asian Studies. Looking for a text to write a paper on, I stumbled across *The Story of the Immortal Han* (Han xian zhuan 韓仙傳), a novella from perhaps the Yuan or early Ming dynasty. Intrigued by the subject matter, I decided to pursue it further in another seminar the next semester by translating two chapters (6 & 7) of the late Ming dynasty vernacular novel *The Story of Han Xiangzi* (Han Xiangzi quanzhuan 韓湘子全傳; lit., *The Complete Story of Han Xiangzi*) and analyzing their key theme of the trials and tests a candidate for immortality needs to undergo. The instructors of these two seminars, Gary Arbuckle and Daniel L. Overmyer, gave valuable comments on these papers, which ultimately provided a foundation for the present book.

Over the next years, my mind was focused on other things, primarily my dissertation work on a spirit-writing cult in central Taiwan. However, even then Han Xiangzi did not completely vanish from my mental horizon. It so happened that he was the "immortal teacher" (*xianshi* 仙師) of the cult's spirit-writing medium, and his carved image sat in a glass case on a side altar. My affinity with Han Xiangzi was strengthened when during my field work at the spirit-writing temple I was adopted as a disciple by the immortal Lü Dongbin. As Lü was also the teacher of Han Xiangzi, we were now practically brothers!

However, it was not until 2000 that the seeds planted eight years earlier finally germinated in a summer research project in which I explored the possibility of a broader study of Han Xiangzi and his legends. I produced a draft translation of *The Story of Han Xiangzi*—and was hooked. Since that summer I have pursued the traces of the immortal more or less constantly, though at different levels of intensity, depending on how much time my other obligations left me. The largest chunk of work was completed during a year of research leave between 2001 and 2002, two months of which I spent as a visiting scholar at the Institute of Chinese Literature and Philosophy, Academia Sinica, in Taipei. There I continued working on the translation, even while making good use of the marvelous library collections of the Academia Sinica to gather data on other aspects of the Han Xiangzi story cycle. My advisor at the Institute of Chinese Literature and Philosophy was Lee Fong-mao 李豐楙, whose contributions to this work cannot be overstated. An extremely busy and prolific scholar, Professor Lee still devoted many evening hours at his house near the campus of Cheng-chi University to go over the translation manuscript with me and discuss difficult issues. He was not required to give up so much of his personal time for the benefit of a junior visiting scholar, but he did. His zeal for scholarship and his infectious enthusiasm know no bounds, and extend far beyond his office and office hours. I am forever in his debt.

Many other people in Taiwan helped with advice and friendship, and in many practical ways. I would especially like to mention Daniel Altschuler, Paul R. Katz, Li Shih-wei 李世偉, Meir Shahar, Wang Chien-ch'uan 王見川, and Zhou Zhiren 周志仁. Lu Xianghua 盧祥華 is a good friend who has rendered selfless assistance numerous times since I met him and his delightful family during my very first stay in Taiwan in 1989–90. This time he was again invaluable in facilitating my visits to temples in southern Taiwan, where Han Xiangzi is worshiped to the present day. Cheng Meng-hsun 鄭孟訓 and many other members of the Wumiao Mingzheng Tang 武廟明正堂 in Taichung contributed their friendship and support in many ways, linking this project with my earlier work on Taiwanese spirit-writing cults.

After my return from Taiwan, I shared parts of my work with many colleagues, either individually or as part of workshops and conferences. A particular thank you goes to Robert Hegel and Wilt Idema, whose detailed comments on the manuscript helped to greatly improve the final version. Many other colleagues contributed advice, ideas, sources, and other materials, among them Robert Ford Campany, Steve Eskildsen, Monica Esposito, Vincent Goossaert, Rania Huntington, Dan Lusthaus, Dan Overmyer, Elena Valussi, and Richard Wang. Nobumi Iyanaga came to the rescue when the publisher's software proved incompatible with mine. His expert advice and provision of a conversion script solved the problem very elegantly. More expertise, this time in photo reproduction, came from my uncle, Gerhard Prasser. As a professional photographer, he prepared the text's woodblock illustrations for print. Lorri Hagman of the University of Washington Press believed in this book right from the beginning. Her enthusiasm greatly encouraged me to redouble my efforts and get it done. In this task I was aided by the Press's able editorial staff, especially Marilyn Trueblood and Rachel Scollon. Of course, none of the above-named is responsible for this book's remaining shortcomings, which I hope its readers will point out to me in a spirit of constructive criticism.

Crucial financial and institutional support was provided by the Chiang Ching-kuo Foundation for International Scholarly Exchange, the University of Missouri Research Board, the Research Council of the University of Missouri–Columbia, the Department of Religious Studies (University of Missouri–Columbia), and the Institute of Chinese Literature and Philosophy, Academia Sinica.

All of the above help and assistance, however, would have come to nothing if I did not have the support of my family: my wife Uschi, my daughters Anna, Laura, and Sarah, and my mother Inge. Their gifts of time and encouragement were indispensable. To them I dedicate this book.

PHILIP CLART

TRANSLATOR'S

INTRODUCTION

The present volume offers to the English-speaking world the first translation into any Western language of the early seventeenth-century Chinese novel *Han Xiangzi quanzhuan* (韓湘子全傳, lit., "The complete story of Han Xiangzi"), by Yang Erzeng 楊爾曾, a writer and publisher from the beautiful city of Hangzhou in southeastern China. Before reading of Han Xiangzi's adventures, the reader will benefit from learning something of the story's protagonist and of elements of Chinese popular and religious culture.

HAN XIANGZI

The hero of this story is the Daoist immortal Han Xiangzi 韓湘子. This figure is nowadays best known as one of the "Eight Immortals" (Baxian 八仙): Zhongli Quan 鍾離權, Lü Dongbin 呂洞賓, Zhang Guolao 張果老, Li Tieguai 李鐵拐, He Xiangu 何仙姑, Lan Caihe 藍采和, Cao Guojiu 曹國舅, and Han Xiangzi. These immortals came together as a group by the late Song dynasty (12th–13th cent.), with only occasional variations in their composition.[1]

Probably the earliest appearance of an Eight Immortals group is in a wall painting of a Jin dynasty tomb (Taihe 泰和 period, 1201–09), reflecting a popularity that continued into the Yuan dynasty (1279–1368), with the immortals as motifs on incense burners, clothing, and folk art.[2] Dramatists of the Yuan period also picked up the Eight Immortals theme and produced the first literary codifications of their lore. In Yuan drama, the Eight Immortals appear in "deliverance plays" (*dutuoju* 度脱劇), which usually focus on only a few members of the group, most prominently Zhongli Quan and Lü Dongbin.[3] By the Ming dynasty (1368–1644), the Eight Immortals had come to occupy a firm place in the dramatic repertoire. They appeared both in full-length plays[4] and in short skits performed on auspicious occasions such as birthdays (*Baxian qingshou* 八仙慶壽),[5] works which, especially the latter, remain a fixture in local opera traditions across China. The Ming period also saw the first full narrative development of the Eight Immortals complex in the form of a novel, *Journey to the East* (Dongyou ji 東遊記) by Wu Yuantai 吳元泰.[6] Much of the later Eight Immortals lore is linked with this important text, including the famous story of their crossing of the ocean (*Baxian guohai* 八仙過海). This became a staple motif in folk art and can still be found today painted on Taiwanese temple walls and stitched on bright red cloths (*baxiancai* 八仙彩) that are hung over entrances to bring blessings to buildings and their inhabitants.[7] Thus, since the Ming dynasty the Eight Immortals have found a firm place in Chinese popular culture, their stories transmitted through the theater, folk art, storytelling,[8] novels,[9] and popular literature such as "precious volumes" (*baojuan* 寶卷).[10]

Each of the Eight Immortals also is the center of an independent story cycle outside the Baxian collective, though the extent of these cycles differs greatly for individual immortals. The most developed lore attaches to the figure of Lü Dongbin, who has been the object of many plays, stories, ballads, novels, and even of religious veneration in important Daoist movements.[11] Han Xiangzi has not received as much attention as Lü Dongbin, but probably more than any of the other six immortals.[12]

Han Xiangzi[13] is said to be a nephew or grandnephew of the famous Tang dynasty Confucian scholar Han Yu 韓愈 (768–824). And indeed there are reliable indications that Han Yu did have a relative named Han Xiang, a son of Han Yu's nephew Han Laocheng 韓老成. In 819, Han Xiang and his brother Han Pang 韓滂 followed Han Yu into his exile to Chaozhou 潮州, where he had been banished for criticizing the emperor's worship of a Buddha relic. In 820, the brothers followed their great-uncle to a new post in Yuanzhou 袁州, where Han Pang died at the age of nineteen.

According to the historical records, Han Xiang was born in 793 and passed the *jinshi* examination in 823. His style (a name taken upon reaching adulthood) was Beizhu 北渚 and his highest official appointment was assistant minister in the Court of Judicial Review. His death date is unclear. *The Complete Poems of the Tang Dynasty* (Quan Tang shi 全唐詩) contains a handful of poems addressed to Han Xiang by various authors. The most famous of these is the one that is immediately connected with the appearance of the Han Xiangzi legend. Han Yu composed it in 819 at Blue Pass 藍關 on his way into exile in Chaozhou, Guangdong:

> *"Demoted I Arrive at Blue Pass and Show This Poem to My Brother's Grandson Han Xiang"*
>
> *A sealed epistle submitted at dawn to Ninefold Heaven—*
> *Exiled at dusk to Chaozhou, eight thousand leagues to travel.*
>
> *Wishing to save His Sagacious Brilliance from treacherous evils,*
> *Could I have cared for the years that remain in my withered limbs?*
>
> *Clouds straddle the mountains of Qin—where is my home?*
> *Snows crowd the pass at Blue Pass—my horse will not move.*
>
> *I know what the reason must be that makes you come so far—*
> *The better to gather my bones from shores of miasmic water.*[14]

The poem expresses Han Yu's relief on seeing his nephew arrive amidst the heavy snow at the Blue Pass in the Qin mountain range south of Chang'an. Nothing in the sparse existing biographical data on Han Xiang indicates any deeper meaning, yet this poem was to become central in the evolving Han Xiangzi lore. It was taken to refer to Han Xiangzi's arrival at Han Yu's side to rescue him by means of his supernatural powers, and to deliver him from his worldly delusions and allow him to become an immortal.

In terms of historical sources there is of course a serious problem. The historical Han Xiang seems to have led a fairly conventional life, enjoyed a moderately successful official career, and apparently had no particular Daoist leanings. So what does he have to do with the Daoist immortal who delivers Han Yu at Blue Pass? Well, possibly he was conflated with another relative of Han Yu's who indeed is said to have possessed magical abilities. Among Han Yu's writings we find a poem (dating to the year 799) in which he records the visit of a distant relative who claimed to possess extraordinary skills. The relevant passages are found in verses 15 through 22:

"Presented to a Distant Nephew"

[...]

Who is that knocking on the door?
To my inquiry he replies that he is of my clan.
He claims to possess magical powers,
That he has investigated the marvels of the cosmos and understands
*   the workings of Heaven.*
It is of no use to regret the past,
But I shall be glad to have success in the future.
If indeed yours are not just artful words,
I should become a man who is useful to his times.[15]

Han Yu thus receives a visitor who claims to be of his lineage, obviously of a lower generation than Han Yu, as the latter addresses him in the poem's title as a "distant nephew" (*zuzhi* 族侄, a nephew in the generalized sense of a distant relative of a younger generation). The visitor claims to have magical skills and to be able to predict the future. Han Yu himself was thirty-two at the time of this event.

These two poems, one mentioning the visit of a supernaturally gifted "distant nephew" in 799, the other about Han Yu's encounter with his grandnephew Han Xiang at Blue Pass twenty years later, together are the starting point for the Han Xiangzi legend. Its core features are Han Xiangzi's prediction of Han Yu's predicament at Blue Pass, from which he then comes to rescue him. Chronologically it is impossible for Han Xiang to be the "distant nephew" mentioned in the 799 poem (he would have been about six years of age at the time), but attention to detail is not a great concern of myth-makers. And so, very early on we find tales about an unusually gifted relative of Han Yu. The first instance occurs in a text composed by a near-contemporary of Han Yu and Han Xiang, Duan Chengshi's 段成式 (803–63) *Miscellaneous Morsels from the South Slope of You Mountain* (Youyang zazu 酉陽雜俎).[16] Duan records that a distant nephew of Han Yu has been taken into his household to be educated. The nephew, however, turns out to be unruly and unwilling to study. When Han Yu confronts him, the nephew claims to have another skill, namely that of growing multicolored peonies. He prepares such a plant for Han Yu, and when after several weeks it blossoms, on its petals are inscribed the fifth and sixth verses of Han Yu's poem of 819. The nephew then declares his unwillingness to enter officialdom, and leaves. The nephew is not named, but the verses appearing on the flower petals become a part of later Han Xiangzi lore.

Through the Five Dynasties and early Song period we find more stories (in the anecdotal literature and also in Daoist hagiography) about the mysterious relative of Han Yu, whose magical powers grow over time. The earliest explicit linking of the themes in the two poems appears in the famous Daoist Du Guangting's 杜光庭 (850–933) *Supplemental Collection of Immortals' Biographies* (Xianzhuan shiyi 仙傳拾遺),[17] where the nephew prepares the peonies and departs. Han Yu is banished and encounters the same nephew at Blue Pass. The next spring the peonies open and are found to be inscribed with the two verses. Here, for the first time, it is also claimed that the nephew later transmitted the Dao to Han Yu.

This version contains an implicit identification of the nephew with Han Xiang. (Problematically, the nephew here is called a *waisheng* 外甥, i.e., a nephew through a female member of Han Yu's lineage, which does not fit Han Xiang's profile. But again, historical exactitude is not the first concern here.) The first time this identification is made explicit is in Liu Fu's 劉斧 (ca. 1040–later than 1113) collection of anecdotes, *Remarkable Opinions under the Green-Latticed Window* (Qingsuo gaoyi 青瑣高議).[18] From here on the core of Han Xiangzi lore is established: Han Xiangzi as an unconventional and Daoist-leaning nephew who by means of a magical flower trick predicts Han Yu's banishment, saves him in his predicament at Blue Pass, and later transmits the Dao to him. Later sources elaborate on this core and add elements such as Han Xiangzi's earlier existence as a numinous white crane, his apprenticeship with Zhongli Quan and Lü Dongbin, his unconsummated marriage, and his later deliverance of his wife and his aunt.

Most of these themes probably came together for the first time in the popular performance genre of the "Daoist songs" (*daoqing* 道情), which emerged during the Song period.[19] Thematically, these songs either express Daoist sentiments and ideas concerning self and society, or narrate the lives and deeds of Daoist immortals. *Daoqing* are sung by one or more performers, accompanied by two instruments: the fisher drum (*yugu* 漁鼓) and the clappers (*jianban* 簡板). The frontispiece of this book shows Han Xiangzi holding these two instruments. A typical fisher drum is cylindrical and is made of bamboo or wood with a leather membrane covering one end. It is usually at least one meter in length and thirteen to fourteen centimeters in diameter. The clappers are two slats of bamboo or wood, sixty to seventy centimeters long and about four centimeters wide. While the right hand strikes the drum, the left hand shakes the elastic clappers so that they strike against each other, providing rhythm and emphasis to the song.

For their tunes, early *daoqing* mostly drew on the popular songs that also influenced the *ci* 詞, poetry of the literary circles of the Song and the operatic arias (*qupai* 曲牌) of the Yuan. In fact, some of these tunes may have started out as *daoqing* (e.g., the "Shuahai'er" 耍孩兒 and the "Zaoluopao" 皂羅袍 tunes). The songs were often performed publicly by itinerant Daoists as a way of spreading their religion and collecting alms. Some of the early patriarchs of the new Complete Perfection (Quanzhen 全真) School of Daoism composed *daoqing* that are still preserved in their collected writings. There also existed local groups of Daoist laypeople who performed *daoqing* at temple festivals for the creation of merit and the entertainment of the gods. Over time, professional performers adopted the genre and developed its thematic range beyond its Daoist focus, including less obviously religious story lines. However, even to this day, Daoist themes still figure prominently in all regional *daoqing* traditions, and stories about the exploits of Han Xiangzi are among the most widespread. In fact, it has been suggested that the Han Xiangzi stories were one of the earliest thematic complexes of *daoqing*. If, as Wu Yimin hypothesizes, the regional origin of the genre as a whole truly is in the Zhongnan Mountains south of Xi'an, Shaanxi, a focus on Han Xiangzi would make a lot of sense, since much of his story takes place in this area.

The *daoqing* genre, especially in its narrative variety, influenced the development of Chinese theater. As already mentioned, some operatic tunes may have been adopted from *daoqing*, while *daoqing* over time gradually adopted more theatrical features. Around the middle of the Qing period (18th cent.), we witness the emergence of local opera traditions that are closely based on *daoqing* tunes and conventions ("*daoqing* drama," *daoqingxi* 道情戲). Here *daoqing* music and song are combined with an acting out of the narrated story. The Han Xiangzi motif figures prominently in the earliest such plays. While this development for the most part occurs fairly late in Chinese history, there survives one local tradition of *daoqing* drama that may arguably go back as early as the thirteenth century: the "Blue Pass drama" (Languanxi 藍關戲) of Ye County 掖縣, Shandong, an area with strong historical links to Complete Perfection Daoism. The Han Xiangzi story cycle is a centerpiece of the repertoire in this local tradition.[20]

Daoqing remained a popular genre throughout the Late Imperial period. For the Ming period we have at least two interesting pieces of evidence for *daoqing* performances of Han Xiangzi stories. The literatus Li Xu 李詡 (1505–93) mentions that Daoist priests sing *daoqing* such as "The Blue Pass" (Languan ji 藍關記) and "The Journey to the West" (Xiyou ji 西遊記).[21] The other source is a scene in the novel *The Plum in the Golden Vase* (Jinpingmei 金瓶梅) where young actors perform a *daoqing* called "Lord Han is Blocked by Snow at Blue Pass" (Han Zi gong xueyong Languan 韓子公雪擁藍關).[22] As *The Plum in the Golden Vase* was completed around the turn of the seventeenth century, this demonstrates that *daoqing* on Han Xiangzi's exploits were popular in the lifetime of Yang Erzeng, the author of *The Story of Han Xiangzi*. In fact, the preface to *The Story of Han Xiangzi* explicitly mentions that Han Xiangzi's story is only transmitted by the blind storytellers, who either sing in a loud voice while holding documents like officials, or recite ballads in a wild manner dressed up as Daoist priests, sighing three times for every line they chant. These stories everywhere delight the hearts of ignorant people and village matrons, and are listened to by school teachers and their pupils.

The preface's author bemoans the vulgarity of these renditions, and praises the novel's author for his more elegant treatment of the theme. It is implied that popular ballads such as *daoqing* were one important source for the novel, and their influence is still clearly visible in the numerous *daoqing*-style songs incorporated into the text.

However, *daoqing* were not the only source Yang Erzeng could draw on. We have two surviving Han Xiangzi texts that antedate Yang's novel. The first is a novella called *The Immortal Han* (Han xian zhuan 韓仙傳), which may date from somewhere between the late Yuan and middle Ming periods.[23] The second is a southern-style drama from the Ming period, *Ascension to Immortality: How Han Xiangzi Attempted Nine Times to Deliver Wengong* (Han Xiangzi jiudu Wengong shengxian ji 韓湘子九度文公昇仙記).[24]

While the novella has a more generalized influence on the novel, there exist very concrete overlaps with the drama *Ascension to Immortality*. Dialogues in the novel occasionally resemble those in the drama, and at least three songs in the novel are identical with or (in one case) very close to arias in *Ascension to Immortality*.[25] The novel also incorporates structural features of the southern-style (*chuanqi* 傳奇) dramatic tradition, such as the typical reunion of all actors in the last scene/chapter. A study of the songs appearing in *The Story of Han Xiangzi* has led one scholar to surmise that the novel is based on one southern-style and three northern-style (*zaju* 雜劇) dramas, a hypothesis that is further supported by the novel's frequent use of theatrical idioms.[26]

Drawing thus on both existing literary elaborations of the Han Xiangzi story and on popular traditions, *The Story of Han Xiangzi* weaves these strands together into the hitherto most complex and developed version of Han Xiangzi lore. Its earliest surviving edition dates to 1623.[27] The storyline begins in the Han dynasty, where Han Xiangzi's previous incarnation is a beautiful but haughty woman, who is consequently reborn as a white crane. The crane cultivates himself and meets Zhongli Quan and Lü Dongbin. They deliver him to be reborn as the son of Han Yu's elder brother Han Hui 韓會. After Han Hui's and his wife's death, Han Xiangzi is raised in Han Yu's household, where he is treated like a son (as he is the only male offspring of the Han family). Han Yu has great expectations of Han Xiangzi, but the latter follows his destiny and runs away from home to join his masters Zhongli Quan and Lü Dongbin in the Zhongnan Mountains. There he practices inner alchemy and becomes an immortal. The Jade Emperor sends him back to earth to deliver his uncle Han Yu, his aunt, and his wife, Lin Luying 林蘆英. After many failed attempts to break down Han Yu's Confucian obstinacy, he delivers him at Blue Pass, and later does the same for his aunt and wife.

The story has a strong anti-Confucian element, and was clearly written by an author knowledgeable in matters of inner alchemy. The prose narrative alternates with an unusually large number of poetic passages, many of which give rather profound summaries of alchemical wisdom. It is a didactic novel that teaches the superiority of Daoism over Confucianism and provides quite practical lessons in Daoist cultivation.

This novel is the great summa of Han Xiangzi lore, and as such had an enormous influence on the Han Xiangzi literature of the following Qing period (1644–1911). Here we find the Han Xiangzi theme being taken up in various forms of popular literature: precious scrolls (baojuan),[28] ballads (tanci, dagushu),[29] local theater.[30] The focus remains on the theme of deliverance, though in the popular texts attention often shifts from the deliverance of Han Yu to that of Xiangzi's wife Luying, or Lin Ying 林英 as she is usually called in the popular genres. Given the large female component in the audience for this literature, such a shift is understandable. There exists a significant enough number of such popular works to show that Han Xiangzi remained a well-known figure through the Qing period. Among the Eight Immortals, he is perhaps second only to Lü Dongbin in the number of surviving texts devoted to him as an individual.

To the present day, the story of Han Yu and Han Xiangzi is well known in many areas of China, in particular in those regions that served as backdrops to events in the legend. French scholar Adeline Herrou encountered many of its plot elements in the local lore of southern Shaanxi province, an area close to the Zhongnan Mountains where Han Xiangzi and Han Yu pursued their spiritual journeys. At the center of her study is the Wengong Temple in the city of Hanzhong, whose principal deity is Han Yu. Local knowledge of Han Yu emphasizes his relationship with Han Xiangzi. Both laypeople and resident Quanzhen Daoist monks recount life stories of their deity that owe more to the Han Xiangzi story cycle than to official history.[31] The nearby Zhongnan Mountains are dotted with temples, caves, and landmarks that are linked in some way or another with Han Xiangzi and his uncle. Another major center of worship for Han Yu, with a secondary cult of Han Xiangzi, is to be found in Chaozhou, Han Yu's place of banishment in the southern Chinese province of Guangdong. Emigrants from Chaozhou have carried this cult to the island of Taiwan, where both figures are worshipped to the present day in a handful of temples in the south.[32]

The pivotal work in the whole Han Xiangzi tradition clearly is the *Han Xiangzi quanzhuan*. In addition to its importance in the development of Han Xiangzi's lore, this novel deserves closer attention, first because it is a well-crafted and entertaining work of literature whose literary qualities have been considerably underrated so far, and second because it is a fascinating attempt to package Daoist inner alchemy in a belletristic format. Thus the present translation should be of interest to students of Chinese folklore, literature, and religion, as well as to those who simply seek a good read.

THE AUTHOR AND HIS TIMES

The earliest editions of *The Story of Han Xiangzi* are ascribed to a certain Man of Mt. Pheasant-Yoke (Zhiheng Shanren 雉衡山人), one of Yang Erzeng's *noms de plume*. Yang's biography is not recorded in the standard collections, and his life dates are unknown. However, pulling together bits and pieces of evidence, we can at least provide a sketch of our author and his social context.

Yang's style was Shenglu 聖魯; he lived in the city of Qiantang 錢塘 (modern-day Hangzhou 杭州) around the turn of the seventeenth century.[33] Yang was a scholar and printer who ran two publishing houses in Qiantang. One was called the Hall of Purity in Poverty (Yibai Tang 夷白堂), the other the Thatched Abode of Mysteries (Caoxuan Ju 草玄居).[34] The former is the source of another sobriquet of his: Master of Purity in Poverty (Yibai Zhuren 夷白主人). He was an educated man who could write an elegant hand and counted well-known literati among his acquaintances. While he was modest about his erudition ("I have only very few classical works at home and my knowledge is very lowly"[35]), the well-known historian Chen Bangzhan 陳邦瞻 (d. 1623) praised him as a "learned and accomplished man of many parts, leisurely and reclusive in manner."[36] A certain Fang Menglai 方夢來 concurs that his "friend Yang" was "learned and accomplished" and adds that he "took delight in seeking out unusual things."[37] While Fang may have spoken here with specific reference to Yang's project of collecting maps and landscape prints from all over China, the diverse nature of Yang's publications does show both catholicity of taste and a pronounced interest in the "unusual."

The two characterizations of Yang just cited are found in prefaces to Yang's *Extraordinary Sights in China* (Hainei qiguan 海內奇觀), a collection of pictorial materials on famous Chinese mountains and temples, with accompanying texts. In effect, this is what we would today call an "armchair traveler's book," written explicitly for the person who wants to see the sights of China without having to leave the comforts of home. The Chinese term for "armchair travel" is *woyou* 臥遊 (traveling while reclining), and Yang's love of this activity explains his sobriquet Daoist Who Travels while Reclining (Woyou Daoren 臥遊道人). *Extraordinary Sights in China*, in ten volumes (*juan*) and with more than 130 illustrations, was printed in a lavishly appointed edition in Yang's Hall of Purity in Poverty around 1610. It had been preceded in 1607 by another upscale "coffee-table book," an anthology of reproduced paintings: *Tuhui zongyi* 圖繪宗彝, in eight *juan*, also printed at Yang's shop. Thus, one strain of Yang's interest in the unusual found expression in his fascination with pictorial art and its reproduction.

Two other strains are more immediately relevant for the background of *The Story of Han Xiangzi*: Yang's Daoist leanings and his interest in vernacular novels. His Daoist interests are documented by his involvement as compiler or editor of at least two Daoist works. The first is titled *Records of Immortal Beauties* (Xianyuan jishi 仙媛紀事); it is a collection of hagiographies of female immortals, with a post-face by Yang dated to 1602.[38] While *Records of Immortal Beauties* was compiled by Yang himself, he apparently merely edited and corrected *Record of the Ancestral Teachings of the Perfected Lord Xu's [Way of] Purity and Light* (Xu Zhenjun jing-ming zongjiao lu 許真君淨明宗教錄), in fifteen *juan*. This is a collection of texts by and on the third century immortal Xu Xun 許遜, published in 1604.[39]

Yang's forays into the world of vernacular novels yielded two results: *The Story of Han Xiangzi* and *Romance of the Eastern and Western Jin Dynasties* (Dong-Xi liang Jin yanyi 東西兩晉演義). *Romance of the Eastern and Western Jin Dynasties* is a fictionalized account of the battles and intrigues of the third and fourth centuries. Yang's preface reveals that this was not an original work of his, but the result of the editorial efforts he expended on a manuscript offered him by a friend and colleague, the Master of Great Peace Hall (Taihe Zhuren 泰和主人).[40]

Yang's final trace in the literary world of the late Ming period is, to my knowl-edge, his function as copy editor of an anthology of Chan poetry by the Song poet Su Shi 蘇軾 (1036–1101).[41] This nicely rounds off our picture of a scholar-publisher of the early seventeenth century who thrived on the vibrant cultural scene of Qian-tang. In the open-minded atmosphere of a major cultural center away from the capi-tal, Yang was part of a world of literati who pursued highly eclectic interests untrammeled by overly strong concerns for orthodoxy. As copy editor of Buddhist poetry, compiler and editor of Daoist hagiographical collections, publisher of expen-sive art albums, and—last but not least—writer and editor of vernacular novels,

Yang Erzeng likely moved easily among the literati of Qiantang and beyond. Notable scholars of the time contributed prefaces to Yang's works, and these men seemed to share Yang's wide-ranging and rather unorthodox interests. For example, Feng Mengzhen 馮夢禎 (1546–1605), who wrote a preface to Yang's *Records of Immortal Beauties*, composed commentaries on the Daoist classics *Laozi* and *Zhuangzi*, compiled a collection of miscellaneous notes on supernatural phenomena, and was a disciple of the famous female Daoist "saint" Tanyangzi 曇陽子.[42] Ge Yinliang 葛寅良 (*jinshi* 1601) was the author of a preface to Yang's *Extraordinary Sights in China* and of commentaries to Confucian classics, and also compiled an important gazetteer of Buddhist monasteries in Jinling 金陵 (now Nanjing 南京).[43]

Yang Erzeng thus moved in exactly the kind of social circles that Andrew Plaks regards as the cradle of the literati novel, and his *Han Xiangzi* explicitly emulates the paradigmatic works of this new genre: *Record of the Three Kingdoms, Water Margin, The Journey to the West,* and *The Plum in the Golden Vase.*[44] Yang's intellectual and social background provided ample opportunity for the pursuit and discussion of very diverse and less than orthodox interests, and he took full advantage of these circumstances to delve into the history, lore, and practice of Daoism. His two hagiographical collections are evidence of these pursuits, but they really come to fruition in *The Story of Han Xiangzi*, a novel written with a clear didactic purpose: to extol the wonders of the inner alchemy tradition of Daoist cultivation over any transient glories that the world might offer.

DAOISM AND THE STORY OF HAN XIANGZI

As mentioned above, prior to writing *Han Xiangzi*, Yang Erzeng had been involved in the publication of two Daoist collections: one hagiographical (*Records of Immortal Beauties*), the other combining hagiographical and systematic-doctrinal elements (*Record of the Ancestral Teachings of the Perfected Lord Xu's [Way of] Purity and Light*). *The Story of Han Xiangzi* combines both Daoist styles: it narrates the exploits of a Daoist immortal and instructs in a key method of Daoist cultivation—inner alchemy (*neidan* 內丹).[45] To elucidate *Han Xiangzi*'s double function as hagiography and introduction to inner alchemy, we need to take a brief look at these elements of the Daoist tradition.

But first: what is Daoism? Though used in the singular, Daoism is not a single thing. It is a general term for a uniquely Chinese religious tradition that has produced over the centuries a large variety of movements, practices, and ideas, and has had a profound influence on Chinese culture as a whole. Daoism comes in many shapes and sizes, and its representatives include philosophers, alchemists, diviners, poets, priests, magicians, monks, and nuns. The unifying element for all of these diverse expressions is the idea of the Dao, the Way, the conviction that the multiplicity of phenomena in the visible world is rooted in a unitary ultimate reality. Although the *Daodejing* claims in its very first chapter that "the Dao that can be spoken of is not the eternal Dao," the following definition by Livia Kohn may still give us an idea of the concept's scope of meaning:

> The [D]ao, if we then try to grasp it, can be described as the organic order underlying and structuring and pervading all existence. It is organic in that it is not willful, but it is also order because it changes in predictable rhythms and orderly patterns. If one is to approach it, reason and intellect have to be left behind. One can only intuit it when one has become as nameless and as free of conscious choices and evaluations as the [D]ao itself.⁴⁶

If such is the Way, Daoism can then be understood as the large diversity of ways to approach and harmonize with this Dao. These ways include the philosophical mysticism of Zhuangzi, the statecraft of the *Daodejing*, the alchemy of Ge Hong, the millenarianism of Zhang Daoling and the early Celestial Master movement, and the visualization meditations of the Supreme Clarity adepts, to name just a few. Daoist ritual, alchemy, and meditation served to harmonize communities with the Dao and enable individuals to merge with it, thus ultimately coming to share in its eternal constancy—in other words, becoming immortal.⁴⁷

To rise up into the ranks of the immortals (*xian* 仙) was already an ideal in the classical period, when Zhuangzi praised the absolute freedom of these wondrous beings—freedom from death and all other limitations. Throughout Chinese history, emperors sent out searches for such immortals and their mythical lands, such as the Kunlun Mountains or the Isles of Penglai, in the hope of obtaining from them the secret of immortality. Stories about immortals, their adventures in the heavens, and their appearances in the world of humans were featured in popular lore, hagiographical collections, poetry, and the "records of the strange" (*zhiguai* 志怪)—a genre that began in the third century CE and is generally regarded as the earliest form of narrative fiction in China.

The pursuit of immortality is the driving force in the plot of *The Story of Han Xiangzi*. The principal means employed for its attainment is "inner alchemy," a reformulation of the more ancient operative alchemy ("external alchemy," *waidan* 外丹) as a meditational-physiological practice. Here the metals and minerals of external alchemy are reinterpreted as substances and energies within the human body, whose careful manipulation can lengthen a person's life and ultimately lead to immortality. Alchemy is predicated on the reversal of the cosmogonical process described in chapter 42 of the *Daodejing*:

> The way begets one; one begets two; two begets three, three begets the myriad creatures.[48]

If the Daoist's goal is union with the primordial, unified, and unchanging Dao, this can then only be achieved through the reversal of this process, i.e., by reducing the multiplicity of phenomena until one merges them and guides them back into the single source from which they arose. To this end, the multiple energies of the human body are fused and circulated in cyclical movements (orbits, *zhoutian* 周天), which pass through two channels, one ascending along the spine from the coccyx to the head, and one descending in the front of the body. These channels have nodal points, called "passes" (*guan* 關), which need to be kept free from obstructions for the circulation to function. In *Han Xiangzi*, the "double spinal passes" (*jiaji shuangguan* 夾脊雙關), located between the shoulder blades, are particularly emphasized as crucial. These channels connect three energy centers of the body, viz., the lower, middle, and upper elixir fields (*dantian* 丹田). These are located, respectively, below the navel, in the chest, and in the head, and contain the "furnaces" (*lu* 爐) in which the body's three forms of energy, "essence" (*jing* 精), "pneuma" (*qi* 氣), and "spirit" (*shen* 神), are progressively refined in complex "fire phases" (*huohou* 火候). What are fused are yin and yang energies that are described in a vast variety of oppositional terms, such as Mercury and Lead, Dragon and Tiger, White Snow and Yellow Sprouts, or Lovely Maid and Baby Boy. The purpose of this process is to first isolate pure yin and pure yang, then to reduce this last (and cosmogonically first) duality to the Pure Yang force that arose in the undivided primordial chaos. Finally even this Oneness is transcended to reach the non-being of the primordial Dao.

In addition to the rich imagery just described, *The Story of Han Xiangzi* also employs the more abstract trigrams of *The Book of Changes* to talk about this procedure. These trigrams consist of combinations of broken (yin) and unbroken (yang) lines. The trigram *kan* 坎☵ illustrates true yang hidden within yin, while the trigram *li* 離☲ shows true yin hidden within yang. The exchange of the central lines between these two trigrams yields the pure yang trigram *qian* 乾☰ and the pure yin trigram *kun* 坤☷, thus describing the regression to the original duality, which then needs to be overcome in the next reversal by fusing *qian* and *kun*.

As "essence" is transformed into "pneuma," which again is refined into "spirit" by progressive alchemical transmutations, a "pearl" is formed which, with proper nourishment, grows into an immortal embryo that will eventually leave behind the body's husk and join the ranks of immortals. The exact instructions on how to perform this practice were a closely guarded secret and were only supposed to be passed on by masters to carefully chosen disciples whose cultivation enabled them to handle the powerful forces unleashed by this discipline. Although these teachings were written down, the resulting texts were often couched in such esoteric and indirect language that the eager reader still needed the guidance of an accomplished master to put them into practice.[49]

Perhaps the most influential text on internal alchemy is Zhang Boduan's 張伯端 (984–1082) *Chapters on Awakening to Perfection* (Wuzhen pian 悟真篇). It is one of the more cryptic presentations of inner alchemy, and has fascinated Daoists through the centuries as they encased it in layer after layer of commentary. One of those captivated by the suggestive poetry of Zhang Boduan's magnum opus was the author of our novel, Yang Erzeng. The novel's heavy reliance on this text is quite unmistakable. Many of the poems that open its chapters are drawn verbatim from the *Chapters on Awakening to Perfection*, and the descriptions of alchemical procedures follow the guidance (and often the language) of this key text and its commentaries quite closely.[50] The allegorical and technical language used in these passages can be confusing to the uninitiated reader, but should be comprehensible in its general outlines if the above summary of alchemical principles is kept in mind. In the present translation, alchemical terminology is therefore annotated only sparingly. A detailed study of the novel's alchemical language and thought will be included in a future companion volume to this translation.

One needs to "lay a foundation" (*zhuji* 築基) to be able to conserve the energies needed for alchemical work. Foundational practices include celibacy (to avoid the loss of semen, i.e., primordial yang forces), vegetarian diet, abstention from alcohol, and generally a way of life designed to lessen external distractions, desires, and emotional attachments. Such a reclusive lifestyle is greatly extolled in this novel and contrasted with the emotionally exhausting and insecure life of the average worldlings represented by Han Xiangzi's stubborn family members. Much attention is given in *The Story of Han Xiangzi* to these foundational requirements, which are more accessible to the average reader than the arcana of alchemical cultivation. The idealized lifestyle of the Daoist practitioners bears a distinct similarity to that of Buddhist clerics and thus it should not come as a surprise that the alchemical discourses are shot through with phrases and images derived from a Chan-Buddhist context. As Chan (Zen) shares the concern of inner alchemy with the transcendence of dualities, mutual fertilization between the two schools of thought was quite common in the late Imperial period. In *Han Xiangzi*, this affinity manifests itself in citations from the sayings of Chan masters and, perhaps most prominently, in the frequent use of the ox as a stock symbol of the desire-driven ego that needs to be overcome on one's path toward salvation. Thus *The Story of Han Xiangzi* reflects the religious syncretism that dominated the intellectual scene in the early seventeenth century and is apparent in other novels of the age as well.[51] Where our text differs from others is in its clear Daoist partisanship. Confucianism appears mostly as a worldly entanglement that needs to be overcome, while Buddhism is given a more favorable treatment, but is also explicitly relegated to a subordinate position vis-à-vis Daoism. The syncretism of the novel is a hierarchical one, in which Daoism is given pride of place.

Which school of Daoism are we dealing with in the pages of *Han Xiangzi*? This question is rather difficult to decide, as by the seventeenth century inner alchemy had become the dominant form of self-cultivation in pretty much all forms of Daoism. At the time, the institutionally most visible Daoist movement with a strong focus on inner alchemy was the already mentioned Complete Perfection School. Founded by Wang Zhe (1113–70) in northern China, it syncretically combined Confucian and Chan-Buddhist elements with a core of inner alchemy. It had gained great influence during the Yuan dynasty, when its patriarchs enjoyed imperial patronage, but lost much of its political clout under Ming rule.[52] Still, the itinerant Complete Perfection monk was a common sight in Yang Erzeng's time and makes several appearances in the story.

However, the author's treatment of these figures is somewhat ambivalent. In chapter 1, the crane and the musk deer disguise themselves as Complete Perfection monks to hide the fact that they are really just animals. In chapters 13 and 17, Han Xiangzi appears as a monk of this school, but at the same time challenges his audience not to "mistake [him] for an ordinary, mortal monk of the Complete Perfection School, who begs in remote places, eats vegetables, serves demons, and wanders from monastery to monastery."[53] The image of Complete Perfection Daoism is thus ambiguous. Yang Erzeng endorses many of its tenets, such as inner alchemy and celibacy, and makes heavy use of *daoqing* songs, a favorite vehicle of Complete Perfection proselytization; at the same time he shows mistrust of the movement's clergy, who often are not what they seem or what they should be.

In terms of textual references, Yang is clearly leaning toward the so-called "Southern Lineage" (Nanzong 南宗) of inner alchemy. Zhang Boduan's *Wuzhen pian* is the foundational text for this loose assortment of teachers and teachings, and all of the other alchemical texts referenced in the novel also belong to the corpus of writings associated traditionally with the Southern Lineage. Yang's involvement in the publication of a key anthology of the Jingming School may provide a unifying element. This particular movement combined a pronounced interest in inner alchemy with an emphasis on ethical conduct. It is perhaps this combination that shaped Yang's religious perspective in his novel: a focus on the Southern textual lineage of inner alchemy coupled with a rejection of the sexual practices advocated by some in this lineage in favor of Quanzhen-style celibate reclusivism.

THE STORY OF HAN XIANGZI AS A DAOIST NOVEL

Daoism is an ancient religion with a huge corpus of sacred texts. This corpus never stopped growing, as new revelations produced new texts, and new insights and methods required new explications. Periodically efforts were made to gather Daoist texts into authorized collections. Up to the time of Yang Erzeng, several major such efforts had been made. Canonical collections had been published in the eighth, the eleventh, the twelfth, and the thirteenth centuries—only to be lost again. In the Ming dynasty, a more lasting effort was made with the compilation of the *Daoist Canon* (Daozang 道藏) in the fifteenth century.[54] This massive work in 5318 *juan* has remained the canonical basis of Daoism to the present day, but was never regarded as the final word in Daoist scripture. New texts were composed on an ongoing basis, while some older texts had been left out of the *Canon*, with the result that in the following centuries various supplemental collections were published. Yang Erzeng himself was involved in this effort through his editing of the writings of the immortal Xu Xun and his compilation of the *Records of Immortal Beauties*.

Thus, the canonical collections never served to limit the creative impulse in Daoism, and new scriptures, commentaries, and hagiographies kept being added to the textual basis of Daoism. Beyond religious texts in the narrow sense, Daoist ideas also came to be reflected in the various belletristic genres. For example, Daoist imagery suffused the writings of many Chinese poets, and Daoist themes defined a subset of Yuan dynasty (13th–14th cent.) drama: the already mentioned "deliverance plays" (*dutuoju* 度脱劇). Of course, the Daoist content in such works varied greatly, ranging from mere ornamentation to a thorough dominance by Daoist concerns.

The great contribution of the Ming dynasty to Chinese literature was the vernacular novel, i.e., a long narrative written in the vernacular (rather than the classical) language and divided into chapters. As with earlier literary genres, this new one also came to reflect Daoist elements in the background of its authors and audience. This impact is most visible in the subgenre defined by the famous writer and historian of literature Lu Xun 魯迅 (1881–1936) as "novels of gods and demons" (*shenmo xiaoshuo* 神魔小説), to which he devoted three chapters of his seminal "Brief History of Chinese Narrative Fiction" (Zhongguo xiaoshuo shilüe 中國小説史略).[55] In fact, for Lu Xun these novels constituted one of two thematic mainstreams in the Ming novel, the other being novels dealing with human relationships (*renqing xiaoshuo* 人情小説).[56] Later historians of Chinese literature have offered more differentiated typologies of the Ming novel, but in all of these schemata religious novels under various designations have remained a major category.

Not all of these "novels of gods and demons" count as Daoist novels, a term I would like to reserve for those works whose plot serves as a vehicle for Daoist thought, in other words, where the author uses the format of the novel to transmit Daoist truths to the reader. There are many works that focus on the exploits of immortals or battles between gods and demons, but only a few integrate such storylines into a larger scheme of Daoist thought. The most famous example is *The Journey to the West* (Xiyou ji 西遊記), whose story of the Buddhist monk Tripitaka's journey to the Buddha's land serves (on one level of meaning) as an allegory of alchemical cultivation.[57] Clearly Daoist plot structures have also been demonstrated in the novels of Deng Zhimo 鄧志謨, a contemporary of Yang Erzeng.[58]

To be successful, a Daoist novel has to perform a balancing act between a religious message and an entertaining story line. If the latter dominates we end up with a lightly Daoist-flavored adventure story; if the former pushes itself to the foreground, we get pious sermonizing, which is unlikely to attract a wide readership. *The Journey to the West* is the prime example of a successful balancing act: the processes of inner alchemy are placed at an unobtrusively allegorical level where they do not detract from the riveting narrative of the surface plot. As a result, the novel can be (and has been) read purely for its considerable entertainment value. The deeper message is left to the discerning reader of Daoist inclination.

Yang Erzeng's *Han Xiangzi* is certainly not as sophisticated as *The Journey to the West* in its layering of levels of meaning. While the reader of *The Journey to the West* can easily forget the novel's Daoist substructure and just become immersed in the fantasy world of Tripitaka and his companions, in *The Story of Han Xiangzi* the Daoist structure is always visible on the surface of the plot. Strongly influenced as Yang's work is by the example of the deliverance plays, cultivation and conversion are the driving forces in the story, and thus quite naturally the Daoist message is made very explicit and unavoidable throughout the novel—the reader unsympathetic to Daoism is given no escape to another interpretive level. If we use a layered semantic structure as a measure of aesthetic appreciation, *Han Xiangzi* certainly does not play in the same league as *The Journey to the West*.

However, if we compare it to other works in Lu Xun's "novels of gods and demons" category, it cuts a much more favorable figure. It possesses a coherent and well-organized plot structure and a defining message, and is written in a fluent prose style interspersed with highly original rhymed passages, many of them in the style of popular *daoqing*. The story moves along at a good pace, and a liberal infusion of humor makes its insistence on the futility of worldly pursuits much easier to swallow. A comparison with its closest thematic cousin, the Eight Immortals novel *Journey to the East* (Dongyou ji), clearly shows the relative merits of *Han Xiangzi*. Wu Yuantai's *Journey to the East* is a loose collection of episodes about the Eight Immortals, as individuals and as a group, that lacks a strongly developed continuous storyline. The episodes are fun to read and a few have caught the popular imagination, but the work as a whole is rather poorly integrated. Yet since the Ming dynasty *Journey to the East* has outdone Yang's novel in the reading public's favor. While Lu Xun devotes a section of his "Brief History of Chinese Narrative Fiction" to *Journey to the East*, he does not even mention *The Story of Han Xiangzi*. Why the neglect of the artistically superior of the two novels?

Part of the problem may have been *Han Xiangzi*'s consistent and insistent Daoist message. The story's obvious religious partisanship may have offended both the relaxed syncretist who believed in the equivalence of China's three teachings and the staunch Confucian or Buddhist. The reader in search of purely literary enjoyment also may have had problems with a work that tried to harness literature for missionary purposes. One modern historian writing about Ming "novels of gods and strange phenomena" (*shenguai xiaoshuo* 神怪小説) places the *Han Xiangzi* in a large category of "proselytizing works" (*zongjiao xuanchuanpin* 宗教宣傳品), which are said to be of generally low quality. While he admits that "among these novels there are a few that are quite good, such as the *Han Xiangzi quanzhuan*," ultimately Yang Erzeng's opus is excluded from further consideration.[59]

The underlying rationale for the relative neglect of the work becomes visible in the preface to a modern edition. After praising the careful construction and originality of the novel's plot, the editor goes on to criticize it on two counts: (1) the irregular meters of some of its poetry, and (2) "the preposterous and superstitious nature of some of its contents."[60] In the eyes of modern(ist) critics, *The Story of Han Xiangzi* ultimately fails the litmus test of compatibility with science and progress by cleaving to a supposedly backward and degenerate Daoism whose superstition had slowed down China's march into modernity. The even more outrageous "superstitions" in a work such as *Journey to the East* are presumably less of a problem, as they primarily serve ornamental and entertainment purposes and do not merge into a coherent Daoist message. Thus, the seriousness of its religious purpose may continue to affect *Han Xiangzi*'s critical reception today as it did in late Imperial times.

However, there are signs that this attitude may be changing. Yu Deyu 余德余, the editor of yet another modern edition, explicitly recognizes the work's function of promoting Daoism, yet frames his evaluation in purely literary terms. He credits it with a smoothly flowing style, lively language, a tight structure without repetitiveness, as well as clever use of devices such as wordplay. On the downside, Yu criticizes the author's overreliance on dialogue and the insufficient exploration of the main characters' psychology.[61] Fang Sheng 方勝 praises the novel's use of humor, satire, and fantasy. While upholding *The Journey to the West* as the masterpiece and model and pointing out *Han Xiangzi*'s indebtedness to its illustrious predecessor, Fang still sees it as the most outstanding work among all the religious novels inspired by *The Journey to the West*.[62] As the modernist master narrative gradually breaks down in Chinese academia, we may be seeing more such balanced assessments of *The Story of Han Xiangzi* on its own merits, and perhaps it will someday gain the place it deserves in the history of Chinese literature.[63] That place will certainly not be the one the author of the novel's preface claims for it—excelling even the four masterworks of the Ming dynasty—but it does belong in a larger group of well-crafted works that have stood the test of time and deserve serious attention.[64] It is my hope that the present translation will help this process along.

ON THIS TRANSLATION

Obviously, translating a seventeenth-century Chinese novel into twenty-first-century English involves more than a word-by-word transposition to transport meaning from the semantic and syntactic structures of one language, culture, and age, into those of a completely different language, culture, and age. To bridge the gulf between source and target languages, there are basically two strategies available: literal translation with heavy annotation, or creative translation involving a lot of paraphrasing. Under the former option, annotation is needed to elucidate phrases that do not by themselves make sense in a literal English rendering. The notes serve to supply the necessary cultural and linguistic context. With the latter option, such phrases are replaced by close English equivalents, which of course are not direct translations. Obviously, creative translating makes for a smoother read as it does not require the reader to break the flow of the story by continuously having to look up notes. On the other hand, a more literal translation is truer to the original. Of the two target groups of the present translation, the casual reader will prefer the creative option, while the scholar would much rather have the literal one, with all its scholarly apparatus.

I decided to go with what I hope is a reasonable compromise. I aimed to produce a smooth, readable translation, unencumbered by a heavy appendage of scholarly annotation, without however completely shortchanging the serious scholar. Whenever possible I tried to make the translated text stand on its own, i.e., without the crutch of notes. Occasionally this required careful paraphrasing of passages in the original. Annotation has been provided wherever paraphrasing would have required greater departures from the original than my scholarly conscience would brook, or where it would have obscured important semantic elements of the original. The annotation is deliberately limited and does not amount to a running commentary on and analysis of the text. This will be provided in a future companion volume in which I shall address in more depth the textual, intertextual, and religious issues raised by *The Story of Han Xiangzi*, as well as its relation to popular and religious culture in Late Imperial China.

The base text of this translation was a microfiche copy of the edition published by the Jiuru Tang 九如堂 in Hangzhou (preface dated to 1623) and held as a part of the van Gulik collection at Leiden University. I supplemented it with various modern editions.[65] Somewhat confusingly, another Jiuru Tang edition exists that differs from the van Gulik version by adding to it commentaries at the end of each chapter.[66] These commentaries are not reproduced in modern editions of the text and are also omitted in this present translation. However, a few words on their authorship are in order. The commentator is a certain Immortal Guest of Great Peace (Taihe Xianke 泰和仙客) from Wulin 武林 (modern Hangzhou). He is likely the same person as the author of the novel's preface, who signed his name as the Private Historian of the Mists and Vapors at the Hall of Great Peace (Yanxia Waishi ti yu Taihe Tang 煙霞外史題於泰和堂). I have been unable to discover the identity of this person, but in his preface to *Romance of the Eastern and Western Jin Dynasties* Yang recounts how the original manuscript of the novel was given him by a Master of Great Peace Hall (Taihe Tang Zhuren 泰和堂主人). Apparently someone had submitted the manuscript to the Master of Great Peace Hall, who now wanted Yang's help in polishing it up for publication. From the description of this Master of Great Peace Hall, we may surmise that he was a friend of Yang Erzeng's as well as a fellow book publisher—and was most likely the same person as the author of the preface and commentary to Yang's *Han Xiangzi*.[67]

Chinese names and terms are rendered in pinyin romanization. Wherever possible, English equivalents are used, even if they are not exact matches. For example, because none of the measurements in the novel are meant to be exact, for the sake of readability I took liberties such as rendering *sui* as "year" and *li* as "mile." Age is counted differently in traditional China, so that someone of eighteen *sui* would actually be seventeen years of age. I still render it as "eighteen years." Similarly, a Chinese *li* is less than a mile—in fact, it is only a bit more than a third of a mile. However, again, as measures of distance are mostly used in the novel with poetic hyperbole, there was no point in exact conversion, and "mile" henceforth is to be read as standing in for the Chinese *li*.

I have also standardized to some extent the names of some characters appearing in the novel. In traditional usage, both men and women used different names in different social contexts. Thus, Han Yu is variously referred to by his style, Tuizhi; his posthumous title, Wengong; or more generally as Lord Han or Master Han. His wife appears as Mme. Dou or Lady Han. To a traditional reader the use of these variant names would have been meaningful as expressing a specific social context. Thus, Han Yu's posthumous title is used more frequently (though not exclusively) in the novel after the world has come to believe him dead; his wife Mme. Dou is regularly referred to as Lady Han after she has become a widow. Since for the Western reader these issues of nomenclature are rather irrelevant, for ease of reading I have taken the liberty of simplifying the matter somewhat by replacing Lady Han with Mme. Dou and Wengong with Tuizhi or Han Yu throughout. Similar simplifications were made for other names as well.

With these technicalities out of the way, there is nothing more to delay the telling of the story. As the traditional Chinese novelist might have said: "Dear reader, if you do not yet know how the story begins, please turn the page and start reading."

THE STORY OF HAN XIANGZI

韓湘子全傳

PREFACE

When Heaven and Earth were split in two, the unified primordial pneuma began to ferment. By virtue of this pneuma, Heaven and Earth appeared; sun and moon emitted their light;[1] the stars shone forth; the thunderbolt reverberated among the clouds; lightning streamed across the sky; plants and trees produced blossoms and fruits. For birds and beasts, this pneuma became their voices and hides; for reptiles and fish, it became their scales, armor, and wriggling movement. Some animals soar and fly, some hunker down and walk, others again glitter in five colors and sing in the harmony of the eight tones. And at the pinnacle of the animal kingdom, we have the turtle who regulates its breathing so skillfully that it lives through the ages, and the crane who so refines its spirit that it soars up to Heaven and flies afar. All of their abilities are due to this pneuma!

Yet while mountains can rise high and rivers can flow forever due to this pneuma, when it is obstructed mountains may collapse and rivers may overflow or dry up. When humans obtain this pneuma, they are born between Heaven and Earth. If they know how to control it, they may rise to the Mysterious Capital of the immortals, to dwell on high adorned with their vermilion insignia. But if they lose control over it, then they are like soldiers who have lost their general, like the fog about to disperse in a rosy dawn—they will become exhausted and wither away, wearily going to their death. What hope have they of achieving eternal life?

Therefore it is said: Without this pneuma, Gong Gong could not have knocked over the mountain holding up Heaven, nor could Nü Gua have mended the sky.[2]

As for those in the world who are called immortals, they wisely obtain the pure beginnings of this pneuma and profoundly understand its marvels. Ceaselessly transforming along with the transformative force of the cosmos, they merge the myriad phenomena into mystic contemplation.[3] Ceaselessly drawing their vital forces from the apex of the Dao, they control the six dragons and their spiritual nature is strengthened.[4] They perceive that this succession of worlds is a great dream and refute the deep confusion of the unenlightened masses.

Thus they soar above the nine divisions of the realm and still the surging waves in the sea of suffering. Carefree they roam in all the eight directions and extinguish the blazing flames on the mountain of doubts. They ride blue phoenixes above Cinnabar Hill; leaving behind traces divine and marvelous, they transcend the world. They drive chariots pulled by striped unicorns in the Mysterious Garden; their tracks are rare and surpass all human limitations.[5] In the morning they travel over the Round Ocean, in the evening they feast in the Fangzhu Palace.[6] They abstain from grains and eat immortality mushrooms so that throughout their existence they never age. One may compare them to mountain peaks and towering islands where the trees are forever green, and to gardens and parks where the plants are forever luxuriant and elegantly planted. Investigating the red tablets, they reveal the golden records on the Charts of the Five Marchmounts. Evenly examining the purple documents, they divulge the elixir scriptures in their nine tubes.[7]

There is an immortal named Xiangzi who hails from Changli. He was a nephew of Han Yu, during the prosperous age of the reign of Emperor Xianzong in the Tang dynasty. He understood the Three Perfections of inner practice, he comprehended the Eight Minerals of alchemy. Outside he treasured the Five Brilliances, inside he preserved the Nine Essences. Cloud-clad he took off his sash and gradually attained the highest ranks of the immortals. Riding the mist with flying duck shoes, he completely realized the rewards of the way of unified perfection.[8]

His degrees are not noted in the family records, nor are his deeds recorded in the official biographical accounts. Reading in Han Yu's *Collected Works*, we find a "Sacrificial Essay for the Twelfth Gentleman," but Xiangzi is not mentioned.[9] Looking up Han Yu's poetry, we find the line "clouds straddle the mountains of Qin," but its true meaning is not made clear.[10]

His story is only transmitted by the blind storytellers, who either sing in a loud voice while holding documents like officials, or recite ballads in a wild manner dressed up as Daoist priests, sighing three times for every line they chant. These stories everywhere delight the hearts of ignorant people and village matrons, and are listened to by school teachers and their pupils. Yet their style is disorderly and erroneous, their poems are inept and awkward. If they are sung by boatmen while rowing their oars, those who listen will forget their fatigue. But if one were to ascend with them the stage of poetic appreciation, the audience would close their eyes in embarrassment.

As for those who nowadays transmit the story of Xiangzi, could there be one who, having a grasp of the marvels of pneuma ingestion, has thereby succeeded in lengthening his years, and who uses the figure of Xiangzi to divulge the general outline of such successful practice? Or, if this Xiangzi really exists, is there one who might use his story to express the wondrous insights of his own mind?

Imitating romances and drawing on local traditions, such a writer compiled this book, telling the story in its general outlines. Having only limited experience, he spent three years pursuing Xiangzi's traces. He marked and divided his manuscript into chapters and published it as an original work. Its style is extraordinary, being written with a liberal brush and broad-minded intentions. Its contents have both breadth and depth, being composed with a powerful pen in elegant diction.

The author traces Xiangzi's numinous cultivation back to Mount Pheasant Yoke. After he takes the form of a white crane, he undergoes innumerable transformations until he escapes from the wheel of life and death and his fame reaches the stars. He is compelled to drink the nuptial cup, but still he realizes for all eternity the state of no rebirth. From Gold Sprinkle Bridge to his long wait at the city gate, everywhere he manifests the Dao. Cutting the hibiscus and transforming it into a beautiful woman, everywhere he applies his divine powers.

When you see him beheading a demon with perfected fire, you know that the elixir cauldron can be guarded. When you witness a herdboy recognizing a divine immortal, you see how Daoist songs move people. He changes a stone lion into gold and obtains propitious snow through his prayers, thus showing the vastness of his divine abilities. With a wave of his hand he makes the Dragon Sage come, and with his feet he steps on auspicious clouds, thus displaying the perfection of his magical skills.

Well versed in nourishing his original yang, he is no aimless idler, though he sleeps and snores on the snow-covered ground. Roaming at will in the underworld, he has good cause for escaping from the emotional entanglements of his worldly life. When the Buddha bone is received in the imperial palace, the Tathagatha manifests Xiangzi's transformative powers. When Han Yu has to cross the river of love on his way into exile, a beautiful woman awakens him from his confusion. Han Xiangzi divines Han Yu's destiny and exorcizes the violent crocodile of Chaozhou. Having benefited from his ascetic cultivation, Xiangzi goes home once more to complete his return to authentic perfection.

In a dream a marriage proposal is made—but isn't all life a dream? A fake man exacts revenge—but isn't everything just lie and rumor leading to disaster? Fortunately, master and servants meet again and Lord Wood gets to lead the way. Happily, mother and daughter-in-law encourage each other and the Metal Mother gets to engage in her amours. A man-bear obeys orders submissively, while a black-hearted musk-deer escapes from his difficulties and becomes a deity.

This book explains the secret scripts of the Perfected Man Zhuowei Mumu; exhaustively explores the illusory realms of humanity and Heaven, in water and on land; explicates the profound purposes of way and virtue, nature and life; and displays extraordinary tidings from the realms of gods and ghosts. In this book the parts and the whole do not conflict with each other, beginning and end do not contradict each other. It has the sternness of *Record of the Three Kingdoms* and the wondrous transformations of *Water Margin*, while lacking the cruel satire of *The Journey to the West* and the indecent license of *The Plum in the Golden Vase*.[11] It may be said that except for the bequeathed writings of the great historians Sima Qian and Ban Gu, there is nothing that can measure up to this work. Now that the craftsmen have finished carving the printing blocks, and the book is to be published, it shall be praised and achieve fame in the capital.

On the first day of the 6th month in the *guihai* year of the Tianqi reign period,[12] inscribed by the Private Historian of the Mists and Vapors at the Hall of Great Peace.

PROLOGUE

When primordial chaos first separated, the world came into being.
As yin and yang merged, humanity was created.
Yellow Sprouts and White Snow repeatedly renew themselves,[1]
Sun crow and moon rabbit rotate without ever stopping.
One moment I see a mulberry field changing into an ocean,
The next I observe pine and cypress fallen down and withered.[2]
Black ox and white dog bellow at the Milky Way,
In the twinkling of an eye, chess pieces respond to each other.[3]

1

AT MOUNT PHEASANT YOKE, A CRANE REFINES HIMSELF

∾

AT THE BANKS OF THE RIVER XIANG, A MUSK DEER

RECEIVES HIS PUNISHMENT

Between Heaven and Earth, there are nine continents and eight directions. The dry land has nine mountains; the mountains have nine passes. Marshes have nine different pneumata, winds come in eight different degrees, of rivers there are nine classes.

What are the nine continents? In the southeast is Shen Province, called the land of agriculture. In the south is Zi Province, called the land of fertility. In the southwest is Rong Province, called the land of abundance. In the west is Yan Province, called the land of ripeness. In the center is Ji Province, called the central land. In the northwest is Tai Province, called the land of plenty. In the north is Qi Province, called the land of consummation. In the northeast is Bo Province, called the land of seclusion. In the east is Yang Province, called the land of beginning again.

What are the nine mountains? They are Mount Guiji, Mount Tai, Mount Wangwu, Mount Shou, Mount Taihua, Mount Qi, Mount Taihang, Mount Yangchang, and Mount Mengmen.

What are the nine passes? They are the Taifen Pass, the Min'ou Pass, the Jingruan Pass, the Fangcheng Pass, the Yaoban Pass, the Jingxing Pass, the Lingci Pass, the Gouzhu Pass, and the Juyong Pass.

What are the nine marshes? They are the Juqu Marsh of Chu, the Yunmeng Marsh of Yue, the Yangyu Marsh of Qin, the Dalu Marsh of Jin, the Putian Marsh of Zheng, the Mengzhu Marsh of Song, the Haiyu Marsh of Qi, the Julu Marsh of Zhao, and the Zhaoyu Marsh of Yan.

What are the eight winds? The northeast wind is called the intense wind. The east wind is called the protracted wind. The southeast wind is called the luminous wind. The south wind is called the balmy wind. The southwest wind is called the cool wind. The west wind is called the lofty wind. The northwest wind is called the elegant wind. The north wind is called the cold wind.

What are the six rivers? They are the Yellow River, the Vermilion River, the Liao River, the Black River, the Yangtze River, and the Huai River.

The expanse within the four seas measures 28,000 miles from east to west and 26,000 miles from south to north. There are 8,000 miles of watercourses, which pass through six valleys and 600 named streams. There are 3,000 miles of roads and paths. Yu employed Tai Zhang to measure the earth from its eastern extremity to its western extremity. It measured 233,500 miles and 75 paces. He also employed Shu Hai to measure from its northern extremity to its southern extremity. It measured 233,500 miles and 75 paces. Concerning floodlands, deep pools, and swamps greater than 300 fathoms in area: within the expanse of 233,500 miles, there are nine deep pools.

Yu also took expanding earth to fill in the great flood, making the famous mountains. He excavated the wastelands of Kunlun to make level ground. In the center of the world is a manifold wall of nine layers, with a height of 11,000 miles, 114 paces, two feet, and six inches. Atop the heights of Kunlun are tree-like cereal plants thirty-five feet tall. To the west of these are pearl trees, jade trees, carnelian trees, and never-dying trees. To the east are found sand-plum trees and *lang'gan* trees. To the south are crimson trees. To the north are *bi* jade trees and *yao* jade trees.[1] On one side is Mount Bear Ears, on the other Mount Pheasant Yoke. A poem rightly says about them:

> *Clouds hover over Bear Ears—how graceful its peaks.*
> *Water gushes forth from Pheasant Yoke—how lofty this mountain.*

Truly, they are impressive mountains, and here is a lyric to witness to it:

> *A rocky range seen from afar,*
> *Lofty peaks viewed from nearby.*
> *This majestic mountain*
> *Stands firm among the vast waters, the sea churning in snowy waves*
>   *against its sides.*
> *This lofty rock*
> *Subdues the scaly dragons and sea serpents, who let silvery billows gush*
>   *forth from their dens.*

> Here the earth dragon is located in the corner marked by the phases of
>   wood and fire,
> While the cloud mother is hidden at its southeastern border.[2]
> Among high cliffs, steep precipices,
> Strange ravines, extraordinary peaks,
> Constantly one hears pairs of phoenixes singing in unison,
> And everywhere sees single simurghs dancing by themselves.
> Amidst wafting fog,
> Leopards hide in the depth of the mountain;
> In the slight rustling of the wind,
> Tigers come to the lofty ranges.
> There are jasper grasses and wondrous flowers that never die,
> Blue pines and green cypresses in eternal spring.
> Immortals' peaches in gorgeous red,
> Tall bamboo in luxuriant green.
> A streak of rosy clouds merges with the shade of the trees,
> Two mountain torrents splash the roots of vines.

Indeed the scenery resembled

> A thousand mountains rising loftily as pillars supporting Heaven,
> Ten thousand ravines criss-crossing the Earth like scars.

On the peak of Mount Pheasant Yoke there was a great tree. On that tree there stood a white crane whose essence had been endowed with the phases of metal and fire and whose pneuma had received yin and yang. His crown was red, his wings a pure white; the throat was well-rounded, the feet delicately formed. He was a womb-born immortal bird, senior among the feathered creatures.[3] Here is a lyric to illustrate it:

> A slender head and protruding eyes,
> Luxuriant feathers and sparse flesh.
> Phoenix wings and tortoise back,
> Swallow breast and turtle belly.
> Their cries warn of the falling dew.[4]
> Stopping at Gold Cave Mountain, cranes hover and wheel in the air,
> The whiteness of their plumes not due to the bathing sunlight.
> Gathering at Orchid Cliff Mountain, they lower their heads and regard
>   their feet.

At Mount Pheasant Yoke, a crane refines himself.

Some rode in noble chariots in the state of Wei,[5]
While others served as mounts at the Tower of Jiangxia.[6]
Others again fetched arrows for immortals at Ye Brook,[7]
And were fed millet from the marshes.[8]
Their legs' length contrasts with the shortness of ducks' legs,[9]
When in groups, they do not peck about like chicken.
With simurghs and phoenixes as companions they travel afar,
Reaching the clouds, they preen their feathers on high.
Truly, this crane is a descendant of Master Wang of Mount Kou,[10]
Of the same kind as Ding Ling of Liaodong.[11]

This white crane on Mount Pheasant Yoke was just a common bird, yet in the past the cries of ordinary cranes on Mount Eight Lords subdued invaders,[12] and the calls of wild cranes in the Ninth Marsh penetrated Heaven.[13]

It so happened one day that from the Tushita Palace in the Thirty-third Heaven a crane from the team that pulled the carriage of the Heavenly Worthy of Primordial Beginning flew down to this mountain.[14] When the white crane saw her flying in, his mind cleared up in the presence of such good fortune and he went over and engaged in intercourse with her. Afterwards the immortal crane revealed to him one by one the marvelous principles of the immortals and the true way to study the Dao.

Following the instructions given him, the white crane engaged in serious cultivation for three or four hundred years. On his tree in the mountains he swallowed solar sap in the mornings and sought lunar efflorescences in the evenings, drank dew and ingested wind, ate cloud vapors and absorbed dew. However, as he was studying without having been properly inducted as a disciple, it was like having wings but still being unable to fly. He could not escape from his feathery body and reach the garden of the Jasper Pool above.

As it happened, on that same mountain there lived a musk deer, who had also lived for more than one hundred years. He liked to play tricks and do mischief, riding on the mists and mounting the clouds. He struck up an acquaintance with the white crane and they became sworn brothers. Every day they roamed leisurely at the river and played in the mountains. Truly they wandered at ease without restraints, fearing neither Lord Yama nor Heaven itself.

When telling a story, one should recount all the details from beginning to end. In this wide world, there must exist hundreds of thousands of white cranes and musk deer. Why was it then that this particular crane and this particular deer acquired illicit powers and engaged in sinful behavior?

Between Heaven and Earth there are four forms of birth and six paths of rebirth. The Buddhist sutras say that these four forms of birth are birth from the womb, from an egg, from moisture, or by metamorphosis. As for the six paths of rebirth, the Buddha tells us that they are those of immortals, Buddhas, ghosts, humans, beasts, and demigods. If one is placed in a good womb, there will be good results; if the womb is not good, neither will be the results—this is the wheel of rebirth spun by retribution, the impartial principle of Heaven and Earth.

Originally the crane and the deer had lived as humans in the Han dynasty, but their misconduct caused them to be reborn in their present state. How did it happen that humans of the Han period became spirits after a lapse of three or four hundred years? Reader, listen closely—once I have recounted to you this prologue, you will realize what an astounding story is behind this.

During the Han dynasty there was a Counselor-in-chief of the Left named An Fu. When his daughter was four years old, her mother died, and he gave her to a wet nurse to raise. By the age of seven, the girl was able to master all kinds of skills without need for instruction by anyone.

One day when Counselor An returned from court, he heard someone strumming the zither and playing the flute in his daughter's room. He asked who it was, and a slave answered that it was the young lady. Having listened to the music a while, An Fu entered the room and asked his daughter, "When I got back from court, I heard you playing the zither and flute. Who taught you to play?"

The girl replied, "I mastered the hundred arts without need for instruction by anyone."

"I have only this one daughter," An Fu said. "As you are so intelligent, I will call you Bright-Bright. When you're ten I'll look for a husband for you, but I won't settle for anything less than your becoming second wife of the prime minister. Even if the top graduate of the palace examinations comes to ask for your hand, I won't give you to him."

"Why won't you give her to a top graduate, but would rather have her become the prime minister's second wife?" interjected the wet nurse.

An Fu said, "If she marries a top graduate as his first wife, it will be years before she is a lady of the first rank, but if she marries the prime minister as a second wife, she'll receive first rank the moment she enters his household."

"Things don't always turn out the way you plan," the wet nurse said. "I am afraid you're doing your wife a disservice, and will lose a lot, too."

An Fu scolded the wet nurse and sent her away. After that, many asked for the hand of his daughter, but An Fu would not agree to any match.

One day the Han emperor called An Fu to the palace and told him, "We have a nephew, only twenty-two years old, who has been widowed and has not yet remarried. Now We have heard that you have a daughter named Bright-Bright whom you are willing to give in marriage as the prime minister's second wife. Why not have her marry Our nephew instead?"

An Fu replied, "Years ago I made a pledge to give her in marriage only as the prime minister's second wife. I wouldn't dare marry her to an imperial nephew."

"How could marriage to the prime minister be better than to Our nephew?"

"As soon as she enters the prime minister's household, she will become a lady of the first rank. An imperial nephew, on the other hand, may only be a general or a commander. There would be quite a difference in rank."

"What if I granted her first rank in accordance with your wishes?" the emperor asked.

"Such a grant would be at odds with propriety and my daughter's station in life. She would still be better off marrying the prime minister," An Fu said.

The emperor was greatly enraged, and wanted to have An Fu beheaded at the execution grounds as a warning to the other officials. He was set free only after two other officials pleaded for clemency on his behalf. The emperor demoted him and banished him to a faraway place. Furthermore, he sent a messenger to summon Bright-Bright to court for an audience.

When Bright-Bright heard the summons, she was greatly alarmed, knowing that her father had almost lost his life on her account. So, without combing her hair or washing, her eyes filled with tears, she went to the audience with the emperor. The emperor commanded her to raise her face, and truly, her beauty and elegance were matchless.

Thereupon he ordered that she be sent to Red Copper Mountain in Shanxi, there to marry a villager called Stiff Neck, who was only three feet tall and exceedingly ugly. His neck did not extend above his shoulders and was completely inflexible, so that his head and body had to turn together. It was for this reason that people had given him the nickname Stiff Neck. That Bright-Bright, a girl perfect in beauty and talent, should be married to such a dolt truly accords with the saying "A noble mount often carries a stupid fellow, a beautiful wife often sleeps alongside a dull husband."

Bright-Bright's heart was filled with grief, and within a few years she fell ill and died. Seeing her dead, Stiff Neck hanged himself from the roof beam so that his soul might follow that of his wife.

Both drifted far and wide, arriving eventually in the underworld at the court of Yama.[15] The ox-headed and horse-faced demons blocked their way and asked, "Who are you? Who arrested you and brought you here? Why didn't you come with the messenger?"

"I am Bright-Bright, the daughter of the counselor-in-chief An Fu. I died of grief just because the Old Man Under the Moon made a wrong match and married me to this person Stiff Neck.[16] My soul comes for an audience with King Yama to explain the matter," Bright-Bright told them.

"I am Stiff Neck from Red Copper Mountain in Shanxi," Stiff Neck said. "I received a decree from the Han emperor to marry Bright-Bright. I did everything I could to please her, but she still wasn't satisfied and escaped by way of her grief. I couldn't give her up, so I followed her on this road, hoping that she would come back."

"You really are a stiff-necked fellow!" the ox-headed and horse-faced demons said. "Your wife is dead now—how do you think she could return to you?!"

Only when Stiff Neck heard these words did he fully realize that he himself was also dead. He broke into loud wails, startling King Yama.

King Yama ascended the hall and asked what sort of people were outside, wailing so pitifully. The demons were afraid and did not dare utter a sound, but a judge came forward and reported what Bright-Bright and Stiff Neck had said. King Yama called on the two to enter and kneel before his desk. Crying, they told him what they had suffered in their lifetime and asked Yama to send them back to the world of the living.

King Yama said, "You came here of your own accord; it's not as if my runners had brought you here by mistake. Therefore it is not possible for you to go back. I now sentence you to be reborn together, so as to fulfill your hearts' wishes."

Then he pronounced the official judgment, "The husband is the wife's heaven;[17] husband and wife are the beginning of humankind. When a wife has received him who is heaven to her, she should acquiesce and maintain her wifely duties. She must not cause quarrels by being resentful. By harboring resentments toward her superiors in her lifetime, Bright-Bright had already perverted the proper order of human life. Now that she is dead, she makes reckless pleas—for this she ought to be reborn as an animal. Fortunately her spirit is not darkened and there still remains life-force in her bones. Therefore she should not be reborn in a womb. Instead she shall be transformed into a noble bird, first among its kind. After three hundred years she will meet an immortal and be transformed by his instruction, whereupon she will once more become human. As for Stiff Neck, he is ugly in appearance and stupid in constitution, fit only to live in poverty and make a living in the countryside. By rights he should have renounced marriage forever, resigning himself to his ugliness. Yet he dared hope to marry into the family of a high minister and love a beautiful woman, with the result that she died of grief. He threw away his insignificant body to pursue her, unwilling to give her up, thus darkening his nature even further. He should be reborn as an animal, and shall by way of punishment be transformed into a musk deer. After three hundred years he will become acquainted with the white crane to complete his karmic destiny."

When the judgment had been pronounced, Bright-Bright and Stiff Neck lowered their heads and, without uttering a word, each went their own way. This then is the story of the previous existence of the white crane and the musk deer. Today, however, we are to tell how Han Xiangzi saved Han Yu twelve times, so let's leave this story of karmic retribution aside.

Let us instead reveal that in the palace of the Jade Emperor there once was an Attendant Great General on the Left[18] called Chonghezi. At an immortality peach banquet he fought with a certain Yunyangzi over a peach, and in the course of the struggle they broke a crystal cup. Greatly enraged, the Jade Emperor banished Chonghezi and Yunyangzi to the human world.

Chonghezi was born into the Han family of Changli County in Yongping Prefecture and was given the name Han Yu, while Yunyangzi was born into the Lin family of the same location and was named Lin Gui.

The Han family had accumulated merit for nine generations, focusing single-heartedly on the recitation of *The Yellow Court Scripture*.[19] Old Master Han had two sons. The elder was named Han Hui; he married a woman of the Zheng family. The younger was named Han Yu, styled Tuizhi; he married a woman of the Dou family.

The two brothers got along well, their marriages were harmonious, and their household was at peace. Everything was perfect, except for the fact that neither of them could beget a son. All his life Han Hui was saddened by this and often said to his brother Tuizhi, "Those who enjoy a long life have no wealth. Those who have wealth do not have an official position. Those who have an official position have no sons. The allotments of fate are uneven, but to be childless is the saddest of them all. What could be worse than still to be without children at our age?" A poem shall illustrate his state of mind:

> In silence often sighing,
> In darkness lost in confusion.
> All because he has no descendants—
> Day and night his suffering is difficult to bear.

Tuizhi said, "That may be so, but please don't be despondent. Our family has accumulated merit for nine generations. Surely Heaven will give you a worthy son by way of retribution, and won't leave you without so much as a tail to chase away the flies. There is no reason to worry. If only we burn incense and worship all day long, and pray to Heaven, Earth, and our ancestors, we are sure to get a response."

Following Tuizhi's suggestion Han Hui thereupon prayed piously every day. His prayers moved the local city and earth gods, as well as the six fate-supervising spirits of the kitchen, who together submitted a memorial to the Jade Emperor, requesting him to grant a son to Han Hui. This is how the memorial was phrased:

> Your ministers, the six fate-supervising spirits, the earth gods and city god of Changli County in Yongping Prefecture, knock their heads and submit the following memorial to the Jade Emperor, the Exalted Worthy of the Golden Palace in the Vast Heavens: We have heard that, being seated high and august as the jade pinnacle, Your Majesty has the authority to bestow blessings on the common people; that as the Golden Worthy of Great Veil Heaven, Your Majesty opens the way for all beings to renew themselves. Whenever someone reaches out in prayer, he is certain to receive a response. Now there are Han Hui and Han Yu of Changli County whose family has accumulated merit for nine generations and who have revered the esoteric scriptures all their life. Because they are without a son, they have earnestly implored Heaven. We respectfully request that Your Majesty will testify to their reverence by extending your auspicious light to them, that in view of their respectfully sincere hearts you will bestow on them a handsome son. In this way they will forever receive the shelter of the Dao and the sincerity of their minds will not be disregarded. They will fully benefit from your abundant grace, which will further strengthen their worshipful reverence. As the disc of the moon keeps turning in eternity, so the strength of a vow is limitless. Your ministers look up to Heaven with intense reverence, earnestly awaiting the arrival of Your Majesty's orders. Respectfully we submit this memorial for your consideration.

After perusing the memorial, the Jade Emperor gave an imperial commission, as well as magic methods and divine techniques, to the divine immortals Zhongli Quan and Lü Dongbin. These two were to go to the lower realm to save a meritorious person to be used by Heaven for its purposes. If there was to be found one whose cultivation was not yet complete and who needed to be reborn as a human once more, they should dispatch him to the household of Han Hui, there to attain deliverance and final transformation by first entering a womb. Later, when he had accumulated sufficient merit and was no longer confused by his previous karma, they were to go again and save him, so that he might reap the fruits of his efforts. Having received their orders, Zhong and Lü descended from Heaven on a cloud.

On the way the immortal Zhong said to the immortal Lü, "When someone becomes an immortal, he is released from the corpse and ascends to Heaven. There he goes to the immortality peach banquet, where he eats *jiao* pears and fire dates. As a result he enjoys a life-span of ten thousand years and all his descendants and ancestors ascend to the realm of the immortals together. Why is it then that so many people in this vast world only know how to sink into the sea of desire, drown in the river of love, savagely indulge in wine and sex, and arrogantly abuse wealth and power? Why are they unwilling to abandon wife and children and leave their family like cast-off shoes so as to compound the reverted elixir of the nine cycles, and enjoy eternal life without aging?"

"Humans live in the world like fish in water," the immortal Lü replied. "At first they spend their life at ease until, alas, the line plunges into the water from the fishing rod. They throw themselves on the delicious bait until they swallow the hook and are drawn out by it, are cut up and cooked. How many are there who can quench the fire of their mind, still the waves of consciousness, firmly maintain the vast and diffuse primordial pneuma, grasp the seeds of Former Heaven, and hold up sun and moon with both hands?"

"The five turbidities confuse the mind, the three paths lead the feet astray, and as a result people get entangled in lust and resentment," the immortal Zhong said. "If they do not get to swallow a golden elixir pill, they will find it hard to slip their mortal frame. The two of us have today descended into the world of mortals with an imperial commission. In which prefecture and which county will we get to meet an appropriate person?"

Before the immortal Lü could reply, they suddenly saw in the southeast a ray of white pneuma rising up and penetrating the clouds, somewhat like a rainbow. What was so unusual about this pneuma?

> Neither smoke nor mist, yet cloudlike. Neither smoke nor mist, yet
> casting a haze over the clear air. Cloudlike it rose to fill the blue sky.
> Reaching the empyrean, penetrating the Milky Way, striking the sun
> and shading the sky. No thunder was heard and there was no trace of
> wind or rain. Yet the sky was filled with pure and bright white light,
> gathered into an arc. Those who divine by examining pneumata
> would not see in it the Emperor's Pneuma, nor the Pneuma of Divine
> Immortals, nor the Demonic Pneuma, nor the Sea Monster Pneuma.

Those who observe clouds would not recognize in it the Royal Cloud, nor the High Minister's Cloud, nor the General's Cloud, nor the Retired Scholar's Cloud. It is just a ray of white—pneuma or cloud? Looking at it carefully, it is a coiled mass suspended in mid-air, and it is not clear whether good or ill portents can be read from it. A waft of immortal's wind will blow it away, forcing it to drift along exposed roots on the flat ground.

Pointing to the phenomenon, Lü said to Zhong, "This white pneuma rising to the sky seems to come from Cangwu Prefecture by the banks of the Xiang River. Being neither divine nor ordinary, it is likely of demonic origin. Let's blow our immortal pneuma toward it. If it is of immortal quality itself, the pneuma will deflect our wind; if it is demonic, it will itself be deflected."

Thereupon the immortal Zhong lifted his beard to one side, opened his great lion-like mouth, and blew a mouthful of pneuma towards the southeast. It turned into a strong gust of wind which completely deflected the soaring ray of white pneuma.

When Lü opened his eyes of wisdom and peered toward the place where the ray had arisen, he saw two animals spouting pneuma. One was a musk deer doing mischief, the other a white crane playing tricks. Needless to say, the two immortals flew there quick as the wind.

The white crane and the musk deer there on the bank of the Xiang River were just showing off their magical powers, playing to their hearts' delight, when they suddenly saw the gust of wind blowing past and deflecting their white pneuma. They realized that two divine immortals were about to arrive. Quite unhurried, they shook themselves and changed into the shape of Complete Perfection Daoists, and then stood beside the river to await the immortal masters.

How were they dressed?

One wore on his head a cap made from bamboo sheaths, the other had his hair dressed in a yin-yang pattern. One wore a robe trimmed with black down, around his waist a silken sash; the other a gown of yellow cloth, bound with a soft belt. One wore on his feet tied shoes of hemp, looking like Kuafu of ancient myth who pursued the wind and chased the sun.[20] The other was shod with straw sandals and had the appearance of a divine immortal who rides the clouds and paces the moon. Truly, their faces were lighthearted and fresh, their attire original and strange.

When they saw the two masters approaching from afar, they stepped forward, knocked their heads and repeatedly honored them, saying, "Masters, we are two followers of the Way of Complete Perfection cultivating ourselves on the bank of the Xiang River in Cangwu Prefecture. We were slow in welcoming you, please forgive us."

Master Lü pointed to the white crane and said, "You actually are a companion of phoenix and simurgh, how dare you hide your head and tail?"

Again he pointed at the musk deer and said, "You actually are kin to foxes and dogs, how dare you conceal your name?"

When the crane heard his true identity spoken, he lowered his head and remained silent, not daring to reply. The musk deer on the other hand came forward and said, "We really are practitioners of Complete Perfection—do not mistake men for animals, masters!"

"Lying wretch, wanting to hoodwink me with crafty words!" Master Lü said. "Do you think my sword isn't sharp?"

These words frightened the white crane greatly. Lowering himself on both knees he said, "Master, a human body is hard to obtain, a prosperous lifetime is hard to come upon. Although I am an animal, my refined spirit has already undergone transformation. Now my skeleton of immortality is already complete, but I have not yet escaped from this feathered body. Day after day I have faced the wind and absorbed the dew, but have not yet reaped the final reward. I hope that you will take pity on me and spare me a pill of golden elixir, enabling me to shed my feathers and be reborn through your grace."

Hearing the white crane's words, Master Zhong said, "This crane's knowledge of nature and spirit is quite advanced and he fully understands human thinking. His rebirth would fulfill a prophecy. Let us deliver him and take him to the Jade Emperor for further deliberation. This musk deer's bad karma, on the other hand, is as heavy as a mountain. I have no use for you. For now be forgiven and be off, but if you continue to behave recklessly and out of accord with your proper lot, I have my sword of wisdom and my divine lance with which I can get at you as I wheel in the air."

"If you won't deliver me, that's fine with me," the musk deer said. "The scenery here by the river is just as good as at the Three Isles of the Immortals or Mount Kunlun. I'll keep to my proper lot, as you said, and pass my days here."

"Why do you think the scenery by the Xiang River is as good as that of the Three Isles of the Immortals or Mount Kunlun?" Master Zhong asked.

"I'm not just bragging," the musk deer answered. "Here in Cangwu, by the river, ducks float in the mornings and geese in the evenings. Below them black-

and white-scaled turtles dive and frolic. A clear light suffuses everything at sunrise, and the setting sun illuminates the landscape with its slanting rays. In winter lines of frost give off a blue shine that dazzles the eye. In summer elegant flowers and wild herbs are covered with fog and surrounded by mist. My love for this place is deeper than that of the birds which inhabit its skies and the fish which dwell in its depths. It is so much better than the Penglai Isles of the Immortals or the Weak Water of Mount Kunlun, which by comparison are an endless sea of suffering—difficult for a boat to cross or the dreaming soul to traverse."

"From what you say, it does not seem to be at all superior to our land of the immortals. Your bragging is quite useless," Master Lü said.

The musk deer retorted, "Let me offer a poem to prove my point:

"The scenery in Cangwu is refreshing,
In the mountain mists at the Xiang River I sleep well fed and well clad.
White gulls are floating, aware of the setting sun,
Purple swallows twitter of the fine mist against a clear sky.
Swaying red in the light breeze, flowers are opening with a smile,
A luxuriant green, the grass stretches away before my eyes.
Venerable masters, if you came to this place,
You too would forsake Great Veil Heaven."

"Sinful beast, you are utterly devoid of manners," Master Lü said. "Only after ridding ourselves of love and desires do we immortals succeed in completing perfection and realizing our rewards. You are unprincipled and sinful; your mind is filled with greed for profit. What good is there in your reckless boasts?"

At the same time he thought to himself, "He doesn't understand life and death and is just puffing himself up with deceitful words. I'll deliver the crane and take him up to Heaven, while banishing this musk deer to a deep pool where he cannot see the light of day. Once the crane has become an immortal, he'll come to save the deer and make him a great guardian deity of the mountain. This will display the marvelous schemes of which we immortals are capable."

Then he recited some words under his breath and shouted, "Quickly!"

A bright heavenly light shone forth; a black fog gathered. In mid-air a celestial general appeared in a flash and stood in front of the assembled group. How was this general dressed?

On his head was an iron helmet, lacquered black and red; in his hand was a steel rod inlaid with silver threads. Golden dragons writhed on his gown of black gauze, jade pendants dangled high from his lion-buckled belt. His face was as black as the soot under a pot, his lips blood red as if painted vermilion. To his left stood a strong man with a yellow headcloth, to his right the Great Black Tiger Spirit. Flaming fire wheels circled him, fluttering black flags heralded his coming. Truly, it was Marshal Zhao of the Dark Altar, who subdues dragons and tigers—he has no fear of your tricks, you mischievous musk deer![21]

Arriving in a gust of wind, the celestial general bowed and inquired, "What is your command, my master?"

"This musk deer has committed sins that cannot be tolerated by Heaven," Master Lü said.

With one hand the general took up his steel rod and with the other grasped the musk deer. He was just about to get to work on him, when Master Zhong called, "Let us spare this sinful beast's life and banish him to a deep pool among the rivers and lakes. He shall not be allowed to so much as poke out his head until the crane has achieved his proper reward and has ascended to the ranks of the immortals. Then he will come to save the musk deer so that he may serve as guardian of the gate to this grotto-heaven. However, if you do not behave in accordance with your proper lot, but again stir up wind and thunder and harm passing travelers, you will right away be cast into hell."

Following his orders, the celestial general picked up the musk deer and took him to a deep and secluded spot among the rivers and lakes. There he locked him up tightly, giving him no slack whatsoever.

Unable to employ any of his powers, the musk deer wailed and beseeched the general, "I have offended the immortal masters and deserve to die ten thousand deaths. This banishment surely satisfies the desire for retribution. But I am an animal used to roaming the mountains, passing its days eating grass and flowers. Now that I am buried below the water, I will surely drown or die of hunger! Please save me!"

"You do not understand the schemes of immortals," the celestial general replied. "If they spared your life, of course you won't die. So why fear drowning or starvation? Just collect your mind and absorb pneuma, manifest your nature and complete your spirit, while you wait for the crane to save you."

The musk deer bowed. "Many thanks for these instructions, but I don't know how long it will be before the crane comes to save me!"

After the general had left, the musk deer remained locked up in this place, where truly he was submerged in water on all sides. There was no food and he could not roam freely, so he faced upward and stretched, looked down and contracted, closed in his breath, and swallowed his essence. No longer did he dare engage in reckless behavior, which might bring further punishment upon him. It is just as stated by the following poem:

Quarrels are caused by talking too much,
Trouble comes from willfully sticking one's head out.
Now he has learned the way of the turtle,
To pull in his head at the right time.

What happened afterwards? Hear it all explained in the next chapter.

2

DISCUSSING ASTROLOGY AND PHYSIOGNOMY, ZHONG AND LÜ
CONCEAL THEIR NAMES

I sigh at the bustling business of the world,
I laugh at this floating life, so like a restless shuttle shooting back and
forth.
Their sable coats dyed,
Their teams of horses moving in a stately manner,
People fight for fame and grasp for profit without pause for thought,
Caught in reckless thoughts, greed, and anger, and deranged by their
lack of human feelings.
Heroes may have arisen and fallen since olden times,
And poor scholars still keep to their own cold windows day and night.
All this is still no match for a ride on the clouds and mists,
Seeking out a recipe for long life without death.

After Master Lü had banished the musk deer to the bottom of the lake by the Xiang
River, the celestial general bowed with folded hands, reported on his mission, and
left. Master Zhong then took a golden elixir pill from his bottle-gourd and gave
it to the crane to eat. The crane forthwith changed his form and became a young
lad clothed in a green robe. Together with his two immortal teachers, he proceeded
to Changli County in Yongping Prefecture.

Just as they approached the gate of the Han family's mansion, it so happened that Han Tuizhi came out to greet a visitor at the door. The two immortal masters saw that his countenance was dignified and his clothes were orderly and proper. Invisible to all but them, above his head there was a rosy ray of light, and he was followed by a boy carrying an incense pot. They knew right away that he was Chonghezi, the Attendant Great General of the Left, who had been banished to be reborn in this family because of his drunken and disruptive behavior at the immortality peach banquet. Unfortunately, unaware of his previous existence, he later would turn to slandering Daoism and criticizing Buddhism.

The two immortals turned around and conferred with each other. "Chonghezi is already nearly forty years old, yet he still hasn't looked back and become awakened. If he again falls into the fiery pit, into this bustling world full of greed, hankering, and distractions, there may be no escape for him. His older brother Han Hui burns incense and lights candles all day long, praying for a son. Let's go back and submit a memorial to the Jade Emperor, proposing to give the crane boy to Han Hui as a son. Once he has grown up, we will come again to deliver him so that he may become an immortal and complete the Way. Then he in turn can deliver Chonghezi so that he may resume his original position. Wouldn't that solve two problems in one stroke?"

Having made their decision, the two masters turned their cloud around and ascended to the heavenly realm, taking the crane boy along. In no time at all they arrived at the Gate of Southern Heaven and reported on their mission, describing how they had received the imperial commission, traveled to the banks of the Xiang River in Cangwu County, delivered the crane, and so on. The Jade Emperor issued a new decree ordering the two masters to convey the crane boy to the Han family of Changli County in Yongping Prefecture, to be reborn there as a human and to await his later employment.

Having received the decree, they said to the crane boy, "We shall give you another elixir to swallow, which will transform you into an immortality peach. Then we'll convey you to the womb of Madame Zheng, the wife of Han Hui in Changli County of Yongping Prefecture. One month after your birth we shall come to see you and give you a magical elixir and charm water. Once you are sixteen years old, we will teach you how to complete the Way and ascend to the ranks of the immortals to enjoy eternal life without aging. So as not to violate the Jade Emperor's decree, do not divulge this heavenly secret."

In tears the crane boy pleaded with his masters, "When I finally escaped from this body that I had received by way of punishment, I looked forward to achieving perfection and its attending rewards, and to roaming at ease with you, my masters. I didn't expect that I would first have to be reborn as a human, becoming immersed in the river of blood and bound up in the dusty nets of the world. I don't want to go."

"The imperial decree has already been issued," the two masters said. "Who would dare disobey it? Besides, although you have shed your animal hide, you have never compounded the great elixir. The only way for you to attain your goal of immortality is to go through the ten months of gestation, relying on your parents' essence and blood—just like the Most High Lord Lao, who was born from the womb of a jade maiden and only then appeared to cultivate himself and realize his rewards."

"If I have to be reborn before I can become an immortal, then why didn't you have me reborn right away when you transformed me on the banks of the Xiang River, rather than taking me to an audience with the Jade Emperor and only then sending me back to the human world? It would have saved a lot of suffering and hassle."

"We did not dare act without an imperial decree," Master Lü replied.

"I would like to present a poem to you, " the crane boy said.

> "On the bank of the River Xiang I met my honored teachers.
> Delivered by them, I flew to Heaven for an audience with the Jade
>   Emperor.
> Now that I already have escaped from my feathered body,
> Why do I have to descend to earth to become a human once more?"

"I also have a poem," Master Lü said. "Listen closely:

> "You must not worry over the delay,
> But serve your turn in the Han family.
> Your merit completed, you will go to the Jade Palace,
> As sure as the river in Cangwu will still be flowing east."

The crane boy realized that the masters had given him their final instructions. He had no choice but to swallow the golden elixir pill, which transformed him into an immortality peach. The peach in hand, the two masters flew straight to the Han family's mansion. It so happened that it was the third watch, and so the two masters dispatched a spirit to bestow a dream on Han Hui's wife, Mme. Zheng. She dreamt that as the sun rose in the east like a precious mirror suspended high in the sky, an immortal crane came flying down; in its beak it carried an immortality peach, which it let fall into her womb. Beside her there appeared in a flash of light a Daoist wearing a green headcloth and a cotton gown and carrying a precious sword on his shoulder. In a loud voice he called out, "Mme. Zheng, wife of Han Hui, I am Master Two Mouths.[1] I have received an imperial decree to give you this immortality peach for a son. Remember well the command I will give you:

> *"Mme. Zheng, look up and listen to what I say.*
> *The words of immortals are never false.*
> *I send you a son to continue your ancestral line,*
> *But later he will ride the wind to the Nine Heavens."*

Startled, Mme. Zheng awoke from her dream. Overjoyed, she awakened Han Hui and said to him, "At the first watch I couldn't sleep. At the second watch I was still tossing and turning. When I finally went to sleep at the third watch, I had a dream. I dreamt that as the sun rose in the east like a precious mirror suspended high in the sky, an immortal crane came flying down; in its beak it carried an immortality peach, which it let fall into my womb. There was also a Daoist wearing a green headcloth and a cotton gown and carrying a precious sword on his shoulder. He told me that the peach would become our son. Don't you think this dream was extraordinary?"

Joyfully Han Hui replied, "I had the same dream! I am now forty-two years old and still without a son. I think divine Heaven has observed our hidden sincerity, and, having decided that we should not be without posterity, has sent us a son to continue the family line. Surely this is why the divine immortal from Heaven has given this clear and explicit order. Let's burn incense to thank Heaven and then wait and see what happens."

"You are right," Mme. Zheng said. She dressed hurriedly, combed her hair, and washed herself so as to look seemly. Together with Han Hui she burnt precious candles and expensive incense and bowed to Heaven eight times.

At daylight, Han Hui told the dream in all detail to his brother Tuizhi. Delighted, Tuizhi said, "According to this dream omen, my sister-in-law will certainly give birth to a worthy son who will continue the Han family line. Truly, it was not in vain that our family accumulated merit for many generations." A poem proves a fitting illustration:

> *Those who accumulate goodness have a surplus of blessings.*
> *How could misfortune not follow evil deeds?*
> *For nine generations the Han family's hidden merit has been abundant,*
> *And so Heaven has bestowed a baby on their humble household.*

Suffice it to say that time flew like an arrow, the days and months raced by like a shuttle on a loom, and joy filled this meritorious household. In no time at all, Mme. Zheng gave birth to a son. The boy's earlobes were so long that they touched his shoulders; his hands reached further than his knees; his face looked as if it were powdered, his lips as if painted vermilion. Truly he was a beautiful boy. Great joy filled the household and all the relatives came to offer their congratulations. It really was like the saying "A unicorn has its seed in Heaven; in the human world, the most joyful thing is when an oyster gives birth to a pearl."

As it turned out, however, throughout the first month of his life the baby cried incessantly day and night. When Han Hui saw the state of things, he became very worried. "This is no ordinary child," he said to his wife. "I am sure he'll be fine later on, but this crying reminds me of a passage I read: 'If a baby cries at night, he will cause the downfall of his parents.' It's probably because I was not fated to have a son. I think we should get a relative to adopt him. Once he is grown up, we can take him back. That should work, shouldn't it?"

"Before, we couldn't have a son, and prayed day and night to Heaven, Earth, and the ancestors, fearing that the family would remain without posterity," Mme. Zheng replied. "Thanks to Heaven's protection and the ancestors' merit, we have this child now and everything is well. I don't think his incessant wailing means that he won't make it to maturity and that I suffered the misery of my pregnancy in vain. If we give him up for adoption to another family, people will slight him for it later. It would be better to give him as a son to your brother. I am just afraid that my sister-in-law won't be happy about it."

As they were talking, they heard someone out on the street walking past their gate, striking a fisher drum and chanting a Daoist song.[2] As soon as the child heard the sound of the fisher drum, he stopped crying; when he could not hear it any more, he started to cry again. It was really very strange. Reader, what were the words of the fisher drum singer that caused the child to stop crying and listen? The Daoist who struck the fisher drum was Master Lü, and he sang a song to the tune of "Cassia Fragrance," which reminded the baby of his previous existence as the crane boy. The child awakened with a start, stopped crying, and listened to the song:

> "*Crane Boy, awaken!*
> *Your teacher has come to look after you.*
> *From when I delivered you to Changli last year*
> *Until today,*
> *I was absent from your noble dwelling.*

Don't cry,
Don't cry,
But listen to my command.
Are you now at ease?
Though you suffer restrictions for a while,
Later you will ascend to the Purple Empyrean,
And your name will be engraved in the Grotto Court of Heaven.
Crane child, be patient,
While for now you dwell outside of Heaven.
You may sigh at the slow rotation of summer and winter,
But in the turn of a hand, two years will have passed.
Think, little child of the Han family, think!
You have extraordinary ability,
Truly the stuff of which great ministers are made.
Originally you were a guest in Great Veil Heaven,
From whose jade-paved streets you descended because you hankered for
  the mortal world."

When Han Hui saw that the baby had stopped crying and was listening to the song, he remarked to Mme. Zheng, "I think the child likes to listen to fisher drum music. Let's call in this musician to entertain him for a while. I'll ask him—he probably knows some music that might make the child stop crying."

Mme. Zheng summoned the servant Zhang Qian and said, "Go and ask this fisher drum player inside."

Zhang Qian hurried out to the street and called, "Daoist, come back! My master wants to have a word with you."

"Would that be the Lord Han?" the Daoist asked.

"Such foreknowledge is like that of a divine immortal," Zhang Qian replied.

"I am not quite a divine immortal," said the Daoist. Then, following Zhang Qian, he entered the gate with a proud bearing, knocked his head in front of Han Hui, and inquired, "In what matter did you call upon this humble Daoist, my lord?"

Han Hui replied, "I have only one son, who since his birth a month ago has cried incessantly. I was deep in worries just now, unable to think of a solution, when I heard the fisher drum. The boy stopped crying and seemed to listen to it. So I asked you in to play the fisher drum and sing a Daoist song to entertain him for a while."

"Nothing could be easier than to make this child stop crying," said the Daoist. "Bring him here and let me have a look at him. I guarantee he will cry no more."

"If you really succeed, you will be richly rewarded," Han Hui told him. From behind the screen, Mme. Zheng gave the child to Han Hui, who handed him to the Daoist, saying, "This is my son."

The Daoist felt the child's forehead and said, "You need not cry. You will pass sixteen uneventful years before you look for me in the Zhongnan Mountains. When your merit is full, you will ascend to the Jade Emperor's capital, and assist your family below."

The boy seemed happy when he heard these words, and stopped crying.

"Sir, what is your name and home district?" Han Hui inquired.

"I am a poor Daoist who has abandoned his family to cultivate himself. People call me Master Two Mouths, and that's my name. As for a home district, I do not have one," Master Lü informed him.

From behind the screen, Mme. Zheng whispered to Han Hui, "The dream foretold that a Master Two Mouths would bring the child. Could this Master Two Mouths be the divine immortal from the dream?"

"Wandering ascetics are always using assumed names," Han Hui said. "Why should we believe him?"

The Daoist laughed. "The name is identical, but the person may not be the same. Why do you look down on people, my lord?"

"Please forgive me," Han Hui said. "The child is happy and has stopped crying. May I trouble you to choose a childhood name for him?"

"In a distinguished scholarly family, why bother with a childhood name? Let's choose a school name for him," the Daoist suggested.

Han Hui thanked him. "That would be even better," he said.

"I walked here on the road along the Xiang River and saw its billowing fog and rushing water, flowing east and turning west," the Daoist began. "In ten thousand years it has never dried up, a truly eternal river. Now I choose for your son the name Han Xiang; his childhood name shall be Xiangzi. I pray that he will grow up easily, without calamities and disasters. Later he will become as famous and rich as the Xiang River is vast. His longevity and good health shall be as uninterrupted as the flow of the Xiang."

"Many thanks for your instruction. Will you stay for a vegetarian meal?" Han Hui offered. But the Daoist spread out his sleeves and vanished in a ray of golden light. He left behind the fisher drum, which stood up straight on the floor. When Han Hui went to pick it up, he found that he could not lift it. Mme. Zheng came forward and tried, but she could not pull it up either. They called others to try and move it, but not even with four, five, or even ten people pulling at it could it be budged. It was as if it had taken root.

"That Daoist surely was a divine immortal!" Mme. Zheng exclaimed. "He was offended because we didn't recognize him, and left this fisher drum as proof. Face to face with an immortal, we did not recognize him. Hurry, ask your brother to come and look. Then we'll know for sure."

Han Hui quickly sent someone for Tuizhi. When he arrived, Mme. Zheng said, "This is why we asked you here: Your nephew just wouldn't stop crying. Luckily a Daoist striking a fisher drum and singing songs came by. When the child heard him, he finally quieted down. Your older brother invited the Daoist in to play the fisher drum and sing Daoist songs for the child's amusement. The Daoist said that this boy will become a man of great talents. He spoke to him, and chose for him the school name Han Xiang. Your older brother invited him for a vegetarian meal, but he just shook his sleeves, transformed into a ray of golden light, and disappeared. He left behind this fisher drum, which neither your older brother nor several men together can lift. So we called you to have a look and see if you have an explanation."

Tuizhi went forward and pulled lightly at the drum. It lifted off the floor with no resistance, as if it were drifting duckweed or rootless grass. On its bottom, lustrous as jade, was written "Master Chunyang."[3] Tuizhi said, "This was Lü Dongbin descended from Heaven. Naturally your mortal eyes would not recognize him. Divine immortals are not willing to explain themselves clearly, but leave behind clues for mortals to figure out." The whole family lit incense and candles, faced toward Heaven, and gave thanks.

A year went by, and Xiangzi's first-year test was soon to come. Han Hui was still full of joy, but ever since Xiangzi had encountered the Daoist, he seemed struck dumb, as if he were made of clay or wood. He did not cry, but neither did he laugh. It was as if (as the saying goes) they had bought him a mouth that wouldn't open. If they gave him his three meals a day, he would eat them, but if they didn't give him anything, he would not insist. While on the outside he thus appeared confused, within his mind he understood everything that was going on. Everyone called him "the mute little master." Mme. Zheng did not know what to do.

Soon the boy was three years old, but still he did not make the slightest progress. Han Hui thought to himself, "At this age, Xiangzi still can't even speak half a sentence. People are going to make fun of him unnecessarily. Truly, it's like the saying 'You shouldn't insist on asking for a son, if it is your fate not to have one. If you do insist, you may get one, but your worries will then only increase.' In the past Bodao didn't have a son and could cast off all his worries."[4]

Han Hui was very unhappy. Worrying day and night, he contracted a disease and died. Weeping, Tuizhi performed the mourning rites, prepared the coffin, ceremonially placed Han Hui's body in it, and buried him in the ancestral tomb.

One day Tuizhi ordered Zhang Qian, "My deceased brother had only this one child. He was hoping that his son would grow up, marry, and have children of his own, who would continue the Han family line. Who would have expected that at three, he would still not be able to speak? He must be mute, and it is useless to raise a mute child. Go out and find a good fortune-teller who can calculate his fate on the basis of his eight characters.[5] If I later have a son of my own, he can become the one to sweep the family tombs."[6]

Up in the clouds, Master Lü heard Tuizhi's words. He traveled down on a cloud and took the form of a fortune-teller, walking up and down the Han family's street and shouting in a loud voice, "Fortunes told! Fortunes told!"

How was this fortune-teller dressed?

> A folded headcloth, crooked in front, rucked up in the back. A green cotton gown, skewed on the left and wrinkled on the right. Two restless eyes regarding the blue sky, two nervous hands swinging an abacus.
> He shouted, "I can explain the original fate and understand its roots and sources. If one of my fate calculations turns out to be wrong, I'll happily pay a penalty of two cash."

Zhang Qian quickly invited him into the house to see Tuizhi. "What is your name and where do you come from?" Tuizhi asked him.

"I am called Kai Kouling.[7] I have been traveling for many years and am very skilled in calculating accurate fortunes. When I meet a crown prince, my calculations reveal him to be a member of the imperial family. When I meet a divine immortal, I can calculate that he is a descendant of Lord Lao. When I meet a wife, I can calculate that her husband is the prime minister or some other high official. When I meet a monk, I can calculate that he is destined to lead a celibate religious life."

"The way you put it, fortune-telling seems to be a meddlesome business," Tuizhi commented.

"The way I put it, a person's eight characters hold many obscure marvels," countered Master Lü. "What would be your question, my lord?"

"Please divine my nephew's fate. If you get it wrong, I will fine you two cash."

"Since I set out this morning, I haven't had much business," complained Master Lü. "If you want to fine me, pay me my fee first. That way I can pay the fine if I go wrong."

"If you come out with this kind of obnoxious talk, I won't trouble you for your services."

"Please tell me his eight characters," Master Lü said.

"First year of the Jianzhong reign period, the noon hour of the first day of the second month,"[8] Tuizhi replied.

"That makes a *gengshen* year, *jimao* month, *xinyou* day, and *jiawu* hour. *Gengshen* is the position of the white monkey sitting on the immortality peach tree. *Jimao* denotes the jade rabbit returning to the Penglai Isles of the Immortals. *Xinyou* means the golden chicken entering the Sun Palace. *Jiawu* is the simurgh flying to the Jade Palace. These eight characters are not those of an ordinary mortal. Their owner has the lot to serve three emperors as a high minister, and the talent of seven generations of top graduates in the metropolitan examinations. By the age of twenty, he will have had his name entered in the Purple Office and at the Jasper Pool; all of his relatives will achieve perfection, and the whole family will attain divine status. However, if he is willing to study, he will achieve the highest official position, but then his life span will be short. Currently the owner of these eight characters is undergoing the effects of a 'tomb store' fate constellation; as a result his mind is darkened and his tongue mute, so that he is like a useless, discarded object. When he is seven or eight, his fate will change and he will naturally excel over others."

"Right now he is like a mute and cannot even read," Tuizhi said. "As for studying to become an immortal, the world holds only celestial immortals, terrestrial immortals, divine immortals, ghost immortals, and—at the lowest rank—the so-called obtuse immortals.[9] How could there be a mute immortal?"

"His face is clear and extraordinary, his appearance of classical simplicity; his mind is highly perspicacious, and his nature is endowed with high intelligence. The day he opens his mouth to speak, it will be as if Confucius's disciples Yan Hui and Zigong were born again," Master Lü replied. The two men were immersed in animated conversation when Master Zhong, who had descended on a cloud and transformed himself into a physiognomist, called in a loud voice outside the mansion, "By examining face and shape, I can recognize a future emperor in the yellow mud of an impoverished hovel. By examining words and studying expressions, I can recognize a future high minister in a commoner's household. If it is an immortal descended into the world of dust, I also know his past, present, and future."

When Zhang Qian heard these impressive words, he hurried inside and said to Tuizhi, "My lord, this fortune-teller isn't that extraordinary. Outside there is a physiognomist who claims to be Tang Ju reincarnate and Xu Fu reborn.[10] Why not invite him in?"

Master Lü knew that it was Master Zhong, who had come to the human world. He said, "My lord, you say that my fate calculation is not accurate. Let's invite this physiognomist in and see whether what he says accords with my own judgment."

So Tuizhi ordered Zhang Qian to invite him in. Zhang Qian brought the physiognomist into the hall, where he seated himself opposite the fortune-teller. Tuizhi then pointed to Xiangzi and said, "Please read the face of this child."

The physiognomist peered at him closely. "His earlobes hang down to his shoulders; purple mist coils around him. His hands extend below his knees; a golden light is manifest. The corners of his eyes are rich and full; his lower cheekbones are upright and rounded. His spirit is clear and his pneuma bright. His bones are firm and complete. If he does not become a personal retainer of an emperor, he will certainly become an immortal of the Penglai Isles. This boy is not a common person."

"The arts of astrology and physiognomy are different in their techniques, and each arrives at its own conclusions, yet today they agree," Master Lü said. "How could that not be due to the young gentleman's eight characters and physique?"

"I would ask you, my lord, to sit upright so I can examine your physiognomy," Master Zhong added. "How about it?"

"I was just going to request it," Tuizhi replied.

Master Zhong lifted Tuizhi's headcloth. "Your forehead is high and broad; the lower cheek bones are square yet rounded. The ears are high above the shoulder. The nose is well developed. The upper cheek bones point heavenwards, a sign that you will wield authority over ten thousand miles. The bones of your brow rise up, which shows your complete loyalty to one school of thought. Forehead, cheekbones, chin, and nose all bow toward Heaven—your name will be on the yellow list of top examination graduates. The temple bones show that you will suffer few illnesses in your life. The tread of a crane and the breathing of a turtle are signs of a celestial immortal. Bones and spirit tell me, however, that in the end you will suffer misfortunes. In my humble opinion:

> *"Dragon and Tiger are difficult to part,*
> *But phoenix and simurgh must leave the flock.*
> *After eight thousand miles in wind and frost,*
> *There will be a certain person waiting for you."* [11]

"Thank you very much for your instructions, but what do your words mean?" asked Tuizhi.

"These four verses contain the course of your life and will be verified by later events," Master Zhong told him.

"My nephew Xiangzi is four years old, but still can't speak, just like a mute," Tuizhi said. "What can be done about this?"

Discussing astrology and physiognomy, Zhong and Lü conceal their names

The Masters said, "What difficulty is there in getting the young gentleman to speak? Here is a pill. Tomorrow at the fifth watch, have the young gentleman take it with some 'rootless water.'[12] He will then be able to speak."

Overjoyed, Tuizhi received the pill. He ordered Zhang Qian to divide up two ounces of silver into two packages and presented them to the two masters, but they just laughed and would not accept a single coin. Into Xiangzi's ear they whispered the following order:

> "Do not worry, Crane Boy.
> You need to understand earlier causes and their later effects.
> The elixir drug will sweep clear your demonic obstructions,
> And you will be sure to ascend to the Isles of the Immortals soon."

With these words, they walked out the door with their heads held high. When Tuizhi sent someone to run after them, they had disappeared mysteriously. He could see only auspicious clouds swirling in the sky and a propitious crane flying and calling beyond the clouds. Tuizhi thought to himself, "Perhaps these two were immortals, but perhaps not. Let's wait until the fifth watch when my nephew takes the pill, and see if it works. However, he said that my name will be on the yellow list of top examination graduates and that I will be appointed a minister. I wonder how many years this will take. Tomorrow I'll gather my travel money, go to the capital, and sit for the examinations. Then I will know more."

A poem puts it well:

> When your time comes, the wind will convey you to the Pavilion
>   of King Teng,[13]
> But when your destiny retreats, lightning will destroy the Stele of Rec-
>   ommended Blessings.[14]
> One day just like the flood-dragon achieving his wind and rain,
> A young talented scholar will reach his ambitions and return home
>   clothed in brocade.

Did Tuizhi go to the capital or didn't he? Listen to the next chapter to find out.

3

HAN YU INSCRIBES HIS NAME ON THE TIGER PLACARD

XIANGZI DRINKS THE WEDDING CUP IN THE NUPTIAL
CHAMBER

Riches and rank are like dew on a twig,
Success in the examinations like a bubble on water.
Gold at your girdle and robes of purple—these are as halters for
    a horse,
And a rope through your nose won't be far behind.
The lucky groom's arrow hits the peacocks on the screen;[1]
As he pulls the silk thread, the beauty behind the screen blushes.[2]
In the nuptial chamber the newlyweds meet in bliss,
But once the play is over, the puppets are just wooden images after all.

At the fifth watch, Tuizhi quickly stirred the pill into pure rootless water and gave it to Xiangzi to drink. It felt like thunder in his stomach, and his throat seemed to become unlocked. Soon he spat out all kinds of unclean matter, then opened his mouth and called out, "Uncle!"

His heart filled with joy, Tuizhi said, "Thanks be to Heaven and Earth—this drug truly is of divine effectiveness!"

However, when Mme. Zheng and Mme. Dou came to question Xiangzi, as before he did not say a word. Tuizhi said, "Stop chattering and worrying! Since he has already spoken once, of course he will speak again. Quick, pack my luggage! I will travel to the capital to seek success in the examinations. If I secure even the smallest appointment, I will return home to glorify the ancestors and justify the long years I spent studying."

Then Tuizhi took leave of the whole family. Pressing on relentlessly during an arduous journey, he arrived and sat for the examinations—but unexpectedly he failed. He was ashamed to return home and so remained in the capital, doing all kinds of odd jobs to survive and living on other people's pity. In the meantime Xiangzi still did not utter a word. There was nothing Mme. Zheng could do about it, but she still hoped that when he had grown up, he would marry and beget a son to continue the Han family line.

When Xiangzi was seven years old, Mme. Zheng fell ill and died. As Mme. Dou took it upon herself to take care of all the funeral arrangements, Xiangzi wept like an adult, deeply aware of the loss he had suffered. In front of Mme. Zheng's coffin, Mme. Dou prayed, "Brother and Sister-in-law, in life you were humans; in death you have become spirits. The Han family has only one descendant—why is he mute? It cannot be because the ancestors have not accumulated merit. It must be because we have some hidden failings. I pray that your spirits in Heaven may protect Han Xiang, that Heaven may bestow intelligence upon him, that he may daily grow in wisdom, that he may escape all calamities, and that he may overcome all obstacles so that the family line shall be continued." Having finished praying, she wept again.

At night Mme. Zheng appeared to Mme. Dou and told her, "Although my child Han Xiang can't speak at present, he will be able to do so when he reaches the age of fourteen. A time will come when our family will depend on him for its deliverance. Please be patient, my sister-in-law." Mme. Dou awoke with a start, realizing that it had been a dream. She thought to herself, "If my sister-in-law's spirit is so perspicacious after death, then Han Xiangzi definitely is not an ordinary mortal. Let us raise him carefully, see how he turns out as an adult, and then take it from there."

Tuizhi was still tarrying in the capital, his purse empty, his clothes worn out. He had received the news of his sister-in-law's death, but could not return home, though his heart was filled with limitless sorrow. He failed three more times, but then to his joy he passed the provincial examination. After the official celebration banquet, he quickly returned home, pressing on through day and night.

Just as he arrived at the gate of his house, he ran into his mute nephew Xiangzi, who had just turned fourteen. He greeted Tuizhi with the words "Congratulations, Uncle! Congratulations!"

When Tuizhi saw him speaking and making a very courteous bow, he took him by the hand, and they entered the house together. Mme. Dou came out to welcome him. The greetings over, Tuizhi asked, "When did my nephew begin to talk?"

"From the time you left the house until today, I have never heard him utter a word," Mme. Dou replied. "Even when his mother died, I only saw him shed tears profusely, but didn't hear him wail."

Tuizhi said, "Just now when he saw me, he said, 'Congratulations, Uncle!'— surely that counts as speaking! Unworthy though I am, I had the good fortune of passing the examinations. It was out of joy that my nephew was able to speak— this is a great blessing for the family. The only sad thing is that my brother and his wife died so early that they could not see me pass the examinations and see Xiangzi grow up."

"Please do not grieve," Mme. Dou said.

From the side Xiangzi put in, "Ever since I swallowed the Daoist's pill, I've understood the shrinking and growing of yin and yang, the waxing and waning of sun and moon, the prosperity and decay of ages, the successes and defeats of ancient and present times. The scriptures of the sages and traditions of the worthies are just words floating from the mouth. The canon of the emperors and the counsels of the kings are not the truth I feel in my heart. The whole world is before my eyes; blessed places and grotto-heavens are right in front of me. In my humble opinion, as a human being living in the world, one should aim to transcend the three spheres and rise from this ordinary world to become a divine immortal."

"Knowledge has limits, but learning is endless," Tuizhi told him. "These words of yours smack of smugness and self-content, of unwillingness to make an effort to succeed. What can be done about this? We need to invite a tutor to teach you how to study the *Odes* and *Documents* diligently; only then will you succeed in the examinations."

"There's a poem I'd like to present to you," Xiangzi said.

> "I do not study the Odes and Documents; I do not seek fame.
> My whole mind looks toward the Dao. I delight in the mountain forests.
> One day I will master the arts of the divine immortals;
> Then you too will believe in the perfection of the numinous elixir."

"Who taught you to compose poetry?" Tuizhi said.

"If you think you must test me—well, why would I have to ape others?" asked Xiangzi.

"If you are so clever, why do you say you don't want to study?" Tuizhi said.

"The learned man dresses in a purple gown and a golden girdle, he eats roasted phoenix and boiled dragon, in his hands he holds an ivory tablet, and his feet are shod with black court shoes. He rides in a high chariot pulled by a team of four steeds, and when he rests he enjoys the company of dancing and singing girls. He has only to shout and the waters of the Yellow River will flow upstream. He has only to laugh and the flowers of the imperial gardens will overflow and fill the forests. Look, I am now enjoying prestige and glory, but ten years ago I was just a student admired by no one."

"I do want to study," Xiangzi replied. "But in my former existence I didn't plant the seeds for a body to be girded with gold and clothed in purple, a tongue to taste phoenix and boiled dragon, a spirit to travel in chariots and ride horses, or the skill to dally with courtesans. So I'd better engage in quiet contemplation of a hibiscus in the mountains, or discuss the scriptures under a pine tree while breaking off a dew-covered twig. I have a little lyric to the tune 'Ascending the Little Tower'—please listen:

> "What I love is the calm beauty of mountains and waters.
> What I love is to live in seclusion in a humble cottage.
> What I love is to pass my days quietly in a thatched hut at the end
>   of a winding trail.
> What I love is to joyfully drink a few cups.
> What I love is to snore and slumber and not get up even when the sun
>   is already in the sky."

"This is all idle and artful talk with no substance to it, " Tuizhi said. "With this attitude, how will you ever amount to anything?"

Xiangzi said, "Please listen to me":

> *(To the tune "Nezha")*

> "If I were to become a great man,
> I'd be wearing golden fish pendants on my girdle and dress in a purple
>   gown.
> If I were to become a retainer to an important man,
> I'd have to resemble Qin Zhuang in recklessness.
> If I were to study the Three Histories and the Documents,
> I'd have to emulate the labors of Che Yin.[3]
> But if I were to become a Daoist,

I'd be pacing the mists and sleeping on the clouds.
Of these three options, only the Daoist is worth honoring."

(To the tune "Magpie on a Branch")

"I just yearn to go and live in the mountain forests,
There to arrange my fishing lines,
Become a Daoist,
And spend some years in a thatched hut.
The villas of the wealthy and
The emblems of high office
Do not equal straw sandals and a black headcloth."

"Though a little child, you are bright and clever. Why should you want to go from door to door and beg for your food?" Tuizhi asked.

Xiangzi replied, "Uncle!

"By regarding me as a prodigy
You actually belittle me!
I see being a child prodigy as child's play.
I see the great Confucians as vulgar men.
How could a son from a rich family be the equal of me, Han Xiangzi?
You want me to become a high official,
But I fear that one day my fine horses will be dead and my gold used up."

"I won't listen to your extravagant talk!" Tuizhi told him. "I want you to study, improve the family's standing, and give honor to your parents. Then and only then shall I be satisfied."

"There is no need to be anxious, Uncle," Xiangzi replied. "Your wishes are easily fulfilled."

"You will be a blessing to the Han family only if you agree to make an effort to better yourself. I talked with the scholar Lin Gui, while we traveled to the capital together. He has a daughter named Luying, who is only about fifteen years old. Her father has promised her to you as a wife. Right away, I shall choose an auspicious day and hour for you to marry her and bring her to our house. My mind won't be at ease until you have become husband and wife and have produced offspring."

"As you wish, Uncle," Xiangzi consented.

Then Tuizhi called on Zhang Qian to say to the local diviner, "My master wants to complete a marriage agreement with Scholar Lin. May I trouble you to select an auspicious day that will ensure good fortune for many generations to come?" Having received his orders, Zhang Qian went to speak to the diviner.

That master's name was Yuan Zixu, with the adopted name Ruoyou. In earlier years he had been an idle loafer, sponge, and philanderer, who wore on his head a gaudy cap. One day as he was traveling in some county away from home, he was insulted by an official wearing the square cap of a scholar. Greatly angered, Yuan said, "Anyone would like to wear the scholar's square cap. I don't have a square cap like you, but only get to wear a headscarf. Is that a reason to bully me?" At that time he decided to begin studying. He bought some books on astrology, physiognomy, geomancy, and the choosing of auspicious days, and spent day after day at home reading them. He also got hold of a copy of *The Annals of All Dynasties*, which he recited at home from morning to evening.

Having memorized these books, he began to speak in a grandiose manner in front of others, mixing in classical expressions and peppering his speech with tidbits from his bagful of learning. He boasted that there were no books he had not read, there was nothing he did not know, and that he understood past and present and was well versed in the ways of the world. However, the times were not favorable to him and he never passed an official examination. In fact he was like a three-legged cat—not particularly good at anything. However, the rich and powerful of Changli County lacked cultivation and learning, and usually just relied on their money and power to intimidate others. As soon as they heard Yuan Zixu's clever speech, they were amazed by it and were hoodwinked into flocking to him. There was none who did not praise him, saying how talented he was, that he had hardly a peer in the world.

Zixu then began to wear a square cap and fashionable clothes. Outside his door he posted a placard saying, "The diviner Ruoyou lives here, who has received his knowledge from an immortal he encountered. He selects auspicious days for weddings so that the husband will achieve fame and the wife prestige. Also skilled in geomancy to help with official careers and financial distress."

Thereafter everyone in Changli County came to him for their weddings and funerals. When he was lucky, the marriages were successful and the burials proceeded in an auspicious fashion. When he was unlucky, nobody realized how much they were cheated by him. People never blamed him, and even sent him gifts of wine and rice, money, linen and cotton, firewood and coal, household goods, books, and paintings. Some people even presented expensive liquor and delicacies to him. He was a man who could make a living out of thin air with his bare hands, which explained the good fortune he seemed to enjoy for the time being.

On the day when Zhang Qian sought him out and spoke to him, Yuan Zixu replied, "Having received your master's command, I will select an extraordinarily good day and will report to his home. I only ask for your master's deep gratitude for my services."

"If only you choose well, I will return and talk to the master, and he certainly will not treat you lightly," Zhang Qian said.

"Friend Zhang, if you put in a word for me, I will give you a portion of the gains," Yuan Zixu promised. Zhang Qian assented, took his leave, and departed.

Yuan Zixu went into his house and said gleefully, "Han Tuizhi is a man who knows tact and recognizes a worthy person, quite unlike these commoners around here. Now that he has retained me for the selection of the wedding day, I must exert myself to pick a particularly good day for him. That way I can milk him for at least three to five ounces of silver. However, it's easier said than done. I am not sure what the best thing to do is, as lucky and unlucky elements are changing all the time. Let's get out all the almanacs and carefully choose a day for him, making sure that I don't ruin my reputation."

Yuan Zixu indeed took out many almanacs and spread them out on the table. What kinds of books were these?

> There were *Shortcuts to the Almanac*, *Encyclopedia for Choosing Days*, *Marriage Charts of the Nine Heavens*, and *Universal Marriage Calendar*. Lined up in front and back were *Yin-Yang Charts* and *Exposé of the Hidden Jia*. To the right and left were placed *Scripture of Marriage* and *Yellow Register Liturgy*. Turning the pages, one finds that each author's opinions are different. Looking through them, it turns out that the views of each book are unlike those of the others. Although the diviner piled up the books and went over them again and again, he could not merge these divergent opinions into a date that would yield good fortune for many generations.

Yuan Zixu browsed back and forth, but could not find a good day. Eventually he sighed, "Although the thirteenth day of the second month is a Divine Immortal Day, it clashes with the Lodge of the Widowed Simurgh. On the other hand, it harmonizes with the Hall of Zhou. Let's write it down and give it to Han, but make sure that he himself endorses it." Quickly he took out a card of costly Nanjing Double Red paper and wrote, "The *wuzi* hour of the *bingchen* day, in the *yimao* month of the *jiashen* year. The joy of Heaven will arrive at the gate, and a precious star will illumine the household. Prospects for official honors and the blessed virtue of the Purple Empyrean all come together on this day. After the completion of this wedding, your son will certainly be adorned with the precious jade ornaments of officialdom, ascend the phoenix pavilions and dragon towers of the high ministers, amass riches greater than mountains of copper and seas of pearls. Not for several decades will you find another such day."

When Tuizhi saw this message, his heart was filled with joy. Right away, he gave Yuan Zixu three ounces of silver. Having received the money, Yuan returned home very happy. From the sum he gave six cash to Zhang Qian as a sign of his gratitude, whereupon Zhang Qian too brightened right up. Tuizhi called Zhang Qian and ordered him to prepare soup and fruit for the betrothal ceremony, and then discussed the arrangements with Mme. Dou. They prepared hairpins and earrings, satin and cloth, and had the matchmaker Xu go to the house of Scholar Lin to tell him that they wanted to send the chest of betrothal gifts and arrange a wedding.

Scholar Lin raised no objections whatsoever. On the auspicious day, they invited all the relatives to open the chest and view the sumptuous presents:

> The flower clasps to bind the hair were all made of rhinoceros horn,
> pearls, and precious stones, their golden flowers and five-fold
> stamens tinkling with a clear sound. The inlaid bracelets and hairpins
> were all of white and red jade, complemented by dark jades with a
> flashing raven-black sheen. There were hairpins to encircle the face
> like flying dragons, phoenixes hovering over jade trees with a tinkling
> sound. Precious hats spewed flames, golden fish inhaled billows,
> azure leaves greeted the wind. Sixteen kinds of broth, sixteen kinds of
> fruit, all elegantly arranged in bowls. A hundred feet of satin, a thou-
> sand ounces of silver, all laid out in profusion inside the chest. Up
> front went bearers of golden drums and flags, striking up a great
> noise. Held high above was a yellow silk umbrella. It was an impres-
> sive scene, arranged in perfection to the last detail.

When Scholar Lin saw these many gifts, his joy was limitless. He rewarded the messengers and sent back an acceptance notice, while preparing the trousseau to give his daughter Luying in marriage to the Han family, and have her become Xiangzi's wife.

What did Luying look like?

Straight eyes bright like autumn floods,
a brow light in outline like a distant mountain.

Straight eyes bright like autumn floods, resembling Guanyin gazing
at the moon's reflection in the water. A brow light in outline like a
distant mountain, just like Maid Mao of the Han palace. She was
dressed in a gown delicately traced and embroidered with a hundred
flowers. Her feet were shod with slippers adorned with flying and
dancing pairs of phoenixes. She walked slowly in her fine skirt, her
silken stockings suspended low. The variegated sleeves swayed gently,
her rainbow garments floating gracefully. She really was a shining
beauty, with a face whose loveliness was staggering. She was of a
warm and yielding nature, possessing the virtue of complete submission to her husband.

When Tuizhi brought Luying into the house, he was overjoyed, because now
Xiangzi's drifting nature would be steadied and the Han family could hope for
descendants. He expected that Xiangzi's dreams of Daoist cultivation would sink
away like a stone in water. However, when the banquet was over and the newly-
wed couple had retreated to their room, Luying removed her make-up and sat
facing the wall, but Xiangzi would not take off his clothes. He lay down on a bench
and slept there, and so the night passed without anything happening between
them.

The two feasts of the third day and the first full month after the wedding went
by, and Luying in accordance with custom returned for a visit to her father's home.
One day Mme. Dou said to Xiangzi, "It is already many days since Luying
returned to her family. You should go and call on her."

Xiangzi retorted, "Luying and Xiangzi are two separate persons. We are not
pair-eyed fish or trees whose branches interlock. What good would it do if I went
to visit her?"

"The relationship of husband and wife is a constant part of the human way,"
Mme. Dou said. "One leads, the other follows. It is the highest realization of human
sentiment. Even mandarin ducks sleep with their necks entwined, while the *jian*
birds combine their wings to fly. If even birds have the sentiment of marriage,
can humans be inferior?"

"Aunt, you only know that animals feel the love that makes them entwine their
necks and combine their wings, but you don't know the sorrow of fleeting time
and approaching death," Xiangzi responded. "Please listen to me:

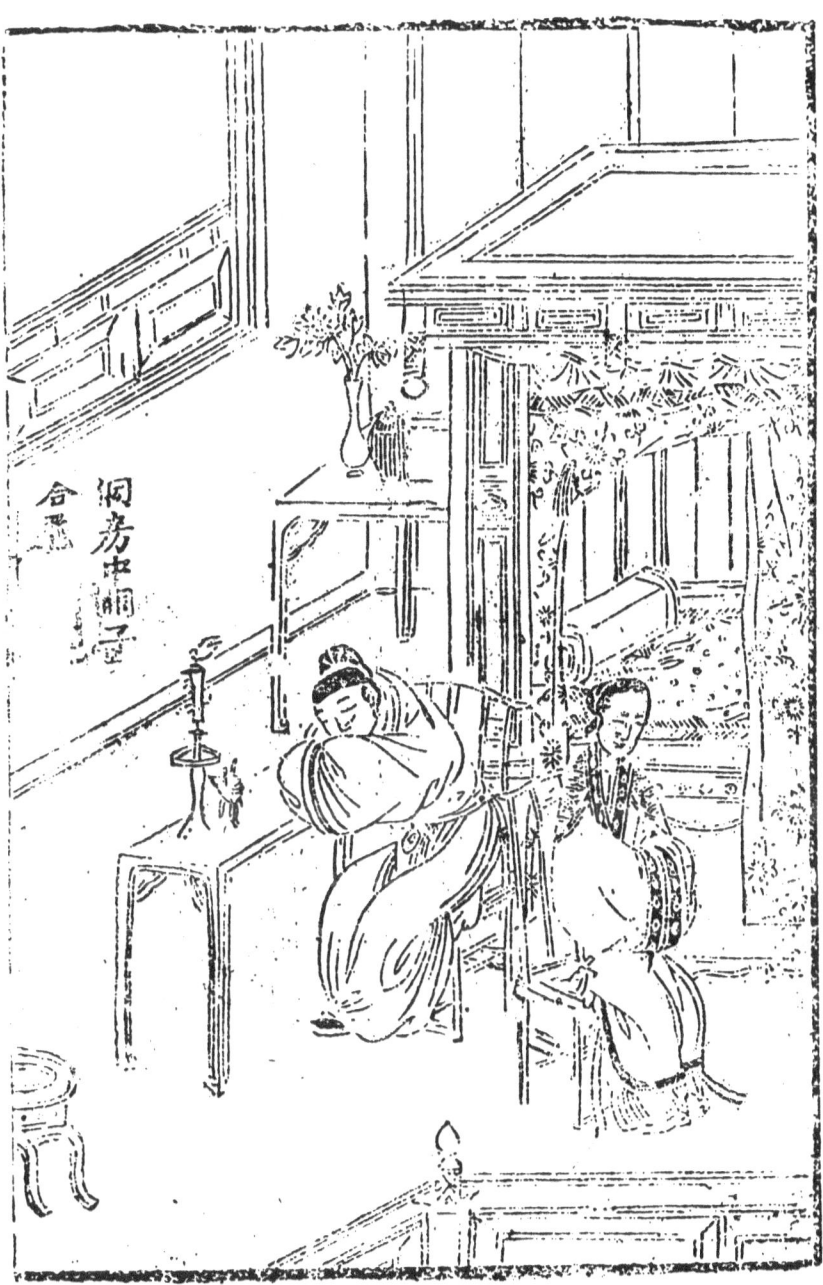

Xiangzi drinks the wedding cup in the nuptial chamber.

"Geese and ducks come and go in swarms.
The purple mandarin duck has to find a partner.
But why should humans follow the example of animals?
Husband and wife are originally birds of the same forest,
But when death catches up with them,
They will suffer deep distress and anxiety.
As their voices become silent and their vital energy ceases,
The two become separated.
Marriage thus seems short-lived like a bubble on water or frost on the
    grass,
And you will look back on it in loneliness."

Mme. Dou said, "Since ancient times there has never been one who did not die—what remains is the historian's record of one's sincere heart.[4] What is there to fear in death? When your parents died when you were young, I took you into my care, raised you, and found a wife for you. My only hope is that you will have many blessings and many sons who will continue the Han family line, worshipping at and sweeping the ancestors' graves. How can you now utter such words, fit to kill me?"

"Do not grieve, Aunt, I will do as you command," Xiangzi said.

"If you will do as I bid, then you are a filial and obedient child," Mme. Dou said. "You are certain to pass the examinations soon, giving your wife a title and extending privilege to your sons. This way you won't have been given life in vain by my brother and sister-in-law. However, if you do not listen to me, but cultivate yourself and debate the Dao, then you are just an unfilial son. And I am afraid there are no unfilial immortals in Heaven. Since ancient times it has been put very well:

"He who is filial begets filial children;
Unfilial wretches beget unfilial sons.
If you can be filial and brotherly, as well as loyal and trustworthy,
What need is there to pace the Jasper Pool up in Heaven?"

Did Xiangzi agree in the end to call on Luying? To find out, listen to the next chapter.

4

ZHONG AND LÜ APPEAR ON GOLD SPRINKLE BRIDGE

HAN XIANG STUDIES THE DAO ON SLEEPING TIGER MOUNTAIN

The Three Isles of Penglai are my home;
I don't care about the hubbub in this world of dust.
When the time is ripe, there are revealed to me
Ten thousand miles of misty clouds.
Green bamboo casts its shade on jasper grasses and extraordinary petals.
Suddenly,
I am completely free of cares,
And in my grotto appears the white deer with a flower in its mouth.

After Mme. Dou spoke to Xiangzi that day, he had no choice but to obey her and escort Luying back home.

Several months seemed to pass very quickly. Tuizhi traveled to the capital to sit for the metropolitan examination, which he passed with distinction. As his first assignment he was sent as an investigating censor to Sichuan. Not even two years later, he was promoted to Vice Minister of Justice and moved to Chang'an together with Mme. Dou, Xiangzi, and Luying.

One day on his way back home from court, he walked across Gold Sprinkle Bridge. At the eastern side of the bridge he saw a Daoist of fierce appearance, with a leopard-like head and ferocious eyes, a back like a tiger's, a torso like a bear's, a dark complexion, and a full beard. His hair was parted in a yin-yang fashion, and he wore a gown of black silk. In his hands he held a steel flute. By

洒金橋鍾呂現形

Zhong and Lü appear on Gold Sprinkle Bridge.

the looks of him, he was strong and energetic enough to lift a heavy bronze tripod or smash a bridge. Surely he would surpass even such heroes as Wu Yun and Zhang Fei.

At the west side of the bridge there sat another Daoist, this one of refined appearance. His brows were clear, his eyes graceful, his hair cut back at the temples, his complexion light as if powdered, his lips red as if painted. On his head he had a Nine Yang cloth and he wore a yellow gown trimmed with crane feathers. One might have mistaken him for Zhang Liang, who helped establish the great Han dynasty, or for Zhuge Liang, who supported the imperial Liu family of the Han.

Lighthearted and in good spirits, and intrigued by these unusual figures, Tuizhi approached them and asked the first, "You, Sir, at the east side of the bridge—where do you come from and where do you live? Why did you leave the family to cultivate yourself?"

"You and I are of the same rank, but not of the same dynasty," the Daoist replied.

"What do you mean by that?"

"You are a Vice Minister of Justice under the Tang dynasty. I was a great general under the Han dynasty, commanding the military forces on the strategic roads and residing in the office of the high command. Aren't we then of the same rank, but of different dynasties?" the Daoist said.

"If you exerted yourself for the imperial family, conquering new lands, and doing your duties to the nation according to your oath of fealty, then why did you abandon your family to cultivate yourself, and dress up in this manner?" Tuizhi asked.

"You don't understand," the Daoist said. "I had no choice but to withdraw to a faraway place, because my ruler did harm to three worthies."

"Which three worthies did he harm?" asked Tuizhi.

"Han Xin, the king of Sanqi; Peng Yue, the king of Daliang; and Ying Bu, the king of Jinjiang. These three worthies slept in their saddles and quenched their thirst with the blood off their swords. During the day they repaired the board path along the cliff; in the dark they crossed the river at Chencang. At Nine Mile Mountain they drove Tian Heng into the sea; at the Black River Ford they compelled Xiang Yu to commit suicide. They helped the first Han emperor to snatch the empire from Chu and Qin, but later they suffered deaths worse than pigs and dogs. For this reason I resigned my duties and withdrew into reclusion in the Zhongnan Mountains, where I studied the Dao with the Imperial Lord of Eastern Florescence until I gained entry to the ranks of the immortals. I am

Zhongli Quan of the Han dynasty and hail originally from Renqiu County in Hejian Prefecture."

Turning to the other Daoist, Tuizhi asked, "You, Sir, at the west side of the bridge—where do you come from and where do you live? Would you be of the same rank as Master Zhongli?"

"I am a scholar of the present dynasty and hail from Xia County in Hezhong Prefecture," the second Daoist said. "In my time I have studied row upon row of books. My writings excelled those of my contemporaries, and my ambition soared high. Then one day, as I was traveling with Li Ziying to the capital to sit for the examinations, I met my future teacher Zhongli under a weeping willow at the Yellow Flower Store, ten miles outside the city of Handan. He tried again and again to deliver me, but I was unwilling to change my mind. So he transformed a coarse rush mat into the underworld, complete with the Ten Great Yama Kings, who placed my numinous perfect nature inside a bottle gourd. It was only when I awoke from this dream that I realized that being an official was not the final aim, and that riches would not last long. Thereupon I abandoned Confucianism and cultivated myself until I achieved my proper rewards. I am Master Two Mouths." Here is a poem to illustrate his words:

> *In the morning I roam over the azure sea, in the evening over Cangwu.*
> *My sleeves hold my sword Green Snake, which I wield with fierce*
> *courage.*
> *Though three times drunk in Yueyang, people did not recognize me.*
> *Singing in a clear voice, I flew across Lake Dongting.*[1]

"Judging by your words, the two of you truly surpass Confucius and Mencius in literary talent, and Sun Wu in military skill," Tuizhi said. "Such a combination of the civil and the military is rare indeed! My family has favored learning for many generations. I would like to invite you to my humble house for a vegetarian meal. What do you say?"

"Having received your undeserved affection, naturally we should go to your house to pay our respects, but how could we dare accept a meal?" Master Zhong said.

Taking Master Lü's hand, Tuizhi said, "Let's walk to my home together, shall we?"

"You are an important magistrate, while we are just rustics from the mountain wilderness. It would not be seemly for us to walk in a group. Please walk ahead and we will follow," Master Lü replied.

"You wouldn't stand me up, would you?" Tuizhi asked.

"We wouldn't dare to deceive you," Master Lü assured him.

Indeed, Tuizhi had been home just a short while when the two masters arrived. He came down the stairs to welcome them, and they sat down to drink tea.

Suddenly Xiangzi walked by in front of them; noticing the two masters, he bowed.

"Who is this?" Master Zhong asked. "He looks like a person who might be a hindrance and source of misfortune to his parents."

"This is my son," Tuizhi answered.

"If it is your son, then I apologize for my ill-considered words," Master Zhong said.

"In fact he is my nephew," said Tuizhi. "He is called Han Xiangzi. At the age of three he lost his father, and at seven his mother. Since then it has fallen to me to raise him."

"This boy has the destiny of a high minister to three successive emperors, and the talent of seven generations of top examination graduates," Master Lü said. "If he doesn't bring the whole family celestial emoluments, at the least everyone within nine generations will ascend to Heaven. With him, there will be no need to worry about fame and riches."

"There is, however, one problem," Master Zhong added. "Right now, this child's destiny moves in the 'tomb store' field, and as a result he meets with many adversities. Only at the age of sixteen will he escape from it. You should hire a good teacher to take charge of his education and to arouse his spirits so that he won't stray from the right path."

"I intended to do just that, but I have not yet been able to find a qualified person," Tuizhi said. "May I ask you two gentlemen, what is it we call 'Nature'?"

"'Nature' is the nature of beings, such as the ox having two horns and the horse four hooves," Master Zhong answered.

"What is a 'human being'?" pursued Tuizhi.

Master Lü replied, "A human being is the one who puts a ring through an ox's nose and who slings a saddle round a horse's middle. Not to use human concerns to destroy one's Heaven-endowed nature, not to destroy one's destiny willfully, not to harm one's perfection by desires, to maintain one's endowments diligently and not lose them—this is what I call being in harmony with one's perfected nature."[2]

"Having been honored by your inquiries, I in turn would like to ask for your instruction," Master Zhong requested.

"Please do," Tuizhi replied.

"Heaven, Earth, and Humanity are called the Three Powers," Master Zhong continued. "Heaven and Earth remain unchanged throughout the eons, while humans live between Heaven and Earth, combining yin and yang, cultivating their nature, and establishing their destiny. Now, some live to an old age like Peng Keng, while others die young like Yan Hui, or even as infants. Why are there these differences in life span?"

Tuizhi thought deeply for some time, but in the end remained silent and could not give an answer. Master Lü said, "Everyone can be as long-lived as Heaven and Earth, people are just not aware of it."

"Shun and Yu taught that the mind of humans is restless and its affinity for the Dao is small,"[3] Tuizhi said. "Can humans be without such a fickle mind?"

"The Sword Path is dangerous, yet even more people walk it at night than during the day," Master Lü said.

"Can humans have a constant mind that holds fast to the Dao?" Tuizhi asked.

"Gold dust may be precious, but still it is harmful when caught in the eyes," Master Lü returned.

"How can I have a constant mind by being mindless?" Tuizhi asked.

"One who once suffered from snow and frost will be startled by willow blossoms falling to the ground," was Master Zhong's reply.

Tuizhi said, "How can I be mindless by having a constant mind?"

"Don't bother hanging up the old mirror. When the sky brightens, the rooster will crow by itself," Master Zhong said.

"Is the conscious mind completely false?" Tuizhi then asked.

Master Lü said, "Without the spring wind the blossoms do not open, but once opened they are blown down by the same wind."

"Is being without a conscious mind alone to be sought after?" was Tuizhi's next question.

"When the light of the sun has not yet risen above the horizon, everyone awaits it with expectation, but once broad daylight is here, it is taken for granted," Master Zhong answered.[4]

When Tuizhi saw how well the two masters could debate, he realized that they were eminently qualified to instruct Xiangzi. He said, "In my garden there is a hill called Sleeping Tiger Mountain. On this hill there is a hut arranged after the pattern of the Nine Palaces and Eight Trigrams, a peaceful and leisurely place. I would like to trouble you to take up residence there, one of you teaching him literary, the other military skills. If you can get my nephew to master both arts, he will be employed by the emperor, and my dearest wish will be fulfilled. What do you think?"

The two masters said, "We are just rustics from the mountain wilderness and really have no talents. Now that we are honored by your patronage, how could we not attend diligently to the young gentleman's education? We would just request that you stick to your decision and that you don't listen to slanderous words and seek fault with us."

When the two masters had eaten their vegetarian meal, Tuizhi called Zhang Qian and Li Wan to guide them to the hut. Needless to say, he also ordered Xiangzi to study hard so as to give honor to his ancestors.

When Zhong and Lü reached the hut with Xiangzi, they passed the whole day without giving him a word of instruction, be it literary or military. Instead they sat cross-legged in silent meditation, their lips sealed and their eyes half closed. When Xiangzi saw them like this, he did not dare address them.

Another day passed like this, but looking in on them on the third day, he saw that Master Zhong was playing his flute as Master Lü sang a Daoist song:

> *"Alas, water and fire have no affection for each other;*
> *If you fry in the fire of your desires, you will injure yourself.*
> *So you must take care and be very cautious.*
> *As yin and yang arise by themselves,*
> *Build a foundation and refine your spirit.*
> *Vanquish the dragon and subdue the tiger; don't let them run wild.*
> *Nourish your body,*
> *Adjust your spirit, and circulate your pneuma.*
> *Inside and outside must not interact,*
> *Inside and outside must not interact."*

The song ended, they finally called to Xiangzi, "Master Han, come closer. We want to ask you some questions."

Xiangzi bowed and stood before the two masters.

Master Zhong said, "Your uncle has employed us to instruct you, and naturally we will make every effort in this assignment. However, we do not know what you would like to study for: immortality, or success in the examinations?"

"May I ask what the outcome of studying for success in the examinations will be?" Xiangzi countered.

"If we teach you the classics as well as the books of military strategy, you can use this knowledge to protect the nation and pacify the people, to suppress the wicked and bring order where there is disorder," Master Zhong said. "At some point you will meet your ruler, and you will be given a respectable official appointment. You will live in a magnificent mansion, wear light furs, and ride well-nourished horses. Soon you will give honor to your ancestors, have titles bestowed on your wife, and have privilege extended to your sons. Everyone will applaud you. This is what an official career would be like. However, once death catches up with you, everything you've done will have been futile and you will be left empty-handed."

"What about immortality?" Xiangzi asked.

Master Lü said, "If you choose immortality, we will teach you how to build a foundation and refine yourself, as well as the secret formulas of the cyclical fire phases. You will learn how to spit out the impure and take in the pure, how to feed on clouds and swallow pneuma. You will ascend to Heaven in broad daylight and proceed to the immortality peach banquet. White hair will become black again; lost teeth will grow back. You will dwell together with sun and moon, and live forever without aging. These are the results of studying for immortality. The two are as different as sky and mud. Which one would you like to study?"

"I want to study immortality," Xiangzi said.

"This practice is quite different from the civil arts," the two masters told him. "If you are careless, you won't succeed. If you lack perseverance, you won't succeed. As the saying goes, 'In exercising your will, do not let it be diverted; rather, concentrate your spirit.'"[5] Here is a poem to provide an illustration:

> Alas that ordinary mortals should ask me
> About immortality peaches, clouds and mists and rosy hazes.
> I do not speak lightly of the fire phase hidden behind the brow;
> I do not boast of the golden lotus planted in my hand.
> A three-foot flute to earn my keep,
> A pot of good wine to make my living.
> On a dragon I travel afar to the Three Isles,
> In the quiet solitude of night, I play with the essences of the moon.

The two masters called to Xiangzi, "Disciple, what is the time now?"

"Masters, the drum has beaten the first watch," Xiangzi replied.

"There are several grades of immortals—which one would you like to study for?" asked the two masters.

"At the prefectural Cultivated Talent examination, they distinguish first, second, third, fourth, fifth, and sixth grades," Xiangzi said. "How is it that there are also grades among the immortals?"

"It's not that kind of grading," Master Zhong answered. "Among the immortals we distinguish celestial, terrestrial, human, divine, and ghost immortals."

"I would like to hear more about it," said Xiangzi.

"Ghost immortals are those whose yin-spirit is most numinous and who have no form," Master Zhong told him. "Human immortals are those who live in the human world without disease or aging. Terrestrial immortals are those who do not suffer thirst or hunger, are unaffected by heat or cold, roam the Three Isles, and live forever without dying. Divine immortals are those who fly across the sky and walk on the mists, journey through regions beyond this world, are here one moment and gone the next, and engage in countless transformations. Celestial immortals are those whose spirit and form are equally marvelous, who exist in harmonious perfection with the Dao, walk under sun and moon without throwing a shadow, go through metal and rock without hindrance, have many transformations, and are hard to grasp, whether hidden or manifest; they appear sometimes as old, sometimes as young. They are the most sacred and divine, unknowable to ghost immortals, unfathomable by milfoil and tortoise shell divination."

Master Lü continued. "Those who cut off their desires, cultivate the embryonic breath, are willing to lead their spirit into samadhi, escape their body and are reborn, support the transformations of yin and yang, and live without decaying physically—they can become the lower-ranked ghost immortals. Those who have achieved the Dao by receiving the talismans and registers of the Orthodox One School, the marvelous methods of the Three Grottoes of the Supreme Clarity School, as well as sword techniques and the method of release from the corpse— they can become the middle-ranked human and terrestrial immortals. Those who refine the perfectly unified pneuma of Former Heaven, cultivate the great drug of the golden elixir, make the mercury dragon rise and the lead tiger descend, and congeal the grain-sized pearl—they are the highest-ranked divine and celestial immortals."[6]

Xiangzi said, "I once heard an old saying, 'If you are going to study immortality, then it must be celestial immortality; only the golden elixir is the most appropriate goal.'[7] Thus I sincerely hope that you will transmit to me the Great Way of the Golden Elixir."

"If you wish to begin the study of celestial immortality, you show the right ambition indeed," the two masters returned. "However, we fear that you might go about it in a careless and haphazard manner and give up halfway, wasting our efforts at universal deliverance and cutting off your own future path of cultivating the school of perfection."

"If you agree to teach me, how could I dare be remiss?"

"Sit down and we will tell you," the two masters commanded. "Remember it well, and do not divulge any of it."

Xiangzi remained standing reverently and listened. The two masters chanted to the tune "Five Watches of the Night":

"At the first watch sit upright.
Slowly adjust the Dragon and the Tiger,
Have them suffuse and revolve through the Three Passes,
And penetrate the Niwan Road.
The Dragon coils round the Golden Tripod;
The Tiger blocks the Gate of the Yellow Court.
Once you master this practice,
Relax and cease your worries,
Relax and cease your worries.

"At the second watch,
When the drum strikes twice,
The true pneumata of yin and yang become marvelous.
Among the Three Passes above and below,
Do not let them go astray.
Once the Young Boy and the Lovely Maid reach the Yellow Matron,
Naturally they form a pair,
Naturally they form a pair.

"At the third watch,
The light of the moon illuminates qian and kun.
The roots and shoots for the production of the drug
Are found only on the Southwestern Path.
When Lead is encountered among the emerging lesser water,
Quickly gather it![8]
The Dragon and Snake at the bottom of the sea
Will naturally come to coil around each other,
Will naturally come to coil around each other.

"At the fourth watch, yet more marvelous,
Kan and li must be inverted.
At dawn and dusk the Fire Phases harmonize with the Celestial Pivot.
The Child is in the Womb,
And a rosy light shines ten thousand fathoms high.

In this position is created the Mysterious Pearl.
This method is truly marvelous and subtle,
This method is truly marvelous and subtle.[9]

"*At the fifth watch the sky lights up,*
The golden rooster crows in its cage.
The weary youth claps his hands and laughs out loud.
Having fed the Ox, he may happily sleep a while.
His task is fulfilled and his merit complete.
By itself a mandate in vermilion script will arrive,
By itself a mandate in vermilion script will arrive."

Xiangzi listened and committed everything firmly to memory.

The two masters said, "Xiangzi, we have transmitted to you the secret of eternal life, but we fear that your uncle will hear of it and treat us with contempt."

"Naturally, I'll take responsibility for it. Don't worry too much," said Xiangzi.

They taught him for three nights in a row. On the fourth night the two masters again struck fisher drum and clapper and instructed Xiangzi with a lyric to the tune "Parasol Tree":

"*At the first watch,*
Adjust spirit and pneuma.
The mind monkey and will horse must be firmly tied up.
Do not let them play around idly,
Play around idly.
Quietly refine the embryonic breath.
Open the Gate of Heaven, while the Door of Earth is closed.
Then you will penetrate the mysterious principles,
Penetrate the mysterious principles.

"*At the second watch,*
Throughout the universe
A ray of numinous light gradually penetrates.
Dragon and Tiger first unite in copulation,
First unite in copulation.
Guard the Three Passes so that none may leave,
So that none may leave.

"At the third watch,
The single yang moves,
And the Golden Tripod comes to join the Jade Tripod.
You refine True Mercury and Lead;
Wu and ji unite in Primordial Redness.
In the Tripod the Golden Flower reverberates,
The Golden Flower reverberates.

"At the fourth watch,
The moon stands in the sky,
A jade mirror suspended on high, reflecting every place equally.
Reflected in it you see the reddening of the Eastern Sea.
As you fetch water beyond the mountain, there is great noise,
There is great noise.

"At the fifth watch,
The clouds are gathered completely,
And the marvelous jade plays with the new moon.
Everywhere the jasper flowers form,
The jasper flowers form.
If the Fire Phase is withdrawn and augmented with the proper timing,
Red snow falls from the primordial mists.
Do not leak out the secrets of Heaven,
Leak out the secrets of Heaven."

At daybreak the two masters said to Xiangzi, "We have taught you for several days how to cultivate and refine yourself. You must practice it diligently. Today your uncle is sure to chase us away."

Xiangzi said, "Let my uncle scold and punish me, I have no regrets whatsoever. But with you gone, whom shall I rely upon for instruction?"

"This is how things are," the two masters said. "A proverb says, 'Husband and wife are originally birds of the same forest, but when disaster looms they each fly away in their own directions.' How much more does this apply to masters and disciples? If only you remain firm of heart and will, we will of course come to deliver you."

As they were speaking, one of Tuizhi's servants came to summon Xiangzi.

Tuizhi asked Xiangzi, "Have you now memorized the civil and military classics that you have been studying for the last several days?"

"I do not dare keep you in the dark," Xiangzi said. "What the two masters taught me was *The Yellow Court Scripture*. I didn't study any civil or military classics."

Angry and displeased, Tuizhi asked the servant on duty, "What did Xiangzi and the two masters practice over the past few days? What books did they lecture on?"

"The two Daoists taught Xiangzi to meditate at the first watch, and to ascend and fly at the second watch. The third and fourth watches they just struck the fisher drum and sang Daoist songs."

When Tuizhi heard this, his heart suddenly seemed to erupt in angry flames, and his face swelled up all purple. Beating Xiangzi with a bamboo cane, he shouted, "When your father died, he entrusted you to me so that I might look after and educate you. His only wish was that you would grow up to give honor to your ancestors. Little did I know that you were so silly as to want to study Daoist cultivation. You are a disgrace to our family. Oh, this is killing me."

Xiangzi said, "It was you who invited the two masters to instruct me. I didn't seek them out myself. So why are you beating me?"

From the side Mme. Dou admonished Tuizhi over and over, saying, "He must have been lonely after his parents died so early. It is we who raised him, but maybe we should think the matter of his education through thoroughly. We don't want people to gossip."

Crying, Xiangzi said, "As I owe you my upbringing, from now on I won't dare disobey your orders again."

"Because my wife admonished me, I won't beat you any more, beast," Tuizhi said. "Get inside, diligently study the *Documents* and *Histories*, and stop pursuing that business of leaving the family."

At the same time he ordered the servant on duty, "Go and call in those two Daoists. I am going to drive them out, and cut off the root of this problem. Then I won't have to fear for Xiangzi's education any longer."

The servant went and called to the two Daoists, "Sirs, the master wants to see you."

"Master Chunyang, that Chonghezi has forgotten his previous existence. He is calling us to chase us out the gate. Let's go and see what he has to say," Master Zhong said.

Following the servant, they arrived in front of Tuizhi, knocked their heads and said, "Our greetings to you, my lord Han."

"Who would exchange courtesies with the likes of you? Haven't you even a shred of human decency?" Tuizhi shouted angrily.

"You invited us to educate the young gentleman," the two masters said.

"How can you disregard the respect due to a teacher? Why don't you treat us with courtesy?"

"I retained two men to instruct my nephew in the civil and military arts so that he would advance in his career," Tuizhi said. "Why did you teach him all day long to strike the fisher drum and sing Daoist songs? How could that not be, as Confucius says in his *Analects*, 'harming another man's son'?[10] Or do you claim that they are good men who sing these Daoist songs?"

"My lord, when did we ever teach him to sing Daoist songs?"

"My nephew has already confessed to it. Why are you two still denying it? Get out now and stop talking rubbish in my presence!"

"We ascetics follow our karmic affinity," the two masters said. "If there is affinity, we stay; if not, we leave. What need is there to get upset?"

Then they called to the inner rooms, "Han Xiangzi, today we leave. If later you want to look for us, come to the Zhongnan Mountains, more than ten thousand miles away. We will await you there."

Xiangzi came running out and said, "Do not leave, but teach me here. If you leave now, it will be difficult to meet again when I come to look for you."

"Your uncle has already evicted us. What face have we left to remain in your household?"

"It is my heartfelt wish to go with you," Xiangzi said.

With one hand Tuizhi pushed Xiangzi back, calling, "Zhang Qian and Li Wan, throw out these uncouth Daoists!"

"You, sir, have the upper hand, " the two masters said. "We will chant a little song for you to thank you for your undeserved affection, and then we shall leave." The song was set to the tune "Buying Good Wine," followed by "Clear River":

> "You think being an official is so desirable,
> But we regard wealth and status as fleeting waves,
> No match for our detached purity and torn robes.
> We close our door in quietude,
> And do not hanker after a nagging wife or an official's gown.
> Such quiet is preferable to the hubbub in the puppet theatre of the
>   world,
> While glory and fame clearly resemble auspicious snow in hot water.
> Leisurely we accompany divine youths picking medicinal sprouts.
> When melancholy, we play the jasper zither.
> What we play are ancient tunes—

A crane crying in the Ninth Marsh.[11]
We do not care if others laugh at us."

Tuizhi shouted, "Get out! I don't want to listen to this kind of talk." The two masters chanted,

"One day you will be stripped of your office and disaster will be hard to
    escape.
At the Blue Pass the snow will pile up while you are on a long journey.
It is then that you shall finally realize the truth."

Having finished chanting, they shook their sleeves and left. A poem says,

A great sleeve can cover the Three Worlds,
As its owner roams freely in the Nine Heavens.
A vulgar scholar has not the eyes to see;
He does not recognize an immortal from Great Veil Heaven.

When Tuizhi saw that the two masters had left, he led Xiangzi to the study hall and locked him into a side room. He ordered the servant on duty to keep careful watch and not to let him out to commit any more foolishness. A poem describes his view:

He bore a grudge against the two Daoists, who at first
With beautiful and cunning words deceived the boy.
Now he pulls up these weeds by the roots,
And casts down The Yellow Court Scripture.

Though locked up, Xiangzi did not harbor any resentful thoughts. He just cultivated himself with great earnestness, sat, and sang Daoist songs. By way of illustration, here is a lyric to the tune "Golden Oriole":

Slowly he chants to himself,
Establishing profound merit,
Enduring suffering,
Passing the days and nights without sleeping deeply.
He tightly binds up the mind monkey,
Lets his pneuma revolve through the Three Passes,

And delves into The Yellow Court Scripture.
As he refines the Perfected Essence without the Elixir Measure,
The celestial principles give rise to each other naturally.

Suddenly he sees that ox charging,
Its nose reared towards Heaven,
Giving a loud roar.
Swaying and reeling, he cannot seize it.
Pull on that rope,
Do not let him run wild,
But make him follow you closely day and night.
Ox-herder,
In the realm of the Elixir field,
Make sure the grain blossoms.

Xiangzi diligently cultivated himself day and night, but if you don't know what happened later, then look at the next chapter.

5

WHILE WAITING AT THE CITY GATE, THE CROWDS

TEASE XIANGZI

While white hair grows sadly at both temples,
The blue hills and green waters remain unchanged.
What difference is there between human life and the dream of Southern
  Bough?[1]
You snap your fingers and eighteen years have gone by!
Yet after eighteen years this scenery is still fresh,
Separated from the dusty world by sandalwood and purple bamboo.
Soon the Dragon's Daughter will offer up her pearl, and
A crane mount will come circling down from the Nine Heavens.

Mme. Dou thought to herself, "When my brother-in-law was still alive, he prayed to Heaven and Earth mornings and evenings. In return he received Xiangzi, but after his birth the baby cried all day long, exhausting his mind and spirit. Fortunately, we were able to raise him, and married him to Luying, the daughter of Scholar Lin. The wedding took place three years ago already, yet still there are no children. It certainly looks as if the Han family line is about to end. I have often heard that when the rhinoceros gazes at the moon, its horn produces auspicious signs; and that when an oyster contains a pearl, it will frolic in the morning sun.[2] Yet Luying shows no sign of becoming pregnant—what is to be done about that?"

Then she had an idea. She ordered her servant Plum Fragrance to fetch Luying, and, when she arrived, asked her, "What kind of tree is the one at the foot of the stairs?"

"Mother-in-law, it is a hibiscus," Luying said.

Mme. Dou said, "I will order Plum Fragrance to get a blade and cut it down."

"Mother-in-law, don't cut it down!" Luying said. "Leave it there so I may look at it mornings and evenings."

"I have only ever seen it blossom, but it never produces any seeds, " Mme. Dou said. "What use is it to me?"

"Flowers and humans are alike, and human life is like a flower, " Luying said. "Male flowers do not produce seeds, and male bamboo does not produce shoots."

"Daughter-in-law, listen to what I say to you:

> *"If I plant a hibiscus against a rock,*
> *Making sure its roots take firm hold in the soil,*
> *But then it only has pretty blossoms but no seeds,*
> *I have wasted my effort."*

Luying said,

> *"You may have a fertile field,*
> *But if the lazy bull won't plough it at night*
> *And you don't sow the seeds in spring—*
> *Then where would the sprouts come from?"*

"So that's how it is!" Mme. Dou said. "Plum Fragrance, quickly fetch Xiangzi. I have something to ask him."

"The master has locked Xiangzi up in the study, and nobody dares let him out," Plum Fragrance reported. So Mme. Dou handed Plum Fragrance the key and told her again to fetch Xiangzi.

When Plum Fragrance opened the door, Xiangzi asked, "What does my aunt want from me?"

"She was in the hall talking with Luying, I don't know about what. She sent me to bring you so that she may question you," Plum Fragrance replied.

So Xiangzi had to go and see his aunt, who said to him, "Nephew, I gave you Luying as a wife, hoping that she would produce sons and daughters to continue the family line. Three years have passed already, but no child has been born. This has caused me considerable concern. Just now when I asked your wife about it, she said that you have never come close to each other. Why is that?"

Mme. Dou criticizes Luying by cutting down the hibiscus.

Xiangzi answered, "I will explain it to you with a poem:

"*Taking care of essence and pneuma, I nourish my primordial spirit.*
Nourishing essence and spirit, I nourish my own body.
In the cauldron I refine the great elixir drug;
I won't produce descendants in the world of humans."

When Mme. Dou heard these words, she cried and said, "My son, you are so wrong! From ancient times, people have always hoped for their sons and daughters to have families of their own. You and your wife are young. Instead of speaking such heartless and immoral words, why don't you give some thought to continuing the family line? Though your parents are dead at the Yellow Springs, they won't be able to close their eyes in peace."

Xiangzi said, "The Buddha said that if a man is tied to wife and children, though he may live in a house made of seven kinds of jewels, his suffering is worse than in a prison. In a prison at least one still has leisure, but with wife and children one has no hope for peace of mind. To love with emotional desire casts a man in the mire, there to drown himself. If a man can get through this pass, he will leave the world of dust. This is why Luying and I treat each other respectfully, like guests. I hope you will forgive me."

"This is unbearable! How can he speak like this?" Luying cried, and swiftly ran to her room. Mme. Dou held Xiangzi back and admonished him over and over again.

"Aunt, don't you know that life and death are an important matter, not to be trifled with?" Xiangzi said. "The ancients put it very well:

"*Three fish with one head,*
Swimming in the water with a shared heart and gall.
The dull do not understand the fishes' meaning—
Without predestination no union would be made."

Just as Mme. Dou and Xiangzi were arguing, Tuizhi returned from court. On seeing them, he inquired, "What are you talking about, my wife?"

"I am admonishing Xiangzi to study," Mme. Dou replied.

"I locked Xiangzi up in the study," Tuizhi pursued. "Who let him out?"

"I took the key and let him out," said Mme. Dou.

"Xiangzi, come here and let me ask you: which books have you studied and what have you done the last few days?" Tuizhi said.

"Confucius's disciple Zhongyou said, 'The prefecture of Bi has people in it and has the altars to the soil and grain in it. Why is it that only by reading books one can be considered learned?'"[3] Xiangzi quoted.

Tuizhi struck Xiangzi a blow with his bamboo cane. "You fool, do you also know that Confucius replied to Zhongyou, 'It is for this reason that I hate those people with a glib tongue'?"[4]

"Confucius inquired after the rites with Lao Dan, who is the founding father of the immortals and the leader of the Daoists. Didn't Confucius once say that one should 'withstand others by means of smart speech'?[5] Why then do you call me 'glib'?" Xiangzi said.

"To know the male but keep to the female, to know the white but keep to the black—those are the teachings of Lao Dan. When did Lao Dan's writings ever serve to conceal faults and gloss over wrongdoings? If you want to study the Dao and cultivate perfection, you must study and understand principles. Why do you throw away gold to pick up a moldy brick? I'll just beat you to death, you useless beast, and be done with you!" He raised the stick and gave Xiangzi a savage thrashing.

Xiangzi cried out, "Aunt, save me! Uncle is beating me too hard!"

Mme. Dou knelt down and admonished her husband, "When your brother and his wife were close to their deaths, they repeatedly ordered you to take loving care of Xiangzi. When today you beat him like this, those who understand will say that you're teaching an unfilial son a lesson, but those who don't understand will say that you're violating the orders given by your late brother and his wife, and that you are not taking proper care of Xiangzi. I hope that you will forgive him this time."

"Everyone who raises a son hopes that he will grow up to achieve success in the examinations and bring honor to the family," Tuizhi said. "Our family has only this unfilial child who refuses to study and strive for advancement. Instead he studies the calling of those vagrant beggars, wasting the precious time of his youth. Alas that I am already old. Who is to blame for this? A proverb says, 'If mulberry branches grow in a bushy cluster when small, they will remain entangled and crooked later.' How can you tell me not to beat this beast?"

"The Han family has only this one descendant," Mme. Dou told him. "If there are to be regrets, then regret that you made the mistake of employing the two Daoists who led him astray."

"When I hired the Daoists, my hope was that he might practice the civil and study the military arts. He was to become a well-rounded man in both spheres, so that he could exert himself for the court and for the Han family. Who could have known that the Daoists would beguile him into leaving the family, leading him astray for the rest of his life? Now let's talk no more about it. The only thing to do is to subject him to intensive instruction. Then he will come to change his mind quite by himself," Tuizhi said.

"Please spare yourself the trouble," Mme. Dou said. "Leave it to me to urge him to study properly." Finally, Tuizhi let go of Xiangzi.

Xiangzi returned to the study, depressed and unhappy. He sat down to adjust his spirit and circulate his pneuma. Two servants came forward and said, "Don't fret. We'll find a way to lift your spirits, all right?"

"What is there in the world that could lift my spirits?" Xiangzi asked.

"Playing cards and games of chance should work," they replied. "Chess. Throwing dice. Football."

Xiangzi said, "For all these types of gambling one needs to dissipate one's essence and spirit, and waste one's time. I do not like to engage in them."

"Then wine might cheer you up," one servant proposed.

"If wine is all right, let's fetch some right away and you can drink a few bowls to chase those worries away," agreed the other.

"What help would wine be?" Xiangzi said.

"Wine was invented by Yi Di," the servant said. "Good wine is sweet and fragrant, clear and pure. People call it the 'Administrator of Qing Province.' Bad wine is turbid and muddy, weak and sour, and is named the 'Inspector-General above the diaphragm.'[6] In the springtime there are green leaves and red blossoms to find pleasure in. In the summer you'll find cool arbors and pavilions by the water where you can escape the heat and enjoy the shade. The autumn brings chrysanthemum blossoms and cassia fragrance, which you can smell as you crumple the flowers in your hands. In the winter there are the days of clearing skies deep in the mountains, where you can relax in idleness and pleasure. Taking advantage of the fresh and beautiful scenery of the four seasons, you take along a wine jug and raise your cup. If you invite two or three friends and pleasant female company, then amid the toasting and convivial merriment all worries are soon lost and all sorrow is thrown off. That is what is meant by this poem:

> "To dispel all the worries of your life, there is only wine.
> To break the ten thousand sorrows, nothing surpasses wine.
> Black lines like the contours of distant mountains let me dip into the
>   autumn waters,
> If I don't drink from them, bystanders will laugh at me."[7]

"Wine can confuse one's perfection and throw one's nature into disorder," Xiangzi retorted. "It attracts disasters and calamities. That's why the Great Yu disliked wine and rejected Yi Di. Only poets, and dissolute fellows who willfully forget common decency, use wine as a broom to sweep away sorrow and as a hook to fish for poetry. I don't like to drink it."

One of the servants said, "In the sky there is a Wine Star, on earth there is a Wine Spring. Among the sages and worthies there is the 'virtue of wine.' Yao and Shun could drink a thousand cups, Confucius a hundred goblets. Zilu drank in small sips, but he could still drain ten tankards.[8] Li Bai attained the Dao by hankering for the cup. Liu Ling became an immortal through his love of drink. From ancient times to the present, not only sages, worthies, and gentlemen wouldn't let go of wine, but even the divine immortal Lü from Heaven on high got drunk three times in Yueyang without anyone recognizing him. There's never been one who abstained from drink—why then do you say that it is so bad?"

"How do you come to realize that wine is not good?" Xiangzi answered. "There is an old poem that makes the point. I'll recite it to you:

> *"In his day Yi Di created the roots of calamity—*
> *Unbearable how he confused perfection and disordered human*
>   *nature.*
> *When drunk, a man foolhardily embraces the universe,*
> *While in fact bringing upon himself calamities and disasters."*

"If wine won't lift your spirits," one of the servants said, "let's take you to the pleasure quarters, and invite along a few friends who understand your heart and want to help with your troubles. You'll have delicacies prepared, and engage in ribald conversation. You'll softly chant poetry while sipping wine and dallying with courtesans. By late morning, simurgh and phoenix will still be tumbling about in bed. Like the butterfly in love and the bee wild with lust, you'll feel the joy of sexual union penetrate your heart and bones. This is sure to lift your spirits!"

"Since you mention lust," Xiangzi commented, "this is another trap for men to fall into. How could it lift anyone's spirits? An ancient poem is to the point:

> *"At sixteen a beautiful maid's body is white and soft as butter,*
> *But in her loins she carries a sword to decapitate an ignorant man.*
> *Though you don't see a head roll,*
> *Secretly she sucks your marrow dry."*[9]

"The ancients have another poem, which speaks especially of the ills of wine, lust, wealth, and temper. I'll recite it to you:

"Wine, lust, wealth, and temper are four high walls—
How many lost souls are imprisoned within them?
If only a mortal can jump over them and escape—
That is the divine immortals' recipe for eternal youth."

The servant said, "The way you talk, it would seem that people all pass their days in the city of sorrow. How could they be happy for even a day?"

"Humans indeed pass their days in the city of sorrow," Xiangzi said. "There is a song to the tune 'Goat on the Mountainside' to illustrate it. Please listen:

"In my view it is in vain that people busy themselves all their life.
What will it help you to amass the family's fortune?
See, as you age, your looks fade away gradually.
Your sons and daughters may be dear to your heart,
But when one day death arrives,
Who will take your place on the wheel of rebirth?
Alas! How much longer will you wait before you turn back?
Alas! Where will the falling leaf finally end up?"

"You are still young," the servant said. "Where did you learn to talk so much? You should not be ungrateful for your uncle and aunt's kindness in raising you."

"Stop worrying and go to sleep; don't keep gabbling on," Xiangzi retorted.

The servants obeyed and withdrew, but held a secret discussion.

"The master has ordered us to guard Xiangzi carefully. We must take care not to make a mistake."

"Let's pretend to be asleep, and listen outside his door to what he is saying. If he comes out, we'll grab him, and report to the master."

"You're right. Let's be careful."

Inside the room Xiangzi thought to himself, "My uncle is so strict and fails to understand how important cultivation is to me. As I reckon it, out of the thirty-six moves, moving on is the best. If I don't make a run for it now, when will I have another chance?"

When the second watch struck, he took off his clothes, bound his hair in a yin-yang pattern, and changed into a cotton gown. Softly he walked to the door of Mme. Dou's room, knocked his head and said, "From an early age, I, Han Xiang, have received your favor. You brought me up, yet I never repaid you. Today I am unfilial and desert you. When will we meet again?"

Then he went to Luying's door and said, "Although we have been married for three years, all this time we have shared the same bed, but not the same pillow; the same mat, but not the same blanket. We were married in name only, and in this I have done you a great wrong. This morning I take my leave from you to cultivate myself. You must not be sad at our separation."

Having said his good-byes, Xiangzi heard the drum on the look-out tower strike the third watch. He wanted to leave by the front gate, but found it locked. So he had to climb over the wall, but not before leaving the following poem:

> Unwilling to study, afraid to become an official,
> Though the sun stands high I am still asleep, cradling my zither.
> This morning I escape the ranks of confused souls,
> And place my trust in that other world inside the immortal's pot.

When at daybreak the two servants could not find Xiangzi, they clutched their robes and pretended to cry.

Tuizhi came and asked them, "Why are you two crying? Where is Xiangzi?"

One of the servants called out, "Master, I hardly know how to say it—it's so strange! A toad has grown wings! Yesterday he was locked securely in the room, but at some point he must have quietly flown off."

"It's extraordinary!" the other chimed in. "A headcloth can walk! Yesterday evening it hung properly on the wall, and this morning the only thing that remains on my head is a patch of hair."

"You two dogs, what were my orders to you?" Tuizhi said. "You let Xiangzi get away, and now you try to shirk responsibility? You think you'll get a reward from those Daoist crooks—that's why you set him free to follow them. I'll hand you over to the magistrate to be questioned on Xiangzi's whereabouts."

"Please don't be angry any more, Master," the two replied. "Now that Xiangzi has run away, we will take his place."

"How could you take his place?" Tuizhi said.

"You don't have a son, and the two of us are almost like adopted sons to you. If you looked at us with different eyes and raised our status, we'd be the same as Xiangzi."

"This dog has gone crazy!" Tuizhi said.

"I am not crazy," the servant said. "You have not been successful in the union of the Young Boy and the Lovely Maid, and you couldn't keep your only nephew— how can you be the head of the family?"

When Tuizhi heard these words he let go, wailing, "Xiangzi, you have forsaken your family! Where have you gone? I am fifty-four years old and without sons or daughters. Once King Yama summons me and ghost emissaries come to take me away, who will wear the hempen garb of mourning for me and sacrifice at my tomb? The pain is unbearable!"

A poem may illustrate his plight:

> *The hair at both temples resembles silver threads,*
> *A half-withered tree fears to be swayed by the wind.*
> *The family may have innumerable ounces of gold,*
> *But without a son, all is in vain.*

When Mme. Dou and Luying heard Tuizhi's wails, they quickly came to see what was going on. When she saw Tuizhi lying on the floor, crying, Mme. Dou hurried to help him up and said, "What's going on?"

"Xiangzi has left the family," Tuizhi said.

"Is this true?" asked Mme. Dou.

"Aren't these clothes his? He stripped them off, scaled the wall, and left."

Crying, Luying said, "Although never close, he and I respected each other like guests, and there was never a bad word between us. A proverb says, 'A woman without a husband is like a body without a soul.' Now that he has left to cultivate himself, how can I still look people in the eye?"

"You will have to endure the disgrace, my daughter-in-law," Mme. Dou said. Crying, Luying retreated to her chamber.

"My wife, it is obvious that our nephew has betrayed our kindness in raising him," Tuizhi said. "It saddens my heart to look at his clothes and things. Let's light a fire and burn them."

"It would be a pity to burn them," Mme. Dou said. "Let's give them to the servants."

So Tuizhi handed the things to Zhang Qian and Li Wan, and then sent them out to post handbills for Xiangzi everywhere, in all prefectures, subprefectures, counties, inside and outside the cities, at passes and fords, in streets and markets, in all kinds of places, even at mountain monasteries and other secluded locations. The announcement read as follows:

> Vice Minister of Justice Han posts the following search notice: In the Han family of this prefecture (originally from Changli County in Yongping Prefecture), unfortunately, on this day in this month at the fifth watch the family's main son Han Xiangzi climbed over the wall and ran away, looking for his Daoist masters. His hair is

bound in a yin-yang pattern. He wears a dark brown patched robe. He beats a fisher drum, sings Daoist prayers, and wears tied hemp sandals. Whosoever detains him will receive a cash reward. Whosoever brings news of his whereabouts to my home will receive one hundred ounces of silver. The above notice be made known to everyone.

However, in spite of the wide distribution of this handbill, there was not a trace of Xiangzi, and Tuizhi was greatly saddened.

After Xiangzi had left the study and scaled the wall, he ran in the darkness to the city gate. The gate was still closed, and many traders and dealers were crowded in front of it, waiting for it to be opened. Some talked about their household affairs, others about official corruption. There were those who discussed business plans and those who debated the affairs of other families. Some were trading bawdy ballads, others hummed popular opera tunes to themselves. There was great confusion and noise, and everyone was in a bustle. Only Xiangzi calmed his mind, settled his nature, and sat on a rock without making a sound.

Among the crowd was a man who held a small lantern in his hand and walked back and forth. When he saw that Xiangzi made no sound and showed no emotions, he called out, "Master, since ancient times it has been said very well, 'The ministers at court are in the audience waiting hall in the cold of the fifth watch and the iron-clad generals cross the passes at night, but the monks in their mountain monasteries have not yet risen when the sun stands high, reckoning that fame and profit are not equaled by leisure.' For the little bit of profit our livelihood offers, the likes of us need to get up early in the morning and go to bed late. You ascetics, on the other hand, eat anywhere and dress however you like. As you don't desire fame or profit and are not concerned with honor or shame, gain or loss, at such an hour you should be in your plum-blossom tent on your mat of soft grass, stretching out your legs and slumbering peacefully. Why do you bother getting up so early and waiting for the gate to be opened?"

Before Xiangzi could reply, someone in the crowd cut in, "Friend, how can you know what's in the mind of this Daoist? He is a beggar who travels from place to place, speaking of true recipes and selling false medicines in the street, swindling people out of their money with a glib tongue. If you ask me, he's dressed up this way because he is too timid to be a robber and too lazy to be a burglar. Friend, how can you compare the eminent monks in the mountains with him?"

Another man said, "Friends, your roads are different, but your home is the same. You seek to benefit yourselves, but surely this little master is no immortal either. If he gets up early and goes to sleep late, it's because his own mind is full of desire to benefit himself. Why do you say he isn't fit to be a robber or a burglar?"

"Maybe he's a convict who has scaled the walls of his prison and escaped. He's disguised himself like this, and is afraid to speak in case he gives himself away. That's why he keeps his mouth shut tight," someone else suggested.

"He's so young," another man said. "Probably he didn't study hard, was beaten and scolded by his parents, and couldn't bear it. Or perhaps he failed in an examination and couldn't stand the shame. Or perhaps someone slept with his wife and he couldn't stand the anger, and crept away in disguise, swallowing his humiliation."

Another cut in, "Brothers, everyone has his own opinion. Why bother gossiping about others and worrying about other people's troubles? The *Thousand Character Essay* says it well, 'Don't speak of the shortcomings of others and don't presume upon your own superiority.'[10] There's also a verse that runs, 'Everyone should sweep the snow in front of his own door and not concern himself with the frost on other families' roofs.' Once the gate is open, everyone will be rushing out gaily. Let's not stay here and waste our breath with idle talk."

"This brother is right!" the others said. Everyone clapped their hands, stomped their feet, and laughed. His eyes open and his mouth speechless, as if he were deaf and mute, Xiangzi did not dare reply.

They were still talking when a city official came and opened the gate. Everyone ran out, struggling to be the first. Only Xiangzi remained behind, thinking to himself, "Today I am like a big fish who has escaped from the net, like a bird in distress that has left its cage. Now is the time to leave!" And so he hurried forth, singing a Daoist song to the tune of "Cassia Fragrance":

> "Finally today,
> I leave the city,
> To visit the immortals
> And become a better man.
> Just look at you officials—
> What are you scheming for?
> I have left my relatives,
> I have leaped out of the fiery pit.
> I speak no more of wine, lust, wealth, and temper—
> I have made a clean break with them.

Luxurious halls and fine houses I do not love,
What I love is to sleep in the shade of a pine.

"The sky is clear, the moon bright.
The white clouds play their tricks.
I have extracted myself from the waves of the karmic sea,
Paying no attention to the old and young in my family.
I have cut the ties to my family, I have cut the ties to my family!
I travel to the mountains to study the Dao,
Exerting myself every day.
If only I succeed in my efforts,
I shall fly up to the Nine Heavens."

If you don't know what happened after Xiangzi's departure, then listen to the next chapter.

6

ABANDONING HIS FAMILY BONDS, XIANGZI

CULTIVATES HIMSELF

A TRANSFORMED BEAUTY TEMPTS XIANGZI

FOR THE FIRST TIME

> *Discarding his home he roams dissolutely,*
> *Regarding the nobles with cold, indifferent eyes.*
> *In the end, great literary talents return to the yellow earth;*
> *Eventually, great military heroes grow white-haired and frail.*
> *After a bowl of cold rice he takes leave of the wilderness temple;*
> *Sorrowed by the passing of the ages, he sheds tears for the early autumn.*
> *Clad in a torn cassock, he sits on rush mat,*
> *Resting whenever he reaches a place to rest in.*

Xiangzi marched along the road for two days, eating when hungry, drinking when thirsty, resting at night, walking on at day, even though he did not know in which prefecture, which district, and what place the Zhongnan Mountains might be.

His masters Zhong and Lü had seen him climb over the wall and run away on his quest to seek them, but they feared that there might come a time when he would regret his decision, and then he would not be able to ascend to perfection and realize the fruits of his efforts. So they lowered their clouds, called forth the local earth god, and ordered him, "We received the Jade Emperor's command to enter the human world and deliver Han Xiang. Because Han Xiang agreed to follow us and cultivate himself, he abandoned his family bonds and gave up his relatives. Although he is now on his way looking for us, we are afraid that his determination may not be firm, so that it will be difficult for him to achieve success. During his journey you are to transform yourself many times and test him repeatedly. If he really has a true heart set upon studying the Way, and if he is not moved by lust and desires or confused by gain and loss, then we shall deliver him to the best of our ability. However, if he is lustful and filled with regret, then we shall send down heavenly thunder, and throw him into the darkest corner of hell, where he shall never be saved."

The old earth god bowed and promised, "I shall reverently obey your command."

When the two masters had given their orders to the mountain and earth god, they returned to the Zhongnan Mountains.

The old earth god got up and, by pointing with one finger of his hand, made a house appear. Outside its door there were three stalls. On one side were laid out new fruits of the season, fresh game, chickens and geese, seafood and mountain delicacies, meat and vegetables to go with the rice of one's meal. On the other side were displayed Hemp Maiden wine, Three Whites wine, Source of Kindness wine, Perfumed Snow wine, and both fresh unfermented and old fermented liquor, their aroma striking the nose and exciting the senses.

Between these shop counters sat a maiden neither tall nor short in stature, neither fat nor thin. Her eyebrows were knitted like the twigs of spring willows, her eyes shining like the ripples of autumn waves. Her two hands were soft and delicate, tender and white. Her feet were fine and small, pointed and curved. She was not dressed in rare brocade or extraordinary silks; still, she was so refined and delicate in her plain attire that it startled people's hearts and made them rub their eyes in wonder. It really seemed as if the ravishing Xishi of the state of Yue had been reborn in her native village of Zhuluo, or as if the famed beauty Flying Swallow of the Han dynasty had come again to enchant people with her bird-shooting dance.

When you entered the house there were carved balustrades and painted beams, beautiful shelves and lattice windows, embroidered curtains and vermilion blinds, colorful screens and ornamented mats. On the walls hung poems and paintings by renowned artists; on the tables were placed antiques and curiosities. Though the wealth thus displayed may not have surpassed that of a Wang Kai or a Shi Chong, neither did it fall short of the riches of a Dao Zhu or an Yi Dun. Leaning on a long staff, an old man wearing a blue headcloth and cotton gown sat in front of the entrance, letting the sun shine on his back.

As he came up the road, Xiangzi stopped before the old man in the doorway, bowed low, and said, "Old grandfather, I venture to ask which road I should take for the Zhongnan Mountains."

The old man shook his head and asked back, "Little master, why do you ask for the road to the Zhongnan Mountains?"

"I come from Changli County, and want to go to the mountains to look for my two masters," Xiangzi replied.

The old man shook his head again and said, "You won't be able to get there."

"What do you mean, I won't be able to get there?" asked Xiangzi.

The old man continued, "From here to the Zhongnan Mountains is 108,985 miles by road, plus another 3,000 miles by waterway. All along the way there are steep mountains and dangerous paths, winding cliffs and deep valleys, stone walls thousands of feet high, rocky hills in multitudes, curving streams tens of thousands of yards wide, swirling and beating up great waves. The traveler has to clamber along, pulling himself up by means of ropes. Furthermore, these mountains are full of ghosts and demon kings, poisonous snakes and fierce beasts, monstrous and evil birds, who devour anyone who comes along. Even a divine immortal passing through this area would become paralyzed with fear. You, wee little Daoist, are not even enough to make these monsters a full meal—how could you get that far?"

Xiangzi said, "Old grandfather, though you are so advanced in years, you can't even give a few honest words of guidance to your juniors, but instead try to scare people with improper talk. You don't expect me to listen to you and give up halfway, do you?"

The old man laughed, "Your words, little master, are foolish. Even though I am so advanced in years, and neither see nor hear very well, I do know that the road to the Zhongnan Mountains is difficult to travel. If you say my words are dishonest, all right, let me be wrong then."

"Old grandfather, it's not that I blame you for your words. It's just that my heart is firm and determined in the Way, and so I'm not afraid of your ten thousand rivers and thousand mountains, your snakes and tigers, spirits and ghosts. I am afraid only that there might be no such place as the Zhongnan Mountains in this world. If it does exist, then my masters are there. And in that case, nothing can keep me from getting there."

"If you say so," the old man said, "I won't get in your way. However, it is already getting dark, so how about staying in my house for the night and continuing your journey early tomorrow?"

"Having received your command, old grandfather, how could I disobey it?" Xiangzi replied. He got up, put his cloth bundle on his back, and walked into the inn. The old man remained sitting on the chair at the entrance and did not come inside.

Xiangzi stepped straight inside without first looking in, and so he was caught by surprise when a young woman come forth from beside the counter with smooth, swaying steps, in her hands a cup of fragrant, strong tea. She called out, "Sir, you had an arduous journey; please have some tea."

When Xiangzi received the tea in his hands, the girl lightly pressed them and said, "Sir, in which room would you like to rest?"

Xiangzi answered, "For us ascetics, a simple place with a mat is enough to pass the night. Why should I care what room I take?"

The girl made a low and gentle sound and said, "Sir, we have three classes of rooms. Cloud-traveling leaders of the immortals and officials who are passing through stay in the first-class rooms. Traveling merchants with ten thousand strings of cash hanging from their waist stay in the second-class rooms. Those who travel carrying burdens with a pole over the shoulder, who daily eat what they daily earn, settle down in the third-class rooms."

Her voice was high and clear, just like the twittering voice of the oriole warbling beside a flower. It pierced the heart and penetrated the marrow, driving men mad with desire.

"Madam, your house may have several classes of rooms, but I do not love luxury and will simply rest in a third-class room."

"I am a virgin and have never been given in marriage to a husband," she said angrily. "Why are you calling me 'madam'?"

"In addressing you I inadvertently made a mistake. I am sorry. Older Sister, do not be cross with me."

"We don't know each other, and don't belong to the same family either," the girl screamed at him. "How can you call me Older Sister?"

"As you aren't married yet, I erred in addressing you as 'madam,' so I called you Older Sister instead. What does that have to do with knowing or not knowing each other?"

The girl's face changed color as she said, "You ascetics don't know the difference between high and low and have no discrimination whatsoever. I heard that those girls in brothels are called 'older sisters.' I am a virgin of good family, so why do you call me Older Sister rather than 'maid' or Miss?"

"You are right, maid; it is I who was wrong," Xiangzi acquiesced.

The girl said, "I too received my essence from my father and my blood from my mother. Like any human being, I was nurtured in the womb for ten months, not baked out in a tile kiln. Calling me 'maid,' as you did just now, enrages even a sweet-tempered person like me!"

Xiangzi said to himself, "This girl is excessive in her moods and difficult to talk to. She is really embarrassing."

Laughing, the girl drew Xiangzi towards her and said, "A handsome little mas-

A transformed beauty tempts Xiangzi for the first time.

ter like you must be the child of a wealthy and noble family. Why do you want to go and stay in a third-class room? Trust me, you don't want the first or second class either. Go instead to my hall; it's a very quiet, elegant, and clean place. Wouldn't it be nice for you to spend the night there all by yourself?"

"I spend my time begging for alms, and pass my days following my destiny without so much as half a penny in my pocket," Xiangzi replied. "Like everybody else I'll make my bed in the cheapest room and set out early in the morning."

"Adjacent to that hall is my bedroom, which no man has ever entered," the girl said. "Now, sir, today I want to open my charitable heart, and won't take any of your silver. How about I trick the old grandfather and lead you to bed, sir?"

Xiangzi protested, "I am an ascetic. I do not enter the women's quarters, and in my affairs I do not deceive and do not act contrary to my conscience. How could I dare enter your room, maid?"

"There is a confidential matter that I want to tell you about. You must trust me," said the girl.

"I am listening."

"This year I am fifteen years old. I have neither brothers nor sisters, only my grandfather, who is more than ninety years old and almost deaf and blind. He has gathered a fortune of a million strings of cash, but it is of no use, because there is no one to take over its management and inherit it. I am here every day, receiving the guests and merchants who come and go, but there's never been one as young and handsome as you, sir. Now I'll tell Grandfather that I would be willing to turn over my bridewealth to take you into the family as a son-in-law and husband, to be head of the family and take charge of the accounts. That we have met today proves the saying 'If they are destined for each other, two people will meet even if they are a thousand miles apart. Without predestination, they won't meet even when facing each other.' I don't know if in your heart you will consent or not?"

Xiangzi blushed and his ears got hot; he couldn't bring out even half a sound in response.

"Little master, stop putting on airs and throwing poses!" the girl pursued. "Whenever ascetics see a woman, they're like leeches stinging for blood—all they want is to penetrate inside. Why don't you say anything when a virgin like myself is willing to receive you as a husband? Is it that you still have parents and elders and you fear the crime of marrying without their permission? In ancient times, the Great Shun married without telling his parents. You're not a Great Shun, are you? If you commit this little wrong, your parents won't blame you. The magistrate won't find fault with you either, and even if there should be some trouble with the officials, I'll arrange for a few hundred taels of silver in bribes to guarantee that the magistrate won't bother you. Why worry about him?"

Xiangzi exploded angrily, "I just said that you are a daughter of good family, but in fact you are a shameless, lewd, debased person. My uncle is Minister of Justice. My father-in-law is a scholar in the Hanlin Academy. My beautiful wife is the daughter of a respectable official family. I gave up all of this to become an ascetic. How can I respect a wretch who has so little regard for face?"

"You are a vagrant and vagabond," the girl shot back, "an uncouth Daoist who goes from door to door. As I meant well and did not want to despise you, I offered to give you some family property and receive you as my husband, but you berated me as shameless, lewd, and debased. You really are a hapless fellow who doesn't recognize his good fortune."

"The good fortune that I enjoy is of a pure kind that can never be used up," Xiangzi said. "Why should I value your filth and your stinking money?"

"Pure or not, enjoyment or not—that's not up to me," the girl retorted. "What I need to know is, do you want an official settlement or a private settlement?"

"What do you mean, 'official or private settlement'?" Xiangzi asked.

"Well, I won't let you go," the girl replied. "If you want the official settlement, I'll start screaming and say that you, an ascetic, have raped a girl of good family. I'll have the local official send you to the magistrate. He'll give you a few thousand lashes with the thorny stick, display you in a cangue in some marketplaces, revoke your Daoist diploma, and return you to lay status. That's the official settlement. If you agree to enter my family as a son-in-law and marry me, you will become a model husband like Liang Hong and I will imitate that perfect wife Meng Guang and never utter an idle word. That's the private settlement."

"There is a cauldron of seething oil in front of me, knives and saws behind me, tigers and wolves on my left, and a great flood on my right," Xiangzi said. "But I will maintain my original nature and destiny, and my inborn character. Why be afraid of settling officially and not privately, or settling privately and not officially?"

The girl then grabbed Xiangzi with one hand and shouted, "Grandfather, come quickly. The Daoist wants to rape me."

The old man came in, grasping a stick, his head shaking with rage, and said, "What's that you say, Granddaughter?"

Xiangzi was frightened out of his wits, but he managed to say "I, Han Xiang, have one former life less than you. This morning I am willing to make good the difference. It's up to you, old grandfather. Whatever you may do with me, I won't object."

"My little gentleman, you really are foolish," the old man said. "A young lad like you ought to be somebody's son-in-law, manage some family property, beget sons and bring up daughters, thus connecting the ancestors and later generations. You didn't get your life in exchange for a little salt—it's too precious for you to speak of dying."

"Grandpa," the girl interjected, "When he saw that I was alone, he held me in his arms, kissed me, and touched my waist. Since I cried out, now he's trying to deceive us by pretending he wants to die. But really he's by three parts fiercer than a robber."

"All I have to say is, why do you want to die?" the old man said. "If my granddaughter is acceptable to you, I will have her marry you and make you a grandson-in-law. You'll manage the shop outside the front door and keep me fed until I die, that's all. Why do you have to seek death?"

"Old grandfather, I removed myself from my family bonds. When I walked away, I left my life behind me. How can you say I don't need to die?" Xiangzi said.

"If you seek death, there are several kinds you can get," the old man said. "If you owe money to the officials on one side and private debts on the other, you will be pressed, flogged, and beaten until you can take no more. No clothes will cover your body, no food will fill your mouth. You won't be able to stand the hunger, cold, poverty, and suffering. All kinds of diseases and pains will assault you until you are neither dead nor alive. Lying on the bed, struggling to get up, groping about and falling down—you won't be able to endure it. If you do evil and commit crimes, your legs will be fettered and your hands manacled. You will suffer unbearable ordeals before finally you go in search of the road of death. If someone has a beautiful daughter and a well-endowed household and wants to take you in as a son-in-law, won't you then agree to follow your heart? Why do you have to die?"

Xiangzi replied, "I want with all my heart simply to lead an ascetic life and cultivate myself. Don't bring up entering the family as a son-in-law again."

The old man said, "If you want to know the way in the mountains, you have to ask people who have been there. I, too, when I was young, once encountered two itinerant Daoists who bragged that they possessed divine powers that could lift up the heavens and pull up the earth, as well as magical methods that could stir up the sea and overturn the rivers. They would tip over their gourds and let out a thousand rays of auspicious pneuma. They would swish about their fly-brushes and gather up ten thousand kernels of golden elixir.

"When they saw that I was good-looking, they deceived me by praising the benefits of self-cultivation. I was so impressed by them that I reckoned that if they were not heavenly divine immortals, they must at least be Daoists who had come from the three islands of Penglai. If I went with them to cultivate myself, that would be better than to be an ordinary person in this world of red dust, a dull peasant in a thatched hut.

"Thereupon I turned my back on father and mother and went away with the Daoists to seek eternal life. Who would have known that these two were charlatans and crooks, out to deceive people? They had tricked me into following them. The whole journey they used me, by day as a slave, by night as a wife. We traversed prefectures and crossed districts, passing through countless places. All the while they made such game of me that I was at a loss what to do.

"Eventually I decided it was best to abandon them without saying anything and return home. I was an only child, so you can imagine how my parents had cried and wailed when they discovered that I was gone. They put up search notices everywhere, asked the oracle sticks, and paid for divination, spending untold sums of money. When they saw me return home, what great joy there was—just as if they had found a treasure!

"Behind my back, my parents discussed the situation and said, 'Our child spent a lot of time with the two villainous Daoists, and surely was corrupted by them. How could he, in his heart, not know about sex? If we don't get him a wife soon, and somebody takes him away again, this time we may not hope for his return.' They hurried to find a go-between, who mediated a betrothal for me. She got me a wife, who gave birth to a son.

"Years and months went by and my son grew up. He married and brought in a daughter-in-law. He had only one child, the granddaughter that you see here. When she was three years old, my son fell ill and died. My daughter-in-law remarried and left, and my wife and I underwent innumerable hardships until we succeeded in bringing up our granddaughter. My wife also passed away two years ago. There's all this family property, and not one relative to come and inherit it. Therefore I want to take a son-in-law into the family.

"Now, you ponder becoming an ascetic and cultivating yourself, probably because you met some vagrant Daoists who moved your heart by deception. Why put yourself to so much trouble? It is better to do as my granddaughter says, remain in my family as a son-in-law, continue this bloodline, and take charge of this family's property. Wouldn't this be convenient for both of us?"

"The words you speak, old man, are all confused," Xiangzi retorted. "It is in vain that you were allowed to live to such an old age. Now I am going to leave this inn, and that will be it."

The girl spoke to him again, in a seductive tone. "It is already dusk, sir. Everywhere on your way you'll run into jackals, wolves, tigers, leopards, snakes, scorpions, spirits, and demons. If you leave my door, it will mean uselessly throwing away your life. If you don't agree to marry in as a son-in-law, at least rest for a night in the third-class rooms and set out again when it's light outside. What do you say?"

"Whether snakes harm me or tigers maul me—this has been predestined in a former life. Whether I die well or violently, I'll be equally dead. I won't bother you to concern yourselves with me," Xiangzi said.

"Whenever you say something, one hears foolishness," the old man said. "You want to become an ascetic and look for your masters, yet you need to preserve your present life before you can reach that eternal life. If you now are going to die, what was the point in becoming an ascetic and seeking immortality? I'll explain it to you with a story."

"What story, old man?" Xiangzi asked.

"As an old man, I have eaten a bit more salt than you have tasted soy sauce in your life. I read in a book that Emperor Wu of the Han dynasty once heard that there were several pecks of magical wine in a cave on Mount Jun. Anyone who drank it would enjoy eternal life and would never die.

"So the emperor fasted for seven days, then looked for and found the wine. His minister Dongfang Shuo said, 'I've heard of this wine. I would like to taste it first.' He took the wine and drank it all up in one draught. Emperor Wu was very angry and wanted to kill him, but Dongfang Shuo said, 'What your minister drank was a magical wine of deathlessness. Now, if Your Majesty kills me, then it is actually a wine that speeds up death, and it would have been no use to Your Majesty. If it really is magical wine, even if Your Majesty tried to kill me, I still would not die.' Emperor Wu laughed and pardoned him.

"As you can see, it was a magical wine of deathlessness only because Dongfang Shuo's life was spared. You hope for eternal life, yet you first set off on the road of death. This way you'll just speed up your own demise. So why become an ascetic? Why cultivate yourself?"

"After all your talk, I am all the more determined to leave. I won't listen, I won't!" said Xiangzi.

"Grandfather, don't waste your breath on an uncouth Daoist who doesn't appreciate the favors people do for him," the girl said angrily. "It's like blowing hot air against a wall. Get a rope, hang the villainous Daoist from a rafter at the back of the house, and let him starve to death. I don't expect there are any relatives to come and plead for his life."

"Since he does not know good from bad, there is no point in hanging him," the old man answered. "Let's just chase him out the door and let him throw away his own life!"

The girl did as she was told, and with one push shoved Xiangzi out the door. As she did it she chanted,

> "Ten fine fingers came to serve tea,
> A golden bowl full of peonies.
> The fool did not realize the flowers' meaning.
> Disappointed I go to the balcony, but I do not sigh."

Xiangzi was extremely happy to find himself outside the inn's door. Quickly he answered,

> "You say your face is beautiful like a flower;
> In my view it is more like a rotten white gourd.
> A flowery face will not be pretty for even a thousand days;
> A rotten gourd is cast away without anyone sighing for it."

How did Xiangzi fare after he left this place? Listen to the explanations of the next chapter.

7

TIGER AND SNAKE BLOCK THE ROAD TO TEST HAN XIANG

MONSTERS AND DEMONS FLEE FROM PERFECT FIRE

Do not laugh at brambles,
They produce iris and orchid.
Remove the brambles' thorns,
And view iris and orchid in your palm.
Up close, iris and orchid are fragrant.
At a distance, brambles stick in your garment.
In the courtyard one plants iris and orchids,
But the brambles remain beside the road.

As it happened, when the girl pushed Xiangzi out the door, the moon and stars were not shining and he could not make out the road. All he could do was to concentrate his spirit, stabilize his breathing, sit under a big tree, and wait for the daylight.

However, he did not take into account that the girl would grumble to her grandfather, "Such a handsome little master. Surely he is suffering unbearable hardships. You should have let me hang him from that rafter, then he would have come round to marrying into our family as a son-in-law. It makes no sense that you drove him out, Grandfather. If he met a tiger or a wolf on the road, wouldn't it maul and kill him? Then how could we find him again? It was such a handsome little master that came to me."

But the next moment she was cursing Xiangzi again, saying, "That villainous little Daoist doesn't look people in the eyes and treats them with complete disrespect. He must have been born from a hollow mulberry tree, or else come into the world by bubbling up from a river. Outside at night, if he isn't mauled by a tiger, he's sure to be injured by a snake. Then he'll be dragged about by pigs or gnawed at by dogs—all because he was ungrateful for my warm solicitude toward him."

The next moment she again cried out, "How can such a handsome man be, at heart, so stupid? Why are you so obstinate? Are you Liuxia Hui born again, or Lu Zhonglian come back into the world?"[1]

A minute later she called the old grandfather and said, "Grandfather, you are sending him to his doom! Quickly light a torch and bring him back. He mustn't uselessly throw away his life." But a minute after that she said, "You are old, and almost blind and deaf. In the darkness you won't find him. I expect he hasn't gone far. Although my shoes are curved and my stockings small, let me go myself and ask him to come back."

These seductive tones, delicate expressions, and soft words were all blown into Xiangzi's ears by a favorable wind, in the hope of touching him. However, Xiangzi's ambition to cultivate himself was firm as metal and stone, and was not affected in the least. When he heard her words, he became all the more impatient. Without concern for the darkness he marched off blindly.

He had not walked thirty or fifty paces when he suddenly heard the voice of the wind weeping in the trees, the sound of water flowing. A tiger ghost called out, and a mountain elf responded.

He had been running for two or three miles when ahead he saw two lanterns shining brightly. A great gust of wind roared up behind the lanterns, but the lights shone straight at Xiangzi, not shaking at all in the wind.

Xiangzi chanted to himself, "My masters are powerful and perceptive. Seeing me unable to walk in this darkness, from afar they sent two lamps to give me light." By this time, the lamps had come slowly up in front of him, just half an arrow-shot away.

But they were not two lamps at all, but the gleaming eyes of a fierce tiger. When the tiger saw Xiangzi, he threw himself into a mighty pose.

> The head lowered, the tail moving, from his mouth a roar like thunder. His body tense, the claws scratching the ground, beating up dust. The whole body covered with stripes and dots, the silky hairs hard like needles of steel. His eyes full, his teeth densely lined up like swords and lances. When foxes and rabbits in the mountains hear his voice, they go into hiding. When musk deer and bucks in the valleys

smell his scent, they conceal themselves. This truly is the king among beasts with golden eyes and white forehead. He does not yield to the black roars of the dark panther and the yellow lion.

Xiangzi had not realized that it was a tiger, but still took it for two bright lanterns. When he saw from afar that they were the eyes of a tiger, he was so startled that he fell to the ground paralyzed with fear.

The tiger moved all around Xiangzi's body, circling to the left, coming round to the right, sniffing here and snuffling there, but it seemed he would not eat dead meat. Suddenly he turned Xiangzi's body around with his paw.

Finally Xiangzi's soul returned to his body, as if he was just awakening from a dream. Trembling with fear, he got up and said, "My masters possess the magical powers to subdue dragons and suppress tigers. Now that I have given up all family affairs and am looking for my masters far away, it makes no sense that I should lose my life in the mouth of a tiger."

With an effort he stepped forward and shouted, "Tiger, as the chief of all beasts in the mountains, you should understand something of human nature. I, Han Xiang, have abandoned the graves of my parents and the love of wife and child. The masters I am seeking are lords who are willing to forsake their bodies and lose their lives. They're not the sort of itinerant Daoists who covet life and are afraid of death. Now you put up this mighty pose, but I won't be afraid of you. Nor will I follow the example of the old Buddha who cut his flesh to feed the eagles and forsook his body to feed the tigers. If you frighten me to death, beast, my masters won't forgive you. Besides, I'll make sure to accuse you when I arrive at the palace of King Yama. If you eat me, don't think you will get off unscathed."

When the tiger heard this, he looked as if he understood human language. He shook his head, swung his tail, and ran off into the flowing mists of the mountains.

At this point, Xiangzi finally understood his mind, realized his nature, and returned to his original self. This poem puts it well:

> Do not say that there are no spirits—they do indeed exist.
> Look up: they are just three feet above your head.
> Had he still made the smallest distinctions in his mind,
> In the fierce tiger's jaws his life would have ended.

When Xiangzi saw that the tiger was gone, he hurried on a few paces, only to see soaring clouds subduing the peaks, the high morning red winging the mountain ranges. The peaks were soaring, the ravines plunging deep, filled with mist.

The sky gradually lightened. Xiangzi was just about to walk ahead to look for human habitation, beg some vegetarian food, and after eating set off again, when suddenly a bright flash of fire lit up the darkness of clouds and mist. He could make out a broad road.

It so happened that there were no inns in the vicinity, and few people traveled in this area. When Xiangzi focused his eyes and looked closely, he saw a poisonous serpent, as thick as a house pillar and seven or eight fathoms long, lying on the ground and blocking his path. So great was the serpent's fierceness that travelers did not come close. Here is a rhapsody to illustrate it:

> The whole body covered with scaly armor like a red dragon appearing in the mountains; the whole body gleaming like a brush fire scorching the foot of high ranges. Head aloft, tongue protruding, fierce and unyielding, it faced now south, now north. Hollow eyes and cruel jaws, ugly and evil, it darted east and west. At the end of its tail there was a hook—get hit and it's all over. Among the scales it had spurs—they inflict grievous injury. Could it be the white dragon who, disguised as a fish, fell into Yu Qie's net?[2] It was certainly more than the drunkenly drawn bow shape to which the retainer of Chu added feet.[3] At that point Han Xiang had not yet lived up to Sunshu Ao, who buried the double-headed snake and became renowned in all three parts of Chu,[4] or Peigong of Han, who punished with his sword the snake who blocked the road, securing the three territories of Qin.[5]

When the snake saw Xiangzi, it blew out a mouthful of poisonous breath, and Xiangzi fell to the ground in a state of alarm and fright. However, unexpectedly, the snake slithered off into the grass and bushes.

The reader will ask, "The snake and the tiger had come to pursue and attack Xiangzi. Why didn't they eat him instead of going quietly away?" The only reason was that Xiangzi had turned his back on uncle and aunt, had given up wife and child, had traveled over land and water for ten thousand miles, had cultivated himself and discerned the Way.

The two masters Zhong and Lü were afraid his mind of the Way might not be firm and his fickle human mind might burst forth suddenly, so that it would be difficult for him to renounce and transform his wordly body and ascend to the heavenly realms. Therefore they materialized the snake and the tiger to frighten him in order to see if he would backslide and regret his decision. Since Xiangzi did not do so, the snake and tiger naturally did not dare injure him.

Masters Zhong and Lü, with their eyes of wisdom, immediately saw that Xiangzi was chaste, unafraid of snakes and tigers, and undaunted by hardship and labor. He truly was a disciple of the School of Mysteries. They were willing to deliver him, but were still afraid that his demonic obstructions to enlightenment were not yet removed, that the roots of sin were not yet purified. So they commanded a demon judge, "Test him under the Yellow Sand Tree. If he spews out the true fire of samadhi, we will finally allow him to come and see us. Should he shrink back in fear, withdraw, and hide, we will throw him into the underworld and he shall never again be reborn."

The demon judge received the order and went under the Yellow Sand Tree, where he blocked the road. How did this demon judge look?

> A hideous head, his face fierce and evil. A hideous head, like that of a snake-dragon coming out of an earth hole. His face fierce and evil, like that of a guardian spirit standing by the temple gate. His body an indigo color overlayed with red, long teeth in his blue face. On his hands and feet the muscles lay bare and the bones shone through, his hooked fists covered in red hair. Seeing him from afar, he seemed to reach the sky and cross the earth, more awesome than a fierce guardian spirit. Seeing him from nearby, he extended wide and round like a winnowing fan and a rice peck. If he was not Death himself from the netherworld, chasing after souls, he surely must have been that iron-shod and bronze-headed pilgrim in search of the sutras.[6]

As soon as Xiangzi saw the demon judge blocking the road, he thought, "I have come ten thousand miles over land and water in the search for my masters. My only wish is to meet the ones who may satisfy my long-harbored ambition. Who would have expected that all along the way I would encounter so many obstacles? It's not that the masters don't come to save me—no, the reason must be that my mind of the Way is not firm. That's why I haven't succeeded in finding my masters. I'll step forward and ask what kind of demon this is, and then decide what to do."

Xiangzi straightened up, quickly put his clothes in order, and shouted, "Where do you come from, strange spirit? What is your place, evil demon? How dare you come and block my way?"

"I am an upright and unselfish general of awe-inspiring reputation, a divine lord, majestic and fierce, just and possessing the Way," the demon judge answered. "At the place I occupy, I have received temple sacrifices for a thousand years. I particularly like to eat the liver and gall of living people, as well as whole bodies of blood and flesh. You, little Daoist, are not enough to give me a full meal. What do you want here?"

Xiangzi said, "The world holds only the Heavenly Emperor, the gods, the immortals, the city gods, and the earth gods who assure that wind and rain are seasonable and who protect the common people. How can there be someone called 'divine lord,' who indulges his nature by being greedy and rapacious, and who gives rein to the passions of his mouth and stomach? Judging by your words, you are nothing but a demonic spirit and a ghostly apparition, pretending to possess divine efficaciousness and recklessly devouring living people, arrogating to yourself heavenly authority. I, Han Xiangzi, not shirking hardships, have been looking for my teachers over ten thousand miles. I escaped with my life from the mouths of snakes and tigers; why should I be afraid of an evil demon blocking my way?"

When the demon judge heard his words, he raised the flames of desire and fanned the smoke of passion, causing the sky to be covered until it was so dark that one could not see the palm of one's extended hand. The broad road was black, as if blocked by a bronze wall or iron masonry. In the smoke and flames appeared strange forms and abnormal shapes, monstrous things long and short, big and small. I don't know how many thousands or hundreds there were altogether, all laughing and tittering, rushing straight at Xiangzi.

Xiangzi having come to this place was just like a chicken having fallen into the latrine. Ten thousand maggots crowded together, a rank odor fell onto the earth, and a thousand ants accumulated. In such a situation, one's mind might easily be seized by anxiety and one's will might become disoriented, like a dog who has lost its master. But fortunately Xiangzi's nature was firm and his spirit clear, like that of a dragon hibernating in a cave. Immediately he straightened up and without retreating a single step he spat out a flaming red Perfect Fire, which rushed against the evil demon. What did this Perfect Fire look like?

> Without furnace and without stove, it emerges from the Cinnabar
> Field and passes out through the throat. Without flames and without
> smoke, it jumps from the Niwan Palace, its brilliance shaking the
> silvery sea. Blazing without the help of sulphur, dazzlingly red, it
> shoots straight up to the constellations of Dipper and Herdboy.
> Why bother with boxes and drums to draw wind? Soaring red, this

fire distantly rushes into the Milky Way. Hit by it, your head gets scorched and your forehead boiled, both transformed into swirling ashes. All nearby flee in a hurry and hide out of sight. Truly your mind's spirit terrace has its own seeds—why beg them from your neighbor? As they are produced in the heart's vermilion palace, do not let all your yang be exposed to the light of day.

When Xiangzi spewed forth this Perfect Fire, three feet and three inches high, it scattered all the demons. Only then did Xiangzi set his mind at rest and say, "If I hadn't received the secret formulas from my masters and produced a Perfect Fire to scatter these evil demons, they would have overwhelmed me and carried me off to the netherworld." Thereupon he walked ahead with great steps and resumed his journey.

After several peaceful and uneventful days, he saw a high mountain in the distance ahead. What did it look like?

Green cliffs and azure ranges many feet high, soaring loftily to touch the layered clouds. Red precipices and blue peaks tens of thousand feet high, rocky summits linking up with the higher realms. On the top of ranges pines and cedars stand in close array, on the flanks and in the hollows grass and iris grow luxuriantly. Among flying birds there are dark cranes and blue phoenixes, yellow orioles and long-tailed fly-catchers. Among walking beasts there are black bears and blue deer, dark panthers and gray musk deer. Flying falcons and chasing with hounds, in winter hunters set their traps everywhere. Seeking stillness and searching for the mysterious, Daoists stay here in all seasons. It really is the place of the grottoes of gods and immortals, a ladder to the Penglai Isles.

When Xiangzi saw it, he said, "The high mountains ahead must be the Zhongnan Mountains. That must be where the two masters live." He ran up the mountains, seeking to find the masters. Only then would his mind be satisfied. As the following poem puts it:

If one is sure to attain the Way, why worry that the road of immortality is long?
If one's literary talents are great, why fear that success in the examinations may come late?

Monsters and demons flee from Perfect Fire.

As Xiangzi hastened up the mountain, he said to himself, "Why is it that after walking so many roads, I still see no sign of my masters? I don't know on which peak they live."

Just at that moment he happened to look up. In the dark forest undergrowth a signboard with golden letters was visible. "That place must be their hermitage," Xiangzi said.

Hastily he walked on in great strides, pulling himself up on climbing plants and holding on to creepers. He saw layers of pines adorning the rocks, rows of cedars leaning against the walls. Around the mountain ranges clouds swirled. On a strangely shaped peak in the sunlight there stood a lonely tree, surrounded by a multitude of mountains. In a cave in the distance he saw an immortal sitting on a stone bed.

When Xiangzi turned his gaze, he could no longer see the gold-lettered signboard, nor the grotto of the divine immortal. Looking left and right, he did not see the road either. Suddenly he was anxious. He looked up to heaven and shouted, "Masters, Han Xiang today walked to this place, yet still he does not get to meet you. It must be because my determination for the Way is not firm that you do not come to receive me. However, my determination to cultivate myself will end only when I die. If that is not sufficient then I will commit suicide here, and let my soul go find you."

Just then he heard the sound of a flute in the distance. When he looked carefully, a herdboy, astride a black ox, was riding by in the woods. Xiangzi shouted, "Elder Brother Shepherd, come over here. I want to ask you for some information."

"It's full of the nets of dust and desire over there," the herdboy answered. "What sort of man are you that you willingly walk there and don't turn back? I know that trap, and I won't walk into it."

"Older Brother Shepherd, please show me the road of life," Xiangzi implored him mournfully. "Once I have escaped from these nets, I will give you many thanks!"

"In that case, my black ox knows the way," the herdboy said. "Wait until I have led him over to you, then we will ride together on his back. Thus I will lead you slowly out to the road of life."

"Elder Brother, do not deceive me," Xiangzi said.

And really, the herdboy rode the ox straight over to Xiangzi and called on him to climb up on its back. The herdboy sat before him, playing on his flute in birdlike tunes the following poem, even as they rode on:

> *The ox roars and acts wildly,*
> *Control it with a rope through its nose.*

If it is even a little relaxed,
Confusion and desires will expel your original yang.

When Xiangzi heard the sound of the flute, a thought suddenly struck him and he asked, "Older Brother Shepherd, who taught you to play this flute?"

"It is my master who taught me," the herdboy said.

"Who is your master?"

"My master is no common man, but a divine immortal of Heaven."

"It wouldn't happen to be the master Zhongli?"

"If you are talking about that Zhongli," replied the herdboy, "He's a hot-tempered, covetous demon. He kills people without batting an eye. He is certainly no divine immortal!"

"It would not happen to be Master Lü Dongbin?" Xiangzi then asked.

The herdboy laughed and said, "Daoist Lü got drunk three times in the tower of Yueyang, played selfishly with White Peony, sold false ink in Dingzhou, and hawked poor combs in Xunyang. Every time, he used trickery to cheat people. He is even less a divine immortal than Zhongli."

"You have eyes, but you do not recognize Mount Tai, and you just use your mouth to talk nonsense," Xiangzi scolded him. "These masters of mine, Zhongli and Lü, are the leaders of the heavenly immortals, the superiors of the divine sages. If you've never met them, then leave it at that. How dare you slander them?"

"In these mountains, there is hardly a day or an hour when I do not see divine immortals," the herdboy said. "Since you esteem these two unworthy Daoists, I will be honest with you. If you want to meet my master, there will be many difficulties. But if you only want to seek Zhong and Lü, they are not far from here. I can take you there all right."

"Elder Brother, I only want to meet masters Zhong and Lü," Xiangzi said. "May I trouble you to show me the way?" The herdboy pulled at the ox's nose-rope, and they rode off toward the east.

At this moment it was as if Xiangzi was awakening from a dream. It was just as described in this poem:

By clearly pointing out the even road,
He lifted a man out of the nets of Heaven and Earth.

If you do not know where Xiangzi went, listen to the explications of the next chapter.

8

A BODHISATTVA MANIFESTS A NUMINOUS SIGN AS HE

ASCENDS TO THE UPPER REALM

HAN XIANGZI GUARDS THE ELIXIR CAULDRON WITH FIRM

CONCENTRATION

> *Shakyamuni was a Buddha from the west,*
> *The Lord Lao was an eminent worthy of the east.*
> *The words of the Buddha and Laozi are ancient,*
> *And need not fear disturbance in east or west.*
> *If the spirit is settled, the Jade Cauldron will be firm and settled.*
> *If the mind is busy, the Elixir Stove will be unfocused.*
> *If a bodhisattva will ascend to Heaven,*
> *Why fear that an ordinary mortal will not turn back?*

Together with the shepherd boy, Han Xiangzi rode into the mountains astride the black ox. Along the road he saw high mounds and tall cliffs, around which clouds descended to merge with the mist. The green cliffs were dotted black; the hematite rocks showed their red hue.

When they arrived at a windy mountain with a wheel-shaped cave, a flow of cold air, bleak and chilly, struck Xiangzi so violently that he almost lost his balance. The shepherd, however, was not afraid at all. On the back of the black ox he waved joyously, like an eagle or hawk greeting the wind, like an osprey spreading its wings.

Having turned in a northwesterly direction and traveled another twenty miles, they saw a bodhisattva, his pearly cap reflecting the light of the setting sun, his face solemn. He was sitting facing east under a *pattra* tree, auspicious herbs growing all around him. Xiangzi thought to himself, "Although the two teachings of Daoism and Buddhism are different, their source is the same. If I am really to become a golden immortal, the bodhisattva will confirm it by a numinous sign."

As this thought occupied Xiangzi's mind, a Buddha image appeared on the rock face, the hair gathered in blue spirals, the golden face round and radiant as the full moon, the body thirty or forty feet tall. When they had walked on another fifteen paces, five hundred blue birds came flying, circled around the bodhisattva three times, and left again. After a while, celestial standard-bearers led the bodhisattva up to the heavenly realm. Xiangzi thought to himself, "The numinous sign manifested by the Buddha means that I shall achieve the Dao and become an immortal."

The shepherd said, "Among the Five Phases and the Three Realms the Dao alone is to be honored. This bodhisattva was the Buddha Shakyamuni. Once our Most High Lord Lao left the Han Pass riding on a black ox. He delivered the Buddha and brought him to China. It is only for this reason that he possesses this extraordinary numinosity."

"How did you come to know him?" Xiangzi asked.

"Sages may differ in their outward majesty, but in their minds they are the same. I know this bodhisattva because he and my master often visit each other," the shepherd said.

"If you know him, why don't you ascend with him to Heaven?"

The shepherd boy laughed. "If I went with him, who would take you to meet my master?"

"It is just like in the saying 'Unless you are guided by a fisherman, you won't see the waves,'" Xiangzi said.

While they were talking, they crossed several mountains. The shepherd boy said, "Han Xiang, this is the grotto palace of the patriarchal masters, the jasper shrine of sages and immortals. Why aren't you already hastening towards it, instead of sitting there at your self-satisfied ease? Could it be that you are becoming a bit disrespectful?"

"How could I dare be disrespectful?" Xiangzi said.

"If you have a faithful heart, then step forth courageously," the shepherd directed.

Obediently Xiangzi descended from the back of the ox and ran on for several miles, skipping like a swallow and leaping like a snow goose in his excitement. Eventually he arrived at a place where mountain peaks with layered cliffs spread out, torrents meandered, and precipices plunged deeply. Blue cedars shaded the peaks, green pines lined the banks. Foaming and swirling rivers wound through the land like strips of white silk, and trees grew in profusion. The cries of flying birds and soaring fowl harmonized with each other.

The double-leafed door to the grotto was half open, as a young Daoist stood in front of it. Xiangzi quickly approached and greeted him. The youth asked, "Would you be the crane boy from the mouth of the Xiang River in Cangwu Prefecture?"

"My name is Han Xiang, and I am no crane boy," Xiangzi replied.

"If you are not the crane boy, you are not allowed to meet my masters. Please go away," the youth said.

Xiangzi started to protest. "I have come ten thousand miles in search of my masters. Now I've got to this place, how can you make fun of me in this manner?"

The shepherd admonished the young Daoist, "Elder Brother, just report him to the masters, and leave it to them to decide whether they will see him or not. Relax, don't get all tensed up."

"If you say so, Elder Brother, I will go in and make a report," the Daoist said. "If the masters don't allow you to come in for a meeting, then be off and stop making trouble."

Xiangzi nodded and remained standing, not daring to say too much. The Daoist youth went inside and reported Xiangzi's presence to the two masters Zhong and Lü. They said, "Han Xiang is the crane boy. How could there be another? Bring him in."

When he came inside, Xiangzi bowed to the two masters eight times. Kneeling on the floor he said, "Masters, you caused me much suffering when you abandoned me. After a thousand difficulties and a hundred troubles, I have finally arrived here to meet you. I hope that you will take pity on me."

"Han Xiang, you come too late. We have no use for you here," Master Zhong told him.

"When you were about to leave, you told me that if I wanted to see you again I could come to the Zhongnan Mountains, ten thousand miles away. Therefore I abandoned my family, scaled the wall, and fled to look for you. How can you now say that you have no use for me?" Xiangzi said.

"I told you to come quickly and look for us. By now you are too late. I have delivered another person and therefore have no use for you," he replied.

"After I turned my back on my uncle and aunt, I lost my way and barely escaped with my life from ten thousand deadly dangers. That is why I got here late. I hope that you will find it in your hearts to deliver me—that truly would be an act of outstanding mercy."

Master Zhong called to Master Lü, "I have no use for Han Xiang—you take him on as your disciple."

"If you will not retain him, how could I dare do so?" Master Lü protested.

When Xiangzi saw the two masters arguing about whether to keep him or not, he cried and said to them, "You don't want to retain me as a disciple—surely it is because I didn't plant any seeds in my previous existence that I deserve such suffering! Talking any more about it is useless. I want to crack my head on a rock and die to show my sincerity. I am ashamed to go home and face my elders."

When Master Lü saw Xiangzi so broken-hearted, he knelt down and said to Master Zhong, "As Han Xiang is so determined, please retain him. He could guard our hut. That way he won't have wasted his long journey here."

"All right," Master Zhong said, "But come forward, Xiangzi, and listen to my words." Xiangzi knelt in front of him. "These Zhongnan Mountains of ours have always been a short-cut to official appointments.[1] There is a sort of person who gives himself high-minded airs. He withdraws into these mountains and never enters the city or the gates of officials, so as to increase his reputation. Important personages who meet him on the road treat him respectfully, like a lucky star or an auspicious cloud, while in truth he is always scheming and worrying, seeking all day only to increase his reputation and advantage in the city.

"When he gets hold of some official affair to meddle in, he doesn't say that relatives and friends have come to ask his advice, nor does he mention that he has given some of his own money to pay for some religious festival, including wine and the release of captive animals. No, quite modestly he just says, 'This affair has come to my ears. Outraged by this iniquity and being straightforward and honest of character, I cannot keep quiet. Therefore I dare write this letter to clearly expose this matter.' When a high official on the road sees this letter, he will say that the old gentleman has rather the air of a Tantai Mieming,[2] and he will inquire into the matter. Secretly gratified, the man then receives gifts of acknowledgment, buys himself fields, and builds a house. And everyone will say that he is a good fellow. This nowadays is the road to petty officialdom.

"There is yet another kind of person, the crafty official who, on seeing that he has suffered some setback in his career and is about to be impeached, preempts his accusers by resigning his office and quickly returning to private life. He retires into the Zhongnan Mountains, saying, 'I have no wish for official honors. Let them impeach me, I just won't serve as an official anymore.'

"When the judicial officials see that he has resigned his office, they drop the impeachment. When he notices after a year or so that people take no notice of him anymore, he schemes and intrigues until he gets to resume his position. When he meets people, he brags, 'I never intended to seek riches and prestige; who could have known that riches and prestige would come after me?' This is the road of groveling at night and treating others arrogantly in the daytime.

"Therefore the Zhongnan Mountains are no match for the purity and stillness of the realm of the Three Isles of Penglai. Since you have come to this point, I shall lock up this pass of fame and profit for you, which would otherwise cause you to dash around madly all your life in search of honor and enjoyment."

"Why are they called the Three Isles of Penglai?" Xiangzi asked.

"Penglai is located at the center of the ocean," Master Zhong explained. "The distance between its eastern, western, southern, and northern shores is five thousand miles each way, so that it is square in shape. Because it is wide on top, it is called Mount Kunlun.

"On that mountain there is a copper pillar, its height reaching into the sky. This is the so-called Pillar of Heaven. Its circumference is three thousand miles, and it is perfectly round, as if it has been pared off. At its foot there is a stone building, which houses the nine government offices of the immortals. On the pillar's top there is a great bird, whose name is Rare. Facing south, its extended right wing covers the Royal Lord of the East and its left wing the Queen Mother of the West. On its back is a narrow area without feathers which stretches for nineteen thousand miles.

"Once a year the Queen Mother of the West ascends its wings to go to the Royal Lord of the East. Therefore the pillar carries the following inscription: 'The copper pillar of Kunlun is so high it reaches into the clouds. It is perfectly round as if pared off, beautiful within and without.' On the bird the inscription says, 'There is a bird named Rare, its beak red and its golden eye glittering. It does not cry and does not eat. To the east it covers the Royal Lord of the East, to the west the Queen Mother of the West. When the Queen Mother wants to go east, she ascends this bird and passes over. Yin and yang are dependent on each other; only their union benefits creation.'

"Above there is a palace of gold, jade, and crystal, surrounded by embroidered clouds that dazzle the eye and a vermilion mist that gives off nine rays of light. This is the office of the Overseers of Destiny of the Three Heavens, where all those among the immortals who do not want to ascend to Heaven come."[3]

Xiangzi said, "I have abandoned ready-made riches and prestige like drifting clouds. I only ask that you lead me to the Three Isles of Penglai to become an immortal at leisure. That would be the greatest grace you could afford me. I decidedly do not want to emulate those high-minded or crafty fools who covet honor and enjoyment, and yet only end up enslaved to their descendants."

"Since your heart is determined, I will do my best to teach you," Master Zhong said. He sang the following song to the tune "Cassia Fragrance":

> "The sky is clear, the moon bright.
> Cultivate perfection and study the Dao.
> As you were led into the mountains this morning,
> I will transmit to you the mysterious marvels of the perfected
>   scriptures.
> Extinguish darkness, extinguish darkness!
> Do not speak, do not laugh, practice reversal,
> And guard the door firmly.
> On the day when the Five Marchmounts face Heaven,
> The Golden Elixir will burn within the fire."

Master Lü also struck the fisher drum and sang,

> "The mind is clear, thoughts are bright.
> The work is not insignificant.
> Thanks to karmic affinity inherited from previous lives,
> You have encountered the true Way of immortality.
> Vanquish the Three Worms! Vanquish the Three Worms!
> Your body and spirit will attain marvelous perfection and roam
>   freely.
> Only if you drink the wine of eternal spring slowly,
> Will you realize its excellent taste."

Xiangzi lowered his head, bowed, and said, "It was my karmic affinity to have met you, my masters." And he also chanted a lyric:

> "The masters are clear, their methods are bright,
> Holding incense I say my prayer.
> Only if I can realize my nature and make clear my mind
> Will a merciful teacher appear and transmit the teachings to me.
> I take joy that Heaven knows me! That Heaven knows me!
> My mind inside and my feelings outside all show that this morning
> Qian and kun have exchanged places,
> And li and kan have merged in the middle."

When Xiangzi had finished his song, Master Zhong said, "Xiangzi, do you know the secret of the great way of the Ninefold Returns and Seven Reversions?"

"I am ignorant. Please instruct me," Xiangzi replied.

"The Golden Elixir is composed of the unified pneuma of Former Heaven," Master Zhong said. "It is the mother and the ruler, and is therefore called the Lead Tiger. One's own perfected pneuma came into being after the separation of Heaven and Earth. It is the son and minister, and is therefore called the Mercury Dragon. It is little known that although these two things have different names, the trigrams *qian* and *kun* are their body, yin and yang are their roots, dragon and tiger are their symbols, male and female are their form, lead and mercury are their perfection, others and self are their differentiation, essence and pneuma are their function, and the Mysterious Female is their gate. The primordial, perfectly unified pneuma of Former Heaven actually is produced within these two things.[4] The Mercury Dragon and the Lead Tiger combine in the Divine Chamber to produce a sacred embryo in limitless divine transformations. The knowledge of ordinary mortals is limited and cannot distinguish Dragon and Tiger. They are like frogs in a well or quails in a hedge—unable to see the grand scheme of things.[5] They try to measure the ocean with a ladle or gaze at a leopard through a narrow pipe. How could people of such limited perspective realize the highest degrees of perfection and complete the Supreme Liquid and Golden Elixir?"

Master Lü said, "An elixir formula says, 'The spirit's work and the fire's circulation do not require a whole day.' It also says, 'At dawn and dusk, the Fire Phases accord with the Celestial Pivot.'[6] Fire is the pneuma of the first and last quarters of the moon. Its circulation is due to the application of the tally. The *zi* hour is the first of the six yang hours, hence is called "dawn." The *wu* hour is the first of the six yin hours, hence is called "dusk."

"At dawn the *tun* hexagram is in control; it is the time when fire is added. At dusk, the *meng* hexagram is in control; it is the time when the tally is withdrawn. Thus two hexagrams are in control in the course of one day; it begins with *tun* and *meng*, and finishes at the *jiji* and *weiji* hexagrams. And then the circulation begins again and keeps revolving ceaselessly.

"With two hexagrams per day, we arrive at sixty hexagrams in a month. Each hexagram has six lines, which (together with the four hexagrams of *qian*, *kun*, *kan*, and *li*) yields a total of 384 lines, which correspond with the number of days in a leap year. *Qian*'s first line, with a numerical value of nine, arises from *kun*'s first line of six. Thirty-six yarrow stalks yield the hexagram *qian*. If we multiply thirty-six by the six of the six lines of a hexagram, we arrive at the number 216. *Kun's* first line of six arises from *qian's* first line of nine. Twenty-four stalks yield the hexagram *kun*. If we multiply twenty-four by the six of the six lines of a hexagram, we arrive at the number 144. Adding these two figures together, we get 360, which corresponds to the number of the celestial cycle.

"The paths of sun and moon, merging, rising, and falling, thus do not exceed the numerical scope of the hexagrams. The moon moves fast and takes one month to complete one cycle. The sun moves slowly and takes one year to complete one cycle. The celestial pivot is the pole star. One day and one night are one cycle, and after one month there occurs one shift, such as, for example, establishing *yin* as the cyclical sign for the first month and *mao* as the cyclical sign for the second month.

"Therefore it is said: If month by month you continuously strengthen your armor, then hour by hour you see the army defeated. The accomplished person knows the waxing and waning of sun and moon, and understands the rising and falling of yin and yang. If he moves *zi* and *wu*, the tally and the fire, in accordance with the sun's varying lengths of day and night and the moon's increases and decreases over time, then he will secretly unite with the Great Dao and complete the Great Elixir."[7]

"Having received your instruction, I shall not dare forget it," Xiangzi said.

"We have to go up to Heaven for a while," Master Zhong said. "In the meantime, you sit here in meditation, warming and nurturing your elixir cauldron. We will return to look after you in two days."

Then they took Xiangzi to a pure house, quite unlike the dwellings of ordinary mortals. Variegated clouds hovered about its roof; simurghs and cranes soared above it. In the main room there stood an elixir cauldron, only an inch in height and width. From it, purple flames gave forth a light that brilliantly illuminated the windows. Several jade maidens sat around the cauldron, and a green dragon and a white tiger were placed at its front and back. Master Lü took a rush mat and placed it by the room's western wall. He ordered Xiangzi to sit there facing east, carefully watch the furnace, and not let anything leak out. Having given their orders, the two masters closed the door and flew off.

When Xiangzi looked carefully around the room, he saw that it was now completely empty. Thus he realized that everyone has this most precious treasure,[8] and it is not necessary to withdraw to the stillness and solitude of the deep mountains to gain it. Those who regard it as far away have no grasp of it. Those who want to employ it recklessly reveal their attachment to the world of forms. Thereupon he closed his mouth, lowered his eyelids, and sat down cross-legged.

After a short while ten thousand chariots and a thousand horsemen, in a profusion of banners, lances and armor, suddenly covered the cliffs and valleys all around, their shouting so loud it startled Heaven and shook Earth. Among them was a man more than ten feet tall, his body covered in golden armor, its brilliance dazzling the eye. He was accompanied by a personal guard of several hundred armored knights, wielding swords and bows. Pushing open the door, he came straight in, his angry voice like thunder, his retainers pressing forward with raised swords. When Xiangzi saw him, he remained unmoved. The golden armored giant gave a signal to his followers and, suppressing his anger, left.

Suddenly thousands of fierce tigers and poisonous dragons, lions, vipers, and scorpions struggled forward, roaring and brawling, striking and biting. Some jumped over his head, others coiled around his arms. After a short while they disappeared. Then thunder rolled and lightning struck. The sky darkened, heavy rain poured down, lightning flashed, and a storm whirled all around. Within a very short time the courtyard was filled with water ten feet deep. It was as if the mountains were collapsing, the deluge flooding everything up to Xiangzi's seat. Xiangzi continued to fix his gaze ahead, without fully opening his eyes.

After a while the rain stopped and ox-headed underworld soldiers and horse-faced ghost kings surrounded him on all sides, holding spears and lances, knives and tridents. They set a large cauldron in front of Xiangzi, filled with a hundred gallons of seething oil, and made moves to place Xiangzi inside it. They had already seized Xiangzi's wife Luying and held her at the bottom of the stairs. They flogged her until the blood flowed, shot her, hacked her, and burnt her.

Unable to stand the pain, Luying cried out to Xiangzi, "It isn't my fault that we have never been close. It was you who went off to cultivate yourself and study the Dao, while treating me as if I were ugly and coarse. Now I've been seized by ghost soldiers and cannot bear the pain. I prostrate myself before you and beg you to please say a word to save me. Who among humans is without feelings? Are you devoid of them?" Her tears fell like rain in the courtyard as she scolded and cursed.

Suddenly Luying vanished and the ghost soldiers scattered. Instead Xiangzi now saw King Yama of the Tenth Court of Hell. He was seated solemnly in the room, and a hundred prisoners were kneeling at the margins of the courtyard, among them Xiangzi's mother, Mme. Zheng, and his father, Han Hui. He heard King Yama give the order to smelt copper and iron and pound and grind the prisoners to sharpen their suffering. The sounds of screaming and wailing reached everywhere.

After a short while the sky cleared and the stars shone forth. All of the extraordinary phenomena had vanished. Suddenly a man pressed near. He was covered

Xiangzi guards the elixir cauldron with firm concentration.

from head to foot in ragged clothes, malignant boils and pus, so stinking and dirty that no one would go near him. He lay down on Xiangzi's mat and demanded that Xiangzi massage him and wipe him clean. Whenever Xiangzi paused ever so slightly, the man would scream and kick madly, seeming ready to die on the spot. Xiangzi had no choice but to continue massaging him.

The pus gradually soaked Xiangzi's skin, infecting and irritating his hands. The man shouted at him to suck and lick his hands clean and then to continue massaging him. Xiangzi was just bending over to treat the fetid man, when suddenly he saw Master Lü approaching, leading a beautiful woman by the hand. "What kind of demon are you that you dare make game of an immortal's disciple!" Master Lü shouted, to chase the man away.

The man, scared, crawled off into hiding. Pointing to the beautiful woman, Master Lü told Xiangzi, "This woman is like the famous White Peony. If I hadn't obtained White Peony to supplement my essence, I could not have become an immortal and entered the Dao.[9] Now that your practice is almost complete, you need to supplement your original nature of Former Heaven; only then can you complete your ninefold returned elixir and ascend to the Jasper Terrace and the Purple Palace. Therefore I am presenting you with this woman. Make good use of her and don't let Master Zhong know about it—he might think I harbored selfish intentions in delivering you."

Xiangzi laughed and said, "My mind is steadfast like metal and rock; my thoughts are not affected by outside influences. You should know my mind. Why are you beguiling me with talk of white and black peonies?"

"The Yellow Emperor plucked yin to supplement yang," Master Lü said. "When he ascended from Tripod Lake, all his ministers followed him. Qian Geng married fifty-three wives, had eighty-one sons, and lived to eight hundred years of age, roaming the Isles of Penglai. Since ancient times, none among those who became immortals did not use beautiful women to supplement his primordial yang. Furthermore, the elixir scripture says, 'The gate of the Mysterious Female is called the root of Heaven and Earth.'[10] It also says, 'The gate that gave birth to me is the door of my death—some understand this, and some don't.'

"This explains that women's yin is the true Mysterious Female. The student of the Dao will easily cross the Yellow River if he cleanses his mind, completes his spirit, and knows the meaning of the Three Peaks as well the Secret Formula in Five Characters. I shall explain the Three Peaks to you. A woman's mouth, nose, and tongue are her Upper Peak. The two hollows beneath the tongue correlate with the heart, and connect with the meridian of the lower intestine. Therefore the heart produces the liver and the lungs produce saliva. The saliva comes out as a liquid.

When you gather it, you have to suck fast to the tip of the woman's tongue while seizing the underside of the tongue. Then the Jade Spring will surge forth from the Flowery Pond and saliva will fill her mouth, from which you will draw it into your own mouth. Taking the clear pneuma in her nose, you send it down to the Elixir Field to irrigate your five organs. This is called the Upper Lotus Flower Peak.

"A woman's two breasts are her Middle Peak. When you copulate, you knead her nipples with your hands. As the breasts are massaged, the body tingles all over and the milk ducts open. Inside there is a perfected pneuma, which is part of the drug derived from the gallbladder among the Three Cavities. As the milk juice flows out you swallow it. This is called the Middle Lotus Flower Peak.

"A woman's vagina is her Lower Peak. As the numinous turtle enters the tripod, you have to advance very slowly and wait for the woman to become aroused. Then the vaginal ducts will open and their liquid will flow out. With both hands you firmly embrace the woman, and pulling in your ribs and raising your loins you draw in her essence. This is called the Lower Lotus Flower Peak.

"As for the Secret Formula in Five Characters, it is 'Concentrating, inhaling, locking, absorbing, and contracting.' 'Concentrating' means stabilizing one's pneuma. Let the mind think of the Niwan Palace and stabilize the double spinal passes. As you swallow one or two mouthfuls of pneuma, keep thinking of the celestial cycle, and your pneuma will naturally be stabilized. This way your bodies will have intercourse, but not your spirit.

"'Inhaling' means that at the time of copulation you have to think of your jade stalk as a conduit of pneuma. You use your mouth, nose, and jade stalk to inhale her essential pneuma, transport it to the spine and have it penetrate the Niwan Palace. 'Locking' means that you must tightly lock the Human Gate. The Human Gate is connected with the Celestial Gate and this in turn is connected with the Gate of Destiny. If the Celestial Gate is not locked, the primordial spirit will escape and be lost. Like a turtle controlling its pneuma, you must not make a single mistake.

"'Absorbing' means to take her essential pneuma while entering very slowly, and neither deeply nor hastily. 'Contracting' means that during copulation you must pull in your ribs and raise your loins, making the essence move upwards, but not letting it flow down. The formula says, 'Inhale after concentrating, lock after inhaling, absorb after locking, contract after absorbing.' The five steps must not be employed simultaneously, but one after the other. If you observe the required speed at each stage, you will naturally attain immortality and live forever like the sun and the moon."[11]

When Xiangzi heard these words, his face went red and his ears became scarlet. He shouted with a loud voice, "What kind of demon are you that you dare impersonate my master and utter these heresies designed to lead people of the world astray?"

Xiangzi's words were as loud as thunder, shaking the sky and reverberating through the valley. The two masters Zhong and Lü descended from Heaven, and the so-called Master Lü and his beautiful woman vanished. The two masters said, "Xiangzi has come through the trials without turning back. The great elixir is completed."[12] Then they opened the cauldron and looked inside.

They saw the light of the moon and the glitter of the stars, the curtains brilliantly illuminated, the pearl completed, the size of a millet grain, and a dazzling golden flower. It truly was an extraordinary treasure not of this world, like countless tons of gold, a wealth impossible to find anywhere. It was an immense treasure within the body, whose value would hardly be exaggerated if one compared it to that white jade of antiquity for which fifteen cities were once offered.

The two masters took it up in their hands and placed it in a dish one inch square on the elixir platform. They ordered Xiangzi to give courteous thanks to Heaven, and then to inhale the elixir through his nose and let it rise to the Niwan Palace. His perfected pneuma then naturally descended into the sea of primordial pneuma, where it surged up in waves, merging with the elixir. Thereupon his ordinary body was changed, his turbid pneuma and dusty roots were expunged and transformed. Truly it was as described in the following poem:

> If you are going to study immortality, make it the celestial kind;
> Only the golden elixir is the most appropriate goal.
> When the two things come together, emotions and nature merge,
> Where the five phases are complete, dragon and tiger entwine.
> From the outset rely upon earth to be the matchmaker,
> Then cause husband and wife to be happily conjoined.
> After the work is completed, pay court to the Northern Palace;
> In the light of nine-colored clouds ride soaring simurghs.[13]

If you do not know what happened afterwards, listen to the next chapter.

9

HAN XIANGZI'S NAME IS RECORDED AT THE PURPLE OFFICE

TWO SHEPHERDS RECOGNIZE A DIVINE IMMORTAL

Having spent a hundred and two autumns in the world of dust,
He joyfully gathers all the seeds of the mushroom field.
The light arises in the silver sea, Heaven is limitless,
Pneuma is gathered in the Flower Pond, the water flows upstream.
The Golden Tripod is filled with the Dragon and the Tiger,
In the Jade Pot Mercury and Lead are distinguished.
When the elixir is completed, he will soon return to the Isles of Penglai,
Now believing that there is another world hidden within the world of
humans.

After Xiangzi had escaped his mortal body and transcended the world, he roamed the mountains at ease and without constraint. One day the two masters Zhong and Lü led him on a journey beyond the seas, traversing famous mountains and visiting the immortals and perfected of many generations, as well as the Daoists of the Penglai Isles. They traveled across the sky mornings and evenings, roaming widely in the clouds, their shapes lost in the universe, their traces hidden in the mountains of Great Earth, gazing at the scenery of the realm of the immortals. Truly,

Their spirits traveled to the Purple Office in the Jasper Pond,
Their names were inscribed in the grottoes of the Cinnabar Terrace.

Then one day, all of a sudden, the Jade Emperor ascended his throne in the Precious Palace of the Dragon Empyrean. Bells rang without being struck, drums sounded without being beaten to summon the celestial immortals of the upper eight grottoes, the divine immortals of the middle eight grottoes, the terrestrial immortals of the lower eight grottoes, and the numberless unassigned immortals. They all arranged themselves in lines and proceeded to the Great Immortality Peach Assembly.

The two masters Zhong and Lü, together with Xiangzi, also left their grotto-heaven, to first have an audience with the Jade Emperor, and then proceed to the Jasper Pool to attend the Assembly. However, when the divine general who guarded the gate of Southern Heaven saw Xiangzi approaching from afar, he locked the gate with his golden key and would not let him in. The other immortals in the group said, "Xiangzi, the Jade Emperor blames us for arriving late and has ordered the gate to be locked and entry to be refused to us. What shall we do?"

"Please, move aside. I shall open the gate of Heaven with my bare hands and let you in," Xiangzi said.

"Do you possess such powerful magic?" asked Master Zhong.

Xiangzi advanced with the steps of Yu and blew off the golden lock with a breath of perfected pneuma of Former Heaven.[1] The immortals ascended to the Golden Palace, where they saw a magnificent scene:

> Jasper Heaven high and wide, the Jade Throne majestic and severe;
> emperors and kings seated upright, empresses and concubines lined
> up in orderly ranks. On both sides stars were arrayed in rows, and
> immortals were in attendance in front and in back. Jade ornaments
> were wound around the halls; on the Jasper Terrace fluttered color-
> ful festoons. Auspicious clouds hovered; in the Precious Pavilion
> fragrant smoke stirred the senses. Indistinct the shapes of phoenixes
> and simurghs; floating and sinking the shadows of gold and jade.
> Above were set beacon towers, emitting purple lightning of eightfold
> preciousness. In the middle were arranged several layers of green
> jade tables, bearing a thousand flowers in blue-green pots. On the
> feast tables were placed phoenix marrow and dragon liver, monkey
> lips and bear paws. In the flasks were Precious Pearl and Amber
> brew, purple wine, and fragrant liqueur. Truly there were precious
> delicacies of a hundred flavors from the celestial kitchen, as well as
> all sorts of extraordinary fruits and savory foods from the imperial
> park.

The Jade Emperor asked, "Who are you that you dare break open Our heavenly gate?"

"We are divine immortals of the upper eight grottoes, come to attend the Great Immortality Peach Assembly," Master Zhong said.

Opening his golden mouth and showing his silver teeth, the Jade Emperor asked, "There are only seven divine immortals in the upper eight grottoes, but you are eight. Who is this one?"

"My disciple Han Xiang," Master Zhong answered.

"You and Lü Dongbin have descended into the human world by Our orders. How many humans have you led to complete the Dao? How many living souls have you delivered?" the Jade Emperor said.

"Having received our orders, Lü Dongbin and I descended into the ordinary world," Master Zhong reported. "Seeing that in Hongzhou a dragon drove people from their lands with a flood, Dongbin flew down and beheaded it. In Western Yue a snake demon riding in the clouds and mists was devouring the common people and harming the crops. I vanquished it and managed to restore peace. Proceeding to Changli County in Yongping Prefecture, we delivered Han Xiang, who has now come for an audience with Your Majesty."

"We have heard that when one becomes an immortal, all one's relatives within nine generations ascend to Heaven," the Jade Emperor said to Xiangzi. "If that were not really so, it would give the lie to all the immortals. Now that you have become an immortal, why didn't you deliver your relatives and come together with them to Our audience?"

"I received the attentive instruction of the masters Zhong and Lü," Xiangzi said. "They tested my determination several times before I could complete perfection and realize my reward. My relatives, however, have not yet received an immortal's instruction by your decree. How could they escape the ordinary world and have an audience with you?"

Master Zhong reported, "The Attendant Great General Chonghezi was banished to earth because, on the third day of the third month, at the Immortality Peach Assembly, he drunkenly fought over an immortality peach with Yunyangzi. In the course of the quarrel he broke a crystal cup and offended the Celestial Worthy of Primordial Beginning. He was reborn as a son of the Han family called Han Yu, the uncle of Han Xiang. After Yunyangzi was banished to the human world, he was born as a son into the Lin family, and is now called Lin Gui. Now their period of banishment is almost over, and both could return to their former positions, except that there is no one to go and deliver them."

"Since you know everything within a span from five hundred years ago to that far into the future, and thus were aware that Chonghezi's period of punishment was about to come to an end, why couldn't you go and deliver him so he could become an immortal, fulfill the Dao, realize his reward, and ascend to the Primordial Center?" the Jade Emperor said.

"Taking the appearance of Daoists, Dongbin and I went to instruct him several times," Master Zhong said. "However, at present he serves as an official at court, and therefore he is filled with greed, emotional attachment, a short temper, and a desire for wine, sex, and wealth. He wouldn't agree to change his heart. Therefore we were only able to deliver Han Xiang, who previously had been a crane boy on the banks of the Xiang River in Cangwu Prefecture. By your decree he was given to Han Hui as a son. Fortunately his primordial spirit was not scattered, and his nature remained bright. For this reason, Dongbin and I delivered him and brought him here for an audience with Your Majesty."

"Since you cultivated yourself at home, why didn't your uncle join you?" the Jade Emperor asked Xiangzi.

Xiangzi replied, "My uncle Han Yu once said,

"'The way of Confucius is like the sun in the center of the sky. After the decline of the Zhou dynasty, the death of Confucius, and the burning of his books under the Qin dynasty, Daoism dominated in the Han, and Buddhism in the Wei, Jin, Liang, and Sui dynasties. Among the people of the empire those who did not adhere to Daoism adhered to Buddhism. Acknowledging these teachings as their masters, they made Confucianism a lowly slave. They followed their own teachings and vilified the tradition of Confucius. Adhering to the one and rejecting the other—who will set this right? What Laozi called the Dao was only the Dao as he saw it, and not what I call the Dao. What he called virtue was only virtue as he saw it, and not what I call virtue. The Daoists and Buddhists teach people to reject the idea of ruler and subjects and of father and son, to cease activities which sustain life and seek for some so-called purity and Nirvana. It is fortunate for such doctrines that they appeared only after the time of the Three Reigns, and thus escaped suppression at the hands of Yu and Tang, kings Wen and Wu, the Duke of Zhou and Confucius. But it is unfortunate for us that they did not appear before the Three Reigns so that they could have been rectified by those same sages.'[2]

"Therefore he wouldn't consent to cultivate himself together with me. In the middle of the night at the third watch I scaled the wall and escaped. Only after I found my two masters Zhong and Lü did I complete my reward."

"Although Han Yu would not cultivate himself, you should descend to the human world to deliver him so that he may resume his position in Heaven," the Jade Emperor said.

"I have long harbored this desire, but did not dare act without an imperial decree," Xiangzi said.

"We bestow upon you three golden writs which give you control, above, of the thirty-three Heavens; in the middle, of good and evil in the human world; and below, of the underworld. Leave forthwith!"

"I cannot," said Xiangzi.

"We have bestowed upon you the golden writs. What do you mean, you cannot leave?" the Jade Emperor said.

"I cannot leave because I do not have the divine power to penetrate the transformations of yin and yang, nor do I possess the Orthodox One School's magical technique for beheading demons," Xiangzi replied.

"We bestow upon you a headdress representing sun and moon, the purple eight trigrams robe of the immortals, and a densely woven flower basket which contains nonfading flowers and fruits of eternal spring; furthermore you shall have a heaven-reaching fisher drum whose two ends represent yin and yang, and two clappers with which you can subdue dragons and tigers. Now you can leave right away," the Jade Emperor said.

"I still cannot leave," Xiangzi said. "My uncle Han Yu is a great minister at court and is constantly in the presence of the emperor. Without an official appointment, it will be difficult to deliver him."

"We enfeoff you as the Immortal of Universal Deliverance Who Opens the Primordium and Performs Magical Techniques, Greatly Initiating Transformation by His Teachings. Now go quickly!"

"I still cannot leave," said Xiangzi.

"You delay and obstruct left and right and keep on saying that you cannot go. Is it perhaps that you do not wish to deliver Chonghezi?" the Jade Emperor asked.

"How could I dare disobey your command and not deliver my uncle? It is just that when officials move about, a hundred attendants follow them, and when immortals travel, ten thousand spirits protect them. How could I go all alone?"

"We shall order the two generals Ma and Zhao to accompany you and be at your disposal."

Xiangzi thanked the Jade Emperor, received his orders, and forthwith went to an audience with the Queen Mother of the West. Bowing down he declared, "A thousand years to you! I, the divine immortal Han Xiang of the upper eight grottoes, have received the treasure of a golden writ from the Jade Emperor to go to Changli and deliver my uncle Han Yu, the Attendant Great General Chonghezi, so that he may become an immortal and fulfill the Dao. I have come especially to inform you and to discuss some aspects of this mission."

The Queen Mother said, "I bestow upon you three golden tablets. The first lets you investigate the thirty-three Heavens, the eighteen levels of Purgatory, good and evil, life and death. The second golden tablet gives you authority over the dragon kings of the four seas, and over the thirty-six celestial generals, who will all follow you and obey your commands. With the third golden tablet you control wind and clouds, thunder and rain, the city and earth gods of all districts, regions, counties, and cities, as well as the Yama Emperors of the ten courts of Purgatory. Now go forth carefully and do not tarry."

Having thanked the Queen Mother, Xiangzi finished the Immortality Peach Banquet with the other immortals. Then he gathered up clouds and mists, mounted them with his sleeves flying, and descended to the world of dust.

Xiangzi thought to himself, "I am not afraid of a thousand people looking, but I am afraid of one person seeing. If someone were to recognize me as a divine immortal, it would startle the whole prefecture and divulge heavenly secrets. Then it would be difficult to deliver my uncle." So he changed into a yellow-faced and skinny Daoist, unspeakably ugly, and sat down cross-legged under a weeping willow.

It so happened that two shepherds, one called Wry Neck Zhang, the other Straight Leg Li, were herding oxen in a nearby meadow. In the distance ahead of them, they saw a ray of light shooting up to Heaven.

Wry Neck Zhang said, "Elder Brother Li, I think that ray of light there originates from a hidden deity. Our good fortune has arrived!"

"It's no deity," Straight Leg Li said.

"Could it be a will-o'-the-wisp?" Wry Neck Zhang speculated.

"Elder Brother, it isn't a demonic fire either," Li said. "The red and sparkling light of a clear early morning is the sun-wheel just entering from Fusang and illuminating the earth with its dazzling light. This is called daybreak. If it is a bluish and shining light in the evening that moves back and forth above the ground, now closer, now further away—that's a demonic fire. This light now is a shiny yellow, and it penetrates the Heavenly Court. Besides, it's just noontime. From these circumstances we can tell that a divine immortal is in that place."

"You're right," Wry Neck Zhang said. "Let's go and look for him. Wouldn't it be great if we requested immortalhood and inquired after the Dao with him?"

"Sounds good," Straight Leg Li said. The two left their oxen behind and hurried forward hand in hand.

When they reached the place, they really saw a Daoist sitting cross-legged under a weeping willow. What did that Daoist look like?

> On his head he wore a court official's cloth of black silk, with two
> rings in the shape of an old dragon's eyes dangling from the back,
> burnished as bright as sun and moon. From above were suspended
> two green gauze bands representing yin and yang. He was dressed in
> a purple ribboned robe, inlaid with the seven stars, and adorned with
> the patterns of the Northern Dipper and the Eight Trigrams. Around
> his waist was tied a Lügong sash made of the beards of nine dragons
> woven together into a double grain ear pattern. His feet were shod
> in flat-soled[3] boots for climbing mountains, traversing seas, and
> walking on clouds and mists. In his hand he held a brightly polished
> fisher drum made from a sturdy pine branch that had braved the
> wind. His appearance was that of an itinerant Daoist, but his clothes
> were those of a companion of the immortals, who drinks dew and
> feeds on clouds.

The two shepherds came forward, knocked their heads, and said, "Greetings to the divine immortal!"

"How did you recognize me as a divine immortal?" Xiangzi asked.

"From afar we saw above your head ten thousand rays of rosy light, as well as auspicious clouds spreading over a thousand miles. Thus did we know that you are a divine immortal," Wry Neck Zhang replied.

Xiangzi laughed and said to himself, "My uncle, who studied and passed the examinations, didn't realize that Zhong and Lü were divine immortals, but these lowly shepherds recognized me as one. That's really strange." Then he called to the shepherds, "I have come from the Zhongnan Mountains and am hungry and thirsty from walking. In this basket I have a gold-threaded jade bowl. If you take it down to the brook and fetch me some water to drink, I promise to deliver you."

"Elder Brother Zhang, I'll go fetch the water," Straight Leg Li called. "You stay here and watch the divine immortal. Don't let him get away."

"Very well, but hurry a bit," Wry Neck Zhang replied. So he remained behind and guarded Xiangzi with unflinching eyes, never turning his head away.

Xiangzi thought to himself, "He may have recognized me, but now I shall smear my face with some earth and ashes and change into an old man who looks already

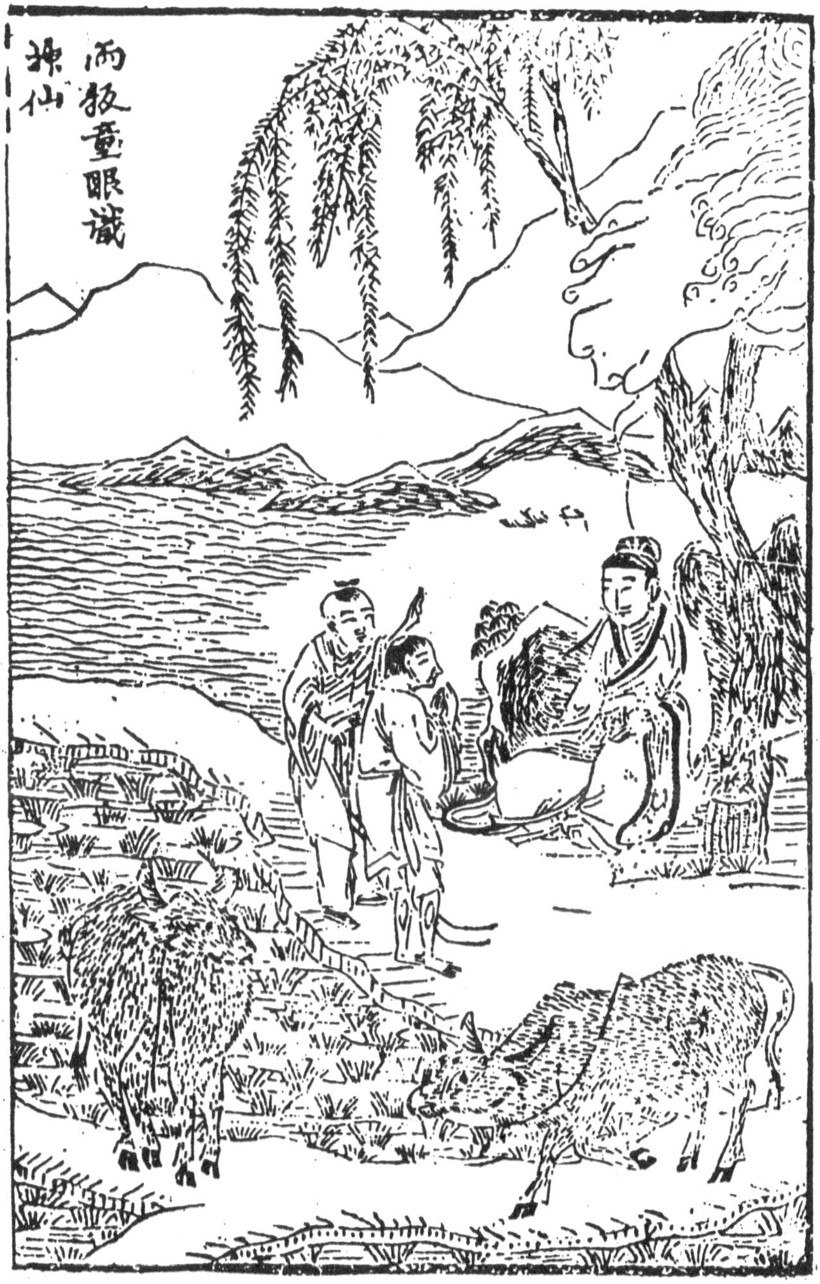

Two shepherds recognize a divine immortal.

more like a ghost than a human being. Let's see if he still knows me then." When Zhang was distracted for a moment, Xiangzi changed into an old man:

> On his head he had a rotten headcloth, askew on the left and crumpled on the right. He wore a torn cloth jacket, patched in a thousand places. In front he had fastened a goat skin, on his back hung a piece of felt, with various parts of his body showing through the gaps. Around his waist he had tied a rotten grass cord, barely hanging together by shreds. His feet were shod in hempen shoes with barely an upper or a sole remaining. His face was like chicken skin, his eyes sticky with mucus. Snot hung long from his nose and saliva spurted from his mouth. What a farce! The eight hundred years of Patriarch Peng after all cannot compare to a tiny fraction of Chen Tuan's precious golden elixir!

When Straight Leg Li came with the water, he didn't see the divine immortal anymore; instead there was a half-dead old man sitting under the tree. He beat his breast, stomped his foot, and said angrily to Wry Neck Zhang, "I wasted all that effort fetching water, and now the divine immortal has vanished. Whom shall I give it to now?"

"I stood here all the time and didn't even move my head. I don't know who exchanged that old man for the divine immortal," Wry Neck Zhang said. "As you've already fetched the water, let's give it to the old man to drink—it'll count as a good deed for us."

"I'd rather pour it out than give it to him to drink," said Straight Leg Li, bursting with anger. "How much merit could we gain from letting him have it?"

"Haven't you read that the Five Hegemons recorded in their pact of alliance that one should respect elders and be kind to the young?[4] Let's give this bowl of water to the old man to drink. Why do you insist on pouring it out and spoiling it?" asked Wry Neck Zhang.

"Someone has switched the divine immortal, but we still have this bowl, which should be worth some pieces of silver. Should we break it in half and divide it up, or should we sell it whole and share the proceeds?" Straight Leg Li said.

"You shouldn't talk of dividing it up," said Wry Neck Zhang. "Objects belonging to immortals are hard to come by. Let's take turns keeping it in our homes, as a treasure for the protection of our households."

When Xiangzi saw the two of them arguing, he called, "Shepherds, you are mistaken. If I'm not a divine immortal, where else is there one?"

"Shut your trap, you old wreck!" the shepherds scolded him. "You're like neither man nor ghost, and should have died a long time ago. To be old and not die is to be a pest, not a divine immortal!"[5]

"Shepherds, people of the world cannot be judged by their faces, the water of the ocean cannot be measured with a grain peck," Xiangzi told them. "Confucius said, 'I judged people by their appearance—and made a mistake in the case of Ziyu.'[6] How can you be so sure that the old man you see before you is not an immortal? So I ask you, why are you looking for the immortal?"

The shepherds said, "We wish to cultivate ourselves with him and become men at ease and happy with their lives."

"That Daoist just now was one of my disciples. If you agree to follow me, leave your families and cultivate yourselves, I will deliver you so that you can become immortals," Xiangzi said.

The two shepherds clapped their hands and laughed. "Your own life is a candle in the wind. In the morning you don't know whether you'll see the evening, yet you think of delivering us—that's really too much of a blessing for us!"

"When a ripe yellow plum falls to the ground it makes a full sound. When the green plum falls to the ground—thump!—it splits apart. I may be old, but fortunately I started cultivating myself early, otherwise things would look even worse for me by now. How dare you bully an old man?" Xiangzi said.

"Stop bothering us with your chatter, old man," the two shepherds said. "Go home and take a rest. We'll come along in twenty or thirty years to leave the family with you."

"If you are unwilling to cultivate yourselves at your age, when do you plan to do so? I am afraid you won't reach my age, and wouldn't that then have been a waste of valuable time?"

The two shepherds put their heads together and sighed, "We are truly out of luck. First a divine immortal vanishes, and now we have to suffer this old fool's babbling."

Xiangzi took advantage of their distraction and changed back into his previous appearance, sitting completely still. When Straight Leg Li lowered his head and looked, he clapped his hands and called out, "Elder Brother, is that the divine immortal come back? But who has switched him with the old man?"

"Elder brother, you don't know the divine immortals' art of transformation," Wry Neck Zhang hastened to tell him. "They want to see if we have the disposition of immortals and the bones of the Dao, so they transform themselves to test our minds. You shouldn't have scolded that old man just now."

Straight Leg Li thereupon bowed with full courtesy and offered the water to

Xiangzi, saying, "When a divine immortal receives a gift of water, he repays it by nourishing and preserving the giver. I brought water for you to drink—how will you deliver me?"

"I will deliver you by having you both leave the family," Xiangzi said.

"What's the good of leaving the family? It would be better if you could make sure that I will become an official," Wry Neck Zhang said.

"So you want me to make you an official?" replied Xiangzi. "But your disheveled hair is not fit to wear a cap of black silk. Your meager waist is not fit to be girded with a golden belt. Your naked feet will not be shod with black court boots, and your blackened hands will not get to hold the ivory tablet. It is better for you to remain here among the soft grass and moss, dressed in rags and sleeping on the back of an ox, or sing your tuneless songs as you hold the ox's muzzle. One morning King Yama will summon you and ghosts will come to fetch you. Your eyes will stare empty, your body will seize up, and you will die. Why even think of becoming an official?"

"You are right—I wish to follow you and leave the family," Wry Neck Zhang said.

"No hurry," Xiangzi said. "Look—another immortal is on his way to this tree."

When the two turned their heads to look, Xiangzi disappeared into thin air.

Wry Neck Zhang stomped his feet and called out, "Elder Brother, this wasn't a divine immortal, it was a daytime ghost."

"Are you sure?" Straight Leg Li said.

"A divine immortal wouldn't tell lies. Only these daytime ghosts play tricks on people. Without any scruples, they just trick people to death with impunity."

"We've wasted half the day on that ghost—let's just go back to herding our oxen," Straight Leg Li said. This poem describes it well:

> The mountains have roots, the waters their sources,
> So it truly was a divine immortal after all.
> Just because he wouldn't clearly explain himself,
> He mistakenly rejected many living beings.

Where did Xiangzi vanish to? Listen to the next chapter.

10

BRAGGING AND BOASTING, TURTLE AND EGRET BRING

CALAMITY UPON THEMSELVES

SINGING DAOIST SONGS, HAN XIANGZI MOVES THE CROWD

If you reach a place of freedom and ease, then be free and at ease;
Do not imitate others who run on the two roads of birth and death.
By the time you have hastened east, you have already lost the west,
Before you can face south, you have to abandon the north.
Master Zhuang would rather drag his tail in the mud and disregard
*   worldly honors,*
Master Lie rode the wind and cherished his thatched hut.
Good and bad fortune all derive from the changeable glitter of the
*   world;*
How could the affairs of this world be compared to the eminence of the
*   Dao?*

The willow under which Xiangzi sat stood by a cave at the Xiang River—the very place where in his previous existence as a white crane he had frolicked with the musk deer.

It had been almost eighteen years now since the deer had been banished by Master Lü to the bottom of a deep pond, years that the musk deer had passed in controlling his pneuma and swallowing essences. He looked forward to the day when he would emerge again, but as the white crane had not come to deliver him, he was at a loss what to do.

Just then he saw a rosy light and cloud-like pneuma by his cave. Realizing that a divine immortal was passing by, he stretched his head, stirred up waves, and cried out, "Destiny has given me the opportunity to meet a great immortal. In your compassion, please deliver me!"

When Xiangzi heard the voice, he knew very well that it was the musk deer calling to him, but he deliberately asked him in a loud voice, "What kind of demon are you that you dare to raise winds and stir up waves deep in the water, thus obstructing my immortal's chariot?"

The musk deer said, "I am a musk deer who eighteen years ago roamed and frolicked here with my partner, a white crane. Suddenly one day the two immortals Zhong and Lü passed by. They delivered the white crane and transformed him into a green-clad boy. Me, on the other hand, they banished to the bottom of this pond, because my words had offended them. I am to wait until my older brother crane has become an immortal and completed the Dao, realized his rewards, and ascended to Heaven. Only then will he come to deliver me. I have been expecting him anxiously, but he has never come. Today I have the good fortune to meet you, great immortal—this truly is the kind of fortunate encounter that happens only once in three lifetimes. I hope desperately that you will save and deliver me so that I may escape from my animal's body and cross the river of emotional attachment. Knowing full well that I have brought this calamity on myself, I will never again dare to do wrong."

Xiangzi thought to himself, "The Jade Emperor never gave me a decree to deliver him. My masters didn't order me to set him free, either. How could I dare act on my own authority?" Then he said, "Today I have descended into the world on a mission from the Jade Emperor. Because I came in haste, I didn't bring any golden elixir. How am I to deliver you? Around here *jiao* pears and fire dates are growing. For the time being I will give you one of each. The crane boy has already become an immortal and will come soon to deliver you. Be calm and patient and do not let your temper get the better of you, so as not to accumulate additional sins."

Having spoken, he dropped a fire date and a *jiao* pear in the water. When the musk deer received them, he swallowed them in three gulps. Suddenly he felt his body becoming clear and pure, and his five viscera becoming quiet and still. As he bowed and said thanks, the wind calmed down and the waves subsided. Thereupon Xiangzi gathered in the auspicious light that had attracted the musk deer, and as before sat under the green willow.

In the same river and pond there lived a turtle with a gold-threaded, green-haired carapace. It had nourished its life forces for more than a hundred and ten years, but never having grown wings under its forelegs, it could not fly up to Heaven.

Previously it had joined in the mischief practiced by the musk deer and the white crane. Ever since the musk deer had been banished and the white crane had slipped his body and left, the turtle spent its time sunning itself and playing in the pond. If people came by, it quickly dived under so that no one could catch it.

On this day, although it was hot, the air still felt fresh, and so the turtle happened to be floating on the surface of the water. When it poked out its head and looked around, it saw Xiangzi sitting under the green willow tree. It did not recognize him as its master from earlier days, but thought he was a fisherman out to catch it. Quickly it pulled in its head and drifted under water without moving. It was just as in this poem:

> It carried a gourd on its back,
> And gathered its feet into its fat waist.
> It is difficult for winds and clouds to meet,
> Even with an immortal basking on a nearby bank.

Floating in the water, the turtle looked just like a submerged stone. Xiangzi considered whether to instruct it, but feared that it could not be awakened.

While he was still undecided, suddenly an egret flew down from the sky. It had also been living for a hundred and ten years. Throughout these one hundred and ten summers and winters, innumerable fish and crabs in the ponds had been devoured by it. Now it had come again to look for food.

When it saw something green floating submerged at the water's surface, the egret thought it was a stone with luxuriant green moss growing all over it. So it spread its wings and landed on it. Standing on the turtle's back, it drank water.

When the turtle felt a weight on its back, it thought it must be the water snake come for some gossip, and poked out its head to look. When it saw that it was a white egret, it was not angry, but still shouted in a loud voice, "Who are you that you dare stand on my back?"

The egret was startled and said, "In such peaceful surroundings, what kind of beast are you that you dare speak in human language?"

"I am a gold-threaded, green-haired turtle, who has lived here for many years," the turtle said. "Where do you come from, rascally bird, that you dare speak in human language? Clearly you have come to bully me."

"I was born and grew up in the Hua Mountains, and have spread my wings in the blue sky above the Jasper Pool," said the white egret. "Sensing the approach of humans, I take flight, and soar about before alighting.[1] Ugly creature, although you may appear in dreams to King Yuan of Chu, you cannot avoid the suffering of seventy-two holes being drilled into you. You can just pull in your head and neck and drag your tail in the mud.² Who allowed you to drift in the blue waves and float on the clear ripples, all the while speaking human language, startling people, and offending animals?"

"Among the 360 hairless beings, man is the first," the green-haired turtle answered. "Among the 360 feathered beings, the phoenix is the first. Among the 360 scaly beings, the dragon is the first. Among the 360 shell-covered beings, I am first. Although you may soar to the Milky Way and reach the sky, you are only the last among the birds. What right have you to speak such grandiose words?"

"Among the animals of the world only the parrot can speak, and only the mynah can recite the Buddha's name. I have never met a talking turtle," the egret remarked.

"A rock once spoke in Jin—if even non-sentient beings can talk, why regard it as strange when a numinous being such as I can do the same?" the turtle replied.

"I won't laugh at your shortcomings, and you won't speak of my strengths— let's become brothers, shall we?" the egret said.

"Each of us will spell out his strengths. Whoever has more to offer will become the elder brother," the turtle agreed.

The egret said, "I'll go first:

> "My body is covered in white feathers,
> I am free and comfortable,
> And do not yield to a thousand-year-old redheaded crane."

The turtle said,

> "My body is covered with golden threads,
> Glittering and shiny.
> What is there to distinguish me from the hundred year old purple-clad
>   sea-turtle?"

The egret said,

> "As I stand in the water watching for fish,
> My shadow falling on the cold pond
> produces patterns like uncut jade."

The turtle said,

> "As I turn towards the sun,
> My shell on the pond's bank competes in preciousness with that
>   of a pearl-bearing oyster."

The egret said,

> "I raise my wings near the red clouds,
> In my embroidered nest I give birth to an Immortal of Supreme
>   Perfection."

The turtle said,

> "I stretch my body and float in the green water,
> In a secluded place among the algae and duckweed I bring forth
>   a blue-eyed barbarian."[3]

The egret said,

> "My crown is covered thickly with feathers,
> Which surely resembles dazzling embroidery on the river bank."

The turtle said,

> "My chest harbors the eight trigrams;
> Are not their canonical principles inscribed on my heart?"

The egret said,

> "If I swallow a pill of golden elixir,
> I shall right away become a feathered immortal in the land of Cinnabar
>   Mound."

The turtle said,

> "If I am delivered by the Eight Immortals,
> I shall leave the world of dust in a moment."

The egret said,

> *"As I stand by the pond's clear water,*
> *My pure white plumes are worthy of being painted."*

The turtle said,

> *"When I climb up to the foot of that green willow,*
> *The green sedge on my armor greatly amazes people."*

As the two animals were arguing, they did not pay any attention to their surroundings, and so were not aware that a hunter was drawing closer step by step. He saw the white egret standing there, its head stretched out, its wings spread, as if it were talking to someone. The hunter lifted his golden-stringed bow, inserted a wolf's tooth arrow, and picked off the egret. This poem describes it well:

> *The left hand drawing the bow, the right pushing,*
> *He pierces a willow leaf at a hundred paces—such is his marksmanship!*
> *Although he hasn't hit the tiger of the Southern Mountain,*
> *The white egret collapses and loses its life.*

As the green-haired turtle was still sighing on seeing the white egret being shot down, a fisherman appeared, punting a small boat and drifting on the deep pond near the cave. When the turtle saw how rapidly the boat was coming on, it stretched out its four legs and hurriedly swam towards a deep place in the water.

When he saw the turtle flee, without undue haste the fisherman took an iron trident and thrust at the turtle. It cracked open the turtle's shell and fresh blood gushed out. Again a poem puts it best:

> *A steel trident twelve feet long,*
> *Its tip and edge sharper than those of a deity's spear.*
> *Thrust with a clear eye and a quick hand, it doesn't miss its aim—*
> *Today the turtle meets King Yama.*

Within a short time both animals had died at the hands of the hunter and the fisherman. Only now did Xiangzi make himself visible and sigh, "Every drink and every bite of food are predetermined. Life and death are up to fate, wealth and rank are up to Heaven—truly, these are not empty words." As he was sighing, a thought came to his mind: "After I had received the Jade Emperor's decree and left the Golden Palace, I went to an audience with the Queen Mother. Afterwards I should have gone and taken leave of my two masters. I have sinned by descending into the world without even saying a word to them."

Hurriedly he ascended a cloud and hastened to their grotto palace. He called upon Cool Breeze and Bright Moon to announce him to the two masters Zhong and Lü.

The two masters said, "You have received an order to deliver Chonghezi. Why are you here again?"

Xiangzi knelt down and said, "I have received the Jade Emperor's command, as well as treasures and golden writs. I was also given three golden tablets by the Queen Mother. I am on my way to Changli County in Yongping Prefecture to deliver my uncle Han Yu so that he may ascend to perfection and complete the Way, realize his rewards, and ascend to the Primordial Center. I have come especially to take my leave of you, hoping for one or two pieces of advice."

"He is now a high official on a big salary—he won't agree easily to abandon it and cultivate himself," the two masters said. "You must use a variety of methods of instruction. Do not fail in the Jade Emperor's mission!"

"What should I do if he won't change his mind?" Xiangzi asked.

"If he still has not changed his mind after you have tried three times to deliver him, return the golden decree."

"I will diligently obey your strict command!" Xiangzi said. It was as in this poem:

> As clouds drift outside the ancient grotto, the pass is already closed.
> A fragrant wind mistily suffuses the world of dust.
> Why would a divine immortal approach the world of mortals?
> He makes the journey to deliver Han Yu.

When Xiangzi had descended from the mountains, he took off his nine-clouds headcloth, stuffed it into his basket, and replaced it with a yin-yang headdress. He changed his gown, which was adorned with the Nine Palaces and Eight Trigrams surrounded by dragons, into a Daoist robe of coarse cloth. He smeared some dust and dirt on his face and changed himself into a sallow-faced, skinny Daoist with a crazed expression. In his hands he held a fisher drum and a clapper, singing Daoist songs as he walked along the road. What did these songs, to the tune "Shoals amid the Waves," speak of?

> "A poor Daoist, I have come down from the mountains,
> Short of rice, without any firewood.
> A fisher drum in my hand, I walk the main street,
> Begging for money to buy good wine,
> Which I will pour and drink by myself.
>
> "The fisher drum sounds again and again,
> Not false and not true.
> I do not seek some small profit or a famous reputation,
> But just let wild gusts blow through the wild grasses,
> Scattering their pure blossoms."

Xiangzi beat the fisher drum, clapped the clapper, sang his Daoist songs, and laughed loudly. Everyone in the street, young and old, male and female, gathered to hear him sing. When they heard that he sang well, they called, "Crazy Daoist, where did you learn these songs? Sing us another!"

Xiangzi said, "The proverb says it well, 'Better to fail in business than to suffer hunger.' Singing on my way, I haven't made a single copper coin to buy myself a bowl of noodles. Now my stomach is hungry and I have no strength left to sing. If you would just give me some vegetarian food so I can eat my fill, I will sing you a good song. How about it?"

Together the people said, "We have some wine and vegetarian food. If only you sing well, we'll see to it that you can eat your fill this morning."

Xiangzi beat his fisher drum and his clapper, and sang to the tune "Brocade Covering the Ground":

> "A child of ten years is just the right age to cultivate himself,
> His original yang has not leaked out and can be preserved whole.
> A pill of golden elixir is truly mysterious and marvelous,
> Body and mind purified, he will pace the land of the immortals.
>
> "At twenty he will marry a wife;
> He'll sleep with a living ghost, yet will not fear her.
> What he should fear, though, is that the Cinnabar Sand may escape
>   from the Golden Tripod,
> Toppling that splendid seven-jewelled pagoda.

"At thirty he will become entangled in the affairs of the world,
Just like a silkworm asleep in its cocoon.
His body will be bound by silk threads all over,
Not allowing him to spread out a rush mat or a felt rug for a rest.

"At forty he will have many sexual relations,
His essence and spirit will be wasted and scattered, his balance and har-
    mony impaired.
Thinking of his misery, he'll realize it is derived from previous misery,
But even if he were to quickly cultivate himself, he would find no shelter.

"At fifty he is old and close to death,
Because in his young years he wouldn't cultivate himself in time.
He waited until his primordial yang was exhausted;
Now he seems like sesame seed whose oil has been completely roasted out.

"At sixty he is all wizened,
His grandsons and granddaughters are just blurs before his eyes.
Why worry that everyone should live to a hundred?
The honey locust pods are crushed to a pulp.

"At seventy he is fearful every moment,
Wife and sons seem like tigers, he like a goat.
If there is joy, they are joyful together,
If there are worries, he is on his own.

"When an old man is seventy-seven,
Four more years and he is eighty-one.
The eyes blind, the ears deaf, and no one there to support him.
With such misery, what good is there in still being among the living?"

Having heard the song, the audience all praised him. Some gave him fruit and cakes to eat, some wine and meats. Some gave him copper and silver coins, saying, "Crazy master, take it and buy yourself something to eat." Others gave him cloth and silk, hempen shoes and straw sandals, saying, "We wish to be friends with you, master."

Xiangzi accepted everything, but ate only a little of the fruit. The remaining wine and meats, copper and silver, cloth and silk, and shoes he distributed among the beggars at the market.

The people admonished him, "We gave these things as alms to you. Why are you giving them to the beggars? Do you think our things aren't good enough? Or don't you know to honor other people's gifts properly?"

"I have left the family and rely completely on alms gladly given," Xiangzi said. "How would I dare bear a grudge because some give much and others little, or because some treat me lightly, while others show me respect? It is just that ever since ancient times, wine, lust, wealth, and temper have been things that are best avoided. How could I dare drink wine and accept money? It would only create trouble." Then he again struck the fisher drum and sang a song to the tune "Jade-Entwined Branches":

> "Insatiable greed for the wine cup,
> Every day you recklessly fill it with Scattered Clouds wine.
> Ziyun's satire was to battle the spread of drunkenness,[4]
> Yet with a wine skin in one hand and a painter's brush in the other,
> Jiying liked to cheer himself up with drink.
> Thinking back to the vegetable and fish dishes of his home district and
>   interested only in the strong liquor made from grapes,
> He tipped over drunk—what a disgrace![5]
> Incessant drinking
> Pickled the Immortal Ge,
> And buried the graduate Zhang in liquor.[6]
> When you rave deliriously,
> Who will heal you?
> You brag about heroism,
> But leave wealth and honor to others.
> There are calamities for you on the margins of the grave,
> And danger at the rim of that jade vat.
> Wine!
> Let the world be warned against it.
>
> "Who are you hankering after?
> At first they are all cherry cheeks and almond faces,
> But the beauty of the river goddesses of Mount Wu and of the
>   banks of the Luo River is not real.
> If we compare the gorgeous Xizi to the ugly Wuyan—
> Where will we find one who combines beauty and perfect virtue?
> Dragon spittle among the bedsheets marks the beginning of struggle,
> Brocade petals are like a defeat at the enemy's hands on the field.[7]
> Have you ever worried about your beloved's figure?

Broken simurgh hair pins,
Unused trousseaus—
Why get all worked up about such trifles?
With your own eyes you have seen the concubine cast herself
    from the tower,
Yet still you dwell in the Pavilion of Linchun.[8]
I laugh at you men
Who bring the whip onto themselves.
Alas that the young girl
Should conceal a sword.
Lust!
Let the world be warned against it.

"The stinginess of the wealthy and the excesses of luxury are all results
    of acquisitiveness.
Wang Rong and Guo Kuang had insatiable minds,
Embracing hoards of gold,
And grasping ivory tablets.
What did they know of the modesty of Bao Shuya, who shared his gold
    with Guan Zhong?
An attitude infinitely better than owning a mountain of copper.
He Qiao of the Jin dynasty was much criticized for his avarice,
Just as Zhu Yi came to grief because of his greed.[9]
The elephant is killed for its ivory tusks,
Much wealth thus requires humility.
If you measure your pearls in pecks,
And hang your trees with precious silk,
You will be killed by one who lusts after your beautiful women,
Or slain by one who desires your precious sword.
Those ten thousand strings of cash of yours are all in vain
When you perish in a ditch.
Wealth!
Let the world be warned against it.

"A hero with passions aflame,
Like a leopard or tiger, is unable to control himself.
Yet the capitals of Daliang and Yan were usurped
In spite of all their heroes' curses and impressive posturing.
They draw lots, sharpen their blades, and guffaw,

But as they laugh and talk, they fall into a ditch.
Soaked and red-faced
They become the laughingstock of bystanders.
With nothing but disdain for the cozy comfort of nobles,
These heroes hold on to their military seals.
As their hair stands up in anger,
Their demeanor becomes yet more ferocious.
And yet they are afraid of the assassin's awl at Vast Wave Beach,
And in loneliness end their own lives at Black River.[10]
How can you forget this?
Unreal like bubbles and shadows are the dangers to the nation,
Yet these heroes keep fighting each other endlessly.
Temper!
Let the world be warned against it.

"None of these can equal us Daoists! "

(To the tune "Zuixiangfeng")

"As we beat the fisher drum and sing loudly, our cheerfulness increases;
As we pluck the numinous fungus, our happiness knows no end.
We shout aloud,
But at the same time conceal ourselves.
Riding the clouds and mists,
We journey through the Nine Heavens in the twinkling of an eye.
Let bystanders laugh at us as crazy."

At the end of the song, the audience all applauded and said, "Although this Daoist is somewhat crazy, he knows many things of ancient and present times. He is well versed in literature and understands principles—quite unlike those hawkers at the street corners who deceive people with their glib talk."

The man who had given wine to Xiangzi said, "Master, if you don't drink my wine, you disrespect my good will in buying it for you. What's more, wine is a blessing in the human world. Divine immortals have transmitted it for generations. Thanks to wine, Liu Ling and Ruan Ji attained the Dao and became immortals. For sacrifices to Heaven and Earth, 'great broth' and 'dark liquor' are used. It won't do any harm if you drink a few cups today."

Xiangzi could not evade his admonishments and had no choice but to drink

Singing Daoist songs, Xiangzi moves the crowd.

a few bowls. Quickly he appeared to become intoxicated and, feigning drunkenness, he fell to the ground.

When the people saw him drunk, they asked, "Crazy Daoist, where do you live? Lying there drunk like that, who is going to help you home?"

A man in the crowd said, "This Daoist is an interesting fellow. Let's find out his address and carry him there."

When Xiangzi saw the people chattering among themselves, he staggered up, laughed loudly, and sang to the tune "Shoals amid the Waves":

> *"So drunk that I can hardly open my eyes,*
> *I lie on the main street.*
> *Everyone laughs at me, but I give no reply.*
> *May we ask where you live?*
> *My home is on the Penglai Isles!"*

When the people heard him sing, they clapped their hands and laughed, "You sing your Daoist songs so well—are you perhaps from Suzhou?"

Xiangzi said, "I am from Changli County in Yongping, not from Suzhou."

"So you are a local fellow," the people said. "Why weren't you honest instead if making such pretentious boasts?"

"My benefactors, in your presence I have not lied nor deceived Heaven," Xiangzi said. "Everything I said is the truth. Why do you say I am a pretender?" He turned around and left.

The people all said, "Just look at this crazy fellow." And right away they ran after him. This poem is apposite:

> *Mortal eyes cannot distinguish clearly,*
> *Facing a divine immortal they don't recognize him.*
> *Nobody asks about a tiger hidden deep in the mountains,*
> *But everyone is startled when it shows its fangs and claws.*

If you don't know where Xiangzi went, listen to the next chapter.

11

IN DISGUISE, XIANGZI TRANSMITS A MESSAGE

A STONE LION IS TRANSFORMED INTO GOLD

A poor man has a pearl in his clothes,
Round and bright and good in its original state.
Unable to look for it in himself,
He counts instead other people's treasures.
Counting other people's treasure
In the end is of no benefit,
But just lets you spend your efforts in vain.
Better to recognize your own pearl,
Which is worth a million pieces of gold.[1]

For now let us speak no more of how Xiangzi went off, but instead of an old man named Tang who lived in Chang'an. He used to own quite a few strings of cash, but he used up all that money because he did not run a business, but just sat and ate until his coffers were empty. Now he had no choice but to do some sharp calculating and scrape together some funds with which to open a shop for unheated wine.

He had chosen this month and this day to hang up his sign and open his shop, when Xiangzi happened to come along, beating his fisher drum and clapper and singing,

"Sun and moon circle from east to west,
Alas, human life is only a hundred years short,

No match for me who has bound his hair into two knots,
Wears cotton clothes
And straw sandals.
I make my living with the Xu You gourd I carry on me.[2]
What better do you want
Than to travel on clouds to the ocean isles?
Who enjoys such peace and ease as I do?"

When Xiangzi reached the old man's door and saw the red and gold decorations above the shop, he knew that it was a newly opened tavern. Thereupon he went a step closer and said, "I transform only those with the right destiny. Do not mistake a divine immortal for an ordinary person. Venerable benefactor, today you've opened a new tavern. Give me a pot of wine, and you will have good trade."

When the old man saw Xiangzi approaching, he quickly turned away, pretending not to hear or see him. Seeing this, Xiangzi drew another step closer, beat his fisher drum, and sang,

"Grandpa, I see that your temples are as white as cotton.
Today you have opened a tavern,
Just to earn a bit of money.
In doing so, you'll rob young and old of their peace.
If you give me a pot of fragrant liquor to drink,
I guarantee that the crowds will rush in to buy your wine.
If you agree to give joyfully,
I will be for you an immortal of prosperous trade,
And promise that you shall double your capital."

Old Man Tang said, "I was just having a good day opening this shop, until you, Daoist, came along asking for free wine to drink. Do you think I am opening an alms-giving shop?"

"Capital will bear interest," Xiangzi said. "How could an ascetic like me dare to ask for alms from an old man like you? But on this auspicious day, you ought to donate a pot of wine as a 'payment to ensure prosperous trade.'"

"The likes of you have absolutely no sense of decency," the old man said. "I have just opened this shop and haven't yet earned a single piece of silver. How can you ask me to give you a pot of wine to help my trade?"

"When the spirits of wealth come, prosperous trade comes, and with it money comes," Xiangzi replied. "Can you call yourself a human being if you are unwilling to pluck a single hair for the benefit of another?"[3]

"I painfully scraped together some money and opened this shop on a good day," Tang said. "Selling a pot of wine is like selling my own blood, yet you, master, who are strong and well-built, want me to give you alms."

"It's not that I absolutely want you to give me alms. It's just that, as you just newly opened up shop and your wine must surely be good, I ask you for some token that will guarantee a prosperous trade, that's all."

Unable to stand Xiangzi's persistent pleading, the old man considered for a while, his head lowered. Then, with shaking hands, he filled a wine cup more than half full, handed it to Xiangzi, and said, "Master, I offer you this cup of wine. Please drink it quickly, so as not to attract other people to come and bother me."

"If your wine really is good, this cup will make me drunk. If I am not drunk, it means that your wine is thin. Why worry about people coming to bother you?" Xiangzi said.

"I'm giving you free wine to drink, and still you're taunting me?" said Old Man Tang. "No wonder people like you have left the family. Get out, now!"

Xiangzi clapped his hands, laughed loudly, and sang,

> "Alas, the human mind knows no satisfaction.
> Morning and evening,
> One's brow is always knit in worry.
> How can a common man recognize an immortal from Great Veil
>   Heaven?
> He just offends him with foolish talk.
> I laugh at one like you who in his dotage still has not cultivated himself.
> Opening a wine shop is futile labor.
> The human mind wants satisfaction, but when will it ever be
>   satisfied?"

Having finished his song, Xiangzi left.

The old man said, "Look at you! You have no understanding of our times whatsoever. I've just opened my shop and you come to beg for alms. I quickly give you a cup of wine, and you're still not satisfied. Instead you say that I treated you with disrespect."

"Old man, stop grumbling," the onlookers said. "That Daoist is a bad one. Your generosity is wasted on him."

Old Man Tang said, "Gentlemen, please take a seat. I am now seventy-three years old, and I have seen many of this kind of Daoist. Why should I regard this one as unusual? For example, across from my door is the mansion of the vice minister Han. They had a son who was properly studying at home when suddenly two Daoists turned up, claiming to be divine immortals who had come from the Zhongnan Mountains. They lured the young gentleman away, and now many years have passed and he still hasn't been found. Master Han and his wife were distraught with worry. They had people arrested and questioned all the time, but they never found a trace of the boy. If I hadn't put my foot down today, I too would have been swindled rotten by this Daoist."

The people said, "That may be so, but with only a cup of wine at stake, how could he have cheated you?" And so they kept talking back and forth.

Xiangzi paid no attention to them, but went straight to Tuizhi's door. Just at that time his aunt, Mme. Dou, was dozing in her room. When Xiangzi saw with his eyes of wisdom that she had not yet woken up, he sent a sleep spirit to give her a dream. After awakening she would send someone to look for him, and he would use the opportunity to go and instruct her.

Mme. Dou dreamt that she saw Xiangzi standing before her and calling to her. She awoke startled and felt very unhappy. She called Luying to discuss with her whether she should send out someone to look for Xiangzi.

"It is your wishful thinking that caused this dream. Where would you have them search?" Luying said.

Mme. Dou called Han Qing and said to him, "My son, your elder brother Xiangzi just called to me, but then was gone again. Quickly, go look for him and bring him to see me."

"My elder brother left the family many years ago. Do you know where he is that you ask me to find him?" Han Qing replied.

As they were talking, Xiangzi was sitting in the street and beating his fisher drum and clapper. Mme. Dou told Han Qing, "With the sound of a fisher drum, how can you say there is no place to look for your elder brother?"

"It is a young Daoist sitting on the tether stone outside our gate," Han Qing said. "He's beating a fisher drum and singing Daoist songs. A big crowd is listening to him. How could he be my elder brother?"

"Go call him in," Mme. Dou instructed him. "Let me question him. He might have news of your elder brother."

Han Qing quickly went outside. He saw a great number of people crowded together, stretching their necks, tilting their heads, and standing on tiptoe, even leaning on each other to listen. He said, "Don't you have better things to do, and work to look after instead of hanging about and listening to Daoist songs? This fellow passes his days singing songs and begging for alms. Could it be that that you too can get by on Daoist songs?"

At this, the crowd murmured their agreement and scattered in all directions. Only Xiangzi remained behind, sitting on the stone. Han Qing approached him and called, "Young Daoist, my mother wants you to come inside so she can talk to you."

Xiangzi just sat there and did not answer him. Han Qing scolded him, "You're damned discourteous, you blasted Daoist! I am the son of the vice minister Han. I spoke with good intentions. How dare you sit there boldly and not get up?"

Xiangzi thought to himself, "When I was studying in the Fuyang Hall and my uncle saw me carrying my book bag all by myself, he was afraid that people might laugh. So he requested and obtained a son of the Zhang family, Zhang Qing, changed his name to Han Qing, and had him study with me. After I left the family, my uncle and aunt, having no son of their own, must have formally adopted him. That's why he calls himself the young gentleman Han. Ridiculous! When he calls me again, I'll throw some mud in his face. Let's see what he says then."

Just then Han Qing piped up again in that fake sophisticated accent of his, "Damned hateful Daoist. If you won't get up, I'll call my servants to beat you up, you dog."

"I am an ascetic," Xiangzi said. "I haven't begged for alms at your door. I haven't accosted you in the street. How can you scold me, and even beat me, for no good reason at all?" He took some mud and flung it into Han Qing's face.

Boiling with anger, Han Qing ran inside and called his servants to go and give Xiangzi a beating. When Mme. Dou saw him running around, beside himself, she stopped him and said, "I sent you to call in that Daoist. Why are you making that face?"

Han Qing had no choice but to stop and reply, "I went to call in that damned criminal, but he wouldn't get up, and even threw mud at me. Now I'm having him brought in, strung up, and given a sound beating. Only then will my anger be assuaged."

"Surely it was because you browbeat him, relying on the power of your family, that he dared throw mud at you," Mme. Dou said. "Go inside and stop making such a fuss, or you will incur your father's displeasure."

Han Qing had to obey and went inside. Mme. Dou then called Zhang Qian and Li Wan and said, "That Daoist playing the fisher drum outside the gate—ask him politely to come and see me. Don't shout at him or abuse him."

Zhang Qian went and called to Xiangzi, "Little master, my lady asks you to come in and sing a Daoist song to dissipate her sadness. Watch yourself when you enter her presence. Don't be impudent or rude."

Thereupon Xiangzi followed him inside, met Mme. Dou, and said, "My lady, I knock my head in greeting."

"Boy, how many years ago did you leave the family?" Mme. Dou asked. "How old are you now?"

"I left the family when I was sixteen years old and have since gone through several summers and winters, but I have forgotten how many," Xiangzi answered.

"Ascetics don't have as much money in their purses as they had in worldly life, nor do they have as much rice in their jars as before," Mme. Dou said. "They have to go around begging—what's the good of it? At so young an age you abandoned father and mother, wife and children to pursue such a calling!"

"You don't understand," Xiangzi said. "I have a poem I would like you to listen to:

> "One bowl of food can feed a thousand families,
> All by myself I can travel ten thousand miles.
> It is to seek escape from the road of life and death
> That I pass the seasons in begging."

Mme. Dou said, "You speak of food for a thousand families, yet not all food is the same. There is rice and wheat, rotten food, damp food, dried-up food. What's the good of eating that? You are all alone at your young age. You don't live in a temple or monastery, but drift around like a floating cloud, like a lonely crane. Sometimes you eat, sometimes you go hungry—how can that be a happy way to pass your days? Think back to the time when you first had the idea of abandoning your relatives and leaving the family—you acted just like my Xiangzi. I am afraid today your regrets would come too late."

"I have no regrets. I have only left my mountain temporarily and come here to deliver the parents who raised me," Xiangzi said.

"From which mountain do you come?"

"I come from the Zhongnan Mountains."

"How many Zhongnan Mountains are there in the world?" Mme. Dou asked Zhang Qian.

"In all the fifteen circuits and all the 358 prefectures, there is only one Zhongnan mountain range," Zhang Qian answered.

Then Mme. Dou asked Xiangzi, "How far is that mountain from here?"

"It is 108,785 miles by road, plus another three thousand miles by waterway."

"How long did you travel to get here?" Mme. Dou asked.

"I am not deceiving you when I say that this morning at the sixth watch I was still on the mountain taking leave of my masters. By the noon hour I arrived in Chang'an."

Mme. Dou laughed and said, "Did you travel on a cloud, then?"

"I can't ride clouds. I just caught hold of some mist and thus was able to get here so quickly," Xiangzi explained.

"If you can straddle clouds and mists and travel in the sky, you must surely be a divine immortal," Mme. Dou said.

Xiangzi said, "The crown of my head is like Mount Tai, my feet tread the Great Earth, my hands carry the sun and the moon, I wear the blue sky at my waist as a cudgel. Walls do not obstruct me; nothing in this world affects me. Fearing that I might inadvertently lose my essence, I established a foundation and refined myself. My merit has already reached the number of three thousand. I subdue dragons and tigers, and do not yield to an immortal from Great Veil Heaven."

"What is your name?" Mme. Dou said.

"My surname is Zhuo, my personal name Wei."[4]

"As you have come from the Zhongnan Mountains, I'd like to ask you for some news."

"What do you want to inquire about?"

"Several years ago two Daoists lured my nephew away to the Zhongnan Mountains," Mme. Dou said. "To this day I've had no news of him, and don't know if he's still alive. I am kept in uncertainty from morning to evening. Therefore I'd like to ask you about him."

"What is your nephew's name?"

"His name is Han Xiang; his childhood name was Xiangzi."

"On the mountain there are two Xiangzis, but I don't know which of them is your nephew," Xiangzi said.

"About how old are they?"

"Big Xiangzi is a man from the country of Aolai east of the ocean. He is a disciple of the long-browed great immortal Li and is about a thousand years old," Xiangzi said.

"You must be mistaken. He surely is only a hundred," Mme. Dou remarked.

"Little Xiangzi is a man from Changli County in Yongping Prefecture," he went on. "He is the disciple of the masters Zhongli and Two Mouths on the mountain, and not yet thirty years of age."

"Little Xiangzi must be my nephew. How sad! When will he come back?" Mme. Dou said.

"I heard him saying that he would never return," Xiangzi replied.

"What are his clothes like? What does he get to eat?"

"Xiangzi imitates the Three August Emperors, wearing clothes made of grass and eating leaves. He passes his days in hardship, just like myself."

"Xiangzi, you are suffering so much in these foreign parts," Mme. Dou wept. "If only your family knew, your uncle, who wears the golden belt and purple robes of a high official, wouldn't hesitate to have you brought home."

"My lady, do not cry," Xiangzi replied. "I almost forgot. When I got up this morning, Little Xiangzi begged me to take along a letter to his family."

"Thanks be to Heaven and Earth, there is a letter! Then we can send people to look for him," Mme. Dou said. "Where is my nephew's letter, sir? Give it to me and I will reward you handsomely."

Xiangzi pretended to feel around his waist and then said, "Oh, because I got up rather early this morning, I took a nap on that rock where the immortals gather and must have dropped Xiangzi's letter. What am I to do?"

"My nephew went through endless difficulties to send a letter to his family and you lose it? You betrayed his trust!" Mme. Dou said.

Xiangzi thought for a while and then said, "Although the letter is lost, I was watching when Little Xiangzi wrote it. I can still remember it and will recite it to you."

"What was written in the letter? Quick, I can't wait to hear it."

Xiangzi said, "He wrote a poem to the tune of 'Painted Eyebrows.' Please listen to my recital:

> "A letter sealed by the son to be opened by the mother.
> My brush not yet inked, but my tears already like pearls.
> In my youth misfortune struck; my parents died.
> Yet I was blessed to be taken in by my uncle and aunt,
> Who raised me to the youthful age of sixteen.
> Although I married Luying of the Lin family,
> I abandoned her to leave home and cultivate myself.
> More than six years have passed since then,
> Which I spent refining cinnabar sand in the Azure Sky grotto palace.
> I respectfully send this letter asking for reply.
> My aunt, you must not worry,
> You must not worry!"

When Mme. Dou heard these words, she wailed and cried loudly. Truly,

湘子假形傳信息

In disguise, Xiangzi transmits a message.

Among all the sad things in the world,
Nothing is sadder than to be separated in life or by death.
Today as she suddenly heard Xiangzi's message,
The matron cried more sorrowfully than ever.

When Xiangzi saw Mme. Dou wailing and crying, he struck up his fisher drum and clapper, and sang a song to the tune "Shoals amid the Waves":

"When I first left home,
I was full of anxiety.
I abandoned my wife's love and cast away my parents.
Spurning even ten thousand ounces of gold,
I left to hide from Death."

Mme. Dou said, "I can see that you, too, have not a piece of good clothing on you. It is very sad. There really is no need to leave the family."
     Xiangzi sang again,

"I am dressed in tattered clothes,
Patched in a thousand and stitched in a hundred places.
A begging bowl in hand, I have come to your door,
Asking you to be compassionate towards me
And give me some vegetarian food, give me some vegetarian food.

The Caoxi River flows vastly, right up into the Hall of Light.
After ten days, the embryo body gives off a fragrance.
When there is a body outside the body, the perfected being manifests
     itself.
What Death do you fear, what Death do you fear?"

When Mme. Dou heard this, she laughed and said, "A Daoist like this is in such dire straits he must pass his days begging for food, but still he boasts and brags of his abilities. Where there is life, there is always death. Even the Buddha did not avoid nirvana, even the Lord Lao could not forgo release from the corpse. Why do you hide from Death?"
     "Fortunately I was successful in this endeavor," Xiangzi said.
     "Confucius left behind the virtues of benevolence, righteousness, propriety, wisdom, and trustworthiness. Lord Lao left behind the Five Phases. The Buddha

left behind the ideas of birth, old age, illness, death, and suffering. Please sing me a song about the five Buddhist concepts," Mme. Dou said.

Xiangzi lightly struck the fisher drum and sang to the tune "Shoals amid the Waves,"

> *"To be born and leave the mother's womb*
> *Is as difficult as blossoms opening on an iron tree.*
> *Embracing me, my mother would suffer dampness to keep me dry.*
> *Without the protection of deities and Heaven,*
> *How could I have become a child?"*

"Once people are born, what happens when old age comes?" Mme. Dou asked.

Xiangzi sang,

> *"White hair hastens to the temples,*
> *Gradually one weakens.*
> *The waist is bent, the back stooped; walking becomes difficult.*
> *The ears are deaf and do not hear the words of others;*
> *The eyes fear the blowing of the wind."*

Mme. Dou asked, "What happens when you fall ill in old age?"

Xiangzi sang,

> *"When you fall ill, you lie on your inlaid bedstead,*
> *Depressed by the pain.*
> *Wife and children are all very worried.*
> *Day and night you don't sleep, but only keep screaming in pain,*
> *And offer worship to the God of Medicine."*

Mme. Dou asked, "What happens when you die?"

Xiangzi sang,

> *"When a man dies he is all alone;*
> *Husband and wife are separated.*
> *His head to the south, his feet to the north, his hands east*
>   *and west.*
> *His ten thousand ounces of gold he cannot take along,*
> *As his body is buried in the soil and mud."*

Mme. Dou asked, "How about the suffering after death?"
Xiangzi sang,

> *"Having died, you meet King Yama.*
> *In pain you move back and forth restlessly.*
> *Two lines of pearly tears fall on your breast.*
> *You implore King Yama, 'Show me compassion,*
> *And send me back home.'"*

Also:

> *From a melon seed buried in the ground*
> *Will grow forth a blossom.*
> *From red roots and green leaves a purple flower opens.*
> *When that flower undergoes all manner of suffering,*
> *Who is there to grieve for it?"*

"Master Zhuo, what do you have to say about our time in this floating world?" Mme. Dou said.

"People in the floating world bustle anxiously about, competing for fame and grasping after profit, all to feed and clothe this body," Xiangzi said. "Sons and daughters are pits of fire, which bind and press us. When will it ever end? An old saying goes, 'A hundred years are like a fire flaring up, a lifetime is like a floating bubble in the water.' When you come to think of it, a person may own a hundred thousand acres of good fields, eat a pint of rice every day, possess a thousand houses, and sleep in a bed seven feet wide. Why does he have to betray Heaven and Earth in his heart by his refusal to cultivate himself? The reason is the love between husband and wife, and between children and mother. But when it is time to part, suddenly he becomes incoherent with anxiety and has to do the bidding of others. What advantage is there in this?"

"Master Zhuo, as my nephew doesn't want to come back, I'd like to help you out with your travel expenses and trouble you to carry a letter to my nephew, calling upon him to return home soon so as to spare us further worry. Are you willing to carry the letter?" Mme. Dou said.

"I'll carry the letter, but I have no use for travel expenses," Xiangzi said.

"Your clothes do not cover your body; your food does not fill your mouth. If you accept some travel money, you can save yourself begging for alms on the journey. Why do you have no use for it?"

"I will explain it with a poem:

"I don't serve a ruler, I don't plant any fields;
Though the sun stands high I am still asleep, cradling my zither.
After getting up, I transmute myself some gold.
I don't have to earn the money of sin among ordinary mortals."[5]

"What is it you call 'the money of sin'?" Mme. Dou asked.

"The money of officials is all beaten with cudgels out of hapless prisoners subject to excessive punishment and wrongful interrogation," Xiangzi said. "The money of Buddhists and Daoists is all swindled out of the pockets of lay benefactors. The money of dealers and pedlars has all been accumulated by tortuous means and devices. The money of butchers has all been exchanged for the lives of many animals killed. The money of gambling hall owners is gained by shameless fraud. All of these I call 'money of sin.' I will not touch it."

Mme. Dou said angrily, "I meant well and wanted to help you with your travel expenses, yet you respond with such offensive nonsense."

Xiangzi chanted another poem,

"I am never a bother to others,
When I am hungry I beg, when I am full, I sleep.
I can sell wind, thunder, rain, and snow,
I can change stone to gold and silver, I can change soil into
     money."

Angrily, Mme. Dou said, "Wind, thunder, rain, and snow are divine things of Heaven. How could they be sold to suit your needs? Stones and soil are base things. How could you change them into gold and silver? Zhang Qian, chase this uncouth Daoist out of the house!"

"Please, don't be angry," Zhang Qian objected. "If this Master Zhuo says he can change stone into gold, why not let us see him do it? If he can't do it, we'll send him to the police station and charge him with vagrancy and swindling, as well as with confusing the world and misleading the people. With such big crimes, he will have to give in."

"You're right," Mme. Dou said. Then she called to Xiangzi, "Since you say you can make gold, will you let me see you transmute some stones?"

"Go ahead and have some stones fetched and I'll transmute them," Xiangzi said.

Mme. Dou called to Zhang Qian, "Go to Sleeping Tiger Mountain and fetch a few big stones."

Zhang Qian chose several others to accompany him. "Elder Brother, where are we going?" they asked.

"The young Daoist says he can turn stones into gold," Zhang Qian said. "If he succeeds, we'll ask if we can keep the gold." Having heard this, they couldn't wait to carry a whole load of stones, and rushed hot-headed to Sleeping Tiger Mountain.

Xiangzi said to himself, "My aunt has sent people to fetch stones. I have to come up with a plan, or she won't believe that I am a divine immortal. I'll make all the stones on Sleeping Tiger Mountain disappear. Let's see how she handles that." Then Xiangzi manifested his divine powers and blew a mouthful of pneuma towards Sleeping Tiger Mountain. And really, not one little stone was left. The servants looked all over the mountain, but there was not a single stone of even the smallest size.

At first they were struck dumb, then they said, "Who carried off all the stones on this mountain? If they weren't stolen by deities or taken by ghosts, it surely must have been that young Daoist, who knew he could not transmute them and therefore used a magic trick to make them vanish." They had to return and report to Mme. Dou, "We looked everywhere, but there is not a single stone to be found."

"If there are no stones on the mountain, I'll have that stone lion carried in," Mme. Dou said.

"We don't want to exhaust the men by having them carry the lion," Xiangzi said. "I just need a handkerchief and a bowl of pure water. If you burn incense and pray, I'll make that stone lion come walking in by itself."

And so Mme. Dou told Zhang Qian to quickly fetch a handkerchief, pure water, and an incense burner. When Zhang Qian had brought them, Xiangzi placed the handkerchief on the lion. Mme. Dou knelt down and offered incense. Xiangzi blew a mouthful of immortal's pneuma on the lion, which moved as if it were alive and came bounding inside. What did this lion look like?

> On his head his mane swirled and curled; golden pupils peered from the corners of his eyes. The fur covering his body resembled copper needles; his paws clawed about restlessly. His teeth were arrayed terrifyingly like swords and lances, his tongue licking his chops menacingly. Tigers and leopards would all be startled by him; he was afraid only of being bound by the bodhisattva Samantabhadra.

When Mme. Dou saw the lion bounding in, she jumped up in alarm.

"Beast, stop! You mustn't startle respectable people," Xiangzi ordered. Whereupon the lion stopped and became again a gate-guarding stone lion, completely motionless.

Mme. Dou said, "Although I am just a woman, I also know a bit about Daoist principles. If you want to turn stone into gold, you need to use some herbs. Quickly say which ones and I will send for them."

"Turning stone into gold is not easy, but just watch, please." Xiangzi once more placed the handkerchief on the lion. He let a grain of golden elixir roll from his bottle gourd and placed it in the lion's mouth. He spat a mouthful of water on the lion, recited something under his breath, and then, pointing with his right hand, shouted, "The white tiger of the western mountain goes wild. The green dragon of the eastern sea cannot be kept in check. Grasp them in both hands and have them fight to the death—thereby they are transmuted into a lump of purple-gold frost.[6] Transform now!"

Suddenly Heaven and Earth turned dark. After a while, a rosy light appeared, so intense one had to shield one's eyes from its glare, and auspicious pneuma abounded in many colors. When Xiangzi removed the handkerchief to look, the lion had turned into gold. Here is a song to the tune "West River Moon" to illustrate it:

> It had been an insentient stone from the deep mountains,
> Which a skilled craftsman had chiseled into shape.
> With a fierce and vicious expression
> It quietly guarded gate and courtyard.
> Today destiny and fortune will have it
> That its skin and fur have changed into gold.
> Do not laugh at this as a clever trick;
> The affairs of this world can change in a moment,
> And this event is no different.

When Mme. Dou saw it, she said, "It truly is a golden lion."

Zhang Qian objected, "On the outside the lion is golden, but on the inside it's still just stone. Don't believe him."

"Master Zhuo, this gold is false," Mme. Dou called to Xiangzi.

"Chisel off a piece and have a look. Then you will see whether it is genuine or false," Xiangzi responded.

Mme. Dou told Zhang Qian, "Fetch a hammer and chisel to see whether it's gold or stone. If it is gold, I shall believe that this gentleman is a divine immortal."

Zhang Qian hurriedly fetched hammer and chisel and knocked off one of the lion's claws. When he looked inside, the interior was an even deeper gold than the outside.

Zhang Qian was so surprised that he stared open-mouthed and drew back three steps.

Mme. Dou said, "How extraordinary!"

Zhang Qian knelt down and suggested to Mme. Dou, "This divine immortal has, by transformation, produced an excellent golden lion. You should reward him with food and wine."

Mme. Dou told the cook to prepare a table of vegetarian food for Master Zhuo. Zhang Qian set up a table in the study and then went to invite Xiangzi.

Originally Xiangzi was not going to eat the meal, because he knew that Zhang Qian and Li Wan wanted to use the opportunity to steal the immortal elixir in his bottle gourd. However, as he could not very well show that he knew of their designs, he followed them to the study and sat down. Zhang Qian and Li Wan stood against a side wall.

Xiangzi said, "I cannot eat and drink so much wine and so many delicacies. If you do not detest my company, why don't you sit down and drink a cup with me?"

"Poverty and wealth, high and low rank are all determined by destiny," Li Wan said. "You are a divine immortal and we have been fated to meet you. We offer you some wine so that you may drink your fill."

"My capacity for wine is small. I get drunk after just three to five cups," Xiangzi said.

Eventually the two servants also took some wine and drank merrily, toasting Xiangzi and being toasted by him. After drinking several cups, Xiangzi feigned deep drunkenness, fell to the floor, and pretended to sleep soundly, snoring like thunder.

Zhang Qian right away untied Xiangzi's bottle-gourd, but Li Wan said, "If the bottle-gourd is gone when he wakes up, he'll search everywhere and we will have to return it. It would be better to steal some of the elixir drug. Let's just take out some golden pills for our use."

So Zhang Qian tipped the gourd and let a pill roll out. However, when it rolled into his hand, it changed into a flame, which he tried in vain to drop. Li Wan did not believe it and poured out another pill, but it changed into a variegated snake which coiled around his palm.

Frightened out of their wits, they dropped the things on the floor. The snake and the fire returned into the bottle-gourd.

Just then Xiangzi awakened and asked innocently, "Why are you making such a noise?"

Zhang Qian said, "You were sleeping, master, and we hadn't yet reported back to Mme. Dou. We were afraid she might scold us and were discussing what to do."

Then Xiangzi went with them to thank Mme. Dou. She said to him, "We have another stone lion outside the gate. You might as well turn it into gold as well. When my husband comes home, he'll present it to the court and request an official appointment for you. What do you think?"

"I don't want him to do that," Xiangzi said. "Here is a poem to explain myself:

> "Official rank is not so eminent after all—
> It is like a sash made from a paper cord.
> It looks good while it's dry,
> But in water it falls apart."

Mme. Dou said, "This uncouth Daoist just keeps messing up his chances for advancement. How dare you hurt my feelings with every word you speak? I'll give you a poem in return:

> "To be an official displays your achievements,
> Your reputation is spread all within the four seas.
> If you are a withered willow tree,
> How can you become a ridgepole?"

Xiangzi said, "Although the willow may be withered now, once it is spring it will put forth blossoms and leaves. I will present you with another poem. Please listen:

> "Although the willow may be dead,
> It can still become a ridgepole.
> But if you are an official and a turn of fate comes about,
> Failure will be difficult to face."

When Mme. Dou heard this, she became very angry and ordered Zhang Qian to chase Xiangzi out.

Xiangzi said to himself, "Although my aunt is so old, she doesn't understand life and death, and her attachments have no end. What shall I do? For today I shall leave and think of another approach." Truly,

> When you drink with an intimate friend, a thousand cups are not
>   excessive,
> But if you speak at an inopportune time, half a sentence is too much.

If you don't know whether Xiangzi came back or not, listen to the next chapter.

12

WHEN TUIZHI PRAYS FOR SNOW, XIANGZI ASCENDS THE SOUTHERN SHRINE

THE DRAGON KING BOWS AND FOLLOWS ORDERS

Yellow sprouts and white snow are not hard to find;
The adept must rely upon profoundly virtuous conduct.
The four signs and the five phases completely rely upon Earth;
The three primes and the eight trigrams cannot be separated from water.
Purifying the numinous substance is hard to understand;
It dissolves all yin spirits and then demons can no longer attack.
I wish to pass on to others these secret formulae,
But have not yet encountered a single soul mate.[1]

Ever since Xianzong had ascended the throne, the harvests had been abundant and the people at peace. However, in the last two years a terrible drought had reigned. No rain or snow had fallen, the wells were empty, the trees withered and prone to burning, and the people had nothing to live on. Eventually the emperor promulgated a decree to all his high officials:

> For four years after Our ascension to the throne the harvests were plentiful, but for the last two years We must have been lacking in virtue and Heaven has therefore sent warning signs. As a result the trees have withered, the wells and springs are dry, no green grass grows in the meadows, and the cooking fires in the households have been extinguished. Who among you military

and civil officials agrees to accept Our command to go to the Southern Shrine and pray for rain and snow? If within half a month your prayers are successful, you will be promoted. If you fail, then it is because Heaven refuses Our command. We will have a pyre built and will immolate Ourselves as an apology to the people and a response to Heaven's punishment.

Tuizhi said, "I, Han Yu, am willing to accept the commission to go to the Southern Shrine and pray for snow. If I cannot bring snow, I shall gladly immolate myself to apologize to Your Majesty."

The scholar Lin said, "I, Lin Gui, am willing to accept the commission and supervise the altar. If Han Yu's prayers do not bring rain, I shall immolate myself with him to repay Your Majesty."

When Xianzong heard them, he was overjoyed and said, "Give your best effort to assist Our concerns."

When Tuizhi and Lin Gui had left the court, they sent Zhang Qian to the Chang'an county authorities, ordering them to prepare the flags of the five directions and appoint functionaries to attend at the Southern Shrine. All the lower officials and the common people were to burn incense, light candles, and pray to Heaven.

When Xiangzi heard this up in the clouds, he said, "So my uncle and my father-in-law want to go to the Southern Shrine to pray for rain and snow. With the present weather situation, how could they succeed? Tomorrow I'll go there and make an effort to deliver Han Yu. Let's see what happens." After a pause he added, "Ordinary mortals have no idea of the marvelous means at the disposal of divine immortals."

And forthwith he transformed his shape and changed his garments. Hanging a flower basket from his wrist and grasping fisher drum and clapper in his hands he proceeded to the Southern Shrine, singing Daoist songs all along the way. From afar he already saw the multicolored flags on the Tower of the Five Phoenixes, as well as the majestic altars. In front of every house tablets with the dragon king's name were set up for worship, alongside small jars filled with water. All around, willow branches and leaves were attached; incense sticks and candles were well arranged in orderly rows. In the streets old and young all faced Heaven and prayed.

Xiangzi went forward and called mockingly, "My dear sirs, I knock my head in greeting. Could it be that you set up these altars to welcome me, the great immortal?"

The people raised their heads, and seeing that Xiangzi was sallow, emaciated, and ugly beyond words, they said, "Shut up! You know the saying 'improper words can destroy luck for a whole lifetime,' don't you? We currently have a drought and the people have nothing to live on. The emperor sent Master Han to ascend the shrine and pray for rain and snow. That's why we've set up altars and are praying to Heaven and Earth—isn't that Master Han coming now?"

When Xiangzi moved aside and looked, he saw Tuizhi in his court robes, holding the ivory tablet, sitting very solemnly on a horse, preceded by heralds shouting to clear the way. It was very orderly and impressive. The scholar Lin followed behind, also in court robes and with an ivory tablet.

Having watched them for a while, Xiangzi went into a tavern and bought a pot of good wine. Pouring wine and drinking it by himself, he sang a Daoist song to the tune "Wild Geese Descending":

> *"Look how deep the blue mountains and the green waters are.*
> *See the pines and cypresses standing unchanged forever.*
> *Shi Chong possessed wealth of ten thousand strings of cash,*
> *Patriarch Peng longevity of a thousand years.*
> *When they went to their deaths, what was left to them?*
> *I am happy every day,*
> *Free all the time,*
> *Joyful and without worries;*
> *Everything I do succeeds.*
> *To expand this freedom,*
> *I drink a few cups of immortality wine."*

As Xiangzi was drinking his wine, he laughed and said, "Uncle, uncle, you are a very ordinary fellow. How could your prayers bring about snow? But so as not to waste the court's money and grain, and the people's efforts, I shall go in a few days and pray on your behalf for a day's worth of snowfall. Manifesting my abilities to you should make you amenable to being delivered."

True enough, Han Tuizhi and Scholar Lin prayed earnestly at the Southern Shrine day and night without interruption, but after twelve days there was not even half a cloud in the sky, let alone any snow. Their worry and distress increased greatly, but they could do nothing except post a placard with the following general announcement:

Concerning the prayers of the Vice Minister of Justice Han and the Hanlin Academician Lin:

A drought prevails and the springs and watercourses are dried up. The sedentary population and traveling merchants all flee for their lives and cannot follow their calling. Because the present prayers have not elicited a response, the following announcement is made:

No matter whether he is a civil or military official, traveling or resident merchant, itinerant Buddhist or Daoist, recluse or mountain hermit—anyone with true merit and magical abilities who can pray for rain and snow shall lead the assembled officials and be courteously asked to ascend the shrine. If he receives an efficacious response, a memorial for his reward shall be submitted.

This notice is made known to everyone concerned.

Just after the placard was posted, outside the eastern gate an old man named Wang Fu stood and read it. Once he understood what it was about, he turned around to return home.

Just at this moment Xiangzi came ambling along, holding his drum and singing a song. On his clapper was written: "Auspicious Snow for Sale."

Wang Fu was walking along without paying attention to his surroundings, but when he raised his head and saw Xiangzi's clapper, he stopped him and said, "Master, if you have snow for sale, then sell me some."

Xiangzi said, "If you really want to buy, come up with some money and I'll order it to come flying down to be sold to you."

"You must be mad," Wang Fu said. "It's such a bad drought the emperor has ordered two officials to pray at the Southern Shrine. After more than ten days, they still haven't brought down a single snowflake. And you dare to tell me that you'll just order it to flow down to be sold to me. Truly mad!"

"I am not mad," Xiangzi said. "The wind, clouds, snow, and moon are all in my sleeves. I am afraid those officials won't be successful with their prayers and the Tang emperor will be very angry."

Wang Fu said, "If you really have such a skill, then go to the Southern Shrine and bring about a big snowfall by your prayers. Then Master Han will memorialize the court to have you appointed a Preceptor of State and a Daoist temple will be built for you to live in. That way you would earn riches and status."

"I don't want such honors. I only want Master Han to pay me ten million ounces of gold and a thousand pecks of bright pearls. Then I'll get him his great snowfall."

"Master, even bottles and jars have ears, yet you haven't heard that Master Han is as pure as water, completely honest and incorrupt. Where would he get so much gold and pearls to give you?"

"If he really is incorruptible and therefore without money, I'll be generous," Xiangzi said. "If he will come to me leading the assembled officials and bowing at every step, and in this manner invite me to ascend the shrine, I guarantee that there will be wind as soon as I raise my hands, and snow as soon as I bring them together."

"Master Han has received an imperial command and acts in compassion for the people. He will agree to your demands, but I am afraid you have no such powers," said Wang Fu.

"I have the powers," Xiangzi said. "But no one goes to tell Master Han about them and call on him to come and invite me in the most respectful manner."

"Where did you come from? What is your name? If you explain yourself, I will gladly go and report it to Master Han."

"I have come from the Zhongnan Mountains, and I am the Daoist Zhuo Wei."

"How far are the Zhongnan Mountains from the capital?" Wang Fu asked.

"More than 100,000 miles," he answered.

"If you have made your way here while begging for alms, it must have taken you several months."

"If I start out early, I arrive early," Xiangzi said. "If I start out late, I arrive late. Why would I need several months?"

"I have heard people speak of immortals who ride the clouds and mists, but have never seen one with my own eyes. You are so young, you wouldn't be able to ride clouds, would you?" Wang Fu wondered.

"Clouds I cannot ride, but I can produce clouds under my feet," Xiangzi said.

"Don't make me the butt of your jokes," Wang Fu said. "I am an old man who has eaten more salt in his lifetime than you have tasted soy sauce in yours. Why cheat me with this baseless talk?"

"Since childhood, I have always been honest and never told a lie," Xiangzi told him.

Then Wang Fu ordered some people in the street, "Watch this master carefully. Get some wine and food for him and keep him here. Don't let him leave. I am running to report to Master Han so that he may come and invite him."

The people in the street said, "As you wish, but hurry up and don't strike roots anywhere gossiping with people."

Wang Fu took to his heels and ran straight to the gate of the Southern Shrine. Truly,

> When one is all in a hurry like an arrow,
> The feet run as if taking flight.

Wang Fu ran until he was red in the face and out of breath. He could no longer stand firmly on his feet and so squatted in a heap on the ground. When the official who guarded the gate saw him in this state, he stepped in front of him and asked, "What lawsuit do you want to lodge, with which official, that you come running here in such a hurry? Right now the two officials are fasting in seclusion and are not allowed to deal with any suits. You have exhausted yourself in vain."

Panting, Wang Fu replied, "I don't want to lodge a lawsuit and have no accusations. The court's vast blessings fill Heaven and the assembled civil and military officials produce so much good fortune that the present star of calamity besetting the people will surely withdraw. This has moved Heaven and it has sent down a young Daoist from the Zhongnan Mountains, his hair bound into two knots, his body dressed in coarse cloth. In his hands he holds a fisher drum and a clapper on which is written "Snow for Sale." He is not more than twenty or thirty years old. He says that when he ascends the shrine, wind will arise as soon as he raises his hands, and snow will fall as soon as he brings his hands together. I did not dare hide this information and came running especially to report it to the two officials so that they may quickly go and invite him to perform his rituals."

"What's your name?" the guard asked him.

"I am called Wang Fu."

The guard then led Wang Fu straight to the foot of the audience hall, knelt and said, "I report that just after we posted the placards, this old man came to say that in the streets of Chang'an there is a young Daoist who has written on his clapper that he is selling wind and clouds, rain and snow. The old man asked him whether he really had such powers. The young Daoist said, 'If you invite me to ascend the shrine, I guarantee that snow will fall.' Therefore this old man came here to see you."

When Tuizhi heard this, he was very pleased and asked Wang Fu, "Where is the young Daoist now?"

Wang Fu came forward and replied, "He is at my home."

Tuizhi then ordered a guardsman to go with an imperial agent to invite Xiangzi to the shrine. They left the Southern Shrine with Wang Fu and arrived outside the eastern gate only to see a hundred or so people surrounding Xiangzi. Pushing their way through the crowd, they caught a glimpse of him.

Startled, they seized Wang Fu and said, "There are many ritual officials at the Southern Shrine, among them one of powerful spirit and high Daoist cultivation, yet even he does not have the magical techniques to bring about snow. How could this young Daoist, who looks as if he didn't have long to live, have such powers? Do you vouch for him?"

When Xiangzi heard the guardsman's words, he laughed out loud and said, "Stop looking down on people! It is in vain that you have so many ritual officials at the Southern Shrine. If you gave them to me as disciples, I'd have no use for them."

Changing his tone, the guardsman replied, "The officials ordered us to invite you to ascend the shrine and pray for snow to relieve the suffering of the people. Please move a little quicker, so as not to keep them waiting."

"As you have invited me, how could I not go?" Xiangzi said. "Please go ahead and I will follow behind."

"This is a trick. You are trying to get away," the guardsman said. He hadn't finished speaking when Xiangzi vanished into thin air.

The guardsman went gray with fright. He pulled Wang Fu along and said, "I am not going to take the blame for this. You go yourself and explain this mess to Master Han. We will not shoulder this trouble for you."

Unable to close his mouth, Wang Fu had no choice but to go with the two. The whole way they led him like a sheep to the marketplace, he unwilling to walk on, they pulling and dragging, until they arrived at the Southern Shrine. And who should they find there but Xiangzi already sitting at the great gate.

When the guardsman saw him sitting there, he pointed him out to Wang Fu and said, "The one sitting there—isn't that the young Daoist? That's really strange."

Wang Fu rubbed his eyes, stepped forward, and said, "How did you arrive here first? You scared me out of my wits."

"You need not be worried," Xiangzi said. "We ascetics move like the wind.

How could you keep up, with your shaking and swaying pace? When I say something, then it is so. I never lie. Guardsman, release this old man and let him go home."

As he was bid, the guardsman released Wang Fu, who hurried off home like a fish that has escaped from the net, or a bird that has gotten out of its cage, paying no attention to where he was stepping or whether he lived or died.

Xiangzi asked the guardsman, "Why is one of the three gates high and the other two low? And what about that little side door?"

The imperial agent said, "The high gate in the middle is the Dragon-and-Phoenix Gate. Only the emperor enters through it, and it is only opened once a year. The other two are the chief gates, through which the civil and military officials pass."

"Through which gate am I to enter today?" Xiangzi asked.

"None of these three gates is for you to go through," the agent said. "We'll take you in by the side door."

Xiangzi said, "As an ascetic I have a green dragon on my left shoulder, a white tiger on my right shoulder, a red bird in front of me, and a dark warrior behind me. How could I enter through the side door? No, I'll only go in if you open the central gate."

The guardsman went pale with fright. "The vice minister of Rites has specifically regulated that Buddhist and Daoist clerics are not to use the central gate. You are just a young Daoist. Who would dare open the central gate and let you enter through it?"

"Among Buddhist and Daoist clerics there are also differences in rank," Xiangzi said. "Don't lump them all together. If you don't open the central gate, I will turn back, and who will dare stop me?"

The guardsman said to himself, "Whatever his powers may be, if he can't produce snow, we'll have the authorities deal with him. No fear that he may fly off to Heaven." Then he ordered the agent, "You watch him closely. I'll go in to report to the officials, and then we'll decide what to do."

The guardsman went straight inside and reported, "The young Daoist from the Zhongnan Mountains is already outside the gate. However, he has made such an impudent demand that I dare not speak of it."

"Tell me what this impudent demand is," Tuizhi said.

The guardsman said, "When he came to the gate, he stopped and asked why the middle one of the three gates was higher than the others, and why there was a little side door. I explained to him that the central gate was for the use of the emperor and was therefore higher. The two other gates were used by officials, the eastern one for the civil and the western one for the military officials. The little side door was used by all kinds of ordinary people. He was to enter by the side door to meet with you. The young Daoist said he would only go in and ascend the shrine if I opened the central gate. If I did not open it, he would on no account come in and I was to tell you to ask someone else to pray for rain. I did not dare act on my own authority, but have to rely on your decision."

When Tuizhi heard this, he became very angry and resentful. He ordered his attendants to bring the young Daoist in and give him forty serious blows with the big stick. His priest's diploma was to be withdrawn and he himself returned to lay status.

With his hands clasped in salute, Scholar Lin said, "Don't be upset. If the young Daoist dares talk so big, he must be of big use to us. At this point we are in urgent need of talent. Why haggle with him over petty issues? A saying puts it well: 'He is accomplished who can slaughter oxen and sell wine illegally without getting caught.' You and I have received an imperial commission to act for the benefit of the common people. If today we violate the law by opening the forbidden gate and inviting him in, and if he then brings about a good snowfall, the emperor is welcome to blame us for our action. Furthermore, the civil and military officials are all observing, so we aren't deceiving anyone. Who will dare oppose us in front of the emperor? However, if the emperor should get to know about it and fault us, I will take the blame."

In accordance with Scholar Lin's suggestion, Tuizhi ordered Zhang Qian to tear off the seals and open the central gate to let the young Daoist in.

When Zhang Qian walked out the gate to invite Xiangzi in, he saw that he was extremely ugly, not at all like a divine immortal. "Today we are in urgent need of a talented person, sir," Zhang Qian said. "Your luck is in and the two lords have specially opened the central gate and are waiting for you to clamber in."

"I am not a turtle," Xiangzi said. "Why do you say I should 'clamber' in?"

"You are young and short of stature," Zhang Qian said. "The threshold of this central gate is very high. I feared you might not be able to step over it. Therefore I spoke of 'clambering.' I meant no offense."

"In the mountains I see mostly trees, but few people, sir," Xiangzi said. "Now that I have the good fortune to enter through the forbidden gate, could I bother you to go and ask the two lords to come out and welcome me?"

"If one gives you ascetics one thing, you want two. They have agreed to open the central gate and allowed you to come and leave through it. That already is way beyond your station. Now in addition you want the two lords to come out and welcome you. Aren't you just asking for your own death?" Zhang Qian said.

Xiangzi laughed and said, "Your master came and wanted something from me, not I something from him. If he welcomes me, I shall enter the gate and cause snow to fall. That will be your master's good fortune. How can you say I'm looking for my own death?"

Zhang Qian had no choice but to go back inside and report to Tuizhi, "That hapless Daoist is not content to be allowed in through the great gate, but wants you gentlemen to go welcome him and lead him in."

Enraged again, Tuizhi said, "What uncouth Daoist dares give himself such airs? Quickly, clap him in irons and bring him before me."

Scholar Lin said, "Don't upset yourself. We've already opened the central gate for him. If we welcome him, it is only for the sake of the state and the people. It won't break the wings off our black silk caps. Can it be that you don't know the story of Han Xin in the Han period? He was a shameful fellow, yet Gaozu built a shrine and asked him to be a general. Later he forced Xiang Yu to commit suicide at the Black River and chased Tian Heng out to die on the ocean isles. Thereby he laid the foundation for over three hundred years of Han reign. Although this young Daoist does not compare to Han Xin, we should still follow the example of the Duke of Zhou, who would spit out his food three times during a meal, or twist up his wet hair three times during a bath, to go out and receive guests, treating worthies with consummate courtesy. What harm is there in humbling ourselves to welcome the fellow this time?"

Following Lin's advice, Tuizhi walked out of the shrine with him to welcome Xiangzi. In the side corridors about a hundred civil and military officials were lined up; in the courtyard more than a thousand ritual specialists, Buddhist monks, and Daoist priests stood in orderly rows.

The imperial agent ran up and called to Xiangzi, "You are lucky, master. Master Han is coming out to welcome you. Quickly come forward."

Xiangzi paid him no attention whatsoever. He waited until Tuizhi and the other officials had come right up in front of him. Only then did he get up and say, "My lords, I knock my head."

Scholar Lin and the other officials returned the greeting, but Tuizhi just pretended not to notice and did not follow suit.

Xiangzi pointed at the courtyard and asked, "What are all these Buddhists and Daoists doing here?"

"They are all ritual officials praying for snow. Don't treat them with contempt," Scholar Lin said.

Xiangzi clapped his hands and laughed, "That lot doesn't even know how to lie down when they sleep. When they eat they don't know if they're still hungry or already full. How could they pray for snow?"

"It's because they weren't successful that we're asking you to ascend the shrine," Scholar Lin said.

"When do you want the snow?" asked Xiangzi.

Scholar Lin said, "The emperor has given us half a month. We have already prayed for thirteen days, so it would have to snow by tomorrow."

"Daoists have twenty-four different approaches to prayer. To which school of ritual do you belong?" Tuizhi asked Xiangzi.

"I belong to the Celestial Heart Orthodox Method of the Five Thunder Spirits," he replied.

"What paraphernalia do you need prepared?" Tuizhi asked.

Xiangzi said, "All I need, sir, is ten new tables, ten yellow flags, ten flag-bearers, ten earthen jars, and ten rush mats, all arranged in front of the shrine. In addition I need a pig's head, a pot of wine, and ten steamed buns which I will use when I ascend the shrine."

"How can you sacrifice a single pig's head to all the divine generals of the whole shrine?" Tuizhi said.

"Don't concern yourself with what to sacrifice and what not, so long as it snows," Xiangzi told him.

"If you really cause snow to fall, I'll memorialize the court to give you a banquet and a noble title. You definitely won't be neglected," Tuizhi said.

"I have long lived in the mountains and am only used to eating yellow leeks and thin rice," Xiangzi replied. "I couldn't eat the dregs from an imperial banquet. I only know how to raise my hands in salutation, not how to flatter and fawn."

Half angry, half laughing, Tuizhi said, "This young Daoist utters nothing but insults." Then he left Xiangzi behind and went to rest in the shrine's fasting room.

The next day all the different paraphernalia were ready. Tuizhi and Scholar Lin, at the head of a hundred officials, courteously asked Xiangzi to ascend the shrine.

Xiangzi ordered that the tables be set up at the points of the five directions, two tables stacked on top of each other at each point. Both on the upper and the lower table an earthen jar should be placed, filled with clear water. The rush mats were to be placed on the upper tables. Two servants holding flags with the appropriate colors were to stand beside each set of tables and attend while Xiangzi performed the rituals.

Xiangzi ascended the shrine with solemn, dignified steps, rolled up his sleeves, and drank a cup of wine. He ripped the pig's head and the big steamed buns to shreds and wolfed them down until everything was gone. The officials and the Buddhist and Daoist clerics said he was just eating these things for himself, not knowing that secretly he was rewarding the celestial generals.

Xiangzi called out, "I am drunk and full. I want a new mat, a pillow, and a blanket. Wait until I have taken a nap. When I wake up, I will get you your snow."

"Just look at that young Daoist," Tuizhi said. "The only ability he has is to get wine and food by cheating. How could he obtain snow?"

"Don't rush to judgment, just ask when the snow will arrive," Scholar Lin said.

So Tuizhi asked him, "When you have slept, at what time will the snow fall?"

"At the sixth watch a wind will start to blow, and at the noon hour it will snow until exactly three feet and three inches have accumulated. Then it will stop," Xiangzi said.

"In that case, please sleep well," Tuizhi said.

Everybody was laughing secretly, unaware that Xiangzi did not intend to sleep, but was performing a sleeping prayer. While he was asleep on the mat, snoring loudly, his sweat pouring like rain, his yang spirit went straight to the gate of Southern Heaven.

The celestial general guarding the gate asked, "Immortal Han, how are you getting on with the deliverance of Chonghezi?"

"It is still early days!" Xiangzi said.

"What are you here for?" asked the celestial general.

"I need to see the Jade Emperor about an urgent official document," Xiangzi replied.

The celestial general led Xiangzi straight up to the Precious Palace of the Numinous Empyrean for an audience with the Jade Emperor. Xiangzi reported in detail on Tuizhi praying for snow at the Southern Shrine. The Jade Emperor quickly transmitted a decree commanding the dragon kings of the four seas, as well as the Rain Master and Wind Count, all to obey Xiangzi. When he raised his hand, without fail there was to be wind, and when he brought his hands together, snow was to fall. Xiangzi led all the deities to the Southern Shrine, where they were to await his signal.

Tuizhi, the officials, and the ritual specialists were all waiting for a wind to blow at the sixth watch and snow to fall at noon. When they saw that the sun was already approaching the noon hour, while Xiangzi was still snoring and no wind stirred, everyone started to chatter and make jokes. The ritual officials said, "We have studied and practiced the Celestial Heart Orthodox Method of the Five Thunder Spirits since we were young, but couldn't bring about a bit of snow. That fellow hasn't even looked at books or charms or chanted invocations. You would need to find a great roc or a golden-winged bird to cover that bright red sun. Otherwise, even if he were an immortal, there would be no chance of snow by noon."

As they were joking, suddenly Xiangzi awoke. Standing on the shrine he called to Tuizhi, "My lord Han, you and the others should withdraw to the corridors below, kneel facing northeast, and wait for the dragon king of the Eastern Ocean to send snow."

Tuizhi said, "Since ancient times snow could only fall if red clouds covered the sky and a north wind blew. How can there be snow when the sun is shining brightly, the sky is clear, and no wind is blowing?"

"Sir, you say there is no wind and you want wind. Why the haste?" Then Xiangzi took a flag from the hands of the attendant in the west, waved it toward the northwestern corner, and called, "Dragon King Ao Ying of the Western Ocean, why is there no wind?"

He had not yet finished speaking when red clouds gathered halfway up the sky and the wind soughed. In the southeast the clouds grew tall and the trees swayed. In the northwest mists developed and dust swirled up, forcing people to shield their faces. The dragon king Ao Ying of the Western Ocean bowed and said, "Immortal Han, is this not wind?" A howling gust grew into a strong wind. Here is a poem to illustrate it:

> *Blowing the dust about,*
> *Soughing over the forests.*
> *On the ocean silver waves are churned up;*
> *In the mountains boulders roll down the slopes.*
> *Noble steeds are neighing on the highways;*
> *Beautiful women drop their bronze needles.*
> *Flying ducks lower their wings;*
> *In the ponds fish struggle against the restless water.*

壇上南雪祈之退

While Tuizhi prays for snow, Xiangzi ascends the Southern Shrine.

Yellow leaves swirl, dancing in the air.
Mountain forests are swept clear, exposing the roots.
Clay images of the gods are blown against the temple walls,
Suspended bells ring in golden palaces.
Walking on the road, it is hard to turn one's head,
It is impossible to let down screens.
When such a wind produces snow,
One needn't fear that it won't be plentiful.

In a gust of western wind ten thousand leaves swirl,
Tree branches in the gardens are broken off.
Above, the wind blows over the saha tree,
Below, it topples the bridge of Zhaozhou.

When the wind had passed, Xiangzi asked, "Sirs, where did that wind come from?"

"It was due to the vast blessings of the emperor, the numinous responsiveness of Heaven and Earth, and the good fortune of the people," Tuizhi said.

Xiangzi laughed and said, "I haven't yet made it snow, and you are already denying me all credit."

"The sun is about to cross its zenith and we have wind, but no snow," Scholar Lin said. "What are you going to do about it?" Xiangzi took a blue flag from the hands of the attendant in the eastern corner, waved it toward the southeast, and called, "Dragon King Ao Run of the Eastern Ocean, why haven't you sent snow?"

As soon as that blue flag unfurled, snow started to fall like a vast mass of white butterflies, like clouds of egret feathers scattered in profusion. The dragon king of the Eastern Ocean came forward and said, "Divine Immortal Han, isn't this snow?" And indeed it was a great snowfall, as displayed in this rhapsody:

Like willow catkins spreading,
Like innumerable pear blossoms,
Everywhere goose feathers seemed to be fanned about chaotically,
And the ground was covered with broken snippets of white silk.
Seeking refuge in the forest, birds lose their way,
Their eyes covered by the snow's white jade.
Dragons coming out of their grottoes don't recognize the landscape

As the Five Lakes appear to have become narrow and shallow.
Jade ground to powder,
White it covers buildings and terraces.
Silver made into make-up,
As silver silk it lies on kiosks and pavilions.
It presses down the plum blossoms without releasing them,
It buries innumerable nameless plants.
If it were shaped like a lion,
It would be of fierce and majestic aspect.
If it were formed like Maitreya,
He would laugh with open mouth.
Truly it was
A cold pneuma arising in the absence of sun or moonlight,
Lead and mercury scattered to cover the red dust.
Cold rivers freeze up the paths of fishing boats;
Covering houses, it casts out spring.

And a poem adds to this:

The flakes are dancing far and wide,
Falling from the sky ceaselessly.
Horses neigh on the lightly powdered ground;
Wagons roll over the gullies filled with white mud.
Nobles in their high houses watch it with appreciation,
But traveling merchants are worried in their lodging houses.
The sun's light is glittering on the silver sea;
The frozen mass causes concern.[2]

The snow fell for half a day, though it seemed like several days as it piled up high and wide, blocking up wells and obstructing rivers. All who saw it were overjoyed and sang Xiangzi's praises.

Xiangzi said, "There are now three feet and three inches. That should be enough."

Scholar Lin called Zhang Qian to take a yardstick and measure how much there was.

Laughing, Zhang Qian said to Xiangzi, "If it is too little, all your efforts will have been in vain." Zhang Qian inserted the yardstick into the snow at an elevated place—it was not a bit too much. He tried it in lower places—

it was not a bit too little. Everywhere it was exactly three feet and three inches.

The officials said, "Who made this snow fall?"

"It was the emperor's virtue and the people's piety that moved Heaven to send down this great snowfall," Tuizhi said.

"I called upon the dragon kings to send this snow. Why don't you say a word in my favor?" Xiangzi asked.

"Where are the dragon kings? Stop telling lies!" Tuizhi told him.

"The dragon kings are in the sky above us right now," Xiangzi said. "If you do not believe me, I'll call upon them to manifest themselves so you can see them. I am just concerned that it might frighten you."

"What is there to be afraid of?" Tuizhi said. "If the dragon kings do not manifest themselves, we shall burn you alive on a pyre so as to counter heresies and demonic practices which confuse the world and lead people astray."

Thereupon Xiangzi waved a yellow flag toward the sky and shouted, "Dragon kings of the Four Oceans, quickly manifest your true appearance!" Before he had finished, the four dragon kings could be seen in the sky, writhing and dancing, flanked by innumerable prawn spirits and turtle generals, crab masters and fish earls. The people inside and outside the city, old and young, all saw them and were so frightened that they fled in screaming confusion. The civil and military officials were all struck dumb and stood rooted to the ground.

Xiangzi said, "My lord Han! Are these dragon kings or aren't they?"

"If these dragon kings were to raise wind and waves in this manner, they would certainly harm the people," Scholar Lin said. "You are a great immortal from the upper realm. Why should you pick a quarrel with ordinary mortals? Quickly, ask the dragon kings to withdraw."

Accordingly, Xiangzi again waved the yellow flag and shouted, "Leave!" The next moment the sky was clear, and for ten thousand miles around the wind abated.

Remorseful, Tuizhi ordered Zhang Qian to fetch ten rolls of cloth and present them to Xiangzi.

Xiangzi said, "I have no use for these. Please keep them and give them as rewards to the generals guarding the borders."

"Take them and make some clothes to cover yourself," Tuizhi recommended. "That would be better than to bedeck yourself with sheep skins and leaves."

"Though my clothes are torn, my person is not," Xiangzi said. "When I am hungry, I eat. When I am full, I work. When I have little firewood and no rice, I don't have to bother with cooking. Wide robes and long sleeves are just impractical."

"If you don't want the cloth, let me submit a memorial to the court and have you richly rewarded."

"I do not desire rewards either. The only thing I want is for you to abandon your office and follow me to cultivate yourself and study the Dao. Then my heart's wish would be fulfilled."

Tuizhi became very angry and called people to seize and beat Xiangzi.

"Don't waste your time beating me," Xiangzi said. "If you don't agree to cultivate yourself, then that's that. I just fear that the snow you encounter as a calamity on another day will be greater than today's. Remember this well. Later, on your birthday, I will come to congratulate you. On no account refuse me again then."

"Our ways are different, but we shouldn't scheme against each other," Tuizhi said. "I won't celebrate my birthday, and you can save yourself the trouble of attending."

Xiangzi clapped his hands, laughed, and walked away across the great expanse of snow. Truly,

> This morning his prayers caused snow to cover the sky,
> Manifesting the abundant blessings of ruler and subjects.

If you don't know whether Xiangzi went to congratulate Tuizhi on his birthday, please listen to the next chapter.

13

RIDING AN AUSPICIOUS CLOUD, XIANGZI IS SALUTED BY
EMPEROR XIANZONG

DISCOURSING ON COMPLETE PERFECTION, XIANGZI
CHANTS A POEM

If you do not know the inverted inversion within the mystery,
How can you understand how to plant the lotus within the fire?
Lead the white tiger back home to be nurtured,
And you shall produce a bright pearl like the orb of the moon.
Constantly guard the elixir furnace and observe the fire phases,
Attentively observe spirit and breath and let them be natural.
With all yin stripped away and the elixir completed,
You shall leap from your worldly cage and live ten thousand years.[1]

When Tuizhi and Lin Gui returned to court to report on their mission, Xiangzi
went with them. Tuizhi memorialized,

> Having received Your Majesty's vast blessings from above, and below
> relied upon the sincere intentions of all officials, we managed to find
> a Complete Perfection monk from the Zhongnan Mountains whose
> prayers caused a snowfall of three feet and three inches. Snow covers
> mountains and forests. Springs, brooks, rivers, and marshes, as well
> as the irrigation channels, are all full. Grasses and trees are lush again.
> The people all sing and dance for joy. This is all due to Your Majesty's
> plans. The Complete Perfection monk is awaiting your summons
> outside.

Truly,

The holy Son of Heaven alone holds the strings of government,
His ministers and officials together harmonize its principles.

Xianzong was overjoyed and said, "If the Complete Perfection monk is here, he may be called in for an audience. We have a reward for him."

The attending officials quickly transmitted the command, and in no time at all Xiangzi arrived. He did not call out the appropriate greeting, nor did he kneel and kowtow. He remained standing erect in the Hall of the Golden Simurgh and did not perform the rites proper for a subject towards his ruler.

Angrily Xianzong said, "All under Heaven is the king's land. All living on this land are the king's subjects. We are the ruler of all under Heaven. From nobles, ministers, and officials above to the common people below, all who have an audience with Us call out the greeting, kneel, and kowtow. You are just an itinerant Daoist who lives within the king's land—how dare you be so lacking in propriety?"

Xiangzi said, "I live in the immortals' gardens and the Penglai Isles, not in the king's land. I ingest the essences of sun and moon and do not eat ordinary food. I do not seek glory and do not hanker after profit and fame. In me the Son of Heaven does not have a subject, and the feudal lords do not have a friend. Why do you want me to practice the vulgar rites of the human world by calling out a greeting and kowtowing?"

"You prayed for snow at the Southern Shrine, you lodge at monasteries, and now you stand in the Hall of the Golden Simurgh. You can hardly say that you do not live in the king's land," Xianzong said.

"If you don't want me to stand on the ground, what's the problem?" Xiangzi said. He waved his hand and a multicolored cloud lifted him up into the air. "Let me ask you officials: am I the king's subject?" he called.

When Xianzong saw Xiangzi in the air, his face went gray with fear. He stepped down from his throne, waved to Xiangzi, and said, "Immortal Master, please come forward. We wish to become your disciple."

"Immortals do not exist!" Tuizhi protested. "The Qin emperor and Emperor Wu of the Han dynasty were led by the nose all their lives by Xu Fu and Li Shao-jun, and in the end it did them no good whatsoever. This Complete Perfection monk just knows a few magical tricks with which to confuse the world and cheat the people. He is definitely not a true divine immortal. If you treat him as your teacher, how can you avoid elevating other people's ambitions and destroying your own authority?"

駕祥雲憲宗頂礼

Riding an auspicious cloud, Xiangzi is saluted by Emperor Xianzong.

Xianzong said, "We had such a severe drought that everything dried up and withered, but by his prayers he caused a great snowfall. When We criticized him somewhat, he floated up into the air. If he is not a divine immortal, how can he have such powers?"

"It is a law of nature that it will rain and snow after a long drought," Tuizhi said. "I think this Complete Perfection monk understands weather patterns and took advantage of the opportunity. He was just lucky. As for floating on clouds and riding on mists, these are heretical tricks of unorthodox schools, designed to hoodwink the people. If you spray him with the unclean blood of pigs and dogs, he will come crashing down and break every bone in his body. What is unusual about it?"

"You may withdraw temporarily. We shall handle this Ourselves," Xianzong said.

Chagrin filling his face, Tuizhi angrily left the court.

Only then did Xiangzi come down to stand on the ground and say, "I will return to the mountain wilderness for the time being, and come again for an audience on another day."

Xianzong said, "The Qin emperor and Emperor Wu of the Han dynasty exhausted their wealth and efforts, but did not get to meet an immortal. Today fate would have it that We meet a master descended from Heaven. How can you not say a word of instruction to Us?"

"You already have the utmost wealth and rank. What else do you want?" Xiangzi asked.

"We seek eternal life," Xianzong said.

"Eternal life is obtained by people with leisure and without obligations," Xiangzi said. "They abandon their family bonds, cast away grace and love, hide in the deep mountains and valleys, cultivate and refine themselves from morning to evening, spit out the old and take in the new. Now, your family includes everything within the Four Seas; the people are your children. You have your own discipline of rectifying your mind and making your intentions sincere, and that is enough to benefit the people and preserve your body. How could you seek the way of eternal life, casting away the concerns of rulership as if they were just so many trifles?"

"We suffer many illnesses and drugs are without effect," Xianzong said. "We request of you an elixir pill to heal Our chronic ailments."

"Every day you weary your spirit and waste your essence in the river of love and the ocean of lust," Xiangzi told him. "To try to make up for these losses with drugs made from grass roots and tree bark is as if you had a bagful of gold and every day replaced some of it with iron. After a long time the gold is used up and the useless iron is left. At that point you want to change the iron into gold—how could that be easy?"

"You are right," Xianzong said. "Please instruct Us what to do."

"I am just a mountain rustic and commoner," Xiangzi replied. "I cannot correct faults, make up for deficiencies, or repair omissions. If from now on you will purify your mind and lessen your desires, nourish your pneuma and preserve your spirit, an extraordinary person will come from the western land to protect your reign for ten thousand years and prolong the people's blessings for a hundred million years."

"What kind of person?"

"Although he has died, his bones still exist. If you treasure them and have them stored carefully wrapped up, miraculous events will occur."

When Xiangzi took his leave, Xianzong was very sad, sighing that he was not destined to have immortality bestowed upon him. Indeed,

> With destiny you will meet an immortal a thousand miles away;
> Without it, he won't stay even though he is facing you.

After several days it was Tuizhi's birthday. The officials of the Five Garrisons and the Six Ministries, the nine Chief Ministers and the four Grand Councilors, the officials of the Twelve Terraces, the Supervising Secretaries of the Six Offices of Scrutiny, and the Twenty-Four Directors—members of officialdom high and low in rank all came to congratulate him. Here is a song to the tune of "Flying on Clouds" to illustrate it:

> As the longevity banquet opens,
> There are longevity fruits on platters in many fresh colors.
> Longevity inscriptions appear on golden cauldrons;
> Longevity wine sparkles in cloudy cups.
> Among the Five Blessings longevity is the foremost.
> Longevity of unbroken years,
> Longevity comparing to that of hills and mounds,
> Longevity whose count of years stretches on without end.
> If only you are willing to seize it,
> Your longevity will compare to the ageless immortals of the Southern
>   Mountain.

Longevity clouds swirl,
Longevity candles burn on high, illuminating the banquet.
The longevity star of the South Pole manifests itself;
Longevity peaches are proffered at the Western Pond.
Longevity cranes dance gracefully,
Promising longevity of ten thousand years.
Longevity comparing to that of lofty pines,
Not afraid of the shears of wind and frost.
If only you are willing to seize it,
Your longevity will compare to the ageless immortals of the Penglai
    Isles.

Birthday congratulations wish longevity like that of the Southern
    Mountain,
Ten thousand years without end, and all blessings complete.
Longevity flowers, gorgeous one and all;
Longevity speeches uttering praises with every word.
May the count of your years be increased in the land of the
    immortals,
Longevity without end.
The days roll by,
Year by year turns over.
If only you are willing to seize it,
Your longevity will compare to the ageless immortals of the East.

Longevity wine is poured again and again,
The guests are numerous at this sumptuous feast.
Longevity comparing to the vigor of the numinous chun *tree,*
Longevity that allows you to observe the changes of the universe over
    eons.
If you obtain longevity, you meet each New Year with joy,
Knowing you will enjoy longevity all year long.
Longevity is a good fortune,
And your life will be limitless.
If only you are willing to seize it,
Your longevity will compare to the ageless immortals of Kunlun.

On this day Tuizhi invited the officials to drink wine in the main hall. Although
there were no extraordinary delicacies or unusual fruits, the food was all palat-

able and filled the stomach. Flute and zither were played to give joy to heart and eyes. Tuizhi ordered Zhang Qian and Li Wan, together with a group of servants, to guard the main and side doors and not let any idlers disrupt the banquet.

When Xiangzi, up in the air, heard this, he lowered his cloud. Fisher drum and clapper in hand, he went straight to Tuizhi's gate and wanted to walk inside.

Zhang Qian stopped him and said, "My master likes to beat Buddhists and scold Daoists. Fortunately, as today is his birthday banquet and a hundred officials are in the main hall drinking wine, he hasn't seen you, otherwise you would have gotten yourself a beating and a dressing down. You'd better leave right away."

"Why does your master dislike these two classes of people?" Xiangzi asked.

"Formerly the master liked the Dao," Zhang Qian said. "But a number of years ago two uncouth Daoists from the Zhongnan Mountains lured the master's nephew away. Thereafter the master ceased his interest in Daoism and no longer trusted Buddhists or Daoists."

Xiangzi laughed and said, "I am not a disciple of Buddha or Laozi. In fact, I am the ancestor of all critics of Buddhism and the first of all detractors of Daoism. It's only because I have no taste for studying and cannot make a living any other way that I beat the fisher drum and sing Daoist songs in this disorderly fashion, disguising myself as a Daoist. If today is your master's birthday, may I trouble you to put in a word for me and let me beg some wine and food to appease my hunger? It will be a good deed on your part."

"Letting you inside is not the problem," Li Wan said. "The problem is that I might get implicated and get a beating."

"Tell him that the Daoist Zhuo Wei from the Zhongnan Mountains requests to see him," Xiangzi said. "This will definitely not create trouble for you."

"Brother Li, this young Daoist comes from the Zhongnan Mountains," Zhang Qian said. "Perhaps he knows the young gentleman. If today we do not announce him, we'll be blamed later if the Daoist stops the master on his way to or from court to tell him about it, and the master then investigates who guarded the gate today. It might be better to announce him and let the master make his own decision."

"You're right, Brother," Li Wan said.

Zhang Qian thereupon went slowly into the banquet room and in an unoccupied moment reported to Tuizhi, "Outside there is a young Daoist who says he is from the Zhongnan Mountains and wants to see you."

"It must be that snow-praying Daoist Zhuo Wei," Tuizhi said. "If it's him, don't let him in."

"He doesn't look or sound like him," Zhang Qian said.

"It doesn't matter whether it's him or not," Tuizhi said. "This morning I ordered you to carefully guard the gates and not let any idlers come in and disrupt the banquet. Why do you come and report to me on behalf of this young Daoist? You should get a sound beating, but I will forgive you this once."

Zhang Qian gathered his courage and in a low voice said again, "How would I dare report to you in contravention of your orders? However, since ancient times it has been said, 'In the whole world only the Dao is to be honored.' Today is your birthday and the fact that this Daoist has come from afar to seek a meeting clearly means that you alone are to be honored."

So Tuizhi saluted his guests with folded hands and said, "Please remain seated for a while. I will fetch a young Daoist to join our company."

Zhang Qian quickly ran to the gate and said, "The master is coming out." He seized Xiangzi and said, "I have gone to a lot of trouble to put in a word for you. I almost got to feel the bamboo stick for it. If I hadn't been able to talk my way out of it, I would have gotten into trouble on your account. Now, when the master comes out, you will answer him carefully. If he gives you something as a reward, you will share it with me, giving me 30 percent of the gains. Don't hog it all for yourself."

At that moment they saw Tuizhi coming out. Everyone moved aside and arranged themselves in orderly rows, pushing Xiangzi behind their backs. Xiangzi said to himself, "How sad! Away from home people are worth little, while things become more valuable. When I lived here formerly, everyone feared me. Today they push me behind their backs."

Tuizhi opened his mouth and called, "Where is the young Daoist from the Zhongnan Mountains?"

The others pushed Xiangzi roughly in front of Tuizhi. When Tuizhi saw Xiangzi, he recognized him as the young Daoist who had prayed for snow and said, "Where do you live? Why have you come here from the Zhongnan Mountains?"

Xiangzi said, "My home is under the astral palace of the Northern Dipper, and I play leisurely among the white jade towers of Southern Heaven. Formerly I cultivated myself with my masters in the Zhongnan Mountains, and thus I came from there."

Tuizhi laughed and said, "This Daoist is young, but he talks big. I think my Xiangzi, who is drifting around in the world, must be similar in demeanor."

Xiangzi had already known what Tuizhi was going to say and so said, "The clothes worn by the young gentleman are not even as good as mine, sir."

"Let me ask you," Tuizhi said, "You ascetics die without descendants to see you off after a life of a hundred years. What good is in this that it should be worth imitating?"

"People raise good-for-nothing children who just do mischief so that they become the object of gossip and cause their ancestors to lose face," Xiangzi replied. "This is no match for the unfettered life of cultivation. Though you may love your sons and daughters dearly, when one day Death arrives, who will take your place on the wheel of rebirth?"

"In my view, family life and taking care of the affairs of the world are more important than personal cultivation," Tuizhi said.

"Sir, do you know that days pass quickly like the shuttle on the loom and that time flies like an arrow? The spring of youth will never come again when white hair covers the head. You must know that

> Health in old age is like the lingering cold of the spring or the remaining
> heat of autumn,
> Like a bright lamp that has burned all night, like the moon at dawn,
> Like dew on branches, like frost on a wooden bridge,
> Like floating bubbles on water, like snow on mountain peaks."

"As you are standing here outside the gate, I'll give you a riddle," Tuizhi said. "If you can solve it, I'll give you wine and food. If you can't answer, get away quickly and don't talk rubbish here."

"I am listening," Xiangzi said.

"The minister asks the Complete Perfection monk: Why did you come here?"

"I can divine the moon on the horizon and light the lamp under water."

"If there is no dust on the rock, how can you come to a conclusion?"

"By having the body riddled with a thousand iron awls."

"Can there be an inextinguishable fire in a stove?"

"Pull down a great river and pour it over the fire."

Tuizhi quietly ordered Zhang Qian, "Put two stalks of grass on your head and go sit on the wooden crossbeam of the second gate. Let's see what he says."

Zhang Qian did as he was told and sat firmly on the gate, two stalks of grass on his head. When Xiangzi saw him he walked inside. Li Wan stopped him and said, "Where do you think you are going?"

Xiangzi replied, "My lord Han has invited me to drink tea."[2] Tuizhi could not keep from laughing and returned to his seat at the banquet.

Xiangzi entered after him, remained standing before the stairs, and chanted a poem.

"Building a thatched hut in front of a mountain,
I escape the bonds of golden cangues and jade locks.
Light heartedly dwelling at the forest spring truly is to be at
*   peace,*
The bright moon's disc is suspended from the tip of my staff."

Having finished chanting, he took the fisher drum and sang to the "Golden Oriole" tune:

"The bright moon's disc is suspended from the tip of my staff,
When it comes to pure leisure,
Who can compare to me?
Green pines and cypresses are my constant companions.
I observe the wild monkeys in front of the cliff,
I listen to cuckoos in the branches.
The green mountains and waters are truly exquisite.
Thinking of the forests and springs,
The mind has no worries.
Among the mountain torrents,
I can give myself up to pleasure."

Then he stepped forward, saluted, and said, "Sirs, I knock my head."

Scholar Lin hurriedly left his seat to return the greeting.

"What high official or prince has come to attend my birthday party that we should leave our seats to receive him?" Tuizhi said.

"I am just being polite to this Daoist," Scholar Lin said.

"You are demeaning yourself," Tuizhi said. Then he called to the servants, "Pour a golden goblet and put it here. Anyone who wants to commend the Daoist first has to drink three cups."

"Sir, today you have three causes for joy. Do you know what they are?" Scholar Lin said.

"What three causes for joy do I have?"

"When during this great drought the people were all afraid, at the Southern Shrine you prayed for and got three feet and three inches of snow. In his joy the emperor promoted you to Minister of Rites. Is this no cause for joy?"

"It was brought about by the emperor's vast blessings and the officials' pious hearts. What merit do I have?" Tuizhi replied.

"Today is your birthday. Except for the emperor, all the court officials have come to celebrate. This is the second cause for joy," Scholar Lin said.

"For your misplaced affection for me, my gratitude knows no bounds."

Scholar Lin continued, "When everyone had just congratulated you, a divine immortal appeared singing of 'the bright moon suspended from the tip of his staff.' That surely is the third joy!"

"In ancient times the Queen Mother had her immortality peach banquet and the Eight Immortals wished her long life. A single thread does not make silk, a single tree does not make a forest. We have here a single Daoist—what divine immortal are you talking about?" Tuizhi said.

"You have long studied Daoism. Can you solve the riddle of 'the bright moon suspended from the tip of a staff'?" asked Scholar Lin.

"I do not know it," Tuizhi replied.

Scholar Lin said, "The character for 'bright' consists of the sun and moon, which together pace the sky day and night. The staff is the kind of staff old farmers lean on, or the Chan staff of the Buddhist monk, or Laozi's immortal's staff. 'To suspend' means 'to hang.' Formerly Laozi plucked down the words 'bright moon' and hung them from his immortal's staff. He carried the staff as he rode on the black ox out through the Hangu Pass to deliver, in the east, the great sages to become immortals, and, in the west, the barbarians to become Buddhas. In the south he answered Confucius's questions about the rites, and thus began the long series of immortals through the ages. I have a poem to praise him:

> "The bright moon's disc suspended from the tip of his staff,
> Roaming freely, he leaves his grotto-heaven.
> A green simurgh flies elegantly,
> A white crane dances gracefully.
> Wine overflows the golden cups in sparkles,
> Flowers open on jade trees in fresh colors.
> He wishes you many blessings and longevity,
> Yielding not to Patriarch Peng of old."

"You praise him too much," Tuizhi said.

Xiangzi stepped forward and said to Tuizhi, "My lord Han, I respectfully come to congratulate you on your birthday."

"As an ascetic you do not shoulder worldly responsibilities, and you do not understand when to advance and when to withdraw," Tuizhi said. "Because the other day your prayers caused the auspicious snowfall, I specifically petitioned the emperor to reward you, but you refused over and over again. At this banquet today all the guests are retainers and ministers of the emperor. How could we tolerate an ascetic like you in such a place? You surely know that the Daoist priests and Buddhist monks in the empire all receive their ordination certificates from the Ministry of Rites. Listen to this:

"In the mountains, jungles grow profusely;
Living on thin rice and yellow leeks is very bitter.
I let you, divine immortal, be a Daoist,
But you must submit to the control of the Ministry of Rites."

"My lord Han, stop bragging," Xiangzi said. "The Buddhist monks and Daoist priests of the empire may all submit to the control of the Ministry of Rites, but I am an immediate retainer of the Queen Mother, and Inner Minister in the Palace of the Jade Emperor. Human rank is not as high as celestial rank. How would you control me? I too have a poem that I would like you to listen to:

"The Son of Heaven of the Tang dynasty sits in his throne hall,
His officials all aligned in orderly rows.
The Buddhists and Daoists of this world submit to official control,
But how could an ordinary mortal dare control a divine immortal?"

Tuizhi said, "Divine immortals have always had an extraordinary appearance. They are endowed with an extraordinary destiny. Their brows and eyes are clear; their earlobes touch their shoulders. Their spirit is brilliant and their pneuma full. Their essence is complete and their body well nourished. Only then are they divine immortals. You are a sallow, skinny, and unbearably ugly fellow, nothing but an unlicensed, vagrant Daoist. How dare you speak such grand words?"

"I have some more grand words for you," Xiangzi said. "In the time it takes to turn my back, Heaven and Earth become narrow; in the twinkling of my eyes sun and moon darken. In my hand the pillars of Heaven are lined up; under my feet the waves of the ocean are calmed. The mountains are my teeth; moss and plants are my hair roots. The sands of the River of Eternity are my food; through my pores shine the stars. If you raise your head to look, you will realize how rare such persons are."

"These are the words of begging proselytizers. I don't want to listen to them," Tuizhi said.

"You call me a proselytizer, but I am unable to live up to that designation," Xiangzi said.

"What's so good about proselytizing that you say you can't live up to it?" Tuizhi pursued.

"The Most High Lord Lao manifested himself as the Ritual Master of the Ten Thousand Methods in the Upper Era of the Three Sovereigns, while in their Middle Era he was known as Sir Pan Gu," Xiangzi replied. "In the time of Fu Xi, his name was Master Denseflower, and in the reign of the Divine Farmer it was Master Great Attainment. Under the Yellow Emperor, his name was Master Far-reaching Attainment; under Shaohao, Master Following Response; under Zhuanxu, Master Red Essence; under Emperor Ku, Master Lutu; under Emperor Yao, Master Who Has Completed his Striving; under Emperor Shun, Master Yinshou; under Yu, Master Who Has Perfected His Practice; and under King Tang, Master Xize.

"At the time of Tang Jia he divided his spirit and transformed his pneuma and lodged in the womb of the Jade Maiden of Mystery and Wonder for eighty-one years, until he was born under a plum tree in Quren Village of Lai District of Ku County in the land of Chu. Pointing to the plum tree, he took Li ('plum') as his surname; his personal name was Er ('ear'), his style Boyang, and his posthumous name Dan. In the time of King Wu of Zhou, he served first as palace librarian, then as archivist. In the time of King Zhao, he crossed the Hangu Pass, on which occasion he delivered the guardian of the pass, Yin Xi.

"Later he descended at the Black Sheep Shop in Shu to meet again with Yin Xi and together with him deliver the barbarian lands beyond the desert. It was only in the time of King Mu that he returned to China. In the age of King Ping, he left China again to bring transformation to the kings of Su and Lin. Again he returned to China.

"In the twenty-first year of King Ling, Confucius was born. In the seventh year of King Jing, Confucius inquired after the Dao with Lord Lao. As he withdrew, Confucius sighed that Lord Lao was 'like a dragon.'

"In the time of King Lie, he traversed the state of Qin. After Duke Xian of Qin had inquired with him after his destiny, Laozi left by the San Pass. In the reign of King Nan, he flew up to Mount Kunlun. In the Qin dynasty, he descended to the banks of the Gorge River, where, under the name of Elder on the River, he instructed Master Anqiu.

"Thus, the Dao was honored, and its virtue cherished through the ages—that's what being a proselytizer is about! For my part, I dwell in the turbid world, and turbid words leave my mouth as I move among common humans—how could I therefore deserve the appellation of 'proselytizer'?"

"The words of a good man are few, those of a coarse man many," Tuizhi said. "The words of him whose heart harbors doubts are scattered.³ You are clearly a pauper who relies on his tongue to earn himself some alms. Get out of my sight!"

"The ancient sages and worthies also used to beg for food. Why do you demand that I do not do so?" Xiangzi said.

"When did the sages and worthies ever beg for food?" Tuizhi asked.

"Confucius roamed the empire with three thousand disciples and seventy-two worthies. At Chen, when their grain ran out, do you think the sage and the worthies did not go out to beg for food?"

"I ask you again: between Heaven and Earth what is called the Dao? What is called man?"

"The Dao is that which embraces Heaven and Earth," Xiangzi said. "He whose body exists in emptiness is called man. As for such 'men,' there exists not a single one between Heaven and Earth."

"Gentlemen, this young Daoist is mad," Tuizhi said.

"I am not mad," Xiangzi replied.

"This banquet room is full of court officials and ministers. Quite a few people are here. If you are not mad, why do you say there is not one man?" Tuizhi asked.

"There are men, but they are false men," Xiangzi said.

"If we are false, who is true?" Tuizhi said angrily.

"Only I am a true man," said Xiangzi.

"How do you distinguish true and false?" Tuizhi asked.

"I come without a shadow, I leave without a trace. I disperse myself to become pneuma, I gather myself to become form. I pass through metal and stones and suffer no obstruction. I endure as long as Heaven and Earth. The time it takes for rocks to rot and oceans to dry up is just a moment for me. Lord Yama and his ghostly judges all submit and acknowledge their lower position. Am I not then a true man? As for ordinary people, they use a single breath for ten thousand things, but when one day Death comes, all their affairs come to an end. They may be famous and rich, but who of them can overcome death? Are they not false men?"

The officials did not know how to reply to these words. Tuizhi asked, "What does 'complete perfection' mean?"

"When one's essence and pneuma are not wasted, and the yang spirit is not dispersed; when one supplements the elixir fields and opens the stomach lodge; when one lives without disease in eternal youth for a thousand years—this is 'completeness,'" Xiangzi said. "When in the winter one needs no stove and in the summer no fan; when cold and heat do not affect one and water and fire cannot harm one—this is 'perfection.'"

"When birds fly and fish dive, do you consider that they do it with or without deliberation?" Tuizhi asked.

"If they did it with deliberation, they would have to struggle and would inevitably fall or sink," Xiangzi answered. "If they did it without deliberation, they would forget what they were about and would also inevitably fall or sink. The space between the presence and absence of deliberation is called the movement of the heavenly force. If it didn't move it couldn't be called a force. That by which the force is moved is Heaven. All things are moved by the force and sent to oblivion by the force. And in each case it is due to their Heaven-endowed nature."

"Although this Daoist is young, he knows how to talk," Tuizhi said.

"What have you come here for?" Scholar Lin asked Xiangzi.

"I have come to congratulate the lord Han on his birthday, and to beg alms from the other lords."

"If you have come to beg for alms, why don't I see you give us a kowtow?" Tuizhi said.

"Because yesterday I was very drunk and got back late, I didn't make it in time to the gate of Southern Heaven," Xiangzi said. "Next I tried the Penglai Isles, then the Peach Spring Grotto, but each time I was too late. When I finally got to the Chaoyang Grotto at Mount Hua in Shaanxi, its gate also was closed. Those two idlers Cool Breeze and Bright Moon wouldn't let me in. I hurried towards the Bixia Grotto at Mount Wudang, but on the way I happened to see the goddess Bixia Yuanjun, who told me she was on her way somewhere else. And so I returned to the gate of Southern Heaven and napped for a while on the Seven Stars Rock. All that strenuous walking has overtaxed my back. Therefore I hope you won't blame me if I cannot kowtow."

"Crazy Daoist, can you chant a poem?" Tuizhi said.

"In my youth I used to study, and I can chant some verses."

"Then describe the affairs of the immortals to us in a poem."

Xiangzi chanted,

> *"A mulberry orchard changes into an ocean, an ocean into an orchard—*
> *Such words may seem hard to believe.*
> *Riding the mists and mounting clouds, why would I count the days?*
> *Eating clouds and swallowing pneuma, I don't notice the passing years.*
> *As the moon moves, flower shadows come to my window,*

While the wind brings the sounds of the pines to my pillow's side.
Having danced with my long sword, I brew some tea for tasting,
Having chanted a new poem, I go to sleep embracing my zither."

"Han, this poem really has merit. Tell him to sing a Daoist song and then we'll give him his alms," Scholar Lin said.

Xiangzi lightly drummed on his fisher drum and clapper and sang:

"Lord Han, do not worry,
Death is just about to come.
I may eat yellow leeks and thin rice,
But they are superior to choice delicacies.
Though you may own ten thousand strings of cash,
This wealth cannot be relied upon.
Think of Shi Chong's prosperity and Deng Tong's money;
When death came, it all returned to emptiness.
I am better off playing the zither when in a melancholy mood,
Playing the song of the cranes crying in the ninth marsh,
Without glory, without shame, without troubles.
Roaming freely, I slowly beat the fisher drum,
Visiting the fisherman and the woodcutter,
My old friends.

"And here is a poem:

"A long line of nobles in purple gowns,
In their grand chariots, they give themselves heroic airs.
Though they receive a thousand bushels of grain as salary,
They have not yet lessened the people's suffering by one little bit.
The good wine in their glasses is the people's blood,
The rich mutton they have minced is the people's fat.
If those in office do not aid the people,
Then they wrongly receive the court's emoluments."

Tuizhi said angrily, "The words of this crazy Daoist are not fit to be listened to. Zhang Qian, throw him out and don't let anyone else come in."

"Although I am a crazy Daoist, I have sung a Daoist song in return for some wine with which to toast the gentlemen present. Why are you having me thrown out?" Xiangzi said.

However, Zhang Qian and Li Wan allowed him to say nothing further, but quickly pushed him out the door. Indeed,

> When you drink with an intimate friend, a thousand cups are not
>   excessive,
> But if you speak at an inopportune time, half a sentence is too much.

If you do not know whether Xiangzi left or not, listen to the next chapter.

14

RUSHING IN AT A BIRTHDAY BANQUET, XIANGZI ENGAGES
THE GUESTS IN CONVERSATION

HEARING OF NOURISHING PRIMORDIAL YANG, TUIZHI DOES
NOT BECOME ENLIGHTENED

Three, five, one, all of these three numbers—
Truly, those who understand them have always been rare.
East is three, south is two, and together they make five;
North is one and the West, being four, completes it.
Earth in its proper place gives rise to the number five;
When the three meet, they form an infant.
The infant is one and contains the perfected pneuma;
In ten months the fetus is complete and enters the sacred realm.[1]

As Xiangzi was being pushed out the door by Zhang Qian, he let his shadow body
return inside and stand again in front of the banquet company.

"I have sent you off—how did you come back in?" Tuizhi said. "Let me ask
you: there are three kinds of Daoists in the world. Which kind are you?"

"My lord, I am a 'cloud-water' Daoist of the four lakes and the five oceans."[2]

"I always ask Daoists about this term 'cloud-water,' but none has ever been
able to explain it to me. Why don't you give it a go?" Tuizhi continued.

"After you, sir," said Xiangzi.

"'Clouds' are the yellow, black, blue, white, red, and auspicious clouds in the
sky," Tuizhi began.

"These are all imperfect clouds," Xiangzi said.

"'Water' is rainwater, well and spring water, the water of the Five Lakes, brook water, and the water of the Four Oceans," Tuizhi said.

"The clouds you speak of are all imperfect clouds, and the waters are imperfect waters," Xiangzi told him.

"Well, then, you try explaining 'cloud-water' to me."

"The cloud-water I speak of originates in Aolai of the Eastern Ocean. A white monkey had kept it in a stone casket, but I released it by blowing my immortal pneuma on the box. Seated on this cloud-water, I travel west at great speed when the east wind blows, and south when the north wind gusts. Like a white cloud, my mind is free, while my thoughts roam east and west at will like flowing water."

"All waters in the empire flow east—what do you mean by waters flowing west?"

"Ordinary waters only flow east, while this immortal water of mine can flow east or west."

"When clouds disperse and water dries up, where do they go?"

"When the clouds disperse, the moon stands in the sky. When the water dries up, the pearl appears."

"On your journeys across the seas, some tall tales seem to have washed up in your belly. I won't ask you any more. Just get yourself out of here!" Tuizhi said.

"I came to beg for some food to still my hunger," Xiangzi said. "Now that I've talked with you all this time, surely you won't dismiss me without giving me some vegetarian food?"

"Zhang Qian, reward him with a bowl of cold food!" Tuizhi directed.

"If you first tread upon your alms, even a tramp will not accept them; or if you offer them in an insulting voice, even a beggar will not stoop to take them. If you do not want to give me any alms, then that's that. Why speak of 'rewarding' me?"[3] Xiangzi said.

"My lord, in this case you are in the wrong," Scholar Lin said.

Zhang Qian called to Xiangzi, "Master, your rice is here. Shut up and eat it quickly!"

"How about accompanying my rice with a gourd of wine?" Xiangzi said.

"You ascetics are forbidden to drink wine," Tuizhi said. "I've already given you food, but now you want wine too. Does your greed know no end?"

"The wine is not for me, but for my master, who is cultivating himself in the Bixia Grotto," Xiangzi explained.

"Zhang Qian, give him some wine as well," said Tuizhi.

"Now that I have wine, please also give me a table," Xiangzi said.

撞子嬰筵湘子談天

Rushing in at the birthday banquet, Xiangzi engages the guests in conversation.

"My dear Han, do give this Daoist a table," said Scholar Lin.

Tuizhi ordered Zhang Qian and Li Wan to carry in a table for Xiangzi, who said, "Sir, may I bother you with another request? Now that I have a table, I can't very well eat while standing. I need something to sit on."

When Zhang Qian passed this request on to Tuizhi, the latter said, "Fetch a low stool. Let's see if he will sit on it."

Zhang Qian fetched the stool and handed it to Xiangzi, who said, "I want an armchair, not a stool."

Tuizhi said to Zhang Qian, "Give him my tiger-skin armchair. Let's see if he dares sit on it."

Zhang Qian quickly placed the armchair behind Xiangzi. Xiangzi immediately recognized it as the chair used by Tuizhi for official functions; he sat on it very straight, struck the fisher drum, and sang:

> "A cassock beats a gauze robe,
> A golden girdle does not equal my straw cord.
> While I clap my hands and laugh merrily on my reed mat,
> You have to grovel at the Court's morning audience.
> A double hair knot beats a cap of black silk;
> I roam in leisure and happiness,
> My joy overflowing all day long."

Tuizhi said, "You don't honor your ruler above, or nurture your parents below. You are a drifter and vagrant, dressed in a ragged cassock, which covers your front but not your back, your east side but not your west. How dare you behave so rudely?"

"My lord, don't laugh at this cassock of mine," Xiangzi said. "I'll sing you a song about an old cassock:

> "This cassock is not worth looking at,
> Being made of neither fine gauze nor thin silk,
> Neither damask nor satin.
> Yet it keeps me as warm as padded cotton in winter,
> And it keeps me cool like a fan in summer.
> Neither dyed nor softened,
> Untouched by safflower and indigo,
> It helps me succeed in all my endeavors.
> It contains 84,000 stitches

And 670 patches.
Never unpicked and washed,
Nor ever replaced,
Yet wearing it I do not fear the wind driving snow into my face.
Burned it does not scorch;
Soaked it does not rot;
Wearing it I do not fear blades or arrows.
Severe frost and violent rain are all the same to me,
Cold wind and humid heat do not bother me.
The three closed lines of the qian trigram,
And the six broken lines of the kun trigram,
The Nine Palaces and Eight Trigrams all turn along with my body.
My thousand merits complete, I am equal to Heaven and Earth.[4]
Yin is within,
Yang is without;
Between them are arrayed the stars in their brightness,
Outside are worlds without end.
Always comfortable and wide,
It truly is a precious thing to wear.
In no prefecture or district
Will any merchant dare to trade in clothes such as these.
If you lift a side
Or let down a piece,
Inside it a perfected man will be seen.
Wearing it, I once proceeded to the moon palace,
Wearing it, I also once went to the immortality peach banquet.
Do not laugh at my tattered cassock,
Or I shall fly straight up to the Palace of the Dragon Empyrean."

"Crazy Daoist, the assembled lords brought goats and wine to celebrate my birthday," Tuizhi said. "You, on the other hand, come here in this ragged cassock of yours just to talk nonsense. What is this all about?"

"What's so special about goats and wine?" Xiangzi said. "I can offer you an immortal goat and an immortal crane on your birthday. If only one particular lord agrees to resign his office and follow me in leaving the family, I shall call down the immortal goat and the immortal crane."

"There are 360 lords here—which one do you want to deliver to the life of an ascetic?" Scholar Lin asked.

"The one who presides over this banquet," Xiangzi said.

"Lonely and forsaken as you are, you dare speak of delivering others! Zhang Qian, Li Wan, throw him out!" Tuizhi said.

Xiangzi clapped his hands and, singing a song to the tune "Breaking a Cassia Twig," went out the door.

> *"Life is never perfect,*
> *But if it is,*
> *It is a wonder beyond words!*
> *Throughout the seasons of the year,*
> *There are those who have little to eat and nothing to wear.*
> *Some who enjoy wealth and prestige*
> *Die early,*
> *While others who suffer poverty*
> *Grow as old as pines and cypresses.*
> *Think back to all those heroes and worthies—*
> *If you consider it carefully, everything is up to Heaven."*

Indeed,

> *They met without drinking together; he left empty-handed.*
> *From the peach-blossomed cave he laughs at those who missed their*
> *   chance.*

The next day, Tuizhi again arranged a banquet for a hundred officials. And Xiangzi came again and called, "I knock my head to the assembled lords."

"Yesterday I was annoyed by you all day long, and the guests were displeased. Why are you here again today?" Tuizhi said.

"To liberate you for an ascetic life," Xiangzi replied.

"I am an official of the second rank, with just one person above me, and many below me," Tuizhi said. "There is no comparison in rank with a Daoist like you. Why do you go on about wanting to deliver me?"

"We immortals have many advantages," Xiangzi said. "If you don't believe me, here is a poem to prove it:

> *"A cloud-water cave in the blue mountains;*
> *This place is my home.*
> *At midnight the elixir liquid flows;*

At dawn I nibble at red clouds.
On my zither I strum melodies of blue jade;
In the stove I refine white elixir sand.
In the golden tripod I preserve the white tiger;
In the fungus field I nourish the white raven.
One gourd contains a whole world.
With my sword I behead evil demons.
I can make wine in an instant,
And open flowers in a trice.
If there is one who can follow my example,
We shall go together to gaze at the immortal plantains."[5]

"All this Daoist can do is talk—why haven't we ever seen him perform any feats?" Tuizhi said.

"It is not that I don't have these powers," Xiangzi replied. "If you make a firm decision to leave the family, I'll conjure an immortal crane and an immortal goat to congratulate you on your birthday."

"If such a crane and goat really do appear, I shall willingly follow you and leave the family," Tuizhi said.

"If you swear an oath to Heaven, I'll call down the crane and goat," Xiangzi said.

Tuizhi pointed to Heaven and swore, "If I refuse to leave the family, may I perish under many feet of snow."

Xiangzi said to himself, "Uncle, Uncle, now that you have made an oath, I am afraid your regrets will come too late." Then he raised his head and called, "Celestial generals and guards, go now to Blue Pass and make a record of this oath."

"I made my oath, but I don't see these immortal cranes and goats of yours. Clearly this is a hoax," Tuizhi said.

"Fetch me a bowl," Xiangzi said.

Tuizhi ordered an engraved red bowl to be brought and handed to Xiangzi. Xiangzi took it and vomited into it in the most revolting manner until it was full, and then set it on the ground.

Covering their faces, the officials said, "How disgusting! The Daoist knows no propriety whatsoever!" Very angry, Tuizhi ordered Zhang Qian to take the bowl and throw it away. Li Wan was to chase the young Daoist out and not let him in again.

Tuizhi was still shouting when a dog darted in from the side and ate the vomit, licking the bowl clean. When Xiangzi chased and beat the dog, it fell to the ground, made a somersault, changed into an immortal crane, and flew up into the air. Xiangzi said, "Is that an immortal crane or isn't it?"

The officials saluted Tuizhi and said, "My lord, we once heard an ancient saying that a man who eats an immortal's golden elixir becomes an immortal himself. If a chicken eats it, it becomes a phoenix. And if a dog eats it, it becomes a crane. Never have we heard, though, that a dog can also change into a crane by eating a Daoist's vomit. Surely the young Daoist must be an immortal!"

"These are all heretical tricks—nothing extraordinary about them at all," Tuizhi said. Then he called to Xiangzi, "Daoist! How can we tell whether this crane is true or false, if it flies up there in the sky? Call it down and let the lords have a look. Then we shall see about your powers."

Xiangzi obeyed, waving toward the sky and saying, "Immortal crane, come down quickly so that together we may deliver the lord Han."

The crane, who had been calling and dancing in the sky, came down to the ground. Seeing it, the officials laughed and said, "How extraordinary! He truly is a divine immortal!"

Tuizhi said, "I have ten or twenty pairs of this kind of 'immortal crane' on Sleeping Tiger mountain. What's extraordinary about it?"

"If you had a thousand pairs of cranes, I wouldn't exchange them for a single feather of this immortal crane," Xiangzi said.

"What's so special about it?" Tuizhi asked.

"It has special abilities," Xiangzi answered.

"All a crane can do is walk around with a stilted gait, fly, dance, and whoop over the Ninth Marsh," Tuizhi said. "What special abilities can it have?"

"There is nothing unusual in whooping and dancing. This crane of mine knows the movement of destiny, thoroughly understands human nature, and can compose poetry and songs. If you order it to, my lord, it shall compose a poem for you."

"If it can compose poems and songs, then I may accept that it is an immortal crane," Tuizhi said.

"But how could an animal chant poems and compose elegies?" Xiangzi pursued.

"Just now you claimed that it could compose poems, if I ordered it to," Tuizhi said. "Now you say it can't. You are uttering nothing but lies and rubbish. 'Who am I deceiving? Heaven?'"[6]

"Do not be hasty, my lord. Try giving it an order and see if it will respond."

"Immortal crane, the young Daoist claims that you can speak," Tuizhi said. "I will now compose a verse. If you can match it, I'll believe that this Daoist is a divine immortal. If you can't match it, I'll indict him for making false claims."

The crane straightened up, looked at Tuizhi with its round eyes, and nodded three times as a threefold salutation. Letting its wings hang down, it extended its neck, and answered in a clear voice, "Please compose the first verse."

When the officials heard human language coming out of the crane's beak, they were greatly frightened and grumbled against Tuizhi. Tuizhi said,

> *"If a bird's wings are so wide that it can follow the phoenix,*
> *It can be called first among all winged creatures."*

Looking at Tuizhi, the crane replied,

> *"If the fox did not borrow the tiger's authority,*
> *He could hardly attain the highest rank among mammals."*

All the officials applauded. Tuizhi said, "Chant me a poem."

The crane said, "I shall chant both a poem and a song. Please listen:

> *"The poem:*

> *"A white crane comes flying down from the Nine Heavens,*
> *Its clear cries ringing forth as it emerges out of the auspicious clouds.*
> *Time passes without hurry, yet men have already grown old.*
> *Wouldn't it be better to seek the Dao and study the way of immortality?*

> *"The song:*

> *"Although you are an official,*
> *You know nothing of human affairs.*
> *Although you are a man,*
> *You do not equal animals.*
> *Withdraw into reclusion,*
> *So that you may avoid calamities.*

> *"My lord,*
> *Haven't you heard of Zhang Liang, who resigned his office and with-*
> *   drew to the mountains,*
> *Or of Fan Li, who went to roam the lakes at the right time?*
> *If you do not soon turn back,*
> *I fear that you will be soaked by rain on your horse,*

Lose your way at Blue Pass,
And will be helpless to advance or retreat."

Tuizhi said, "You have come to congratulate me on my birthday, yet I didn't hear you speak of long life, peace, riches, honors, and fame. Instead you sing this ill-omened mountain song. You are just an animal after all, who doesn't understand the customs of the world."

"The crane's words will be fulfilled in the future. Why then do you say they are not auspicious?" Xiangzi asked.

"A man can't even take care of the things at hand. Why should he worry about past or future?" Tuizhi replied.

"Confucius said it well: 'If a man takes no thought about what is distant, he will find sorrow near at hand.'[7] You, my lord, are petty-minded," Xiangzi said.

"It's not that I am pettily concerned only with the present, but how can anyone have foreknowledge of the future? Your words are not worth listening to, and I don't want to argue with you. Get out!"

"If you agree to follow me and leave the family, I will go. Otherwise I refuse to leave."

"Throw him out. If he comes back in, give him forty blows," Tuizhi ordered his servants angrily.

Xiangzi, however, performed an immobility spell, and though the servants might push and pull at him, they could not budge him at all. "Daoist, what is the point of that immobility trick?" Tuizhi asked.

"My lord, I can travel on clouds, but I can't do immobility spells," Xiangzi told him.

"If you can travel on clouds, why do you come to my house for alms?"

Xiangzi beat the fisher drum and sang to the tune "Ascending the Little Tower":

"I have come today only to deliver you.
Quickly cast off your family bonds and livelihood.
We shall be inseparable,
As we discuss the mysterious principles—
Cling to confusion no longer!
Quickly extract yourself,
Hide from all conflict,
Withdraw to a secluded place.
Like the hermits of old you will live as long as Heaven
On Mount Shouyang."[8]

"The five phases go through their natural cycles. A man's life span is determined from birth. You are no divine immortal, so how could you live as long as Heaven?" said Tuizhi.

"If I am no divine immortal, who in this world is?"

"If you're a divine immortal—well, you just said there would be an immortal crane and an immortal goat. Why have I only seen a crane so far, but no goat?"

"Once the immortal goat comes, it immediately wants to leave. It's not that simple," Xiangzi said.

"I haven't even seen the goat yet, and already you're talking about it leaving," Tuizhi said.

"My lords, carefully guard your primordial yang, as I call it out," Xiangzi warned. With a wave of his hand, he called, "Immortal goat, come quickly!"

All of a sudden, with a rumbling noise, a goat passed through the Double Spinal Passes, ran up to the Niwan Palace, descended straight down the Twelve-Storied Tower, stepped on the Elixir Terrace, and then came shooting straight out of the pneumatic sea of the Elixir Field.

On seeing it, the officials all said, "Its head is red, its tail scarlet; the hooves are white, the back green. With all these colors, this is indeed an excellent goat. Where do you keep it that you can make it come with a single call?"

"I have raised this goat from childhood, and not far away, but very close nearby," Xiangzi responded.

"It is not unusual for ascetics to keep chickens and deer, but when did they ever keep goats?" Tuizhi said.

"Keeping deer is just an idle pastime. The goat, on the other hand, is the seed of Former Heaven, the foundation of Dragon and Tiger. If you nurture it to completion, white hair will become black again, lost teeth will grow back, and you will never die. The goat is exactly what ascetics should raise."

"In my family, we also raise goats," Tuizhi commented. "When they are fattened, we slaughter them. Their manure is useful for fertilizing the fields, but I've never heard that they have so much use beyond that."

"What you raise are external goats that eat wild grass and drink muddy water, fit only to still the cravings of people's stomachs," Xiangzi said. "What I raise is an eternal goat that eats the grass of no-mind and drinks the liquid of the Jade Pools. I keep it in a pen and don't let it roam the mountain meadows. It is not as easy to raise as your external goats."

"How much do you want for this goat? Sell it to me," Tuizhi proposed.

"Once, Emperor Wu of the Han dynasty wanted to buy this goat and was willing to give seventy-two cities for it, but that still wasn't enough by half. You, my lord, are a mere minister. You couldn't afford to buy even one hair of this goat," Xiangzi told him.

"How much does a goat's hair weigh? Don't be ridiculous. Of course I can afford it."

"Even if you got the goat, you wouldn't know how to nurture it."

"You tell me how and I shall follow your instructions," Tuizhi said.

"We Daoists have a song about goat husbandry:[9]

"It is very easy to raise a goat—
Do not lock it up, do not tie it.
When it is hungry, let it eat the blossoms of No-Mind grass.
When it is thirsty, let it drink the eternally flowing water of the torrent.
When it is fed it is bound to act wildly,
Do not let it play around at random.
Your ordinary furry horn bearer
Is quite able to understand human affairs.
Do not let it go off into the wilderness,
Do not sleep,
But keep it penned up and don't let it out of town.
Call it to you,
Send it off,
But never abandon it, whether you use it or not.
If I were to sell it, no one would buy it;
If someone had gold to buy it, he could find it nowhere.
Build a high wall,
And sleep alone.
Women are ravenous like wolves.
Having eaten the kid, their mouths are not soured;
Having devoured the original yang, no taste is left.
Men may not be aware of this,
But animals are—
Who understands what I mean?
I have learned to roam at ease,
While you haven't even mastered The Token of the Union of the Three.
When a few thousand white hairs grow at your temples,
King Yama will have you apprehended.
Even if you had supreme skill in magic,
When your pneuma has leaked out, what is there to save you?"

Having finished his song, Xiangzi said, "My lords, this is the way to nurture the goat—remember it well."

"Sir, what abilities does this goat have?" asked Scholar Lin.

"It also composes songs and chants poems," Xiangzi said.

"Tell it to come up with a song for us," said Tuizhi.

Xiangzi pointed at the goat and said, "Goat, what are you waiting for?"

Having given itself a shake, it raised its head and sang:

"Alas that people of the world do not raise goats,
But vie in greed, trying to best each other.
When wine and sex are excessive, spirit and pneuma are scattered,
And a hundred diseases assault the defenseless body.
The waist hurts,
Tears flow from the eyes,
Coughing incessantly, they lie on their ivory beds.
They call in physicians and shamans,
They call upon the spirits,
Promising to sponsor rituals and offer pigs and goats.
They implore the gods and pray to Buddhas—but all in vain.
With needles and moxa they treat their boil-covered bodies.
Yet they do not awaken,
But blame Heaven.
They spend their days and nights in feverish thought, afraid of Death.
They should have known earlier that their clever schemes would come
    to naught.
Why didn't they learn to raise goats at the outset?
If you want to raise goats,
You must think hard,
Find an enlightened master,
And seek the marvelous recipe
To nourish the goat's essence and pneuma and with it supplement the
    halls of your kidneys.
When the goat is fed, it goes wild—keep it from running away.
You must not sleep day or night, but watch and guard the goat.
Tie it up tightly in its pen,
Erect a high wall—
There are wolves and tigers you need to guard against.
If the goat is dragged off by wolves after all,

All your labors will have been in vain.
If you don't awaken,
But remain dumb,
Your lustful mind will lead you into the land of the Ghostly Gate.
Then your hair will turn white at a young age,
And you will lose your Elixir Field and your yang.
Whoever understands the method of nurturing the goat
Holds the recipe for eternal life."

When the goat finished his song, the officials said, "Lord Han, if the young Daoist is not a divine immortal, how is it that this goat can talk?"

"Its words are all those of the Daoist—do not listen to it," Tuizhi said.

Xiangzi stepped forward and shook his sleeves, whereupon the goat and the crane vanished.

Tuizhi said, "See, he made the goat and crane disappear into the sleeves of his tattered cassock. This is just a trick."

"Sir, where did the goat go to?" Scholar Lin asked.

"It has been carried off by a wolf," Xiangzi said.

"We were all sitting here, but we never saw a wolf," Tuizhi said.

"Those two in red dresses at the back of the hall—aren't they wolves?" Xiangzi asked.

"One is my wife, the other is my nephew's wife Luying," Tuizhi said angrily. "Why do you say they are wolves? Your eyesight must be bad, and yet you claim to be a divine immortal."

"They are wolves all right. Let me explain it to you, my lord." Striking his fisher drum, Xiangzi sang a Daoist song:

(To the tune "Goat on the Mountainside")

"Always keep the goat in its pen,
Don't attract the wolf to come and play with it.
When the goat is fed, fear that it might go wild.
If it does, don't let it run away.
I ask you, my lord,
Do you understand this news?
Who could have known that the Baby Boy and the Lovely Maid you
nourished

Were all the pneuma of your original yang.
Alas!
You have lost your essence and your marrow.
Alas!
The painted skeleton is a ghost that goes after your life,
The painted skeleton is a ghost that goes after your life!"

(To the tune "Clear River")

"Nourish the goat in the elixir field;
Don't allow the wolf to steal it.
By hankering after beautiful women,
You lose your perfected original pneuma.
Such profound words I speak to you,
Such profound words I speak to you!

"Nourish the goat in the elixir field;
Don't wait for the wolf to carry it off.
Wealth is a murderous knife;
Lust is a ghost that steals goats.
I ask you, my lord,
Have you ever heard this news?
Have you ever heard this news?

"In the rivers, in the oceans—everywhere is this water;
Where will you find a place to rest?
If you run, you cannot run away.
If you walk, you cannot leave.
I admonish you, my lord,
Find a secure place,
Find a secure place!

"I have traveled all over the empire, but few know me.
How many comprehend the mysterious marvels?
If you want to buy it, it is nowhere to be found.
If you want to sell it, no one wants it.
Thus you are wasting good time.

"And here is a poem as well:

> "*The triangular field is below;*
> *Defenseless, you are plowing and hoeing it day and night.*
> *When one day your original yang is gone,*
> *Your marrow is exhausted, your essence withered,*
>   *your life lost.*"

Tuizhi flared up in anger and shouted to his servants, "Throw him out!" Zhang Qian and Li Wan pushed Xiangzi out the main gate and then stood close guard at the second door.

Xiangzi thought to himself, "Uncle won't listen to well-meaning words. What am I to do?" Truly,

> *You refuse to cultivate yourself and study immortality,*
> *No matter how hard I try to persuade you.*
> *When suddenly the ghostly emissaries arrive to seize you,*
> *In panic, you will kick your feet and pound your fists.*

Did Xiangzi come back to deliver Tuizhi? Listen to the next chapter to find out.

15

MANIFESTING HIS DIVINE POWERS, XIANGZI LIES SNORING
ON THE GROUND

A FALSE DAOIST DRINKS MERRILY BEFORE THE ASSEMBLED
GUESTS

> *Human life everywhere is like a crooked path;*
> *The affairs of this world are full of anxiety, like catkins blown away by*
>   *the wind.*
> *Within the transformations of the universe, we are children who have*
>   *nothing firm to hold on to.*
> *Coming and going,*
> *Up and down, back and forth,*
> *Everything in sight is like this.*
>
> *Why admire the achievements of Yi and Zhou*
> *Instead of imitating Yuanming and returning to your home?*
> *Halt in your dangerous drift, and seek shelter.*
> *Whether it is jade halls and golden horses*
> *Or bamboo fences and thatched huts,*
> *Any of these are places of no-mind.*[1]

When Xiangzi had collected the immortal crane and goat and gone out the gate, he considered that he still had not delivered Tuizhi and fulfilled his mission. So he returned to the gate and called, "Open up, open up!"

Zhang Qian and Li Wan blocked his way and said, "The master ordered twenty blows of the bamboo for us if we let you in. How come you aren't afraid of the embarrassment, but just insist on making trouble? If you give no heed to the reputation of ascetics, we shall first give you a beating and then send you to the warden's office to have you charged."

"Stop this chattering," Xiangzi said. "The ancients said, 'In the monk that comes you see the face of the Buddha.' How can you speak of beatings? I'm not afraid that you might beat me. I have things to discuss with you. Don't be so obstinate."

"The master doesn't want to cultivate himself with you, so perhaps you think can deliver us, eh?" Li Wan said. "No offense, but rather than spend my life without food to eat or clothes to wear until I die of cold and hunger, I prefer to die at home. I certainly won't go and cultivate myself with you, so save your breath."

"Even if you bribed us to let you in, we wouldn't do it, so don't waste your time arguing," Zhang Qian said.

"I haven't come to deliver you, and have no bribe to give you," Xiangzi said. "If the problem is that your master has ordered you to be beaten if you let me in— well, come to think of it, if you let me in, you won't necessarily get beaten, but if you don't let me in, you will definitely get your twenty blows of the bamboo."

"Why should we be beaten if we don't let you in? I don't believe a word you are saying!" Zhang Qian said.

"I am not a three-and-a-half-year-old-child to be hoodwinked by you. I don't believe a word!" Li Wan added.

"Do you dare say 'I don't believe you!' three times?" Xiangzi asked.

"What if I said it not just three, but three thousand times?" Zhang Qian said.

"In that case, say it!" Xiangzi said.

Together the two said, "We won't let you in! We won't let you in! We absolutely won't let you in!"

Using his divine powers, Xiangzi shook his sleeves, fell to the ground, and with his drum as a pillow fell fast asleep, snoring and motionless. His primordial spirit, however, went straight into the banquet room and said, "My lords, here I am again."

As soon as Tuizhi saw Xiangzi, he became so angry that his hair stood up under his cap and his heart burned with wrath. "How did you get in?" he shouted.

"I had gone quite a way when your two servants came and said that you wanted to speak to me. So I came back," Xiangzi replied.

"Go sit in the side room. I have business to take care of," Tuizhi said.

Xiangzi obeyed, and played his fisher drum in the side room. Meanwhile Tuizhi called Zhang Qian and Li Wan and asked, "Has that young Daoist left?"

Zhang Qian said, "He is so drunk he can't walk and is now sleeping on the ground outside the gate."

Manifesting his divine powers, Xiangzi lies snoring on the ground.

"Prick up your donkey ears and listen!" Tuizhi said. "Who is beating the fisher drum?"

"I don't know who it is," Zhang Qian said.

"You detestable dogs! You let in a Daoist and claim at the same time that he is sleeping on the ground outside," Tuizhi shouted. "You're lying straight to my face. Twenty strokes each!" Other servants dragged and pulled Zhang Qian and Li Wan to the ground.

The two wailed and said, "A Daoist really is sleeping on the ground outside. Master, if you don't believe us, we request all of you gentlemen to see for yourselves. Then it will become clear. Don't beat us unjustly!"

The officials said, "These two are detestable, but the Daoist is indeed a strange fellow. You really mustn't beat them undeservedly."

When Tuizhi walked out the gate with the officials to take a look, there really was a Daoist sleeping on the ground and snoring like thunder. And yet inside, in the side room, there was another Daoist beating a fisher drum and singing Daoist songs. The officials all said, "Although there are two different people, their faces and clothes are exactly alike. Clearly he is a divine immortal who can divide his body and appear in several places at once. Lord Han, you must not treat him rudely."

Thereupon Tuizhi said to the Daoist, "Leaving the body is nothing but a fraudulent trick. How dare you come here and cheat me? I will burn this body of yours—let's see what abode your primordial spirit will go to then."

At that moment, the Daoist in the side room came walking out, and the Daoist sleeping on the ground woke up. The two merged into one.

On seeing this, the officials all dropped down and saluted him. "Today we have the good fortune of meeting a divine immortal. Please save and deliver us!"

Tuizhi rushed to hold the officials back and said, "Do not let your eyes be deceived. Don't fall for the tricks of a swindler."

"Lord Han, I am no swindler," Xiangzi said. "I am a blood relative of yours, who cannot endure that you should fall into the fiery pit. Therefore I have gone to a great deal of trouble to deliver you. My spirit-souls may go to purgatory and my body-souls may be scattered through the Nine Heavens, but this drop of primordial spirit will never perish. How could that ordinary fire of yours burn me?"

"You are nothing but a vagrant, uncouth Daoist. What blood relationship could we have?" Tuizhi said.

"Related or not, we are still from the same native place," Xiangzi said. "Beautiful or not, it is still our home. Even the mountains and waters will meet some day; why should humans be fated never to meet? Why do you say such unkind things?"

"The lord Han wanted to punish you several times, but each time we asked him to forgive you," said Scholar Lin. "If you are a divine immortal, why don't you fly high and do great deeds in faraway places, so that people hear of your reputation even without getting to meet you? Why go to so much trouble to disturb people's banquets and annoy their guests?"

"In the mountains I heard that the family of lord Han had accumulated merit for many generations," Xiangzi said. "Furthermore, I heard that he had good steamed buns at his house. I specifically came to beg for some to take back to the mountains and give to my master to still his hunger."

"You should have said earlier that you wanted to beg for steamed buns," Tuizhi said. "By all means, go and take some with you. Why do you have to talk so much and do all these tricks?" Then he ordered Zhang Qian to go to the kitchen, get some buns, and send the Daoist off with them.

Zhang Qian led Xiangzi into the kitchen and said, "How many do you want? What kind of container do you want to fill?"

"I have this flower basket," Xiangzi replied.

"That little flower basket will hold only a few buns," Zhang Qian said. "I'll give you a piece of silver so you can hire a carrier to carry a big basket for you, all right?"

But Xiangzi answered, "How could I eat them all up? It'll be enough if you just fill this flower basket."

So Zhang Qian brought a big basket of steamed buns and started to fill the flower basket. Xiangzi performed a vanishing spell, and so Zhang Qian emptied basket after basket until he had put 356 buns in the flower basket, which was still not full. When Zhang Qian realized that no buns were left, he stood open-mouthed with amazement. He seized Xiangzi and began to shout, but Xiangzi shook his sleeves, stepped on top of the flower basket, and floated up into the air. From above he let a piece of paper flutter down.

Looking up, Zhang Qian said, "Daoist, your mind is too devious. After filling your flower basket with so many of our household's steamed buns, you don't even thank the master but just drop a written complaint. Who do you want to accuse? You don't want me to fill another flower basket, do you?"

Xiangzi came down and said, "Let's go together and see your master."

Zhang Qian seized him again, whereupon Xiangzi protested loudly.

"Why are you holding onto the Daoist and shouting like this?" Tuizhi asked.

"He didn't obey your orders at all, but instead seized me and shouted at me," Xiangzi said. "I'm not an important person, but how can you govern the important affairs at court if you can't even control two servants?"

Zhang Qian handed the piece of paper to Tuizhi and reported, "You ordered me to reward the Daoist with some steamed buns. He filled a small flower basket with 356 of them, and it wasn't even full then. Then he wrote an accusation against me. Therefore I seized him and brought him to see you so that he can explain himself."

When Tuizhi looked at the paper, he saw that it contained a poem that simply stated the miraculous properties of the flower basket:

> *A bamboo rod broken into splinters,*
> *Woven exquisitely by an ingenious craftsman.*
> *Diminutive on the outside, spacious inside,*
> *It can hold the whole world, sun and moon.*

When Tuizhi had finished reading the poem, he said, "Daoist, you really are lacking in manners. The 356 buns were intended for my guests. I meant well by rewarding you with a few. Why did you use a vanishing spell to cheat me out of all of them?"

"Don't be so petty-minded," Xiangzi said. "The buns are all in the basket. If you don't want to donate them, I'll take them out and return them to you."

"How could this tiny flower basket hold 356 buns?" Tuizhi inquired.

"It looks small on the outside, but inside it is as deep as a dried-up well," Zhang Qian said.

"Don't underestimate this basket," Xiangzi said. "Here is a song to the tune 'Shoals amid the Waves' to illustrate it":

> *"A small flower basket,*
> *Which had long been at the Peach Spring.*
> *A purple bamboo rod in front of the Jade Emperor's palace.*
> *The Queen Mother broke it into splinters for three full years;*
> *Lu Ban wove it for ten full years.*
> *This flower basket*
> *Has special origins.*
> *Though it may hold the universe and Heaven and Earth,*
> *It is still just a basket."*

"Extolling the flower basket is just another trick to confuse me. I don't believe you at all," Tuizhi said.

"It's up to you whether you believe me or not," Xiangzi said. "As for me, let me ask you once more for some wine."

"I already rewarded you with wine and a table. Why are you begging for wine again?"

"The truth of the matter is, my master in the mountains is about to concoct the Elixir of Ten Thousand Spirits, but he still doesn't have any good wine. That's why I'm trying to get some."

"I also know how to concoct that recipe," Tuizhi said. "How much wine do you need?"

"Just one gourd full will be enough."

"A gourd doesn't hold much. How could it be enough to concoct the elixir?"

"Don't underestimate this bottle-gourd," Xiangzi said. "Here is a poem to show why:

> "A tiny gourd just three inches high,
> But it grew at the foot of the Penglai Mountains.
> It can hold all the water of the Five Lakes and Four Oceans,
> And still not be even half full."

"Stop blabbing," Tuizhi said. "Zhang Qian, hurry and give him his wine."

"Master, where is your bamboo tube? Bring it here so I can give you wine," Zhang Qian said.

"I have tied your skin onto the bamboo tube and made a fisher drum out of it. I have only this bottle-gourd here," Xiangzi said.

"If you intended to beg for alms, you might as well have brought a large container, so we could give you a few jugs more," Zhang Qian said. "How much can this small gourd hold? It will reflect badly on us as alms-givers if we give so little."

"I don't want much," Xiangzi said. "Just fill up the bottle-gourd."

Zhang Qian poured in more than ten vats of wine, but the gourd still wasn't full. "Strange, why doesn't it fill up?" he said.

"Pour in a few more vats, that should do it," said Xiangzi. Then he struck his fisher drum and clapper and sang,

> "A tiny gourd,
> Narrow in the middle,
> Thick at the ends.
> Having expended much effort on the practice of Nine Cycles,
> It can measure itself with Lake Dongting.
> Stop deriding the small size of my gourd,

> *It can take in liquid until the oceans are exhausted and the rivers*
>   *dried up.”*

Zhang Qian reported to Tuizhi, "Master, the Daoist used the same trick again. The wine is all used up, but still hasn't filled this bottle-gourd."

"Young Daoist, a true divine immortal both takes and gives," Tuizhi said. "To only take and not give does not fulfill the great Dao. It's quite enough that you performed the trick with the steamed buns. Why did you cheat me out of my wine as well?"

"Don't worry," said Xiangzi. "Just bring me some empty vats and I'll return it all to you. If a single drop is missing, I'll give you an extra vat. Bring some big bamboo baskets and I'll return your 356 steamed buns. If even one is missing, I'll give you a hundred extra, all right?"

And true enough, when Zhang Qian brought the empty vats and baskets, Xiangzi rolled up his sleeves and lightly picked up the bottle-gourd, as if it were empty. He inclined it over one vat after another, until several dozen were full. Not even a drop was missing, and there was still wine left in the gourd. Nobody understood how so much wine could have been stored in the bottle-gourd.

When the officials saw this, they all applauded and praised Xiangzi. Tuizhi alone did not believe it and said, "These are just some heterodox magical tricks of the Maoshan School, fit only to deceive fools. How could a divine immortal consent to covet wine and food, and to employ his magical powers in a frivolous manner?"

When Xiangzi heard Tuizhi's words, he again displayed his divine powers by taking out of the flower basket 356 steamed buns. Not one was missing. The officials said together, "Such magic is truly unique!" They sighed in boundless admiration.

Suddenly, Xiangzi returned the wine to the gourd and the steamed buns to the basket and secretly dispatched a celestial general to deposit them below Blue Pass. The general gave them to the local earth god to keep in storage for later use when Tuizhi came this way and needed to eat and ward off the cold. Then he beat the clapper and sang a song to the tune of "Ascending the Little Tower":

> *"People say I covet flowers and hanker after wine,*
> *But in the wine I penetrate the Mysterious Pass.*
> *Among the flowers I meet divine immortals;*
> *In the wine I obtain the ancient Dao.*
> *I refine the cinnabar sand,*

> Revolving it nine times to return to a perfect yang body.
> I only care about awakening to eternal life,
> To grow as old as Heaven."

"You're just bragging," Tuizhi said. "I was enjoying the good company of my guests and we were going to discuss important political matters, but you keep disturbing us. This isn't the kind of skillful means you ascetics like to employ." He called to the servants, "Throw him out."

"Don't bother having me thrown out," Xiangzi said. "Just drink a few cups of wine with me and I won't come again to disturb you."

Tuizhi laughed. "How much wine can you take?"

"Just make sure I get drunk. Don't worry about my capacity for wine," Xiangzi said.

"Can you drink a hundred large cups?"

"With twice fifty I'll be only half drunk."

"Such stamina is quite good," Tuizhi said. "Today I have 356 guests. Each one will drink a cup with you. Start with me."

"I obey your command," assented Xiangzi.

Tuizhi ordered wine to be served. After just three cups Xiangzi fell drunk to the floor. Tuizhi said, "Look at this Daoist, so drunk after three cups of wine. He is all big words and has no shame. How could he be a divine immortal? Zhang Qian and Li Wan, carry him out, drop him outside the gate, and pay no more attention to him."

Zhang Qian and Li Wan used all their strength, but they could not lift him off the ground. Tuizhi got very angry and shouted, "Get several dozen more people and drag this uncouth Daoist out!" Zhang Qian called two units of police runners to drag Xiangzi out. However, Xiangzi did not seem like one fallen down drunk, but rather as if he were made of iron and copper. They could not budge him one inch.

"You dogs are all useless," Tuizhi said angrily. "Let him sleep, and when he wakes up, throw him out right away before he can say anything." Zhang Qian and the others bowed and withdrew.

After half an hour, Xiangzi scrambled up with a great deal of noise and said, "My lord, how is my capacity for wine?"

"You fell down drunk after three cups—do you have any capacity to speak of?" Tuizhi replied.

"My capacity didn't measure up and I couldn't drink with the lords," Xiangzi said. "However, I have a fellow disciple who won't even refuse the sort of wine that makes one drunk for a thousand days and completely intoxicated until the day the realm of Great Peace comes. How about inviting him to drink a cup with us?"

"What is his station in life, and where is he now?"

"He comes from a cellar and lives in a palace, fills his belly with wine, and will die drunk on the road. If you will permit him to see you, I'll call him."

"Go call him," Tuizhi said.

"I can call him from here."

Using a magical technique employed by immortals, Xiangzi waved his hand toward the sky and called, "Brother, come quickly." Suddenly, an auspicious cloud appeared and carried a man to the ground. What did he look like? Here is a lyric to the tune "West River Moon" to show it:

> A black face,
> Glistening eyes.
> A head like a mortar and a wide mouth, large yet spiritual.
> His teeth bared and his Adam's apple prominent.
> A Nine Yang cloth on his head,
> Two tasseled sashes around his waist.
> With the red face and the staring eyes of a drunkard,
> He could be compared to Li Bai or Liu Ling.

This Daoist stood in front of the stairs and called a greeting to the officials, "My lords, I knock my head."

Tuizhi said, "Your brother claims that you are a hardy drinker. How much can you really take?"

"When the guest of honor is in his seat, with servants at the sides; when people bow and yield to each other in a pleasant manner, and clothes are complete and proper; when the seating mats are uncomfortable and sweat trickles down my back—on such formal occasions I can drink two or three pints," he said. "When I am among good friends and we roll dice and gamble; when a red-skirted beauty holds my goblet and a jade hand lifts my cup; when we sing together and watch marvelous dances at the banquet—then from morning to evening I can drink two or three pecks full. When it has gotten late and the drinkers are few and the guests have dispersed; when the host sees off the last guests and only I remain; when I am led to a secluded room where lamps and candles shine, skirts and sleeves link behind the bed-curtains, and shoes become mixed up; when a jade-like body is close in my embrace and a powdered face snuggles up to my soft chest; when the host is so merry he doesn't recognize me, and I so exhilarated that I forget the host, but throw off my clothes and go wild without restraint—at such a time I can drink two gallons."

"How can an ascetic speak the words of that crazy Chunyu Kun?[2] Disgusting! I have no use for you here—get out!" Tuizhi said.

"I don't stand for idle words either, but you should by all means drink some wine," said Scholar Lin. "If you drink a lot, you will confirm your brother's recommendation. If you don't drink much, we'll have your brother punished."

"All right, fetch the wine and let me drink it," the Daoist said. Thereupon Tuizhi ordered Zhang Qian and Li Wan to set two or three jars of good wine before him.

He quickly drank up one after the other until he had finished several dozen flasks. Then he finally nibbled some fruit, stretched out, and said, "Good wine! In less than an hour I finished three jars. Now I feel a little drunk."

Tuizhi said to Scholar Lin, "Such capacity for wine is more like it."

"You look like you're drunk. Can you still drink more?" Scholar Lin asked the Daoist.

"If you keep it coming, I'll drink it," he replied. Tuizhi then ordered Zhang Qian and Li Wan to carry in a large jar of wine. The Daoist did not use a flask or a bowl, but drank to his delight directly from the jar. Very quickly he finished it and fell to the ground motionless.

"My brother is drunk," Xiangzi said. "It is not seemly for him to sleep on the ground. If you have a blanket, I would like to borrow it to cover him. When he wakes up, we'll leave together."

Tuizhi ordered a blanket brought to cover the Daoist and then said to Xiangzi, "You've performed a lot of false tricks. Only this drinker was real. I won't argue with you, just leave quickly and don't come back. If you do return, I will have you dealt with by the law."

"The law only applies to officials," Xiangzi said. "I don't covet fame or profit, don't hanker after the world's red dust, and pay no heed to the passing of time. Why would I fear those fetters and shackles?"

"If you keep talking rubbish, I shall fast and bathe and then submit a memorial to the Jade Emperor, requesting that the criminal Daoist who covets wine and food and confuses the world and its people be sent to purgatory and forever sink into the realm of suffering," Tuizhi said.

Xiangzi laughed to himself and said, "You say I brag and talk bigger than I act, but you, Uncle, can make empty threats as well. Only I can have an audience with the Jade Emperor. How could an ordinary mortal like you submit a memorial that would actually reach his desk? Such grandiose words wouldn't even frighten a ghost, let alone someone like me." Alas,

Many words have been spoken,
But all in vain.
The clever awaken only by way of stupidity—
Why do the clever not become immortals?

If you don't know what Xiangzi did next, please listen to the next chapter.

16

XIANGZI ENTERS THE UNDERWORLD TO EXAMINE THE

REGISTERS OF LIFE AND DEATH

HE SUMMONS IMMORTAL MAIDENS TO DELIVER

BIRTHDAY GREETINGS

> *Truth is illusory, illusion true, so truth is also illusion;*
> *Illusion is true, truth illusory, yet illusion is not truth.*
> *Your original nature knows no distinction between truth and*
> *   illusion;*
> *Once you laugh at the world of dust, illusion and truth become*
> *   clear.*

Earlier on, when Xiangzi had drunk three cups of wine and lay sleeping on the floor, everyone around thought he was drunk, while in fact he had sent out his yang spirit to go directly to purgatory.

Reader, let me tell you why Xiangzi went so hurriedly to visit King Yama. The Jade Emperor had ordered him to deliver Tuizhi so that he could achieve perfection and resume his previous post, but Xiangzi realized that it was Tuizhi's nature to be pedantic and shallow, clinging to his own views. Tuizhi coveted high official position and a big salary and would not agree to turn back.

Fearing that Death would come quickly to Tuizhi once he was punished for a mistake, Xiangzi proceeded to the underworld palace of Lord Yama to examine Tuizhi's file and see how many years were left to him and how much longer his official career was going to last. When his destiny was broken and his career finished—that would be a good time for a vigorous effort at delivering him. The right timing would allow Xiangzi to avoid wasting his efforts. So,

Having respectfully received the court's mandate, he left Southern Heaven,
And proceeded straight to the subterranean offices of the underworld,
There to examine the lord Han's file of life and death,
To deliver him that he might complete the Dao and become a golden
   immortal.

When Xiangzi's primordial spirit came to the Ghost Gate Pass, thirty-six celestial generals crowded around him and seventy-two merit officers and earth gods hastened along the road to welcome him. White cranes and blue simurghs flew in pairs, and flags and banners fluttered in great numbers. Suddenly a flash of light appeared, illuminating the dark Capital of the Dead and breaking through the Blade Mountain Hell. It startled the ox-headed and horse-faced demons so much that they quavered and took fright. The ghost soldiers and underworld officials gesticulated nervously and ran back and forth. The Buddha Ksitigarbha forgot to grasp his nine-ringed pewter staff; in vain the Eavesdropping Spirit pressed his highly sensitive ears to the ground. The sweepers could not find their straw brooms, and the dust piled up in the palaces. Those responsible for burning incense destroyed their aquilaria and sandalwood, and the golden censers went cold. The Assistants to the Left carried the Registers of Good and Evil upside down, so that long and short life spans became difficult to differentiate. The Assistants to the Right held the containers of iron brushes sideways, so that life and death could not be determined.

Forthwith the ox-headed demons hit the drums and their horse-faced colleagues struck the bells to summon the Yama Kings of the Ten Palaces: Qinguang, Chujiang, Songdi, Wuguan, Yama, Pingdeng, Qinshan, Dushi, Biancheng, and Zhuanlun. Together they came to welcome Xiangzi, but they had come in such haste that their clothes were disordered and their courtesies were rushed. Baffled, they walked on tiptoe and whispered to each other, wondering why a divine immortal from the Upper Eight Grottoes had descended into the underworld.

Xiangzi spread his sleeves and stood comfortably. He held a golden tablet in his hands, proclaimed the imperial decree, and then said to Lord Yama, "Seven days in the mountains are a thousand years on earth. One day and night among humans are twelve years in the underworld. I would not come to your palace, breaking the door bolts and opening up the underworld, if I didn't have serious business. The Jade Emperor has dispatched me to deliver my uncle Tuizhi so that he may become an immortal, complete the Dao, realize his rewards, and ascend to the Primordial Center. I tried to deliver and transform him several times, but he wouldn't change his mind at all, remaining as obstinate as before. I fear that sooner or later he will

入酆司查勘
生死

Xiangzi enters the underworld to examine the Registers of Life and Death.

suffer a calamity and his worldly possessions will vanish into thin air. When one day the ghost emissaries come to chase him to purgatory, my efforts will have been in vain. Therefore I came to examine how many years are left to my uncle and what career is still ahead of him, so that I may better go about his deliverance."

Having heard these words, King Yama ordered a ghost assistant, "Quickly fetch the Register of Retribution and Rebirth and let the divine immortal examine it."

The Assistant to the Left hastened to hand the ledger to Xiangzi. When Xiangzi opened and read it, the first page turned out to be about Pei Du, the Duke of Jin; the second page was on Huangfu Bo; and the third about Li Sheng. On the fourth page was written:

> Han Yu of Changli County in Yongping Prefecture. Orphaned at three years of age. Later attains the degree of Presented Academician and becomes Surveillance Commissioner in Xuancheng. Transferred to posting as Investigating Censor. Demoted to Magistrate of Shan-yang. Reassigned as Administrator of Law Section in Jiangling. At the beginning of the Yuanhe reign period selected as Erudite of the National University branch in the Eastern Capital. Reassigned as Vice Director of the Criminal Administration Bureau. Then appointed Magistrate of Henan. Transferred to a posting as Vice Director of the Bureau of Operations. Then again Erudite. Transferred to posts of Director of the Bureau of Review, Historiographer, Senior Compiler, Assistant to the Director of the Bureau of Evaluations, and Procla-mation Drafter. Promoted to Secretariat Drafter. Reassigned as Men-tor to the Right of the Heir Apparent. Becomes Adjutant in Huaixi. Transferred as Vice Minister of Justice. Moved to Vice Minister of War. Promoted to Minister of Rites. Submits a memorial strongly remonstrating against the Buddha bone. Demoted to Prefect of Chao-zhou. On the journey there, wolves block the road and snow accu-mulates up to his horse's head. Suffers from hunger and cold. Almost loses his life several times. Reassigned as Prefect of Yuanzhou. Sum-moned to the capital and appointed Chancellor of the National Uni-versity, then becomes Metropolitan Governor and Vice Minister of Personnel.[1]

When Xiangzi had finished reading, he said, "My uncle still has so many appoint-ments ahead of him—that's why he won't change his mind. I will now cancel his official prospects and remove his name, so as to save him further rebirths in the

Register of Good and Evil, and to resolve his calamities and extend his years in the Account Book of Life and Death." Indeed,

> When you remove a name in King Yama's palace,
> It gets listed in the Purple Palace and the Jasper Pool.

The Assistant to the Right quickly dipped a brush in thick ink and handed it to Xiangzi. Xiangzi rapidly blotted out Tuizhi's whole page. When he turned to the fifth page, it happened to contain the fate of Scholar Lin.

Xiangzi said, "My father-in-law is a reincarnation of Yunyangzi. If my uncle regains his former position, my father-in-law should also return to his post in Heaven. I might as well blot out his page to spare him another rebirth."

The Yama Kings of the Ten Palaces together saluted Xiangzi and said, "In the six paths of rebirth, Heaven has deities and Earth ghosts. The Five Phases produce transformations; within life there is death, and within death life. By yin and yang male and female are differentiated; their combination and separation distinguish longevity and early death. Therefore the Southern Dipper records births and the Northern Dipper deaths. We carefully maintain the files as they are constituted and do not dare alter them. Now, however, you, blessed immortal, blot out entries without consulting us. We are afraid we'll get the blame if the Emperor on High gets to know of it."

Xiangzi said, "My uncle Han Tuizhi was the Attendant Great General Chonghezi and the academician Lin was Yunyangzi. Because they drunkenly fought over an immortality peach, broke a crystal cup, and offended the Lord of Supreme Clarity, they were banished to the world of mortals. Thus they are not ordinary humans who go through the cycle of rebirth and have their souls extinguished and scattered. Now their period of exile is almost over, and they are to resume their posts. The Jade Emperor fears that they are unaware of their previous existences and have adopted evil tendencies since falling into the realm of suffering, so he dispatched me to come down and deliver both of them. Therefore I first expunge their names to avoid having their souls punished and seized, which would create a lot of trouble."

The Yama Kings of the Ten Palaces all bowed and said, "Unaware of these circumstances, it was discourteous of us to interfere. Now that you have clarified the imperial mandate, our minds are put at ease." Then they followed Xiangzi to see him off.

All the ox-headed ghost soldiers and horse-faced assistants, with their green faces and long fangs, indigo-colored bodies and red hair, were lined up orderly in two rows. Prostrating themselves and kneeling down, they saw him off. Xiangzi took up his fisher drum, concealed his auspicious light, left the underworld, and returned to the world of humans. There he feigned to awaken from his drunken slumber, without letting ordinary mortals realize what had really been going on.

After Xiangzi had asked Tuizhi for a blanket to cover the little Daoist, he talked with Tuizhi for some time longer and then stepped forward again and said, "Lord Han, if you have wine, give me some more to drink."

"You fell to the ground after just three cups," Tuizhi told him. "The other Daoist has not yet awakened after getting solidly drunk. And yet you want to beg for more?"

"I didn't fall down drunk, but instead went before King Yama in the underworld to examine a lord's career prospects and lifespan," Xiangzi explained. "That's why I went to sleep. My brother, who drank with you, left a long time ago already, while we were talking. How can you say he hasn't woken up yet?"

"Nonsense," Tuizhi said. "If your brother has already woken up, who then is that under the blanket?"

"Lift up the blanket and you will see," Xiangzi said.

When Tuizhi ordered Zhang Qian to lift up the blanket, he didn't see a drunken Daoist, but instead a large vat of good wine. Startled, he went to tell Tuizhi, "He has vanished—there is only a large wine vat."

"I acknowledged that that wine drinker had a real capacity for liquor, and now it turns out to be another trick," Tuizhi said. He called to Xiangzi, "Let me ask you, you uncouth Daoist, which lord's career and life-span did you examine in the underworld?"

"One of those present here," Xiangzi said.

"There are 356 officials present here. Be more precise as to who it is; then we can see later whether you spoke the truth. Who will believe what you say if you are so muddle-headed and discourteous?"

"I only examined the records of Lord Han, Minister of Rites," Xiangzi said.

"Why did you examine mine?" asked Tuizhi.

"I want to deliver you so that you will cultivate yourself, but I was afraid your life span wasn't long enough. Therefore I went to the underworld to gain clarity."

"I am now fifty-seven years old. What did you find out about my career and life span? Out with it or I shall certainly have you punished as a criminal Daoist who boasts shamelessly and confuses the world with his aberrant talk."

"Well, don't blame me for speaking openly. If you want to continue in your official career, you will be exiled next year and there will be little more than a year left of your life span. If, however, you agree to follow me and cultivate yourself, you can live as long as sun and moon and will never age."

"Since my childhood I have seen countless fortune-tellers and physiognomists," Tuizhi said. "All of them said I would become an official of the first rank and single-handedly govern the affairs of state. I would live to be a hundred and pass my days in good health. How dare you talk such nonsense?"

"A life span is difficult to calculate, and it is up to you to prolong it. If you do not cultivate yourself, you throw yourself into the snare of Death."

"You're just a vagrant Daoist," Tuizhi said. "You are not Death himself living in the world, nor have you ever died and returned as a ghost. How could you get to see the Registers of Life and Death in the underworld?"

"While I was lying here, my spirit traveled to the underworld," Xiangzi said. "At the Ghost Gate Pass, the Yama lords, ghost assistants, hell wardens, and underworld soldiers all came to welcome me. I sat in the Senluo Palace, took the Register of Life and Death, and examined it thoroughly. I saw your name in it. It said that you are now fifty-seven years old and that at fifty-eight you will pass away and go to the realm of the dead. Word for word, line for line, I saw that it was true. As for dying and returning as a ghost—if I didn't have enough time to save myself, how would I have the leisure to examine the records of other people?"

"These are clearly the words of a ghost! I don't believe it!" Tuizhi said.

"It's up to you whether to believe it or not. I'm just afraid that next year when you want me to come, you won't find me anywhere," Xiangzi said.

Tuizhi's wrath rose like thunder and he shouted at Zhang Qian to throw Xiangzi out. Only one step out of the gate, Xiangzi turned back once more and called, "Let me in to see your master. I have something important to talk about with him."

Zhang Qian said, "Daoist, you really are too shameless, aren't you? Not only is the master annoyed, but the two of us also detest you. Off with you."

"Why do you detest me, too? This is what is meant by 'A dog biting Lü Dongbin does not recognize the heart of a good person,'" Xiangzi said.

"The sage put it well: 'Blind is he who speaks without watching the countenance of his superiors.'[2] You aren't blind in both eyes. Having seen that the master was so angry that he had you chased out, you should know to get lost. By blabbing on you'll just bring further humiliation upon yourself," Zhang Qian told him.

"I have a face like the husk of a bamboo shoot—you can peel off layer after layer, and still I can take more humiliation. Have a heart and let me in. Once I have spoken to Master Han, I will leave."

"You may scold or beat me, but I won't let you in," Li Wan said. "You'll just pester the master and mistress for tea and food. I won't suffer all that trouble on your behalf."

When Xiangzi heard him speak like this, he blew a mouthful of magical pneuma in their faces, whereupon Zhang Qian and Li Wan sank into a deep slumber. Xiangzi dashed inside and beat his fisher drum.

"This vulgar Daoist has come again to bother me," Tuizhi said. "This really is revolting. I'll order the servants to give him forty strokes and then display him in a cangue outside the gate to serve as a warning to vagrant Buddhists and Daoists."

When the servants moved to seize him, Xiangzi calmly blew a mouthful of magical pneuma at Scholar Lin's horse groom Wang Xiao'er, whereupon the latter changed into the likeness of Xiangzi.

When Tuizhi saw his men running around in confusion, he shouted, "Are you blind? The Daoist clearly is standing in the corridor over there. Go seize him and stop chattering and prevaricating!" When the servants saw Tuizhi's anger, they right away seized Wang Xiao'er, pinned him to the ground, and beat him with the bamboo stick. The real Xiangzi they did not see.

When Wang Xiao'er was seized and beaten, he screamed angrily, "I am Wang Xiao'er of the household of Scholar Lin! Why are you beating me?"

"That is the voice of my servant," Scholar Lin said. "Lord Han, what business do you have beating him? If my servant has offended you, you should explain it to me before beating him. A proverb says, 'When beating a dog, pay attention to its owner's face.' Why do you treat my servant in such an irregular fashion and without regard for propriety?"

"My apologies, but I am not to blame," Tuizhi said. "I just ordered that criminal Daoist beaten. How would I dare beat your servant Wang Xiao'er? I believe the Daoist used the trick of 'transferring the staff' to deflect the strokes onto the body of your servant."

"The vile scoundrel!" Scholar Lin said. "Where is he now? Let me lay hands on him and give him a sound beating in return."

Xiangzi came forward and said, "Here I am."

"We wanted to beat you because you came to disturb the lord Han's banquet," Lin shouted. "If you couldn't bear the shame or pain, you should have escaped quickly—that would have been the proper course of action for an ascetic. Why do you insist on making trouble here and even let my servant be beaten in your place?"

"My lord, please do not blame me," Xiangzi said. "This was a miraculous technique of the immortals, called 'the golden cicada escapes its shell.' I only dared to have your servant beaten in my place because he deserved it anyway. In this way I have helped him pay off some sins which otherwise would have brought him further calamities."

"Wang Xiao'er had given no offense," said Scholar Lin. "He suffered this beating for nothing, and yet you speak of paying off sins. I reckon you will now find it impossible to avoid your own calamities. Why don't you just do some paying off on your own account?"

Wang Xiao'er said, "You and I both have skin and flesh given us by our parents, and being beaten hurts us both. You are generous at the expense of others, and you just do as you please. Take care not to overdo it!"

"He is a cunning and criminal Daoist. Don't waste your breath on him," Tuizhi recommended. "I'll just chase him out. Only then will we have any peace."

"It so happens that I won't go," said Xiangzi.

"If you refuse to go, what is it that you are waiting for?" asked Tuizhi.

"I will leave once you agree to leave the family with me," Xiangzi told him.

"Agreeing or declining to leave the family depends on a person's conviction," Tuizhi said. "If you keep trying to force people into it, who will want to listen to you?"

"It isn't that I don't understand proper conduct and am trying to force you," Xiangzi said. "It's just that if you go wrong this time, you will suffer innumerable calamities and I will have no way of fulfilling my imperial mission. You, my lord, will fall into the realm of suffering to die and be reborn—I really have no choice."

"Fulfill what imperial mission? Fall into what realm of suffering? Your words are irksome. Let me ask you something. In the four or five days since my birthday, you've disturbed my banquets every day, all the time claiming that you are a divine immortal. I have only heard you saying inauspicious things, but not seen you offering me any extraordinary object of the immortals as a birthday present. Shame on you!"

"You're right," Xiangzi acknowledged. "I have a magical painting to present to you. I wish you ten thousand years without end."

"I have many good paintings, each worth at least 110 ounces of silver. In what way is your painting magical?"

"My lord, you may have many good paintings, but they are all dead. This painting of mine is alive. If you want it to grow, it grows. If you want it to shrink, it shrinks. The people in it can all be called out. Surely you have no such painting in your collection."

"Where is it now? How big is it? Get it and hang it up here in the middle of the hall, so that my guests can appreciate it."

"It's twelve feet long and eight feet wide. It should just fit into your hall," Xiangzi replied.

"Zhang Qian, get the picture fork and hang up this Daoist's painting for me to look at," Tuizhi directed.

Zhang Qian took the picture fork. "Sir, where is the painting?" he said.

"In my sleeve," Xiangzi said. "Let me take it out."

"You said it was twelve feet long and eight feet wide, and yet you claim to have it in your sleeve. Are you sure that you can make good on your boast?" said Zhang Qian.

"Don't laugh at me," Xiangzi responded. "Let me take it out and you'll understand."

In a leisurely manner Xiangzi pulled a painting from his sleeve and handed it to Zhang Qian, who hung it up. And indeed it was twelve feet long and eight feet wide. On it were painted many beautiful women, each one very lifelike and ravishing. Here is a poem to describe them:

> Leaning on chiseled balustrades, they stroke their feathered headdresses,
> Famous flowers who bring down nations by their seductiveness.
> Beautiful eyebrows sweep the moon with their even, blackened lines;
> Their cloud-high and raven-piled hair surpasses the Two Qiao Daughters.
> On the bank of the Luo River an exquisite courtesan leaves a jade
>   pendant;
> On the phoenix terrace an immortal bestows a jade flute.
> Although for lifelike portraits there is the brush of Sengyou,
> Even in his paintings Mount Wu is cut off from the onlookers and the
>   road is far.[3]

"I must admit, the painting is excellent," Tuizhi said.

"As you have to come to congratulate the lord Han on his birthday, why haven't you painted something with a longevity theme instead of these beautiful women? Do you want to compare the lord Han to Shi Chong?"[4] asked Scholar Lin.

"The lord Han stands at court with a correct expression," Xiangzi replied. "He walks his path uprightly. How could I compare him to that money-grabbing and petty miser? Just for the lord Han's birthday, I went to the Bixia Grotto in the Zhongnan Mountains and borrowed these immortal maidens of the Eight Grottos from the Perfected Lady Bixia to congratulate him."

"The beautiful women are well painted, but they are merely the works of a gifted artist. Why should they be immortal maidens of the Bixia Grotto?" Tuizhi said.

"All I desire is to deliver you, so that you may leave the family. So I borrowed the immortal maidens to serve wine to the assembled lords."

"Only if you call them down will I believe that they are immortal maidens," Tuizhi said.

"Nothing could be easier." He pointed toward the picture and called, "Immortal Sisters, come down and offer wine to the guests." And indeed, two of the beautiful women stepped down from the painting. What were they like?

> Golden hairpins pointing downward at an angle, hair piled high
> like clouds obscuring the sun. Kingfisher-blue sleeves ingeniously
> tailored, lightly covering skin as white as auspicious snow. Cherry
> mouths, a light mist of delicate red. Spring bamboo hands, light
> and tender. Graceful, with slender waists; skirts of green gauze,
> showing the tips of golden lotus feet. White bodies, light yet full,
> red robes favoring their jade-like wrists. Their faces lovely as all
> the peach blossoms of the third moon, their eyebrows excelling the
> poplars and willows of early spring. Their fragrant flesh celebrated
> in songs to the tune "Jasper Terrace Moon," their temples enveloped
> in kingfisher-like hair like clouds on the peaks of Chu.

The two maidens stepped forward and said, "Ten thousand blessings to you, lords."

When the guests saw their matchless beauty, they said, "Lord Han, if Chang'e from the Moon Palace isn't among them, they must at least be immortals from the Penglai Isles. If the Daoist were not a true divine immortal, how could he have invited them to descend?"

Xiangzi beat the fisher drum and called to the maidens to sing a song to the tune "Graceful Steps" and offer wine to the guests. The immortal maidens sang,

> "The sea of suffering is vast, and many fathoms deep.
> In all ages many were those who perished there—
> Even heroes could not avoid it.
> We steer the boat of compassion,
> Securely carrying you away from the stormy waves.
> If today you do not awaken to the threat of Death,
> In the end you will like ordinary fish fall into its nets of green silk."

(To the tune "Fresh Water")

> "If you are willing one morning to wave good-bye to your ruler,
> Shed your court robes,
> Don a cotton gown,
> And leave the imperial palaces,

You will reach the land of waters and clouds.
Your sleeves fluttering,
Your sleeves fluttering,
Seek a recipe for eternal life without aging."

Having finished their song, they suddenly disappeared and were seen no more in the painting. Xiangzi waved to the remaining immortal maidens in the painting and said, "Again I ask two immortal sisters to come down." With an elegantly swaying gait two more maidens stepped down. A poem describes them well:

Eight lengths of gauze skirts, shoes three inches long,
Their seductive bodies betraying their immortal nature.
Jade maidens from the Nine Heavens have come to the ordinary world
To deliver Han Yu so he may return to his original home.

Slowly the immortal maidens stepped forward and uttered a greeting. Then Xiangzi beat the clapper and called, "Immortal Sisters, the lords are assembled here to celebrate a birthday and drink wine. How about singing a song to the 'Mistletoe' tune?" The immortal maidens put a cup of wine to Tuizhi's mouth and sang,

"Alas, wealth and prestige are like candles in the wind,
A fleeting reputation like a bubble on water.
We admonish you: exchange your black silk hat for a cotton
    headcloth,
A patched robe, a fisher drum, and a blanket of auspicious
    clouds.
Who can reach the marvelous realm of the immortals?
Yet roaming free among the Five Lakes and Four Seas
Is better than a royal family's patent of nobility.

"Strong winds make the waves foam;
Mice nibble until the withered cane falls.
Time is running out for you to let go and turn back.
Don't wait until the mats are cold, the feast has broken up,
    and everyone has left.
Once you sink into the sea of suffering,
It will be difficult to drag you out and save you from eternal
    calamity.

Once your spirit is dispersed, your body will be changed beyond
  recognition.
How often will you find yourself in the den of ghosts?
In life your will is strong,
But you can't win against time.
At that point, what use will high rank and office be?"

"Please return to the grotto palace," Xiangzi said. "I ask two more maidens to come down and give their birthday congratulations." The previous two maidens suddenly vanished, and two more danced in front of the assembled guests. Looking at them, the guests felt that they were even more elegant and beautiful than the last ones. How beautiful were they? Just look:

Loose hair in cloud-like fashion, pinned with azure jade. Graceful, slender waists, bound with six lengths of crimson silk skirt. Pure white gowns enveloping their snow-white bodies, light yellow soft stockings in curved shoes. Beautiful eyebrows knit in a pretty frown; alert phoenix eyes rivaling bright pearls. Painted faces looking down; fine, fragrant skin putting auspicious snow to shame. If it is not Chang-e of the Moon Cave, it must be the Xiang Empress or the Consort of the Luo River Banks.

Swirling and dancing in the air, they sang,

"Alas, throughout their lives people busy themselves for nothing.
Before they notice it, their temples have become frosted.
Although you may have accumulated a thousand loads of rice,
And gathered many thousand ounces of gold,
You ponder in vain,
And waste your energies in worrying.
You would hate not to own as much property as Shi Chong,
Not to be as rich and powerful as Wang Kai,
And not to have the Lord of Mengchang's long rows of retainers.
But, when all is said and done, it is difficult to sleep in two beds,
Or eat a peck of grain in a day.
When one day the Great Limit is upon you,
Which of your own sons

And your own daughters
Can enter Death in your stead?
A recipe for not dying cannot be bought;
Not being subject to Death cannot be bought.
Even if you had the Venerable Lord Li's elixir,
The face of the Buddha Shakyamuni,
The literary skills of Confucius,
The divinatory abilities of the Duke of Zhou,
The magical recipes of the famed physicians Bian Que and Cang
  Gong—
Each and every one of them has perished!
Who among the people of the world will dare measure his strength with
  King Yama?
Say you were to imitate the king of Liang,
And buy fields
To leave to your sons.
What if you beget a wastrel
Who will squander everything?
In the third month, when the flowers open,
Everyone hangs paper money outside the cities,
A hundred kinds of offering will be carried out and set out before the
  graves,
Where filial sons shed streams of tears.
Yet how many of the dead have ever been moistened by them?
Today you still have things to eat
And things to wear.
Quickly turn back and study immortality;
Then you will attain freedom.
If you refuse to soon extract yourself,
You won't avoid a deep slumber in the realm of shades."

"Whichever way you change it, it is always just two maidens. What's special about that?" Tuizhi said. "You say this and you say that, but it always just comes down to saying that it isn't good for me to be an official—not really novel, either! From now on anyone arguing against officialdom will be slapped on the mouth ten times—not excluding that young Daoist."

"My lord, why do you have to get annoyed?" The immortal maidens said. "Let us sing you a song to the "Golden Oriole" tune:

> *"We admonish you not to be angry*
> *And explode in fury.*
> *Good and bad luck, calamities and blessings, are sent down by Heaven;*
> *Even among those standing in the halls of the court,*
> *Who dares to resist?*
> *How long can high office last?*
> *Think about it carefully:*
> *Once the ruler's wrath is roused,*
> *You will be banished to a faraway place."*

"I am upright at court and honest and frugal in my private life," Tuizhi shouted. "For what offense would I be banished? Even these girls talk in a disorderly fashion. Throw them out, and don't allow them to stir up trouble here!"

"My lord, don't be angry," Xiangzi said. "Another immortal maiden is coming to drink with you." To the tune "Dragon in a Turbid River," the maiden sang,

> *"Your seat is at the top of officialdom,*
> *Placed at the highest rank, you enjoy honor and glory.*
> *True, you are honest and frugal,*
> *And serve the court with uprightness.*
> *At the palace you attend upon the ruler wearing your jade-hung girdle;*
> *At home you feast guests for days in a row.*
> *You trust to your power and might,*
> *And your reputation in all quarters.*
> *Great men in high office have always faced calamities equally great.*
> *While traveling through dangerous waters, it is difficult to turn your*
>   *boat around.*
> *I am afraid one morning you will submit a memorial,*
> *And in the evening be banished without mercy."*

Tuizhi was greatly enraged and called to his attendants, "Take this girl and deliver her to the Judicial Office on the charge of fabricating lies and insulting an official."

Xiangzi said, "As a former Vice Minister of Justice, you surely know that for any offenses of a woman her husband is held responsible. However, this girl is right in saying that it is risky to hold a high office. She did not mean to be disrespectful to you. Furthermore, she doesn't have a husband here. How would you find him and send him to the Judicial Office? Please don't be angry. Here's another immortal maiden. How about listening to her sing a song to the tune 'Black Gauze Robe'?"

"Sir, you need not upset yourself," Scholar Lin said. "These people are like birds in a basket or fish in a cauldron—if you want to detain them, you can do so at any time. Where could they escape to? Why not listen to this girl sing?" Xiangzi beat the fisher drum and the immortal maiden sang,

> *"Those who are soft and weak can live in peace and freedom,*
> *Those who are hard and strong bring calamities and disasters upon*
>   *themselves.*
> *If you idly fight and like to struggle, trouble will come;*
> *If you shut your mouth and hide, no harm will come to you.*
> *If you peacefully keep your lot,*
> *Your worried frown will relax and open up.*
> *Time is limited;*
> *If success does not come in youth,*
> *You need to be patient."*

"A well-sung song," Scholar Lin said. "Have another cup."

"This girl admonishes people to patience, which is quite right. Sing another song and I will reward you richly," Tuizhi said.

"You can't make up previous omissions by wearing fur coats in summer," the immortal maiden said. "The wastrel son can't be reformed with a thousand pieces of gold. I'd rather drag my tail in the mud and take up residence in Elysium and the Penglai Isles. I am not sullied by a mind keen on profit, so why do you speak of rich rewards, sir?" Xiangzi beat the fisher drum and she sang once more:

> *"I admonish you, sir, to be calm.*
> *How long can spring flowers remain red?*
> *What use are piled up gold and jade?*
> *I sigh at the fate of Shi Chong of the Golden Valley.*
> *I laugh at Zhuge Liang, the Sleeping Dragon of South Yang.*
> *Present and past are all but dreams.*
> *Study it carefully and you will find*
> *That Fan Li who returned to the lakes*
> *Attained true peace and honor."*

"You got talk like this from that vulgar Daoist," Tuizhi said. "It's revolting! I don't want to listen to it here. Throw her out, now!"

As soon as Tuizhi said "Throw her out," Zhang Qian, Li Wan, and many others crowded in to chase the immortal maiden and evict her. She, however, vanished into thin air. On the wall there was left hanging an empty sheet of white paper, without a single immortal maiden, or any poems or landscape. Hanging there just like the funerary scrolls made in scroll-mounting shops, it excited Tuizhi's rage. Viciously he said, "This criminal Daoist is clearly out to bully and insult me by acting in such an inauspicious manner. Disgusting!" Truly,

> *Seeing off guests with pleasant words keeps one warm through the*
> *winter months.*
> *Harming others with malicious talk makes you shiver in summer.*

What was the outcome of Tuizhi's wrath? Please listen to the explanations of the next chapter.

17

BY HIS DIVINE POWERS, HAN XIANGZI MANIFESTS

TRANSFORMATIONS

LIN LUYING IS ENTANGLED IN LOVE

> *The divine powers of transformation cannot be resisted.*
> *Entanglements in love are the most difficult to guard against.*
> *The mind monkey and the will horse must be firmly tied up;*
> *Once released, they dash about wildly like the east wind.*

Tuizhi was angry. He yelled at Xiangzi, "These goats and cranes and maidens of yours are all illusions and nothing to marvel at. Earlier you said you knew how to produce wine and flowers on the spot. If you can produce these now for me to see, I'll believe that you are an immortal."

"To make such wine and flowers one needs to open the bellows of Heaven and Earth's yin and yang forces, and appropriate the scales of the creative forces of the spirits. It is a rare feat. However, if you, my lord, will agree to leave the family with me, I will produce them and show them to the assembled lords," Xiangzi said.

"Don't talk so much. Just do it, so that we may witness your powers," retorted Tuizhi.

Xiangzi requested an empty jar from Zhang Qian and recited under his breath:

> *"Let's try to make from scratch a goblet of good liquor,*
> *Wine never served by the ancient emperor Fuxi.*
> *A color of flowing amber and a fragrant flavor.*
> *Do not decline getting drunk by drinking three cups."*

"Quickly!" he shouted, and lo and behold, the empty jar filled up with wine. Xiangzi called, "My lords, behold the wine!"

The officials were all greatly surprised. Xiangzi took the wine jar and, starting at the seat of honor, poured out wine until he got to Tuizhi's host seat. Altogether he poured 356 cups from a single jar. Who would have thought that the jar could hold so much wine? When the officials had emptied their cups, they all said that it was excellent.

Only Tuizhi refused to drink it and said, "This wine has just been taken from my own stores. What's special about it?"

Scholar Lin said, "You shouldn't misjudge this wine. It is sweet dew from Heaven, nectar from the Purple Palace, quite unlike the wine from your cellar."

Tuizhi ordered Xiangzi, "Produce the flowers for everyone to see. That will show your true abilities."

"The Empress Wu Zetian, earlier in this dynasty, was just a usurper of the throne, but when she chanted poems in the imperial gardens, she could make a hundred flowers open brilliantly," Xiangzi said. "How much easier is it for us immortals, who hold the lever of the universe in our hands and have the secrets of Heaven before our eyes? However, when you look at the flower, you must not get annoyed, that's all I ask."

"If I see the flower with my own eyes, why should I get annoyed?" Tuizhi said.

Xiangzi pointed to a stone slab at the foot of the stairs and recited under his breath,

> "A fresh flower shall open immediately;
> No need to plant it laboriously in earth.
> Divine immortals have their subtle mysteries,
> And sow their flowers on the Penglai Isles."

He had just finished reciting when, lo and behold, out of the slab grew several green leaves with a stem rising from them. On top of the stem a lotus flower opened, golden and fresh. The officials all applauded and said, "It really is an instantaneous flower." When everyone drew nearer to look at it, they saw that on the petals two lines were inscribed:

> Clouds straddle the mountains of Qin—where is my home?
> Snows crowd the pass at Blue Pass—my horse will not move.

When Tuizhi saw the lines, he asked, "What is the meaning of this couplet? Why is it written on the flower petals?"

"It hints at your future, but you must not ask about it," Xiangzi replied. "But I would encourage you to follow me and leave the family so as to avoid future regrets."

"Rascally Daoist! You don't know anything at all!" Tuizhi said, greatly enraged. "Your so-called instantaneous wine and flower are nothing but tricks to deceive the eye and cheat people out of their money. Zhang Qian, hurry and pour some unclean pig and dog blood on him, then grab him and give him a sound beating. And make sure he doesn't use a substituting spell again."

"Sir, please do not be angry," the officials admonished him. "The Daoist is young and doesn't understand the rules of proper conduct. Let us take his written deposition for now; there will still be time to take him to court later."

"Zhang Qian, Li Wan!" Tuizhi shouted. "Seize the rascally Daoist and take his deposition. Make sure to include that he intruded into an official's home, disturbed a banquet, performed tricks, and cheated people. Once I have dealt with him according to the law, he shall be deported back to his home district."

"If you want a deposition, I'll give it," Xiangzi said. "Give me paper and brush. Why bother seizing me?"

"Make sure your deposition is complete—there is no escape to Heaven for you!" Tuizhi said.

"But my home is within the Gate of Southern Heaven," Xiangzi objected.

"Lord Han, if you want to deport him to his home district you'll have to find a prisoner's escort who can ascend to Heaven," said Scholar Lin.

"There are places called Gate of Southern Heaven on Mount Hua in Shaanxi, in Shenzhou of Tai'an, on Mount Wudang in Xiangyang, and at the Qiyun Cliff of Taizhou," Tuizhi said. "I think this Daoist must hail from the Gate of Southern Heaven at Qiyun Cliff. Surely it isn't the celestial Gate of Southern Heaven?"

"This Gate of Southern Heaven where you live—is it east or west, north or south of here?" Scholar Lin asked Xiangzi.

"It is just beside the Great Ultimate Palace of the Dragon Empyrean," he replied.

"Only the Jade Emperor's residence is called the Great Ultimate Palace of the Dragon Empyrean," the scholar said. "Daoist, do you have cold and heat there?"

"It is always pleasantly warm there, never cold. Five-colored auspicious lights are constantly present as deities assemble. Immortal cranes circle in the air, and blue simurghs fly and dance. Monkeys present fruit, and deer hold flowers in their mouths. It is completely different from the ordinary world, where smoke and dust swirl in dangerous confusion and turbid pneumata rise in thick, hot vapors."

"Uncouth Daoist, this idle talk won't help you," Tuizhi interrupted. "Quick, write down your deposition."

Xiangzi took paper and brush and wrote the following deposition:

> The deponent declares his rank among the immortals. His date
> of birth is not recorded. I have resided all my life between Heaven
> and Earth, with my constant residence in the Penglai Isles. I rely on
> the sun, moon, and stars to aid my life, and on the Five Pneumata
> to complete my body. I have received the Dao methods transmitted
> by the Lord Lao and have become enlightened to the Mysterious
> Perfection. By day I travel on simurghs and cranes to the Penglai
> Isles, at night I fly on clouds to stay at the immortals' pavilions. I
> honor the lords of the South Pole and the Eastern Florescence as
> my landlords, and the Northern Dipper and the Western Mother as
> my neighbors. I have refined the cinnabar sand, saved others from
> suffering, and brought relief to humans. Today I have come to the
> world of mortals to attend to those who are deaf to the truth. I am
> the Immortal Minister of Great Veil Heaven Who Widely Brings
> Relief, Greatly Propounds Transformation by the Teachings, and
> Opens the Primordium to Apply the Techniques of the Dao. Do
> not mistake me for an ordinary, mortal monk of the Complete Per-
> fection School, who begs in remote places, eats vegetables, serves
> demons, and wanders from monastery to monastery. This deposi-
> tion accords with the facts.

When Xiangzi had finished writing, Zhang Qian handed the paper to Tuizhi. Tuizhi looked at it and said, "I just wanted you to clearly state your name, ancestral home, the names of your parents, whether or not you have brothers and uncles, what your original profession was, and how many years ago you left the family. That's what giving a deposition means. Instead you keep prevaricating and writing this rubbish. If you continue like this there will be no leniency for you!"

Xiangzi beat his fisher drum and sang,

> *"My home is halfway up the mountain slope.*
> *The rivers are my neighbors,*
> *The mountains my companions.*
> *All around no people pass,*
> *No one to levy taxes,*

Not even fishermen and woodcutters to keep me company.
In my patched clothes I seem a madman,
As I throw in my lot with tigers, leopards, and wolves."

Tuizhi said, "In your deposition you claimed to be one of the celestial deities, a companion of the high sages. Now you say you congregate with wild ghosts and mountain spirits. By now I am already all too familiar with this kind of nonsense. Zhang Qian, Li Wan!" he shouted. "If he doesn't give a clear statement, put iron shackles around his neck, hands, and feet and start punching him with the club. Then he will surely relent."

When Xiangzi heard these words, his eyes filled with tears. Tuizhi shouted, "If you cry out for fear of being beaten, why don't you just tell the truth? If you prevaricate right and left, nobody will have pity on you even if blood flows from your eyes."

"I am not crying out of fear of being punched and beaten," Xiangzi said. "Because you wanted me to make a truthful deposition, I suddenly remembered my parents. This thought brought on tears and pain."

"You made no effort to study and get on in the world, causing your parents to lose face. Your tears come too late."

"My home is in Changli County, Luanzhou City, in the prefecture Yongping," Xiangzi said.

"Where do you live within the city?" Tuizhi asked.

"At the crossroads by the eastern gate, in a north-facing house. The drum tower is on its western side."

"What is your family background?"

"My family has collected merit for many generations. My uncle is a Minister of Rites."

"What is your uncle's name? Under which dynasty did he serve as Minister of Rites? What other people are there in your family today?"

"My uncle is Han Yu, styled Tuizhi. My aunt is Mme. Dou, who has been appointed a wife of the second rank."

"According to the Daoist's testimony, he is your nephew," Scholar Lin said.

The officials were overjoyed. They saluted Tuizhi and said, "Congratulations, Lord Han, the young gentleman has returned today."

Shame filling his face, Tuizhi said, "My nephew had a clear brow and fine eyes. How could he be so haggard and ugly, quite unlike a human being? This Daoist has merely heard that I yearn for my nephew and is using his name to get himself some wine and food. How could he be my nephew?

"If your surname is Han, what is your personal name?" he asked Xiangzi.

"My study name is Han Xiang, my style Qingfu. At three years of age I lost my father, at seven my mother. From then on I was raised by my uncle and aunt. At nine I studied books, at twelve I studied the Dao. At fifteen I married Luying, the precious daughter of the scholar Lin. This is my truthful deposition."

"You really are my son-in-law Han Xiangzi!" Scholar Lin cried.

"Not so hasty," said Tuizhi. "If you mistake another person for your son-in-law, people will laugh at you behind your back. As I see it, this Daoist probably met my nephew on his journeys. My nephew told him things about my family, which he memorized for the specific purpose of coming here to swindle us."

In tears, Scholar Lin said, "If he weren't your nephew, his words would have given him away in some manner. How can it be that every detail is correct?"

"What you said appears to have been told you by my nephew," Tuizhi said to Xiangzi.

"Han Xiangzi and I came down from the mountains together," he replied. "On the road he told me these things and asked me to go and congratulate you on your birthday. In a few days he will come back in person."

"As you said, it is more than ten thousand miles from here to the Zhongnan Mountains," Tuizhi said." Do you know whether my nephew is coming by boat, by chariot, or by horse?"

"Alas, alas! For us ascetics, alms are our grain stores and our two feet are our post-horses. Where would we find the silver to hire a boat, chariot, or horse? The two of us walked here hand in hand."

Tuizhi cried and said, "My nephew grew up in a wealthy family where he had light chariots and fat horses at his disposal. It pains me to hear of him traveling in such hardship."

"If your nephew is returning, send out someone with this Daoist to look for him and bring him in," suggested Scholar Lin. "What is the need for further worry?"

"Where is my nephew now?" Tuizhi asked. "Why didn't he come with you to see me?"

"Right now he's outside the eastern gate. Because his clothes are in tatters, he didn't want to face you," Xiangzi said.

"Bring a suit of new clothes and go with the Daoist to invite the young gentleman home," Tuizhi ordered the servants.

"My uncle doesn't recognize my immortal nature," Xiangzi said to himself. "I'll leave for the time being, and meet him tomorrow in my original appearance." He turned to Tuizhi and said, "My lord, you don't need to send anyone to invite him in. It is enough if I go to call him." Then he strode out the door with his head held high.

Tuizhi hurriedly told Zhang Qian to follow the Daoist secretly wherever he went, but after turning a corner, he had vanished without a trace. Zhang Qian ran back and reported this to Tuizhi.

Scholar Lin said, "Clearly he was an immortal descended from Heaven, yet you just kept taking him for an ordinary mortal. Truly this is like standing before Mount Tai and not recognizing it. As I see it, it might well be that your nephew has already become an immortal and changed his form just to come and test us."

"That may be so or it may not," said Tuizhi. "Let's wait until he comes again. Then we will see for ourselves." It is as described in this poem:

> *He departed the home district several years ago.*
> *Suddenly there is news of him, and for now the worried frown is*
>   *lifted.*
> *In a muddy pond one cannot distinguish bream and carp;*
> *Only in clear water does one see that they are two kinds of fish.*

After the guests left, Tuizhi became more and more depressed and listless, and spent the night worrying. At dawn the next day, Mme. Dou ordered Zhang Qian, "The young gentleman has been gone for many years. When that person yesterday said he would bring the young gentleman back, he added to the master's vexation and troubles. Go quickly and stand outside the gate. When the young gentleman comes, pull him inside. If you only see that Daoist, detain him so we can get the truth out of him. Make no mistake!"

Zhang Qian acknowledged the command and took up his position.

As Tuizhi would not recognize him, Xiangzi shook himself and assumed his original appearance. When he walked to the gate of his home, Zhang Qian was there on the lookout for him. When he saw Xiangzi approaching, he pulled him inside, shouting, "Master! Mistress! The young gentleman has returned!" Here is a poem to describe the scene:

> *His eighteen-year-old face was unchanged,*
> *The lips red, the teeth white, the hair at the temples newly cut.*
> *Although he let uncle and aunt see him again,*
> *Their furrowed brows were not to open up yet.*

When Tuizhi and Mme. Dou heard that Xiangzi had returned, they were over-joyed and came running outside helter-skelter. Seizing his garments, they said to him, as their tears flowed freely, "Where have you been all this time? When you abandoned us, we could not face people for shame. How distressful it was! Why are you dressed in such tatters? It makes our hearts ache to look at you."

"Dressed in rags have I passed the years."

"What did you eat?" Tuizhi asked.
    Xiangzi said,

> *"When I cut firewood in the mountains I saved the leaves.*
> *I boiled sealwort and wild vegetables with their roots,*
> *And ate my fill of them without sauces or salt."*

"What joy is there in such food?" Tuizhi said.
    Xiangzi said,

> *"Without playing the reed pipes,*
> *I was at ease in cold and warm weather.*
> *In a stone gong there always bubbled a clear spring,*
> *In an earthen bowl often floated mysterious wine.*
> *These flavors*
> *I savored without bothering over right and wrong."*

Mme. Dou called Luying and said, "Daughter-in-law, your husband has returned. Quick, seize him and don't let him leave again."
    Luying obeyed and tried to grab Xiangzi. Xiangzi evaded by dashing aside. When Luying pursued him, he darted to the other side so that she could not get ahold of him. "Mother-in-law, I cannot catch him. What shall I do?" she said.
    "Leave it to me to retain him," replied Mme. Dou.
    "Let me ask you where you were all that time," Tuizhi said to Xiangzi.
    Xiangzi sang:

> *"I lived in that excellent place, the Zhongnan Mountains,*
> *Where the scenery is most pleasant.*
> *Whenever there was a disturbance,*
> *I leisurely guided my immortal crane elsewhere.*

林盧英思愛
李緹

Lin Luying is entangled in love.

When I found a convenient place,
I read the Yellow Court Scripture from beginning to end.
I understood the Mystery and discussed the Dao,
Becoming completely awakened to the Unborn.
In eternal spring I rested in myself, my mind completely pure."

"With whom did you have contact there?" Tuizhi asked.
Xiangzi said,

"Han Zhongli opened his shrine and expounded the
   teachings,
Lü Dongbin transmitted the methods and taught the Dao.
I penetrated the mysterious secrets and subtle marvels.
I ascended as a companion of the immortals,
Shed the dusty vessel of my body,
My mind carefree,
My thoughts roaming."

Tuizhi said, "Looking at you, you don't seem like a divine immortal. But even if
you looked the part, I still wouldn't believe it."
Xiangzi continued,

"Even below the rank of divine immortal,
You will still manage to hide from troubles.
When difficulties come,
You can just snore and sleep.
Clothed in cotton robes,
Tied with a hempen sash.
In a thatched hut,
You drink some cups of Wengtouqing wine,
Going by the maxim, 'Get drunk while you can!'"

"How could you have been happier in the mountains than I in my official career?"
Tuizhi said.
Xiangzi said,

"Do not say that it is good to be an official,
When studying the Dao is clearly superior—

No worries, no humiliation, no vexations.
People know little of the mountain scenery,
Where flowers bloom constantly throughout the four seasons.
You just let sun and moon jump incessantly across the sky,
While your longevity will be like that of Heaven,
And you will joyfully attain eternal life without aging."

Mme. Dou said, "All the time that you were gone, did you think at all of our kindness in raising you and of your wife's deep-felt love for you?"

Xiangzi said,

"Aunt, your kindness is not small,
And often I was vexed with myself.
To be adopted as a son truly is a debt hard to repay.
But as for conjugal love, there never has been much.

"Aunt, please tell Uncle!

"Leave your office so you may cultivate yourself soon.
Thus avoiding being snowed in on the road at Blue Pass."

"What's this about a Blue Pass or White Pass?" Tuizhi said. "Wu Zixu once traversed a Zhao Pass."[1]

"The Zhao Pass was very easy to cross, but I am afraid the Blue Pass will be somewhat more difficult. Uncle, listen to what I say:

"Take for example Zhang Liang, who retired from his office,
And Fan Li, who returned to the lakes.
They both escaped from the realm of tigers and wolves,
And never rejoined the ranks at court.
Instead they loved to view
The pines on lofty mountains many fathoms high,
And the waters swirling green in the mighty Yangtze.
As the Seven States struggled for hegemony,
The famous strategists Sun Bin and Pang Juan matched their wisdom
*   against each other.*
When the tripods of Shang were moved to the Central Plains,
Boyi and Shuqi starved themselves to death.

Fear those who pass off a deer as a horse,
Or a phoenix as a chicken.
If wealth is extensive it harms its owner;
A high official injures himself.
Therefore I raise my gourd and do not dispute right and wrong;
Completely drunk,
I spare myself the worry of asking after the affairs of the world of red
*   dust.*
If I had gold, piled as high as the Northern Dipper,
I still could not buy any extra time to live.
When rebirth is imminent,
Chickens fly,
Hares rush about—
Until their eyes are fixed in the stare of death.
Those with white hair have always been rare—
At the end regrets are futile."

When Tuizhi heard him speak, great wrath rose in his heart and he scolded, "You parentless, neglected, unfilial wretch! Coming back after having been away for so long, you still don't utter one good word, but speak nonsense to my face. What kind of behavior is that? As an official I have to govern the people under Heaven. If I can't even put a single nephew in order, how can I govern the nation or pacify the empire? If it weren't for your parents' face, I'd beat you to death like an animal. I'd rather cut off the family line than be laughed at and shamed by others."

Xiangzi laughed and said to himself, "As I have already become an immortal, how could you beat me to death?"

Mme. Dou called to Han Qing, "Quickly go and order Zhang Qian to prepare a banquet. Once your older brother has changed clothes, he will come out to drink wine with us."

"Uncle, I haven't yet congratulated you on your birthday," Xiangzi said. "I have a little present I would like to give you on this occasion."

"356 officials came to congratulate me on my birthday, but because you weren't here, my heart was not completely happy. Now that you are back, I am filled with joy—why would I want a present from you?" Tuizhi replied.

"I have already sent someone to fetch it," Xiangzi told him.

"Where is the present? Who has gone to get it?"

"It's in the Azure Grotto-Heaven."

"All the court officials and relatives brought presents on my birthday," Tuizhi said. "There is hardly a thing that I don't have. I won't accept your gift. Why would I hope for things from you? Who do you think you're deceiving with these absurd words?"

"How would I dare lie to you?" Xiangzi said. "I've already dispatched the immortal youths Cool Breeze and Bright Moon to the immortality peach banquet in the Azure Grotto-Heaven to borrow forty dishes with which to congratulate you on your birthday. They'll return before a stick of incense has burned down. Quickly invite the court officials to a banquet."

"I don't believe you," Tuizhi stated.

"If the immortal youths haven't come within the stipulated time, I will take the blame," Xiangzi replied.

Thereupon Tuizhi ordered Zhang Qian to fetch and light an incense stick, at the same time inviting the scholar Lin and many other officials.

Soon the officials had all arrived. Tuizhi stepped forward to greet them and explained the matter of Xiangzi's invitation. They all smiled secretly and seated themselves in order of rank. Tuizhi rose several times to look at the lighted incense. When he saw that it was about to go out, he said, "Nephew, the incense is almost burned down, but I haven't seen the immortal youths arrive. Could it be that you invited our guests in vain?"

"Please make ready to receive the immortal youths," Xiangzi said, looking up toward Heaven.

Tuizhi and the officials got up to see two youths, who possessed the ineffable appearance of immortals, descend from the sky into their midst. "Young Daoists, what do you have in that flower basket?" Tuizhi asked.

"Dishes to congratulate you on your birthday, my lord."

"Such a small basket doesn't hold enough for me alone to eat, yet you had me invite all these lords?" said Tuizhi.

"In our flower basket there are precious delicacies from Heaven and jade nectar from the Jasper Pool," they replied. "These are not flavors that are to be had in the ordinary world. If the lords will just try them, it will be a limitless blessing to them. May they eat their fill."

Then Cool Breeze took the things out of the flower basket one by one, and Bright Moon arranged them one by one on the tables. Although there were no dragon lips or dried meats, bear paws or camel hooves, the dishes were all extraordinary things rarely seen or heard of. Tuizhi said, "Such things are fit for use in the mountains. Why lay them out in my hall? They appear rather bland and tasteless."

"Uncle, if you want a mountain, nothing is easier," Xiangzi said. "What if I paint a mountain on that partition wall there and we go for a walk with the lords?"

"The partition wall already has a unicorn painted on it," Tuizhi told him. "If you paint a landscape scene on it as well, I'm afraid you'll ruin the wall."

"I'll call down the unicorn first, before I paint the landscape."

"A unicorn painted with ink has shape, but no life force. How could you call it down?"

"I won't talk about it, but just do it," Xiangzi retorted. "Lords, please watch closely.

"Beast, what are you waiting for that you still haven't come down?" he shouted loudly.

With a sound as if Heaven fell down and Earth collapsed, the unicorn jumped down from the wall, ran out the door, and stood guard in front of it without moving. Xiangzi then took a straw broom and randomly swept it over the partition wall. And, lo and behold, there appeared blue mountains and green water, blue cypresses and dark-green pines. Deer were moving about; phoenixes and simurghs danced in flight. Waterfalls plummeted from high cliffs, the water draped like a white sheet across the rock face. There were boulders of many hues, and the air was warm as dew. It had clearly been a partition wall, but now it was transformed into real mountains and real waters.

When the officials saw the scene, they were overjoyed. What were the miraculous features of this mountain scene? Here is a lyric to the tune "Blossoming Branch" to illustrate it:

> In the mountain forests birds flew;
> On the mountain tops pheasants cried;
> The mountain was covered with banana plants.
> A shady green the high pines and ancient cypresses,
> A gleaming red the mountain fruits and peaches.
> In shimmering brightness green simurghs, blue cranes, dark swallows,
>   black vultures came floating down.
> I saw
> Pheasants coming and going,
> And mountain macaques leaning against green kai trees.
> As divine dragons passed,
> Thunder and lightning flashed in the east.
> A tiger left its den,
> Swishing its tail and stretching its back.

I heard
The incessant sounds of bells in mountain monasteries,
The hurried beating of drums in mountain cloisters.
The mountain monks discussed sutras and the Buddhist
  dharma,
While the mountain Daoists coveted purity and elevation.
I also saw
A woodcutter
Holding an axe in his hand and laughing loudly,
Laughing at the height of the peaks and the beauty of the
  summits.
Suddenly looking up,
He beheld the banner of a tavern fluttering,
In the inn a beautiful village maid.
She called to him,
"Quickly buy a calabash of wine,
And let us eat together."

"My lords, what do you think of this mountain?" Xiangzi said.

"Indeed it is excellent," said Scholar Lin. "You could display your powers as an immortal by leading us up onto the mountain, there to enjoy ourselves for a while."

"Nothing easier!" Xiangzi said. He waved to the officials and called to Tuizhi, "I'll go ahead. Uncle, why don't you and the other lords climb the mountain and walk around for a while." Very excited, the officials all followed him up the mountain.

After a while they had to cross a river by way of a single log. Below, the water fell into an abyss with a sound like roaring thunder, the foam white as snowy silk. It was very frightening to tread on this log. "Lord Han, you need to step carefully," Scholar Lin cautioned.

When Tuizhi heard this, he did not dare go on.

"Uncle, just ahead of you are the Penglai Isles," Xiangzi said. "Wouldn't it be a pity if you refused to go on?"

"You performed this trick to deceive us, on what is clearly just a partition wall. You enticed us inside the picture, and now if we make a single wrong step we shall fall down and be injured grievously, if not die. Why should I throw my life away in this place?" Tuizhi said.

When Xiangzi heard this, he pushed once with his hand, and Tuizhi and the officials were suddenly back in the hall. On the partition wall there was as before a unicorn, and the immortal youths and Xiangzi were gone. Truly,

> *Clearly the divine immortals' road was at hand,*
> *But alas, ordinary mortals would not walk it.*

If you don't know whether or not Xiangzi returned, please listen to the explanations of the next chapter.

18

EMPEROR XIANZONG OF THE TANG RESPECTFULLY WELCOMES
THE BUDDHA BONE

HAN TUIZHI'S INDIGNANT PROTEST GETS HIM BANISHED

Days and months race by like shuttles on a loom;
The sword of time strikes at people's faces and beheads them.
A cool breeze and a bright moon are around every morning,
Miasmic vapors envelop the body and must be endured day after day.
In the limitless sea of suffering it is difficult to reach a shore.
The boat of compassion can cross it—in vain you labor for other means.
Are you stronger and I weaker?—it does not matter,
None of us will avoid having his name marked in King Yama's register.

When Xiangzi, the immortal youths, the dishes, and the landscape all vanished, the officials blamed each other, saying, "We didn't recognize a divine immortal when he stood before us. What use are these eyes? Better to be a blind man who at least has some understanding in his mind."

But Tuizhi said, "Don't worry, my nephew is sure to come back."

At that moment, Xiangzi appeared before him and called, "Uncle, here I am again."

"Now that you have come back, you need to make up for your mistakes and make a fresh start by studying diligently, so as to give honor to your ancestors and lineage and procure appointments for your wife and protection for your children," Tuizhi said. "Don't say it's enough that you're good-looking—you're not the only one with good looks in here. Quickly go change your clothes and come back."

"I have returned to congratulate you on your birthday. As you disliked my dishes and would not eat them, how about a magical peach as a birthday present?" Xiangzi proposed.

"Magical or not, I don't want to eat it," Tuizhi said.

"While you are at it, bring some more magical peaches so that we all may have a taste," Scholar Lin told Xiangzi. "That way you'll earn yourself the goodwill of everyone present."

"How could magical peaches be that easy to get ahold of?" Xiangzi said. "On the mountain where I live there is a magical peach tree in the northwest with fruit as large as bushels, all striped and dotted in scarlet. If a human being eats one, he becomes an immortal. In the southeast there is a magical peach tree with fruit the size of a pint. If a horse eats one, it becomes a dragon. In the southwest there is a magical peach tree with fruit the size of tea cups. If a dog eats them, it becomes an immortal crane. However, if you do not possess karmic affinity, you must not speak of eating them—you won't even get to see their shadows."

"If we have the affinity to meet you, then surely we also have the affinity to eat magical peaches," Scholar Lin said. "It's only because you're stingy that you talk in this evasive manner."

Xiangzi laughed and said, "I give in. Let me order the immortal youths to fetch some. Depending on how many there are, you may have to divide them up among yourselves."

"As long as we get to eat them, who will argue about the amount?" Lin said.

Xiangzi then looked up to Heaven and called, "Cool Breeze, Bright Moon, quickly bring down some magical peaches."

Right away two immortal youths descended from the sky, each carrying a tray of peaches which he handed to Xiangzi. Having received them, he held two peaches, prostrated himself, and congratulated Tuizhi, "I have no present with which to wish you and my aunt a long life. I wish that you may have a long life—as long as the life-span of a crane. Furthermore I wish that you will soon change your mind, resign your official positions, and follow me to cultivate yourself and discuss the Dao."

He offered the remaining peaches to Scholar Lin and the other officials, saying, "I wish that you, my lord Lin, may withdraw from worldly affairs and resign from your office. The other officials shall take care of their careers and repay the nation with utmost loyalty."

"My son, you have done what your heart desired by presenting me with the magical peaches," Tuizhi said. "Now abandon fisher drum and clapper, change into cap and gown, and drink with my guests. Do not speak again of 'leaving the family.'"

Xiangzi beat the fisher drum and sang,

"Uncle, why are you not anxious?"

"I wear silk brocade and dine on delicacies every day," Tuizhi said. "I live in a finely painted and ornamented house and go about in high chariots drawn by noble steeds. What should I be anxious about?"

"I am afraid that disaster will come to you.
Once you have incurred your ruler's ire, it is hard to stop.
You have worked single-mindedly for the nation,
Yet you end up making enemies for yourself.
I admonish you to turn back soon and seek a friend beyond this world."

"You have been away for a long time," Scholar Lin remarked. "Now that you have returned, you should offer a cup of wine to your uncle and show your proper feelings as a nephew for him, instead of speaking of things that annoy him."

Xiangzi sang again,

"If you once cultivated yourself in a previous life,
You reap the rewards in this life,
Yet I fear that the bridles of fame and the chains of profit are difficult
*   to shed.*
Is it not better to be like Zhang Liang, who retired from his office
And went to roam with Master Red Pine?
When Emperor Gao of the Han dynasty wanted to harm him, he
*   could not."*

Tuizhi said, "Your words are very irksome. Listen to what I have to say":

(To the tune "Mistletoe")

"Talk no more nonsense;
It is futile to admonish me to cultivate myself.
I occupy a high and honorable position in the Ministry of Rites;
I have a close relationship with my ruler that is praised by everyone;
My family has enjoyed a wide reputation in officialdom for many
*   generations;*
I enter the imperial presence every morning, holding my tablet of office.

In such a position, who will agree to laugh and give up success and fame,
And instead suffer hunger and cold to study immortality?"

Xiangzi said, "Uncle, though that may be so, I am afraid that once your relation-ship isn't as harmonious any more, no one will save you if you make even just a little mistake."

"Beast!" Tuizhi said. "Your words show that you understand nothing about the intricate ways of officialdom. You must be insane. How can there be insane immortals in the mountains of Penglai? You'd better leave rather than continu-ing to disturb everybody's peace."

"Uncle, I have admonished you time and again, but you won't change your mind," Xiangzi said. "On the contrary, you even get upset. I believe it must be that you blame me for having eaten your food and drunk your wine. I will spit out the wine and food and return it to you." Thereupon he vomited into a bowl and said, "Here it is."

Tuizhi held his nose and said, "Stop being so disgusting."

As these events were unfolding, Luying was standing behind the screen with Mme. Dou. When she saw what Xiangzi had done, she thought, "Perhaps my hus-band is a true immortal, after all." She hurried forward, took the bowl, and was about to eat its contents when Mme. Dou snatched it away, poured it on the ground, and said, "You should be ashamed of wanting to eat such filth."

Suddenly a white cat belonging to the household ran in and ate it all up. Imme-diately it changed into a white phoenix and flew off into the sky. Indignantly Luy-ing said, "Mother-in-law, look, the cat turned into a phoenix after eating the vomit. Clearly we have made a mistake and my husband really is an immortal."

Mme. Dou was also startled. "Yes, we really made a mistake!" she said.

"Since ancient times innumerable people have been deceived by such tricks," Tuizhi said. "You must not believe him, my wife."

When Xiangzi saw that Tuizhi remained stubborn and would not listen, he pointed toward the sky and said, "Uncle, look, immortals are coming."

When Tuizhi looked up, groups of immortal youths and maidens were lined up in mid-air, holding banners and canopies. Riding on auspicious clouds, they descended from Heaven. Xiangzi took his seat among the clouds and gradually ascended to Heaven, vanishing from sight. Tuizhi improvised a lyric:

"Crafty fellow, you deserve my anger,
As you came to mislead me with frivolous words.
Where in this world is there a road to eternal life?

Who can reach the Clear Capital?
Though they set up golden statues holding bowls in immortal hands
    to catch the morning dew,
The emperor of Qin and Emperor Wu of the Han never realized their
    foolishness.
Their stories make people laugh to the present day!
Their stories make people laugh to the present day!"

Xiangzi flew on his cloud straight to the Zhongnan Mountains to visit his teachers Zhong and Lü. "Xiangzi, how is Tuizhi's deliverance coming along?" the two masters asked.

Xiangzi bowed low. "Masters, I am ashamed to say that I have descended into the world of mortals and attempted to deliver and transform my uncle five or six times already. But he just won't change his mind. What am I to do?"

"Which magical powers did you display to him?" the two masters asked. Xiangzi described one by one the many miraculous feats he had performed since he received the imperial decree and descended into the ordinary world—how he had prayed for snow at the Southern Altar, had an audience with Xianzong, and intruded into his uncle's birthday banquet.

As soon as they had heard what Xiangzi had to say, the two masters ascended with him to the gate of Southern Heaven and reported to the Jade Emperor, "Our disciple Han Xiang received an imperial decree to descend into the mortal world to deliver the Attendant Great General Chonghezi. This Han Yu, however, is so firmly caught in his greed for fame that he cannot be awakened. We await Your Majesty's new directions."

When the Jade Emperor heard this report, he became very angry and sent out the ministers of the Celestial Office to check the records. They reported back that according to the records, Han Yu of Changli County in Yongping Prefecture had originally been the Attendant Great General of the palace. Because he drunkenly quarreled with Yunyangzi over an immortality peach and in the course of the altercation smashed a crystal cup, he had been banished to be reborn in the human world. At age sixty-one he would face many obstructions and difficulties and would only then resume his earlier position.

The Jade Emperor said to Xiangzi, "Han Yu's term of banishment is not yet over. Descend again to deliver him, and don't be late."

"Xianzong prefers Buddhism to Daoism, while Han Yu prefers Daoism over Buddhism," Xiangzi replied. "Lan Caihe and I will take the shape of two foreign monks, and I'll transform my clapper into a bone of Shakyamuni Buddha.

Together we will go to the imperial court and present the bone to Emperor Xianzong. Once my uncle Han Yu remonstrates with Xianzong, the emperor will become very angry and will exile him as a prefect to Chaozhou. On the road in the Qin Mountains, I will make his horse die and his servants scatter. Then I will deliver him."

The Jade Emperor approved the proposal and sent Lan Caihe off to accompany Xiangzi.

When Xiangzi and Lan Caihe had left the Gate of Southern Heaven, they changed into foreign monks. This is how one of them looked:

> Clothed in a cassock embroidered with Buddhist treasures, a Vairocana cap set at an angle on his head. From his ears hung glittering golden rings. In his hand he held a metal staff as he made his way into China. His breast concealed a marvelous divine light; his feet were shod with boots of extravagant cut. He seemed like an arhat descended into the world, truly like a living Buddha come among humans.

This is how the other looked:

> Wearing a woolen embroidered cap fastened on the left with a pin; clothed in a thin robe made of Turkish wool. His long earlobes touched his shoulders; his black eyes were round and shone like silver. In his hand he carried a box wrapped in golden silk, and he kept reciting foreign sutras in a heavy accent. Although he was a divine immortal in disguise, he looked just like a lama on a road in a western land.

When the two monks arrived at the Jinting post house, the post commissioner welcomed them, bade them sit down, and asked, "Where do you come from? What tribute are you bringing?"

The two monks replied in a foreign language, which the commissioner did not understand at all. At his side an interpreter appeared, who translated the monks' words. Only then did the commissioner understand that they were foreign monks come to present a bone of the Buddha to the emperor.

"It is already late," he told them. "Please stay at the post house for the night and continue your journey tomorrow." He hastened to order that a vegetarian meal be prepared for them free of charge.

Xiangzi and Caihe secretly planned their next move. Xiangzi said, "Seeing the way people are, we may not have much of an effect on them if we don't manifest some of our divine powers. Let's send a dream to Xianzong tonight. When he ascends his throne tomorrow morning and orders his officials to interpret the dream, we will abruptly enter his presence. This approach should be of benefit to our mission."

"Excellent plan," Caihe said. Xiangzi sent a dream spirit to the palace to give a dream to the emperor. Just around the first watch, Xianzong saw in his dream the rice from a granary all scattered over a field. Beside the field stood a deity in golden armor, holding a bow in his left hand and two arrows in his right. He shot the arrows at Xianzong and they hit the center of his golden crown.

Xianzong awoke with a start, his body covered in cold sweat. The next morning he summoned his officials and said, "We had a dream last night in which We saw the rice from a granary all scattered over a field. Beside the field stood a deity in golden armor, holding a bow in his left hand and two arrows in his right. He shot the arrows at Us and they hit the center of Our golden crown. Does this bode ill or well?"

Holding his tablet of office before his chest, Scholar Lin knelt before the throne and reported, "This dream is highly auspicious. It indicates the arrival of tribute and extraordinary persons from a foreign country."

"Explain in detail so that We may understand it," Xianzong said.

"Rice in a field combines into the character *fan*, meaning "foreign." A man holding a bow and two arrows is the character *fo* ("Buddha"). *Fan* are foreigners; *fo* is a foreign treasure. Your dream means that today foreigners will present an extraordinary object."

Just then, two foreign monks arrived in front of the Palace of the Five Phoenixes. They were carrying a large, gold-threaded casket, inlaid on top with a purple pearl. The casket contained a bone of Shakyamuni Buddha and was surrounded by rosy light and auspicious pneuma. In loud voices the monks called, "Emperor of the Great Tang, listen! The Buddha lived in the West and never came east. However, he took pity on all living beings of the Four Continents, who are afflicted by greed, murder, lust, heresy, lies, and deceit; who are neither loyal nor filial, neither benevolent nor righteous; who don't honor the sun, moon, and stars, and don't cherish the Five Grains, thus creating boundless sins and transgressions that will affect them throughout their existences.

"Therefore he sent the Bodhisattva Guanyin in the thirteenth year of the Zhenguan reign period of Emperor Taizong to instruct the Elder Gold Cicada, who ascended the Thunder Clap Monastery in Western Heaven to worship the Buddha and seek sutras, deliver the souls of the departed, and instruct those who are

Emperor Xianzong of the Tang respectfully welcomes the Buddha bone.

deaf and blind to the dharma.[1] However, those that can be enlightened by means of the sutras are few, while the number of those who benefit from the powers of the Buddha is inexhaustible. Now here is a finger bone left behind by the World-Honored One when he returned to Heaven. It weighs nine pounds and six ounces and was located at the Phoenix Soaring Monastery. It is said that it was displayed once every thirty years and that year was always one of bountiful harvests and peace. We have come especially to present it to Your Majesty so that all sentient beings under Heaven may honor the Tathagatha and widely cultivate good karma. May it protect the nation's blessings for all eternity and secure the emperor's plans."

When the eunuchs heard the words of the foreign monks, they quickly memorialized the emperor. In addition, the commissioner of the Jinting post house submitted his report. Having heard this testimony, the emperor said, "That Daoist who prayed for snow said that an unusual person would come from the West who would preserve Our person and the blessings of the nation for countless years. Today his words are proven true." Immediately he summoned the foreign monks for an audience.

Offering the Buddha bone, the foreign monks stood at the foot of the throne. When Xianzong saw the auspicious light and swirling pneuma, he was overjoyed. He stood up, descended from his throne, and accepted the Buddha bone. He placed it on the dragon and phoenix table and bowed before it. He ordered the Monastery of Shining Prosperity to prepare a vegetarian feast for the foreign monks. Every imaginable kind of delicacy was arranged, and though they were of the human world, they seemed to excel the immortal cuisine of Heaven.

When the two monks had eaten, they knocked their heads and took their leave from court. Xianzong wanted to reward them with ten ounces of gold, ten pairs of white jade ornaments, a thousand rolls of silk, and a bushel of bright pearls, but the two monks just waved their sleeves and walked out, their heads held high, not accepting any of it.

Xianzong respected them all the more for it and wanted to keep the Buddha bone in the palace. In the second month he promulgated a decree that the bone was to travel from monastery to monastery throughout the empire. Wherever it arrived, everyone should recite the Buddha's name, and every household should feast the monks. Those who uttered slanders and were disrespectful were to be prosecuted for blasphemy. Everyone from the court officials and imperial relatives down to the common people hastened to give alms reverently, afraid only to do less than was expected of them. Some gave away all their possessions; others worshiped by burning incense on their heads and arms. There was none who did not bow to Heaven and praise the name of Buddha.

Only Minister of Rites Han Yu would not worship the Buddha. He held forth, "As a high minister, I am responsible by office for the reform of customs. Buddhism is the nirvana teaching of the West. The Buddha is a filthy thing of the West. Besides, what evidence is there that this is really the Buddha's finger? That an enlightened age can be duped like this—how can I not feel anger in my heart?" Then he submitted the following memorial to Emperor Xianzong:

I humbly submit that Buddhism is but one of the religious systems obtaining among barbarian tribes, that only during the later Han dynasty did it filter into the Middle Kingdom, and that it never existed in the golden age of the past.

In remote times, the Yellow Emperor ruled for a hundred years and lived to the age of a hundred and ten; Shao Hao ruled for eighty years and lived to the age of a hundred; Zhuan Xu ruled for seventy-nine years and lived to the age of ninety-eight; Emperor Gu ruled for seventy years to the age of a hundred and five, Emperor Yao for ninety-eight years to the age of a hundred and eighteen; while both emperors Shun and Yu lived to be a hundred. During this time the empire was in a state of perfect equilibrium and the people lived to ripe old age in peace and prosperity; but as yet the Middle Kingdom did not know of Buddha. After this, Tang of Yin lived to be a hundred. His grandson Taimou ruled for seventy-five years, and Wuding for fifty-nine years, and though the histories do not tell us to what age they lived, it cannot in either case be reckoned at less than a hundred. In the Zhou dynasty, King Wen lived to be ninety-three, while King Mu was on the throne for a hundred years. As Buddhism had still not penetrated to the Middle Kingdom, this cannot be attributed to the worship of Buddha.

It was not until the reign of Emperor Ming of the Han dynasty that Buddhism first appeared. Emperor Ming's reign lasted no longer than eighteen years, and after him disturbance followed upon disturbance, and reigns were all short. From the time of the Song, Qi, Liang, Chen, and Yuan-Wei dynasties onward, as the worship of Buddha slowly increased, dynasties became more short-lived. Only Emperor Wu of Liang reigned as long as forty-eight years. During his reign, he three times consecrated his life to Buddha, made no animal sacrifices in his ancestral temple, and ate but one meal a day of vegetables and fruit. Yet in the end he was driven out by the rebel Hou Jing and died of starvation in Taicheng, and his state was immediately destroyed. By worshipping Buddha he looked for prosperity but found only disaster, a sufficient proof that Buddha is not worthy of worship.

When Emperor Gaozu succeeded the fallen house of Sui, he determined to eradicate Buddhism. But the ministers of the time were lacking in foresight and ability; they had no real understanding of the way of the ancient kings, nor of the things that are right both for then and now. Thus, they were unable to assist the wise resolution of their ruler and save the country from this plague. To my constant regret, the attempt stopped short. But you, Your Majesty, are possessed of a skill in the arts of peace and war, of wisdom and courage the like of which has not been seen for several thousand years. When you first ascended to the throne, you prohibited recruitment of Buddhist monks and Taoist priests and the foundation of new temples and monasteries, and I firmly believed that the intention of Gaozu would be carried out by your hand, or if this were still impossible, that at least their religions would not be allowed to spread and flourish.

And now, Your Majesty, I hear that you have ordered all Buddhist monks to escort a bone of the Buddha from Fengxiang and that a pavilion be erected from which you will in person watch its entrance into the imperial palace. You have further ordered every Buddhist temple to receive this object with due homage. Stupid as I am, I feel convinced that it is not out of regard for Buddha that you, Your Majesty, are praying for blessings by doing him this honor, but that you are organizing this curious spectacle for the benefit of the people of the capital and for their gratification in this year of plenty and happiness. For a mind so enlightened as Your Majesty's could never believe such nonsense.

The minds of the common people, however, are as easy to becloud as they are difficult to enlighten. If they see Your Majesty acting in this way, they will think that you are wholeheartedly worshipping the Buddha, and will say: "His Majesty is a great sage, and even he worships the Buddha with all his heart. Who are we that we should any of us grudge our lives in the Buddha's service?" They will cauterize the crowns of their heads, burn off their fingers, and in bands of tens and hundreds cast off their clothing and scatter their money, and from daylight to darkness follow one another in the cold fear of being too late. Young and old in one mad rush will forsake their trades and callings and, unless you issue some prohibition, will flock round the temples, hacking their arms and mutilating their bodies to do him homage. And the laughter that such unseemly and degenerate behavior will everywhere provoke will be no light matter.

The Buddha was born a barbarian; he was unacquainted with the language of the Middle Kingdom, and his dress was of a different cut. His tongue did not speak nor was his body clothed in the manner prescribed by the kings of old; he knew nothing of the duty of minister to prince or the relationship of son to father. Were he still alive today, were he to come to court at the bidding of his country, Your Majesty would give him no greater reception than an interview in the Strangers' Hall, a ceremonial banquet, and the gift of a suit of clothes, after which you would have sent him under guard to the frontier to prevent him from misleading your people. There is then all the less reason now that he has been dead so long for allowing his decayed and rotten bone, this filthy and disgusting relic, to enter the Forbidden Palace. 'I stand in awe of supernatural beings,' said Confucius, 'but keep them at a distance.' And the feudal lords of olden times when making a visit of condolence even within their own state would still not approach without sending a shaman to precede them and drive away all evil influences with a branch of peach wood.

But now and for no given reason Your Majesty proposes to view in person the reception of this decayed and disgusting object without sending ahead the shaman with his peach-wood wand, and to my shame and indignation none of your ministers says that this is wrong, none of your censors has exposed the error.

I beg that this bone be handed over to the authorities to throw into water or fire, that Buddhism be destroyed root and branch forever, that the doubts of your people be settled once and for all and their descendants saved from heresy. For if you make it known to your people that the actions of the true sage surpass ten thousand times ten thousand those of ordinary men, with what wondering joy will you be acclaimed! And if the Buddha should indeed possess the power to bring down evil, let all the bane and punishment fall upon my head, and as Heaven is my witness I shall not complain.

In the fullness of my emotion, I humbly present this memorial for your attention.

Ever since the age of the Warring States, Daoists and Confucians contended for dominance and disputed each other. By the end of the Han, Buddhism was added, but its followers were still few. Since the Jin and Song dynasties, it has flourished more every day, and from emperors and kings down to the officials and commoners, there is none who does not honor and believe in it. Those below do so out of fear of punishment and desire for blessings, while those above like to debate about emptiness and being. Only I, Han Yu, abhor how Buddhism robs the wealth of the nation and confuses its people. Therefore I forcefully reject it.[2]

When Han Yu had submitted the memorial, Xianzong became greatly enraged and said, "This menial Han Yu insults the court and slanders the worthies and sages. How disgusting! The commander of the Imperial Bodyguard shall bind him and lead him to the Yunyang execution grounds, where he is to be publicly beheaded. If anyone remonstrates, he shall go with Yu."

Twenty to thirty executioners appeared who ripped off Tuizhi's court robes and led him in chains to the execution grounds. When Tuizhi saw the many flags fluttering, the sun gleaming on the swords and spears, and the place filled with a hundred people or more, he became very frightened. He looked up and called, "Heaven! I, Han Yu, have served my country with a loyal heart. What would be the hardship if I alone were to die? However, my nephew Xiangzi has not yet returned home, and so my death could not but be unfilial."

As they arrived at the execution grounds, suddenly a man stepped forward to speak up on his behalf.

If you do not know whether Tuizhi survived or not, listen to the explanations in the next chapter. Truly,

> *When King Yama has set death for the third watch,*
> *On no account will he let a person live on until the fifth.*
> *Green Dragon and White Tiger walk together;*
> *Good and ill fortune are never guaranteed.*

19

Looking back longingly to the birds on the Eastern Gate,
An injured string abhors crooked wood.[1]
When the Duke of Zhou's merit was hidden in a metal-bound
*   coffer,*
Rumors recklessly spread their poison.
Such malice might uproot trees and bend the autumn crops,
Yet the grace of August Heaven was deeply enriching.
When the new ruler ascended the throne, he opened the coffer,
And, ashamed, everyone admitted their error.
Once the truth about the Duke became known,
No one at all meddled idly any more.[2]

From among the lines of civil and military officials, Cui Qun, Li Gui, and others stepped forward together. They took off their black silk caps, laid down their ivory tablets, discarded golden girdle and purple robe, and knocking their heads memorialized, "Yu's words were recalcitrant and truly deserve punishment. However, it only came to this because in his heart he harbors the utmost loyalty. We hope that Your Majesty will grant some leniency, so as not to discourage future remonstrations by officials."

Xianzong said, "What Yu said of Our worship of the Buddha was excessive, yet this sentiment We could still tolerate. However, when he said that ever since the Eastern Han dynasty worshipped the Buddha, the emperors all suffered premature deaths, what was that but perverse criticism? Though just a minister, Yu challenged Us with reckless words. Under no circumstances can he be pardoned."

All within and outside the court were startled, and many nobles related to the emperor by marriage also spoke up for Yu. Thereupon Xianzong approved the memorial and leniently annulled Yu's death penalty. Instead he was to be banished to a most foul, malarial, and remote place, never again to be promoted. From among the ranks a minister of personnel rushed forward and, holding his tablet, memorialized, "These days Chaozhou in Guangdong Province is afflicted by a crocodile, whose depredations affect the people's livelihood. This place just happens to lack a magistrate, but all whom I have recommended for appointment to this post have tearfully requested another assignment. Why not demote Han Yu and send him to fill this post?"

"If there are strange aquatic creatures in this place, it must be a malarious area. How far is it from the capital? How long does the journey take?" Xianzong asked.

"The distance is eight thousand miles, and it takes at least five months to get there," the minister of personnel replied.

"In that case, let Han Yu travel alone with a single horse, setting out tonight," Xianzong said. "He has to assume his post within three months. If he is late by a single day, he shall be enlisted as a common soldier on the borders. If he is late by two days, he shall be decapitated and his head publicly displayed. If he is late by three days, his whole family shall be executed."

When Tuizhi was released, he thanked the emperor for his mercy and left the court, covering his face and crying loudly. Indeed,

> Because he did not believe the immortal's words,
> Disaster and calamity struck today.
> In a single morning the walls have tumbled,
> Crushing him who might have been a ridgepole.

When Tuizhi arrived home in a hurry, he said to Mme. Dou, "My criticism of his reception of the Buddha bone incurred the emperor's wrath. My body and head almost found themselves in different places. Fortunately all the high court officials intervened on my behalf, so that I managed to keep my life. However, I have been banished to Chaozhou as a magistrate. I am to travel alone with a single horse and must set out immediately. I have to assume my post within three months. If I am a day late, I will be sent as a soldier to the borders. If I am two days late, I will be decapitated. If three days, my whole family will be eradicated. Even if I could fly, a journey of eight thousand miles would take me three or four months. What shall I do?"

On hearing this, Mme. Dou at first beat her chest and wailed loudly, but then she hurriedly packed the luggage and ordered Zhang Qian and Li Wan to set out together with Tuizhi.

Giving Mme. Dou his instructions, Tuizhi said, "Take care to look after my daughter-in-law Luying and to restrain my adopted son Han Qing. At home and outside, be careful that they don't stir up any trouble which might bring calamity upon you all." As they struggled to part, they shed bitter tears.

Just then they heard horses neighing and men shouting outside. When Zhang Qian, all flustered, ran out to see what was going on, it turned out that a large group of officials had come to see Tuizhi off. Originally they had intended to bid him farewell at the ten mile waystation, but Emperor Xianzong had ordered that any official who accompanied Han Yu out of the city to see him off would be demoted by two ranks. Therefore the officials had come to Tuizhi's home to say their good-byes.

When Tuizhi saw this scene, his grief deepened even more, and tearfully he took his leave of them one by one. Only Scholar Lin accompanied him to the waystation. He said, "If a high official cannot leave behind a fragrant reputation for a hundred generations, he might as well bequeath the stench of dishonor for ten thousand years. Although today you have suffered banishment, you will clear your name in the future and everyone will look up to you. Just put your mind at ease as you are leaving. The emperor's wrath will dissipate and he will certainly reinstate your old rank."

"Many thanks for the trouble you have taken," Tuizhi said. "Someday I will repay you for your efforts on my behalf." Indeed,

> Distress amidst the scenery of rivers and mountains
> Is the result of the ubiquitous hunt for wealth and fame.
> Why not drink another cup of wine?
> Beyond Yang Pass you have no friends.[3]

Tuizhi and his two servants wanted to hurry on to the next relay station to spend the night there, but quite unlike his previous travels on this route, no station was to be found in that desolate land. Here is a lyric to describe their plight:

> Quickening their pace they walk ahead.
> A high lamp gleams in the far distance.

All around people are silent
As master and servants hurry by.
Is that perhaps a monastery, a thatched hut, a tavern, or a tea
house?
But all around is deserted and desolate,
And there is no one to ask.

But for now let us speak no more of Tuizhi's journey, but instead relate how Han Xiangzi and Lan Caihe observed Tuizhi shedding profuse tears at the unbearable parting from his home, and Scholar Lin alone accompanying him to the ten mile waystation to drink a farewell cup of wine. They clapped their hands, laughed, and sang,

"Alas, Lord Han,
That you do not understand our marvelous powers.
Recklessly you tried to be a hero,
But the mountains are hard to shake.
In the halls at court you bragged of your high position,
And all the officials deferred to you.
Your power extended everywhere within and without the palace.
Who did not obey you?
But who could have known that your memorial on the Buddha bone
would offend the emperor,
And that you would be dragged in chains to the execution grounds,
where you almost lost your life?
Luckily the other officials memorialized on your behalf and you were
banished to Chaozhou,
A journey with endless suffering.
Today the marvelous powers of the immortals finally can be seen."

When Xiangzi saw that on the journey Tuizhi's brow was always knitted in sorrow and that his face carried a constant expression of distress, racked with grief and quite unlike his former haughty self, he said to Lan Caihe, "Brother, let's ride ahead on a cloud to the Blue Pass road and wait there for my uncle's arrival. What do you think?"

"In my view, we should go again and ask the masters Zhong and Lü to prepare a device to help us deliver him," Lan Caihe said.

Xiangzi said, "You're right, Brother," Xiangzi said. "If I can trouble you to go to their grotto palace, I in the meantime will wait by the Blue Pass road." When Lan Caihe had left, Xiangzi sang,

> *"To deliver you is not easy—*
> *Why do you cling so dearly to your delusions?*
> *You make me exert myself in vain,*
> *If you will not change your way of thinking.*
> *The only choice I had was to change into a foreign monk,*
> *And deliver you by hidden means.*
> *If you are still unwilling to turn back,*
> *How much time will there be left for you?*
> *Once King Yama has arrested you,*
> *Your regrets will be too late!"*

Xiangzi had just finished his song when Lan Caihe arrived with the masters Zhong and Lü.

Xiangzi bowed to them and then said, "My uncle is already on the way to Chaozhou. We should let some wind blow and snow fall and frighten him with tigers and wolves. Unless we let him taste the bitterness of suffering to the full, his dedication to the Dao will not be steadfast. I have ordered a messenger deity to call on the wind god to raise a storm, and the snow god to let snow fall for one month, sometimes more, sometimes less heavily, but never ceasing completely for even a moment. Master Lan and I will change on one occasion into ferry boatmen, on another into fishermen angling in a mountain torrent; then we'll change into woodcutters come to fell trees in the mountains, and then into farmers with bamboo hats and hoes on our shoulders. On yet another occasion we will materialize a village full of beautiful women looking for a live-in husband. On this occasion my uncle will suffer being bound and hung from a tree.

"All along the way we'll display our divine powers and produce transformations in many places. If after that he still doesn't have a change of heart, we'll have to order the earth god of Blue Pass to send the spirits Thousand Miles Eyes and Wind Ears in the shape of fierce tigers who will carry off Zhang Qian and Li Wan into the mountains, where they shall cultivate themselves. Then, only my uncle will be left with his mount to climb Blue Pass. At that point we'll materialize a thatched hut at a convenient place near Blue Pass, where he can stay the night. When his horse is dead and he is all alone, then we will deliver him. Do you think this is feasible?"

"It's a very suitable approach," the two masters said. So,

Both astride blue simurghs descending from the Jade Stairs,
They see each other off at the White Cloud Stairway of Jasper Heaven.
Why are divine immortals willing to approach the profane world?
It is to deliver Han Yu that they journey hither and thither.

Having deliberated with the other immortals, Xiangzi proceeded to put the plan into practice. He drew a river on the ground that would block Tuizhi's way. He changed his clappers into a boat, which he punted across to the other shore and anchored in the shade under some trees. When Tuizhi came, he would move him with some apposite words.

This river was a very dangerous place. Here is a poem to show it:

The vast waters rushed by in roaring waves,
Flowing sands swirling like golden shuttles.
Like the Yangtze's misty waves rising to the sky,
Like the ocean's stormy billows enveloping the land.
Frolicking reptiles and serpents burst forth from their caves;
Surging lizards and turtles turn about in large numbers.
Needless to say a small skiff could hardly move its oars,
But how could even a dragon boat get across?

Traveling along the road, Tuizhi said to Zhang Qian, "When we left home the weather was still hot, but now it looks as if we are deep in autumn. The leaves are red, the blossoms yellowed. An autumnal wind has suddenly started to blow, and it is quite cold and bleak. Truly this poem describes it well:

"In the desolation of an ancient road next to the wild jungles,
A western wind blows against my horse, its gusts cutting like knives.
Who will take pity on the lonely traveler,
A gray-haired man buffeted by cold dew and chilly frost?"[4]

"Master, you are suffering the anguish of lonely banishment from the capital, of being cast a thousand miles out into the wilderness," Zhang Qian said. "But don't sigh and blame yourself. When you loyally admonished the ruler, who could have foreseen the troubles it would bring you?"

As they were lost in gloomy thoughts, they happened to pass by a house, above whose door was written "Yellow Blossom Inn." "Here's a waystation. Let's enter and put up here for the night. We'll continue on tomorrow," Tuizhi said.

However, the station master would not let them stay. "I have received new orders from the emperor that I am not to let you stay overnight in the station. Anyone who lets you stay will be prosecuted for violation of an imperial decree," he said.

When Tuizhi heard this, tears streamed down his face. "I am already far from the capital—who will know about it?"

"The only way for no one to know about it is not to do it," the stationmaster replied. "I am just a lowly official and am afraid that my superiors would learn of it."

Tuizhi was just going to vent his anger when suddenly Li Wan came to report, "Master, ahead of us a great river is blocking the road. The bank on this side is all empty without a single ferry boat. How will we get across?"

Tuizhi lifted his head and looked on up the road. Sighing, he said, "There really is a great river. With its stormy waves dashing so violently, how will we cross to the other side?" Then he asked the stationmaster, "If you are unwilling to let us stay overnight, at least find us a ferry to carry us across the river."

"There isn't any ferry. If you can swim, then swim across," the stationmaster said.

Tuizhi became very annoyed and angry on hearing these words. He ordered Zhang Qian, "There must be a ferry in a place like this. Go look for the local headman and tell him that I wish to hire a boat to take us across. Don't be long!"

"There are no houses around here except for the waystation," Li Wan said. "There are a few station attendants, but they work under the stationmaster and just follow his orders. Where do you want us to look for the local headman? Maybe we've taken the wrong road and reached the end of the world!"

"Nonsense!" Tuizhi said. "It's no more than forty days since we started out. How could we have reached the end of the world? Quickly, go look for a boat, and don't waste time."

Pulling Li Wan along, Zhang Qian went in search of a boat. They searched east, they searched west—not a soul to be seen anywhere. They searched south, they searched north—they didn't see even one little skiff. After searching for a long time, they returned to report to Tuizhi. Feigning a bellyache, the stationmaster went inside and did not come out again.

All alone, Tuizhi sat on the porch of the waystation, while Zhang Qian had to run off again to look for a boat. Just then in the distance a boatman steered a little boat downstream. Zhang Qian pointed to it and called to Li Wan, "Brother! Isn't that a boat coming there?"

"Where?"

"Isn't the dark shadow moving there a boat?"

渡愛河湘子撐船

Crossing the River of Love, Xiangzi rows the boat.

"Looks like an old crow spreading its wings to me," Li Wan said. "That's no boat. And even if it were a boat, it's floating downstream. With no one on board to work the sculls, it's useless to us."

"What you mistook for a crow spreading its wings is actually a man," Zhang Qian said.

The two were still arguing when the boat appeared before them. "You have good eyes," Li Wan said. "It really is a boat, and a man is working its sculls. I'll go report to the master while you wait for the boat and keep him here. Tell him that we want him to take us across."

Li Wan had just left when the boat reached the bank. Zhang Qian called from the bank, "Boatman, take us across, will you!"

"No crossing! No crossing!" the boatman said.

"Boatman, if you take us across, we'll pay you more than the usual fee," Zhang Qian said.

"My boat is too small. I can't ferry anyone across," the boatman said.

"There are only a few of us, you can manage to get us across. Don't be difficult!" Zhang Qian said.

"Who is the man on the horse there in the distance?" asked the boatman. "Do you want me to ferry him across?"

"That is our master Han," Zhang Qian said.

"Autumn has only just begun. Why do you call him Master Han?"[5] the boatman asked.

"Boatman, haven't you ever been to school?"

"Well, I have read a few lines."

"If you can read, how come you don't know the character *Han*?" Zhang Qian said. "In the *Surnames of the Hundred Families* it says, 'Jiang, Shen, Han, Yang.' My master's surname is that Han, not the character for 'cold.' The character *han* you spoke of is the one in the passage from the *Thousand Character Essay*, 'Cold comes and heat leaves.'"[6]

"I can tell cold and heat apart all right," the boatman said. "As for this man sitting so pompously on his horse, he seems to be a person of power and distinction. How am I to ferry him across?"[7]

"My master is a very good man who does not presume upon his power and distinction," Zhang Qian said. "If you take him across, he will reward you richly."

"An old saying goes, 'Those who come to your door are in no position to bargain,'" said the boatman. "If your master is such a good man, why doesn't he lead the good life at court, instead of coming to this river bank, seeking me out to ferry him across?"

The two men were still conversing when Tuizhi on his horse and Li Wan with the luggage on his shoulders arrived. Zhang Qian reported, "The boatman claims his boat is too small to take us across."

Tuizhi got off his horse, went to the bank, and called, "Boatman, it won't be your loss if you take me across the river."

"Master, this boat of mine has the same problem as those who are officials: when it was a good time to repair it, I wouldn't do so.[8] If it sprang a leak in midstream, there would be no way to patch it. Where would I get an enlightened person to save us?"

"Enough idle talk, just get me across!" Tuizhi said.

"Master, just look at this river," the boatman said. "Only a divine immortal could get you across. If I ferried you over, you still wouldn't have faith."

"How could there be a divine immortal to come to our aid?" Tuizhi asked.

"The divine immortal exists all right. It's just because you, master, relied on that power and distinction of yours and didn't heed him when he was at your home that now he won't come to take you over to the other side," the boatman replied.

"Let me make it clear to you," Zhang Qian said. "If you are willing to row us over, then do so. If not, my master will use the authority of his travel warrant to have the local people pull your boat onto the bank, and you won't be allowed to make a living with it anymore."

When the boatman heard this, he pushed the boat off the bank with his foot and said, "You're just trying to bully me. I won't take you across!"

"Brother boatman!" Li Wan put in. "Don't be annoyed, my brother was only joking. How can you take it seriously?"

"Let me ask you, Master: what is your purpose for wanting to go to the other bank?" asked the boatman.

"It's on official business," Tuizhi replied.

"A man should not follow the example of the pheasant, who thinks himself clever as he hides his head, even while leaving his feet exposed," the boatman told him. "I'm afraid you are in a situation where it's too late to pull in the reins, as your horse has already walked onto a narrow and dangerous path, and too late to patch a leak now that your boat has already reached midstream."

Tuizhi blushed and said nothing for a long time. Zhang Qian said, "Brother boatman, our time is limited. After crossing the river, we still have to find an inn. If you keep on chattering idly, you are just like the sitting man who doesn't understand the suffering of one who is standing. Hurry up and row us across!"

"My boat is small. It might just carry men, but it won't hold a horse."

"This horse is my master's means of transportation," Li Wan said. "We'll pay you extra if you'll take it over with us."

"The wind and waves are very big, and the boat really is small," the boatman said. "I can't ferry it across with you, but what if I make a second trip for it?"

"It is easy for you to say you'll take us across first and then come back to bring the horse over," Zhang Qian said. "By that time the moon will be bright in the sky, and then where will we find an inn for the night?"

"Brother, if you worry about the sun setting while it's still early, why didn't you stay at home?" the boatman said. "I'm not worried about the moon. What I'm really worried about is that the wind and snow will be so bad that I can't row my boat."

"There's no chance of a snowstorm at this time of year," Zhang Qian said. "Just row fast and everything will be all right."

"Well, then, get aboard, all of you," said the boatman. "Just be a little careful—this is no simple matter of moving with the current without having to use the oar."

Tuizhi's whole party, including the horse, got on the boat. Tuizhi sat in the middle, the horse was in one compartment, and Zhang Qian, Li Wan, and the luggage were in another. The boat didn't seem so small after all. As the boatman slowly worked the scull, he sang the following song:

> "Off a rock-strewn beach I steer my boat.
> On the banks of the fast stream, the willow shadows are lengthening.
> I sing as the oars creak
> And the waves heave vastly,
> Fearing not the wild up and down of the east wind.
>
> In secluded places among the misty billows I roam at ease,
> South, north, east, west—when I arrive I can rest.
> Career success I detest,
> Profit and fame I frown upon,
> I never swallowed that fish-hook."

When Tuizhi heard this song, he asked, "Boatman, where is your home?"

"My home is in the Dipper Ox Palace of the Azure Cloud Empyrean."

"The Dipper Ox Palace of the Azure Cloud Empyrean is the dwelling place of divine immortals. How could you live there?"

"I'm not much different from a divine immortal."

"If you're a divine immortal, why do you still earn money by rowing a small boat?" Tuizhi asked.

The boatman said,

"*I love my leisure.*
With my little boat
I can roam all over the Five Lakes and the Four Oceans.
Who says I do it to make money?"

"Have you had any schooling?" Tuizhi asked.

"Once I too tied my hair to a rafter and pricked my thigh to stay awake," the boatman answered. "I studied by the light of the moon reflected from the snow and the gleam of fireflies caught in a bag. While sitting at my desk I thought of Yi Yin and Lü Shang; in my dreams I contemplated the Duke of Zhou and Confucius."

"Since you studied so hard, did you ever pass the examinations and become an official?"

"I too once wore the graduate's flowers, drank at imperial banquets, held the ivory tablet, and bowed to the emperor."

"That makes no sense," Tuizhi said. "After you passed the examinations and became an official, which post were you appointed to?"

"First I was appointed Investigating Censor, then I was promoted to Court Gentleman in the Bureau of Evaluations."

"And after that?"

"I was promoted to Vice Minister of Justice. Then I was further promoted to Minister of Rites, because of my merit in praying for snow at the Southern Altar."

"If you reached the rank of Minister of Rites, why did you abandon your position to scull a small boat in this place?" Tuizhi asked.

"Because at court I criticized the emperor's reception of the Buddha bone, I almost had my head cut off at the Yunyang execution grounds. Fortunately, all the officials came to save me, and that same evening I was banished to Chaozhou, eight thousand miles from the capital."

Lowering his head, Tuizhi thought to himself, "Everything this boatman says fits my own person. It's really as if he were a divine immortal."

"Master, who are you thinking of?" the boatman asked.

"Of my nephew Han Xiangzi."

"I have seen a Han Xiangzi. His clothes did not cover his body, his food did not fill his mouth; he was already just an emaciated body in the dust. But I don't know if this was your nephew."

Tuizhi began to cry. "Where did he die?" he asked.

"He is dead, yet not dead; alive, yet not alive," the boatman said. "Neither dead nor alive, he is like Nie Que."

"Nie Que is one who attained the Dao in ancient times," Tuizhi said. "Thus according to your words, my nephew also has attained the Dao. Why then do his clothes not cover his body and his food not fill his mouth?"

"The ancients said, 'If you are full and warm, your thoughts turn to licentious desires. If you are hungry and cold, your mind will focus on the Dao.' If Xiangzi was not lacking in clothes and food, he would again think of becoming an official. Then how could he be willing to discard officialdom in favor of cultivation?"

"Only frivolous and dissipated men are willing to engage in cultivation. Those of solid learning will absolutely refuse to do so," stated Tuizhi.

The boatman said,

> "Stop laughing at those who are frivolous and dissolute,
> But remember well the Village of Beautiful Women.
> If you can pass the Village of Beautiful Women,
> Then you can count as a Gentleman of the Hanlin Academy."

As they were talking, they reached the other bank. Tuizhi and his party jumped out of the boat. While Zhang Qian was fumbling in the purse for money to give to the boatman, the latter and his ferry vanished, as did the great river with its roaring waters. There was just a stretch of flat, wide road.

Tuizhi's face turned ashen with shock. Trying to steady himself, he said, "Strange! Strange indeed!"

"Master, don't worry," Li Wan said. "Knowing you were disgraced in spite of your loyalty and virtue, Heaven deliberately materialized this boatman and ferry in order to test you." Indeed,

> Under this deep blue sky, do not carry grudges—
> Act loyally for the nation, what else is there to ask for?
> Look up and a deity is there to protect you—
> If only the unenlightened became aware of it.

Tuizhi sighed, but he had no choice but to get on his horse and move swiftly on.

Soon they were in a secluded place deep in the mountain forests. No villages or inns were in sight anywhere. All around was an empty wilderness without a trace of human habitation. As fear was creeping into their hearts, suddenly black clouds appeared and a great wind arose. They were cold and shivered all over; their teeth clenched and their heads shook, their lips turned blue and their faces white. They could not stand steadily on their feet. Tuizhi said, "Ever since we left Chang'an, we've suffered a constant succession of adversities and anxieties. Now that we've come to this boundless wilderness, we encounter this storm. How can we not be filled with sorrow?"

Zhang Qian said, "Earlier on, the boatman said that he wasn't worried about the rising of the moon, but rather was afraid there might be a snowstorm. Now the storm is here and we have no place to take shelter. What are we to do?"

Tuizhi said, "Hold my horse, while I compose a 'Rhapsody to the Wind,' with which to dissipate our grief:

> "Cold and soughing,
> Without shape or shadow,
> Screaming and roaring,
> With might and voice.
> It winnows the soil and scatters the dust;
> It breaks forests and snaps trees.
> It gathers clouds and mists;
> It penetrates doors and windows.
> Dimmed, the red sun moves by,
> The ten thousand bright stars all are suddenly dark.
> Within a moment,
> Heaven and earth are covered.
> Within an instant,
> The universe is hidden from view.
> It shakes the Dipper Ox Palace,
> Where the Eight Great Vajra deities stand turned aside.
> It blows over the Palace of Responding to Perfection,
> Where the five hundred arhats can hardly open their eyes.
> It frightens the birds—
> They gather in their feathers
> And hide in the trees and bushes, cowering with their heads drawn in.
> It startles the running beasts—
> They wave their tails and shake their heads,
> And with trembling hearts conceal themselves in the mountains.

Whirling and rolling,
Strange creatures in the Three Rivers overturn boats.
Howling and screaming,
Evil spirits on the Five Marchmounts topple trees.
It blows apart the Eastern Ocean where the Crystal Palace is laid bare,
While on Western Blossom Mountain the Agate Palace shakes.
With a moaning sound,
The stone bridge at Zhaozhou breaks in two.
With thundering anger,
The Precious Palace of Thunderclap collapses completely.
I see the White Parrot and Red Lotus Terraces of Mount Putuo shaking
*   unsteadily,*
And the blue-haired lions and Bailai elephants of the Bodhisattva Court
*   rolling about uncontrolled.*
Amidst rolling rocks and flying sand,
Gods cry out and ghosts are wailing.
Heaven is dim and the earth is dark;
The moon is black and the stars have sunk.
Thousand-year-old pagodas are darkened,
Trembling as if hit by thunder.
Rivers and mountains for ten thousand miles around are dimmed,
Lost and masterless.
What has aroused Erlang's anger,
That he overturns rivers and stirs up the seas?"[9]

When Tuizhi had finished his rhapsody, Zhang Qian said, "Master, the storm has stopped and snow has begun to fall. Which way should we turn?"

"As the storm has ceased, I expect the snow will also let up," Tuizhi said. "So let's move ahead quickly and find a house to spend the night. Then we can make further plans."

"There's not even the shadow of a human being around—how will we find a house to spend the night?" said Zhang Qian.

"Oh dear, oh dear!" Li Wan said. "When the young master returned home, he said he would come, but now I don't see him arriving to rescue us!"

"The young master admonished the master time and again to abandon his official position, but the master wouldn't believe him," Zhang Qian said. "Why should he be willing to come here and rescue us?"

While they were speaking, they had already walked several miles. Suddenly the snowfall intensified. "It is snowing very heavily," Li Wan said. "Let's take cover in the bamboo grove ahead before walking on."

"What shelter is there in that grove?" Tuizhi said. "That won't help us. No, it's better to press on and find an inn where we can stay a few days. We can continue our journey once it has cleared up."

"A man may harden his stomach and struggle on, but the horse needs its fodder. In this cold, how could it be willing to go on?" Zhang Qian said.

As they talked and walked, the snow came beating down onto their heads, until it filled their collars and covered their necks. Tuizhi was sunk in deep gloom when suddenly Li Wan pointed and said, "There is smoke rising from the forest ahead. It looks as if there is a village. Come on, let's go and ask for a night's accommodation. Then we can continue on tomorrow."

Tuizhi fiercely whipped his horse on. Neighing, it broke into a wild gallop.

If you don't know if people really lived there, please listen to the next chapter.

> Alas that this common fellow will not agree to cultivate himself;
> He does not understand the changes of destiny.
> If we reckon it over a period of three hundred years,
> Such people have wasted a good many of your efforts.

20

AT THE VILLAGE OF BEAUTIFUL WOMEN, A FISHERMAN AND A
WOODCUTTER OPEN TUIZHI'S MIND

ON A SNOWY MOUNTAIN, A HERDBOY AWAKENS TUIZHI FROM
HIS CONFUSION

> *Commanding the ether and eating clouds, you'll accompany Lord Lao;*
> *Controlling your pneuma and tired of the world, you cross the border*
>   *of Heaven.*
> *Invert the Five Phases and you will complete the Golden Tripod;*
> *Take refuge in the Three Lumina and you will reach the Purple Vapors*
>   *of Heaven.*
> *As you play an immortal tune on the zither,*
> *In your embroidered bag there is bound to be a text of Jade Vacuity.*
> *If you set your hopes on escaping the world of dust,*
> *Then from the Purple Mansions and Red Jade Palaces crimson clouds*
>   *will emerge.*

The place in the grove was called Three Mountains Village. The only settlement
for three hundred miles around, it consisted of three to four hundred households. As each of them had several daughters, together there were seven to eight
hundred young women, and therefore it was also called the Village of Beautiful
Women.

Reader, shall I tell you why there were so many young women in this place?
Because Tuizhi refused to cultivate himself, Lan Caihe had deliberately materialized this village, complete with an inn. He ordered Bright Moon and Cool Breeze

to change into beautiful women, who were to use their seductive powers to test Tuizhi's heart when he came to the village to seek shelter from the snow.

And indeed, struggling against the wind and snow, Tuizhi together with Zhang Qian and Li Wan hurried to the village gate. When they saw that there was an inn, they were overjoyed. Hastily Tuizhi descended from his horse and whispered in Zhang Qian's ear, "When we are in the inn, don't tell them that I am the Minister of Rites Han, but just say that I am a trader on the way to Chaozhou to settle accounts with my business partner."

Zhang Qian nodded, shouldered the luggage, and went ahead. Tuizhi followed him into the inn, chose a seat, and sat down. The waiter came over and asked, "Would you like some wine?"

"How could I do without wine on such a cold day?" Tuizhi said. "First heat up some top quality wine, and afterward we'll have some food."

"We have first rate wine, and it's hot, too, but it's very strong," the waiter said.

"Drinking wine without getting drunk is like being buried alive," answered Tuizhi. "Who would buy weak wine that doesn't make you drunk?"

"Since ancient times it has been said, 'If wine doesn't intoxicate a man, he intoxicates himself; if lust does not confuse a man, he confuses himself,'" said the waiter. "That's why I don't recommend that you drink our wine."

"What place is this?" Tuizhi asked.

"It is called the Three Mountains Village of Beautiful Women."

"'A beautiful lad can ruin an older head; beautiful women can tangle a tongue.'¹ Since ancient times we have been thus warned. Why was this place name chosen?" Tuizhi asked.

"That's a long story. The three to four hundred families in our village have only been able to produce beautiful daughters, but not a single son. Now grown up, none of these daughters has been given in marriage. That is why it is called the Three Mountains Village of Beautiful Women. For example, the keeper of this inn has a daughter called Bright Moon Immortal. She is now thirty-eight years old, and a fortune-teller has said that any moment a noble man will arrive who will make her his second wife. But when will that noble man come? If he fails to turn up for another year, she'll be thirty-nine, and her hair will soon turn white. Bright Moon Immortal has a younger sister called Cool Breeze Immortal, who is thirty-one this year. The fortune-teller said that her eight characters contain a secure destiny of three sons. The innkeeper is thinking of giving her to someone as a concubine, hoping to reap the blessings later on when she gives birth to sons."

Tuizhi was just going to question him further when Zhang Qian became impatient and shouted at the waiter, "Are you going to serve us heated wine or not?

The way you just go on idly gossiping, you don't seem like someone who has to make a living!"

When the waiter heard Zhang Qian, he turned around in a hurry and brought wine and food, which he placed on the table. He poured a bowl of hot wine and set it before Tuizhi. Tuizhi lifted it and drank.

He had just finished one bowl when a man came in by a side door. When he noticed Tuizhi, he looked more closely and said, "My daughter Bright Moon Immortal dreamt last night of a noble man, wearing a headcloth, dressed in court robes, and holding an ivory tablet. He came into her chamber to celebrate the wedding night. I must pay close attention to all passersby, lest I overlook that person." Then he went back inside.

The waiter laughed and said, "You see, on such a snowy and freezing day, my boss is still asleep and dreaming of spring."

When Tuizhi heard these words, he felt his heart give a jump; he wanted to speak, but did not. The waiter came closer and asked, "Where do you come from? For what purpose are you traveling to Chaozhou?"

"I pooled my capital with a partner who went to Chaozhou to engage in trade," Tuizhi said. "It's been a long time and he hasn't come back, so now I am seeking him out to settle accounts."

The waiter said,

> "Settling accounts, settling accounts
> Will give you nothing but trouble;
> But if you are willing to doctor your accounts,
> Everything will be taken care of."

Just then a beautiful woman appeared on the upper floor of the sumptuous building across the yard. Leaning on the balustrade and twisting the pearly curtain in her hand, she sang,

> "I heard people speak of a meritorious minister praying,
> Whereupon auspicious snow fell in profusion at the Southern Altar.
> He saved the common people from their suffering,
> And the withered stalks of grain received moisture.
> Today a high minister has come,
> Even though since ancient times a noble man has been hard to find.
> With gathered sleeves I bow bashfully,
> Unable not to honor him."

When Tuizhi heard her voice, which was like that of an oriole warbling among high trees, he quickly raised his head to look. Enchanted by the beautiful sounds, his soul flew out beyond Heaven and scattered among the Nine Empyreans. He looked left and right, and then his gaze came to rest on the woman. Her eyes were clear and bright like autumn ripples in finely slanted streams; her eyebrows were blackened and knit in a shy frown, ineffably expressive of her feelings.

Having watched her for a while, Tuizhi called, "Heat up more wine!" When the waiter came over with the wine pot, Tuizhi asked him, "What is the name of your boss?"

"He is called Jia Sizhen."[2]

"How many surnames are there among the households of this village?"

"All are Jia,"[3] the waiter said.

"The upper floor of that sumptuous building over there—does it contain the innkeeper's family's sleeping quarters?" Tuizhi inquired further. "Or are the guest chambers located there?"

"The master's sleeping quarters are in the seventh house in the back," the waiter said. "The upper floor of that building holds the sleeping chamber of his daughter Bright Moon Immortal."

"It is getting dark and it is snowing heavily," Tuizhi said. "Are there any good inns on the road ahead where we could stay?"

"The next inn is far away. In such snow you won't reach it. We have excellent accommodations at this inn, but you have to make your own decision," responded the waiter.

"In that case, clean a room for us and let us stay the night," Tuizhi said. "We'll travel on tomorrow morning."

"The rooms and beds are all clean. There is no need to sweep them. The room on the lower floor of Bright Moon Immortal's house is very tidy and refined. You could stay there," the waiter suggested.

"The lower floor will be fine," Tuizhi said. He ordered Zhang Qian and Li Wan to bring the luggage, and followed the waiter to the room on the lower floor, which turned out to be very elegant and refined indeed. Rejoicing secretly, Tuizhi pulled over a chair and sat by the balustrade.

Soon he heard the creaking sound of a door. A man stepped out. It was none other than the innkeeper Jia. Tuizhi rose to greet him.

Jia Sizhen bowed very courteously and responded, "Greetings to you, my lord."

Tuizhi returned the bow and said, "I am just an old trader passing through and spending a night at your worthy place. Why do you call me 'lord'?"

"My daughter Bright Moon Immortal dreamt last night that a noble man would celebrate the wedding night with her," Jia Sizhen said. "So far no other guests but you three have arrived to stay at my inn. This happens to correspond with my daughter's dream. If they are destined for each other, two people will meet even if they are a thousand miles apart. I wish to give my two daughters to you in marriage, my lord, so as to make this auspicious dream come true."

When Tuizhi heard these words his heart gave a leap. He whispered to Zhang Qian, "I don't have a son. If I marry these two women and they give birth to at least one son, then the Han family will have a descendant to continue its line. But would that son count as coming from the main wife or from a secondary wife?"

"As long as you get a son, who cares about that?" Zhang Qian said. "As long as there's a fertile womb to impregnate, you'll have a son, and that's all that counts."

"I beg to disagree," Li Wan said.

"What is your opinion of the circumstances?" Tuizhi whispered.

"In this heavy snow, we might as well turn this fellow's trick against him," Li Wan said. "You agree to marry into his family and stay here for some time, during which you eat his food and sleep with his daughters. As soon as the weather clears up, we'll be off quickly to go to your posting. If you receive a pardon and return home, you won't even need a waystation, but can come back by this route. If your second wife has in the meantime given birth to a son, you just take him back home, and never mind your old wife's jealousy. If she hasn't yet given birth to a son, you tell her that you'll send someone to fetch her once you are home, without actually doing so, of course. If you conceal this matter from your first wife, you will save your ears the din of noisy complaints. What do you think, master?"

Tuizhi thought for a while, his head lowered, and then said, "What Li Wan says makes sense." Turning around and stepping forward, he said to Jia Sizhen, "I truly should not have deceived you. I was Minister of Rites at the Court. My surname is Han. Because I criticized the reception of the Buddha bone, I am being banished to Chaozhou as a magistrate. I am now more than fifty years old and would thus fit the middle-aged noble man your daughter saw in her dream. However, as my wife is still alive, your daughter could only become my second wife. This you need to discuss with her."

"A fortune-teller calculated that a noble man would soon come to take her as his second wife," Jia Sizhen said. "Besides, it accords with her dream. She'd be content to be your housemaid, let alone a second wife. There is no need to discuss it with her."

When Tuizhi saw the innkeeper accept his offer, a smile spread all over his face, so that he looked like a child eating sugar or a beggar picking up a treasure.

Right away Jia Sizhen called to a slave girl, "Quickly ask my two daughters to come. On this auspicious day they will be married to the noble lord Han."

Soon, amidst the tinkling of jewelry and the fragrant waft of perfume, four slave girls called Biaozhi, Zhibiao, Xiqi, and Qixi led out Bright Moon Immortal and Cool Breeze Immortal to greet Tuizhi. Tuizhi thereupon went through the wedding rites with them and retired to the gauze-screened bed.

In the bedroom on the upper floor a table with wine and fruit was set up. Was this wine false or real?

Dear reader, listen: that wine was the same that Tuizhi had given Xiangzi to drink at his birthday banquet. At the time Xiangzi had dispatched a celestial general to convey it here and set it out on this day to test whether Tuizhi would remember it.

Bright Moon Immortal took up a golden cup, filled it with Green Ant wine, and handing it to Tuizhi said,

> "As we float our cups of Lamb wine,
> Snow falls profusely and the day is not yet over.
> I am glad we were fated to meet,
> To join in union as phoenix and simurgh.
> In that union
> We shall together laugh and be joyful.
> Please loosen your robes—
> Tonight's love
> Will give us overflowing happiness for a hundred years."

Tuizhi accepted the wine and drank it. Cool Breeze Immortal poured another cup and, handing it to Tuizhi, sang,

> "Jade cups and fragrant liquor—
> I am glad that a new friend turns out to be an old relationship.
> I only wish that we will be bound together while our hair is black,
> And harmonize still when it has turned white.
> We must not abandon each other half way.
> Please loosen your robe,
> Take pity on the new and discard the old—
> Storms and downpours pummel the budding spring."

Taking the wine in his hand, Tuizhi asked, "My brides, do these two slave girls already have husbands?"

"If we sisters only today came to serve a noble man, how could the slave girls be married?" Bright Moon Immortal said.

"Since they have no husbands, let's take advantage of this auspicious night to marry Zhibiao to Zhang Qian and Biaozhi to Li Wan, allowing them too a taste of married bliss," Tuizhi said.

"It shall be done as you order," said Bright Moon Immortal.

Right away, Tuizhi called Zhang Qian and Li Wan and said, "My wives give Zhibiao and Biaozhi to you in marriage. Knock your heads and thank them."

Zhang Qian pulled Tuizhi aside and whispered to him, "Master,

> *"You just see their external beauty,*
> *But give no thought to the possibility that these are not human beings.*
> *I remember that the boatman said,*
> *'If you can pass by the Village of Beautiful Women,*
> *Then you can count as a Gentleman of the Hanlin Academy.'*
> *See, this morning's scenery*
> *Clearly was an artificial creation.*
> *If they swindled us out of our travel purse*
> *And disappeared in a gust of wind,*
> *Then we'd be in deep trouble, even if we were divine immortals."*

"Save your breath," Tuizhi said. "This is a stroke of good luck for me."

"Do not speak of good luck. I am afraid it may turn out to be bad luck," Zhang Qian replied.

Tuizhi shouted at him, "When I was a high minister at court, I saw innumerable strange things. What we encountered today was an insignificant incident, but you keep on babbling and complaining because of it! If it weren't that my wife would accuse me of being short-tempered, I would send you back home. So I forgive you this once."

Apologizing profusely, Zhang Qian withdrew.

Bright Moon Immortal bowed with gathered sleeves and said, "Sir, do not blame that small-minded man for his transgression. Please don't be angry any more."

Biaozhi and Zhibiao brought a new headcloth, boots, and clothes, and handed them to Tuizhi so that he could change into them. Tuizhi hurriedly stripped off his old clothes and gave them to Xiqi and Qixi to take away. As he was putting on the new clothes, he ordered Zhang Qian and Li Wan to wait in the corridor outside. Bright Moon Immortal and Cool Breeze Immortal took Tuizhi's hands and sang,

"Whether our family is poor or not,
We shall pass autumn and winter resting at ease.
Although we have no fields or possessions,
Our meager belongings still rival those of Deng Tong."

Looking around him, Tuizhi replied,

"You laugh at my poverty, but my Dao is not poor.
This autumn or winter, the emperor's grace will change.
Although the years of half a century are not few,
To beget a son would be my good fortune."

Bright Moon Immortal laughed and said, "The Jade Maid was eighty years old when she became pregnant with Lao Dan. I am only thirty-eight and my younger sister thirty-one—just the right age for childbirth. Please go to bed first. We will both come to keep you company."

Tuizhi was just going to undress and climb into bed when suddenly his belt grew tighter and tighter, as if someone were pulling it like a rope. He seemed to be pulled up and suspended from it in the air. When he opened his eyes to look again, there was no one around. Terrified, Tuizhi shouted and bellowed like thunder.

"Right about now the master should be enjoying the pleasures of the wedding night," Zhang Qian said. "Why is he shouting? Those two wives are probably difficult to handle."

"I rather think he may be reaching the climax of intercourse," Li Wan said. But when the two of them looked closely, there were no more houses and no beautiful women to be seen. The only thing they saw was Tuizhi, dangling high up in a pine tree. From the tip of a branch hung a white piece of paper, on which was written the following poem:

I laugh at you, stupid and befuddled old Confucian;
Your lust, greedy official, brought this chagrin upon you.
Now that you hang bound from the pine branch,
Why don't you submit another memorial in court?

Zhang Qian climbed quickly up and freed Tuizhi. Shame filled Tuizhi's face, and when he saw the poem he became even more embarrassed. Uncertain what to do, he suddenly heard a voice singing indistinctly. When he looked around, he saw a woodcutter coming along. He carried a bundle of firewood on a pole over his shoulder and sang a song while treading the snow. As he came closer, Tuizhi could hear that it was a mountain song:

> "Holding my ax to gather firewood, I set out early.
> My wife's orders were really worth listening to:
> 'After the morning rain the mountains are slippery,
> So do not walk in dangerous places!'"

When Tuizhi heard this song, two tears flowed down his face, and he called to Zhang Qian, "That woodcutter and his wife may just be uneducated commoners, but they know to avoid dangerous places. The ancients said, 'A high official will always be in danger.' I didn't understand to avoid it and brought this anguish upon myself. I cannot compare myself to these commoners."

Just then the woodcutter arrived. Zhang Qian said to him, "My master has suffered this misfortune because of his efforts on behalf of the nation and the people. As you live in these deep mountains and valleys, your granary must have some grain, and your loom some cloth to spare. As the saying goes, 'A man who has clothes to wear and food to eat definitely won't be one who has no firewood under his stove, no rice in his jar, and gets a meal only every now and then.' Why do you brave the cold and the dew to cut wood?"

"We have special terms for cutting wood in the four seasons," the woodcutter said.

"Mountain wood is cut as the season requires—what special terms would there be?" Tuizhi asked.

"Sir, don't show off your cleverness and laugh at my lack of education," the woodcutter replied. "We call cutting wood in the spring 'making a start.' We call cutting wood in the summer 'advancing onwards.' We call cutting wood in the autumn 'cultivating oneself well.' We call cutting wood in the winter 'pulling out branches in the cold.'"[4]

When Tuizhi heard the words "pulling out branches in the cold," he silently thought to himself, "Very strange. Everything this woodcutter says contains a satirical jab. Now he has also mentioned my name—clearly there is a hidden message somewhere."

"Brother woodcutter! Don't give yourself such literary airs—it's like wielding an ornate axe in front of Lu Ban, the carpenter god," Zhang Qian said. "Let me ask you something: if we want to travel to Chaozhou, which road should we take to find places to stay overnight?"

"All within the Four Seas are brethren; in all four directions there live people," the woodcutter replied. "Choose a place to stay according to your lot and it'll do. Why bother asking me?"

Zhang Qian shouted, "It is exactly because there are no people around here and we have to choose a convenient route that I asked you. What's the point of the rubbish you talk? What's more, my master is a high court official who is passing through here because he has been banished to Chaozhou. He has encountered this great snowfall and asked you the way. He is not a lowly minion—how come you speak so glibly and deceitfully? If we were in the streets of Chang'an, I'd give you a thorough beating with my cudgel and have you exposed in a cangue at the crossroads."

"Zhang Qian, keep it down and hold my horse," Tuizhi said. "I'll ask him myself."

Tuizhi grabbed hold of the woodcutter and said, "When I, Han Yu, was at court, I brought about benefits and removed harm, acted for the nation and was concerned for the people. At the Southern Altar I prayed for snow and brought relief to many places. But now that I suffer adversity, no one comes to rescue me."

"You, sir, say you are a high court official," the woodcutter said. "So why aren't you in those red towers and warm pavilions right now, where they roast lambs and heat wine, burn charcoal and light incense, as they gamble surrounded by courtesans. Instead you have hastened to this place—isn't it rather inconvenient?"

"I am only here because the emperor has banished me as a magistrate to Chaozhou," Tuizhi said. "I've lost my way and cannot travel on. I hope that you, brother, will instruct me as to where I can find the main road to Chaozhou, and whether there are places to stay overnight."

"So, you, sir, are an old scholar, yet you don't even know your way," said the woodcutter. "As for the road to Chaozhou, I'll tell you something. That road is rough, dangerous, and difficult to travel."

"My orders are very strict and I cannot do anything about the situation," Tuizhi said. "Even if it is hard to travel, I still have to go. Let me just ask you one more thing. How much further is it from here?"

"The distance is only two or three thousand miles, but there are few inhabited places and many obstacles," the woodcutter said. "Listen as I explain it to you slowly,

> "Old scholar, don't be hasty,
> Let me explain it to you in detail.
> Ahead there is the Yellow Earth Gorge,
> A dangerous place indeed.
> Your feet have to tread a steep slope,

While your hands need to hold on to creepers and vines.
Your hands need to hold on fast;
Your feet need to tread securely.
If you lose your hold,
You will fall to your death.
Having rounded one mountain,
Walking becomes more difficult with every step.
There are many spirits and monsters,
Who will block your path."

"Who says there are spirits and monsters?" Tuizhi said.

The woodcutter said,

"Dark leopards are the censors,
Black bears the prefects.
Goblins are the assistant prefects,
Sprites the protector-generals.
Wolves are the magistrates,
Fierce tigers the policemen.
Musk deer and muntjacs are the clerks and soldiers,
Rabbits and common deer the subjects.
The lions and goats run shops,
Where they buy and sell human flesh."

"How could animals be officials or merchants? I don't believe a word you are saying," Tuizhi said.

The woodcutter continued,

"There is also an old monkey spirit of many years,
Whose chief stock-in-trade is dried meat.
Strike up an acquaintance with him—
He knows the road to Chaozhou.
If you want to know about good and bad fortune,
The oracle sticks in the temple do not err.
If you receive three inauspicious oracles in a row,
It will strike fear into your heart.
In the Qin Mountains master and servants will be separated;
Your horse will die as you cross the Blue Pass.

At that time things will be out of your control;
Life and death are dealt out by Heaven.
I am a mountain man,
And do not understand the paths of scholars.
If you want to go to Chaozhou,
Ask the fisherman at the mountain river."

When Tuizhi heard these words he was paralyzed with fear. He caught hold of the woodcutter and said, "Brother woodcutter, tell me honestly. Which road should I take? Don't just scare me with your words."

"You're not listening to me," the woodcutter said. "I was speaking in vain. At the river in the east there is a fisherman who is used to traveling the lakes and rivers, visiting cities and markets to engage in trade. He has a good knowledge of roads, go and ask him."

While Tuizhi turned his head to look for the river, the woodcutter vanished without a trace. Fearfully Tuizhi called to Zhang Qian, "Where did the woodcutter go?"

"We were both here, but we didn't see where he went," Zhang Qian and Li Wan said.

"I was just questioning him when he tricked me into turning my head and looking for the river in the east," Tuizhi said. "When I turned around again, he was gone. Did I waste half the day talking with a ghost?"

"Master, forget about him. We have to get going," Zhang Qian said.

"Not so fast," Tuizhi said. "There really is a fisherman at the river. Wait until I've talked to him. There will still be time to leave then."

By and by, Tuizhi arrived at the riverbank and called out, "Brother fisherman, how far is it from here to Chaozhou?"

"If you want to go to Chaozhou, you have plenty of time!" the fisherman said.

"I have heard that the land route is not easy," Tuizhi said. "Is the water route safe?"

"It's possible to take the water route, but this fool is asleep and has not yet awakened," the fisherman said.

"You're a fisherman and you're talking with me right now," Tuizhi said. "How can you say you aren't yet awake?"

"I am no fisherman," the fisherman said, "but there is a fool here right before my eyes."[5]

"Fisherman, may I ask your exalted name?" Tuizhi asked. What is the number of your years? Where is your exalted residence?"

"An exalted name, great age, and exalted residence merely serve to attract mis-

At the Village of Beautiful Women, a fisherman and a woodcutter open Tuizhi's mind.

fortune," the fisherman replied. "I conceal my name and live in a cave. I don't keep count of time and don't fear the wind and waves. I am nothing but a fisherman catching turtles on the ocean,[6] and cannot compare myself to a famous minister at court."

"It's very well if you cherish such high ideals, but you seem to be lacking in knowledge," said Tuizhi.

"I don't argue about right or wrong; I am unmoved by favor or disgrace," the fisherman said. "When I catch fish, I exchange them for a pot of good wine and drink until I fall down helplessly drunk. Using the bow of my boat as a pillow, I sleep as the evening sun sets in the west. It's a very happy life. What knowledge do I lack?"

Tuizhi said, "Haven't you heard that

"In a quiet night and cold water the fish won't bite,
And your boat will return empty under the bright moon.[7]

"In weather such as today's, the rivers and streams are all frozen, yet you are fishing here. Doesn't that show a lack of knowledge?"

"When you speak of fish not biting in cold water, they are those high-placed fish who already had a change of heart," said the fisherman. "What I am fishing for is that cold fish[8] which struggles against the current, thrashes its tail, shakes its head, and swallows the hook without chance of escape."

Tuizhi said to Zhang Qian, "Very strange! A while ago that woodcutter mentioned my name, and just now this fisherman did the same. Strange indeed!"

"What's strange about it?" Zhang Qian said. "He's just talking glib nonsense. Let me give him a beating and he won't dare to shoot his mouth off any longer." When the fisherman heard that Zhang Qian wanted to beat him, he covered his mouth with his hand and gave a great laugh. He crossed the river and vanished on the other bank.

"Damn! Was that another ghost?" Tuizhi said.

"Where's the ghost?" Zhang Qian said.

"A ghost that tricked three clear-eyed men for half a day," remarked Li Wan.

"There are five kinds of ghosts. Which kind was he?" asked Zhang Qian.

"What do you mean by 'five kinds of ghosts'?" Li Wan asked.

"There is one kind that speaks sweet and beautiful words and cheats people into taking a great liking to him, leaving them quite unaware that he's just waiting to stab them in the back," Zhang Qian said. "This kind is called the gentle ghost. Another kind is rough and hard, and his words feign foolishness. In his heart he covets other people's things, but he won't utter a polite request. He just pretends to close his door tightly and to be unconcerned if people won't give him their things. This is called the malicious ghost. Yet another kind is the one who, on seeing other people's possessions, desires them, but can't get himself to ask for them. When he sees these things given to other people, envy arises in his heart and he bears a grudge against them. This is called the resentful ghost.

"The fourth kind wants some possession of another, but when the conversation turns to that object, he talks around it and builds up a situation where the other will fall quite unaware into his trap and end up giving that thing to him. It's like the ant which stealthily snatches people's possessions. This is called the ant ghost. Finally, there is the kind that points east while speaking of the west, and uses the south to mirror the north. He conducts official business on other people's behalf, makes marriage matches, posts security on the sale of land, and adopts sons and daughters. This kind is called the daylight ghost. This fisherman and the woodcutter were probably this kind of confidence-tricking daylight ghost."

"I have seen a ghost—I will probably have to die!" Tuizhi said.

"Everyone knows daylight ghosts like that—they won't drive people to their deaths," Zhang Qian said.

"Master, be in doubt no longer," Li Wan said. "By my reckoning, it was Master Xiangzi who changed into a fisherman and a woodcutter to convert you. Those weren't ghosts!"

And really, the woodcutter was Xiangzi, while Lan Caihe had taken on the shape of the fisherman. With their words they ridiculed Tuizhi, but he did not realize it, and in the end it was Li Wan who guessed correctly.

"Baseless guessing won't do us any good," Zhang Qian said. "We should hurry on and look for an inn to spend the night. Tomorrow we can resume our journey refreshed."

"Zhang Qian, hold my horse," Tuizhi said, "while I compose a rhapsody to unburden my mind:

"*Snow,*
It is the essence of rain and dew,
The auspicious omen of a year of rich harvests.
One flake is called goose down;
Two flakes are called phoenix ears;
Three flakes are called a collection;
Four flakes are called an accumulation;
Five flakes are called a celestial flower;

Six flakes are called a six-petalled blossom.
Pneumata rise and fall;
A chilly wind covers the universe.
The grains' flavors are strong or light,
As the crops grow luxuriantly.
In substance pure, it is transformed;
Riding the ether, it flurries down.
On meeting forms, it makes them new;
Instantly cleansed, they turn to light.[9]
The heavenly artisan cuts water with his scissors,[10]
And the universe is filled with flying cotton.
Snow has four aesthetic qualities:
Its stillness in falling to the ground without a sound.
Its purity that does not stain when it melts on clothes.
Its whiteness which drops from on high to spread out evenly.
Its brilliance whose reflected light falls through windows.
It penetrates curtains and doors,
Is sprinkled densely on houses of song,
Their paired roof tiles seemingly adorned with silver.
It covers the houses and fills the ditches,
Blowing wildly around the monks' huts.[11]
Kingfisher towers all appear to trail white silk.
Formed into a lion, its aspect is strong and virile,
Falling like crowded pear blossoms and metal blades, it adds to the chill.
Like white silk snipped to pieces it glitters brightly;
Piled up like willow catkins and thin gauze it brings forth cold.
I think of the woodcutter who loses his way on the mountain paths,
And of the fisherman who stops fishing and returns to the southern
    bank.
The roads are blocked to the traveler;
The guest does not have a companion.
I see a lonely village,
With a fluttering flag advertising wine for sale.
I hear a lonely wild goose,
But receive no word from anyone.
In confused profusion the white egrets fly in groups,
While the white roc beats its wings.
The whole mountain is covered in layers of jade,
And the wanderer's soul loses its way.

Ten thousand households are sealed in by this powder,
And the traveler must go hungry.
Afraid of the cold, the pauper prays to Lord Heaven that he may reduce
*   the snowfall by a third;*
Enjoying the scenery, the scions of noble families wish that the snow god
*   may add a few feet to the snow cover.*
It is good for old pines,
It is good for cultivation,
And it is good for strangely formed rocks that rise steeply.
It is good for stones in bizarre shapes,
It is good for old plum trees,
And it is good for the seclusion of deep mountains.
Though one may say it is an auspicious omen for a year of good
*   harvests,*
What about this auspicious omen?
For the paupers in the streets of Chang'an,
Good omens are fine, but there should not be too many."

By the time Tuizhi completed his rhapsody, his brush was frozen and his hand stiff; he looked chilled to the bone. Zhang Qian said, "Master, it is snowing more heavily all the time. What are we going to do?"

"The wind sweeps the ground, the snow serves as lighting," Tuizhi said. "In ancient times there were those like Su Wu of the Han dynasty who ate snow and gnawed the felt of their clothing. However, even though I haven't mastered Yuan An's art of sleeping in the deep snow, how could I decline a journey of a thousand miles just because it is hard to travel?"

"Master, previously you wouldn't listen, but remained attached to your position and reputation and refused to cultivate yourself," Zhang Qian said. "Today the snow blocks the road in front of us, and above our heads crows are cawing and owls are hooting."

Tuizhi remained silent and pressed on, feeling miserable and fearful. But the wind blew wilder all the time and the snow fell ever more densely. Hungry and weak, Tuizhi got off his horse and sought shelter from the snow with his companions, even while improvising a song to the tune "Goat on the Mountainside":

"The road is long.
I won't reach Blue Pass.
My regrets are deep;

Hunger and cold are difficult to bear.
In the expanse of white,
The horse cannot go forward.
With slow steps,
I advance and retreat and suffer many falls.
When the dreaming soul is lost,
It is hard to call back from afar with just a few words.
And it is truly hard to foretell what will happen in the end.
My fate is against me, the time inauspicious,
Yet in my heart I remain loyal to the emperor.
On the bleak and wild mountain,
Snow swirls chaotically through forests and across marshes;
As misery meets my eye, the crow calls out."

Having chanted this poem, Tuizhi was overcome by sadness. He got back on his horse and moved on. After several miles they came to a hollow, from which several roads led out. Which was the one to Chaozhou?

While they were at a loss what to do, a herdboy came along, looking all around, searching for his ox. Tuizhi wanted to ask him the way, but feared that he might be humiliated again. Then he had an idea and called to the herdboy, "Boy, what are you looking for?"

"I've lost an ox and I am looking for it here," the herdboy replied.

"Where did you lose it?"

"I followed this ox from Chang'an, and all the way it has been unwilling to turn back. Then, somehow I suddenly lost sight of it."

"I saw an ox, but I'm not sure whether it was yours," Tuizhi said. "If you agree to show us the road to Chaozhou, I'll guide you to the place where you can find the ox."

"Don't try to trick me!" the herdboy said. "My ox looks pure and extraordinary, and its shape is strange. This is an unusual ox—you wouldn't be able to recognize it."

"Your ox, like any other, has four legs and two horns, a thin tail and large head, a rope through its nose, and blinkers over its eyes. What's unusual about it?" Tuizhi said.

"There are many famous oxen in this world, but none can compare to mine," the herdboy said. "I'll describe them to you: If sitting on its back you pull the halter three times and still can't make it turn its towering head, it's a strong ox. When it hangs its head and pulls in its tail, unwilling to push the mill and sleeping on the ground, it's a lazy ox. When it raises its tail to shit, leaving behind its excrement, it's a stinking ox. When, on being beaten with the thorny stick, it's completely fearless and wildly charges left and right, it's a wild ox. When its whole body is covered in sores and its backbone is rotten, its flesh wasted away and its legs weak, then it's a diseased ox. When its head doesn't move when you step on its tail, and it seems to be neither dead nor alive, then it's a dull ox. If it pulls the plough to work the field, without ever stopping, it's a stupid ox. If a person has ten thousand strings of money, but won't spend any, eating only ginger and drinking bitter vinegar, holding on so stingily to his wealth that people shake their heads at him, he is nicknamed 'village ox.' And if someone wears on his head a scholar's cap, gives himself airs as he plays football, and imitates the vices of well-born wastrels, he is called a 'robber ox.' My ox is of a glossy black color unmatched by any other. It's not like ordinary oxen of the human world. If I don't find it today, my master's whip will truly give me cause to be anxious."

"When formerly Laozi left by the Hangu Pass, instructed Yin Xi, and delivered the Tathagatha, he was also riding a black ox," Tuizhi said. "You are no divine immortal—why do you speak of looking for a black ox?"

Laughing, the herdboy said, "Although I am not a divine immortal, neither am I an ordinary man. Why don't you abandon your official position and cultivate yourself with me? Don't go to Chaozhou!"

"My nephew Han Xiangzi admonished me numerous times to leave the family, yet I wasn't willing to follow him. Why would I today agree to follow a boy like you?"

"I know that Han Xiangzi. He's a divine immortal of the Upper Eight Grottoes. If you don't follow me to cultivate yourself, that's your ill fortune," the herdboy answered.

When Tuizhi heard the herdboy say that he knew Han Xiangzi, he said, "Brother herdboy, I would like to meet with Han Xiangzi. Where is he now? May I trouble you to tell him from me that I am calling on him to come and save me? If he tarries another few days, I will certainly have died in this deep mountain wilderness."

"Sir, though you served at court, you don't understand at all," the herdboy said.

"What is it that I don't understand?"

"You want me speak to the divine immortal Han and call on him to come meet with you—that shows your lack of understanding."

"Brother herdboy, what you don't know is that, first, I am under orders from the emperor; second, Xiangzi is my nephew; third, I raised him as a child; and fourth, Xiangzi promised to come to the Blue Pass and rescue me. That's why I ask you to look for him."

"Immortals have escaped from the bonds of fame and profit; they have abandoned father, mother, wife, and children," the herdboy said. "Their mind is not attached to anything anymore. Why would he be concerned about his uncle?"

"If he doesn't agree to come, I'd rather die than go and seek him out," Tuizhi said.

"If that's the case, please suit yourself, but take care not to miss the emperor's deadline," said the herdboy.

"Brother herdboy, you grew up here. Do you know what place this is?" Tuizhi asked.

Pointing with his hand, the herdboy said, "In that forest ahead of you there stands a great stone stele. On it are written some words. Go and look at it and you will know the name of this place."

Tuizhi reined in his horse and looked ahead. On the stele were written the words "Blue Pass, Qin Mountains." Sighing, he said, "When Xiangzi came home, he said that I would undergo suffering when I got to this place, but I wouldn't believe him. Who could have known that today I would meet with such calamity, yet he doesn't come to rescue me. What shall I do?"

"Master, it seems that you came here in this wintry weather not of your own choosing, but because of the time limit set by the emperor," Zhang Qian said. "As an immortal, the young master isn't willing to come and expose himself to trouble."

"Master, don't harbor resentments," Li Wan added. "There must be people living somewhere deep in that forest. Let's hurry on and find an inn to spend the night. Then we can make further deliberations."

> In a long drought I prayed for sweet rain;
> Away from home I hope to meet an old friend.
> If I can be rescued by him,
> This will be my good fortune.

If you don't know whether people lived in the forest or not, please listen to the explanations in the next chapter.

21

INQUIRING INTO HIS FORTUNE, TUIZHI SEEKS AN ORACLE
IN A TEMPLE

SEEKING TO ASSUAGE HIS HUNGER AND THIRST, TUIZHI
STAYS IN A THATCHED HUT

In the distance the Qin Pass rises in manifold layers;
The dust of carriages and the tracks of horses stretch from west to east.
High pavilions cling to cliffs, surrounded by Heaven-towering cypresses;
On an ancient road a Chan hermitage, overgrown by pines
Enveloping the cracked walls, shielding them from the morning sun.
Nearby a cool breeze stirs up ripples in a duckweed pond.
Sitting alone in a thatched hut with no one come to visit,
There is only the slanting sun which reddens the ground.

As Tuizhi's party was struggling through the snow, Lan Caihe said to Xiangzi, "My immortal brother, you see how Tuizhi hasn't met a single soul for ten days and has had no place to rest himself. Yet still he hasn't had the slightest change of heart or any true regrets. Truly his nature is as inflexible as iron or rock. However, while we need to keep up the pressure on him, if he freezes or starves to death in this severe cold, we will defeat our own purpose. Let's go up the mountains and order the local earth god to materialize a temple, where Tuizhi can rest a while and find shelter from the snow. Surely there is no problem with that."

"You're right, my immortal brother," Xiangzi said. Forthwith he called out the mountain and earth gods and ordered them, "My uncle Han Tuizhi originally was the Attendant Great General, but was banished to the human world. The Jade Emperor sent me to deliver him. I have already tried several times, but he still hasn't changed his mind. Traveling in such a snowstorm and on the Blue Pass road in the Qin Mountains, he will be extremely cold and hungry. Go to the fork in the road and materialize a temple there in which he can find shelter. If he uses the divination sticks to ask for an omen, give him three negative oracles in a row. Do not fail!"

Having received their orders, the mountain and earth gods really did materialize a temple at the road fork. What did this temple look like?

> Small, oh so small the three temple halls;
> Low, oh so low the two side wings;
> Surrounded by a wall made of yellow clay,
> The leaves of the doors hanging askew and loose.
> In the center images of the earth god and his wife,
> On the sides the ghost judges striking their imposing postures.
> Passing travelers encountering difficult adversity
> Ask the oracle and draw its sticks, but get only muddled answers.

Having struggled against the wind and snow for half a day, Tuizhi, Zhang Qian, and Li Wan were completely exhausted. When suddenly they spied a temple ahead, Zhang Qian said, "Master, ahead there is a temple! Let's go inside and take shelter for a while. If there is a temple keeper, we can have him prepare some hot soup and hot water, and eat a little."

"Yes, let's go inside and stay there for the night," Tuizhi said. "We shall continue our journey early in the morning."

Li Wan hurried forward to hold the reins. Tuizhi descended and stepped in front of the temple. Looking up, he saw a tablet with the inscription, "Shrine to the God of the Earth and Grain."

Tuizhi sighed and said, "If there is an earth god temple, there should be people's homes nearby. Why haven't we seen a single one on this long journey?"

The party entered the temple. Tuizhi stepped forward, bowed, and announced, "Grandpa Earth, you truly are a selfless spirit. I was banished to Chaozhou for my loyal service to the nation. My whole journey has been arduous, the hunger and cold hard to bear. Today the snow is coming up to my horse's head and I cannot go on. I have no choice but to avail myself of your temple to spend the night. I pray that you will protect us, that the snowstorm will soon clear up, that my career will prosper, and that I will soon be allowed to return home and be reunited with my wife."

"There is a container with divination sticks on the altar, which surely is for

問吉凶廟中求卜

Inquiring into his fortune, Tuizhi seeks an oracle in a temple.

the use of visitors," Zhang Qian said. "Master, how about requesting a stick to divine our fortunes?"

Accordingly, Tuizhi scraped up some soil to substitute for incense, and prayed to the deity, "Enlightened spirit above, I, Han Yu, have been banished to Chaozhou. On the road, I have suffered many setbacks. Now I have reached the Blue Pass in the Qin Mountains. How far is it still to Chaozhou? If from now on our blessings will be many and misfortunes few, I beg that you will grant me a positive divination stick. If our misfortunes will be many and blessings few, please give me a negative one."

He shook the container for a long time and eventually obtained a negative stick. He drew three times, but each time he got a negative response. When he saw this, Tuizhi said, "How sad! I have drawn three negative sticks in a row. My life must be destined to end here."

Zhang Qian and Li Wan went to the rear of the temple and found a keeper, an old man, supporting himself on a staff. As he stepped outside, his head trembling and shaking, he saw Tuizhi and burst into laughter. Tuizhi said, "What are you laughing at? We have come a long way and are hungry. We'd be very obliged if you could prepare us some food."

The temple keeper said, "I am an old man who can't sleep at night and can't get up early in the morning. By the time I rise, it is already late. When I manage to cook a meal, it has to last me for the whole day. If you're hungry, I have some rice here, but you have to cook it yourself, if you want it to reach your bellies any time soon."

"Please give us some cinders, if you have any," Tuizhi requested.

"You seem to be an educated man," the temple keeper said. "How come you don't know that there's fire within stones?"

Thereupon Tuizhi called to Zhang Qian, "The old Daoist is right. Get a flintstone to light a fire and prepare the food."

"I only know to make fire by drilling into wood," Zhang Qian said. "How do you make fire with a stone?"

"Get me one," Tuizhi said. "I'll handle it myself."

Zhang Qian quickly scratched the snow away, picked up a stone, and handed it to Tuizhi. The temple keeper then pulled an iron blade and lighting paper cylinder from his sleeve. Tuizhi took them, but however much he struck the stone, not a single spark came out. When the temple keeper saw his unsuccessful attempts, he came forward and took the stone and blade. With trembling hands he struck them just two or three times, and a bright red fire was started.

Overjoyed, Zhang Qian took the cylinder and went to look for the kitchen stove, only to discover that the kitchen building stood askew, its walls fallen over, and that the stove had collapsed and the pot was broken. There was not even a single basin or bowl. He sighed, caught hold of the temple keeper, and said to him, "Looks like you don't eat, but just swallow pneuma, eh?"

Pretending not to hear him, the temple keeper said, "When I wasn't awarded a degree, I still didn't run around making courtesy calls to my betters, wagging my tail and begging for patronage. When I did receive a degree, I still knew to be content, and withdrew at the height of my success. Why should I get overexcited?"

"This old Daoist is making fun of me," Tuizhi said.

"The old fellow probably ate some leftover clams that didn't agree with him," Zhang Qian said. "As a result he's now all confused and talking nonsense. Pay no attention to him." Then he and Li Wan gathered some stones and built a temporary stove. They dragged down some tree branches and lit a fire. From their travel bags they took a small copper pot, filled it with snow, and set it on the stove.

Unexpectedly, however, the snow melted down to no more than a bowlful of water. They had to melt several pots of snow before they had enough to cook rice. It wasn't until evening that they could eat a meal.

The temple keeper had gone into the rear building and hadn't come out again. As they had no place to rest, Zhang Qian said, "There are no clean guest rooms or beds in the temple. If you don't find it too revolting, we should spend the night in the back with the temple keeper."

"Master, don't go in yet," Li Wan said. "Let me have a look at his room first."

"You're right," Zhang Qian agreed.

When Li Wan ran to the rear to look, he saw only a straw mat on the floor, on which the temple keeper lay, fully clothed. He didn't even have a blanket, let alone a curtained bedstead. Turning back, Li Wan murmured under his breath, "With such sleeping arrangements, perhaps it's better if the master doesn't come in here!"

He gave the whole story to Tuizhi, who said, "We are stranded in a desolate area, and the temple keeper is a man in his dotage, who is content just to survive from day to day. Where would he get a bedstead to sleep on? It is my bitter fate to have been banished to such a place."

"Do not vex yourself," Zhang Qian said. "In this windy and snowy weather, we can count ourselves lucky to have found this temple to rest in. Without it our situation would be even worse." When everything had been said, they had no choice but to curl up and huddle together in a heap in front of the deities' shrine.

Sighing all the time, Tuizhi hardly closed an eye all night. At daybreak he looked around and saw they were all huddled together underneath an old pine tree, the horse standing nearby. All around there was nothing but snow, which luckily had not fallen on them. No temple was to be seen, and no temple keeper. Tuizhi stared open-mouthed, and then quickly called to Zhang Qian and Li Wan, "How come you two are still asleep?"

Li Wan dreamily rubbed his eyes and said, "I am getting up already."

When Zhang Qian looked up, he was greatly startled and said, "That old Daoist is a master robber!"

"What do you mean by that?" Tuizhi said.

"If he weren't, he'd have left tracks to follow," Zhang Qian said. "Why, he even tore down the temple and took it away!"

"The old Daoist couldn't have dismantled it so cleanly," Li Wan said. "He must have had help from some craftsmen."

"Why did we so sleep so deeply that we didn't even hear any noise of axes and saws?" cried Zhang Qian.

"It's because we were so exhausted from the journey and our exertions last evening," Li Wan offered.

"You're both making wild guesses," Tuizhi said. "Surely when a house is torn down, some roof tiles and waste wood will remain. How could it have been cleaned up so thoroughly? No, Heaven took pity on me, because I had been banished due to my loyalty and righteousness, and nearly died of cold and hunger. Therefore it sent the local mountain and earth gods to materialize this temple so that I might stay for the night. Stop talking such nonsense!" Then Zhang Qian fastened the horse's rope, Li Wan shouldered the luggage, and they continued their journey. Indeed,

> Thinking back to the time when he was rich and noble,
> How could he have known his present loneliness and grief?
> The road to Chaozhou is long—when will he arrive?
> Looking back to Chang'an, the road is lost among cloudy trees.

Tuizhi's party had not walked even three to five miles when suddenly the cold wind started again, and snowflakes came beating down into their faces.

"Master, it's snowing hard again," Zhang Qian said. "What shall we do?"

"Xiangzi! Xiangzi!" Tuizhi wailed with deep grief, "If you have forgotten me and my wife's sacrifices in bringing you up, you should at least remember that I am your father's brother. At a time of such suffering, why do you still not come to rescue me?"

"The little master may already be dead, and we don't know where he died," Li Wan said. "We don't even know whether or not someone collected his bones.

You're calling for him now, but he couldn't hear you even if he were a divine immortal. What's the use?"

Actually, Xiangzi was up in the clouds following Tuizhi. When he heard Tuizhi calling for him so grievously, he changed into the shape of a peasant, who came walking along carrying a hoe.

When Tuizhi saw this peasant, he thought to himself, "How can someone plant fields in this wilderness on such a snowy day? Surely this must be a ghost. Earlier those two ghosts in the shapes of a woodcutter and a fisherman already led me by the nose for a whole day. Now I'll recite a passage from *The Book of Changes* to subdue him. Let's see if that frightens him." And right away he recited several times the classic's opening: "Great and originating, penetrating, advantageous, correct and firm."[1]

When Xiangzi heard Tuizhi reciting from *The Book of Changes*, he secretly laughed and said, "As beings of pure yin, ghosts are destroyed by the two lines in *The Book of Changes*, 'The union of seed and power produces all things / The escape of the soul brings about change.'[2] Hence they fear *The Book of Changes*. I, however, am a being of pure yang. It was *The Book of Changes* that awakened me to the Great Way of the Agreement of the Three. Why should I fear this formula? But I'll let him recite it and won't reveal my secrets prematurely."

Tuizhi recited these syllables many times, until he realized that the peasant was standing before him upright and unmoved. He thought to himself, "It is by no means certain that the woodcutter and fisherman were ghosts, but this peasant definitely is a human being." Then he stepped forward, greeted him, and said, "May I ask you, Brother, how far it is from here to Chaozhou?"

The peasant answered,

> "A farmer only knows to plough his fields,
> And doesn't understand the high mountains and manifold peaks.
> He doesn't know, either, how many trees and creeks there are on these
>   peaks,
> Or how many cypresses and pines grow at the foot of these ranges,
> Or where waterfalls and springs come from and where they go,
> Or what drums and what bells Buddhist and Daoist clerics strike.
> Although you wear embroidered clothes and sit on a fine horse,
> Although you drink a thousand cupfuls of wine from jade goblets,
> Although your wealth far exceeds the Northern Dipper,
> Although you are so full of yourself,
> When all is said and done, you are no match for a farmer."

Having spoken these words, without looking further at Tuizhi, the farmer left. Tuizhi wanted to run after him and hold him back, but because he feared that the fellow was simply ignorant and would just grumble away and waste their time, he could not make up his mind whether to go after him.

"We should resume our journey here and now," Zhang Qian said. "What are we waiting for?"

"I think we should inquire further with the peasant and get some information from him," Tuizhi said.

"If you want to know the road down the mountain, you must ask passing travelers, not a peasant who plants his fields in the mountains and probably never travels any distance to other places," Li Wan said. "Why take the trouble to ask him anything?"

Nagged by Zhang Qian and Li Wan, Tuizhi had no choice but to give his horse the whip and move on, but from his eyes tears streamed down. Truly, the limitless pain of the heart is contained in two welling tears.

They had traveled more than ten miles, hoping to find an inn where they could rest, when suddenly ahead of them two fierce tigers jumped out from among the trees, truly frightening to behold.

> In the deep mountains, hidden in the mist, the tiger's fur rivals in
> elegance that of the panther. Amidst a rising storm, its teeth and
> claws compete in sharpness with those of the dark lion. Only on high
> cliffs will it roar, with proud head and waving tail shaking mountains
> and rivers. On precipices it faces the wind fearlessly, with angry eyes
> and frowning brows terrifying woodcutters and shepherds. Even if
> you are Bian Zhuang come back into the world, it is hard to act the
> hero when you are hungry and cold. Suppose you are Feng Fu born
> again, how can you apply your fists and cudgel when you are freezing
> and starved?[3] Tuizhi meeting a tiger today is like having a leaking
> roof and then suffering several nights of constant rain, or running
> into a head wind while traveling by boat. If his soul does not go
> straight to King Yama's palace, it surely is about to fly away into the air.

Zhang Qian turned around and came running back, shouting, "Master! Ahead two fierce tigers are rushing toward us!"

When Tuizhi heard this, he tumbled from his horse and collapsed in a swoon onto the ground, with hardly a breath left in him. The two tigers came rushing on, seized Zhang Qian and Li Wan in their mouths, and carried them off, so that

Tuizhi alone remained behind. Truly, life is transitory, like the moon atop a mountain at the fifth watch, or like a lamp whose oil is used up at the third watch.

Let's digress here to say that after Xiangzi had made the mountain god transform himself into fierce tigers come to carry Zhang Qian and Li Wan off and scare Tuizhi into an unconscious state, Lan Caihe said, "Immortal Brother, your uncle is in a deep coma. Quickly go wake him up, otherwise his perfected nature might be thrown into confusion."

"Immortal Brother, my uncle is of no mind to die, but is still intent on going to Chaozhou and taking up his official duties," Xiangzi said. "I'll create a gust of cold wind to wake him up, and materialize a thatched hut farther down the road. In the hut I'll place the buns and the fine wine that he once gave me, the ones I put in my flower basket. With these he can fill his stomach and warm himself against the cold. The next day I'll collect his horse's soul so that it will die and he will lose his means of transportation. And then I will come to convert him."

"Good," said Lan Caihe.

And indeed, Tuizhi lay in a deep coma for a long time, but then a gust of cold wind made him shiver all over so that he revived and struggled to his feet. He looked around and saw that Zhang Qian and Li Wan were gone and only the horse was left. It stood there exposed to the wind, yet not moving. Two tears ran down Tuizhi's face as he sighed, "I, Han Yu, was loyal and filial to the utmost and acted for the nation and the people. My only wish was that my name would be displayed in the historical records and my reputation would live on after my death. Who could have known that my memorial on the Buddha bone would destroy my household and separate me from my wife? Just a while ago there were still three of us, but now two of them are buried in the bellies of fierce tigers and I alone am left. If I meet another tiger, I will be hard pressed to escape with my life. Well, I guess what I brought upon myself, I should suffer myself. If my life is to end in this place, I might as well find a way to put an early end to it. If someone takes pity on a masterless orphaned soul and digs a hole to bury me in, then at least my body will be in one piece, which is better than being ripped to pieces by a tiger."

Having considered his options, Tuizhi proceeded to a dense cluster of trees, took off his girdle, and tried to hang himself. However, he was not destined to die by hanging. Whenever he fastened the girdle, it slipped off again. Tuizhi then picked a robust tree branch and said, "On that forked branch I can hang it securely." Yet when he hung up the girdle, even that branch broke off.

Tuizhi said, "It appears that I am not to die by the rope, but to perish by the sword. It was for this reason that the emperor wanted to have me beheaded at the execution grounds. Because Scholar Lin and the other officials made such an effort to come to my rescue, I was banished to Chaozhou, but now it seems that I cannot avoid going down that path after all."

Quickly he untied the sword from his luggage, but when he wanted to cut his own throat, the blade was stuck in its sheath as if it had taken root there. He pulled as hard as he could, but he couldn't pull it out.

Distressed, Han Yu called out, "Heaven! I, Han Yu, have come to this place where I can't find life when I seek it, and can't obtain death when I want it. It is no use leaving me behind all alone."

The echo of his voice was still reverberating among the mountains when he heard in the distance the sound of a fisher drum. "Good! Good!" Tuizhi said. "My nephew Xiangzi has come to save me." But when he lifted his head to look all around, he saw only snowflakes whirling everywhere like butterfly wings and goose down, blown about by a strong wind. Where was his nephew Xiangzi? And where the fisher drum and the clappers?

Tuizhi wanted to run, yet there was no road; he looked around, yet there was no one in sight. Quickly untying its tether, he said, "Horse, I have ridden you all this time and we have never been separated for a single day. When I die, as I definitely will soon, don't yearn for me. If you don't want to die yourself, run straight back to Chang'an, lest you be mauled to death by a tiger."

While he was speaking to the horse, two lines of tears streamed down his face, and he sobbed chokingly. Suddenly he heard the sound of the fisher drum again. After listening to it for a while, he said, "It must be my nephew Xiangzi who is beating that drum. Why do I just hear the sound, but not see his shape? Formerly he said he would come to the Blue Pass to rescue me—why then has he still not come, but let me suffer such loneliness and hardship?" Looking up to Heaven, he called for Xiangzi several times in a row, but there was no reply.

Anxious and at a loss what to do, he heard the fisher drum once more, and this time he saw a young Daoist braving the snow to make his way toward him. The youth's hair was bound into double knots, and he wore a single-piece gown of dark cloth. In one hand he held the fisher drum, and on his shoulder he carried a flower basket. Not one of the big snowflakes stuck to his body, and he had the fresh appearance of an immortal, with red lips and white teeth. He was singing these Daoist songs, the first to the tune of "Mistletoe," the second to that of "Goat on the Mountainside":

> "My home is in the wilderness of the deep mountains,
> Where I have no neighbors in the east or west.
> All I see are clear and secluded mountain streams,
> The birds flying and singing,

The deer running.
By evening,
Signs of humans are few,
The birds have stopped singing,
And the air is cold and clear.
My companions are
The waning moon and the morning star sitting on the tree tops.

"Think back
To the time when you used to drive in a noble chariot.
Why have you come to this dangerous place, the Blue Pass?
Where is your heroism now?
You fear your horse may become exhausted and you yourself perish!
Trepidation fills your heart,
You are separated from your wife,
And this snow is piling up,
Piling up in layers of silver.
Turning to look back toward your home district, the road is lost.
Alas!
In this predicament
Who will bear the burden of loneliness and anxiety in your stead?
Even if you were to change your mind soon, it would be too late."

When Tuizhi saw the youth's graceful bearing and refined appearance, and heard his fervent words and urging tone, he prostrated himself before him and said, "Divine immortal, save me!"

The Daoist quickly caught hold of Tuizhi and said, "What kind of man are you? What is your business in coming to this forsaken place?"

"I am the Minister of Rites Han Yu," Tuizhi said.

"If you are a high minister at court, you should be preceded by banners and flags and surrounded by heralds and attendants," the Daoist said. "On such a wintry day, why aren't you in the red towers and warm pavilions roasting lambs and heating wine, sipping liquor and humming songs to give expression to your exuberant spirit? Why do you instead walk all alone with just one horse on this road?"

"I, Han Yu, once knew how to enjoy myself. It is because I refused to follow my nephew Xiangzi's admonitions to cultivate myself that I have come to suffer such hardship in this place. I can't find a store or inn to stay in, and have lost my servants, Zhang Qian and Li Wan. I am left all alone, beset by difficulties left and right. Therefore I sought a way to end my life. Fortunately I met you, Immortal Brother. May I ask you, how far is it from here to Chaozhou?"

Pointing with his hand, the youth said, "Ahead there is the Fortress of Blue Pass."

As Tuizhi lifted his head to look, the youth vanished into thin air. Tuizhi thought to himself, "I am probably not destined to die here, and therefore Heaven has sent down this young Daoist to show me the way. I shall press on a few more steps, find an inn to stay at, and then make further decisions."

However, the snowfall got even worse. Shivering with cold all over, the horse fell to the ground and would not get up. Tuizhi said, "I am suffering this ordeal because of my offense against the court. But, horse! what guilt do you have that you should suffer hunger and cold in this place?" Slowly he helped the horse up, rearranged saddle and reins, and mounted to continue the journey. However, the horse was already too badly affected by the cold, and could hardly walk. As it stumbled with every step, Tuizhi almost fell off. By that time he had almost found his faith in Xiangzi as a divine immortal, and he had almost completely abandoned his ambition to be an official.

After less than half a mile, he saw a thatched hut by the side of the mountain and said to himself, "That hut is not a teahouse or tavern. It must be a place where an ascetic cultivates himself. I shall go there and seek shelter from my misfortunes."

Quickly he led the horse to the door of the hut, only to find that it was shut tightly with no sign of human presence. Tuizhi said, "Strange. How come there is a house, but no one near it? Perhaps the owner is sleeping, or he is ill in his bed and cannot get up. Or he has gone out to beg and has not yet returned. Or he has gone to look for his teacher or visit a friend. Or he is taking a walk in the snow to seek poetic inspiration. Or he has been killed by a tiger or wolf. Or his soul has been confused by sprites."

He went on, "Having said all this, although this is an uninhabited mountain area, there still ought to be a few Daoists to look after this house. It can't be that there is no one in the house, can it?" But when Tuizhi tethered the horse and pushed the door open, there was no one inside.

The only things inside were a table and a chair. On the table stood a flower basket, filled with buns. Steam was rising from them as if they had only just tumbled from the steamer. Beside the basket there stood a gourd filled with hot wine. As Tuizhi was hungry and thirsty, he took a bun and began to eat it.

He had just taken the first bite when a thought suddenly struck him: "This bun looks just like the ones prepared at my birthday." When he looked at it closely, he realized that these indeed were the buns prepared by his cook Zhao Xiaoyi, which he had given that day to the emaciated Daoist. "The Daoist used trickery to fill his flower basket with 356 buns. How did they get here? Why are they so hot? It's really strange!"

Then Tuizhi said, "That Daoist said I would be snowed in at the Blue Pass and that was why he gathered 356 of my buns. Let me count the buns in this basket. If there are 356, I won't have anything more to say. If there are more or less than this number, then these buns were materialized by some other ascetic, sent by Heaven to place them in this house so that I may assuage my hunger and thirst."

Immediately Tuizhi began taking the buns out of the basket one by one. There were exactly 356 of them, not one less and not one more. Tuizhi sighed and said, "I have eyes, yet did not recognize a worthy man. That Daoist truly was a divine immortal and truly had the powers of one. I shall quickly eat some buns to still my hunger, and drink some wine to quench my thirst."

When he had eaten a bun and drunk a mouthful of wine, Tuizhi felt refreshed in spirit, and his body felt relaxed and warm. He thought to himself, "The horse shared my suffering, but I have no hay for it to eat. I shall feed it some buns." However, the horse hung its head, tears filling its eyes, and would not eat anything.

When Tuizhi saw it in this state, he said in his anguish, "Zhang Qian and Li Wan were dragged off by tigers and I only have this horse left as a companion. If anything were to happen to it, what should I do?" As he was stroking the horse and sighing, the sky darkened and dusk fell. He had no choice but to sit inside the hut for the night.

> Even though I know that he is not my companion,
> In an emergency we still have to follow each other.

Please listen to the next chapter.

22

SITTING IN A THATCHED HUT, TUIZHI SIGHS TO HIMSELF

∽

EXPELLING A CROCODILE, THE CELESTIAL GENERALS BESTOW

BLESSINGS ON THE PEOPLE

> *Struck by fierce wind and rain at the twelfth watch,*
> *Tuizhi regrets his earlier errors.*
> *If the trigrams kan and li exchanged their places in the body,*
> *Pure yin would be completely stripped away and pure yang would exult.*
> *Then Tuizhi's lonely desolation would end,*
> *And, like the womb-born crane, he would gather strength in the even-*
>   *ing sun.*
> *Turning back to pick up the Metal in the Water*
> *Is much better than driving away crocodiles in Chaozhou.*

In the hut there was no bedstead, mattress, or coverlet for Tuizhi to use; neither was there the light of a lamp which would give him at least his shadow for company. He was all alone, cut off from Heaven and Earth. The only thing he could do was to fasten the door tightly and take a nap sitting on the chair. However, though he wanted to sleep, his mind was full of sorrow and anxiety. The rattling noises of the wind were in his ear and so he tossed and turned, and couldn't get a wink of sleep. Therefore he improvised a lyric to the tune "Clear River" to pass the long night:

> *"At the first watch,*
> *As dusk is falling I cannot sleep,*

Facing my shadow, I am all alone.
I intended to maintain my loyalty and virtue—
It was nothing but wishful thinking!
Two tears roll down my cheeks.

"At the second watch,
I am unable to stop my flowing tears,
As snow crowds the Blue Pass road.
Looking back toward Chang'an,
The road is long and there is no news.
The words spoken in the beginning surely were not wrong.

"At the third watch,
A wild snowstorm blows again,
And outside the door a ghost is saying:
Your horse will not escape with its life;
Where will you rest all alone?
Han Yu must have created much bad karma in previous
    lives.

"At the fourth watch,
A rooster crows, but the sky has not yet brightened.
I hear a tiger roaring by the mountainside.
My soul is filled with anxious agitation,
Life and death are truly hard to secure.
Having no way of escaping from the maze,
I can only blame the divine immortals.

"At the fifth watch,
The golden pheasant cries three times,
And the east becomes brighter imperceptibly.
Quickly I get up and straighten out my clothes,
Planning to go up to the Blue Pass,
And let the snowstorm bury my body."

The whole night Tuizhi was unable to sleep, but kept sighing until daybreak. He was just about to arrange saddle and reins and mount his horse when he saw it lying stiff and dead on the ground.

On seeing it with its legs stretched out and its eyes without their shine, he stamped his foot, beat his breast, and wailed loudly. "When we started out in Chang'an, there were four of us. Although it was a solitary journey, I did not feel distressed by loneliness. Then Zhang Qian and Li Wan were carried off by tigers, and from morning to evening I had only my horse to rely upon. It rode over rough paths and dangerous roads. It stepped through high snow and layered ice. It was hungry, but I had no fodder to give to it. It was cold, but I had no straw for it to sleep on. I was still hoping to hurry on to Chaozhou and serve in office there for a while. Once I had received an imperial pardon, my horse and I would once more have galloped through the streets of Chang'an. Today it has perished in this wilderness and I am left behind in a thatched hut. This was all determined in a previous existence and so I do not bear a grudge—but how am I to reach Chaozhou?"

Sunk in his grief, Tuizhi shaped the things on his mind into a poem which he inscribed on the wall of the hut:

> A sealed epistle submitted at dawn to Ninefold Heaven—
> Exiled at dusk to Chaozhou, eight thousand leagues to travel.
>
> Wishing to save His Sagacious Brilliance from treacherous evils,
> Could I have cared for the years that remain in my withered limbs?

Having chanted the first four lines, he was thinking about the second half of the poem when he remembered the couplet on the petals of the golden lotus, which fit the events of that day well. So he continued to chant:

> "Clouds straddle the mountains of Qin—where is my home?
> Snows crowd the pass at Blue Pass—my horse will not move."

Tuizhi was just going to compose the final couplet when his brush froze so that he could not write with it any more and had to lay it down. Now he finally came to understand that his own life was as ephemeral as a lamp in the snow, or snow on top of a stove. With his whole heart and mind he was hoping to see Xiangzi coming to his rescue. However, as it was no solution to stay in the hut all by himself, he continued to walk on.

He had not walked half a mile when suddenly a tiger blocked the road again. Tuizhi cried out, "This time I am done for! Nephew Xiangzi, why are you still not coming to save me?"

At that moment he saw a man standing in midair and shouting at the tiger, "Wicked beast, you must not harm people! Get back!" The tiger became as tame as a house cat or a dog. It hung its head and let its ears droop, gave a roar, and left.

When Tuizhi saw this, he desperately called out, "Save me, immortal from Great Veil Heaven, save me! I am willing to follow you and cultivate myself. No longer do I want to be an official."

"Uncle, Uncle, I am not some immortal from Great Veil Heaven," Xiangzi said. "I am your nephew Xiangzi come to see you. Why don't you recognize me?"

Tuizhi embraced Xiangzi and amidst tears and sobs said, "I should have listened to you earlier. On the whole journey I have suffered many hardships—why didn't you come earlier to save me?" He gave Xiangzi a detailed account of the events of the journey, and then said, "I just wrote a poem on the wall of the hut to give expression to my sorrow. Because my brush froze, I could only finish six verses. On this joyous occasion of our meeting, I shall complete the poem."

"Which couplets does your poem consist of?" Xiangzi asked.

"Listen, I'll recite it to you:

"A sealed epistle submitted at dawn to Ninefold Heaven—
Exiled at dusk to Chaozhou, eight thousand leagues to travel.

"Wishing to save His Sagacious Brilliance from treacherous evils,
Could I have cared for the years that remain in my withered limbs?

"Clouds straddle the mountains of Qin—where is my home?
Snows crowd the pass at Blue Pass—my horse will not move.

"I know what the reason must be that makes you come so far—
The better to gather my bones from shores of miasmic water."[1]

"Uncle, do not vex yourself," Xiangzi said. "I know all about it. Let me ask you: do you still want to assume your post and serve as an official, or do you now have other plans?"

With a wave of his hand, Tuizhi said, "Thanks to the protection of Heaven and the ancestors, I have escaped the clutches of death. I shall devote myself fully to cultivation and the pursuit of the Dao in hopes of a fruitful outcome. I no longer want to serve as an official." He improvised a lyric to the tune "Stable Song" to explain his feelings to Xiangzi:

"I earnestly right my former wrongs,
And will no longer be an official and incur troubles.
I will discard my seal of office with its purple ribbon,
My ivory tablet and black boots,
My embroidered court robes.
I will regard the ruler's grace and my friends' amity as flying ashes,
And abandon all dissipations, entanglements, wine, and obligations.
Escaping beyond all limitations,
With all my heart I only wish for pure cultivation in a propitious place."

"Uncle, since you have turned your heart toward the Dao, if you cultivate yourself single-mindedly, you are sure to ascend to the realm of the immortals," Xiangzi said. "However, there is no master in these mountains. Whom shall we ask to transmit the marvelous elixir formulae to you?"

"He who has heard the Dao before me is my teacher.[2] Since you have already become an immortal, I shall honor you as my teacher. Why bother looking for another master?" Tuizhi responded.

"Father and son do not transmit their minds to each other; uncle and nephew find it difficult to transmit the Dao to each other," Xiangzi told him. "This definitely won't do."

"The way you speak you seem to suspect that I have no respect for my teacher or the Dao, and that in my heart I am not sincere," Tuizhi said. "If I ever have the slightest thought of backsliding, may I fall into Avici hell forever!"

"You brought me up—how could I not know your heart?" replied Xiangzi. "There is no need to make oaths. The problem is that if you violate the deadline set by the court, your family will be implicated. What shall we do about that?"

"All my heart is set on cultivating myself," Tuizhi said. "I pay them no heed."

"That's as may be, but your incorruptibility, honesty, and moderation are well known among your contemporaries. How could you change your character just because of your banishment? Come to think of it, the right thing to do is still for you to go and assume your post in time to meet the court's deadline, and only then to go and cultivate yourself."

"It would be useless for me to go all by myself," Tuizhi said. "If I were to meet another tiger on the road ahead, I'd certainly forfeit my life."

"In that case I shall go with you," Xiangzi told him. "Once we've attended to some official business and left a good reputation in Chaozhou, I shall use Former Heaven's Marvelous Method of Release from the Corpse to change your appearance, and announce that you have suffered a stroke and died while attending to your duties. I'll change my shape and return to Chang'an, where I will report your death and request that you be awarded posthumous honors. And then I'll help you seek a teacher with whom you can inquire into the Dao. In this way you will do your duty to the Emperor by not violating the court's orders, even while completing your excellent reputation as an official among the people. In between you will obtain the marvelous formulae of eternal life. Won't that be just perfect?"

Overjoyed upon hearing Xiangzi's words, Tuizhi said, "I completely rely on you; we'll do as you suggest." When they resumed Tuizhi's journey, Xiangzi didn't ride a cloud or walk on the mist, but followed Tuizhi in enduring the hardships of travel and braving the cold.

After walking for two days, they saw a gate tower in the far distance. Xiangzi said, "Ahead is Chaozhou Prefecture. There will certainly be someone to welcome you. You'd better put on your official's cap and girdle to receive them."

Tuizhi put on his official dress and seated himself in the Ten-Mile Pavilion. And sure enough, an agent dressed in a blue robe and a small cap came forward and asked, "Where do you serve in office? For what purpose have you come here?"

"My master is the Minister of Rites," Xiangzi said. "His name is Han. Because his memorial against the Buddha bone offended the emperor, he has been banished as a magistrate to this area. Today he has come to assume his office."

"So you're our new magistrate," the agent said. "Please, sit for a while, as I go to inform the officials so that they may come out to welcome you."

Having thus spoken, he ran into the town as if for his life and informed the local officials. Soon a large number of officials, local elders, teachers, and students came hurrying out of the city to welcome Tuizhi, carrying colorful embroidered banners.

After each of them had performed his greetings, Tuizhi ordered, "This is a highly auspicious day and I therefore want to assume my official duties right away. Prepare for my inspection all registers, regulations, and laws that I need to know about." With one voice the officials acknowledged the order and withdrew.

Tuizhi then took his seat in an official's sedan chair, carried by four men. Surrounded by police runners and bailiffs, preceded by drums and banners, he entered the city and took up residence in the yamen.

The next morning he ascended the reception hall and examined the files and documents. He burned incense at the temple of the city god, calculated the contents of the granary, and inspected the prison. Having acquitted himself of these various duties, he had a public announcement posted that instructed the population to present in detail what great benefits were to be promoted in this area, and what evils to be reformed, so that action could be taken on these issues. Greedy and corrupt officials exploiting commoners; powerful clans and local bullies abusing the people—all who had been wronged without gaining redress should state their cases in detail so that they could be acted upon.

Within two days of this announcement's posting, many commoners of all ages crowded into the yamen's hall, knelt on the floor, and petitioned the magistrate, "Sir, as you have newly assumed your office, we do not dare say too much, but there is a song that's been passed down for a long time that we would like to recite to you, so that you can form your own opinion."

"What kind of song is it? Let me hear it," Tuizhi said. The people sang,

> "Chaozhou once lay on the ocean shore,
> Where the tides took their turns.
> Since ancient times officials never stayed for long,
> And a crocodile has been doing harm for many years."

"The tides have their natural indications. Why talk of it?" Tuizhi said. "As for being an official, every day that one is in office one should take care of that day's affairs. There is a saying, 'Serving as an elder for a day, striking the bell for a day.' Why waste so many words on this?"

"The words of the song have been transmitted for a long time and we do not know how they arose," the people said. "However, since ancient times people have spoken of 'serving as governor of the capital for five days,' which is an example of how short periods of office can be."

"Don't waste my time with idle words," Tuizhi said. "Explain to me in detail the issue of the harmful crocodile."

"This place is close to the ocean," the people said. "Several years ago a large sea creature emerged in great waves from the sea, its body several dozen feet long. From morning to evening it comes in and goes out with the seawater. As it makes the water surge, it overflows and ruins the people's fields. The creature's tail is also several dozen feet long, and when it sees oxen, goats, horses, or other livestock on the shore, it drags them into the water with that tail and devours them. If it sees people lingering behind, it pulls them too into the water with its tail, and eats them. Therefore people fear it greatly and call it a crocodile. These past years it has devoured innumerable people and livestock. Of ten houses nine are empty, and the survivors subsist in loneliness and poverty. None of the previous magistrates could control it. Sir, you must first eradicate this calamity to save the people."

"What does the crocodile look like?" Tuizhi asked.

The people said, "It has the head of a dragon and the mouth of a lion, the tail of a tiger and the body of a snake. When it swims in the sea, its body covers several miles. It devours men and livestock indiscriminately."

"You may withdraw," Tuizhi said. "I will deal with it." The people filed out of the yamen one after another. Tuizhi was about to leave the hall himself and return to his office, when he saw a man with dishevelled hair come in to lodge a lawsuit. The man wailed so loudly that his cries of sorrow reached the sky.

"What lawsuit are you bringing?" Tuizhi asked. "Don't cry, just explain it to me slowly."

The man said, "My surname is Liu, my personal name Ke. I am bringing suit in a murder case."

"Who is the victim?" Tuizhi asked. "What is the name of the murderer? Where does he live now?"

"I fish every day at Qinqiaokou," Liu Ke said. "At home there is only my mother, who every day brings me food to eat. Yesterday it was already past noon, but my mother hadn't come with my lunch. I couldn't wait any longer and returned home along the river.

"I don't know who killed my mother and threw her into the river, but there remained only a pair of shoes on the riverbank. Truly this is a great injustice with no place to find redress. I hope you, sir, will pity me and take on the case."

"This is a murder case with an unknown perpetrator," Tuizhi said. "Quickly fill out a form, and I will dispatch people to look for the murderer and indemnify you for your mother's death."

Liu Ke knocked his head and said, "Your honor, I cannot write. Let me lodge the suit verbally."

"Without a written charge it is difficult to arrest anyone," Tuizhi said. "Since you can't write, just explain it clearly and I'll have a clerk write it down for you."

Liu Ke said,

"The plaintiff Liu Ke brings suit in a murder case: On this day in this month, my mother Mme. Zhang was killed and disposed of by someone. Her body has not been found, and only a pair of embroidered shoes remains as evidence. Submissively I beg that the murderer be arrested and questioned on the circumstances that led to this death, and that restitution be paid for my mother's death. I urgently submit this suit."

As Liu Ke recited this, Tuizhi ordered a clerk to write it down sentence for sentence, and then dismissed Liu Ke. When he returned to his office alone, he thought to himself, "The people all said that the crocodile is wont to devour people and livestock and does no small amount of harm. Could it be that the mother of Liu Ke also was dragged into the river by the crocodile? But in that case, how did she come to take off her shoes on the riverbank?"

He then called Xiangzi and explained what Liu Ke had told him. With his eyes of wisdom, Xiangzi already knew of this matter, and was waiting for Tuizhi's return to his office to discuss ways of solving the problem.

It just so happened that Tuizhi called him, and so Xiangzi told him, "This crocodile has already been bringing disaster for a long time. The previous officials have avoided it assiduously, just waiting to be promoted and reassigned, happy to get away from this place. Who was there to concern himself with driving it away? Thus this great calamity has taken shape. Uncle, tomorrow when you come to your office you should write an official proclamation of warning and sacrifice it to lay plaint with Heaven and Earth. I'll dispatch the two celestial generals Ma and Zhao to put the document in the mouth of the crocodile, drive it into the deep sea, and lock it up there so that it can harm the people no longer. Afterwards you will demonstrate plainly the circumstances of the death of Liu Ke's mother. Then your loyalty will be seen to illumine Heaven and Earth, and your trustworthiness will be seen to affect every creature. As a result the gentry and commoners of the whole prefecture will establish a shrine and arrange prayers in your honor. Won't that be just perfect?"

Following Xiangzi's suggestions, Tuizhi went to his office the next morning, took a sheet of placard paper, rubbed ink, and wielded the brush to compose the "Essay in Sacrifice to the Crocodile":

> On a certain date, Han Yu, prefect of Chaozhou, has his military judge
> Qin Ji take a goat and a pig and throw them into the deep waters of
> Wu Creek as food for the crocodile. He then is to address it as follows:
>
> When in ancient times the former kings possessed the land, they set
> fire to the mountains and the swamp, and with nets, ropes, fish
> spears, and knives expelled the reptiles and snakes and evil creatures

that did harm to the people, and drove them out beyond the four seas. When there came later kings of lesser power who could not hold so wide an empire, even the land between the Yangtze and the Huai Rivers they wholly abandoned and gave up to the Man and the Yi, to Chu and to Yue, let alone Chao, which lies between the five peaks and the seas, some ten thousand miles from the capital. Here it was that the crocodiles lurked and bred, and it was truly their rightful place. But now a Son of Heaven has succeeded to the throne of Tang, who is godlike in his wisdom, merciful in peace, and fierce in war. All between the four seas and within the six directions is his to hold and to care for; still more the land trod by the footsteps of Yu and near to Yangzhou, administered by prefects and magistrates, whose soil pays tribute and taxes to supply the sacrifices to Heaven and Earth, to the ancestral altars and to all the deities. The crocodile and the prefect cannot together share this ground.

The prefect has received the command of the Son of Heaven to protect this ground and take charge of its people; but you, crocodile, goggle-eyed, are not content with the deep waters of the creek, but seize your advantage to devour the people and their stock, the bears and boars, stags and deer, to fatten your body and multiply your sons and grandsons. You join issue with the prefect and contend with him for mastery. The prefect, though weak and feeble, will not bow his head and humble his heart before a crocodile; nor will he look on timorously and be put to shame before his officers and his people by leading unworthily a borrowed existence in this place. But having received the command of the Son of Heaven to come here as an officer, he cannot but dispute with you, crocodile, and if you have understanding, do you hearken to the governor's words:

To the south of the prefecture of Chao lies the great sea, and in it there is room for creatures as large as the whale or roc, as small as the shrimp or crab, all to find homes in which to live and feed. Crocodile, if you set out in the morning, by the evening you would be there. Now, crocodile, I will make an agreement with you. Within three full days, you will take your ugly brood and remove southward to the sea, and so give way before the appointed officer of the Son of Heaven. If within three days you cannot, I will go to five days; if within five days you cannot, I will go to seven. If within seven days you cannot, this shall mean that finally you have refused to remove, and though I be prefect you will not hear and obey my words; or else that you are stupid and without intellect, and that even when a prefect speaks you do not hear and understand.

Now those who defy the appointed officers of the Son of Heaven, who do not listen to their words and refuse to make way before them, who from stupidity and lack of intellect do harm to the people and to other creatures, all shall be put to death. The prefect will then choose skillful officers and men, who shall take string bows and poisoned arrows and conclude matters with you, crocodile, nor stop until they have slain you utterly. Do not leave repentance until too late![3]

Having finished the essay, Tuizhi sent a military judge by the name of Qin Ji to carry it to the riverbank and throw it into the water.

Ever since the crocodile had come to the Chaozhou River, it had surfaced every day to swim around. When it encountered people or animals, it would reach with its tail to the bank, coil the tail around the unfortunate victim, drag it into the water, and devour it. Therefore everyone was terrified and did not dare go to the riverbank. If the crocodile got nothing to eat, it would churn up waves, block the channel, and let the billows rise until the river flooded the land both inside and outside the city. People could neither live nor die, and they had no place to find shelter.

When Qin Ji received Tuizhi's proclamation and thought about having to go to the river, he feared that he might encounter the crocodile, which would rise to swallow him. But when he thought about not going there, he feared that he might receive a heavy flogging and be removed from office, as new magistrates tended to be very strict. He considered it this way and that way, hesitated, and didn't know what to do. Eventually he had no choice but to gather his courage and run to the riverbank, taking along several people and some sacrificial items. When he arrived, the crocodile was already there, watching him, its head raised, its huge mouth open.

Reader, let me say that the crocodile used to come to the riverbank every day to do violent mischief and commit all manner of evil deeds. Why, then, was it so submissive and tame on this day, just staring ahead without moving?

It was because Han Xiangzi had dispatched the two celestial generals Ma and Zhao, who had secretly bound the monster. They were only to wait for Qin Ji to throw the proclamation into its mouth, and then to drive it away into the deep

驅鼊魚天將施功

Expelling a crocodile, the celestial generals bestow blessings on the people.

sea. Qin Ji, of course, did not know this state of affairs; he only knew that the crocodile would eat any people it met. When from afar he saw it with raised head and open mouth, at first he became so frightened that his hands and feet went limp and he could not move. He broke out in a cold sweat all over his body and crumpled into a trembling heap on the ground.

When, after shaking for more than a double hour, he opened his eyes again to look, the monster was still in the same position, and all its awesome power seemed to have gone. Considering this, he said, "The crocodile has always been extremely violent and wild. Why is it that today, when Lord Han has sent me to deliver the proclamation, it's just sitting there dull and staring without moving at all? Isn't that strange?"

As he was still pondering, suddenly the sky darkened, thunder rolled and lightning flashed, and a great rain came down as if poured from a basin. The Chao River looked as if it was pushed about, gushing up high, although not a drop overflowed onto the river bank. Qin Ji had no choice but to gather his courage, brave the rain, and throw the proclamation into the monster's mouth.

Once it had the proclamation in its mouth, the monster lowered its head, closed its mouth, and mournfully passed from sight. As if exorcised, it vanished in an instant.

Qin Ji's eyes were all blurred and darkened with fear, and so he did not know that the crocodile had already left. He grasped the opportunity to quickly push the pig, the goat, and the other sacrificial items into the water, turned around, and ran for his life.

By the time he reached the yamen, Tuizhi was still sitting in the courtroom. Gasping for air, Qin reported, "Pig . . . goat . . . proclamation . . . proclamation . . . pig . . . goat."

"You look startled," Tuizhi said. "Rest a while and catch your breath, and then tell it to me slowly."

After a long time Qin said, "The pig, goat, and proclamation were all swallowed by the crocodile. I barely escaped with my life!"

"Is the crocodile still there?" Tuizhi asked.

"Yes, it is still there!" Qin Ji answered. "After swallowing the proclamation, it swam away."

"If after swallowing the proclamation it moved away into the deep sea, why do you say it is still there?" Tuizhi said.

Qin Ji thought for a long time and then responded, "It almost frightened me to death, and in my confusion my response was wrong." Then he explained in detail how he went to deliver the proclamation, and described the appearance of the crocodile.

"I owe you my gratitude," Tuizhi said. He called for a silver ingot to be fetched from the vault and given in reward to Qin Ji. Then he ordered Qin Ji to return home and rest for the night. Tomorrow he should come again to the yamen to await further orders. Qin Ji thanked Tuizhi and withdrew.

After Tuizhi returned to his office, he told Xiangzi about Qin Ji. Xiangzi said, "Uncle, tomorrow morning you should ascend the hall and write an announcement to be made known to the whole population. It will display the virtue of your administration, which affects even beasts and fish."

The next day Tuizhi wrote the announcement, and sent Qin Ji to post it in many places. This is what he wrote:

> An official announcement by Han, the prefect of Chaozhou: When I first took over the administration of this region, I wished to act on behalf of the nation and the people. Whatever was beneficial was to be promoted, whatever was harmful was to be reformed. If due to my negligence just one man were to lose his home, it would be as if I had pushed him into a ditch myself.[4] Now, there was a crocodile which had been causing harm for a long time already. My predecessors had not expelled it, and as result the people were unable to follow their livelihood. When I learned that Liu Ke's mother had been devoured by the crocodile, I was greatly aggrieved. Consequently I issued a proclamation and dispatched the military judge Qin Ji to throw it into the monster's mouth and thereby drive it out into the sea. Fortunately, Heaven took pity on your unjust suffering, and the Emperor's benevolent mercy worked far and wide, touching both the stupid and the clever. Thus without wasting a single arrow, or expending any miltary forces, within a single day an old menace was exterminated all at once. Overjoyed, I proclaim to you that from now on everyone is to follow his livelihood peacefully, without being disturbed by ill omens or being confused by unnatural deaths and as a result getting into difficulties. As for bringing accusations against others, although Liu Ke has lodged a suit because he was suffering grievously from his mother's violent death, he should calm his mind and accept his fate so as to fulfill his filial piety. He must no longer implicate and harm innocent persons and thereby create a disturbance.

When it was posted, people all over the prefecture gathered in crowds to read it, and there was none who did not sigh in appreciation and say, "If it hadn't been for our magistrate's divine powers, nine out of ten of us would have died, and who could have righted this wrong and redressed this injustice? Such an announcement truly is a mercy bestowed on ten thousand generations."

> A single thought of refined sincerity evokes Heaven's response,
> And so the crocodile has now gone to its demise.
> From now on, Chaozhou will enjoy peace and happiness,
> And in history his name will be fragrant for a thousand years.

If you don't know what happened afterwards, please look at the next chapter.

23

Summer heat and winter cold take turns, spring and autumn alternate;
We all know that Heaven and Earth drift like empty boats.
Although we have fallen into the dust,
Yonder are still the Islands of the Immortals to aspire to.
Like dew on flowers, or bubbles in the water,
How long can you remain in this life?
We come and go in the passing of a shadow as time speeds along;
There is no freedom in the land of birth and death.

After Qin Ji had posted the announcement, the people of Chaozhou, gentry and commoners alike, all admired Tuizhi's virtue. They all sang for joy, honored him like a deity, and felt as close to him as to a parent. Several gentry members took the lead in collecting funds to build a shrine, fashion and set up a tablet, and set out incense, flowers, meat, and beans as sacrifices. On the first and fifteenth of every month, people would come in crowds to celebrate and sing his praises. Even travelers and itinerant merchants from outside the prefecture, on seeing this spectacle, sighed in appreciation and praised him, performing their kowtows with dedication.

In his modesty Tuizhi felt unworthy of such admiration and converted the shrine into the Chaozhou Academy. Inside, a tablet to Confucius was set up, while Tuizhi's own tablet was moved to the rear hall where it stood in the company of tablets for such Confucian luminaries as Yan Hui, Zengzi, Zisi, and Mencius. On the first and fifteenth of each month, scholars gathered here to expound the classics and elucidate what the ancient Confucians had not yet made clear. But let's speak of this no more.

One day, Xiangzi was sitting in meditation on a rush mat when the deity on duty came to report to him, "The emperor has realized that Tuizhi suffered banishment unjustly for his straightforward words; a decree has been issued that he be transferred to the interior prefecture of Yuanzhou."

Xiangzi was startled and said to himself, "Uncle's devotion to the Way is not yet steadfast, and his human desires are still present. If he learns that the emperor has realized his previous error, he will again want to serve as an official. How would he then be willing to cultivate himself with me? I have to do something if he is to complete perfection and realize the Dao."

Quickly he went to Tuizhi and said, "Formerly I told you that you would come to Chaozhou to meet the emperor's deadline and leave behind a good reputation. Then I would use Former Heaven's Marvelous Method of Release from the Corpse to put a substitute body in your place, and would pretend that you died of an illness. I would then report this to the emperor and have you reinstated in your previous position and awarded an honorary tablet. Then you would finally go to cultivate yourself. Now that you have been given a shrine while still alive, and have earned such an excellent reputation, it is time to depart."

"I leave it all up to you," Tuizhi said. "I won't waver in my determination."

Xiangzi took a bamboo staff, changed it into a likeness of Tuizhi, laid it on the bed, and covered it with a blanket. He ordered the two generals Ma and Zhao to escort Tuizhi to the Qin Mountains, where he should wait for Xiangzi so that they could go together to cultivate themselves.

When all his preparations were complete, he began to wail in the yamen and sent out a messenger to notify all the prefectural officials. He also made a report to Tuizhi's superior and submitted a memorial to Emperor Xianzong. As all the high and low officials in the prefecture came to give their condolences, Xiangzi received and thanked them one by one, without giving any hint of the truth. Then he packed up his luggage and set out.

The common people said, "Too bad! Why did such a saintly magistrate die? Why couldn't he have remained with us a bit longer to promote benefits and remove harm, thus bringing relief to us? Truly, August Heaven has no eyes to see."

One man said, "A saying puts it well: 'There are no good people in this world, where bad people bring grief even to the Buddha.' Now that this magistrate has died suddenly, what hope is there for us common people?"

Among the crowd there was a certain Zhang Gua, who blurted out, "This is the crocodile's revenge. How else could he have died so quickly?"

"The good receive good retribution, the bad receive bad retribution," another man said. "Yes, the magistrate has died, but it has been a peaceful death, and so this can still be regarded as good retribution."

"You are all wrong," yet another man said. "In my opinion, having eaten so many people, this crocodile's measure of evil was full. The Jade Emperor wanted to drive it out and sent a divine immortal into the human world specifically for the purpose of subduing it. Once that immortal had subdued the crocodile, he appeared to die and reported back to the Jade Emperor."

Still another said, "It was because we people of Chaozhou were due to be afflicted by disaster that Heaven produced this evil thing to devour countless people and livestock. Now the allotted calamities are fulfilled, and Heaven sent this good official to drive out the crocodile and bring peace to the city. In my view, it was all due to an inauspicious turn in the cosmic order and had nothing to do with karmic retribution and the distinction of good and evil."

"Brother, you may have a point there, but in submitting his memorial on the Buddha bone, Master Han dared to challenge the emperor directly," a scholar put in. "Why should such a man be afraid that the crocodile would not submit to his will and vanish? Evil cannot overcome good, and so the monster went into hiding far away. As for karmic retribution, just look at Master Han's remonstrance concerning the Buddha bone: in spite of its bluntness, his life had been spared until today."

All the people, gentry and commoners, wailed grievously for him as if for a deceased parent. Truly, "only grace received and hatred accumulated do not turn to dust in a thousand or ten thousand years."

When Xiangzi announced that he would be returning to the capital to report Tuizhi's death and packed up for the journey, he would not agree to keep the many condolence gifts arriving from everywhere, but had them transferred into the official treasury in lieu of the people's tax payments. He submitted a report to his superior that this year there was no need to levy taxes. The people of Chaozhou, old and young, men and women, all came to hold the ropes of the hearse and give comfort to Tuizhi's spirit, pulling the hearse for a long distance to see their magistrate off. Xiangzi consoled each of them individually and then sent them home.

After traveling for three days, Xiangzi left the jurisdiction of Chaozhou Prefecture and came to a sparsely populated area. There he ascended a cloud and sped on to Blue Pass in the Qin Mountains to rendezvous with Tuizhi.

Tuizhi thanked Xiangzi profusely. Xiangzi told him, "Now that I've brought you here, you and I need to part and go our separate ways."

"Having saved me, why do you now speak of parting?" Tuizhi asked.

"I received a commission from the Jade Emperor to deliver you, but because you refused to change your mind for so long, I had no choice but to return the commission," Xiangzi said. "Later when I saved your life in that perilous place, I offended the Jade Emperor by acting without his express authority. How could I now dare deliver you once again?"

"If you don't deliver me, I will starve to death in this place, and there will be no one to gather my bones," Tuizhi said.

"You could assume a new name and return to Chang'an to live happily with your wife and daughter-in-law. Why speak of death?"

"Having come so far, if I didn't now change my mind and devote myself to cultivation, I would be worse than an animal. Confucius said, 'Can one be a human being, yet be less than a bird'?"[1]

"If that's how you feel, then I'll tell you that to the southeast of here there is a mountain called Mount Zhuowei," Xiangzi told him. "Below it is a grotto called Zhuowei Grotto, in which dwells the Perfected Man Mumu.[2] He is my sworn friend and is very close to me. I will write a letter that you will deliver to him, asking him to take you into his hermitage and transmit the marvelous formulae of the Great Elixir to you. This way you will not have suffered all this hardship in vain."

"Where will I find refuge if he is not willing to take me?" Tuizhi asked.

"Although he and I are separate in body, we have the same root," Xiangzi said. "Of course he will take you when he sees my letter."

"Where would I find shelter in such a secluded mountain region if tigers or wolves were to appear?"

"If you encounter tigers or wolves blocking your way, just hold my letter over your head and the beasts will back off."

"The peaks are high and the mountains lofty; the woods are dense and deep," Tuizhi said. "There is not a single road—how shall I walk?"

"Cross these mountain ranges, and you will find a wide road that is easy to travel."

Tuizhi took the letter and placed it in his shirt. With one hand he held on to Xiangzi and was going to address more questions to him, when Xiangzi said, "Uncle, there's another immortal coming from the east." When Tuizhi turned his head to look, Xiangzi vanished into thin air and went ahead to Mount Zhuowei to play his role as the Perfected Man Mumu.

When Tuizhi saw that Xiangzi was gone, he had no choice but to obey his nephew's words and scramble step by step over several peaks and round the bases of several mountains. Finally he saw a wide road, but half a mile away a fierce tiger jumped onto it. The tiger roared and came towards Tuizhi.

Tuizhi was so startled that he could not even back away, but then he remembered Xiangzi's letter and quickly threw it in the beast's direction. When the tiger saw Xiangzi's letter, it waved its tail, lowered its head, and in an instant had run off into the woods.

Picking up the letter, Tuizhi said, "That my nephew should possess such powers—he truly is a divine immortal!" Then he struggled on and after several quick paces saw in the distance a high mountain with pure and unusual forests and valleys, its peaks rising in vivid layers of blue. Green pines and cypresses towered toward the sky, and many gulls and ducks bathed in the sunlight.

The farther Tuizhi climbed on this mountain, the more his muscles trembled with fatigue, and the more dangerous the path became. When he finally reached the summit, there was indeed a thatched hut, above whose door was written: "Pure Chamber of Zhuowei." It was surrounded by blue mountains on all sides, and flowers and trees grew around in elegant profusion—a truly beautiful location. However, the leaves of the door were shut tightly, and from inside one could hear a man chanting a poem:

> "I transcend the world and quietly nourish myself on the Penglai Isles,
> Where the fragrant wind does not stir and the pine blossoms are old.
> The immortal youths are not yet back from gathering medicinal herbs;
> White clouds cover the ground with no one to sweep them away."

When he finished this poem, Tuizhi heard him sing the following Daoist song to the tune "Wild Geese Descending":

> "Playing a game of deathless chess;
> Discussing a long-life scheme;
> Eating a pill of ageless elixir;
> Nourishing perfected primordial pneuma for a day;
> Hearing a wild monkey cry at one moment,
> Becoming enlightened to The Token for the Agreement of the Three
>   in the next;
> Traveling on a cloud all over the Five Lakes and Streams in just an
>   hour—
> Who understands the pursuits of divine immortals?

When I obtain my leisure,
I am content.
Alas, those who live to seventy are so few,
I laugh at the fleeting reputation sought after by many—where is it
*   now?*

"Just think: how long does a man's life last?
Yet people do not think of escaping from the fiery pit.
Every day they labor and toil,
And for no good reason strive for fame and profit.
They never let go of their abacus and stop calculating and scheming.
When one day their original yang is all used up,
And impermanence is about to arrive,
They have no more tricks left.
All of this does not equal grasping an early opportunity for cultivation.
Cultivation takes precedence over everything."

Tuizhi twice knocked lightly on the door, but it seemed that the man inside did not hear it. Tuizhi again knocked twice, and finally a voice inside asked, "Who is knocking? What's your business here?"

"I am Han Yu and I am an acquaintance of yours, Master," Tuizhi said.

"This is a place where I cultivate myself and deal with the Dao, a place with no concern for honor or shame, right or wrong. When did I ever make your acquaintance?" the voice replied.

"I have come to be your disciple, Master," said Tuizhi.

"You are a heroic scholar who offended the emperor and was banished. Here is not the place for you to hide," the voice said.

Tuizhi thought to himself, "If he quietly nourishes his nature in the seclusion of the deep mountains, how does he know that I am a banished official? He truly is an immortal."

Then he sighed and knocked again. "I have come a long way. If you aren't willing to open the door and let me stay, I'll bash my head against the door until I die right in front of you. Won't that harm your merit, Master?"

"Tell me, who directed you here?" the voice inside asked.

"It was your friend and my nephew Han Xiangzi who told me to come see you," Tuizhi answered.

"If it was Han Xiangzi, surely he gave you a letter for me."

"I have Xiangzi's letter here," Tuizhi answered.

"In that case, open the door and let him in," the voice said.

When a young Daoist opened the door, instead of creaking its hinges the door emitted a sound like singing simurghs and phoenixes. The inside of the hermitage was clean and expensively appointed, a rival to the jade chambers of celestial palaces. In the middle sat a perfected man, dressed in clothes made of feathers and wearing a bamboo hat and straw sandals. His hair was violet and his face youthful, his skin like ice and snow. He seemed to have the gentle modesty of a recluse scholar. The Daoist youth standing at his side also had a refined air, without the least hint of roughness.

Tuizhi prostrated himself before the perfected man and said, "Master, save me!"

"Why did Han Xiangzi send you here?" the perfected man asked.

"My nephew said that father and son do not transmit the methods from mind to mind, and uncle and nephew find it difficult to transmit the Dao to each other. Therefore he sent me to request that you, Master, may transmit to me the marvelous formulae of the utmost Dao. I am willing to cut firewood and draw water at your hermitage, to serve you and work hard. In return, I only hope for your compassion."

"When you were an official at court, you ate mutton and lamb and drank fine wine," the perfected man said. "Wherever you went, a large crowd followed. Here on this mountain I have nothing but thin rice and yellow leeks. It is so lonely, you have only your shadow for company. I fear that you are unable to endure such solitude."

"Do not worry, master, I can bear it," Tuizhi said.

"In that case, boy, take him to his temporary quarters in the rear of the hermitage. Every day send him to the temple on the mountain out front to sweep the floor and burn incense."

"Thank you, Master, for letting me stay," Tuizhi said. Then the youth led Tuizhi to the kitchen to eat a snack.

When Tuizhi followed him into the kitchen, the boy gave him a bowl of food. Tuizhi ate a mouthful only to find that its taste was almost unbearably bitter, and he had to force himself to finish it. Truly,

> When the mind is at peace, even a thatched hut is stable and secure;
> When the nature is settled, even vegetable roots are fragrant.
> As one penetrates the subtle mysteries,
> One finds intense flavor in the middle of blandness.

Arduous cultivation leads Tuizhi to an awakening.

For now let us talk no more of Tuizhi burning incense and sweeping the floor at the Zhuowei Hermitage, but instead speak of Mme. Dou and Luying, who at that time were at home thinking of Tuizhi.

After his departure there had been no news of him. They knew that the weather had been cold all along the way and his sufferings and labors must have been many, but they did not know at what time he had arrived in Chaozhou to assume his post. They were just about to send someone to the news office to ask for information when Han Qing strode in, his face covered in tears. "Mother, Sister-in-law, have you heard? Today a messenger from Chaozhou submitted a memorial reporting that Father died of illness in his office."

On hearing this news Mme. Dou and Luying burst into tears and hugged each other.

Scholar Lin stepped in from outside and said, "Indeed, Tuizhi has passed away. However, those who are dead cannot come back to life again, and so tears are of no benefit. Please do not vex yourself, Mme. Dou, but take care of your health. You should look after the preparations for the burial."

"Did it say in the memorial what disease he died of?" Mme. Dou asked.

"It said that his prefecture had long suffered from a crocodile that churned up wind and waves and devoured people. The previous magistrates had no way of controlling it. A few days after assuming office, Lord Han sacrificed to Heaven, asking that the crocodile be driven away. Thereupon the monster vanished far away into the ocean, the prefecture was at peace, and its people were content with their lot. The people of Chaozhou erected a shrine in the magistrate's honor, where they performed sacrifices for his praise. One night he died unexpectedly and without a sign of illness; I believe he probably returned to Heaven," Lin reported.

"I was hoping that he would receive a pardon and return home, so that we could grow old together," Mme. Dou said. "Who could have known that we would have to abandon each other so soon? Our family has no male descendants and the sacrifices to the ancestors will be cut off. What can be done about this sorrow? I probably won't be in this world much longer. Your daughter is so young, and it would be useless to stand in her way. It would be better for all concerned if you used the time while I am still here to find a good family to which to give your daughter in marriage."

"Why are you saying this?" Lin replied. "This decision is not mine, but is completely up to my daughter."

In tears, Luying said, "Mother-in-law, don't worry any longer. Although my father-in-law has passed away, my father is still an official, and we won't lack food or clothes. I wish to serve you until you pass away, to requite your great kindness in having raised Xiangzi. Do not bring the issue of remarriage up again. If my father did not let me make this decision, I would throw myself down the stairs and kill myself to give expression to the purity of my heart."

"Daughter-in-law, your knowledge in these matters is not complete," Mme. Dou said. "You are still young and without children. For whom do you maintain your chastity? When your father-in-law was alive, we still had hopes of bringing your husband back so that you could give birth to sons and daughters, who would continue the family line and look after you until your death. Now your father-in-law has died far from home, we have no word from Xiangzi, and I will soon be gone as well; there is no point in you continuing to maintain your widowhood. It's better to use the time while I am still here to have your father find a good family and settle you securely. I don't think Han Qing is the kind of person who would look after you for the rest of your life. If discord should later develop between you and him, you will be ridiculed by others. Have you given careful thought to this?"

"Mother-in-law, you are in your dotage and your words are all confused," Luying said. "As long as I follow you, why should I be unable to pass my days? Furthermore, in a few years I will already be too old for any remarriage."

"You are so young," Mme. Dou said. "Why do you say you'll be too old?"

"Don't worry so much, Mother-in-law. As long as you are alive, I will stay with you. After your demise I'll return to my father's house and keep the mourning period. I will definitely not have your or my father-in-law's reputation be affected in any way."

"My daughter's words are right," Scholar Lin said. "Please compose yourself and take care of the burial. Let me submit a memorial at court that your husband's title be restored and you be given his salary to take care of your material needs for the remainder of your life. Then we can deliberate further."

"Many thanks for your efforts. I shall be grateful even in death," Mme. Dou said. Then Scholar Lin rose and took his leave.

Mme. Dou ordered Han Qing to erect the pole for recalling the soul and to set up a soul tablet in which to install Tuizhi's spirit. All the death and mourning rituals were performed at their proper time. However, whenever Mme. Dou thought of Tuizhi, Xiangzi would come to her mind as well, and she was deeply unhappy day and night. One day she called Han Qing and said, "Since your father died, you've been sitting around at home all day and have given no attention to outside affairs. Why is that?"

"You gave me an order, and I don't dare disobey it. Didn't you command me not to do mischief and incur trouble?" Han Qing said.

"Of course your father is dead, but there is still hope for your elder brother Xiangzi," Mme. Dou said. "Why don't you go out into the street and inquire after some reliable news of him?"

"I went often to ask around, and Scholar Lin also sent people to make enquiries everywhere, but nobody knew of my brother's whereabouts. Therefore I did not dare upset you," Han Qing said.

"You needn't bother to go far to make enquiries. Just stand by the door and watch the people passing by," Mme. Dou said. "If you see a person of extraordinary appearance, it is bound to be an itinerant ascetic who knows a lot of people. It shouldn't be much trouble for you to stop such a person and question him."

Resentfully, Han Qing obeyed Mme. Dou's order and took up position outside the door to look out for a man of extraordinary appearance and question him. However, he saw traders, merchants, carriers, physicians, fortune-tellers, physiognomists, and nuns walking past, but not a single man of unusual appearance.

After standing about for a long time, he was just going to turn around and head back inside when he finally saw two Daoists. Dressed in torn robes and holding fisher drum and clapper in their hands, they came along slowly with a swaying gait. They were Lan Caihe and Han Xiangzi in disguise and were singing this song to the tune "Bushilu":

> "We laugh merrily in joy
> As we descend for a while from Heaven on our cloud
> To travel all over the ocean islands.
> See, in the goblet there is wine,
> And in the box are piled rich meats.
> Now that we have come to Chang'an for a stroll,
> The person we deliver must have much merit."

Han Qing thought to himself, "The appearance of these two Daoists is extraordinary; they certainly are wandering ascetics. I'll ask them about my brother. They'll know his whereabouts for sure." So he called to them, "Daoists, come here!"

"What do you want from us?" they said.

"My mistress wants to ask you something," Han Qing said.

The two followed Han Qing into the main hall to be received by Mme. Dou.

"Where do you two hail from?" she asked. "Where do you live?"

"We live at the Gate of Southern Heaven, and have come from the Zhongnan Mountains," Lan Caihe said.

"Years ago there were two Daoists who said they came from the Zhongnan

Mountains," Mme. Dou said. "They lured my nephew away to cultivate himself, and to this day he hasn't returned. Later, on my husband's birthday, there was yet another Daoist who said he had come from the Zhongnan Mountains. Day after day he practiced many deceitful tricks, but could not cajole my husband into doing his bidding. Later my husband offended the emperor with a memorial against the Buddha bone and was banished to Chaozhou, from where he never returned. Now you two also say that you come from the Zhongnan Mountains. With so many people hidden away in these mountains, perhaps you are frauds just like the earlier ones."

"Those who came previously may perhaps have been false, but the two of us really do come from there," Xiangzi said. "We would never utter a lie."

"As I see it, these Zhongnan Mountains are not a dwelling place of scholars who cherish the Dao and affiliate with the School of Mystery, or of men who refine their essence and ingest the drugs of immortality," Mme. Dou said. "Instead they are a den of frauds and kidnappers."

"Madame, don't mistake us for what we are not," Lan Caihe said. "The Zhongnan Mountains are a place where all noise is stilled and the dust of the world is washed off. If one has not inherited the bones of the Dao and the demeanor of an immortal from a previous existence, the tigers, leopards, and wolves won't let one walk on the mountain paths. Why do you say things fit to cast you into hell?"

"It's not that I don't believe in divine immortals," Mme. Dou said. "It's just that I've been cheated so badly by these false immortals. Since you are traveling from place to place, you must know the saying, 'Once bitten by a snake, for three years one fears withered grass.'"

"Whether you believe or not is up to you," Xiangzi said. "May I ask why your face is so haggard with worry and your hair all white as snow? Is it that you are worried because of your husband's death?"

"On Scholar Lin's recommendation, I fortunately received the court's kindness and will be given my husband's salary every year, so there's nothing to be worried about," Mme. Dou said. "It's just that my nephew Xiangzi has been away for so long, and I think of him night and day. That's why my spirit is weakened and my hair is white."

Xiangzi said to himself, "If my aunt yearns for me so much, I should requite her kindness." And aloud, "You have suffered so much because of Xiangzi's failure to return that you have become lonely, haggard, and fearful. But Xiangzi didn't know of this and did not think of you at all. I have the good fortune of belonging to the same school of Daoism as Xiangzi. What would you say if I healed you on his behalf and thus spared him a sin?"

"What drug is there that could heal me?" Mme. Dou asked.

"The recipe has been brought across the ocean," Xiangzi said. "The drug has been refined in the Dragon Palace. I guarantee that once you swallow it, your withered face will regain its healthy appearance and your white hair will turn black again."

"If you really have an extraordinary recipe from across the ocean, a marvelous drug made of numinous elixir, I will reward you richly," Mme. Dou said.

Then Xiangzi let a pill of rejuvenation elixir roll from his gourd, and handed it to Mme. Dou. She swallowed it, and forthwith her spirits strengthened and she was rejuvenated so that no illness or pain remained anywhere in her body.

Mme. Dou was overjoyed and ordered Plum Fragrance to give silver to the two Daoists to express her gratitude. Xiangzi said, "I don't want a reward. I only wish that you may follow me and cultivate yourself."

"When my husband was still alive, a Daoist once came to deliver him and make him leave the family, but my husband wouldn't believe him," Mme. Dou said. "Now you want to deliver me, and I don't believe you, either."

"Do you still remember what this Daoist looked like?" Xiangzi asked.

"No, I don't."

"I am not deceiving you when I say that it was I who came at that time," he told her.

"These vagrants are experts in deceitful talk," Mme. Dou said. "It is truly detestable. Tell me what present you brought my husband on his birthday. If you get it right, I'll believe that you are a divine immortal."

"In that year the lord Han, together with Scholar Lin, was praying for snow at the Southern Altar. It was only after I sold him snow that he was promoted to Minister of Rites, with a concurrent appointment to the Ministry of Justice. He received permission to absent himself from court for five days. At his birthday celebration I presented him with an immortal goat, an immortal crane, immortal maidens, and forty immortals' dishes. I also created immediate wine and instantaneous flowers, on whose petals was written, 'Clouds straddle the mountains of Qin—where is my home? Snows crowd the pass at Blue Pass—my horse will not move.' Do you remember this?"

"I remember all of it, but my husband didn't believe any of it," Mme. Dou said.

"Although the lord Han did not believe it, later when he was banished to

Chaozhou, he wanted to see me and could not, and was filled with remorse," Xiangzi said.

"Who saw him be remorseful? What you are saying is unsupported by any evidence. I do not believe you," said Mme. Dou.

"If you don't believe me, I am afraid your regrets will come too late."

"Why are you saying these inauspicious words again?" Mme. Dou said. "Let me ask you: Where does your family hail from? What sort of people are your parents? Why did you ascend the Zhongnan Mountains to study the Dao? What is the area of these Zhongnan Mountains? How many people are engaged in cultivation there? Is Han Xiangzi among them or not? You tell me everything from the beginning, and do so honestly. If you conceal anything, I shall have you dealt with by the authorities according to the law."

"My home is in Changli County, west of Drum Tower Alley," Xiangzi said. "My ancestral home is situated in the north and faces south. My father's name is Han Hui, my mother's Mme. Zheng. My uncle is called Han Yu, my aunt Mme. Dou. When I was young, I lost my parents and was raised by my uncle and aunt. I married Miss Luying, a daughter of the Lin family. My uncle was banished to Chaozhou. On the road he suffered many hardships. I have already delivered him to complete perfection, fulfill the Dao, and become an immortal of Great Veil Heaven. Today I have come especially to deliver you."

"If you are my nephew, why do you look so different?"

"Immortals and mortals are different and their principles are not the same."

"If you are Xiangzi, manifest your original body so I can see it," Mme. Dou said.

"There is no problem in manifesting my original body, but I fear that you will cling to illusions and not awaken!" Xiangzi said. Indeed,

> You keep looking out, hoping for your child's return,
> But parents and children go their separate ways.
> Only after the snow has melted on the peaks can the road be seen,
> But the clouds drifting over the green pines hide the mountain.

Then Xiangzi shook himself once and, really, he returned to his old appearance.

Mme. Dou took hold of him and said, "My son, where have you been, that you return home only today? Your uncle has passed away, and things have been so difficult at home that I thought of you day and night. Your return today is a great joy. From now on, comply with the family rules as you did at first, and become a good man. Speak no more of leaving the family!"

"I have now returned with my master Lü to deliver a person with the right karmic affinity," Xiangzi said. "How could I hanker after the vain world of family life, following a calling that would get me nowhere?"

"Immortal Brother, you should stay at home for a while," Lan Caihe said. "In the meantime I'll go back to the Gate of Southern Heaven, and later return to the Zhongnan Mountains with you."

"My son, your elder companion, too, is telling you to stay at home," Mme. Dou said. "Why don't you listen to him?"

Xiangzi took his leave from Lan Caihe and then said, "I haven't been back for many years. Is that garden house on Sleeping Tiger Mountain still in good order? I'd like to go and have a look at it."

"Han Qing, take your brother there so he can have a look," Mme. Dou said.

Han Qing led Xiangzi to the House of the Nine Palaces and Eight Trigrams on Sleeping Tiger Mountain. After Tuizhi's death, Han Qing had changed all the paths, so that they had to walk around many bends and corners before they arrived.

When Xiangzi looked up he saw that, though the paths were different, the house was unchanged. However, the benches and beds were all covered in dust, and the many books on the tables were piled in chaotic heaps. Everything was in a very disorderly condition. Of the good fruit trees around the mountain, half had withered, and only the grass grew luxuriantly, so high that a person lying in it would be quite hidden. Xiangzi said to himself, "When Uncle was an official, there was not a day when he didn't send people here to sweep the dust and cut back the brushwood and grass. In the short time since his death, such a beautiful world has been brought to this state. My aunt's desire for splendor truly is futile."

Then he said to Han Qing, "You go back inside. I will stay here."

"Brother, you haven't been back for so long; today you should spend the night in your wife's room," Han Qing said. "Why do you want to stay here all by yourself?"

"This is my decision," Xiangzi said. "Don't concern yourself with me."

As he was told, Han Qing went to Mme. Dou's room and explained to her that Xiangzi wanted to stay in the garden house. Mme. Dou quickly told the kitchen staff to prepare wine and fine foods and bring them to the garden house for Xiangzi to eat. She also ordered Han Qing, "Wait until your brother has drunk the wine and then take him to his wife's room to spend the night there."

"Mother-in-law, that won't do," Luying said. "The Daoist who once came to see my father-in-law also said he was Xiangzi, and spent two dissolute days here before disappearing again. Can you tell for sure whether this Daoist today is true or false, that he is to be taken to my room?"

"You're right. There are many in this world who can do magic tricks. It's hard to tell what to believe," Mme. Dou said. "Han Qing, go and spend the night in his company. Tomorrow we shall make further plans." And of course Han Qing did as he was told and went to keep Xiangzi company in the garden house.

> *I know that he is not my companion,*
> *Yet today I followed him.*

If you don't know what happened later, please listen to the next chapter.

24

RETURNING HOME, HAN XIANG MANIFESTS HIS
TRANSFORMATIVE POWERS

SHOOTING A PARROT, MME. DOU REMAINS ATTACHED
TO HER ILLUSIONS

Vast the sea of suffering;
Terrifying its stormy waves.
The future consists only of nets cast by greed and ire,
And snares set by lust and malice.
Who can turn around and jump out of the pit of right and wrong,
Becoming a leisurely, carefree, and ever-young matron?

At the third watch a fresh breeze wafted through the garden house and Xiangzi vanished. Reader, shall I say where Xiangzi went at that time?

He went to see Master Zhong and then proceeded with him to an audience with the Jade Emperor, where he submitted the following memorandum:

> Thanks to Your Majesty's grace, my uncle, Han Yu, has already had a change of mind. However, my aunt, Mme. Dou, and my wife, Lin Luying, still cling to their delusions and are difficult to deliver. Obediently I await Your Majesty's decision.

A golden lad transmitted the following decree of the Jade Emperor:

> Mme. Dou was originally a Venerable Dame of the Upper Realm who was banished to undergo suffering in the ordinary world

because she stole a sunflower at the Immortality Peach Banquet. Luy-ing was originally a jade maiden at the Empyrean Palace. Once, when the Dark Emperor dispatched celestial generals to vanquish demons, she stole a peek at the world below before the Gate of Heaven was closed again. Therefore she was banished to the common world, there to sleep alone, without a husband, so as to warn her and others against hankering after the mortal world. Together with Lü Dongbin and Lan Caihe, Han Xiang may make another attempt at delivering these two so that together they may complete their proper rewards.

Xiangzi said his thanks and then went on to an audience with the Queen Mother of the West. She said, "I am glad that Chonghezi has awakened to his previous existence. He will soon resume his former position. However, the Venerable Dame and the Jade Maiden are still on the path of confusion. Who will go once more to deliver them?"

"The Jade Emperor is sending me, together with Lü Dongbin and Lan Caihe, to make another attempt at delivering them. What advice can you give me?" Xiangzi said.

The Queen Mother of the West said, "As these two have been sunk in the world of dust for a long time already, their hearts are filled with greed for splendor, wealth, and honor. You must go to the Mahasattva Guanyin at Mount Putuo and borrow from her some objects used in effecting magical transformations. Only then will you be able to move them."

"The Mahasattva Guanyin is a Buddhist worthy and as such does not agree with our Daoist School," Xiangzi said. "Why should she be willing to lend us such devices?"

"Guanyin's sole concern is to bring order to the world and save people," said the Queen Mother of the West. "Why would she make distinctions between schools in this endeavor?"

"I shall carefully follow your orders," Xiangzi said. He took his leave of the Queen Mother and departed the jasper terraces and purple palaces of Heaven. With his two companions he rode on a cloud to the Southern Sea for an audience with Guan-yin. Having obtained a parrot from her, they left right away for Chang'an. And so,

> Having just left the golden palaces to roam the South Sea,
> They arrive in Chang'an the same day to spend the night.

Let us now recount how the next morning Han Qing came hurrying in to report, "It's my fault for not paying better attention! When my elder brother stayed in the garden house, nothing was wrong at the first watch, and everything was quiet in the second watch. But at the third watch, as the bright moon was in the sky, suddenly a fresh breeze passed through and my elder brother vanished."

"Such strange events prove that it was a divine immortal who had descended from Heaven," Luying said. "It wasn't Xiangzi who had returned home."

"If it were a divine immortal, his actions would be serious and responsible," Mme. Dou said. "He wouldn't engage in such frivolous trickery. This definitely was one of those vagrant Daoists who play tricks on people to cheat them out of their money. He will certainly come again today. We must steel ourselves and not believe him. Whatever he says, be it that Lü Dongbin is coming or that Xiangzi is returning—we'll have nothing to do with this person. Let's ignore him."

"Mother-in-law, you are absolutely right," Luying said.

At that moment, they heard the fisher drum again beyond the side wall. "Han Qing, quickly call my child in," Mme. Dou said.

"You just said that those Daoists are all tricksters and that we should ignore them," Han Qing pointed out. "Why have you changed your mind?"

"It may seem that I contradict myself in one breath, but when I heard the fisher drum, the thought of Xiangzi pained my heart," Mme. Dou said. "Quickly, go bring him in. I want to speak to him."

"It's yesterday's Daoist," Han Qing reported. "He's sitting in front of the gate striking his drum."

"Perhaps he is Xiangzi after all," Mme. Dou said. "Call him in and I will question him."

Han Qing walked out of the great gate and called the Daoist. The latter followed him in and, on seeing Mme. Dou, said, "Aunt, I knock my head."

"My child, when you see me, you should just follow the rules of courtesy appropriate within the family," Mme. Dou said. "Why do you speak of knocking your head?"

"I dwell beyond the Islands of the Immortals and thus do not fall under the usual rules of propriety."

"Why do you always strike the fisher drum?" Mme. Dou asked.

"Because the people of the world are thick-skinned and unwilling to change their ways, I have no choice but to tie that thick skin onto a bamboo tube, which is called a 'drum of stupidity.'[1] Intelligent people are awakened when they hear this drum. Stupid people, on the other hand, won't change their ways, even if you beat the drum a thousand, nay, ten thousand times, until this thick skin rips apart. All the same I keep drumming and singing my Daoist songs to get those stupid people to jump out of this world of dust and noise."

"My son, when you rested in the garden house yesterday, why did you leave in the middle of the night and return only now?" Mme. Dou asked.

"I went to the Gate of Southern Heaven to have a word with my master Zhong," Xiangzi explained. "That's why I'm only here now."

"How far is it from here to the Gate of Southern Heaven?"

"It's 108,000 miles each way," Xiangzi replied.

"If it's that far, how come you are already back, having only left at midnight?" Mme. Dou asked.

"After meeting with Master Zhong, I also went to visit the Mahasattva Guanyin on Mount Putuo in the Southern Sea," Xiangzi explained.

"How far is it from here to Mount Putuo in the Southern Sea?"

"Much closer."

"How many miles?"

"Only a little more than 84,700 miles."

"To travel to both of these places and back would take a year, even if you could fly," she said. "How could you have returned so quickly?"

"I ride the clouds and mists and don't walk on the ground like ordinary people."

"Stop telling such lies," said Luying.

"On the Jade Emperor's orders I have come specifically to deliver you and make you leave the family," Xiangzi said. "How can you say I tell lies?"

"When my father-in-law was still alive, there was a fellow who kept pestering him, claiming to be a divine immortal come to deliver him," Luying said. "But later when he submitted his memorial and the emperor in his anger banished him to Chaozhou, no divine immortal showed himself."

"When at first I admonished Uncle to leave the family, he repeatedly refused to believe me," Xiangzi said. "It was only when, on the road at Blue Pass, his horse had died, he was all alone, and tigers and wolves blocked his path that he called to me in tears to save him. If it hadn't been for me, where would his bones be now? Instead he now enjoys a free and unfettered existence as Chonghezi in the immortals' palaces of Great Veil Heaven."

"Your uncle died in his office in Chaozhou," Mme. Dou said. "The local officials reported it to the throne—who doesn't know about this? Yet you tell wild stories about having delivered him to become Chonghezi and live happily in the celestial palaces."

"My uncle's death wasn't real, but merely staged with the immortals' marvelous method of release from the corpse."

"There is nothing and no one to corroborate your story and we won't take just your word for it," Luying said.

"Many magical objects were used to deliver your uncle, yet still he refused to believe," Mme. Dou said. "What have you brought now to deliver us?"

"Immortal goats, cranes, wine, and peaches you have all already seen, so I didn't bring them along to deliver you," Xiangzi answered. "Instead I made a point of borrowing a white parrot from the Mahasattva Guanyin to show to you."

"I have a green parrot with a red beak who can recite poems and chant the Buddha's name, but I have never seen a white one," Mme. Dou said. "Where is it?"

Xiangzi waved his hand, and a white parrot came flying in front of Mme. Dou. Here is a poem to describe it:

> Hiding in the snow, flying in the snow,
> A maid in a snowy robe surpasses one clad in gold.
> Every sound in the snow calls out "prajna,"[2]
> Establishing a snowy refuge for this School of Compassion.

"What is special about this parrot?" asked Mme. Dou.

"He can fly, sing, dance, and chant."

"Let him sing me a song," she said.

"Parrot, what are you waiting for? Sing!" commanded Xiangzi.

Flying and dancing in circles, the parrot sang to the tune "Heard in the Stable":

> "Of parrots there are many,
> But among them there is none that can equal me.
> I have flown from the Southern Sea
> To admonish you to a change of heart,
> But you still covet laughter and song.
> I am just afraid
> That impermanence will come,
> And though you may possess countless pearls,
> You will find it difficult to avoid.
> If you don't turn back,
> You will suffer for it.
> Even if you were a brave hero,
> You'd have to imitate Han Yu, who suffered hunger and thirst at the
>   Qin River."

"A lot of rubbish," Mme. Dou said. "Pay no attention to him." She ordered a servant to fetch a bow and arrow and had the parrot shot dead.

"If you don't believe, that's up to you," Xiangzi said. "I just fear that when the time of suffering arrives, any regrets will come too late."

"In ancient times it was said that 'it is dangerous to be a high official—it is like sleeping beside a tiger,'" Mme. Dou remarked. "It is because your uncle was an official at court that he suffered adversity. We women don't go out and concern ourselves with public affairs. Thanks to the court, we receive a monthly stipend which allows us to enjoy a peaceful and honorable life. What suffering should there be? What regrets do you speak of?"

"When your emoluments are used up and your horses have fallen down, not even your nephew will come," Xiangzi said.

"Where are you going?" Mme. Dou asked.

"Aunt, you still don't understand: I shall return to the Zhongnan Mountains."

"If you don't want to remain at home, then go wherever you want and don't bother us by your babbling."

"I have told you over and over, yet you won't change your mind," Xiangzi said. "Having wasted all this effort, I shall now rest and make further plans." Whereupon he strode out the door with his head held high. Alas,

> This morning you would not believe a divine immortal's words;
> When later you have regrets, to meet me again will be difficult.

"Clearly this was a Daoist who had assumed my elder brother's appearance," Han Qing said. "He came here to stir up trouble for two days and now he has left again. It's hard to know what to make of this."

"Don't talk so much. Just let him go," Mme. Dou said.

"You're absolutely right, Mother-in-law," Luying said. "Let's not argue with him any longer." They both returned to their rooms right away. An ancient poem shall serve as illustration:

> To take leave from him is easy, to meet him again hard.
> Resentfully she enters her chambers, her fingers plucking a tired tune.
> On the terrace of the twelve-storied tower she spends spring in
>   solitude;
> Behind the crystal curtains, she fears the cold loneliness of this season.

Let's not talk any longer of Mme. Dou and Luying returning to their chambers, but tell instead how Xiangzi turned back to meet Master Lü. He said to him, "Master, Han Xiang knocks his head."

Shooting a parrot, Mme. Dou remains attached to her illusions.

"How is your deliverance of Mme. Dou coming along?" Master Lü asked.

"I went to deliver my aunt, but she wouldn't change her mind," Xiangzi replied. "What can be done?"

"What did you use to convert her?"

"I borrowed a white parrot from the Mahasattva Guanyin at Mount Putuo in the Southern Sea, but my aunt is too attached to the splendors of this world and won't concern herself with the ultimate matters of life and death."

"Tomorrow Mme. Dou and Luying are holding a banquet at the Chrysanthemum Pavilion," Master Lü said. "We'll invite the immortal Lan to accompany us there and give it another try. Let's see how it goes."

"Many thanks, Master," Xiangzi said.

Then the three divine immortals gathered some clouds together and descended into the world of dust. Having manifested their yang bodies and arrived in the city of Chang'an, they saw two old men playing chess by the window of a high building. When one of them made a wrong move and wanted to retract it, the other would not let him, and so they argued until their faces were all red and puffed up. One of the two was surnamed Wo; he was the grandfather of Chang'an's well-known nouveau riche Wo Duicang. The other was surnamed Quan; he was the father of Quan Yunfeng, another well-known character in Chang'an.

As the two were arguing over the chess move, Xiangzi said to Master Lü, "Master, to win a single chess move, neither of these two is willing to give in. We should teach these two greedy fellows how to admit defeat graciously. Would you like to go and arbitrate between them?"

Master Lü gave them a look and then said, "These two old fellows have potential. We could use their chess talents in the Palace of Supreme Purity. I'll convert them, so our journey won't have been in vain."

Then the three Daoists lined up below the window and called, "Venerable benefactors, what chess move are you playing?"

"There is no almsgiving in chess," one of the old men replied. "What do you want?"

"We haven't come to beg for alms," Master Lü said. "My disciple's chess skills are very good, but he hasn't dared to play since he left his family. When he saw you two benefactors playing today, his old habit reasserted itself, and so he's here specifically to ask your instruction."

"We're completely at loggerheads over the retraction of one move," said one of the old men. "If you want, you may play a game with me, Master, but there will be no retracting of moves."

"Which move are you arguing about?" Master Lü asked.

"I moved this horse to take his chariot. He didn't notice it and moved another horse. If my horse takes the chariot, I need only one more move to beat him. Therefore he wanted to retract his move."

"It would useless to take his chariot, as it would only give you a draw. Why would you necessarily be the winner?" Xiangzi said.

"You come play!" the old man said. "If you can bring about a draw, I'll spend a tenth of an ounce of silver to buy the three of you a vegetarian meal."

"If I succeed in a draw, I don't want you to buy us a meal with your silver. Instead, I want you to carry this gourd and shoulder this flower basket and leave the family with me," Xiangzi said.

"Aren't you afraid to give offense? You're so young, yet you want an old man like me to become your disciple. Aren't you rather overdoing it?" one of the old men said.

"Patriarch Peng, who lived to the ripe age of 800, would still have to yield to me before sitting down himself. You're no more than seventy or eighty—how could that count as old?" Xiangzi said.

"I won't argue with you about age," the old man said. "If you can really play to a draw, I am willing to become your disciple and serve you."

"Once a word is out, a team of four horses cannot catch up with it. You must not go back on your word when the time comes," said Xiangzi.

"A man's mouth speaks a man's words," the old man said. "This is not an animal's mouth spitting out a man's words. I won't go back on what I said!"

Xiangzi then let the old man take the chariot and countered him move for move. After more than ten moves the game ended in a draw. The old man said, "I think you three are divine immortals. I willingly become your disciple and follow you as my masters."

"If you can follow divine immortals, surely I can do the same," the other old man chimed in. "As of now I shall carry the gourd and shoulder the flower basket. Let us leave the family together." Having said this, the two old men went with Master Lü, the immortal Lan, and Han Xiangzi to the gate of the Han family's mansion. They sat down, beat their fisher drums, and sang Daoist songs, making a stir among the crowd in the street.

When the Han family's gatekeeper saw Old Wo carrying a gourd, he grabbed him and said, "Old greatgrandpa, you used to spend your days happily playing chess and drinking wine. Why are you carrying the gourd for this vagrant Daoist today? Is this your idea of fun? A saying goes, 'If in youth you don't run wild, you won't be stiff in old age.' You certainly know how to enjoy yourself, old man!"

An onlooker got hold of Old Quan and asked him, "You're a rich man of city-wide reputation. Why don't you show more dignity than to shoulder a flower basket for a vagrant Daoist? I think your sons and grandsons must be unfilial, so that you have gone mad and come to act in this way."

"I am not mad," Old Quan said. "What is there to be unhappy about if I follow a divine immortal?"

The onlookers laughed and said, "Divine immortal!—you're exchanging your gold for moldy bricks."

When the people in the street heard this, they broke out in laughter. Old Wo and Old Quan just let them laugh, acting as if they did not hear them.

The gatekeeper went to report to Mme. Dou, "Outside there are three young Daoists. Although they are not very old, they have managed to hoodwink the old grandfather of the wealthy Wo Duicang, as well as the old father of Quan Yunfeng, into becoming their disciples and carrying their flower basket and gourd for them. They are now outside your gate, beating the fisher drum and singing Daoist songs. They have attracted a great crowd, and I can't chase them away."

"Call the three Daoists in and let me ask them what songs they are singing," Mme. Dou said.

The gatekeeper called to the three Daoists, "Stop singing. The lady of the house wants to have a word with you." When the three rose and went with the gatekeeper, Old Wo and Old Quan followed them inside.

Mme. Dou and Luying were sitting in the Chrysanthemum Pavilion. The three Daoists approached and knocked their heads.

Mme. Dou bowed in return and then asked them, "Where do you come from?"

"I do not deceive you, my lady, when I say that we have come from the Palace of the Eight Luminaries in Great Veil Heaven," Master Lü said.

"This Daoist also claims he is a divine immortal," Mme. Dou said to Luying.

"I am no divine immortal, just an itinerant Daoist," Master Lü said.

"Are you three all of the same surname?" Mme. Dou asked.

"I am Master Two Mouths, this is Lan Caihe, and that is Han Xiangzi," Master Lü replied.

"There is a Han Xiangzi in our family who was lured away by two Daoists. To the present day we don't know where he is," Mme. Dou said.

"This Han Xiangzi here is my lady's nephew," Master Lü told her.

"His face has no resemblance whatsoever," Mme. Dou said. "The other day a Daoist came claiming he was my nephew. He stayed in our house for two days before leaving again. How can you say that this one is Han Xiangzi? Even if he really were Xiangzi, I wouldn't acknowledge him."

"Since he is my lady's nephew, why would you refuse to acknowledge him?"

"Why have you come here?" Mme. Dou asked.

"To deliver my lady so that she may leave the family," Master Lü replied.

"To deliver me? What are you holding in your hand?"

"It is a magical painting," said Master Lü.

Mme. Dou ordered an attendant to hang it up so that she could look at it. "It's nothing but a landscape painting," she said. "What's so special about it, that you call it magical? I have the works of many famous painters in my house, but am tired of looking at them."

"If my lady is tired of landscapes, I will change the painting to one of a blue bird and a white crane," Lan Caihe said. "Please take a look."

"Strange, indeed!" Mme. Dou said. "The picture has changed! However, I am not interested in paintings of blue birds and white cranes either."

With a wave of his hand Master Lü made the birds vanish and instead there appeared a picture of the Immortal of the Rotten Axe-handle. Master Lü said, "My venerable lady, once Master Wang went out to seek immortalhood, to refine the elixir and enter the Nine Heavens. He spent only seven days in the mountains, but on his return a thousand years had already passed in the world outside.[3] In front of the gate white mineral deposits had split the gilded well, and at the entrance of the grotto blue fungus covered what had been a field of white jade. Too bad that today as in the past people age easily, following the slivered moon down the great river.[4] Surely this is a good painting?"

"Perhaps, but I just don't want to look at it," Mme. Dou said.

"If I call down the Immortal of the Rotten Axe-handle to exhort you to leave the family, will my lady believe?" Master Lü asked.

"The Master of the Rotten Axe-handle lived several hundred years ago. From where is he supposed to come?" Mme. Dou said.

"From the painting." He called in a loud voice, "Wang Zhi, come down and admonish the lady Han to leave the family."

His voice had not yet died away when the Immortal of the Rotten Axe-handle stepped lightly down out of the picture, giving Mme. Dou and Luying such a scare that they were dumbstruck and their faces went ashen. Master Lü ordered, "Wang Zhi, kneel down, don't frighten the Sagely Mother."

With difficulty, Mme. Dou said, "Clearly this is trickery. There is no real Immortal of the Rotten Axe-handle. Han Qing, quickly chase them out. Don't let them bother us."

Wang Zhi began to sing a song to the tune "Goat on the Mountainside":

> *"Venerable lady, don't be impatient,*
> *Death will come soon enough.*
> *Though you may own ten thousand strings of cash,*
> *When the end comes they will provide no refuge for you.*
> *Who can compare with me, who knows no honor and no shame,*
> *But lives a carefree, unfettered life without hassles.*
> *Listen to my advice:*
> *Nothing is better than to cast off all luxuries.*
> *Suffering and worries!*
> *Alas, how can you reach eternal life in this world of dust?"*

"Half an empty phrase can destroy a lifetime's luck. You shouldn't speak in this way," Mme. Dou said.

"Wang Zhi, you may return to the grotto palace," Master Lü said. "Now I'll call down a golden lad and a jade maiden to admonish the lady to leave the family."

When Wang Zhi had returned into the painting, suddenly a golden lad and a jade maiden stood in front of Mme. Dou. Master Lü said, "Immortal Brother and Sister, take out your magical fruit and wine and sing a little song to exhort the venerable lady." And together the lad and the maid sang a song to the tune "Old Drunkard":

> *"We admonish you, our lady,*
> *Count your blessings!*
> *Splendor and luxury are like bubbles floating on water.*
> *Although you may enjoy monthly emoluments of a thousand bushels of*
>   *grain,*
> *Why don't you extract yourself from these attachments and turn your*
>   *back on the world?*
> *By turning back soon,*
> *You save your mind many troubles.*
> *If you don't understand when to advance and when to retreat,*
> *When the great floods come flowing in,*
> *Mother and children will be separated like north and south—truly, it*
>   *will be a great sorrow.*
> *When you meet a fierce tiger on the road, it is hard to walk on.*
> *If you do not cultivate yourself when we admonish you to,*
> *In vain will you beg the divine immortals when the time of regret comes."*

When they had finished, Master Lü said, "Immortal Brother and Sister, you may return to the grotto palace."

"The three of you are going to a lot of trouble to admonish me to leave the family," Mme. Dou said. "However, I am a woman, and there is no way I could follow a Daoist whom I don't know at all. Is there no guide I am well acquainted with?"

"Venerable lady, you are absolutely right," Master Lü said. "If you agree to leave the family, I will call upon Xiangzi to be your guide."

"Where is Xiangzi?" Mme. Dou asked.

"Right here in front of you," Master Lü said.

"If you can call him here, I shall be willing to leave the family," Mme. Dou said.

Master Lü pointed with his hand and said, "Immortal Brother, why aren't you showing your original appearance yet?"

Immediately the Daoist took on the exact appearance of Xiangzi. Mme. Dou said, "Do you think you can move me with your tricks?"

"What if I delivered another person to accompany you in leaving the family?" Xiangzi said.

"Who?" asked Mme. Dou.

Xiangzi then scraped some black dirt from his armpit, mixed it with some mucus and saliva, and molded it into a big pellet. Holding it on his palm, he called out, "If there is anyone with the right affinity who will eat this magical drug of mine, I will deliver him to become an immortal."

Old Wo hurried forward, took it, and swallowed it in one piece. Right away clouds lifted up his feet and he floated in mid-air.

Old Quan said, "Master, we both followed you together, why don't you deliver me by means of a pill like this?" Thereupon Master Lü also scraped some dirt from his armpit, rolled it into a pill, and gave it to Old Quan. Old Quan ate it as soon as he received it, and he too was lifted up by a cloud.

Lan Caihe also made a pill of black dirt and called out, "Those with the right affinity, come quickly, don't miss this opportunity." Suddenly a slave girl named Golden Lotus, Luying's personal attendant, dashed forth from behind a curtain, snatched the pill and swallowed it. The moment it went down, auspicious clouds surrounded her and like Old Wo and Old Quan she was lifted about ten feet off the ground.

Golden Lotus called in a loud voice, "Mme. Dou and Miss Luying, don't be angry with me. Having the good fortune to meet an immortal master, I have escaped the fiery pit, and need no longer be a servant." Then a breeze carried the three off into the clouds until they could no longer be seen.

Luying stepped forward and said, "Mother-in-law, if these Daoists are not divine immortals, how could Golden Lotus and the two old men rise to Heaven in broad daylight?"

"This is all black magic. Don't believe them," Mme. Dou said. "I remember when your father-in-law was still alive he often mentioned a certain Cloud Terrace Monastery which was located on a mountain. More than one hundred Daoists lived in this monastery. It was said that whenever five-colored clouds filled the mountain valleys, they were sent by Heaven to welcome immortals. Those among the Daoists in the monastery who didn't want to remain in this world then bathed, changed their clothes, and entered the five-colored clouds. When the clouds dissolved after a while, the Daoists were nowhere to be seen.

"This went on for several years, and people told each other about it. Eventually all who sought to ascend to immortalhood first prepared by means of fasting and bathing and then came to Cloud Terrace Monastery to await the emergence of the clouds so as to fly up on them.

"One day, an itinerant Daoist who was passing by this place saw a great crowd of people, noble and common, high and low, all bowing toward the sky. When he learned the reason for their behavior, he said, 'If becoming an immortal were that easy, there would be no space left in Heaven to accommodate so many immortals.' Right away he took up lodging in the monastery, intending to carefully observe with his own eyes the events on the day that the clouds emerged.

"After several days, he happened to be sitting in the main hall discussing Daoist doctrines with a priest named Wang when suddenly the monk on duty came to report that the many-colored cloud had emerged on the mountain. Master Wang immediately returned to his room, washed with hot water, and changed into fresh clothes. In the meantime the cloud had gathered outside his door. Master Wang slowly stepped into the cloud, which thereupon dispersed gradually.

"When the itinerant Daoist saw this scene, he said, 'This cloud is the breath of a poisonous monster. Alas, my ignorant fellow Daoist is already dead now.' Then he traced the Steps of Yu and uttered a wind and thunder spell. Suddenly thunder rolled and lightning flashed, and when it stopped again abruptly, the five-colored auspicious cloud had vanished without a trace.

"At the head of the monks the Daoist went to investigate the matter. When they crossed a mountain, they found Master Wang lying halfway down its slope. Quickly they had some men carry him back to the monastery. A few steps farther on, they came upon a venomous snake lying in a ravine, struck dead by lightning. It was as thick as a rice peck and several tens of feet long. In its lair was a high pile of bones, and countless hairpins and caps of the kind worn by Daoists. Now they understood that all those who had 'ascended to immortalhood' had in fact been devoured by this poisonous pneuma. As for the clouds we saw today, how do we know whether they are true or false? It is not impossible that these three Daoists are monsters who have transformed themselves. How could divine immortals appear in this world? Daughter-in-law, don't commit an error and fall into the snares of evil people."

"Mother-in-law, your words make sense," Luying said. "I won't believe in them either."

"You made a promise—why are you retracting it now?" Master Lü said.

When Xiangzi saw that Mme. Dou was not going to acknowledge him, he said, "Aunt, you are old, Uncle is not here anymore, and there is no blood descendant to continue the family line. Why do you remain attached to the family and refuse to turn back and change your mind?"

"Although your uncle is dead," Mme. Dou said, "the court still grants me a monthly emolument, and I still have servants to direct as before. I have nothing to be dissatisfied with—what reason would I have to abandon all this and leave the family?"

"Venerable lady, although you live well at the moment, I am afraid that your fate will take a turn for the worse and you will suffer many setbacks," Master Lü said. "Then dissatisfaction will quite naturally set in. I have a poem that I would ask you to listen to, my lady:

"When your destiny is troubled and the times are difficult, do not sigh;
Then the scenery of Chang'an is suddenly not so praiseworthy anymore.
With the ancestral property washed away, there is no refuge for you;
Then you will realize that your earlier views were mistaken."

"The next person to utter such unlucky words shall receive twenty blows with the stick!" Mme. Dou said.

"Mother-in-law, if you are afraid of unlucky words, why don't you leave the family with me?" Xiangzi said.

"Your ancestors must have neglected to collect merit, that they gave birth to one like you," said Mme. Dou. "How could you be my nephew? Get out, now! If you can only talk nonsense here, I'll lodge a complaint with the office of the Ministry of Rites and memorialize the court to eradicate all Daoist establishments in the empire, so that the likes of you have no roof over your heads while alive, and no place to be buried when you're dead."

Master Lü laughed and said, "Xiangzi, Caihe, let's leave quickly, so as not to implicate others and bring the people's curses upon us."

"Such stubborn attachment to confusion—our journey was in vain," Caihe said. The three then gracefully walked out the door. Truly,

> *The road of the divine immortals clearly was close at hand,*
> *Yet hapless and stupid people would not turn around.*

What happened afterward? Listen to the explanations in the next chapter.

25

MASTER LÜ SENDS A DREAM TO THE CUI FAMILY

MOTHER ZHANG TWO MAKES A MARRIAGE PROPOSAL

AT THE HAN MANSION

The affairs of the world are confused like a dream,
A yellow millet dream from which we have not yet awakened.
In the dream we at first say it is a dream,
Then after awakening it all turns out to be false.
The dream of existence is still a dream,
And because it is a dream it does not fulfill itself.
Being and non-being are both dreams,
Spring dreams that are new and fresh only once.

When Master Lü and his two companions had left the Han mansion, they hesitated over what to do next. Then Xiangzi said, "Master, Brother, since my aunt won't change her mind, we should hand back the Jade Emperor's commission, and then think about other alternatives."

"No, the Jade Emperor sent the three of us to go together and deliver them so that they may transcend the ordinary world and enter the sacred realm," Caihe said. "If they refuse to change their minds, we must find other ways to convert them. If we hand back the commission, the Jade Emperor will be furious, and things will get uncomfortable for us."

"From my cloud I saw in Chang'an Cui Shicun, the son of the minister Cui Qun," Master Lü said. "He married the daughter of the viceminister Hu, but she passed away recently, and now he wants to remarry. It might be a good idea to send Minister Cui a dream that tells him to ask for Luying as a second wife for his son Shicun. Mme. Dou will never permit it, and Minister Cui will angrily memorialize the court to annul her emoluments and send her back to her native district. In the meantime you and I will order the Dragon King of the Eastern Sea to raise storms and waves and destroy in a flood the Han family's mansions and fields. When Mme. Dou and Luying find themselves destitute, it will be a good time to deliver them."

"An excellent plan!" said Xiangzi. "If I may trouble you, Master, to go to the Cui household and send the dream, and Master Lan to report to Master Zhong in the Zhongnan Mountains, then I myself shall make the trip to the Dragon King of the Eastern Sea." The three immortals forthwith set off for their respective destinations.

But no more about this for now. Instead let me speak of the minister Cui Qun, who indeed had a dream that night. In the morning he said to his wife, "Around midnight I dreamt of an immortal wearing a blue headcloth and a yellow robe. On his back he carried a precious sword. He called himself Master Two Mouths and said that our son Shicun should marry Minister Lin's daughter Luying as his second wife. I believe Lin Gui has only the one daughter, Miss Luying, and she was given in marriage to Han Tuizhi's nephew Han Xiang. Although Han Xiang has forsaken his family to cultivate himself and has never returned, and Han Tuizhi has died at his post in Chaozhou, Luying effectively is still married. Even if she were not, how could a family such as ours take a widow in marriage? Furthermore, Han Tuizhi was a colleague of mine. If I were to have my son marry his nephew's widow, we would lose face and people would talk."

"My husband, you are wrong!" his wife said. "If a divine immortal sent you a dream, this Luying must be fated to be our son's wife. All along people have been saying that although the Han family brought in Luying in marriage, the marriage was never consummated. Luying is still a virgin, so surely she is no widow in the usual sense? If we could obtain her in marriage, it would be good match. Who would dare talk behind our backs?"

When Minister Cui heard his wife's words, he ordered the servant on duty to call in a matchmaker and have her negotiate with the Han and Lin families.

The servant did indeed go to call a matchmaker. This matchmaker was surnamed Zhang and was her parents' second child. She lived in the Alley of Loyal Purity, and everyone called her Mother Zhang Two. She was very skilled at her profession and gifted with a sharp tongue. She could dupe the groom's family onto one hook with no fear of losing the bride's family off the other. If she chanced

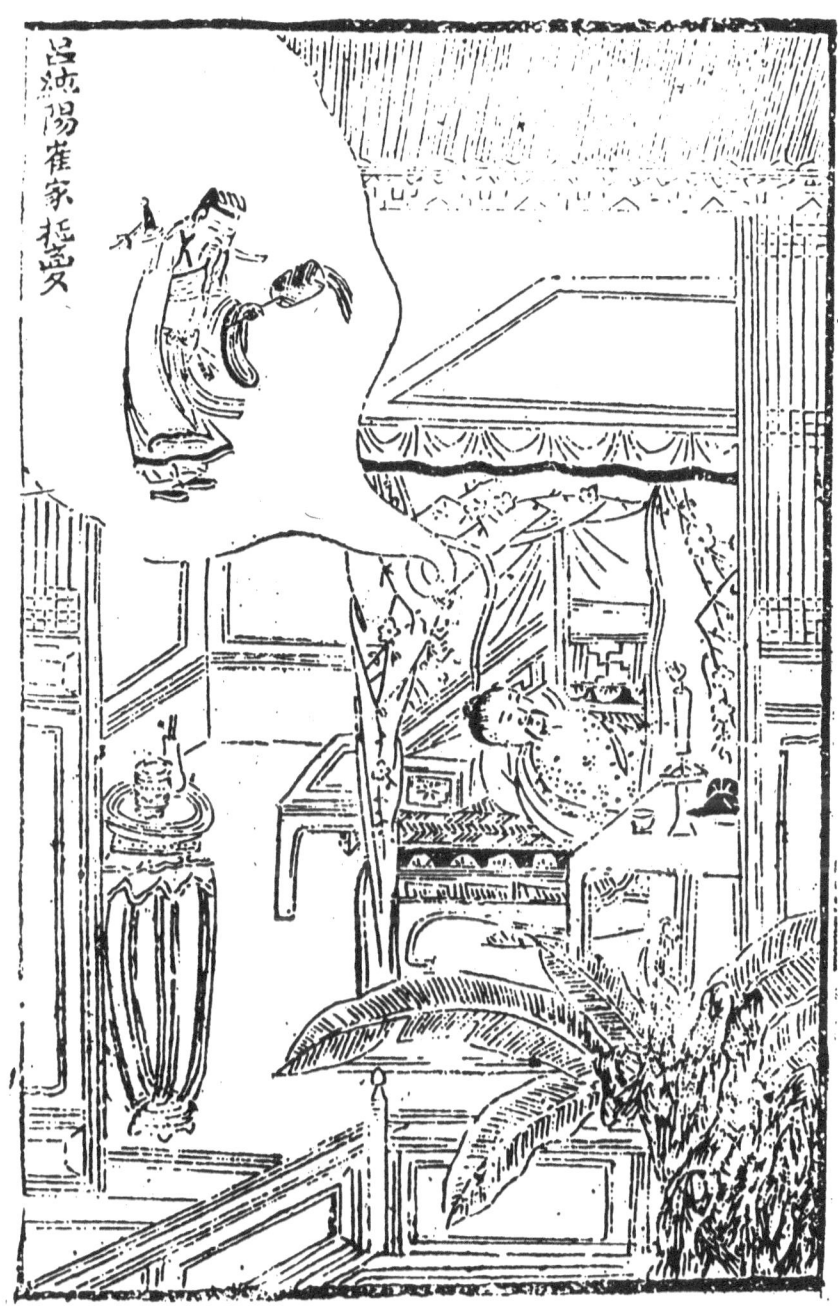

Master Lü sends a dream to the Cui family.

upon people with little regard for propriety between the sexes, she would draw close and entice them to employ her as matchmaker. Everyone knew her, and, truly, in her persuasive skills she was a match for famous disputers such as Sui He and Lu Jia.

When this Mother Zhang Two followed the servant to the Cuis' mansion, Minister Cui happened to be at court, and so she went straight to the inner chambers to see his wife. She said, "I am extremely busy. At the sixth watch, Censor Huang wants to send the bridal presents to the mansion of Commander Guo. Why have you sent for me, my lady?"

"I want you to act as matchmaker," the lady Cui replied.

"Other matches I can all do, but if your husband wants to take a concubine, I am afraid they are impossible to find this year," said Mother Zhang Two. "The harvest was very good, and very few people are selling their daughters."

Lady Cui laughed and said, "You have a quick tongue. No, it isn't my husband who wants to take a concubine, but my widowed son who wants to marry a girl from a family of a standing equivalent to ours."

"Those are available," Mother Zhang Two said. "The Metropolitan Governor Liu Gongchuo has a daughter, beautiful as flowers and jade. The Minister of Revenue Li Yong has two daughters, the elder eighteen, the younger sixteen years old; both are incomparably beautiful and winsome. The Vice Minister of Revenue Huangfu Zun also has a daughter, who is only fourteen years old, but knowledgeable in all kinds of affairs. The daughter of Li Ao, the senior compiler at the Historiography Institute, is nineteen years old and has a very good hand at calligraphy and the zither. All along none of her suitors have met with her approval, which is why she has not yet drunk the wedding tea. But if I propose a match as second wife to your son, she will certainly agree. I will go there to negotiate and then report back to you, my lady."

"No need to contact these families," said lady Cui.

"These families are your social peers," Mother Zhang Two said. "If I don't approach them, where should I go?"

"A divine immortal appeared to my husband in a dream last night and told him that the wife of Minister Han's nephew, Minister Lin's daughter Luying, is destined by Heaven to become our son's wife. Therefore I want you to first speak a word with Minister Lin and then come to an arrangement with Mme. Dou. I shall send the presents to the Han family and bring her over to our family as soon as possible."

Mother Zhang Two laughed. "My lady, your words are extraordinary and strange. It was I who originally escorted Miss Luying to the Han mansion. She is a married woman, and furthermore she is the daughter-in-law of a minister. How could she ever agree to remarry? If I go to make this proposal, it will cause a scandal."

"Of course I know that Miss Lin is married, but if a divine immortal orders in a dream that it should be done like this, then so shall it be done," Lady Cui said. "Furthermore, the minister Han has been dead for a long time and Han Xiangzi has abandoned his family. My husband is in a high and influential position. Who will dare disobey him?"

"That may be so, but this Mme. Dou is a very obstinate and narrow-minded person. How could I dare contradict her to her face? I'd just be snubbed by her," Mother Zhang Two said.

When Lady Cui heard Mother Zhang Two's words, she said angrily, "You detestable old bitch! You're afraid of Mme. Dou, but not of me. I'll have you clapped in irons at the warden's office and employ someone else as matchmaker. Once this marriage is completed, I'll have you displayed in a two hundred pound cangue for a whole month. Let's see if you're afraid of me or not!"

These words so frightened Mother Zhang Two that she stood with her eyes staring and her mouth open. Then she burst into tears and implored Lady Cui, "My lady, don't get upset. I will go, I will go."

"Then I'll forgive you this time," Lady Cui said. "Go quickly, make the proposal, and then report back to me." Here is a poem to illustrate the situation:

> When a matchmaker is sent to make a proposal,
> One expects that it will be accepted.
> When you are in the chamber on the wedding night,
> You will realize that divine immortals do not deceive people.

Having taken leave of the lady Cui, Zhang Two paid no attention to her surroundings on her way home, but just turned over plan after plan in her mind, saying to herself, "I'll go to Master Lin first to get his approval, and only then go to see Mme. Dou. If Master Lin has consented, I have no fear that Mme. Dou won't follow his lead."

Having decided on her plan, she set off right away for the Lin mansion. Another matchmaker, called Mother Jiang Five, was headed in the opposite direction. Originally she had been a concubine in the Chen family, but when after three or four years she still wasn't pregnant, the head wife provided her with a dowry and gave her as a daughter-in-law to the tradeswoman Jiang without asking for a bride price. When the tradeswoman Jiang saw that she was talented and a good talker, she took her along when she made her rounds among the gentry families. In this way she learned the skills required of a matchmaker.

That day, when she encountered Mother Zhang Two and saw her gesticulating and debating with herself, she realized that her colleague must be on a matchmaking mission. She barely managed to avoid a collision with her by stepping aside into a doorway. Then she turned around and followed Mother Zhang Two.

After passing eight or nine houses, Mother Zhang Two suddenly clapped her hands and said, "How stupid of me! I recently heard that that Tradeswoman Jiang Five has been frequenting the Han mansion. I should get her to go with me when I make the proposal. That will be a lot safer. Why didn't I think of it before?"

When Jiang Five heard this, she hurried forward, covered Mother Zhang Two's eyes with her hands from behind, and said, "Where are you going, Mum?"

Trying to free herself, Zhang Two said, "Who is it?"

"I am Li Sanguan," Jiang Five said.

"You little bastard, how can you make fun of me!" Zhang Two said.

Laughing, Jiang Five took her hands away and said, "Mum, see if you recognize Li Sanguan."

Zhang Two turned around and saw Jiang Five. "Jiang Five, it was you who played this trick on me," she said. "Just as well that you are here. I just happen to have something to discuss with you."

"Zhang Two, you are the old hand in this trade. Everyone defers to you. I'm just a fledgling. What is there worth discussing with me?"

"That's not true at all. My time is over, I'm no good any more at persuading people. Your time has come, and I will have to rely on you to make my own living," Zhang Two said.

"Don't make a fool of me, Mum" Jiang Five said. "If you let me take part in your affairs, it is a great kindness on your part."

Zhang Two laughed and said, "You look winsome and you speak winsomely—even I feel affection for you!"[1]

"Don't be so respectful, Mum, people will laugh at us," Jiang Five replied. Then Zhang Two pulled Jiang Five into Pissing Alley and whispered in her ear.

Reader, let me explain why this one of the many alleys opening off the big street happened to be called Pissing Alley. Well, thousands of people passed through the big street, but few people walked along this small alley. Only those with an urgent call of nature stepped into it to relieve themselves, and therefore it came to be called Pissing Alley.

Even though Zhang Two was an old hand at her trade and Jiang Five was her junior, why didn't they go somewhere else to talk, instead of choosing these unrefined surroundings for their conversation? It was because Zhang Two had been humiliated by Lady Cui and she was afraid that people would no longer respect her if they learned of it. So she brought Jiang Five to this secluded place to talk to her in private. Indeed,

> There are ears on the other side of the wall;
> There is always someone outside the window.
> If you intend to speak openly,
> Fear that someone might even be in the sky above you.

After Zhang Two had spoken to Jiang Five for a long time, the latter said, "I'm afraid this can't be done. It's useless to even try it."

"I completely depend on your help to accomplish it. I'm willing to split the fee forty/sixty, with you getting the larger share," Zhang Two said.

Then they went straight to the residence of Minister Lin, who just happened to be on the staircase leading up to the main hall, viewing his flowers. When he saw them, he asked, "What do the two of you want here?"

"Sir, I have something ridiculous to tell you," Zhang Two said.

"What is ridiculous?" he asked.

"Minister Cui has sent us to communicate a marriage proposal to you, sir," Jiang Five said.

"That's really ridiculous," Minister Lin said. "For my only son you, Jiang Five, have already procured me a daughter-in-law, while you, Zhang Two, escorted my only daughter to be given in marriage to the nephew of Minister Han. I don't have any other children, and neither do I have any grandchildren yet. Concerning whom are you supposed to submit this proposal?"

"That's just what is so ridiculous," Zhang Two said.

"If you already know it, just say so to the parties concerned. Why did you come to speak of it to me at all?" Minister Lin said.

"It really is ludicrous," Jiang Five said. "Well, here goes: to be honest, there is a special reason why I could not but accompany Zhang Two to see you."

"What reason are you speaking of?" Minister Lin asked.

Together Jiang Five and Zhang Two replied, "Minister Cui's son married the daughter of Vice Minister Hu. She passed away recently, and now Minister Cui seeks a new wife for his son. He had not yet announced his intentions when a divine immortal appeared to him in a dream, wearing a blue headcloth and a yellow robe. On his back he carried a precious sword, and he called himself Master Two Mouths. He said to Master Cui that your daughter Luying should be his son's second wife. In the morning, Master Cui said to his wife, 'A few years ago Miss Luying married the nephew of Han Tuizhi, so that she already has a husband. Why did I have this dream? If it weren't true, it wouldn't have been so very clear. If the dream really is true, it can't be that a divine immortal doesn't know past events.' The lady Cui said, 'The marriage between Master Han and Miss Luying was never consummated—she is still a virgin. Furthermore, Master Han abandoned her to go off and cultivate himself; it's been many years and he hasn't come back. The maiden has to spend her days like a widow. For someone so young, this won't do.' Therefore she called us matchmakers to approach you, sir. The one she wishes to ask for is this daughter of yours."

When Minister Lin heard these words, he was dumbstruck for some time. Then he said, "Although Master Han has departed this world and his heir has never returned, there is still Mme. Dou at home, so I can't take charge of this matter. Go see Mme. Dou. If she consents, I shall certainly comply with Master Cui's wishes."

"As long as your daughter is in the Han family, you have to worry about her," Jiang Five replied. "If she is married to Master Cui, you too will be able to shed your anxiety. Although Mme. Dou is still at home, she is after all only a woman. You have to take charge of this. One word of encouragement from you is worth more than ten words from us."

"Having given a daughter in marriage is like having sold a field," Minister Lin said. "How could I still act as the owner? You go speak to Mme. Dou. If I see her, I'll put in a word."

"We'll go see the Han family then," Zhang Two said. "On another day we'll come again to pay our respects to your wife."

"If Mme. Dou consents, there will be another occasion to see my wife," Minister Lin said.

In a happy mood, Zhang Two and Jiang Five walked out the gate and made for Han Tuizhi's residence. Talking together, they turned some corners, and soon arrived at the gate of the Han mansion.

"Mother Zhang Two, what wind has blown you to our house?" asked Old Liao, who guarded the gate.

"I have come to propose a marriage," Zhang Two replied.

"You must have gone mad," the gatekeeper said. "Who is there in this household that you want to propose a marriage for?"

"I am not mad," Zhang Two said. "The young lady of your household has no husband."

The gatekeeper laughed. "That's really stupid. The young lady is married to the young master. How can you say that she has no husband?"

"She may be married, but she sleeps alone and her pillow and bedcover are cold," Zhang Two said.

"That's because the young master left her to cultivate himself," the gatekeeper said. "Surely she doesn't qualify for remarriage? There is no need to speak to our young lady—you two matrons really know nothing at all of the affairs of the world."

"Don't concern yourself with things that are none of your business," Zhang Two said. "I will see the old lady and take it up with her."

As they went inside, Jiang Five held Zhang Two back and said softly to her, "Even just getting inside was a big hassle; let's forget about the proposal."

Zhang Two shook her head and said, "If you want to close a deal, you need to act in time. There's no point in worrying and putting it off until the next day." Jiang Five had no choice but to follow Zhang Two to see Mme. Dou.

It so happened that Mme. Dou was playing a game of chess with Luying, with no care other than to distract and enjoy themselves. Zhang Two and Jiang Five stepped forward and called out together. The courtesies completed, Mme. Dou said, "Dear Mother Two, what wind has blown you here today that you tread the unworthy floor of my house?"

"Don't make fun of me, my lady," Zhang Two said. "I'm so tied up with duties here and there that I haven't been able to find the time to pay my respects to you, even though I often think of you. Today I took advantage of some free time to come, along with Jiang Five, yet you deride me, making me feel quite embarrassed."

"Don't be coy," Mme. Dou said. "You're the kind who wouldn't ascend a precious palace if she didn't have some particular business. You wouldn't visit me without some purpose in mind."

Jiang Five gave a laugh and said, "Venerable lady, you really are a living divine immortal. Mother Two does indeed have an urgent matter to discuss with you, and therefore brought me along."

"So I was right," Mme. Dou said. "Well, I depend upon your instruction, Mother Two."

"The two of us have come especially to congratulate you on this joyous occasion," Zhang Two said.

"Ever since my husband departed this world, the household has been immeasurably lonely," Mme. Dou said. "What joy do I have to be congratulated upon?"

"We are joy bugs," said Jiang Five. "We don't go where there is no joy. In such a great mansion the lucky stars must be shining every day. How can you say that you have no joy?"

"Pigeons only fly to prosperous places," Mme. Dou remarked. "The two of you coming to me today—the pigeons must have lost their way."

"Venerable lady, do you know what the pigeons are saying?" Jiang Five asked.

"I am not a Gongye Chang who knows the language of birds, nor a Ge Jielu who understands the braying of donkeys. How would I know what the pigeons are saying?"

"The pigeons say, 'hadagoodoo, hadagoodoo,'" Jiang Five said.

Mme. Dou laughed and said, "That's very clever."

Zhang Two prevaricated for a while and laughed for a while, but then she braced herself and said to Mme. Dou, "I have frequented your house for many years and have never dared utter an idle word. My lady, you know me. Today I received a stern command from Lady Cui, the wife of Minister Cui, and had no choice but to come see you."

"What does the Cui family have to say?" asked Mme. Dou.

"She has sent me to make a marriage proposal," Zhang Two said.

Mme. Dou laughed. "Well, I would like to marry, it's just that no one wants me," she said.

Zhang Two clapped her hands and said, "Some time ago there was a 120-year-old bachelor in Chang'an who wished to marry a virgin of the same age. He said that if there was absolutely no one of his age, a woman of sixty or seventy years would do. If you wish, I could make that match."

Jiang Five giggled and said, "You don't have a proper word to say, but are just gossiping in front of the lady."

"You are right," Zhang Two said. "Well, young Master Cui has recently been widowed, and the daughters of many ministers and vice ministers are trying to negotiate a match with him. Minister Cui was going to cast the oracle tomorrow with utmost sincerity and decide upon a family, but then in the night a divine immortal appeared in his dream who said that Miss Lin should be his son's second wife. And so he sent me to the Lin residence to propose marriage. Minister Lin, not having another daughter, thought that it wouldn't do for his only daughter Luying to remain a widow, young as she is. It would be better if she married someone, and therefore he sent me to see you."

"You have already seen Master Lin?" Mme. Dou said.

"We only dared come to see you after having met with Master Lin," Zhang Two replied.

"What did he say?" asked Mme Dou.

"He said, 'You are absolutely right in what you say. I shall visit Mme. Dou and encourage her to bring this matter to completion,'" said Zhang Two.

When Mme. Dou heard these words, she went purple in the face and screamed, "That this little lewd damsel of the Jiang family doesn't understand the affairs of the world goes without saying, but you, you bitch, you lewd hag, who have frequented my house for many years, whom I have recommended, how dare you bully me now that my husband is dead by speaking such immoral and illicit words? A family such as ours will never allow a daughter-in-law to remarry! Master Lin doesn't deserve to have been an official all his life if he completely disregards all morality and cares only to fawn upon others. Just think about it: would you let your daughter marry first into one family, and then again into another?"

Cursing them repeatedly, she scolded Zhang Two and Jiang Five until their faces turned from red to white, and from white to red, and they stood open-mouthed.

Mme. Dou hadn't finished her tirade yet when Luying stepped forward and said, "The two of you have no human decency! However well my mother-in-law treats you, you don't know good from bad, but are just afraid of those with official position and money. You give no thought to heavenly principles or the human heart. You don't deserve to have been born as humans!"

"Mother-in-law, don't upset yourself," she added. "Even when Father-in-law was still here and things were better overall, we were still bullied by others. That Cui Qun perverts the law and monopolizes power. He abuses his position to browbeat his colleagues. If he tries to force this marriage, surely Heaven will punish him."

"I should give you two a beating and send you back to the Lin residence to shame him," Mme. Dou said. "However, since he has already lost all dignity, I shall forgive you this time. Never come here again, trying to cheat us by pretending to pass on the words of others."

Shame filled the faces of Zhang Two and Jiang Five, and they didn't know where to move. In the end they had to endure their shame and leave.

Zhang Two wanted to drag Jiang Five back to the Cui residence to report, but Jiang refused adamantly and left her halfway. So Zhang Two had to go to the Cui family by herself.

Minister Cui and his wife were waiting eagerly for Zhang Two's report. As soon as they saw her coming, they asked, "Where do the marriage negotiations stand?"

Zhang Two opened her eyes wide, raised her eyebrows, and answered viciously,

"It was for nothing that you made me suffer such embarrassment and denunciation, and now you still ask how it went!"

"Your words are detestable," Minister Cui said. "No wonder my wife wanted to punish you the other day. You have come to report to me, yet instead of a decent word, you just give me this nonsensical talk. Let me ask you, when did you go to see Master Lin and Mme. Dou? What did they say to you that on your return you seem so put out?"

Only then did Zhang Two conquer her temper and say in a low voice, "When I went to see Master Lin, he promised to cooperate and made no trouble at all. It was just Mme. Dou who scolded me so much that I won't repeat it. She also cursed you, saying you were not fit to be human beings. She said if young Master Cui wanted to marry Luying as his second wife, it was really like a toad lying in a covered drain hoping to eat a swan's meat. She also said she would lodge an official complaint to have you, sir, banished as a commoner to a distant prefecture, and that you'd never be allowed to return home. Only then would her anger be assuaged."

"Only I have power in court!" Minister Cui said angrily. "What official will dare defy me? She is only the wife of Han Yu. How dare she talk that way? If she wants to lodge a complaint against me, I'll head her off by submitting a memorial at court tomorrow that her monthly emoluments be annulled and she be expelled to her native district. Then I'll order the local official there to trump up some charges against her and wipe out her property holdings and fields. I will leave them no road to walk and no country to find refuge in—that will demonstrate my power to everyone. That's carrying a thing to its conclusion: come down hard in the beginning, and end by wreaking disaster upon them."

"Lady Han is wrong, but since ancient times it has been said that 'rumor makes much out of very little,'" Lady Cui said. "In all affairs one should hear for oneself whether they are true. How can you injure your colleagues' feelings just on the strength of a matchmaker's claims?"

"Han Yu was a man who only thought of himself and never of others," Minister Cui said. "Just as he was unreasonable and undiscriminating, his wife has no understanding of the affairs of our times. She said those things word for word. How do you expect me to tolerate them?"

"Our son is without a wife. Our first priority should be to find him one. Why does it have to be Lin Luying? Mother Zhang Two, you may go," Lady Cui said.

"If I don't submit a memorial tomorrow to have her expelled, my name isn't Cui!" the minister said.

A poem shall serve as illustration:

A memorial will be submitted to the emperor,
Convincing him that the Han family's guilt is vast.
Thus is made a net of blue silk for simurgh and phoenix,
A cage of azure jade for the mandarin ducks.

If you don't know what happened afterwards, listen to the explanations in the next chapter.

26

A cave high up in the mountains touching the purple empyrean,
The milky water of a hoary cliff dripping on monks and woodcutters.
Quietly sitting on a rush mat, without distractions,
Watching a strange sign arising far off on Mount Tiantai.

Let's speak no more of Mother Zhang Two's departure, but tell instead how Han Xiangzi took leave of Master Lü and went straight to the Dragon King of the Eastern Sea. A great crowd of turtle grand councilors and palace secretaries, dragon advisers and grand masters, all bowed to him. Carp marshals, bream superintendents, mackerel defenders-in-chief, and crab office managers all together hastened submissively to welcome him. Along the sides many sturgeon squad leaders, water-lizard vanguards, shrimp warriors, and culter soldiers turned out; a gaggle of dragon sons and grandsons came hurrying out of the palace to welcome him. They drew near and inquired, "May we ask the divine immortal of the upper realms in what matter he comes to the water palace?"

"This is not for you to know," Xiangzi said. "Where is the dragon king Ao Guang?"

With one voice the dragon sons and grandsons answered, "He received an order to proceed to Guilin Xiang Prefecture to produce rain and has not yet returned."

"I received a decree from the Jade Emperor to go to Chang'an and deliver Mme. Dou and Luying," Xiangzi said. "However, they were so attached to the splendors of this world that they refused to follow me and cultivate themselves. Therefore I memorialized the Jade Emperor, who then sent Master Lü to give a dream to Minister Cui. In it he told him to submit a memorial to Emperor Xianzong that the whole Han family be expelled and sent back to live in Changli.

"Because the Jade Emperor was afraid that they might remain attached to their confusions and not turn back, he also ordered the Dragon King to raise wind and waves, to roll the seas and arouse its billows, so as to wash away all the Han family's mansions, houses, fields, hills, and marshes in Changli County. Nothing must remain, so as to shake their sense of earthly comforts. When they have nothing left around them and can go neither forward nor back, then I shall make my move and deliver them. None of the other habitations, official buildings, mountain fields, and level marshes must be damaged in the least, otherwise the Dragon King will be punished."

The dragon sons and grandsons replied, "Who dares defy the Jade Emperor's decree? As soon as our father, Ao Guang, returns he will put this command into execution and then report on his mission."

Thereupon Xiangzi left the Crystal Palace and stepped on a cloud to meet with Master Lü and Lan Caihe and continue his journey with them.

That night the Dragon King led his sons and grandsons towards Changli. He opened wide his lightning eyes and bristled his red dorsal spikes, manifesting his awesome powers to overturn rivers and stir up oceans. Suddenly a rainstorm darkened the sky, thunder and lightning came in quick alternation, a chaotic mass of mists and clouds appeared out of nowhere, and flood waters flowed turbulently. It was as if the earth split and the sky fell down, as if the mountains collapsed and the rivers overflowed their banks.

The Han family's houses, mansions, and honorific arches by the drum tower in the town, as well as their fields north and south of town and their granaries, were completely washed away. Not a bit remained. Alas, where did all those grasses and trees, grain stalks and seedlings, vanish to without leaving a trace?

When the people of Changli County saw this scene early the next morning, they said, "Since ancient times it has been said that mulberry orchards have changed into oceans, and oceans into mulberry orchards. This morning we realize that such a thing can really happen."

One man, who rushed to the Chaotian Bridge to view the scene, said, "It seems as if Heaven channeled this water by lock-gates in such a way that it only submerged the property of Han Yu's family. That's very strange!"

"If Heaven sent down this flood to destroy his property holdings, it must be that Han Yu must have been lacking in merit," the crowd said in one voice.

One man in the crowd said, "He was a very good official. There is nothing wrong with his merit. It must have been his memorial against the Buddha bone that insulted the buddhas and bodhisattvas. Because they were very angry with him, they manifested their divine powers and destroyed his family property, his fields, houses, and honorific arches, so as to demonstrate their authority. From now on, we should recite the Buddha's name and rely on Heaven for our well-being."

Another opined, "In Guangdong a crocodile had a nice lair until it was chased away without good cause by an official proclamation composed by Han Yu. The crocodile is seeking revenge, that's why this great flood came and transformed the foundations of his walls into deep pits. I think it's quite possible that the crocodile is hiding at the bottom of this water."

"We are not divine immortals," yet another said. "What do we know about the things of the hidden realm? Let's all go home and concern ourselves with our own affairs." Truly,

> Everyone should sweep the snow before his own door,
> And not concern himself with the frost on the roof of others.

The crowd heaved a sigh and dispersed.

In the meantime the minister Cui, having heard the many things that Mother Zhang Two said, was gnashing his teeth as hate penetrated his very bone marrow. After pondering the whole night, the next morning he hurriedly wrote a memorial to submit to Emperor Xianzong. In it he said that Mme. Dou and her family should not be allowed to remain in the capital and enjoy official emoluments. The text ran as follows:

> The minister of revenue Cui Qun, sincere, yet trembling before Your
> Majesty's authority, knocks his head. Your servant has heard that
> ordinary officials should not enjoy hereditary emoluments. If one
> is not a meritorious official with extraordinary achievements, one
> should not be able to receive the favors of golden scripts and iron
> contracts. I now perceive that Han Yu, the deceased prefect of Chao-
> zhou, made no vast contribution to the nation while at court, nor did
> he achieve among the people any great accomplishments in control-
> ling disasters. Instead he recklessly offended Your Majesty and was
> banished for life to a distant prefecture. His nephew Han Xiang has
> turned his back on the teachings of the sages and thrown in his lot
> with the School of Mysteries! He has abandoned his parents' grave,

and there is nobody to perform the periodic sacrifices for them. He has cast away the emotional bonds to his wife, who lives at home with no one to discipline her. Han Yu's adopted son Han Qing has the feeble constitution of the earworm which ends up continuing the line of the sphex.[1] He does not apply himself to the study of *The Book of Documents* and *Records of the Historian*, but lives the life of a reckless wastrel.

Truly, the disorderly human relationships in this family are a disgrace to officialdom and do great harm to public morals. Yet Your Majesty has bestowed upon them monthly emoluments, a hereditary salary for them to enjoy. By means of such favors greedy and blackhearted characters can whitewash their name, and crafty fellows can pretend to be loyal and upright. How will Your Majesty in future treat one whose contributions to the nation and achievements for the people are manifested clearly? With all respect I beg you to apply severely the rule of punishing the criminal for his intentions and to strictly apply the utmost penalties. Strip Han Yu's wife Mme. Dou of her monthly emoluments, send Han Qing to join the border guard at a remote frontier, and convert their house into a shrine to the former worthies. Their gold and silk, corn and rice, should all be used to enhance the granaries of the border troops, and they should not be allowed to secretly carry any of it with them. This way the officials will take warning and the common people will fear the law. Unable to overcome my shame and fear, I fervently await Your Majesty's commands.

When Xianzong perused this memorial, he was filled with joy and said, "Cui Qun really is a supportive minister. When he learns of anything that is of benefit to the nation, he never hides it from Us. This Han Qing and the whole family receive a salary without deserving it. For nothing have they wasted money and grain. He should be made a border soldier and set out as soon as possible. No delays are permitted."

Cui Qun was overjoyed when he saw Xianzong promulgate this decree. Truly, a lance thrust openly is easy to dodge, but a covert arrow is difficult to defend against. To illustrate this point, here is a poem:

> When three men made up wild rumors,
> The mother of Zeng jumped over the wall in fear.

For a wronged woman frost flew to proclaim her sorrow.[2]
For Jing Ke a rainbow gave forth a ray of light.
Melting gold and stripping people of their good names is easy;
A mere fly can do harm by blemishing a white jade token of office.
Just a day's worth of slander
Caused grief to Jia Yi in Luoyang.[3]

When the civil and military officials assembled at court saw Xianzong promulgate this decree, they watched each other with embarrassment, but did not dare say anything. Suddenly an official rushed forth from among their ranks and approached the throne holding his tablet of office. He bowed to the throne and said,

"The Minister of Personnel Lin Gui, sincere, yet trembling before Your Majesty's authority, knocks his head. The Duke of Zhou was a great sage, yet he was slandered by the four states, so that even his ruler became suspicious of him. Zeng Can was a great worthy, yet the words of three rumor-mongers shook and confused even his own mother. Surely this was not because King Cheng was not enlightened, or the mother of Zeng was not a good parent. No, it happened because rumors can melt gold, and slander can strip people of their good names. Your Majesty governs the whole empire, shining like the sun and moon, merciful like a father and mother. Yet among those that you seek to rely upon, how can there be no injustice? And injustice will always engender deep grievances.

"Allow me to explain it to Your Majesty. With his literary talents the former Minister of Rites Han Yu reinvigorated literature after eight generations of decay, and by means of his Dao he saved the empire from doom. All his life he was loyal and blunt and governed with loyalty and uprightness. When he prayed for snow, his sincerity reached the gods. When he expelled the crocodile, his grace was bestowed on many generations. It was only because his memorial against the Buddha bone offended Your Majesty that he was banished to a remote place and died of an illness in his office. Truly, Heaven has lost a proponent of its way,[4] and as a result officials and the people have lost hope. Yet fortunately, when his burial was prepared his loyalty and righteousness still extended far, and because Your Majesty still remembered his former accomplishments, you graciously granted him sacrifices and a state burial, and enfeoffed him posthumously as Marquis of Changli Prefecture. A monthly emolument was granted to assist his family in their grief. Not only is Han Yu in the netherworld comforted by these tokens of acknowledgment, but they have also caused high and low officials to praise Your Majesty's virtue, saying that Your Majesty has not turned his back on Han Yu.

"Now here is Cui Qun, who harbors jealousy in his heart because his marriage proposal was snubbed. He spouts groundless slander like certain vermin spit sand at passing shadows. Recklessly he memorializes that Han Yu in his lifetime never benefited the court, that now after his death he still enjoys undeserved emoluments, and that he should be stripped of all honors and denounced. It was because Your Majesty misheard that you approved this memorial. For my part, when I heard it I was very surprised and startled. Among all the civil and military officials at court there was none who did not sigh. All said that ever since Your Majesty ascended the throne, you have respected the high ministers and shown consideration for your officials. There has never been a precedent for the demands of Cui Qun, who would punish Han Yu to such an extreme degree. In the days of Yao and Shun such a devil as Cui Qun surely would never have been tolerated. With all respect I beg Your Majesty to take back your orders, and to send Han Yu's wife, Mme. Dou, back to her estate only temporarily. His son Han Qing should be spared military duty, so that he may serve his mother to the end of her life. If both the living and the dead were to receive Your Majesty's mercy in this way,[5] your minister Gui would be very happy indeed! I fervently submit this request and await Your Majesty's orders."

Xianzong approved Lin Gui's request and ordered Han Qing to return with his mother Mme. Dou and the others to live in leisure at Changli. All their gold, silk, rice, and corn were to be thoroughly examined by the palace guards and impounded to be given to the officers of the border troops. They were not allowed to take anything with them. If they disobeyed, they were to be subject to threefold punishment. Here is a poem to underline their plight:

The ruler approved the memorial that they be returned to their estate,
To live in peace and leisure in their native district,

Not knowing that the Lord of Heaven had a cunning plan,
And destroyed their property so that they could not support themselves.

Let's talk no more of events at court, but speak instead of Mme. Dou, who was sitting at home when her heart suddenly gave a start and she shivered. Her mind was uneasy. When a flock of crows and magpies flew noisily by, she quickly called Luying and said, "Daughter-in-law, last night I had an inauspicious dream, and today I am confused. All these crows and magpies making noise—is this a good or bad omen?"

"Mother-in-law, it is thinking of Father-in-law that has brought this about," Luying said. "In ancient times they said, 'A magpie's cry has never indicated a good omen, and a crow's cawing surely is not a bad one. Good and bad in the human realm are not to be found in the cries of birds.' Those who have good fortune will always receive Heaven's assistance; there is no need to worry."

At that very moment they heard the clanging of gongs and the rolling of drums amidst the noise of horses and men. When they hurried out to look, a palace guard was outside the main hall, surrounded by a troop of attendants and runners, who seemed like evil spirits and baleful emanations and stood there menacingly with rolled-up sleeves. Mme. Dou and Luying were frightened and their faces turned ashen. They stared with their mouths open, but did not understand the reason for this at all. What crime had they committed? Everyone in the household hid and didn't show themselves.

Han Qing, however, had no choice but to come out, kneel in the main hall, and inquire after the reason for their presence. The palace guard said, "I have received an imperial decree: I order Han Qing to lead Mme. Dou and other members of the household quickly home to reside in Changli. He is to be spared military duty. All family property is to be impounded and given as rewards to the border troops. You are not allowed to take anything along. The house will be assessed by officials from the Ministry of Works today and converted into a shrine for the former worthies, for whom statues will be set up so that they may receive sacrifices during the four seasons." Having finished, the guard turned around and left.

Mme. Dou stomped her feet and beat her chest; she cried until she fell unconscious to the ground. Little did she know that it was Cui Qun who, having listened to Mother Zhang Two's words, had secretly harmed them.

Suddenly Minister Lin arrived. Luying went forward to take hold of his sleeve; crying she collapsed in his arms. Lin Gui said, "My daughter, don't be distressed, but count yourself lucky. If the emperor's original decree had stood, your mother-in-law's life would not have been spared."

When Mme. Dou heard Lin Gui speaking in this manner, she struggled forward and asked, "Ever since my husband's death we have lived a quiet life within our lot. Which slanderous official's words did the emperor listen to that I am being subjected to such humiliation? Thus is my poor husband's lifelong loyalty and goodness repaid!"

"Venerable lady, you don't yet know the inside story," Lin Gui said. "This is the doing of the Minister of Revenue Cui Qun, who memorialized the court that you and all your family be exiled to military service beyond the borders. This is to get back at you for not consenting to the marriage of my daughter. It was only when I took up the impossible task and, at risk of my life, submitted a memorial in your support, that the emperor took pity and allowed you to return to your native district instead. This is a great joy."

"Cui Qun, you old robber!" Mme. Dou said. "You deceive your own conscience when you make designs on other people's daughters, yet you won't admit that you are in the wrong, but instead secretly slander us. Clearly you are deceiving Heaven. Just wait, the gods are always watching, and Heaven will not lightly forgive you. If only I live a little longer, I shall see you receive your deserved retribution with my own eyes."

"Once the ruler is enraged, the heads of men fall to the ground," Luying said. "If it hadn't been for my father, things would have looked bleak indeed. Mother-in-law, upset yourself no more."

Then Mme. Dou ordered Han Qing to quickly pack up and set out. Han Qing hired boats, carts, and horses. He took leave of Minister Lin and led Mme. Dou and Luying home towards Changli County. As they passed the wayside pavilions at the ten- and five-mile markers he looked at the willows along the bank and listened to the calls of the doves outside the forest. It seemed to him that the scenery was very different from when he last saw it as he was traveling towards Chang'an, overlayed with grief as it was now. Truly: Wild flowers are not planted, yet they bloom every year; worries have no roots, yet they appear every day. A poem shall serve as illustration:

> *Up and down, success and failure are unpredictable;*
> *In this world we are flowering willows shaken by spring gusts.*
> *A landscape with neither limits nor compassion—*
> *Pleasant in a painting, but not to travel through.*

Han Qing and his group traveled for several days. It was just the time of transition from spring to summer. The shade was dense, the leaves green. The weather turned hot suddenly and the scenery was captivating.

Luying called to Mme. Dou, "Mother-in-law, many days have flown by since we left Chang'an. My parents are both old. What shall I do if I never see them again?"

"We have traveled for so long and still haven't met a convenient person with whom to send a letter back to your parents to thank them and wish them well," Mme. Dou replied. "As for an opportunity to meet them face to face, the only place is in the dream realm. When we have arrived at home, we'll make plans."

As mother and daughter-in-law were conversing, Xiangzi and Lan Caihe were following them, close by, yet invisible. When they heard the two women speak, they realized that they had not yet changed their minds, and so they took on the appearance of two fishermen, who sat in the shade of a willow tree and cast their lines across from the road on which the Han household was traveling.

When Mme. Dou saw the two fishermen from afar, she called Han Qing and said, "See those two fishing there? They are much happier than we."

"They fish only for profit," Han Qing said. "If they catch fish, they are happy; if they don't, then they have many worries. Why should they necessarily be happy?"

"Go see if they have some fish," Mme. Dou told him. "If they do, we'll buy a few to make soup."

"Fishermen, if you have fish in your basket, sell us a few," he called. One of them waved and chanted a poem:

> "I wouldn't want to be a rich and powerful marquis;
> Instead, I make my living following my lot in a little skiff.
> I spend some time in leisure by the wide misty waves;
> Once I drink maozhai wine, I become drunk and take a rest."

"You are no poet, yet when I ask to buy fish from you, you don't answer whether you have any, but instead start chanting poetry!" Han Qing said. "Ridiculous!" Then he called to the other fisherman, "Fisherman, if you have fish, sell me a few."

That fisherman didn't say whether he had any fish either, but instead chanted a poem as well:

> "A single fishing line on a wide area of misty waves;
> Among the dense trees in the deep mountains white clouds dwell.
> When I catch fish I buy wine and settle under the thatched pavilion;
> Of the confusions of the dusty world I know nothing."

Han Qing laughed and said, "You two are not fishermen, but courtiers!"

Two fishermen sit together as they cast their lines.

"Courtiers trail their long robes in royal households, are unsure whether to step forward or not, are uncertain whether to speak or not, and always wag their tails and beg for pity," the fishermen replied. "We on the other hand do not care for right or wrong, are not moved by favor or disgrace; we are happy men, leisurely and free. Why do you insult us by calling us courtiers? Here is another poem:

"We don't pay our respects at noble doors and thus attain our freedom;
We roam freely among the misty scenery of the five lakes.
Our only concern is that, drunken with wine, we might go wild,
And push over the white jade towers of the celestial palace."

When Han Qing heard the fishermen's poem, he hurried back to Mme. Dou and reported to her in detail what had happened.

"If they speak in this way, these two fishermen are not lowly underlings," she said. "I'll speak to them myself; let's see how they reply." She approached them and asked, "Fishermen, with the two of you fishing you should each have your own place. Why are you sitting together? Haven't you heard that 'Fish that roam in pairs are like bubbles on water; swimming against the stream they never turn their heads.' Fishermen should not fish in pairs. If there are no fish here, try somewhere else."

The fishermen did not respond, but just recited with lowered heads:

"Amid the scattered shade under the green willow there is a ferry;
Holding our rods we wish to board the fishing boat.
Being at leisure, we are not fettered by fame and profit;
Drunk and well fed we roam and laugh at the nobility."

When Mme. Dou heard this, she said, "'Being at leisure, we are not fettered by fame and profit; drunk and well fed we roam and laugh at the nobility'—that's well said. You fishermen are much happier than we." She came yet a step closer and called to one of the fishermen, "Fisherman, where do you live? Why do the two of you fish in one place?"

Turning his head, the fisherman recited:

"When thirsty, we drink from a clear spring; when drunk, we rest.
Throughout the four seasons we roam freely, enjoying pleasing vistas.
What's the use of jade halls and golden horses?
Caves and cloudy mountains remain in everlasting autumn."

Having recited this poem, the two fishermen suddenly vanished.

Anxiously, the lady called, "Han Qing, did you see where the two fishermen went?"

"We were all here, but never saw them leave," Han Qing said.

Imploring Heaven and Earth, Mme. Dou wailed, "When authority is gone, the slave will cheat his master; when the times are in decline, ghosts will play tricks on humans. Today I have seen ghosts—what shall I do?"

"Mother-in-law, please be patient," Luying said. "How can there be ghosts in broad daylight? Those two must have been divine immortals who had transformed themselves. Let's just hurry on and make further plans later."

So the party journeyed on, eating when they were hungry, drinking when they were thirsty. They stopped at night and traveled during the day, in this way crossing several counties in several days.

When he saw that they were approaching Changli County, Han Qing said, "From here it is not far to Changli. Let me hurry ahead to the town so that I can call together the tenants and have them sweep our mansion clean. Afterwards I will come and fetch you and Sister-in-law."

"That's an excellent idea. Make haste!" Mme. Dou said.

Han Qing rented a horse and, taking along one attendant, rushed ahead at flying speed. After an arduous day's journey he reached the county capital of Changli.

By the time he reached the Chaotian Bridge, dusk was already falling. Stopping his horse, Han Qing looked around, but did not see his family's houses. Badly startled he said, "This must be Chaotian Bridge. Why can't I see our houses? Is my eyesight so dim that I can't even see buildings? Or is a thick fog shielding them from my eyes?" Anxious and confused, he rode his horse to Drum Tower Alley, but when he got there, he saw only a wide body of deep, clear water. Where was the main hall, where the half-beamed towers and buildings? Not half a wall, not one stone was left.

Han Qing was so agitated that he shivered and sweated in turn. He had to get off his horse, and ordered his attendant to guard it. He himself made his way to the home of their old neighbor Qian Xinyu, who lived at the entrance to the alley. There he asked, "Is the venerable official Qian at home? I would like to ask him a question."

"Who is asking for me?" Qian Xinyu said. "How come you address me so formally as 'venerable official' rather than as 'old gentleman'?"

"I am the second son of Minister Han," Han Qing said.

"The Han family has only a nephew called Han Xiang, who has never returned since he left to cultivate himself," Qian Xinyu said. "How many years ago did he adopt you as second son?"

"When my father adopted me, did he first have to send a messenger to notify you so that you could recognize impostors?" Han Qing said. "Minister Han was your old neighbor—would it be easy to impersonate his son to you? Come out and look at me closely. Why the idle interrogation?"

Qian Xinyu put on some clothes, came out, and looked at Han Qing in the light of a lamp. Then he said, "So, it is Zhang Erguan. You were with Mr. Han in Chang'an. When did you come back? What do you want from me at this hour? After Mr. Han died, his wife probably couldn't stand you any more and chased you out. Sorry, but I'd bring my own wife's ill will on myself if I took you in."

These words made Han Qing so angry that his face went red and puffy and he couldn't get out a word. To himself he thought, "It's lucky I didn't bring my attendant along to his house. If that old dog bone had opened his stupid mouth in his presence, I would have died of shame."

When Qian Xinyu saw that Han Qing didn't say anything, he added, "I haven't seen you for some years. Erguan, you've developed into a proper and neat young man, quite unlike your former self. Well, it's as they say: live in a different environment and you develop a different appearance."

Han Qing looked around, and when he saw that nobody was in the corridor he said, "Venerable Official Qian, I'll be frank with you. It was because his nephew had abandoned the family to cultivate himself and had never returned, and because he had no son of his own, that Master Han elevated me to become his second son. None of the people who knew me before are around any more, and our present servants were all hired afterwards. Everyone calls me the second young gentleman and nobody knows that I used to be Zhang Erguan. Even the old lady calls me Son, and Miss Luying calls me Brother-in-law. So you, venerable official, should no longer speak of the past."

"I had no idea," Qian Xinyu said. "I just said that you were Zhang Erguan, but truly I gave offense." Quickly he brought out some tea and offered it to Han Qing. Only then did Han Qing raise the matter of the Hans' house. Qian Xinyu recounted to him in all detail that in the third month a thunderstorm had swept everything away.

Han Qing cried bitterly, took his leave of Qian Xinyu, and rushed back onto the road. When he met up with Mme. Dou and Luying, he said, "Mother, Sister-in-law, oh dear, oh dear!"

Startled, Mme. Dou said, "Thanks to our rescue by Master Lin, we have returned to our native land. What is wrong now?"

Han Qing said, "When I arrived in Drum Tower Alley, I couldn't find our house. I was so startled that I just stared open-mouthed. Eventually I inquired with a neighbor, who told me that on the eleventh day of the third month a great flood destroyed all our family's houses and fields. The only thing that's left is a wide, deep pond."

"How many other people were harmed by this flood?" Mme. Dou asked.

"Our family alone was harmed. No others suffered any damage."

"Blessings never come in pairs, calamities never alone," Luying said. "We have neither home nor country to find refuge in. What shall we do?"

"This grievous suffering has been brought about by that old robber Cui Qun," Mme. Dou said. "Have the dragons and Heaven no eyes to see?"

"Mother, Sister-in-law, do you remember?" said Han Qing. "That day in the Chrysanthemum Pavilion there was that Daoist who said,

> *"When your destiny is troubled and the times are difficult, do not sigh;*
> *Then the scenery of Chang'an is suddenly not so praiseworthy anymore.*
> *With the ancestral property washed away, there is no refuge for you;*
> *Then you will realize that your earlier views were mistaken.'*

"Mother, you wouldn't believe him, yet today his words are all proven right."

"You're right," Mme. Dou responded. "It was only because that Daoist pretended to be Xiangzi that I did not heed him. If Xiangzi really returned, I'd be willing to follow him and leave the family."

"It's getting late," Luying said. "Let's think about it again tomorrow. There's a proverb that says, 'Heaven always leaves you a way out.' Besides the choice of death, there must also be an option for life. Please don't upset yourself, Mother-in-law."

Mme. Dou and Luying again spent the night on the boat. Early the next morning, after Han Qing had arranged for and eaten breakfast, he went into town with a servant to rent a house. He temporarily moved all the things they had brought along into the house, and only when everything was properly prepared did he fetch Mme. Dou and Luying. When his mother entered the house, she wailed loudly. It was only when Luying at her side admonished her repeatedly to calm down that she fell silent.

Master Lü was on a cloud nearby, together with Lan Caihe and Han Xiangzi. When he saw Mme. Dou's grief, he laughed and said, "They used to live peacefully in Chang'an. If the Jade Emperor hadn't sent us to deliver them, would they ever willingly have come to this place?"

"Let me send them a dream and see if they awake or not," Xiangzi proposed.

"Yes, do, quickly," Master Lü said.

When Xiangzi went into his aunt's chamber, he saw that she was sleeping soundly. He called into her ear, "Aunt, I am Han Xiangzi, come especially to see you. You said that you dwelled in a great mansion in Chang'an and enjoyed a generous salary. Where is Chang'an now? Why do you still not awaken? Leave the family right away, before you suffer further setbacks."

Mme. Dou awoke with a start and said, "When I dozed off, I saw Xiangzi standing before me and mocking me. When I looked closely, he was gone. What am I to do?

"At the first watch,
I shed many tears
That I had to leave Chang'an.
Turning to regard my native mountains,
The road is far and there are no tidings.
I remember how at first
I misunderstood words of good advice.

"At the second watch,
A strange wind howls,
Pressing in on me.
My eyes regarding the sky,
My soul ascends the paper bridge.
Tell Heaven
That Mme. Dou will soon come.

"At the third watch,
I still have not woken from my dream,
When I see Xiangzi's shape and shadow.
He says that I did not consider
How long the journey would be.
It is my obstinacy
That brought these calamities on us.

"At the fourth watch,
I see that there is no light yet in the sky,
When suddenly I see Xiangzi arrive.
He still looks the same,
But his clothes are all tattered.
With every word he blames me—
It is high time to turn back.

> *"At the fifth watch,*
> *I see Xiangzi coming to save us.*
> *I clearly hear him speak, dumb no more,*
> *But on awakening, I see him not.*
> *I clap my hand and sigh in vain.*
> *In my anger against Cui Qun,*
> *I cannot distinguish true and false."*

When the fifth watch had passed, the sky began gradually to lighten. Luying came forward and said, "Mother-in-law, why were you murmuring all night? You didn't sleep at all."

"Above I own not a single roof tile to shield me, below not enough empty ground to stick an awl," Mme. Dou said. "Having to rent a house to stay in is painful enough. To make things worse, as I closed my eyes I saw Xiangzi before me talking of all kinds of things, but when I opened my eyes he was gone. So I didn't get any sleep all night."

"Events take their course beyond our control," Luying admonished her. "A tree may want to stop the seasons, but the wind still will not cease. You can only be patient, Mother-in-law. You mustn't succumb to sorrow or you will harm your health."

"I do know that sorrow is useless, but it still weighs on my mind," Mme. Dou replied.

"Mother, Sister-in-law, all affairs must be given careful deliberation," said Han Qing. "An ancient saying goes 'Although the garden of Liang is beautiful, it is not a home that one should hanker after for too long.' It is also said, 'If you borrow another man's wife, she will be difficult to control and your stove will remain cold.' Renting this house is no permanent solution. We have to find other housing; only then will we be able to make a living and pass our days. We won't last with just these temporary arrangements. Surely you have heard: if a family has a thousand ounces and uses two tenths of an ounce of silver every day, it won't last for more than thirteen years, unless it is invested."

"In your view, what options are open to us?" Mme. Dou asked.

"I think we should build us some bamboo fences and thatched huts on the beach," Han Qing said. "That would be better than living in another person's house and having to worry day and night about paying the rent."

"Well said," Mme. Dou agreed.

Han Qing thereupon made plans to find timber, buy bricks, erect a work shed, and choose an auspicious day to begin the project.

How sad when a family is scattered like the stars;
When they abandon each other, each one is heartbroken.
Truly this is the point when it is unbearable to look back.
If thinking of home is hard, look ahead to the land of white clouds.

If you don't know what happened next, please listen to the explanations of the next chapter.

27

AT THE ZHUOWEI HERMITAGE, MASTER AND SERVANTS MEET AGAIN

CARING FOR AN OX, HAN YU AWAKENS TO THE DAO

> *To buy a cup of Dongping wine,*
> *We met and discussed the secrets of immortality.*
> *There is a road that gives access to paradise;*
> *Even those without the destiny can fly, transformed into*
>   *cranes.*
> *Do not brood in obscurity among misty clouds;*
> *Instead of family and nation, recognize the ineffable Dao.*
> *Too bad if you should have withdrawn to solitude in vain—*
> *Turn away from the world of dust and its disputes.*

Let us speak no more of Han Qing's efforts to rebuild the house, but note instead that time flew like an arrow.

Tuizhi lived as a Daoist errand-boy on Mount Zhuowei. Day after day he got up early and went to sleep late, burning incense and lighting candles, opening and closing the doors, sweeping the dust, moving things here and there. Whenever called upon, he obliged; there was no duty he did not take care of—with one exception: he had never gone to the mountains to chop wood, cut grass, or water the fields. He felt no resentment at all. Even when the Perfected Man scolded and punished him, as happened often, he was still joyful. He composed a song to the tune "Clear River" to give expression to his happiness:

> *"Who wants to wear linen robes and wide sleeves?*
> *Why speak of golden seals and purple seal-strings?*
> *I eat thin rice and yellow leeks;*
> *I have the blue mountains and the green waters at my disposition.*
> *I regard the fame and profit of human life*
> *As bubbles floating on water."*

More than a year had passed when suddenly one day the Perfected Man called Tuizhi to him. He ordered him, "Tomorrow some Daoist friends will visit me and there is no firewood left in the kitchen. Go cut some."

"I dare not disobey your command, but where does the Master want me to gather wood?" Tuizhi said.

"It isn't far," the Perfected Man said. "A little more than five miles to the southwest of here there is a garden, the flower garden of this mountain. Go cut wood there."

Tuizhi got together carrying pole, axe, and rope, tied everything up properly, took leave of the Perfected Man, and headed out toward the southwest.

He had not yet walked a mile when heavy snowfall set in. Tuizhi said, "Every day that I didn't leave the hermitage, the sky was clear and fine. Today, when I'm being sent to cut wood, I have to run into this heavy snowfall. Han Yu, your fate is hard! At Blue Pass I suffered a lot from snow, and as if that wasn't enough, today some more is added to make my measure full."

Walking on, he suddenly saw a wooden gate on which was written "Flower Garden of Mount Zhuowei." Tuizhi pushed it open and stepped inside. Red-blossomed branches were gently swaying, vying in loveliness with each other, while leafy shadows formed intricate patterns on the ground. It truly was an enchanted world, a separate universe.

As Tuizhi was gazing at it, the snow stopped. He laughed and said, "Although this garden looks very lovely, it would only take a strong gust of wind for all these blossoms to be shaken to the ground." And in fact, after a short while a dark cloud emerged in the southeast that sank everything into a murky darkness. A strong wind arose and blew all the lovely blossoms away and scattered them far and wide. Han sighed and said, "These blossoms are just like me, Han Yu. When I served as an official at court, I blossomed like a beautiful flower; being scattered within an instant, they resemble my own sad fate." And he burst forth into a ballad:

> *"Flowers, I look at you.*
> *When flowers open, people love to look at them.*

> *A thousand shades of red, ten thousand shades of purple show their*
>   *beauty and grace.*
> *Butterflies love them, bees enter them—it is hard to capture in a*
>   *painting.*
> *I just fear a gust might blow*
> *And rain might beat down,*
> *Scattering you, my flowers."*

He wanted to continue contemplating the flowers, but he was afraid that the Perfected Man might accuse him of being lazy. And so he gathered a bundle of dry wood and quickly left the garden. The burden weighed heavily on his shoulder, and the tears welled from his eyes. He said, "Heaven, why do you submit Han Yu to such suffering and tribulations?"

At that moment he saw a tiger bounding down the mountain slope. When it jumped at him, he was almost scared to death and fell into a half-conscious state.

He only came to when he heard Xiangzi beating the fisher drum and calling in a loud voice, "Uncle, your nephew is here. Quickly, wake up!"

Tuizhi grasped Xiangzi and, in tears, told him, "It is already more than a year since you directed me to come here and meet my master, and in all that time I never left the hermitage. Today he sent me to cut wood, and right away I am attacked and thrown to the ground by a tiger. If you hadn't come, I might have been eaten by the beast."

"Uncle, don't cry," Xiangzi said. "In this gourd I have some hot wine. Drink some to keep out the cold."

"If I drink wine, how can I face the master on my return?" asked Tuizhi.

When Xiangzi saw that he refused the wine, he said, "Well, in that case, pick up your wood and go back. In two days I will visit you again."

"If you come to see the master, please put in a word for me, asking him to treat me better than the common crowd. That would make me happy," Tuizhi said.

"If I don't come, I will definitely write the Perfected Man a letter," Xiangzi replied.

"Don't forget!" Tuizhi said.

"When you see an immortal crane in the sky carrying a letter, that will be my message to the Perfected Man," Xiangzi told him.

Then Tuizhi took leave of Xiangzi, shouldered his firewood, and walked towards Zhuowei Grotto to deliver it. On the way he sighed and said,

> *"My tears flow like water*
> *That as an official I received the emperor's proclamations,*

But now have sunk low to become a woodcutter in the mountains.
I have already carried burdens that are painful beyond words,
And now I am threatened by fierce tigers to boot,
So that my soul almost flew to the palace of King Yama.
Luckily my nephew returned;
He will put in a word for me with the immortal of Great Veil
  Heaven."

When he arrived at the grotto with his load of firewood, he found the gate firmly locked. He set down the wood and called in a loud voice, "Master, open the gate."

"The Master won't let us open the gate," a youth answered. "He said you are a prime minister at court; how come you don't know the difference between high and low?"

"The Master sent me to cut firewood," Tuizhi said. "Because I had difficulty carrying it, I am a little late. I hope the Master will forgive me."

"I only told you to cut firewood," the Perfected Man said. "Why did you sigh in the garden at the wind and flowers?"

When Tuizhi heard these words, he broke out in a cold sweat. "The garden is five miles from here. How does he know what happened there?" he thought to himself.

"When I entered the garden I saw that innumerable flowers had opened in red and white, so beautiful that they stirred my heart," he admitted. "Suddenly a gust of wind blew them to the ground. Because of that I made a poem and sighed a few times."

"What did you talk about with Han Xiangzi on the road?" the Perfected Man then asked.

Again, Tuizhi was startled and thought to himself, "Unless he is a celestial immortal, how can he know all these things?"

Again he knelt down and reported, "On the path I encountered a tiger, but luckily my nephew Xiangzi came along and saved my life. My nephew ordered me to serve you attentively. No other words were exchanged."

"If that is so, open the gate and let him in," the Perfected Man said.

Han came in and handed the firewood to the cook. Suddenly he heard the Perfected Man call to him, "Han Yu, you were a high minister at court, and you are still of two minds. I've tried again and again, but my well-meant exhortations are wind blowing past your ears. You've made no progress. Go back to court and become an official again!"

"When I first came here, I didn't know east from west, south from north,"

Han objected. "I relied completely on my Master's support. Please be merciful and forgive my transgressions."

"I don't blame you," the Perfected Man said. "Well, we don't have enough flour in the hermitage. Take two bushels of wheat, grind them through the night, and give me the flour tomorrow."

"Master, where is the mill?"

"Show him the mill," the Perfected Man called to one of the young Daoists.

When Tuizhi had looked at it carefully, he turned back and said to the Perfected Man, "Master, it is not that I seek to shirk the work, but I am sixty-four years old and haven't much strength left. I can't push this mill by myself. Furthermore, there isn't much time in one night. How can I finish grinding two bushels of wheat all by myself?"

The Perfected Man did not answer, but just called to Cool Breeze and Bright Moon, "Go on, you two, encourage Han Yu to grind the flour. But you're not allowed to help him."

Cool Breeze and Bright Moon escorted him to the mill room. Tuizhi said, "My brothers, I am old and my strength is failing. How can I grind two bushels of wheat in one night? Please help me a bit."

Cool Breeze and Bright Moon said, "We would be willing to lend you a hand in grinding the wheat, but the Master's rules are extremely strict. He ordered us to drive you on in your work and not let you be lazy. How would we dare help you push the millstone?"

Tuizhi saw that he would have to operate the mill by himself, and so he turned it until dawn, by which time he had only just ground eight quarts. Together with Cool Breeze and Bright Moon he went to see the Perfected Man and reported, "Master, I inform you that my strength was not sufficient. In one night I ground only eight quarts of wheat. Please forgive me."

"I'll accept it this time," the Perfected Man said.

Han knocked his head and thanked the Perfected Man. Then he returned to the mill room to continue grinding wheat, and there was no resentment, regret, or anger whatsoever in his heart.

Finally, when he had finished grinding the wheat, he carried it to the Perfected Man and reported his work done. As he had some free time, he went for a walk on the mountain behind the hermitage. Suddenly he saw a group of men carrying a lot of firewood to the hermitage. "Where do you come from?" Tuizhi asked them.

One of the wood carriers said, "We are Daoists at the Perfected Man Mumu's hermitage. Every day we go up into the mountains to cut wood and grass and carry it to the hermitage."

"Aren't you afraid of all this hard work?" Tuizhi said.

"You may use innumerable tricks and schemes, but you cannot avoid Death," the wood carrier said. "Ever since we left the family and followed the great immortal Mumu, we no longer fear Death. It is our lot to do this hard work. The only hardship we fear is that the great immortal might not keep us."

"You are indeed right," Han said. "It is in vain that I was a scholar—my knowledge does not equal yours."

Two others among the group added, "Your face is like that of our master Han."

"What master Han?" Tuizhi asked.

"Han Yu, the minister of rites," the two answered with one voice.

"How do you know him?" Han asked. "He's a powerful official at court and wouldn't come to a place like this."

"Because Minister Han submitted a memorial against the Buddha bone, the emperor was greatly angered and banished him as prefect to Chaozhou," the two said. "On the long journey of eight thousand miles, the two of us accompanied him half of the way, undergoing innumerable hardships. Then two fierce tigers jumped out of the bushes, carried us off, and dropped us here at Mount Zhuowei. We just barely got away with our lives. Since then we have been cutting wood and grass for the hermitage. It is thanks to the Perfected Man Mumu that we escaped death."

"Are you perhaps Zhang Qian and Li Wan?"

"I am Li Wan, he is Zhang Qian. Can it be that you are Master Han?"

"In this place we have all left the family and are Daoists. Why do you still call me Master Han?"

"So you really are Master Han," Li Wan said.

"We have come to live here thanks to the Perfected Man Mumu," Zhang Qian said. "We thought that Master Han had frozen to death at Blue Pass. How was he supposed to get here?"

"I really am Minister Han; I am no impostor," Tuizhi said.

"In today's world there are too many who assume the names of others, so I am skeptical," Zhang Qian said. "Tell me, why didn't you go to Chaozhou, but instead come to Mount Zhuowei?"

"I suffered many hardships at Blue Pass, because I didn't listen to my nephew Xiangzi. My life seemed as doomed as a lantern in the wind or snow on a stove, but fortunately my nephew led me here to become a disciple of the Perfected Man Mumu. Therefore I have served here willingly, burning incense and lighting candles, sweeping the ground and brewing tea."

At the Zhuowei Hermitage master and servants meet again.

"Tell me, why did the young master Han Xiang go to cultivate himself? If you can give me the correct answer, I will believe that you are Master Han," Zhang Qian said.

"Xiangzi is the only son of my elder brother Han Hui and his wife Mme. Zheng," Han answered. "At three years old he still couldn't speak, and it was only when I passed the examinations that he opened his mouth. As he was growing up, his only wish was to leave the family and cultivate himself, and he refused to study. Having married Lin Luying, he shared with her the same bed, but not the same pillow, the same mat, but not the same blanket. One day I encountered two Daoists at the Gold Sprinkle Bridge, who claimed that they understood Heaven and Earth and were skilled in the military and the civil arts. I invited them home to instruct Xiangzi. Due to their influence Xiangzi ran away to cultivate himself and didn't come back for a long time. There wasn't a day when I didn't think of him. Everywhere I posted notices inquiring into his whereabouts.

"In the year when I prayed for snow at the Southern Altar, there was a Daoist who claimed to be Xiangzi. He ascended the altar in my place and by his prayers caused a great snowfall. On my birthday, there was again a Daoist claiming to be Xiangzi, who came to deliver me so that I would leave the family. He tried again and again, but I didn't believe him and so he left abruptly. It was only when I reached Blue Pass that I understood that my nephew Xiangzi really is an immortal, and that the two Daoists I once met at the Gold Sprinkle Bridge in fact were Han Zhongli and Lü Dongbin.

"Well, did I answer correctly?"

Zhang Qian broke into tears and said, "We are Zhang Qian and Li Wan. Why didn't you recognize us, Master?"

Tuizhi also began to cry. As the three men were sharing their feelings of sadness, the Perfected Man Mumu suddenly shouted at them from close by, "Grief and joy, reunion and separation—these are all customs of the world of dust; they are pits of fire. Here with me all worries are relinquished, all memories are left behind. Why have you three still not shaken them off, that you indulge in such childish sentimentality?"

When Tuizhi recounted what had happened, the Perfected Man Mumu said, "These are all karmic obstructions from your previous lives, roots of sin in your present lives. Having come to my place, you must hand everything over to nothingness. Never again bring up the past."

"I respectfully obey the Master's command," Han replied. From then on, Zhang Qian and Li Wan happily continued as Tuizhi's Daoist companions.

Two days later the Perfected Man suddenly called, "Han Yu, an immortal crane has come with a letter. Quickly fetch it for me."

Han hurried to collect the letter and handed it to the Perfected Man. Having perused it, the Perfected Man said, "Your nephew Xiangzi writes that you are old and cannot lead such a hard life. Quickly go wash yourself, and then look after this ox."

When Tuizhi looked at the ox, he saw that its mane was ten feet long and its legs eight feet high. It looked as vicious as a fierce tiger. So he objected, "Master, this ox will be hard to control."

The Perfected Man said, "I give you a few words of instruction to remember":

(To the tune "Wild Geese Descending")

"I too once met an enlightened teacher who transmitted to me a mar-
velous formula
By pointing out to me the moon in the sky.
When the moon is full, the Jade Buds are born,
As the moon wanes, the Golden Flower declines.
As Three and Five are applied in their proper time,
Old and young separate by themselves.
Send it into the hut of the Yellow Matron;
Do not let it lightly leak out.
This is my formula.
When you see that the Numinous Turtle has completely absorbed the
Golden Crow's blood,
Make a determined decision
To become a deathless immortal.

"There is an iron ox who supports you across the river;
There is a clay horse set loose in the mountains.
There is a stone lion who holds a rope fast between his teeth.
How can waves lap in a dry well?
There is a clay earth god who recites essays,
A wooden arhat who chants the Diamond Sutra,
A beauty in a painting who can sing songs.
There is a paper door god who can perform a war dance with his lance,
And before your eyes a snake swallows an elephant.
I do not lie: my home is in the Southern Ocean;

But whether you believe it or not—Two and Three all the more manifest
the Great Yang."

"I have memorized everything that you gave me as instruction," Han said. "However, this ox has a vicious temperament. How am I to control it?"

"You have to feed him at the first, fourth, seventh and tenth watches—and don't get the timing wrong," the Perfected Man said. "Furthermore, I give you a sword of wisdom. When the ox is wild and won't submit to your control, chop off his head with this sword, and he will be subdued."

Following his orders, Tuizhi tied up the ox in a shed and fed it with hay and water at the first, fourth, seventh and tenth watches, not daring to be remiss for even a day. For more than three years the ox was submissive and did not rage.

One day, the Perfected Man called, "Han Yu, the cook is out of firewood today. Go once more and fetch some. When you come back, I also have something else to talk to you about."

"Last time I cut wood in the flower garden. Where should I go today?" Tuizhi asked.

"Northeast of here is a mountain called Mount Green Dragon," the Perfected Man said. "On this side it belongs to Mount Zhuowei, but the other side is looked after by other people. You mustn't go there to cut wood. If by mistake you cut other people's wood, you will cause your inner organs all to become inflamed so that even if you had four heads, eight arms, seven mouths, and eight tongues, you would be unable to drive out the resultant evil pneuma. Under no circumstances would I come to save you."

"How could I dare incite evil people and bring trouble upon you, Master?" Tuizhi said. He took carrying pole, axe, and rope, and set out.

After two or three miles he suddenly noticed three old men playing chess on a cliff. He thought to himself, "These three old men seem so happy, yet in my old age I have become a woodcutter in the mountains. It's just like this:

"In old age I work diligently; at night I am busy.
With absolute sincerity I rely on Heaven.
Only if I get taken up by a divine immortal
Will I be sure that I can avoid Death."

He went to the cliff and watched the old men at their game. When one of them saw him standing there, he asked, "You are a woodcutter. Why are you standing there instead of cutting wood? Do you perhaps know how to play chess?"

"I know how to play, but won't," Tuizhi said. "It is said, 'The best move in chess is not to play it.'"

"You sound neither like a woodcutter nor like one of us," one of the old men said.

"Listen to what I have to say, you three masters," Han said. "My name is Han Yu, and I was minister of rites at the court. I was banished, because I couldn't control my tongue. On the way into exile I suffered many hardships at Blue Pass in the Qin Mountains. Fortunately my nephew Xiangzi led me to Mount Zhuowei, where I took the Perfected Man Mumu as my teacher of the Dao. Today I was sent by my master to Mount Green Dragon to cut wood. When I saw you three masters playing chess here, I realized that you are divine immortals descended to earth, and so I came to ask you to deliver me."

"How long have you been with the Perfected Man?" the three old men asked with one voice.

"Already three winters and summers," Han answered.

One old man pursued, "In the long time you've been on this mountain, what has the Perfected Man told you? How does he expound the Dao to you?"

"When I first arrived, he made me burn incense and sweep the ground," Han replied. "Later he sent me to cut firewood and look after an ox. Today he has sent me again to cut firewood. He has not transmitted a single word of instruction to me."

"If the Perfected Man is unwilling to transmit the Dao to you, you should look for another place to stay," one of the old men said. "If you waste more years, you will soon have reached old age. Then how will you achieve your goal?"

"It is my good fortune to have met you today," Han said. "I beg you to instruct me to the best of your ability. To the day I die I shall not forget the mercy you have shown me."

The three old men said, "The Perfected Man Mumu is our Daoist friend, with whom we meet here often. As you are his disciple, we couldn't forgive ourselves if we didn't give you some instruction. Please listen to us":

(To the tune "Luojiangyuan")

"In spring a hundred herbs grow;
Life is growing wherever one gazes.
It would seem a good time to roam,
But I sit in my hut.
In silence, all noise is excluded.

I hope to accomplish the perfect change.
Yet who knows?
If affinity is sparse and your lot shallow, it will be difficult to meet.

"*In summer it gets gradually hotter,*
Yet my mind is in a cool place.
Having abandoned children and wife,
I go to live in a thatched hermitage.
I find some men whose heart is set on the Dao,
And embrace Heaven and Earth each at the right time.
As the simurgh flies and the crane dances, I ascend to the Jasper
*   Pool,*
And see with my own eyes the marvelous significance of the fish and
*   the kite.*[1]

"*In autumn as the days grow gradually cooler,*
Those who have left the family roam at ease.
Having traveled enough after several dozen years,
I finally meet an enlightened master who expounds the Dao to me.
He transmits to me the inner and outer elixir;
In my mind everything becomes bright and shining.
Without noticing it, the yang spirit descends within three years.

"*In winter the snow flies chaotically;*
The mind of him who has left the family knows itself.
Cold and heat do not contradict each other;
Gods and ghosts do not oppress each other.
When fatigue comes, I use my bent arm as a pillow,
When hunger comes, I subsist on dates and fruits.
Water from a mountain brook quenches my thirst.
This is the secret of the marvelous mystery."

When Han heard this, he said, "These views of the four seasons are meant for immortals. I, Han Yu, am a common mortal. How could I get to see these scenes?"

"Minister Han, the Perfected Man Mumu is coming," said one of the old men. When Han turned to look, the three old men had vanished.

He said to himself, "The three venerable immortals instructed me very clearly. I have eyes, yet did not see, and missed another opportunity."

Nothing was left for him to do but to cut and shoulder the firewood. Leaving Mount Green Dragon, he carried his load back to the grotto. When he called to his master to open the gate, the Perfected Man told an attendant to let him in. He carried the firewood to the kitchen and handed it over. He was about to return to his chamber when the Perfected Man suddenly called to him, "Han Yu, did you meet anyone as you went to Mount Green Dragon to cut wood?"

"I met three old men who were playing chess on that rock cliff. When I watched them, they asked me what my name was and where I came from. I said, 'I am a disciple of the Perfected Man Zhuowei and have come from Mount Zhuowei.' The three old men said they were friends of yours, Master."

"What did you ask them?"

"I asked them what yellow sprouts are," Tuizhi said. "They said they were the root of Heaven and Earth, the refined pneuma of the human body. They also taught me how to circulate the pneuma in the four watches, and instructed me about the Eight Trigrams hidden within and the Nine Divisions that exist in union outside. I didn't understand the mysterious marvels that were implied by these terms. Would you explain them to me clearly?"

The Perfected Man said,

(To the tune "Blossoming Branch")

"First understand the secrets of Heaven and Earth,
Then distinguish yin and yang.
If there is Former Heaven, there is the Mother;
Without the Mother there is no Heaven either.
This is the source of our Daoism.
Count the Cosmic Orbit from the beginning;
Reverse qian and kun.
Choose the foundation of Later Heaven;
Refine yourself to seize Former Heaven.
If you know who is after and who is before,
You become a sage and immortal.
The center of li is empty;
The center of kan is full.
In the center of li a thing is lacking;
Seek it in kan to return to the primordium.
As Green Dragon and White Tiger struggle with each other,
See beginning and end in the oral formula;

Obtain the sacred method whose marvel lies in the mind transmission.
Flowing backward one accomplishes the elixir as the Dragon swallows
the Tiger's marrow.
By going with the flow one accomplishes one's humanity as the Tiger
seizes the Dragon's saliva.
Guard against the unsheathed, green-tipped sword in front of your
heart.
Fear that it is difficult to stay in the boat among fast-flowing water and
wind-whipped waves.
Feel, just feel, the Yellow Matron is enticing you;
Wait, just wait, the Maiden is opening the lotus.
These things are difficult to speak of.
After five thousand days, the mind is firm;
After thirty hours, something moves in the dark.
Only when the primordial Embryo is bathed,
And one has sat facing a wall for nine years,
Will one become an immortal beyond the clouds on the Isles of the
Blessed."

"Former Heaven and Later Heaven, Yellow Sprouts and White Snow, Dragon and Tiger, Lead and Mercury—of these I already know a thing or two," Tuizhi said. "But there are also the marvelous practices of the Great Liquid and Returned Elixir, the Nine Revolutions and Seven Reversals. May I ask you to clearly reveal these?"

"You have already learned about eighty to ninety percent of the practice, but there is still the three-word formula, which I shall transmit to you today and which will lead you to enlightenment," the Perfected Man said.

"Will you teach me the three-word formula?" Han pursued.

"The first word is 'sincerity,' the second 'silence,' the third 'softness.' By sincerity you enter; by silence you maintain; by softness you employ. By sincerity you become stupid; by silence you become loquacious; by softness you become coarse."

When Tuizhi heard the word "coarse," he suddenly comprehended. It was as if a key had opened a lock, as if the switch had been turned on a mechanism. It was a complete awakening.

He said to the Perfected Man, "I have awakened in my mind."

"Since you have awakened, what further difficulty is there?" said the Perfected Man. He took up some immortal wine, poured a cup, and handed it to Tuizhi. The latter bowed and drank it in one gulp, whereupon he felt his inner organs purified and his spirit strengthening. The Perfected Man sang a song to the tune "Buying Good Wine":

> "I have transmitted to you the practice of entering the Dao—never stop
>   practicing it.
> I have told you the path of cultivating perfection—you need fierce
>   determination.
> You must maintain your primordial yang and not let it leak out.
> I gave you the moon in the sky.
> When it is full, the Golden Flower will form itself;
> When it wanes, the Red Lead will also wane.
> Let the Lovely Maid and the Baby Boy be joyful;
> Watch the White Snow and the Yellow Sprouts germinate.
> I shout,
> Use this practice to scrape off the dust and dirt,
> And become an immortal of the Penglai Isles."

When Tuizhi heard the Perfected Man's oral formula, he drank another cup of immortal wine. From then on he raised the Dragon and captured the Tiger day and night, nourished the Mercury and preserved the Lead. And really, the two pneumata exchanged their places, the Three Flowers accumulated in the head, the Dragon coiled around the gate, and the Tiger wound itself around the drug cauldron. The lightning flashed that gives life to the self and nourishment to all beings.

Instantly Tuizhi opened the door of the chamber and saw the ox he had been looking after. Now it was violent as thunder, uncontrollably wild. He shouted at it, "You headstrong beast, how dare you be so ill-mannered?" Then he took the sword of wisdom that the Perfected Man had given him. When the ox saw Han with the sword in his hand, it lowered its horns, opened its eyes wide, and rushed at him. Tuizhi brought the sword down on the ox's head. The head fell; the sword dropped to the ground. Then suddenly a ray of white pneuma shot up to the gate of Heaven, startling the Jade Emperor. When with his eyes of wisdom he saw that a white pneuma had struck Heaven from Mount Zhuowei, he dispatched golden lads and jade maidens to summon Zhongli Quan, Lü Dongbin, and the other immortals to welcome Tuizhi. But more about that reception later.

Now let us describe how Tuizhi, after he had chopped off the ox's head, turned around and reported to the Perfected Man, "The ox roared wildly and I chopped off its head with the sword. I have transgressed."

The Perfected Man said,

> *"The ox was always in the dust of the common world.*
> *He was stupidity, dullness, dumbness, confusion, laughter, and other*
> *   ordinary things.*
> *Today you have withdrawn from the body and will go beyond the*
> *   clouds;*
> *Among your companions, who will again dare apply the whip?"*

"Does that mean that the ox has also become immortal?" Han asked.

"The nature of dogs is like the nature of oxen," the Perfected Man said. "The nature of oxen is like the nature of humans. Once it has changed into the utmost Dao, why shouldn't it become an immortal?"

Then Tuizhi suddenly realized that the two characters *zhuowei* together made up the character *Han*, and *mumu* combined became *Xiang*. Looking closely at the Perfected Man's eyes of the Dao, blue and green with square pupils, he saw that they were the same as Xiangzi's. He stepped forward, embraced the Perfected Man, and said, "You were Xiangzi all along, and not some Perfected Man Mumu. If you hadn't instructed me over and over again, I would already have fallen among the ranks of ghosts. How could I have seen this day?"

"Indeed, I am your nephew Xiangzi. I was afraid that your belief was not firm, therefore I split the character *Han* into the two characters *zhuo* and *wei*, and the character *Xiang* into *mu* and *mu*. I deceived you, Uncle, but it was worthwhile, as now your rewards of the Dao are complete. I shall recount to you my past attempts at delivering and transforming you. Please listen":

(To the tune "Shoal among the Waves")

> *"That day down from the celestial gate*
> *I flew on the back of a crane,*
> *And ascended the altar to pray for abundant snow.*
> *I changed a stone into gold and worked many transformations—*
> *All to deliver you and make you change your mind.*

> *"Twice I tried to deliver you at your birthday,*
> *Making flowers grow instantly,*
> *And congratulating you by filling vessels with immediate wine.*

The powers of my magical basket and fruit were great,
All to deliver you and make you change your mind.

"I presented the Buddha bone to the illustrious ruler,
Who banished you to the city of Chaozhou.
As a fisherman, woodcutter, farmer, and herdsman I spoke of your
     whole life,
Wolves and tigers threatened your life,
All to deliver you and make you change your mind.

"In the thatched hut you found temporary shelter;
Your horse died and it was difficult to walk on.
On Mount Zhuowei you met the Perfected Man.
Counting them off on my fingers, twelve attempts
Before I succeeded in making you change your mind."

Then Xiangzi said, "It took twelve attempts at converting you, Uncle, before you completed your proper rewards today. I shall once more summon an immortal crane, and we shall ride to Heaven together."

Lifting his head, Tuizhi expressed his gratitude in the following words:

"Attached to high officialdom, my thinking was mistaken;
How was I to know that life and death are intertwined?
Yet now that I am at ease and roam in happiness,
I realize why Han Xiang wanted me to leave the family."

Did Xiangzi really summon an immortal crane? Please listen to the explanations in the next chapter.

28

ON CHEATING MOUNTAIN, A WOODCUTTER SHOWS THE WAY

MOTHER AND DAUGHTER-IN-LAW CULTIVATE THEMSELVES IN MAGU'S HERMITAGE

Living a hundred years without becoming free—
Such a life was nothing but a floating bubble.
How eternally sad if the golden elixir went to waste;
What perennial sorrow if one became an immortal crane in vain.
Would a flood dragon who finds himself out of water
Dare to call the simurgh and phoenix down from their painted
*   towers?*
Roam at ease without restrictions;
Cross high mountains and watch the water flow.

Han Xiangzi summoned a white crane from the sky. Riding on its back, Tuizhi slowly ascended straight to the gate of the Three Heavens, where he met Zhongli Quan, Lü Dongbin, and other immortals. Here is a poem to illustrate it:

Among the piles of white clouds a crane comes flying
To guide Han Yu up the jade steps.
Auspicious clouds are wafting; immortal music is played;
The immortals jostle to ascend the jasper terrace.

"It has been a long time since I learned that you had left the family," Master Zhong said. "Today you have successfully accomplished your proper rewards."

"Don't bring up what I said before," Tuizhi said. "Though I had eyes to see, I did not."

Then immortals carrying a golden decree written in great vermilion characters led him to an audience with the Jade Emperor. As the Jade Emperor prepared to promulgate a decree, he asked, "Han Yu, as you come here today, do you know why you were banished to earth?"

Silent at first, Tuizhi suddenly became aware of his past and said, "I was originally the Attendant Great General Chonghezi. Because I drunkenly snatched an immortality peach and shattered a crystal cup at the Immortality Peach Banquet, I was banished to the lower world. After that I became attached to my work and coveted official positions, thus spending a long time in the world of dust. Fortunately my nephew Han Xiang received a commission from Jasper Heaven to repay my original sincerity and save me from the entanglements of my human existence. On the occasion of this audience, I respectfully beg that in your celestial mercy Your Majesty will forgive my fatal sins."

Immortals from the Three Offices of Heaven, Earth, and Humanity recommended that Han Yu resume his former post as Attendant General. The Jade Emperor approved the submission, and right away enfeoffed Tuizhi as an immortal of the jade realm and had him resume his former position. The immortals and Tuizhi thanked the emperor and withdrew, but we need talk no more about this. A poem shall provide a summary:

> By eating pneuma and clouds one gets to the origin of the Dao,
> Allowing one to roam freely in the grotto heavens.
> A limitless view of purple fungi and jasper herbs,
> Reversing old age and returning one to childhood and youth.

We will not describe how Han Yu entered the ranks of the immortals and proceeded to a banquet at the Jasper Pool; instead let us relate how Han Qing chose an auspicious day and erected some huts on the beach. Although they were not great mansions, they did provide protection from the wind and rain. Just as he was about to move the whole family in, earth and sky darkened all at once. Thunder and lightning followed in rapid succession, struck the huts, and burned them down completely. They could not even save a single piece of furniture or other property. This is what is meant when people say:

> Withered grass is hit hard by frost;
> Faded flowers are destroyed by rain.

A leaking boat is struck by sky-high waves;
A broken hut is destroyed by a storm.
A man with a broken foot has to cross a high ridge.
A ram gets its horns entangled in a hedge.
When time and destiny are against one,
A single thunderbolt destroys all prospects.[1]

When the people in the Han family's party witnessed this scene, each and every one of them called to Heaven and Earth and cried bitterly. At this point of deepest sorrow, suddenly a fisher drum sounded urgently and a song was heard loud and clear. Listening to the far-off sound, Mme. Dou peered attentively in that direction, and saw a singing Daoist coming towards them.

(To the tune "Golden Oriole")

"As sun and moon alternate between east and west,
Alas, the life of humans is as short as a hundred years.
How about seeking refuge in the School of Mystery?
Your hair combed into a double knot,
Your body clothed in cotton robes,
Straw sandals and fisher drum are all you need to make a living.
I laugh and giggle,
Traveling by cloud to the ocean isles,
Seeing through the stupidity of worldly people."

Reader, shall I tell you where this Daoist came from? He was Lü Dongbin, who had transformed himself to point out the way to them. Therefore he struck the drum and sang his song just at the time of their sorrow, waiting for them to awaken of their own accord.

When Mme. Dou saw Master Lü, she called, "Master, save us!"

"How am I to save you?" Master Lü asked.

"We used to live comfortably in Chang'an, until we were expelled by that robber Cui Qun," she said. "It's his fault that we now have no roof over our heads and not half an acre of land below our feet. We have no clothes to cover our bodies, no food to fill our mouths. What are we to do?"

"On that mountain ahead, not more than a mile's journey, there is the hermitage of a female master. It is very clean, and there is ample space. Go there and stay with her for a time," Master Lü suggested.

"Many thanks to you, Master, for your directions, but I would feel embarrassed to visit her empty-handed," she replied.

"Those who have left the family are concerned only with compassion and skillful means. They use all their possessions to nourish believers everywhere. Why worry about going empty-handed to see her?"

Having spoken, Master Lü turned around and left. Mme. Dou told Han Qing to lead the way, and together with Luying and the others she slowly crossed the beach and made her way toward the mountain.

Having walked for half the day, they saw only dense forests, snarls of brushwood, and grassy paths. The wind sang and the leaves trembled, birds called among the abundant branches, yet no hermitage was to be seen anywhere. Although Mme. Dou was afraid in her heart, she could only press ahead. She called to Han Qing, "That Daoist said it was only a distance of little more than one mile. How come we have walked for half the day and still haven't seen a trace of the hermitage?"

"Mother, don't worry," Han Qing said. "Let's just keep walking; the hermitage is sure to be over there."

However, having walked another few miles, they found themselves surrounded on all sides by high mountains and great ravines, steep walls and precipitous cliffs. Not only was there no hermitage, there was not even a road any more. Greatly frightened, Mme. Dou called to Han Qing, "Let's quickly go back the way we came."

But when Han Qing started to head back, he could no longer find the path among the dense crags, trees, and underbrush. The group wailed in sorrow and cried bitterly, calling out to Heaven. How had they ended up in this dark and forsaken dell in the mountains?

"Mother-in-law, we have clearly fallen into someone's trap," Luying said. "There is no way forward and none back. Are we to die here? Let's pick up some earth as a substitute for incense and pray to Heaven and Earth. If we are not fated to die, a saving star is certain to come to our rescue."

Following Luying's proposal, Mme. Dou was just knocking her head and praying when they suddenly heard, ding-ding, dang-dang, the sound of an axe against wood.

"Mother!" Han Qing said. "There's the sound of wood being cut coming from over there. Someone must be there. I'll go talk to him and beg him to lead us back to the main road."

"If there is someone, do go quickly and ask him!" she said.

As she was speaking, they saw a woodcutter chopping firewood in the dell. "Brother," Han Qing called, "May I ask the name of this mountain? How is it that we could get here, but now we can't leave? We'd be very obliged to you, if we might bother you to show us the way out."

The woodcutter laid down his axe. "This place is called Cheating Mountain and Cheating Valley," he said, pointing. "Only cheating people walk on the cheating road. You are so good at laying plans, why did you come to Cheating Valley in the first place?"

"We made the mistake of listening to the words of a villainous Daoist. That's why we came to these mountains," Han Qing said.

"It was when you lived in Chang'an that you made the mistake," the woodcutter said. "Why do you say you only now made a mistake by listening to this Daoist's words?"

When Han Qing heard the woodcutter speak of a mistake they made in Chang'an, he thought to himself that the woodcutter must be an immortal. Hastily he knelt down and said, "I hope that the divine immortal will show us a way out."

The woodcutter pointed and said, "There in the southeast, two divine immortals are sitting on top of that cliff. If you go there quickly, you will find a road." As Han Qing lifted his head to look, the woodcutter took up his axe, and ran across the high mountain in no time at all. Indeed,

> At first they did not believe the divine immortals' words;
> Today they realize that regrets come too late.

Han Qing had no choice but to lead the family toward the southeast, where indeed there was a walkable path which was not blocked by entangled trees. They felt assured that they would reach the road ahead. In the distance they saw smoke rising from kitchen fires, curling and swirling in the wind.

It looked like there were homes there, but when they arrived, all around were only dense woods and tall bamboos, no huts or shacks. Suddenly they saw two Daoists sitting on top of the rock cliff, before them a tripod cauldron from which the light of a flaming red fire shone forth. "Those two Daoists sitting there must be immortals," Mme. Dou told Han Qing. "Go and ask them to deliver us from this calamity."

Han Qing hurried to the side of the cliff and called in a loud voice, "Divine immortals, save us!"

The two Daoists were in fact Lan Caihe and Han Xiangzi. Earlier on, Lü Dongbin had taken the form of a woodcutter and directed the women to the cliff where the other two immortals were waiting.

Xiangzi saw Han Qing on his way toward them, shouting, and answered, "We

墨床山樵夫指路

On Cheating Mountain a woodcutter shows the way.

are Daoists of the mountain wilderness, not divine immortals. We just begged some vegetarian food at the foot of the mountains and are now cooking it to still our hunger. If you want something to eat, we'll give you some to help you. If you don't want anything to eat, then suit yourself and leave as soon as possible."

"We walked the whole day and would indeed like to eat something," Han Qing said. "But if you give us some, you won't have enough for yourselves. Masters, why don't you deliver us so that we may escape our suffering, rather than sharing your meal with us?"

"The firefly can shine, but its light is not bright," Caihe said. "How could we deliver you? Be off!"

"Oh dear! We have no place to go, either in Chang'an or in Changli County. Where do you want us to return to?" Han Qing said.

"In Chang'an you have grand mansions and an emolument of a thousand bushels," Xiangzi said. "In Changli you have fields in the south and the north, melon patches and vegetable gardens. Why don't you go and enjoy all that? Why do you talk as if you had no options left?"

"Now we only beseech you to save us," Mme. Dou said.

"When first someone admonished you to leave the family, you said you were going to submit a petition to the yamen of the Ministry of Rites to have the Daoist monasteries on renowned mountains and the immortals' dwellings in outstanding places all over the empire demolished," Xiangzi said. "Not one was to be left standing. Those who spoke of leaving the family were to receive twenty-one blows with the stick and would find no mercy. Now that you're in this difficult situation, why don't you submit a petition to the Ministry of Rites to dispatch some men, sedan chairs, and horses and have you return in pomp and style by the main road? Instead you are asking a Daoist of the wilderness for help. What power and splendor do we rustic Daoists have that we could be of help to you?"

"Unenlightened mortals have but ordinary eyes and bodies," she said. "They don't recognize divine immortals. Master, please save our unworthy lives."

"Master, if you don't deliver us, I will tie my handkerchief to a tree and hang myself, forcing the local officials to arrest you and make you pay with your own lives," Han Qing said.

"We ascetics roam the blue ocean in the morning and stay in Cangwu in the evening," Caihe said. "Within a moment we can fly several thousand miles. Why should we be afraid that anyone might arrest us?"

"Saving a human life is worth more than building a seven-storied pagoda," Mme. Dou said. "Why do you refuse to employ the bit of compassion required to save and deliver us?"

"I won't beat around the bush, but ask you directly," Xiangzi said. Are you honestly willing to leave the family today or are you just pretending?"

"Today I have given up all other hope and only wish to leave the family," Mme. Dou said.

"Mother-in-law, earlier, when Xiangzi came home, you refused to cultivate yourself," said Luying, standing beside her. "Today there is no Xiangzi around. How can we two women follow two masters to cultivate ourselves?"

"Well said," Caihe replied. "We just wanted to be certain that you were honestly willing to leave the family. If you are, and want to see Xiangzi, there is no problem."

"Master, where is my elder brother?" Han Qing asked. "If you help us find him, it will count as merit for you."

"I happen to have met Xiangzi and I know where he lives," Xiangzi said. "I can lead you to him."

"We really, really are willing to cultivate ourselves," Mme. Dou pleaded. "Master, don't play any more tricks on us."

"If you think we are tricksters, you better go and be somebody else's disciples," Caihe said.

"Masters, if you are divine immortals, why do you speak like extortionists?" Han Qing said. "It's because we have been fooled so often that we can't get ourselves to trust you now."

"I may not be able to distinguish true and false right away, but if I have Xiangzi before my eyes, I will believe," Mme. Dou said.

"In that case, Immortal Brother, we can reveal our original appearance and see if they recognize us," Caihe said.

"Over there!" Xiangzi called out, pointing. "Xiangzi is coming!"

When Mme. Dou, Luying, and Han Qing turned around to look, they didn't see any Han Xiangzi, but when they turned back again, there stood Xiangzi before them, saying, "Aunt, when I first exhorted you to leave the family, you said that although Uncle had passed away you still had the emoluments bestowed by the court, and that you lived in a grand mansion. Every day you could eat delicacies, drink good wine, dine on fat mutton, dress in silk gauze and finely ornamented cloth, and sleep on blue bamboo shoot mattresses in ivory bedsteads. You had more food than you could eat and more money than you could spend. Wasn't that better than leaving the family? Why, then, are you today thinking of leaving the family?"

"Nephew, don't bring up what I said before," his aunt said. "Just remember that I raised you, and save me!"

"Xu Jingyang's *Zongjiao lu* puts it well," Luying said. "'A loyal man won't deceive. A filial son won't rebel.' Since you are a divine immortal, how come you don't know the way of filial piety?"[2]

"What makes you think that I don't know it?" asked Xiangzi.

"Your uncle educated you, your aunt raised you. The debt you owe both of them is the same. You've already delivered your uncle to become an immortal, yet you refuse to deliver your aunt. Doesn't that look as if you didn't know the way of filial piety?"

"If that's what you say, I shall deliver my aunt only," Xiangzi said. "You can go home."

"I have no home," Luying said. "Where do you want me to go?"

"Go to the Cui family," he suggested.

"Which Cui family?"

"The family of the minister Cui."

"If I had been willing to go to the Cui family, we wouldn't be in this mess today," she responded.

"If you don't go to the Cui family, then return to the family of Scholar Lin,"

"I am not returning to the Lin family either," Luying said.

"If you refuse to return, can it be that you want to remain standing here in these mountains?" Xiangzi asked.

"The ancient saying puts it well," Luying said. "'If you marry a rooster, you have to fly with the chickens. If you marry a dog, you have to walk with the dogs.' I married you, and lived with you. Since you've become an immortal, I am now the wife of an immortal. If I don't go with you, where do you want me to go?"

"I received an imperial decree to deliver one person, not two. I can only deliver my aunt. How could I also deliver you?"

"When Xu Jingyang ascended to Heaven, he took even his chickens and dogs with him," Luying said. "When Wang Lao rose to Heaven, one could still hear the sound of his servants turning the millstone in the sky. Since you are a divine immortal, why do you refuse to take your wife along?"

"The people you mention all already had their names inscribed in the registers of immortals—that's why they got delivered," Xiangzi told her. "You, on the other hand, are a common woman with no name in the immortals' registers. How am I to deliver you?"

"The bond of husband and wife is one of the cardinal human relationships, and divine immortals are persons who completely fulfill the principles of human relationships," said Luying. "You, however, have failed in all five relationships—how can you be a divine immortal?"

"You're speaking in vain. There's no way I will deliver you."

"Brother, Miss Lin makes a valid point about morality," Caihe cut in. "You have to deliver her. If you don't, nobody in the world will listen any more to those who promote morality."

"Brother, don't let yourself be badgered by these Confucian moralists," Xiangzi replied. "Miss Lin's is a feminine morality; she speaks of the five relationships only because she has no other choice. When it comes to masculine morality, she will come up with other tricks. She'll keep quiet about the five relationships, but speak of six relationships instead, until you don't know any more where your head and feet are!"

"How can there be a difference between female and male in morality?" Caihe said. "As long as what she expounds is true morality, then men like us beyond the clouds must not speak of female and male. If we deliver her simply by virtue of that 'morality,' the benefits of expounding it in the world will be made clear."

Xiangzi gave a laugh and said, "Aunt, Miss, I'll deliver you today, but you still have the body and bones of ordinary mortals. You can't proceed to the Purple Palace or ascend to the Jasper Pool directly. You first need to go to the hermitage of Magu, the Hemp Maiden, to cultivate and refine yourself for a few years.[3] Shed this mortal body, change these mortal bones; only then can you complete the way of perfection, realize your rewards, and ascend to the Primordial Center."

"Where is the hermitage of Magu?" Mme. Dou asked. "How far is it from here? Our feet are bound, and we don't know the way. How can we get there?"

"Magu's hermitage is in Nanchang Prefecture in Jiangxi, more than eight thousand miles from here," Xiangzi said. "There are no wild beasts or poisonous insects on the way, nor are there ruffians and robbers, so you should get there within three to five months. As long as you keep a firm heart and a determined will and don't stir up trouble, you won't have problems on the journey."

"I'm not stupid—why would I stir up trouble?" Luying said. "But during those three to five months on the road, how shall we find food to eat and inns to rest at? If we have to go begging from door to door and stay in makeshift quarters, what if we encounter frivolous youths and unrestrained students? An ugly donkey can in a short time change into a bear ready to commit evil deeds. Tell me, from whom are we to seek rescue then? Or perhaps the Master will take pity on us two indigent but determined widows and show us a broad road to salvation. That would be better than cultivating ourselves at the hermitage of Magu."

"You say a journey of eight thousand miles is long and hard to make. When I want to go there, it takes me less than an hour. If only you acknowledge that I am the true Xiangzi, you can go the same way."

"Why are you talking like this again? If our commitment to the Dao weren't firm, we wouldn't be willing to leave the family today," Mme. Dou said.

When Xiangzi saw that their minds and intentions were indeed firmly set, he spread his sleeves, and within a moment two yellow clouds came slowly drifting down. He stopped the clouds, and they touched down on the ground like lotus leaves sprouting roots. Xiangzi then made Mme. Dou and Luying each sit on a cloud, and shouted, "Leave quickly!" The two clouds rose up higher and higher until they could be seen only indistinctly, and then they were gone. Truly,

> From the sky stretches out a hand that takes the clouds
> And lifts humans from the nets of Heaven and Earth.

Han Qing watched wide-eyed as Mme. Dou and Luying flew off on the clouds. He alone was left by the side of the cliff. Feeling embarrassed and not knowing what to do, he broke into loud wailing. Not even the two Daoists were to be seen any more, and he wasn't sure whether they had been real or imagined. Han Qing beat his chest and stomped the ground. Now he cried, now he clapped his hands and laughed, saying, "Strange and absurd things happen in the world. It is really laughable. The lady and the young mistress were clearly standing here and talking, when suddenly two clouds descended from the sky and carried them off. There's no trace to be seen even of those two Daoists, and I alone am left. If they had abducted me as well, I would surely have been lost! I suppose those two criminal Daoists were master pimps who deceived my sister-in-law and will make her a queen of whores. My mother will be the madam. How absurd! But I don't seem to have any way out, either. What am I to do?"

As he was talking to himself, a sudden thundering sound scared him almost to death. When he looked closely, he saw that a large crack had opened in the cliff, from which a flood of water came surging out. While Han Qing, all flustered, sought to save his life, the water had already flowed up to his feet, and he was almost knocked over. Although he crossed two mountains and climbed up a tall tree, when he looked down the water was still rising.

Sitting in his tree he said, "There was an ancient who worried that the sky might collapse and the earth fall down, and that from the rupture a mighty river might spurt forth. People laughed at him and said that he worried too much. This flood today, however, clearly is caused by Heaven and Earth overturning, a kalpic disaster that will be difficult to escape. Who would have known that at such a young age I should suffer such adversity? I just said that when Mother and Sister-in-law ascended to Heaven on their clouds they were abducted by the

Daoists. Now they are no better off than I—even the Daoists are within the world's fate and can't escape."

Looking again, he said, "The water is only filling that space over there, and only the people in that place will be harmed by it. I should be fine over here. But if I jump off the tree, where should I go? If the whole world is flooded and I alone am left, who will serve me? Who will till and plant the fields to feed me and keep me alive? I'll be doomed to die." After a while he added, "Although the Hans adopted me as their son, they also often humiliated me unnecessarily. The other day, that old dog bone Qian Xinyu also revealed my weak spot. Today this great flood has left me alone. In some way this is cause for joy, isn't it?"

Then he said, "With the water rising so high the fierce tigers and poisonous insects all over the mountains will be disturbed and come rushing out. If I climb down from the tree and bump into one of them, I am as good as dead and buried." Once more he spoke to himself, saying, "Hiding in this tree I'm lucky it hasn't rained. If it rains—well, I'm not the Bird Nest Chan Master. How would I shelter from it?"[4] After another while he said, "Up here in the tree I have nothing to eat or drink. If it doesn't rain, I will be thirsty and shrivel up like a dried fish."

After considering innumerable schemes, he still didn't know what to do. Having no other choice, he climbed down from the tree. As it is said,

> Green Dragon and White Tiger always walk together;
> One never knows how things will turn out.

What happened to Han Qing afterward? Please listen to the explanations in the next chapter.

29

A BEAR-MAN CARRIES HAN QING ACROSS

THE MOUNTAIN RANGES

AN IMMORTAL TRANSMITS MYSTERIOUS SECRETS TO MME. DOU

All people have within them the medicine of long life,
Yet self-assured, stupid, and deluded, they vainly toss it away.
When the sweet dew descends, Heaven and Earth unite;
At the place where the Yellow Sprouts grow, kan and li interact.
The well frog responds by saying that there is no dragon's lair;
How can a fence quail know that there is a phoenix nest?
Once the elixir is cooked, the room is filled with gold.
Why bother seeking herbs and learning how to cook water
mallows?[1]

For now let us speak no more of Han Qing climbing down out of the tree, but instead tell you about Minister Lin in Chang'an.

Because Mme. Dou and Luying had been sent back to the Han family's native district due to the memorial Cui Qun submitted to Emperor Xianzong, Lin Gui had not seen his daughter Luying in a long time and missed her very much. One day, he was about to send a man to Changli County to seek news of Luying when a messenger arrived and reported, "The Han family's houses and farms in Changli County have all been destroyed by a flood. Not a single beam or an inch of earth was left. Mme. Dou has no roof over her head and is suffering grievously."

When Minister Lin heard this report, tears sprang to his eyes and he said, "Han Yu was straightforward and blunt; throughout his career he was loyal and incorruptible. His only wish was to protect his descendants and preserve his reputation for a hundred generations. He wanted to live and die in honor. Yet as a result of the one memorial against the Buddha bone, he was separated from his family and died in a foreign place. That his family has now been struck by a flood is a perfect example of the fact that blessings never come in pairs, while calamities never walk alone. Who has eyes in his back so that he can see what goes on behind him? Under these circumstances, my attachment to my office is meaningless." Immediately he submitted his resignation and expressed his wish to return to Changli County.

Fortunately Emperor Xianzong approved his resignation and allowed him to return to his native district via the official courier service. Lin Gui set out on his journey right away. As illustration, here is a lyric:

> Yellow flowers grow all over the ground.
> People half raise their door bars to peer at the traveler,
> But hear only his horse neighing as it canters along the flowery path.
> Listening to the cries of a sorrowful monkey,
> He traverses a wilderness with few villages.
> He sees herdboys in groups of two or three,
> Riding calves with the light of the declining sun among the flowers.
> As he passes post stations and wayside pavilions
> His tears fall like rain,
> His grief beyond measure.

Traveling on the road, Minister Lin became sadder day by day as he contemplated the fickle ways of the world. He often thought of Xiangzi, but never encountered him on the way. One day when he arrived at a place by the Grand Canal, he saw a bustling crowd of people by the water, coming and going, all striving for fame and profit. Among them was a young Daoist, his hair disheveled, his clothes tattered. Over his right shoulder he had slung a bottle gourd and a flower basket; in his right hand he raised a fisher drum and a clapper. Looking toward Minister Lin he sang:

> "You don't follow the example of Tao Qian, who was reluctant to bow to
>   his superior.
> You don't follow the example of Fan Li, who went wandering among the
>   five lakes.
> You don't follow the example of Zhang Zifang, who followed Master
>   Red Pine.

You don't follow the example of Yan Ziling, who fished at Seven Mile
   Beach.
You don't follow the example of Lu Guimeng, who packed up his brush
   holder and tea stove and went to roam the rivers and lakes.
And you don't follow the example of the Marquis of East Mount, who
   abandoned fame and profit.
How can you equal me, who has tied a hempen cord to his cotton robe
And beats on the fisher drum?"

After listening for a while, Minister Lin said, "Once, on Han Tuizhi's birthday, a Daoist came and urged him to leave the family. Tuizhi, however, was obstinate and wouldn't listen, and ultimately this led to the present misfortune. My resignation from office and return home show that good and bad fortune are not predestined, but are brought by human beings upon themselves.[2] Time passes quickly; life and death are difficult to know. The song sung by this young Daoist seems to fit me word for word. Perhaps I have met him before? I shall call him to me and question him."

Forthwith he called, "Young Daoist, step on board. I want to ask you something."

When the passersby saw Minister Lin calling in person to the Daoist, they wondered what the reason might be and pushed towards the boat in a thick crowd. When the Daoist heard that he was being called, he struggled through to the front of the crowd, supporting himself with both hands on people's shoulders, and said, "Sir, I knock my head."

Minister Lin returned the courtesy with a half bow. The onlookers and Minister Lin's servants gesticulated and chattered, saying, "On the way we came through many jurisdictions, circuits, prefectures, and counties, and there were those who repeatedly requested an audience with the minister, yet he refused to see them. What's so special about this filthy Daoist that the minister himself calls him and even gives him a half bow in return? How strange!"

Although Lin heard these whispers among the crowd, he pretended not to notice them and called, "Young Daoist, please take a seat." Without further courtesies, the Daoist youth stepped forward and sat down facing south.

"Where is your home?" Minister Lin asked. "Why did you leave the family to cultivate yourself?"

The youth sang,

"My home is the Zhongnan Mountains,
Where I have a hut with three rooms.

The roof tiles covering it are the blue sky;
There are no walls around it, and there is nothing to impede me.
The ten thousand phenomena in their majesty all bow to the dipper;
Sun and moon I carry on my shoulders.
When I sleep,
I turn over only very carefully,
For fear I might push over Mount Buzhou.
Not to leak one's essence for several thousand years
Is possible only by previous affinity.
Once your merit reaches three thousand,
You can look forward to your deliverance."

"If you are a divine immortal, I am willing to honor you as my teacher," Minister Lin said.

"If you want me to deliver you, that's not difficult," said the youth. "However, I fear that your mind is not steadfast and your spirit not firmly settled, so that my efforts would be in vain."

"I have abandoned my honors of office like garbage, gold and silver like sand and mud," Minister Lin said. "I regard my body as stinking and rotten, wife and children as cast-off shells. I will single-mindedly cultivate the Dao and have no other sentiments."

"In that case, this is not the place to discuss it," the Daoist said. "Come with me." Lin followed him. As the crowd opened before them, they made a run for it. Members of Lin's household pursued, but when they caught hold of him, he drew his sword, cut off his sleeve, and kept running. The onlookers all said that Minister Lin had met an immortal and left.

Reader, shall I tell you who the young Daoist was, and why Scholar Lin agreed to follow him?

Well, the Daoist was Han Xiangzi. Minister Lin was originally Yunyangzi, who had been banished to earth. Now that Chonghezi had resumed his post, Yunyangzi also was to return to his position. This is why Xiangzi played the role of the Daoist to instruct him. Once Lin saw Xiangzi, he recognized him as an immortal, and consequently, giving no further thought to his family and relatives, followed him to the grotto on Mount Zhuowei.

After bowing eight times toward Xiangzi, Minister Lin said, "Your disciple Lin Gui has met his Master. Please instruct me."

"South and north accord with the Source through the inversion of the signs of the trigrams," Xiangzi said. "At dawn and dusk the Fire Phases harmonize with the

Celestial Pivot.[3] You must seal the Earth Cauldron firmly and let the flowing Pearl make a pair with it.[4] Your emotions must be adjusted, your nature unified, the Tiger crouching, the Dragon coiling. In the *Token for the Agreement of the Three* it is said, 'The pneuma of *li* gives nourishment from the inside. When one is empty there is no need for a keen sense of hearing. When understanding meets mind, there is no need for oral exchange of thought—and the fewer the spoken words, the surer and greater the success.'[5] The Elixir Formula says, 'The metal man was originally the eastern family's son, but was sent to lodge with the western neighbor. Having been recognized, he is invited home to be nourished. He is then matched with a lovely maid, and they are brought together in intimacy.'[6] Do you understand?"

"I am dumb and confused. Please instruct me again," Minister Lin said.

Xiangzi sang,

> "The aperture of the Mysterious Pass
> Was first joined in Former Heaven,
> When Metal and Wood invited each other.
> Mercury of yin can fly and travel;
> Lead of yang can submit and adjust.
> Control the obstinate Monkey and the evil Horse;
> Don't give them the least room to move.
> Let the mind be like stagnant water,
> And the emotions like the Nine Empyreans.
> Be firm and nourish warmth,
> Hold fast as you apply boiling heat,
> And you shall behold the radiance of the precious pearl."

"Thanks to your teachings I have become aware of my previous existences—I will submit to your instruction!" said Minister Lin. And he sang:

> "The mysterious marvel of the Golden Pill
> Has been transmitted to me by my Master's teachings.
> Having been stirred from my dumb confusion,
> How would I dare shirk hard work?
> I love the life of the immortals,
> The clear loftiness of the golden palaces.
> The incense dissipates in precious seal script characters,
> Its smoke dissolving into the Nine Empyreans;
> From now on I shall be free and roam at ease."

Xiangzi said, "Since you are now awakened, you must struggle onward and not allow yourself a single moment of slackness. If you let your thoughts roam far afield while sitting still, you will fall back into your evil ways."

"I may not be intelligent, but how could I waste this opportunity?" said Minister Lin. From then on he cultivated himself at Zhuowei Grotto from morning to evening.

But now let's speak again of that day when Han Qing climbed down from the tree. He was just going to set out southward when suddenly he saw a bear-man. His whole body and face were covered with hair, and only a pair of gleaming red eyes were visible underneath. When he saw that Han Qing was about to leave, he came running over so fast that his feet barely seemed to touch the ground.

When Han Qing caught sight of the creature he was so frightened that he collapsed in a trembling heap, unable to open his mouth or move his limbs. His eyes closed, he cowered on the ground. Sensing Han Qing's fear, the bear-man broke out into bellowing and terrifying laughter. Han Qing kept his eyes closed and didn't dare look at him. The creature patted and kneaded Han Qing's body all over, all the while making mumbling sounds as if he were speaking.

Han Qing did not dare move, and when the bear-man realized that Han Qing was not heeding him, he dragged him up, threw him over his shoulder, and strode away across one of the mountains. At first Han Qing feared that the beast would devour him alive, and was scared out his wits. Later he noticed that the bear-man just kept carrying him on, and he recovered somewhat. He broke into tears and told his captor, "Bear-man! You have a numinous nature, consciousness, and perception; you're not a stupid and unconscious beast. I am a stricken man, without father or mother, relatives or friends who would care for me. Where are you carrying me? Is there perhaps a country for stricken men at the end of the sky?"

The bear-man kept going, while at the same time mumbling incessantly, as if he were answering him. When Han Qing saw that the creature seemed to have some human understanding, he told him, "My elder brother is called Han Xiangzi. He is a divine immortal in Great Veil Heaven. My mother and sister-in-law have both been delivered and transformed thanks to him, but me alone he didn't deliver; instead he abandoned me with no place to go. If you really possess a numinous nature, then carry me to Xiangzi."

The bear-man rocked and shook his head as if he were responding to Han Qing, but just kept walking on, with Han Qing on his back. They traversed heights and crossed torrents, went across mountain ranges and through forests—nothing hindered their progress. When they were hungry, they ate, when thirsty, they drank, resting at night and walking during the day. However, as there was no wine or rice available, they ate mountain fruits and drank spring water. At night Han Qing shared the same sleeping place with the bear-man, sometimes by a cliff, sometimes in a cave.

Having traveled for several weeks, they saw in the distance a high mountain. Its walls rose thousands of feet, with huge boulders balanced precariously on them. Anyone who approached this mountain would feel his eyes going blurry and his heart beating wildly, because there were no footholds, and manifold dangers lurked. It was a place that both humans and ghosts would find difficult to cross.

But the bear-man, carrying Han Qing, scaled the mountain and crossed the brooks, passing through many difficult places as if he were treading on level ground or walking on an even road, without ever stumbling. On his back, Han Qing thought to himself, "In the extremity of my loneliness and suffering, I met this bear-man. I was destined to die, yet he carried me over such a great distance. I wonder where he is taking me. I imagine I was supposed to die earlier, yet now I have been given a new lease on life. So I'll just let him carry me to wherever it may be!"

They had passed a few more places when all at once a group of woodcutters came along. When the bear-man saw the woodcutters, he was not at all flustered, but just kept on carrying Han Qing. When the woodcutters saw that he was carrying a man, they didn't come hurrying over either, but just sang a Daoist song.

When Han Qing called for help, one of the woodcutters pulled him off the bear-man's shoulder and asked, "Where do you come from? Where did you meet this creature, that you got carried here by him?"

Han Qing was just going to reply when another woodcutter put down his load and said, "Are you Han Qing? Why have you been brought here? Where are the old lady and Miss Lin?"

"You are Zhang Qian, aren't you?" Han Qing said.

"I am the Daoist Qian," the woodcutter said.

"Daoist Qian my foot! You did recognize me, didn't you?"

"All right, I am Zhang Qian."

"Once you accompanied my father to Chaozhou with Li Wan," Han Qing said. "I heard that you were dragged off by a tiger on the way. How did you manage to escape and hide on this mountain?"

"This place is called Mount Zhuowei," Zhang Qian said. "A Perfected Man called Mumu lives in a hermitage on this mountain. He is an immortal from Great Veil Heaven whose sole purpose is to deliver suffering people. When the tigers carried the two of us here he allowed us to stay, cut wood and grass, and avoid Death. As for the master, thanks to young Master Xiangzi he also was led here.

人熊馱韓清

A bear-man carries Han Qing across the mountain ranges.

He honored the Perfected Man as his master, and learned from him the marvelous Dao. Therefore he realized his rewards and ascended to the Primordial Center. Now he lives at ease and happily in Great Veil Heaven. This bear-man is a servant of the Perfected Man Mumu. You are fortunate that he carried you here. Quickly put your clothes in order and follow us to the hermitage to honor the Perfected Man and become his disciple. He will transmit to you mysterious formulae of the golden elixir, which will allow you to avoid death."

Han Qing thanked the woodcutters for their advice and the bear-man for saving his life. Complacently he followed them to the hermitage for an audience with the Perfected Man. He said, "Your disciple Han Qing knocks his head."

"So you are Han Qing," the Perfected Man said. "What do you want?"

Han Qing bowed again and said, "To take you as my master and be your disciple."

"Where are your mother and sister-in-law?" the Perfected Man asked.

"They encountered two divine immortals who delivered them so that they ascended to Heaven."

"Divine immortals? Didn't you say they were pimps?"

These words frightened Han Qing so much that he prostrated himself on the floor and did not dare raise his head. He called out, "I have committed a mortal sin!"

"In Chang'an, you played the young gentleman Han and wanted to beat up that singing Daoist. Now you are maligning divine immortals behind my back. How can someone like you become my disciple?"

"Standing in front of Mount Tai, I didn't see it. I hope for your compassion, Master!" Han Qing said.

The Perfected Man shook his head briefly, and the bear-man stepped before him. The Perfected Man whispered some orders, and the bear-man carried Han Qing off again. He carried him straight to Chang'an, dropped him in front of the Tower of Five Phoenixes, and left.

When the servants at the Tower of Five Phoenixes saw that a bear-man had brought this person, they hurried to report it to Emperor Xianzong. Emperor Xianzong summoned Han Qing and asked, "Who are you? Where do you live? Where did you meet the bear-man who carried you here?"

"My name is Han Qing, my father was the Minister of Rites Han Yu."

When Xianzong heard the name Han Yu, he inquired, "Where is Han Yu now?"

"He died in his office in Chaozhou."

"Who else is there in your family?" Xianzong asked.

"Only I," said Han Qing.

"Your father was straightforward and blunt all his life and We often think of him. Since you are his descendant, We shall appoint you Erudite of the Five Classics to express Our appreciation of your father's loyalty."

Han Qing thanked the emperor and withdrew. I will speak no further about how he followed in Tuizhi's footsteps. Instead I shall tell you how Xiangzi sent Mme. Dou and Lin Luying on two clouds to the hermitage of the Hemp Maiden. On their arrival, they saw an immortal sitting in the hermitage, her skin like ice and snow, her aspect graceful and virginal. They prostrated themselves, knocked their foreheads, and earnestly requested her instruction. The immortal said, "Those who would study immortality first must efface the seven sins and keep the five prohibitions and the three refuges. Only then will they make their minds bright and behold their original nature, restore their life-force and return to their roots."

"What are the seven sins?" Mme. Dou asked. "Would the Master please enlighten us?"

The immortal said,

"First, a master who presents the heterodox as orthodox, who follows that which is not the true transmission, who transmits false teachings to those of a believing mind—such a master will fall into the Tongue-Tearing Hell, and when her punishment there is full, she shall be reborn as a wolf for a hundred eons.

"Second, a master who transmits the orthodox methods to the wrong person, who is careless and disrespectful so that she does not engender belief in people's minds—such a master shall receive her punishment in the Hell of Iron Staffs.

"Third, a disciple who, having received the orthodox methods from her master, does not engage in cultivation, but slights the methods and her master—such a disciple shall receive her punishment in the Hell of Incessant Tortures.

"Fourth, a disciple who, having received the orthodox methods from her master, backslides and regrets, breaks her fast and violates the prohibitions—such a disciple shall receive her punishment in the Hell of Iron Weights.

"Fifth, a disciple who, having received the orthodox methods from her master, knows the orthodox, but practices the heterodox—

such a disciple shall receive her punishment in the Hell of Iron Bedsteads.

"Sixth, a disciple who maligns the scriptures and canons and scolds the Buddhas and patriarchs shall be reborn as a limbless insect.

"Seventh, a disciple who makes no diligent effort in advancing in the orthodox method, who is close to material wealth, but far from the Dao, who squanders the days and months, who is orthodox on the outside, but heterodox in her heart, who is shining bright on the outside, but dark inside, whose sins are so serious that they implicate all her relatives—such a disciple will fall into hell."

When the immortal had spoken, Mme. Dou and Luying again knocked their heads before her and said, "It is due to our affinity that we got to meet you, Master. We will no longer dare to speak of the right while harboring the wrong in our hearts. We only hope that the Master will lecture and instruct us. What are the three refuges and the five prohibitions?"

"The three refuges and five prohibitions all have to do with unifying the mind," the immortal said. "I shall describe them to you:

"Refuge in the Dao: Looking at it one does not see it and listening to it one does not hear it—that is the marvelous Dao.

"Refuge in the scriptures: The wheel of the methods needs to be turned constantly, without resting day or night.

"Refuge in the master: Morning and evening consider and examine her teachings, be careful to serve her, take pride in nourishing the orthodox, and do not fall into heterodoxy.

"The prohibition against killing: Embody the Lord on High's mind, which loves all living beings. Grasses, trees, insects, and ants all have life.

"The prohibition against greed: Cultivate your body and your self; don't allow greed to arise in your mind.

"The prohibition against lust: Dislike lust and license; make your primordial pneuma, essence, and spirit constantly firm. Regard splendor and luxuries as empty, and do not give rise to desires.

"The prohibition against gossip: Do not speak recklessly; cut off all banter and mocking.

"The prohibition against meat: Drink no wine; eat no meat. Do not let your will become disoriented; do not salivate for food.

"If you fail to follow any one of the eight items, spirits and ghosts will scold you, and the great Dao will be difficult to complete.

> *"Although you may exhaust a thousand schemes,*
> *All will be empty clamor and foolish efforts of the mind."*

Mme. Dou and Luying said, "We will obey each and every one of them. Master, we hope that in your compassion you will soon bestow instruction on us."

The immortal touched a fisher drum and sang a song to the tune "Pacing the Moon":

> *"Kan, li, kun, and dui separate zi and wu;*
> *You need to recognize your own origin.*
> *When thunder shakes the earth, rain falls on the peak,*
> *Cleanse yourself and let the Yellow Sprouts emerge from Earth.*
> *Grasp the Metal Essence and close it up firmly,*
> *Refine geng and shen and give rise again to Dragon and Tiger.*
> *Open the Double Spinal Passes and traverse Kunlun;*
> *When you obtain pneumatic strength, think of me."*

Having heard this, Luying stepped forward and said, "By nature I am dull and confused and cannot free myself. I request the Master to give me one more instruction."

The immortal said, "Essence, pneuma, and spirit are the rulers of the body; the body is the habitation of spirit and pneuma. If the form did not obtain spirit, pneuma would not come into being. If the spirit did not obtain pneuma, the essence would not come into being. If spirit, pneuma and essence did not obtain form, then they could not be established. You must refine the form and make it return to the unified pneuma. By refining the pneuma, in turn you will enter into emptiness and nonbeing. Only then will you attain perfection in union with the Dao and experience limitless transformations. The method for men to cultivate immortality is called 'refining pneuma,' the method for women, 'refining form.' You first need to accumulate pneuma in your breasts before setting up a stove, establishing the tripod cauldron, and practicing the Great Yin method of refining form."[7] Then she sang,

> "Listen to what I tell you:
> The immortals' elixir is not far;
> The Eight Trigrams can be encountered everywhere.
> By the strength of the well-protected Child,
> And the beauty of the following Maiden,
> Ask for and obtain the Yellow Matron as matchmaker.
> Unite li and kan,
> Exchange their central lines,
> Toward the southwest pluck the young medicinal shoots.
> You need to adjust the Fire Phases,
> The Fire Phases need to be adjusted,
> To nourish with warmth Mercury and Lead in the elixir stove."

Mme. Dou stepped forward and said, "I am advanced in years and my strength is failing. I cannot compete with a young girl like Luying. I request the Master to give me one more instruction."

The immortal sang again,

> "Mercury and Lead in the elixir oven
> Can fly and are easily dissipated;
> The fire phases are extremely difficult to adjust.
> Even if you entice the Mind Monkey to behave itself,
> And guard against the arrogance of the Will Horse,
> If you do not switch the central line of li with that of kan,
> How can qian and kun then be linked?
> If you make the slightest mistake,
> The effort was in vain.
> You need to use great care,
> With great care apply heat,
> Until the marvelous mystery of the Golden Elixir manifests itself."

When the immortal had finished singing, she said, "Have you awakened yet?"

"I request further instruction," Luying said.

The immortal said,

> "Immortality is the highest good,
> To cultivate perfection the most valiant endeavor.
> For a thousand years you will attend the immortality peach banquets.
> When metal is broken, it needs to be fixed with metal.
> When a brick is cracked, it needs to be coated with clay.
> If you do not comprehend this message,
> All I said was empty clamor.
> Then to preserve the spirit and circulate the pneuma
> Was a useless effort of body and mind.
> Metal is smelted, rock refined;
> Rock is melted, metal burned.
> In your futility you will be ridiculed by the immortals."

Mme. Dou and Luying immediately experienced a great awakening. They knocked their heads and said,

> "As we are not intelligent by nature,
> We did not understand the principles of the mysterious marvels.
> Fortunately, you, Master, opened up our dullness.
> You gave us directions
> How to enter the secrets of the Dao,
> And comprehend the unified pneuma of Former Heaven.
> Leaving the circle of birth and death,
> We free ourselves from our mortal bodies.
> This message,
> How many know it?
> In the empty sky and the wide sea,
> We fly and dance free as kites and fish."

"Now that you are enlightened, you must on no account be lax," the immortal said. "I will travel for a short while to the Penglai Isles beyond the sea. When I return I shall lead you to an audience with the Queen Mother of the West." Having spoken, she rose into the air and left.

Mme. Dou and her daughter-in-law had obtained the immortal's secret and mysterious words, her profound and marvelous Dao. They knew how to circulate the Firing Phases, how to employ withdrawal and supplementation. To retain the Mercury within the Vermilion inside the Golden Tripod, they first let the Silver within the water descend into the Jade Pond.[8] Thus they obtained a bright golden radiance that filled their bodies, and the Millet-Rice Pearl was complete. It was only because they had not yet been instructed in the proto-elixir that they could not fly up to the celestial realm.

In no time at all two years went by. One evening the moon shone as brightly as daylight, the stars and constellations were scattered majestically across the sky, all sounds were hushed, and nothing moved. When Mme. Dou and Luying stepped out into the courtyard they looked up to Heaven and pleaded, "Master, you have been gone a long time. Why haven't you returned yet?"

Suddenly they saw Xiangzi and Master Lü descend on a cloud and stand before them. "Masters, why haven't you come for so long?" Mme. Dou asked. "There wasn't a day that the two of us weren't thinking of you."

"Your faces have changed and taken on an extraordinary appearance," Master Lü said. "The great elixir is already completed. The only thing not yet fulfilled is the practice of the Nine Transmutations and Seven Cycles."

"Although this practice is not yet fulfilled, if you, Master, will agree in your compassion to give them this already refined transmuted elixir, they will forthwith fly and ascend to Heaven," Xiangzi suggested.

"It is difficult to get hold of the great elixir. I am afraid that their destiny does not provide for such a blessing," said Master Lü.

"Everyone has such an utmost treasure, if only common mortals would look for it attentively," Xiangzi replied. "Master, be compassionate so that they may ascend the shore of the Dao."

Master Lü tipped over his bottle gourd. Two red and three white elixir pills came rolling out. He held them in his hand. "Master, didn't you just say that one pill is hard to get?" Xiangzi said. "Yet now there are two red and three white pills. How are they used?"

"The two red ones and three white ones differ in their use," Master Lü said.

"Red and white seem to distinguish some secret of the immortals," Xiangzi said. "This is something that I don't know. Please instruct me, Master."

Master Lü sang,

> "Immortality is the highest good;
> To cultivate perfection the most valiant endeavor.

> *The one formula of the immortal pass is truly mysterious and*
> *marvelous.*
> *The eyes perceive the Penglai Isles as remote,*
> *But when the elixir is completed, the road is not long.*
> *The cave in the white clouds is sealed,*
> *A feather submerges in the Weak Water,*
> *But with a light body you fly across and proceed to the immortality*
> *peach banquet.*
> *Filling your cup with immortals' wine,*
> *The flaming light by itself rises to the empyrean."*

"I have talked too much. Please forgive me," Xiangzi said.

If you don't know how the two kinds of elixir, red and white, differed, please listen to the explanations in the next chapter.

> *Decocting lead and refining mercury is not done literally;*
> *Ingesting pneuma and eating clouds—all of this happens in the mind.*
> *When your ancestors transcend and rise to the golden palaces,*
> *They roam at ease and enjoy eternal spring.*

30

THE MUSK DEER IS FREED FROM HIS WATER PRISON

∾

THE HAN AND LIN FAMILIES TOGETHER REALIZE THE SACRED
AND TRANSCEND THE WORLD

> *When your merits exceed eight hundred,*
> *And of hidden merit you have gathered three thousand,*
> *You treat as equal others and self, intimates and enemies,*
> *And come to accord with the divine immortals' original vows.*
> *Tigers and rhinoceroses, knives and weapons cannot harm you,*
> *And you can no more be dragged into the great house of Death.*
> *Once the precious tally has descended, you go for a heavenly audience,*
> *Securely riding in simurgh chariots and phoenix carriages.*

As Master Lü held up the elixir, he called to Xiangzi in a loud voice, "Immortal Brother, now that Han Yu has resumed his old post as Attendant General, and Mme. Dou and Luying have already left the world of mortals, your task is almost complete. There is only thing left to do."

"What is that, Master?"

"There is still a companion of yours at the bottom of the deep lake near the banks of the Xiang," Master Lü said. "As long as you don't go to deliver him, you still fall short of your duty."

"Luying is the Master's companion and she is already here," Mme. Dou said. "How come he has another companion who is at the bottom of some deep lake?"

"This is a connection from a previous existence that needs to be concluded in this life," Xiangzi said.

"If you will try to explain it to us, we'll listen respectfully," Mme. Dou said.

"If a drum is not beaten, it gives no sound; if a bell is not struck, it won't give forth its call," Xiangzi said. "If I am to explain my previous existence, please listen well."

And right away he began, "In my previous life I was a white crane at Mount Pheasant Yoke. Through inhaling solar essences and lunar efflorescences, I lived to more than one hundred years of age. On this mountain there likewise lived a musk deer, who also cultivated and refined the pneumatic phases. He often roamed and played with me at the mouth of the Xiang River in Cangwu Prefecture.

"One day, as we were playing, we happened to see the two masters Zhong and Lü descend on a cloud. The musk deer and I changed our appearance into that of two itinerant Daoists and went to welcome them. We told ourselves that our magical powers were so great that we could take on manifold forms and deceive two masters, but we didn't know that the masters with their eyes of wisdom had already recognized our true nature. Thereupon I lowered my head and honored them, requesting from them a golden elixir pill so that I might escape from my animal's body. The musk deer, however, did not grasp the situation at all; he made forced arguments and glossed over his wrongdoings, hoping to conceal his true nature. Master Zhong indulged him, but Master Lü became greatly enraged, drew his sword, and said, 'You sinful beast! Who do you think you are deceiving? Do you think my sword is not sharp?'

"These words struck terror into my very heart, and I fell prostrate and pleaded for mercy. Master Zhong said, 'This crane will do, but for this musk deer I have no use. Quickly, be off!' When the musk deer heard these words, he burst out laughing and said, 'If you won't save me, that's fine with me. The scenery here by the river anyway is superior to that of the Elysium and the Jasper Pool. I'd rather roam freely and be at ease here than ascend to Great Veil Heaven, where I'd be at the Jade Emperor's beck and call.' When Master Lü heard these words he became even angrier, recited something under his breath, and then shouted, 'Quickly!' He summoned Marshal Zhao of the Black Tiger and the Dark Altar and had him banish the musk deer to the bottom of the deep lake, where he was tied up securely and allowed no freedom to move. He ordered him, 'Only after the crane has become an immortal will he come to deliver you and make you a great spirit guarding the mountain.'

"Then Master Zhong gave me a golden elixir pill from his gourd, and I was immediately transformed into a green-robed youth, called Crane Boy, and followed the two masters to an audience with the Jade Emperor. I considered it a lucky occasion such as one rarely encounters in three lifetimes or ten thousand kalpas that I met the two masters and escaped from my animal's body. However, at just that time my future parents were still childless and were praying to Heaven all day long for a son who could continue the ancestral line. The city god and earth gods of Changli County memorialized the Jade Emperor, who then issued a decree ordering the two masters to first send me to the Han family to be reborn as a human. Later they were to deliver me so that I could become an immortal. I refused to leave Heaven, but the two masters said, 'The imperial decree has already been issued—who will dare disobey it? Go and be reborn. We shall come to deliver you.' I had no choice but to do as they said and be reborn as a human being.

"Unfortunately my parents both passed away, but I was raised to adulthood by my uncle and aunt. When my uncle asked the masters to instruct me, they did not teach me the usual curriculum, but instead secretly transmitted to me the great Dao of the Golden Elixir and its mysteries. Only then did I realize my rewards and transcend the ordinary world, happily roaming the universe. Since then I have been exerting myself to deliver my uncle, aunt, and Miss Luying, yet I forgot about the matter of this musk deer. As Master Lü now reminds me, I simply have to bring my task to a final conclusion."

"There are also Zhang Qian and Li Wan to be taken care of," Master Lü said. Forthwith Xiangzi faced southeast and recited something, whereupon a celestial general appeared before him. How did this general look?

> On his head he wore a dipper helmet, twinkling golden in the sun-
> light. In his hand he held a lance wrapped in silk, whose silvery color
> struck the eye. He was clothed in a finely meshed green coat of mail,
> a jade-adorned sash of pure white tied about his waist. Three eyes
> flashed fiercely—no goblins could hide from them. His foot was set
> firmly—fearless of any attack by demons. Surely, if he was not the
> Great Diamond guardian deity of Mount Putuo, he must have been
> the Marshal Ma who served the god Huaguang.

Marshal Ma bowed and said, "Immortal Master, what mission do you have for me?"

"At the bottom of a lake at the mouth of the Xiang River in Cangwu Prefecture a musk deer is tied up," Xiangzi said. "His measure of punishment is full. Quickly go and fetch him!"

Marshal Ma left and returned after a short time with the musk deer. Then he rose up into the air, took his leave, and departed.

When the musk deer saw Master Lü standing over him holding an immortal elixir, he was so greatly frightened that he fell to the ground, knocked his head, and said, "On this day as I see again the sun in the sky I hope the Master won't remember my previous transgressions, but will forgive me."

Master Lü chuckled and said, "Deer, why aren't you enjoying the scenery at the Xiang River? What are you doing here?"

"Those were the vulgar views of a frog in a well, who was trying to measure the ocean with a calabash," said the musk deer. "Master, be merciful and it will count as a blessing for three lifetimes."

"Step forward and hear my orders!" Xiangzi called to the musk deer. The musk deer prostrated himself and listened with lowered head. "It is difficult to be born as a sentient being, and it is also difficult to succeed on the path to immortality," Xiangzi said. "Although you were reborn as an animal, fortunately your numinous nature was not blinded and you are still able to ascend to the Primordial Center. I shall now promote you to great guardian spirit of this mountain. You will administer this mountain area and its grotto palace, and enjoy the people's sacrifices. Are you willing?"

The musk deer knocked his head and said, "When I was submerged in the water, I nourished my nature and concealed my spirit. To be appointed guardian of a famous mountain is more than I could have expected. Why wouldn't I be willing? But on the banks of the Xiang River Master Lü declared, 'Wait until your crane brother has become an immortal; he will deliver you to become the guardian of a grotto palace.' Now that you, Master, are appointing me mountain guardian, the words of Master Lü are proven right. But where is my crane brother now? Did he become an immortal or not? Why didn't he come to deliver me?"

"I was the crane in my previous existence," Xiangzi said. "Now I have completed my proper reward and have become the eighth immortal."

"Master, how long has it been since you became an immortal?" the musk deer asked. "Master, please try to explain to me the chain of causes that brought about this result."

Xiangzi immediately explained the intervening events to him.

The musk deer knocked his head. "Although past and present are not the same, I hope the Master will be touched to remember our past relationship and give me a pill of golden elixir so that I may become an immortal," he said.

"You have not yet escaped the consequences of your past sins, and the obstructions caused by your karma are not yet removed," Xiangzi said. "Just administer the mountain spirits and enjoy the meat sacrifices offered by the people. If from now on you take refuge in the great Dao, change your disposition, become a pure Daoist, and administer your realm without idleness, you will accumulate much merit and your virtue will earn the respect of others. At that stage I shall come again to deliver you so that you may leave the world's dust and reach the realm of immortals."

"I just ask for your compassion, Master," the musk deer said. "I will never again offend, but will stick to the straight path."

> *If only you maintain orthodoxy in your mind,*
> *Why worry that this moment might be too late?*
> *When I obtain a master and the strength to follow his directions,*
> *That will be the time of my good fortune.*

Enough for now about the affair of the musk deer.

Master Lü now said, "This golden elixir of mine is not easy to make. It appropriates the creative powers of the ruler of Heaven and Earth, the powers of the Great Ultimate before its division, the immeasurable powers of yin and yang, the powers of the union of water and fire, the powers of the mutual destruction cycle of the Five Phases, the powers by which all things are born and completed. Everyone has these powers in their fullness. However, while the intelligent regard them as an empty mystery, the dull and confused will become attached to them, so that their primordial yang leaks away and their perfected pneuma dissipates. Now I shall use these two red pills to deliver and transform Mme. Dou and Luying, and the three white pills to do the same for Zhang Qian, Li Wan, and the musk deer. Come forward, each of you, and hear my orders."

"There is something strange in your words," the musk deer interjected.

"What's strange?" Master Lü asked.

"In the Daoist teachings, others and the self are the same, and there should be no preferential treatment," the musk deer said. "Now that you, Master, give the great elixir to save people, why are there two kinds, red and white? Isn't this like treating the brick better than the tile?"

Master Lü laughed and said, "Bricks and tiles are both made of clay and fired in a kiln, but they differ in their thickness. The teachings expounded by the Highest Purity must be mastered step by step by each person according to their ability; no stage may be skipped. It is for this reason that the elixir is divided into red and white. Preferential treatment has nothing to do with it. You beast, you have the audacity to waggle your lips and drum with your tongue, making willful and reckless charges. You are more detestable than ever!"

"Master, be tolerant and forgive the deer," Xiangzi said.

Master Lü then waved once towards the south and shouted, "Come!"

In an instant Zhang Qian and Li Wan arrived. When they saw that both Mme. Dou and Luying were there, they asked, "Lady, Miss, how did you come here?"

"It's good that you're here today, thus putting my mind at ease," Mme. Dou said. Just then Tuizhi also arrived, and the whole family was overjoyed.

> *To part is easy, to meet again difficult;*
> *Wanting to meet, we were blocked by vast peaks.*
> *As we suddenly meet this day,*
> *Joy descends from Heaven and opens our faces in delight.*

Master Lü called to Mme. Dou, "Originally you were a Sagely Mother who entered the mortal world and became tainted by its splendors. All along you were caught in confused attachment, and only now have you escaped the hook. Swallow the golden elixir and recognize your own true nature. Forget future and present."

He called again, this time to Luying, "Jade Maiden of the Lofty Empyrean, do you remember your previous existence at all?"

"I sank into confusion and descended to earth, becoming dark, inferior, and devoid of knowledge," Luying said.

"Originally you were a Jade Maiden of the Lofty Empyrean," Master Lü said. "When the Gate of Heaven was being closed, you stole a glance at the world below and subsequently sank down into it. Fortunately your mortal roots were cut off and you awakened to the karmic causes of your condition. Cleanse yourself of your former affinities, completely erase your old mistakes, return your perfected essence to the Gold Chamber, and nourish your perfected pneuma to complete the Millet-Rice Pearl. Swallow the Golden Elixir and you shall soon resume your original position."

Then he called to Zhang Qian and Li Wan, "You two have been unblessed children, but now you have become blessed disciples. You served your master single-mindedly, not turning back in the face of a hundred adversities, escaping a hundred deaths in this one lifetime, all the while harboring not a trace of resentment. Such loyalty and righteousness is praiseworthy, and so I bestow on you one golden elixir pill each."

Finally he called to the musk deer, "At the outset all your thoughts were mistaken and you could count yourself very lucky to have escaped with your life. Fortunately you cultivated yourself while submerged in the lake, so that you unified and softened your pneuma; your body and mind became immoveable and your souls became controlled. Now I give you the immortals' elixir so that you may shed your animal's body and realize your reward as a deity. If you continue to cultivate and refine yourself, then you can ascend into the ranks of the immortals and your future blessings will be assured."

Gratefully Mme. Dou, Luying, Zhang Qian, Li Wan, and the musk deer received the immortals' elixir and swallowed it.

> *The lightning of kan boils and rumbles in the region of metal and water,*
> *Fire issues forth from Kunlun and yin and yang are united.*
> *If the two things are returned, they will be harmoniously combined;*
> *The elixir will then be ripe and the whole body fragrant.*[1]

"Master, now that they have swallowed the elixir and escaped their mortal bodies, those who resume their posts will return to their former positions, those who rise up will take their places in the ranks of the immortals, and those who walk on earth will roam at leisure among the Penglai Isles," Xiangzi said. "Only my father, Han Hui, and my mother, Mme. Zheng, are still confined to the underworld and have not been delivered. It would be a grave injustice to leave them like this."

"When a son ascends to immortality, all relatives rise to Heaven," Master Lü replied. "Of course your parents will leave the sea of suffering and step up to the Lotus Terrace. Just await the arrival of an imperial decree and don't worry—everything will turn out well." Just then they saw auspicious clouds in the hazy distance, propitious mist enshrouding the horizon, simurghs and cranes soaring and circling, flags and banners fluttering. In mid-air many immortals were approaching.

Master Zhong held up the imperial decree and called, "Immortals, hear the proclamation of the imperial decree!" The decree ran as follows:

> Immortals turn the balancing scales of creative transformation; they
> grasp the pivot of the universe. The work of the spirit and the circu-
> lation of the fire do not require a whole evening before the single orb
> of the sun manifests itself, emerging from the deep pool.[2] When
> Mercury is clear and gold radiant, then in the sky the moon will be
> bright and the stars shining. When Lead is encountered amid the
> emerging lesser water,[3] all things in the human world can be refined.
> By shaping themselves like the Dao that existed even before God,[4]
> they will achieve agelessness in Later Heaven. Han Xiang, you have
> been concerned solely with the Celestial Pass and the Axle of Earth.
> By the method of obversion you moved the sixty-four hexagrams to

韓林盡証聖
超凡

The Han and Lin families together realize the sacred and transcend the world.

the yin talisman. Through reversion you gathered the twenty-four pneumata around the yang fire. Circulating the essences of the seventy-two phases, you gathered them into your chest. Appropriating the 3,600 orthodox pneumata, you circulated them in your womb. By bringing relief to humans and benefiting all beings, your virtue has grown ever weightier, and ghosts and spirits admire you. As you refined yourself and emptied your mind, the Dao rose ever higher, and Dragon and Tiger submitted.

Your uncle Han Yu was originally the Attendant Great General, but was banished to the world of dust. Now he has become aware of the previous causes for his present condition, taken refuge in the great Dao, obeyed Heaven and Earth in their waxing and waning, and employed this practice diligently. Imitating *gengshen* and making up his deficiencies, he carefully achieved entry into the ranks of the immortals. Mme. Dou and Luying brought punishment upon themselves through a single reckless thought. Fortunately their six roots were still clear and pure and their minds not beclouded by the five poisons. As their old obstructions are already removed, they can together resume their original positions.

Xiangzi's father, Han Hui, and mother, Mme. Zheng, planted roots of goodness over nine generations and accumulated hidden merit over three lifetimes. When a son has ascended to perfection, his parents too shall be delivered. They will quickly realize the ignorance of this world and ascend without hindrance to the celestial palaces. Yunyangzi Lin Gui has planted roots of wisdom in Heaven and has abandoned his official honors in the world of dust. As yin and yang are united, the corpse ghosts are all eradicated, water and fire are joined, and his soul and spirit excel. Zhang Qian and Li Wan were born from imperfect wombs, with turbid bones that possessed no affinity for immortality. Although they hankered after luxuries in their early lives, they proved themselves loyal and sincere in the end. Since their hidden cultivation is already complete, their lifespan shall be extended and they shall be sent to Mount Zhuowei to cultivate themselves for a further two dozen years, after which time their progress will be examined.

The musk deer has become aware of the insecurity of an animal's body and hopes for the marvelous formula of eternal life. However, for him it is already a piece of good fortune to enjoy his leisure on earth and receive meat sacrifices in the mountains. Although no further plans are allowed at present, the roots of goodness are inexhaustible. By accumulating merit he can gain rewards, and his karmic sins will be easy to cancel. If this comes about, We shall reverse our present judgment. If he can cut off the smell of sacrificed sheep and goats and pare away his worldly thoughts, I shall give permission for him to record his merits, and be rewarded and inducted into the ranks of immortals. No worries arise when all attachments to the world of dust are extinguished. The true joy of immortals is extraordinary—it is to attain freedom and ease. Be respectful and diligent!

After the proclamation, the immortals knocked their heads, said thanks, and then returned to their posts. Their spirits still clear, the souls of Han Hui and Mme. Zheng returned from the netherworld. The immortals welcomed them, and they got to meet their son Han Xiang. At first they were tearful and sad that they could not be together in their lifetimes, but then their joy at the good fortune of meeting again after death knew no bounds. Here are eight songs to the tune "Blue Sky Song" to recount these events:

The perfected immortals congregate at the Jasper Pool.
Singing to immortal tunes, simurghs and phoenixes descend.
Simurghs and phoenixes fly down in pairs from the purple empyrean;
Immortal cranes dance together, while immortal lads are singing.

Immortal lads are singing, singing of Great Peace,
Having obtained a crane's count of ten thousand years of longevity.
Propitious clouds and auspicious light fill Heaven and Earth;
In their assembly the immortals speak of immortality.

The deathless know the subtle and marvelous formulae,
Which are difficult to put in a few words.
If one carelessly reveals this mysterious secret,
It will frighten people out of their wits.

The tip of the tongue emits a fine jade-colored light,
Dazzlingly illuminating the ten directions.

The spring wind lightly moves the blossoming twigs;
The gardens and forests are bathed in beautiful sunshine.

At a time of beautiful sunshine one gathers numinous sprouts,
And does not wait until the mid-autumn moon stands high.
Overturning the li male to meet the kan female,
The Yellow Matron claps her hands in joy that they are waving at each
    other.

Waving and calling to each other, they pair up yin and yang;
Dense rain and thick clouds enter their bedchamber.
After a thousand years the numinous womb gives birth to a child,
Who will ride on a white crane up to Heaven's azure canopy.

The azure canopy is filled with vast pneuma; a high wind blows steadily,
Blows so that what turned right now turns left.
The firmament and all things are arrayed in majestic splendor;
The immortals' palaces of three realms all face toward the Jade Palace.

Along the golden stairways of the Jade Palace immortals are lined up;
Immortality peaches are presented for the sumptuous banquet.
Immortal wine and immortal flowers shine on immortal fruits—
You will enjoy eternal life without aging for a million years.

Zhang Qian and Li Wan changed back into their human bodies and returned to the world. Twenty-four years later they achieved perfection. While the musk deer was guarding his mountain, he met a master who instructed him; as he had preserved his primordial spirit, he became united with eternity.

It was because of all these events that the "Blue Pass Record of Han Xiangzi, the Divine Immortal of the Eighth Grotto Who Delivered Han Yu Twelve Times" was transmitted through the ages.

Lascivious beauty is then an empty flower,
The floating world is then a scorched grain,
A good marriage is in fine pairing,
But in an instant one becomes single and alone.
One enters service wishing for self-glorification,
But in an instant becomes degraded and disgraced.

Joining together is the start of parting.
Joy! That's where grief is concealed.
Melancholy and remorse most always long,
Joy and glory rushing on in a fraction of time.
Aroused awareness depends on insight;
Delusion's grip comes from authority.

Abundance and brightness entice the moths of darkness;
The bright sun causes the foolish deer to flee.
Greed is the assembly place of pain;
Love is the base of the forest of sadness.
The water agitates the unclear waves;
The wheel turns its spokes of birth and death.
Dust responds to sprinkles of sweet dew;
Dirt awaits the clarified butter's cleansing.

Obstructions—one needs the lamp of wisdom to burn them away.
Demons—one must annihilate them with the knife of intelligence.
An inwardly perfumed nature is easy to imbue,
But an outwardly battling heart is hard to check.
The past is gone—pursue it no more,
But look forward with joyous excitement to what's to come.[5]

NOTES

TRANSLATOR'S INTRODUCTION

1   Wang Hanmin, *Baxian yu Zhongguo wenhua* (Beijing: Zhongguo Shehui Kexue Chu-banshe, 2000), 36.

2   Wang Hanmin, *Baxian yu Zhongguo wenhua*, 37.

3   An example is the play "Zhongli of the Han Delivers Lan Caihe" (Han Zhongli dutuo Lan Caihe 漢鍾離度脫藍采和), which has been translated by Wilt Idema and Stephen H. West. See their *Chinese Theater 1100–1450: A Source Book* (Wiesbaden: Franz Steiner Verlag, 1982), 299–343. See ibid. for an analysis of the thematic structure of deliverance plays.

4   One of the best known examples is Tang Xianzu's 湯顯祖 Lü Dongbin play *Handan ji* 邯鄲記. *Xiuke Handan ji dingben* (Taipei: Taiwan Kaiming Shuju, 1986).

5   On the place of the Baxian in traditional opera, see Idema and West, *Chinese Theater 1100–1450*, 300–308; Wang Hanmin, *Baxian yu Zhongguo wenhua*, chap. 5. Also see Chen Lingling, "Baxian zai Yuan-Ming zaju he Taiwan banxianxi zhong de zhuang-kuang" (M.A. thesis, Wenhua Xueyuan, 1978).

6   Numerous editions exist. See for example *Si youji* 四遊記, comp. Wang Jiquan (Harbin: Beifang Wenxue Chubanshe, 1985). Trans. Nadine Perront, *Pérégrination vers l'est* (Paris: Gallimard, 1993).

7   On the *baxiancai*, see Wang Jingyi's *Shenling huoxian: Jingyan baxiancai* (Luzhou shi: Boyang Wenhua, 2000). The story of the Baxian's crossing of the ocean appears first in the Yuan drama "Struggling over Jade Clappers, the Eight Immortals Cross the Vast Ocean" (Zheng yuban Baxian guo canghai 爭玉板八仙過滄海). On this play see Chen Lingling, "Baxian zai Yuan-Ming zaju," 35–36. Paul R. Katz describes a Yuan dynasty mural with the *Baxian guohai* motif at the Yongle Gong 永樂宮 in Shanxi. See his *Images of the Immortal: The Cult of Lü Dongbin at the Palace of Eternal Joy* (Honolulu:

University of Hawai'i Press, 1999), 188–89. A modern example of a Baxian temple mural is described in Zeng Qinliang's *Sanxia Zushi Miao diaohui gushi tanyuan* (Taipei: Wenjin, 1996), 302–4.

8   Three recent collections of Baxian stories collected in different parts of the Chinese mainland are: *Baxian chuanshuo gushi ji*, ed. Yu Hang (Beijing: Zhongguo Minjian Wenyi Chubanshe, 1988); *Baxian renwu de chuanshuo*, ed. Liu Xicheng, Xiao Rong, and Feng Zhi (Shijiazhuang: Huashan Wenyi Chubanshe, 1995); and *Baxian de gushi*, ed. Chen Delai and Liu Xunda (Taipei: Jiangmen Wenwu, 1995). There is considerable overlap between the books by Yu Hang and Liu Xicheng et al. Yu Hang's book has also been republished in Taiwan by a certain Ouyang Jingyi as *Baxian chuanqi* (Banqiao: Kezhu Shuju, 1992) and *Baxian de gushi* (Banqiao: Kezhu Shuju, 1995).

9   In the nineteenth century, the novel *The Eight Immortals Attain the Dao* (Baxian dedao 八仙得道) by Wugou Daoren 無垢道人 appeared (Shenyang: Chunfeng Wenyi Chubanshe, 1987). A modern example is Chen Sanfeng's *Baxian chuanqi* 八仙傳奇 (Xinzhuang: Mantingfang, 1994). An overview of Baxian-related novels is given in Han Xiduo's 韓錫鐸 *Baxian xilie xiaoshuo* (Shenyang: Liaoning Jiaoyu Chubanshe, 1993).

10 Che Xilun lists six Baxian *baojuan* in his bibliography *Zhongguo baojuan zongmu* (Taipei: Zhongyang Yanjiuyuan Zhongguo Wenzhe Yanjiusuo Choubeichu, 1998), 1–2. Fairly easily accessible is "Precious Volume on the Eight Immortals' Birthday Congratulations" (*Baxian da shangshou baojuan* 八仙大上壽寶卷), which is included in the collection *Baojuan chuji*, ed. Zhang Xishun et al., vol. 28 (Taiyuan: Shanxi Renmin Chubanshe, n.d.). An overview of Baxian motifs in folk art and folk literature can be found in Wang Hanmin, *Baxian yu Zhongguo wenhua*, chap. 4. See also Shan Man, *Baxian xinyang* (Beijing: Xueyuan Chubanshe, 1994).

11 Recent research provides a good overview of the Lü Dongbin lore and cult. See for example Farzeen Baldrian-Hussein, "Lü Tung-pin in Northern Sung Literature," *Cahiers d'Extrême-Asie* 2 (1986): 133–69; Isabelle Ang, "Le culte de Lü Dongbin des origines jusqu'au début du XIVe siècle: Caractéristiques et transformations d'un Saint Immortel dans la Chine pré-moderne" (Thèse de doctorat, Université Paris VII, 1993); and Paul R. Katz, *Images of the Immortal*.

12 A close competitor in popularity may be He Xiangu, who has a number of *baojuan* to her name and appears occasionally as an independent deity in Taiwanese popular religion. In fact, she is certainly a better-known figure nowadays than Han Xiangzi, even though her role in late Imperial literature is less significant. She is the heroine of a recent martial arts novel by Xiao Yuhan 蕭玉寒, titled *He Xiangu chuanqi* 何仙姑傳奇 (Hong Kong: Xinghui Tushu, 1994).

13 I would like to acknowledge my indebtedness to two earlier researchers working on Han Xiangzi: Sawada Mizuho 澤田瑞穗, who published an essay on Han Xiangzi in 1968, and Chen Liyu 陳麗宇, who wrote an M.A. thesis on Han Xiangzi in 1988. Their studies provide the foundation for the following sections. See Sawada Mizuho, "Kan Shôshi densetsu to zoku bungaku," *Zhongguo xuezhi* 5 (1968): 345–80; Chen Liyu, "Han Xiangzi yanjiu" (M.A. thesis, Taiwan Shifan Daxue, 1988).

14 Chen Keming, *Han Yu nianpu ji shiwen xinian* (Chengdu: Bashu Shushe, 1999), 526; Qian Zhonglian, *Han Changli shi xinian jishi* (Taipei: Xuehai Chubanshe, 1985), 1097. This translation follows (with minor modifications) that of Charles Hartman. See his *Han Yü and the T'ang Search for Unity* (Princeton, NJ: Princeton University Press,

1986), 86–87. Cf. Erwin von Zach's German translation in his *Han Yü's poetische Werke* (Cambridge, MA: Harvard University Press, 1952), 276–77.

15 Chen Keming, *Han Yu nianpu ji shiwen xinian*, 92; Qian Zhonglian, *Han Changli shi xinian jishi*, 98. Cf. von Zach's translation, *Han Yü's poetische Werke*, 294–95.

16 *Youyang zazu, qianji, juan* 18 (Taipei: Taiwan Xuesheng Shuju, 1975), 104. On this work see Carrie E. Reed, *A Tang Miscellany: An Introduction to* Youyang zazu (New York: Peter Lang, 2003).

17 Quoted under the title "Han Yu waisheng," in *Taiping guangji, juan* 54 (Beijing: Zhonghua Shuju, 1986), 331.

18 *Qingsuo gaoyi, qianji, juan* 9 (Shanghai: Shanghai Guji Chubanshe, 1983), 85–87.

19 The following account is based mostly on Wu Yimin's excellent overview of the history of *daoqing*, *Zhongguo daoqing yishu gailun* (Taiyuan: Shanxi Guji Chubanshe, 1997).

20 Wang Hanmin, *Baxian yu Zhongguo wenhua*, 109. See also Wu Yimin, *Zhongguo daoqing yishu gailun*, 135, 176–81.

21 Li Xu, *Jie'an manbi* 戒庵漫筆, *juan* 5, 3a–3b, in *Changzhou xianzhe yishu* 常州先哲 遺書, comp. Sheng Xuanhuai 盛宣懷 (Taipei: Yiwen Yinshuguan, 1971). Quoted in Wu Yimin, *Zhongguo daoqing yishu gailun*, 85; Gao Guofan, *Zhongguo minjian wenxue* (Taipei: Taiwan Xuesheng Shuju, 1999), 411.

22 Quoted in Gao Guofan, *Zhongguo minjian wenxue*, 411. The scene in question occurs in chapter 64 of *The Plum in the Golden Vase*. Trans. Clement Egerton, *The Golden Lotus*, vol. III (London: Routledge & Kegan Paul Ltd., 1964), 172.

23 Two editions of *Han xian zhuan* survive. One dates from the turn of the seventeenth century and is part of a Ming dynasty anthology by the name of "The Secret Book Box of Baoyan Hall" (*Baoyan Tang miji* 寶顏堂祕笈), a diverse collection of 226 works in 457 *juan* that share the quality of having been estimated "rare texts" by their editor. This editor is Chen Jiru 陳繼儒 (1558–1639), a somewhat eccentric and reclusive private scholar with interests in all fields of literature. We may surmise that when Chen picked up *Han xian zhuan* it must have struck him as quaint and "rare," and therefore probably old. This would indicate the text came into being quite a while before Chen's lifetime. The *Baoyan Tang miji* version can be found in *Baibu congshu jicheng zhi 18*, vol. 65 (Taipei: Yiwen Yinshuguan, 1965). A reprint of the same edition is included in *Zangwai daoshu*, ed. Hu Daojing et al., vol. 18 (Chengdu: Bashu Shushe, 1992–1994), 802–14. The second edition is in the anthology *Shuofu* 説乎 compiled by Tao Zongyi 陶宗儀 (1316–1403), which would give us a date *ante quem* in the Yuan dynasty. However, the only *Shuofu* edition to contain *Han xian zhuan* is the somewhat dubious early Qing version in 120 *juan* edited by Tao Ting 陶珽. See *Shuofu sanzhong*, vol. 8 (Shanghai: Shanghai Guji Chubanshe, 1989), 5171–81. For an English translation of *Han xian zhuan*, see my "The Story of the Immortal Han (*Han xian zhuan*): An Annotated Translation" (MS, 1992). A modern Chinese rendering of the text can be found in *Baixian chuanqi*, ed. Yuan Lükun (Zhonghe: Jianhong Chubanshe, 1995), 437–62.

24 In *Guben xiqu congkan chuji*, vol. 47 (Shanghai: Shangwu Yinshuguan, 1954).

25 Identical songs include the *Gumeijiu* tune in chapter 27 of *Han Xiangzi* (= scene 35 of *Ascension to Immortality*) and the *Zhuyunfei* tune in chapter 13 (= scene 6). The "Goat-Raising Song" (*Yangyangge* 養羊歌) in chapter 14 seems closely based on its counterpart in the twelfth scene of the drama. Evidence from the novel *The Plum in the Golden Vase* shows that *Ascension to Immortality* was being performed at the end of the sixteenth century, i.e., in Yang Erzeng's lifetime. In chapter 32, we witness the perfor-

mance of four scenes from a drama named *Han Xiangzi shengxian ji* 韓湘子昇
仙記. The translator David T. Roy identifies this title with that of a (now lost) northern drama by Lu Jinzhi 陸進之 (fl. 14th–15th cent.), but in my view this attribution
is likely mistaken and we have here indeed a reference to the surviving southern-
tradition work. See David T. Roy, trans., *The Plum in the Golden Vase, or Chin P'ing
Mei*, vol. 2, *The Rivals* (Princeton: Princeton University Press, 2001), 245, 538.

26   Dai Bufan, *Xiaoshuo jianwenlu* (Hangzhou: Zhejiang Renmin Chubanshe, 1980),
     261–65. Dai also points out that a number of songs have close parallels to arias in the
     Qing anthology *Piecing Together a White Fur Coat* (Zhuibaiqiu 綴白裘), suggesting
     a common source. These close links of *Han Xiangzi* with stage adaptions of the Han
     Xiangzi theme support Andrew Plaks's argument concerning the formative influence
     of drama, especially southern drama, on the genre of the novel in general. See his *Four
     Masterworks of the Ming Novel—Ssu ta ch'i-shu* (Princeton: Princeton University
     Press, 1987), 40–45.

27   Jinling: Jiuru Tang, 1623 (Van Gulik collection microfiche CH-1289). Another edition
     from the Tianqi reign period entitled simply *Han Xiangzi* survives in the Naikaku
     Bunko and is reproduced in Liu Shide et al., eds., *Guben xiaoshuo congkan*, series 34,
     vol. 4 (Beijing: Zhonghua Shuju, 1991). Also in *Guben xiaoshuo jicheng*, vol. 200:1/2
     (Shanghai: Shanghai Guji Chubanshe, n.d.).

28   Che Xilun lists nine Han Xiangzi *baojuan* (*Zhongguo baojuan zongmu*, 101–102, 159,
     203), though it is not clear whether these are really nine independent texts or whether
     some represent mere title variations. I have been able to collect three texts: (1) *Han xian
     baozhuan* 韓仙寶傳 (Taichung: Shengxian Zazhishe, n.d.); (2) *Han Zu chengxian bao-
     zhuan* 韓祖成仙寶傳 (Ciyi: Deshan Tang, 1890; Shanghai: Jinzhang Tushuju, 1930);
     (3) *Xiangzi du Lin Ying baojuan* 湘子度林英寶卷, in Duan Ping, ed., *Hexi baojuan
     xuxuan*, vol. 1 (Taipei: Xinwenfeng, 1994), 1–196.

29   Chen Liyu discusses various ballads on the Han Xiangzi theme. "Han Xiangzi yanjiu,"
     131–62.

30   An overview of Han Xiangzi pieces in local opera traditions is given by Chen Liyu,
     "Han Xiangzi yanjiu," 114–120. A Taiwan opera on Han Xiangzi's deliverance of his
     wife ("Du qi" 渡妻) is included in Chen Xiufang, ed., *Taiwan suo jian de beiguan
     shouchaoben*, vol. 3 (Taichung: Taiwan Sheng Wenxian Weiyuanhui, 1981), 204–13.

31   Adeline Herrou, *La vie entre soi: Les moines taoïstes aujourd'hui en Chine* (Nanterre:
     Société d'ethnologie, 2005).

32   See my paper, "Han Xiangzi: A Story without a Cult," presented at the Annual Meet-
     ing of the Association of Asian Studies (New York, 27–30 March 2003). My research
     on the history and current status of the religious cult of Han Xiangzi (and Han Yu)
     will be treated in more detail in future publications.

33   We have three dated texts by Yang Erzeng. "Shu *Xianyuan jishi* hou" is dated 7 Octo-
     ber 1602. See *Xinjuan xianyuan jishi* (Taipei: Taiwan Xusheng Shuju, 1989), 650. A
     preface to his *Tuhui zongyi* 圖繪宗彝 gives the year 1607 (Wulin: Yibai Tang edition),
     and finally his preface to *Hainei qiguan* 海內奇觀 is dated the 9th moon of the year
     1609. See *Zhongguo gudai banhua congkan er bian*, vol. 8 (Shanghai: Shanghai Guji
     Chubanshe, 1994), 23.

34   Shi Gufeng, "*Hainei qiguan* ba," in *Zhongguo gudai banhua congkan er bian*, vol. 8
     (Shanghai: Shanghai Guji Chubanshe, 1994), 1 (separate pagination at end of book).

35   "*Xinjuan Hainei qiguan* fanli," in *Zhongguo gudai banhua congkan er bian*, vol. 8
     (Shanghai: Shanghai Guji Chubanshe, 1994), 31.

36 "*Hainei qiguan* yin," in *Zhongguo gudai banhua congkan er bian*, vol. 8 (Shanghai: Shanghai Guji Chubanshe, 1994), 1. On Chen Bangzhan see the *Dictionary of Ming Biography*, vol. 1, ed. L. Carrington Goodrich and Chaoying Fang (New York: Columbia University Press, 1976), 176–78.

37 "*Hainei qiguan* tiyu," in *Zhongguo gudai banhua congkan er bian*, vol. 8 (Shanghai: Shanghai Guji Chubanshe, 1994), 13.

38 This work was reprinted in 1989 by Taiwan Xuesheng Shuju in Taipei.

39 A work with this title is available in the Daoist collections *Daozang jiyao* (Chengdu: Bashu Shushe, 1995; vol. 5) and *Zangwai daoshu* (Chengdu: Bashu Shushe, 1992; vol. 7), though it is not clear how far this version overlaps with the one edited by Yang. Qing Xitai ascribes the *Daozang jiyao* and *Zangwai daoshu* editions to Hu Zhimei 胡之玫, a Jingming 淨明 Daoist of the early Qing period (*Zhongguo Daojiao shi*, vol. 4 [Chengdu: Sichuan Renmin Chubanshe, 1996], 193–94). However, Qing Xitai apparently was unaware of Yang's edition of the text, of which a copy (dated 1604) is held at the library of Beijing University (see *Daojiao wenhua cidian* [Nanjing: Jiangsu Guji Chubanshe, 1994], 412). I have been unable to view this edition so far.

40 "*Dong-Xi liang Jin yanyi* xu," in *Dong-Xi Jin yanyi* (Taipei: Guoli Zhongyang Tushuguan, 1971), 3–12. Alternatively, see "*Dong-Xi liang Jin yanyi* xu," in *Ming-Qing zhanghui xiaoshuo yanjiu ziliao*, by Zhang Juling (Beijing: Zhongyang Minzu Xueyuan Keyanchu, 1980), 8–9.

41 This particular edition is (probably erroneously) attributed to the famous literatus Chen Jiru 陳繼儒 (1558–1639), complete with a preface by Chen dated to 1590. See *Su Dongpo xiansheng chanxi ji* 蘇東坡先生禪喜集 (Ming edition from the Wanli period held at the Fu Ssu-nien Library, Academia Sinica). On the textual history of this collection, see *Mount Lu Revisited: Buddhism in the Life and Writings of Su Shih*, by Beata Grant (Honolulu: University of Hawai'i Press, 1994), 3.

42 *Laozi daode jing* 老子道德經 (Taipei: Yiwen Yinshuguan, 1965); *Nanhua zhenjing chongjiao* 南華真經重校 (Taipei: Yiwen Yinshuguan, 1974*); Kuaixue Tang manlu* 快雪堂漫錄 (Beijing: Zhonghua Shuju, 1991). On the cult of Tanyangzi and Feng's involvement in it, see Daria Berg, "Reformer, Saint, and Savior: Visions of the Great Mother in the Novel 'Xingshi yinyuan zhuan'," *Nan Nü: Men, Women and Gender in Early and Imperial China* 1, no. 2 (1999): 243–45. Yang Erzeng devotes a whole chapter of his collected hagiographies of female immortals to Tanyangzi. See *Xianyuan jishi*, *juan* 8, 507–88.

43 *Jinling fanchazhi* 金陵梵剎志. Earliest edition printed in 1607. For a modern reprint edition see *Jinling fanchazhi*, 3 vols. (Taipei: Guangwen Shuju, 1976).

44 *The Four Masterworks of the Ming Novel*, 45. See the hyperbolic statement in *Han Xiangzi*'s preface that Yang's work "has the sternness of *Record of the Three Kingdoms* and the wondrous transformations of *Water Margin*, while lacking the cruel satire of *Journey to the West* and the indecent license of *The Plum in the Golden Vase*" (see below p. 6). This statement nicely corroborates Plaks's claim that these four novels "defined and shaped the serious novel form in Ming and Ch'ing China." *The Four Masterworks of the Ming Novel*, 4.

45 This point is actually disputed. For example, the Chinese scholar Fang Sheng argues (incorrectly, in my view) that in spite of the prevalence of *neidan* terminology in *Han Xiangzi*, the text's emphasis actually lies on external, rather than inner, alchemy. See his "Ping Daojiao xiaoshuo *Han Xiangzi quanzhuan*," *Ming-Qing xiaoshuo yanjiu* 16 (1990): 198–99.

46 *The Taoist Experience* (Albany, NY: SUNY Press, 1993), 11.

47 For a more complete overview of Daoism, a number of handy publications exist. See, for example, Livia Kohn's *Daoism and Chinese Culture* (Cambridge, MA: Three Pines Press, 2001) and Isabelle Robinet's *Taoism: Growth of a Religion* (Stanford, CA: Stanford University Press, 1997).

48 Trans. D. C. Lau, *Tao Te Ching* (Harmondsworth: Penguin, 1963), 103.

49 Overviews of inner alchemy are provided in a number of Western-language publications. See *Science and Civilisation in China*, by Joseph Needham (Cambridge: Cambridge University Press, 1983), vol. 5, part 5; *Introduction à l'alchimie intérieure taoïste: De l'unité et de la multiplicité*, by Isabelle Robinet (Paris: Éditions du Cerf, 1995); *Daoism Handbook*, ed. Livia Kohn (Leiden: Brill, 2000), chap. 16.

50 *Wuzhen pian* (*Daozang* 263.26). All references to texts in the *Daoist Canon* (Daozang) are by the number given the work in *The Taoist Canon: A Historical Companion to the Daozang*, edited by Kristofer Schipper and Franciscus Verellen (Chicago: University of Chicago Press, 2004). Here the reader will easily be able to find additional information about the texts in question. Yang mostly uses two commentators: Weng Baoguang 翁葆光 (fl. 1173–75) and Chen Zhixu 陳致虛 (fl. 1326–86). The *Wuzhen pian* has been studied extensively and has been translated a number of times. See, for example, Isabelle Robinet's *Introduction à l'alchimie intérieure taoïste: De l'unité et de la multiplicité* (Paris: Éditions du Cerf, 1995), Thomas Cleary's *Understanding Reality: A Taoist Alchemical Classic* (Honolulu: University of Hawai'i Press, 1987), and Paul Crowe's "An Annotated Translation and Study of Chapters on Awakening to the Real (ca. 1061) attributed to Zhang Boduan (ca. 983–1081)" (M.A. thesis, University of British Columbia, 1997). Fang Sheng lists some of Yang Erzeng's direct borrowings from the *Wuzhen pian* and its commentaries. See his "Ping Daojiao xiaoshuo *Han Xiangzi quanzhuan*," 197–98.

51 Plaks, *The Four Masterworks of the Ming Novel*, 21–22.

52 On the history and teachings of the Complete Perfection School, see Tao-chung Yao, "Quanzhen—Complete Perfection," in *Daoism Handbook*, chap. 19; Stephen Eskildsen, *The Teachings and Practices of the Early Quanzhen Taoist Masters* (Albany: State University of New York, 2004).

53 See chapter 17.

54 For a concise overview of this history, see Judith Boltz's *A Survey of Taoist Literature: Tenth to Seventeenth Centuries* (Berkeley, CA: Institute of East Asian Studies, University of California, 1987).

55 See Lu Xun, "Zhongguo xiaoshuo shilüe," in *Lu Xun xiaoshuoshi lunwenji* (Taipei: Liren, 1992), 1–273.

56 Ibid.; see also Lu Xun, "Zhongguo xiaoshuo de lishi de bianqian," in *Lu Xun xiaoshuoshi lunwenji* (Taipei: Liren, 1992), 533.

57 See the complete English translation by Anthony Yu, *The Journey to the West* (Chicago: University of Chicago Press, 1977–83). On a Daoist reading of the *Xiyou ji*, see Ping Shao, "Monkey and Chinese Scriptural Tradition: A Rereading of the Novel *Xiyou ji*" (PhD dissertation, Washington University in St. Louis, 1997).

58 See Li Fengmao, *Xu Xun yu Sa Shoujian: Deng Zhimo Daojiao xiaoshuo yanjiu* (Taipei: Taiwan Xuesheng Shuju, 1997). Among English-speaking readers, the best-known didactic Daoist novel aside from *The Journey to the West* is Eva Wong's translation of *The Story of the Seven Perfected* (Qizhen zhuan), published by Shambhala in 1990 under the title *Seven Taoist Masters: A Folk Novel of China*. In her introduction, the translator claims on stylistic grounds that this work was composed "during the middle part of

the Ming dynasty" (p. xvi). And indeed there exist hints that a work of that name may have existed during the Ming (see *Zhongguo tongsu xiaoshuo zongmu tiyao* [Beijing: Zhongguo Wenlian Chuban Gongsi, 1997], 783). However, no such Ming version survives. Wong relied on a late Qing redaction that has no clear relationship with any text composed before the nineteenth century. The only scholar to have produced a thorough study of the text concludes that it is essentially a nineteenth-century work. Hence, while a fascinating work in its own right, it is irrelevant to the interpretation of the *Han Xiangzi*. See *Die Sieben Meister der Vollkommenen Verwirklichung: Der taoistische Lehrroman Ch'i-chen chuan in Übersetzung und im Spiegel seiner Quellen*, by Günther Endres (Frankfurt/M.: Peter Lang, 1985).

59   Lin Chen, *Shenguai xiaoshuo shihua* (Shenyang: Liaoning Jiaoyu Chubanshe, 1992), 83–84.

60   Yin Ming, "Jiaodian shuoming," in *Han Xiangzi quanzhuan* (Beijing: Baowen Tang Shudian, 1990), 1–3. Yin may be echoing the dictum of the famous historian of Chinese literature Zheng Zhenduo 鄭振鐸 that the plot of this novel is very "fantastic and absurd." Zheng definitely preferred Yang Erzeng's more serious historical epic *Dong-Xi Jin yanyi*. See his *Chatuben Zhongguo wenxueshi* (Hong Kong: Shangwu Yinshuguan, 1961), 918–19.

61   See his foreword in *Han Xiangzi quanzhuan* (Shanghai: Shanghai Guji Chubanshe, 1990). See also Yu's entry "Han Xiangzi quanzhuan" in *Zhongguo tongsu xiaoshuo jianshang cidian* (Nanjing: Nanjing Daxue Chubanshe, 1993), 182–85. This assessment is repeated almost verbatim (but without attribution) in Qi Yukun's *Mingdai xiaoshuoshi* (Hangzhou: Zhejiang Guji Chubanshe, 1997), 204–5.

62   Fang Sheng, "Ping Daojiao xiaoshuo *Han Xiangzi quanzhuan*," 204–5.

63   There are signs that the upsurge in interest among scholars in the People's Republic of China in their nation's religious traditions is also bringing *Han Xiangzi* to scholarly attention. In his recent study of religious themes in traditional novels, Wu Guangzheng devotes a whole section to *Han Xiangzi* as a paradigmatic example of a novel arranged around the theme of the banished immortal. See his *Zhongguo gudai xiaoshuo de yuanxing yu muti* (Beijing: Shehui Kexue Wenxian Chubanshe, 2002), 113–22.

64   Among the Chinese-speaking public, the novel has remained popular ever since its first publication in 1623. Modern trade editions in the People's Republic include: (1) Shenyang: Chunfeng Wenyi Chubanshe, 1987; (2) Zhengzhou: Zhongzhou Guji Chubanshe, 1989; (3) Shanghai: Shanghai Guji Chubanshe, 1990; (4) Beijing: Baowen Tang Shudian, 1990; (5) Chengdu: Bashu Shushe, 1999; (6) Beijing: Zhongguo Zhigong Chubanshe, 2001. In Taiwan, we find the following editions: (1) Taipei: Fenghuang Chubanshe, 1974 ; (2) Taipei: Wenhua Tushu, 1983, 1992. An expensive, traditionally bound edition was produced by Tianyi Chubanshe (Taipei) in 1985. An interesting development is the appearance of a simplified retelling of the novel in modern Chinese. See Zhiheng Shanren 制衡山人, *Shuang-Han wuyu* 雙韓物語 (Taipei: Miaolun Chubanshe, 1994).

65   Mostly the Zhongzhou Guji Chubanshe and Shanghai Guji Chubanshe editions (1989 and 1990 respectively). As there is little variance between the Ming editions of *Han Xiangzi quanzhuan* and between those modern editions based on them, text-critical efforts could be kept to a minimum. Unfortunately, the same cannot be said of Qing and Republican period editions or modern editions based on them. These are often severely corrupted and should be avoided by the scholar.

66   See for example the reprint in the *Guben xiaoshuo jicheng* series (Shanghai: Shanghai Guji Chubanshe, 1990 ff.), vol. 200, pts. 1–2.

67 See "*Dong-Xi liang Ji yanyi* xu," in *Dong-Xi Jin yanyi* (Taipei: Guoli Zhongyang Tushuguan, 1971), 6. Alternatively, see "*Dong-Xi liang Jin yanyi* xu," in *Ming-Qing zhanghui xiaoshuo yanjiu ziliao*, by Zhang Juling (n.p.: Zhongyang Minzu Xueyuan Keyanchu, 1980), 9.

PREFACE

1 A paraphrase from the "Great Appendix" of *The Book of Changes. The I-ching or Book of Changes*, trans. Richard Wilhelm and Cary F. Baynes (Princeton: Princeton University Press, 1967), 326; *The Text of Yi king*, trans. Z. D. Sung (Taipei: Wenhua Tushu, 1983), 307.

2 Two well-known ancient myths reported respectively in the "Tianwen xun" (天文訓) and "Lanming xun" (覽冥訓) chapters of *Huainanzi* 淮南子. See Anne Birrell, *Chinese Mythology: An Introduction* (Baltimore: Johns Hopkins University Press, 1993), 69–72, 97–98. Charles Le Blanc and Rémi Mathieu, trans., *Philosophes taoïstes II: Huainanzi* (Paris: Gallimard, 2003), 102, 278.

3 A paraphrase of a line in a poem by Sun Chuo 孫綽 (314–71). See *Wenxuan* 11:10a (Beijing: Zhonghua Shuju, 1977), 166. Cf. David R. Knechtges's translation in *Wenxuan or Selections of Refined Literature*, vol. 2 (Princeton: Princeton University Press, 1987), 253. Also see Erwin von Zach's translation in *Die chinesische Anthologie* (Cambridge, MA: Harvard University Press, 1958), 162.

4 The "six dragons" refers to the six *yang* lines of the *qian* 乾 hexagram in *The Book of Changes*. The sages are said to understand the meaning of these lines and be able to drive their carriage across the sky drawn by these "six dragons." See Sung, *The Text of Yi king*, 3. Figuratively this can be understood to say that a correct grasp of the *qian* hexagram, representing pure *yang* (i.e., the pure beginning mentioned in the text), opens one's mind to a holistic understanding of the universe. In a Daoist understanding, this complete clarity is a quality of the immortals, who of course also travel the Heavens in their free and easy wandering. In Daoist inner practice, the six dragons also refer to the pneumata of the human digestive system (see *Daojiao da cidian* [Beijing: Huaxia Chubanshe, 1995], 308), but the use of the term in the present context is surely on the more general level of *The Book of Changes*.

5 Hill of Cinnabar (*Danqiu* 丹邱) and Mysterious Garden (*Xuanpu* 玄圃) are names for the lands of the immortals used in ancient texts such as *Huainanzi* and *Songs of the South*.

6 A paraphrase of a verse from "Canto on Pacing the Void" (Buxu ci 步虛詞) by Emperor Yang of the Sui dynasty 隋煬帝. The Round Ocean 圓海 and the Fangzhu 方諸-Palace are features of the realms of the immortals. See *Yuefu shiji* 樂府詩集, *juan* 78 (Taipei: Taiwan Shangwu Yinshuguan, 1968), 888.

7 The last two sentences are a paraphrase of Bao Zhao's 鮑照 (c. 414–66) poem "To the Tune of 'Ascension to Heaven'" ("Shengtian xing" 升天行). See *Wenxuan* 28:23b (Beijing: Zhonghua Shuju, 1977), 405. Cf. von Zach's translation in *Die chinesische Anthologie*, 506. Elixir scriptures and the Charts of the Five Marchmounts are sacred texts containing the secret recipes of immortality. These are believed to be stored in the lands of the immortals.

8 The sash was a sign of official rank. Taking it off indicates the rejection of worldly

honors. "Flying duck shoes" (*feifuxi* 飛鳧舄) were said to have been worn by the immortal Wang Ziqiao 王子喬. See Max Kaltenmark, *Le Lie-sien tchouan* (Beijing: Université de Paris, Centre d'études sinologiques de Pékin, 1953), 112.

9 See *Han Changli wenji jiaozhu* (Shanghai: Shanghai Guji Chubanshe, 1998), 336–40. *Xinyi Changli xiansheng wenji* (Taipei: Sanmin Shuju, 1999), 529–36. The Twelfth Gentleman is Han Yu's nephew, Han Laocheng 韓老成, the father of the historical Han Xiang.

10 See *Han Changli shi xinian jishi*, ed. Qian Zhonglian (Taipei: Xuehai Chubanshe, 1985), 1097–1100. The poem's title indicates that it is dedicated to Han Yu's "grand-nephew Xiang." It has been translated by Charles Hartman in his *Han Yü and the T'ang Search for Unity*, 86–87.

11 These four works are generally regarded as the most accomplished novels of the Ming dynasty. See Plaks, *The Four Masterworks of the Ming Novel: Ssu ta ch'i-shu*.

12 I.e., 28 June 1623.

PROLOGUE

1 "Yellow sprouts" and "white snow" are references to lead and mercury respectively. These are the key ingredients in the alchemical process and are associated in internal alchemy with yin and yang.

2 These two lines describe the vast changes affecting the world (fields turning to oceans) and the rapid passage of time, causing the death of even such long-lived trees as pines and cypresses. Emending *cangtian* 滄田 to *sangtian* 桑田.

3 These two lines evoke the setting of an immortal's hermitage and, again, the rapid passage of time. The black ox is a common mount of immortals. Its appearance together with the white dog may be an allusion to a Tang poem by Yu Gu 于鵠 on the dwelling of a recluse. See *Quan Tang shi, juan* 310 (Beijing: Zhonghua Shuju, 1999), 3500. The chess game is one played by immortals; the human onlooker at such a game falls into a dreamlike state, and finds at the end of the game that by human reckoning years have passed.

CHAPTER 1. AT MOUNT PHEASANT YOKE

1 The preceding is a lengthy literal quote (with some minor variations) from the topographical chapter (Dixingxun) of *Huainanzi*, a second century BCE text. With minor modifications, my translation follows that of John S. Major in his *Heaven and Earth in Early Han Thought* (Albany, NY: State University of New York Press, 1993), 145–50. Cf. Charles Le Blanc and Rémi Mathieu, trans., *Philosophes taoïstes II: Huainanzi,* 161–64.

2 The "earth dragon" is an alternative name for the earthworm, while the "cloud mother" is the mineral mica. Found in the ground, both are ingredients in alchemical concoctions and serve here to indicate the mountains' spiritual potential.

3 This description is a pastiche of classical crane lore. The preceding prose passage and the first four lines of the following poem draw primarily on the *Physiognomical Crane Scripture* (Xianghe jing 相鶴經), a brief third- to fourth-century text of which a ver-

sion survives in Li Shan's 李善 (630–89) commentary to Bao Zhao's 鮑照 (c. 414–66) famous "Dancing Cranes Rhapsody" (Wuhe fu 舞鶴賦) in *Selections of Refined Literature* (*Wenxuan* 文選). Bao's rhapsody itself is quoted in the line "a womb-born immortal bird," which makes it likely that Yang Erzeng was using a copy of *Selections*. See *Wenxuan*, 14:8a–20a (Beijing: Zhonghua Shuju, 1977), 207–8; Erwin von Zach's translation of Bao Zhao's rhapsody in *Die chinesische Anthologie*, 208–10.

4   It is said that cranes cry to warn each other when the dew of autumn begins to fall and they need to prepare for their migration south.

5   A reference to Duke Yi of Wei of the Spring and Autumn Period, who was so fond of cranes that he had them ride in chariots usually reserved for high officials. See the *Zuo Commentary to the Spring and Autumn Annals*, second year of Duke Min (659 BCE). Legge, *The Chinese Classics*, vol. 5 (Hong Kong: Hong Kong University Press, 1960), 126, 129.

6   The Tower of Jiangxia 江夏之樓 refers to the Yellow Crane Tower 黃鶴樓 at Snake Mountain 蛇山 in Jiangxia Prefecture (in the modern city of Wuhan 武漢, Hubei). Several stories circulate about immortals visiting this place, riding on cranes. The most famous is that of the innkeeper Xin 辛, who unbeknownst to himself had served wine to an immortal. The immortal reciprocated the favor by drawing a yellow crane on the wall of the inn. The crane often descended from the wall to dance for Xin's guests; as a result, his business boomed and he became very rich. One day the immortal returned and flew off into the skies on the crane. Xin then named his inn Yellow Crane Tower.

7   An allusion to a line in a poem by the Tang poet Luo Yin 羅隱 (833–909). See *Quan Tang shi, juan* 665 (Beijing: Zhonghua Shuju, 1999), 7671; *Luo Yin shiji jianzhu* (Changsha: Yuelu Shushe, 2001), 331–34. South of Shaoxing 紹興 in the present-day province of Zhejiang 浙江 are located the Guiji Mountains 會稽山, to the east of which flows Ye Brook 耶溪, also known as Ruoye Brook 若耶溪, and in spite of the name a sizable river. Two peaks of these mountains are called Target Mountain 射的山 and White Crane Mountain 白鶴山 respectively. It is said that the crane of White Crane Mountain fetches the arrows shot by immortals at Target Mountain. See *Hailu suishi* 海錄碎事, *juan* 13 (Beijing: Zhonghua Shuju, 2002), 688.

8   A reference to the collection *Record of Assorted Remnants* (Shiyi ji 拾遺記), attributed to Wang Jia 王嘉 (4th cent.). *Juan* 2 of this work reports that a barbarian nation sent two pairs of strange birds as tribute to the court of King Zhao of the Zhou dynasty (traditionally dated to the eleventh century BCE). However, in the received text of *Record of Assorted Remnants* the line alluded to in the present poem is not found, nor are the birds identified as cranes. The variant text apparently used by Yang Erzeng is an excerpt from *Record of Assorted Remnants* recorded in *juan* 916 of the tenth century encyclopedia *Taiping yulan* 太平御覽. See *Shiyi ji* (Beijing: Zhonghua Shuju, 1981), 55–56.

9   A reference to a passage in *Zhuangzi* speaking of the shortness of ducks' legs and the length of cranes' legs. See book 8 ("Pianmu") of *Zhuangzi*; *Xinyi Zhuangzi duben* (Taipei: Sanmin Shuju, 2002), 109. Trans. Burton Watson, *The Complete Works of Chuang Tzu* (New York: Columbia University Press, 1968), 99–100.

10 The immortal Wang Zijin 王子晉 (aka Wang Ziqiao 王子喬) ascended to heaven from Mount Koushi (in modern Henan) mounted on a crane. See the entry on this immortal in *Liexian zhuan* (trans. Max Kaltenmark, *Le Lie-sien tchouan*, 109–114). Text emendation: *hou* 猴 to be read as *kou* 緱.

11 Ding Lingwei 丁令威 of Liaodong 遼東 was an adept who became an immortal and

ascended to Heaven in the shape of a crane. See *Soushen houji* 搜神後記, *juan* 1 (Beijing: Zhonghua Shuju, 1988), 1. Cf. the entry on Ding Lingwei in *Yunji qiqian* 雲笈七籤, *juan* 110 (quoted from *Dongxian zhuan* 洞仙傳) (Beijing: Huaxia Chubanshe, 1996), 682.

12 In 383 the invading army of Fu Jian 苻堅 (337–85), the ruler of one of the barbarian northern kingdoms, was defeated by an army of the Jin dynasty at the Fei 肥 River, by the foot of Mount Eight Lords 八公山 (in modern Anhui). As Fu's army was routed, the soldiers were in such a state of terror that they mistook the grass and trees on Mount Eight Lords for Jin troops, and believed the cries of cranes to be the shouts of pursuing Jin units. See Herbert A. Giles, *A Chinese Biographical Dictionary* (London: Bernard Quaritch; Shanghai: Kelly & Walsh, 1898), 231; *Jin shu, juan* 113–14 (Beijing: Zhonghua Shuju, 1974), 2883–2939.

13 See *Book of Songs*, "Xiaoya," "He ming." Trans. James Legge, *The Chinese Classics*, vol. 4, 297.

14 The Heavenly Worthy of Primordial Beginning (Yuanshi Tianzun 元始天尊) is one of the Three Pure Ones (Sanqing 三清), the highest deities of the Daoist pantheon.

15 King Yama reigns over the underworld, the purgatory where the souls of the dead go to be judged.

16 In popular belief, the Old Man Under the Moon (Yuexia Laoren 月下老人) is responsible for bringing together those who are destined to become spouses. He is the patron deity of marriage.

17 *Ceremonies and Rites* (Yili 儀禮), chap. 11. Cf. John Steele, trans., *The I-li or Book of Etiquette and Ceremonial*, vol. 2 (London: Probsthain & Co., 1917), 20.

18 Literally Great Curtain-Raising General on the Left, title of an attendant to the Jade Emperor.

19 A key Daoist scripture (*Daozang* #331) used in visualization meditations and inner alchemy.

20 See *Liezi*, book 5 ("Tangwen"). Trans. A. C. Graham, *The Book of Lieh-tzu* (London: John Murray, 1960), 101.

21 This deity's full title is Marshal Zhao of the Dark Altar of Orthodox Unity (Zhengyi Xuantan Zhao Yuanshuai 正一玄壇趙元帥). He is one of the four celestial marshals guarding the Daoist ritual arena. Among the common people he is better known as a deity of wealth (*caishen* 財神) named Zhao Gongming 趙公明, and is often portrayed in auspicious woodblock prints astride a black tiger.

CHAPTER 2. SEEKING ESCAPE FROM SAMSARA

1 A pun on Master Lü's surname (呂) which is written in Chinese with two *kou* ("mouth" 口) characters, one on top of the other.

2 The "Daoist song" is the *daoqing* 道情, a popular performance genre of the late Imperial period that survives to the present day. The "fisher drum" (*yugu* 漁鼓) is long and fairly narrow bamboo tube, covered with leather at its ends and used to keep the song's rhythm. Its name is derived from the fact that it supposedly was first made and used by fishermen. This instrument is often accompanied by the "clapper" (*jianban* 簡板), two long bamboo strips bound together so that they strike against each other. On the *daoqing* and its musical instruments see Wu Yimin, *Zhongguo*

daoqing yishu gailun (Taiyuan: Shanxi Guji Chubanshe, 1997). Throughout this novel, the fisher drum, the clapper, and the singing of *daoqing* are trademarks of the itinerant Daoist.

3 Chunyang (Pure Yang) is another name of the immortal Lü Dongbin.

4 Bodao is the style of Deng You 鄧攸 (d. 326), a minister under the Eastern Jin dynasty, who abandoned his own son to save the son of his deceased brother. He explained that while he could have another child, his dead brother could not, and thus his brother's only descendant had to take precedence. However, Deng You never had another son of his own. See Giles, *A Chinese Biographical Dictionary*, 723–24.

5 The "eight characters" (*bazi* 八字) are a combination of cyclical signs that identify a person's year, month, day, and hour of birth. Establishing these eight characters is the first step in any astrological divination.

6 I.e., this new son will become the Han family's main descendant.

7 A play on words: the name means literally, "Whenever he opens the mouth, something efficacious comes out."

8 I.e., 11 March 780.

9 "Obtuse immortals" (*wanxian* 頑仙) is a tongue-in-cheek literary rather than a religious category. For example, a work on calligraphy from the Tang dynasty, the *Fashu yaolu* 法書要錄, notes that "a talented ghost usually excels an obtuse immortal." See *Peiwen yunfu* 佩文韻府 (Shanghai: Shanghai Guji Shudian, 1983), p. 698, sec. 2.

10 Emending Tang 唐 for Kang 康. Tang Ju 唐舉 and Xu Fu 許負 were famous physiognomists of the Warring States and Han periods respectively.

11 Reading *mou* 某 for *dai* 呆.

12 "Rootless water" (*wugenshui* 無根水) is a traditional Chinese medication.

13 Reading *wang* 王 for *huang* 黃. The reference here is not quite clear. If the emendation (which is also made in several modern editions of the novel) is correct, the "Pavilion of King Teng" refers to a banquet given by the King of Teng, a son of Emperor Gao of the Tang dynasty (r. 650–84). This feast was immortalized by Wang Bo 王勃 (649–76) in his famous prose piece "Preface to the Pavilion of King Teng" (Teng Wang ge xu 滕王閣序). See *Guwen guanzhi, juan* 7 (Tianjin: Tianjin Guji Shudian, 1981), 597–608; *Le kou-wen chinois,* trans. Georges Margouliès, (Paris: Librairie orientaliste, 1926), 148–55. As Wang Bo was considered a kind of *wunderkind*, this verse hints at precocious literary success, while the following verse speaks of failure. According to legend, a favorable wind brought Wang Bo in one night over a distance of 700 *li* so that he would make it in time for the feast.

14 This line refers to a famous story that exemplifies the vagaries of destiny. An impoverished scholar wanted to make a rubbing of a famous stele at Jianfu (Recommended Blessings) Monastery 荐福寺, planning to sell it so he could afford to sit for the civil service examinations. However, before he could put his plan into action, the stele was destroyed by lightning.

CHAPTER 3. HAN YU INSCRIBES HIS NAME

1 A reference to the way Emperor Gaozu 高祖 of the Tang came to marry his wife. Her father promised her to the man who could hit the eyes of two pheasants he had painted on a screen, an endeavor in which only Li Yuan 李淵, the future emperor, succeeded.

2 Zhang Jiazhen 張嘉貞 (8th cent.), a prime minister of the Tang dynasty, allowed Guo Yuanzhen 郭元振 to choose a bride from among his five daughters. As Guo found it impossible to decide, all five daughters hid behind a screen, holding red silk threads that were visible to Guo. By pulling on one of the threads, Guo obtained the attached bride—the third-born daughter.

3 Che Yin 車胤 (d. ca. 397 CE) was such a diligent (and poor) student that, unable to afford a lamp, he studied at night by the light of a bag of fireflies.

4 A quote from a famous poem by Wen Tianxiang 文天祥 (1236–83). See his "Guo Lingdingyang," in *Wenshan xiansheng quanji, juan* 14 (Taipei: Taiwan Shangwu Yin-shuguan, 1968), 487.

CHAPTER 4. ZHONG AND LÜ ON GOLD SPRINKLE BRIDGE

1 Part of a poem attributed to Lü Dongbin. See *Quan Tang shi, juan* 858 (Beijing: Zhonghua Shuju, 1999), 9756.

2 This dialogue is a paraphrase of an exchange between the gods of the Yellow River and of the North Sea in *Zhuangzi* (chap. 17, "Autumn Floods"). *Xinyi Zhuangzi duben*, 217; Watson, *The Complete Works of Chuang Tzu*, 183.

3 *Book of Documents*, "Da Yu mo." Cf. Legge's translation, *The Chinese Classics*, vol. 3, 61–62.

4 In the above exchange, Han Yu poses his questions in a dualistic mode (being/non-being, mindful/mindless), while his two interlocutors reply with phrases, culled mostly from the recorded dialogues of Chan masters, meant to propel Han's mind beyond its dualistic outlook. I would like to thank Dan Lusthans for his help with this dialogue.

5 *Zhuangzi* (chap. 19, "Dasheng"). Translation from Victor Mair, *Wandering on the Way* (Honolulu: University of Hawai'i Press, 1994), 177.

6 The locus classicus for this division of immortals into five ranks is the *Zhong-Lü chuandao ji* 鍾呂傳道集 (*Daozang* #263.14), a work on internal alchemy supposedly composed by Zhongli Quan and Lü Dongbin, and transmitted by Shi Jianwu 施肩吾 (fl. 815). See *Zhong-Lü chuandao quanji* 鍾呂傳道全集 (Taipei: Ziyou Chubanshe, 1974), 116. Yang Erzeng's direct source, however, appears to have been Weng Bao-guang's 翁葆光 (12th cent.) commentary to Zhang Boduan's 張伯端 (ca. 983–1082) *Wuzhen pian* 悟真篇. With minor deviations, the above description of the five grades of immortals is a literal quote from Weng's commentary. See *Wuzhen pian jizhu* 悟真篇集註, *shang juan*:3a–3b (Shanghai: Shanghai Guji Chubanshe, 1989), 63–64.

7 A quote from Zhang Boduan's *Wuzhen pian*. See Wang Mu, *Wuzhen pian qianjie*, (Beijing: Zhonghua Shuju, 1990), 3. For other translations see Paul Crowe, "An Annotated Translation and Study of Chapters on Awakening to the Real (ca. 1061) Attributed to Zhang Boduan (ca. 983–1081)" (M.A. thesis, University of British Columbia, 1997), 40; Robinet, *Introduction à l'alchimie intérieure taoïste: De l'unité et de la multiplicité* (Paris: Éditions du Cerf, 1995), 206; Thomas Cleary, *Understanding Reality: A Taoist Alchemical Classic* (Honolulu: University of Hawai'i Press, 1987), 28.

8 These four lines are paraphrases of *Wuzhen pian*, stanza 7 (*Wuzhen pian qianjie*, 13). For translations, see Crowe, "Annotated Translation," 44; Robinet, *Introduction à l'alchimie intérieure taoïste*, 211; Cleary, *Understanding Reality*, 39–40.

9   Another paraphrase of a stanza (no. 5) from *Wuzhen pian* (*Wuzhen pian qianjie*, 8). For translations, see Crowe, "Annotated Translation," 42–43; Robinet, *Introduction à l'alchimie intérieure taoïste*, 209; Cleary, *Understanding Reality*, 36.

10   *Analects* 11.24. See Legge, *The Chinese Classics*, vol. 1, 246.

11   See *Book of Songs*, "Xiaoya," "He ming" (Legge, *The Chinese Classics*, vol. 4, 297).

CHAPTER 5. MME. DOU CRITICIZES LUYING

1   A reference to a famous story about a dreamer living a lifetime in the ant kingdom Southern Bough (Nanke), before awakening back in his real life. The Ming dramatist Tang Xianzu 湯顯祖 (1550–1617) based one of his most famous plays (*Nanke ji* 南柯記) on this theme, originally from a novella of the Tang period. The novella has been translated by E. D. Edwards. See *Chinese Prose Literature of the T'ang Period*, A.D. *618–906*, vol. 2 (London: Arthur Probsthain, 1938), 206–12.

2   The locus classicus for the rhinoceros horn allusion is the *Wenshi zhenjing* 文始真經, where the curved shape of the horn is attributed to its impregnation with moonlight. See *Wenshi zhenjing, juan zhong* (Shanghai: Shanghai Shudian, 1985; reprint of Sibu Congkan edition), 11b-12a. In proverbial use, this expression is used to illustrate intense and long-lasting yearning like that of the rhinoceros that stared so long at the moon that its horn took on the moon's shape. The reference to the oyster playing in the sunshine is not completely clear, but may have to do with the joy felt by a woman when discovering her pregnancy. The pearl's growth within the oyster is a common metaphor for human pregnancy.

3   *Analects* 11.24. Cf. Roger T. Ames and Henry Rosemont, Jr., trans., *The Analects of Confucius: A Philosophical Translation* (New York: Ballantine Books, 1998), 148.

4   Ibid.

5   *Analects* 5.4. Cf. Ames and Rosemont, *The Analects of Confucius*, 96. Actually, in this passage Confucius criticizes people who use artful speech to dispute others—quite the opposite of what Xiangzi makes it out to be here.

6   These two terms have their source in a pun recorded in the fifth century work *A New Account of Tales of the World* (Shishuo xinyu 世説新語). See Richard B. Mather, *Shih-shuo hsin-yü: A New Account of Tales of the World*, 2d ed. (Ann Arbor: Center for Chinese Studies, The University of Michigan, 2002), 387.

7   The first two lines are taken from two poems by Han Yu. See von Zach, *Han Yü's poetische Werke*, 69, 261. The last two lines refer obliquely to the pleasures of female beauty. Qian Zhonglian, *Han Changli shi xinian jishi*, 385, 978.

8   A quote from *Kongcongzi* 孔從子, a third-century work. See Yoav Ariel, *K'ung-ts'ung-tzu: The K'ung Family Masters' Anthology* (Princeton: Princeton University Press, 1989), 136.

9   A poem attributed to Lü Dongbin, entitled "A Warning to the World" (Jingshi 警世). See *Quan Tang shi, juan 858* (Beijing: Zhonghua Shuju, 1999), 9702.462

10   See *Ch'ien tzu wen: The Thousand Character Classic*, ed. Francis W. Paar (New York: Frederick Ungar, 1963), 82–83.

CHAPTER 7. TIGER AND SNAKE BLOCK THE ROAD

1   Two paragons of respectability who would not be seduced by female charms. Liuxia Hui 柳下惠 lived in the seventh and sixth centuries BCE, Lu Zhonglian 魯仲連 in the third century BCE.

2   Refers to the story of a white dragon which, when swimming about in the form of a fish, loses an eye when shot at by the fisherman Yu Qie 豫且. The dragon accuses Yu Qie in front of the Celestial Emperor, demanding justice. But the emperor points out that fish are bound to be hunted by men, so if the dragon went about disguised as a fish, he alone was responsible for the risk he took.

3   A reference to a famous story in *Zhanguoce* 戰國策. See J. I. Crump, *Chan-kuo Ts'e* (Ann Arbor: Center for Chinese Studies, The University of Michigan, 1996), 177.

4   As a boy, Sunshu Ao 孫叔敖 (6th cent. BCE) came upon a double-headed snake lying on the road. Because he had heard that anyone seeing a double-headed snake must die, he expected his own death. Since he was concerned others might suffer his fate as well, he killed the snake and buried it.

5   One of the exploits of Liu Bang 劉邦 (247–195 BCE), the founder of the great Han dynasty.

6   The "pilgrim in search of the sutras" refers to the monkey Sun Wukong, the hero of the novel *Journey to the West*. The description of him as "iron-shod and bronze-headed" is a bit puzzling, as is the fact that Sun is here equated with a demon. However, in *Journey to the West* iron and bronze are used several times to describe Sun's strength, for example when he is said to have a "head of copper and a brain of iron" (chap. 19). In chapter 32, Sun transforms himself into a vicious woodpecker with "red bronze-hard bill and black iron claws" and attacks his companion Zhu Bajie. Trans. Anthony Yu, *The Journey to the West*, vol. 2, 108.

CHAPTER 8. A BODHISATTVA MANIFESTS A NUMINOUS SIGN

1   An allusion to a Chinese proverb: *Zhongnan jiejing* 終南捷徑, "the shortcut through the Zhongnan Mountains." In its original context it referred to ambitious men going into reclusion in the mountains merely to attract the attention of the powers that be. Based on a bon mot of the Tang dynasty Daoist Sima Chengzhen 司馬承禎 (647–735). See Liu Su 劉肅 (fl. 806–820), *Da Tang xin yu* 大唐新語 *juan* 10 (Beijing: Zhonghua Shuju, 1997), 157–158.

2   A disciple of Confucius who was ugly, yet very capable.

3   Part of this mythographical passage stems from *Shenyi jing* 神異經, a work of the Six Dynasties period falsely attributed to Dongfang Shuo 東方朔. My translation follows the emendations proposed by Zhou Ciji in his *Shenyi jing yanjiu* (Taipei: Wenjin Chubanshe, 1986), 66–68.

4   A quote from Chen Zhixu's 陳致虛 (fl. 1326–86) commentary to *Wuzhen pian*. See *Wuzhen pian jizhu, shang juan*:4a–4b (Shanghai: Shanghai Guji Chubanshe, 1989) 65–66.

5   A reference to *Wuzhen pian*, stanza 6. See Wang Mu, *Wuzhen pian qianjie*, 11. Trans. Crowe, "An Annotated Translation," 44; Robinet, *Introduction à l'alchimie intérieure taoïste*, 210; Cleary, *Understanding Reality*, 38. The frog in the well motif ultimately

goes back to a parable in chapter 17 ("Autumn Floods") of *Zhuangzi*. See Mair, *Wandering on the Way*, 161.

6 Quotations from stanzas 4 and 5 of *Wuzhen pian*. See Wang Mu, *Wuzhen pian qianjie*, 5, 8. Trans. Crowe, "An Annotated Translation," 42, 43; Robinet, *Introduction à l'alchimie intérieure taoïste*, 207, 209; Cleary, *Understanding Reality*, 32, 36.

7 Master Lü's explication of the two passages from *Wuzhen pian* is based mostly on Weng Baoguang's commentary. See *Wuzhen pian jizhu, shang juan*:7b, 9a–9b (Shanghai: Shanghai Guji Chubanshe, 1989), 72, 75–76.

8 Another quote from Weng Baoguang's *Wuzhen pian* commentary: *Wuzhen pian jizhu, shang juan*:10b (Shanghai: Shanghai Guji Chubanshe, 1989), 78. Cf. also the first verse of *Wuzhen pian*'s sixth stanza (Wang Mu, *Wuzhen pian qianjie*, 11). Trans. Crowe, "An Annotated Translation," 44; Robinet, *Introduction à l'alchimie intérieure taoïste*, 210; Cleary, *Understanding Reality*, 38.

9 A reference to the famous story of Lü Dongbin's affair with White Peony (Bai Mudan 白牡丹). For a description and discussion of this topos, see Paul Katz, *Images of the Immortal* (Honolulu: University of Hawai'i Press, 1999), 189–90.

10 *Daode jing*, chap. 6. Trans. D. C. Lau, *Tao Te Ching* (Harmondsworth: Penguin, 1963), 62.

11 This outline of sexual technique is a paraphrase of *Exposition of Cultivating the True Essence by the Great Immortal of the Purple Gold Splendor* (Zijin Guangyao Daxian xiuzhen yanyi 紫金光耀大仙修真演義), a key text in the Chinese sexual yoga genre. See Robert Hans van Gulik, *Erotic Colour Prints of the Ming Dynasty* (Tokyo: privately published, 1951). Trans. Douglas Wile, *Art of the Bedchamber: The Chinese Sexual Yoga Classics, Including Women's Solo Meditation Texts* (Albany, NY: State University of New York Press, 1992), 136–46.

12 Many of the trials suffered by Han Xiangzi are described in close imitation of those imposed on Du Zichun 杜子春 in the eponymous Tang dynasty novella. The difference is that Du Zichun failed the test, while Xiangzi successfully completes the elixir. See "Du Zichun," in *Taiping guangji*, vol. 1 (Changsha: Yuelu Shushe, 1996), 78–80. Translated in E. D. Edwards, *Chinese Prose Literature of the T'ang Period, A.D. 618–906*, vol. 2 (London: Arthur Probsthain, 1938), 54–62.

13 Stanza 3 of *Wuzhen pian*. See Wang Mu, *Wuzhen pian qianjie*, 3. Trans. Crowe, "An Annotated Translation," 40–41; Robinet, *Introduction à l'alchimie intérieure taoïste*, 206; Cleary, *Understanding Reality*, 28. Reading *xiang* 翔 for *xiang* 祥.

CHAPTER 9. XIANGZI'S NAME

IS RECORDED AT THE PURPLE OFFICE

1 The Steps of Yu (Yubu 禹步) is a sequence of steps that is part of many Daoist rituals and is believed to produce great magical efficacy.

2 Excerpts from Han Yu's famous essay on the Dao ("Yuan Dao"). My translation follows that given in Wm. Theodore de Bary, ed., *Sources of Chinese Tradition*, vol. 2 (New York: Columbia University Press, 1960), 376–79.

3 *Ru* 入 emended to *ba* 八.

4 See *Mencius* 6.2.3. Trans. Legge, *The Chinese Classics*, vol. 2, 437.

5 An allusion to *Analects* 14.46. Cf. Legge, *The Chinese Classics*, vol. 1, 293.

6 Ziyu was a disciple of Confucius, who was of pleasant demeanor, but did not live up to his promise. This citation is lifted from the writings of the Legalist philosopher Han Feizi (*juan* 50, "Xianxue"). Cf. the English translation by W. K. Liao in *The Complete Works of Han Fei Tzu*, vol. 2 (London: Arthur Probsthain, 1959), 303.

CHAPTER 10. A TURTLE AND AN EGRET

BRING CALAMITY UPON THEMSELVES

1 A quote from the *Analects* of Confucius (10.18). Cf. Ames and Rosemont, *The Analects of Confucius*, 141; Legge, *The Chinese Classics*, vol. 1, 236.

2 A play on a famous passage in *Zhuangzi*, chap. 17 ("Autumn Floods"). Trans. Watson, *The Complete Works of Chuang Tzu*, 187–188.

3 The preceding four lines of verse allude to the process in inner alchemy of engendering an immortal embryo within oneself. The egret and the turtle are thus boasting of their alchemical accomplishments.

4 A reference to Yang Xiong's 揚雄 (53 BCE–18 CE) essay "Admonition against Wine" (Jiuzhen 酒箴). Only a part of "Admonition against Wine," or "Wine Rhapsody" (Jiufu 酒賦), has survived. See *Yang Xiong ji jiaozhu* 揚雄集校注, ed. Zhang Zhenze (Shanghai: Shanghai Guji Chubanshe, 1993), 153–56.

5 Jiying is the style of Zhang Han 張翰 (3rd cent. CE), a poet who resigned his official position because he was homesick for the dishes of his home in Songjiang (Jiangsu). See Giles, *A Chinese Biographical Dictionary*, 22.

6 The Immortal Ge is Ge Xuan 葛玄. See his hagiography in the *Shenxian zhuan*, trans. Robert F. Campany, *To Live as Long as Heaven and Earth* (Berkeley: University of California Press, 2002), 152–59. The identity of the "graduate Zhang" is not clear.

7 The two lines refer to sexual affairs and their dire consequences. The first alludes to the birth of the famous concubine Baosi 褒姒, who contributed to the downfall of a king. She was conceived when her mother came into contact with dragon saliva. The allusion in the second line is obscure, but would again seem to refer to a defeat because of infatuation with a woman ("brocade petals").

8 Lüzhu 綠珠, the concubine of Shi Chong 石崇 (249–300), killed herself by jumping off a tower to escape the unwanted attentions of a powerful suitor. Shi Chong himself was executed, in part because of his refusal to surrender Lüzhu. In the next line, the Pavilion of Linchun refers to the private abode of Chen Shubao 陳叔寶 (553–604), the last emperor of the Chen dynasty, who was known for his infatuation with his harem.

9 Emending *yi* 异 for *fang* 方.

10 These lines refer to the attempted assassination of the first emperor of Qin by Zhang Liang 張良 (d. 185 BCE) and the suicide of Xiang Yu 項羽 (232–92 BCE).

CHAPTER 11. IN DISGUISE, XIANGZI TRANSMITS A MESSAGE

1   A quote from the "Pearl-gathering Song" (Caizhuge 採珠歌) in Zhang Boduan's *Wuzhen pian*. See Wang Mu, *Wuzhen pian qianjie*, 189–90. Cf. translations by Crowe, "An Annotated Translation," 120; Cleary, *Understanding Reality*, 171–72.

2   Xu You is a famous recluse of the mythical age of Emperor Yao. He avoided any distractions in his secluded life. Someone gave him a gourd to use as a ladle, so he wouldn't have to drink brook water from his cupped hands. But when he noticed that he liked the pleasant sound made by the wind whistling through the gourd, Xu threw it away so as to rid himself of this disturbance of his senses. See Giles, *A Chinese Biographical Dictionary*, 312.

3   An allusion to the ancient philosopher Yang Zhu, who was said to have advocated "not giving up a single hair to benefit the world." See chapter 7 ("Yang Zhu") of *Liezi*. Trans. A. C. Graham, *The Book of Lieh-tzu*, 148–49.

4   A pun: the characters *zhuo* and *wei* put together give the character *han*, Han Xiangzi's real surname.

5   Part of a poem attributed to Lü Dongbin. See *Quan Tang shi, juan* 858 (Beijing: Zhonghua Shuju, 1999), 9757.

6   *Wuzhen pian, zhong*, 20. See Wang Mu, *Wuzhen pian qianjie*, 60. Cf. translations by Crowe, "Annotated Translation," 61; Robinet, *Introduction à l'alchimie intérieure taoïste*, 226; Cleary, *Understanding Reality*, 79.

CHAPTER 12. WHEN TUIZHI PRAYS FOR SNOW

1   *Wuzhen pian, shang*, 11. Wang Mu, *Wuzhen pian qianjie*, 19–20. Cf. translations by Crowe, "Annotated Translation," 48–49; Robinet, *Introduction à l'alchimie intérieure taoïste*, 214–15; Cleary, *Understanding Reality*, 47.

2   The last two lines are a quotation from a poem by Su Shi 蘇軾 (1037–1101). *Su Dongpo quanji, qianji, juan* 6 (Taipei: Shijie Shuju, 1964), vol. 1, 106.

CHAPTER 13. RIDING AN AUSPICIOUS CLOUD

1   *Wuzhen pian, shang*, 13. Wang Mu, *Wuzhen pian qianjie*, 22. Cf. translations by Crowe, "Annotated Translation," 50; Robinet, *Introduction à l'alchimie intérieure taoïste*, 216; Cleary, *Understanding Reality*, 50.

2   By sitting on the (wooden) gate with two stalks of grass on his head, Zhang Qian represents the Chinese character *cha* 茶 (tea), which consists of the components "grass," "man," and "wood." I have been unable to solve the other riddles.

3   A paraphrase of a passage from *The Book of Changes*. See Sung, *The Text of Yi king*, 337; Wilhelm and Baynes, *The I-ching or Book of Changes*, 355.

CHAPTER 14. RUSHING IN AT A BIRTHDAY BANQUET

1   *Wuzhen pian, shang*, 14. Wang Mu, *Wuzhen pian qianjie*, 24. Cf. translations by Crowe, "Annotated Translation," 51; Robinet, *Introduction à l'alchimie intérieure taoïste*, 217; Cleary, *Understanding Reality*, 52.
2   "Cloud-water" (*yunshui* 雲水) is a traditional term for an itinerant monk.
3   *Mengzi, Gaozi shang*, 10. Trans. Legge, *The Chinese Classics*, vol.2, 412–413.
4   Cf. *Wuzhen pian zhong*, 60. Wang Mu, *Wuzhen pian qianjie*, 125. Cf. translations by Crowe, "Annotated Translation," 85; Robinet, *Introduction à l'alchimie intérieure taoïste*, 242; Cleary, *Understanding Reality*, 118.
5   This poem, ascribed to Han Xiang, is recorded in *Quan Tang shi, juan* 860 (Beijing: Zhonghua Shuju, 1999), 9785.
6   *Analects* 9.11. Cf. Legge, *The Chinese Classics*, vol. 1, 220.
7   *Analects* 15.11. Cf. Legge, *The Chinese Classics*, vol. 1, 298.
8   Mount Shouyang was famous for its hermits.
9   The following song (and the whole goat episode) is predicated on a pun: the vital *yang* 陽 energy (of the yin/yang dualism) has the same pronunciation as the Chinese word for goat (*yang* 羊). Thus, when talking of goats, Han Xiangzi is really expounding how to harness and nourish one's yang forces.

CHAPTER 15. MANIFESTING HIS DIVINE POWERS

1   An anonymous lyric. See *Quan Song ci*, ed. Tang Guizhang (Beijing: Zhonghua Shuju, 1965), 3742–43. Yi and Zhou are two famous loyal ministers of Chinese antiquity. Yuanming is another name of the poet Tao Qian 陶潛 (365–427), a paradigmatic recluse. The juxtaposition extols the contemplative over the active life. The reference to Tao Qian's return home is an allusion to his rhapsody "The Return" (Guiqulai 歸去來). See *Wenxuan* 45: 19a–20b (Beijing: Zhonghua Shuju, 1977), 636–37. Trans. James Hightower, *The Poetry of T'ao Ch'ien* (Oxford: Clarendon Press, 1970), 268–70.
2   淳于　, a famous profligate of the fourth century BCE.

CHAPTER 16. XIANGZI ENTERS THE UNDERWORLD

1   This summary consists largely of (subtly altered) excerpts from Han Yu's biography in *Xin Tang shu, juan* 176 (Beijing: Zhonghua Shuju, 1975), 5255–69. *Han Changli wenji jiaozhu*, 739–56.
2   *Analects* 16.6. Cf. Legge, *The Chinese Classics*, vol. 1, 312.
3   Zhang Sengyou 張僧繇 (6th cent.) was famed for painting extremely lifelike pictures. Legend has it that on one occasion he painted two dragons on a temple wall, but deliberately left them without eyes lest they come alive. And indeed, when someone added the eyes, the wall collapsed and the dragons soared into the sky.
4   His infatuation with a concubine led to his ruin. Shi Chong 石崇 (3rd cent.) is also frequently mentioned as a proverbially rich man.

CHAPTER 17. XIANGZI MANIFESTS TRANSFORMATIONS

1 Wu Zixu 伍子胥 (Wu Yun 伍員, d. 484 BCE), a minister of the State of Wu during the Spring and Autumn Period. See Giles, *A Chinese Biographical Dictionary*, 892–93.

CHAPTER 18. EMPEROR XIANZONG OF THE TANG

1 Elder Gold Cicada is the earlier incarnation of Tripitaka, the fictionalized monk Xuanzang in *Journey to West* (Xiyou ji). See chapter 12 of that novel. *The Journey to the West*, trans. Anthony Yu, vol. 1 (Chicago: University of Chicago Press, 1977), 256–81.

2 *Han Changli wenji jiaozhu*, 612–17. *Xinyi Changli xiansheng wenji*, 970–76. The translation follows that of J. K. Rideout in *Anthology of Chinese Literature*, ed. Cyril Birch (New York: Grove Press, 1965), 250–53. The last paragraph does not appear in the original version of Han Yu's memorial. It is an excerpt from Sima Guang's 司馬光 (1019–1086) monumental history of China, the *Zizhi tongjian* 資治通鑑. See *Zizhi tongjian* (Beijing: Zhonghua Shuju, 1982), *juan* 240, 7759.

CHAPTER 19. BANISHED TO CHAOYANG

1 As Han Yu looks back at the gates of Chang'an, he is resentful of the corruption (the crooked wood of the bow) that did injury to him (the bowstring).

2 Han Yu's troubles are compared here to those of the Duke of Zhou, who was accused of being disloyal to the Zhou king. In fact, when the king was gravely ill, the duke had secretly offered his own life to the ancestors in exchange for the king's health. This offer was recorded and locked away in a metal-bound coffer. The king recovered at first, but then died not long after. After the king's death the duke acted as regent and was slandered by enemies who implied that he was grabbing power for himself. Eventually he was vindicated, when the new king after his ascension to the throne opened the coffer and made public this evidence of the duke's devotion to the dynasty. See *The Book of Documents*, trans. Legge, *The Chinese Classics*, vol. 3, 351ff.

3 The last two lines are from a poem by the Tang poet Wang Wei (701–61). See G. W. Robinson, *Poems of Wang Wei* (Harmondsworth: Penguin, 1973), 104; Tony Barnstone, Willis Barnstone, and Xu Haixin, *Laughing Lost in the Mountains* (Hanover, NH: University Press of New England, 1991), 65.

4 A poem by Wen Tingyun 溫庭筠 (ca. 812–70). See *Wen Feiqing shiji* 溫飛卿詩集, *juan* 8 (Taipei: Taiwan Xuesheng Shuju, 1967), 248.

5 The surname Han 韓 is pronounced the same as *han* 寒, "cold." The boatman understood (or pretended to understand) Master Han (Han *laoye* 韓老爺) as Master Cold (*han laoye* 寒老爺). A close equivalent of the latter might be Old Man Winter.

6 See Paar, *Ch'ien tzu wen*, 42.

7 This is the beginning of a series of double entendres. The character *du* 渡 can mean both "to ferry across" and "to deliver, to save, to bring salvation." The two meanings are closely related in the Buddhist context, where the salvational activity of bodhisattvas is often described metaphorically and depicted iconographically as a ferry carrying

souls to the other shore of the Pure Land. This section of the novel employs the same metaphorical tool.

8 Another double entendre: the word for "repair" (*xiu* 修) is the same as that for "cultivate, cultivation."

9 Erlang 二郎 is a deity well-known for his battles with river-dwelling dragons.

CHAPTER 20. AT THE VILLAGE OF BEAUTIFUL WOMEN

1 A quote from the *Yizhou shu* 逸周書. Trans. J.I. Crump, *Chan-kuo Ts'e* (Ann Arbor: Center for Chinese Studies, The University of Michigan, 1996), 88.

2 A play on words: Sizhen 似真 means "seems true." The surname Jia 賈 is a homonym of *jia* 假 (false), which is written with a different character. The innkeeper's name can thus be read as "false, but seeming true."

3 *Dou shi jia* 都是賈 can be read as "all share the surname Jia," or as "all are false," i.e., illusions.

4 "Pulling out branches in the cold" (*han tui zhi* 寒退枝) is a pun on Han Yu's name (Han Tuizhi 韓退之). The first three phrases allude to the preparatory stages of Daoist cultivation.

5 This dialogue is based on wordplay using the homonyms *yuren* 漁人 (fisherman) and *yuren* 愚人 (fool).

6 In fact, this phrase is not as modest as it sounds. It connotes freedom from restraint and limitations and was often used by famous poets to refer to themselves.

7 A quote from a poem by the Tang dynasty Chan master Chuanzi Decheng 船子德誠. See Shi Puji 釋普濟 (1179–1253), *Wudeng huiyuan* 五燈會元 *juan* 5 (Taipei: Guangwen Shuju, 1971), 436.

8 "Cold fish" (*hanyu* 寒魚) is a pun on the name Han Yu 韓愈.

9 The foregoing four lines are from Yang Fu's 羊孚 (ca. 358 or 373–403) "Ode to Snow" 雪讚. Translation by Richard Mather, *Shih-shuo hsin-yü: A New Account of Tales of the World* (Ann Arbor, MI: Center for Chinese Studies, The University of Michigan, 2002), 151–52.

10 An allusion to a poem by Lu Chang 陸暢 (Tang dynasty). See *Quan Tang shi, juan* 478 (Beijing: Zhonghua Shuju, 1999), 5477.

11 The foregoing lines elaborate on two lines from a poem by Zheng Gu 鄭谷 (fl. 886). See *Quan Tang shi, juan* 675 (Beijing: Zhonghua Shuju, 1999), 7792.

CHAPTER 21. INQUIRING INTO HIS FORTUNE

1 Trans. Z. D. Sung, *The Text of Yi king*, 1.

2 Following the Wilhelm and Baynes translation (*The I-ching or Book of Changes*, 294).

3 Bian Zhuang 卞莊 and Feng Fu 馮婦 are two famous men of valor from the Spring and Autumn Period. Of Feng Fu it is specifically reported that he wrestled with tigers.

CHAPTER 22. SITTING IN A THATCHED HUT

1 Chen Keming, *Han Yu nianpu ji shiwen xinian*, 526; Qian Zhonglian, *Han Changli shi xinian jishi*, 1097. Translated by Charles Hartman in his *Han Yü and the T'ang Search for Unity* (Princeton: Princeton University Press, 1986), 86–87.

2 A quote from Han Yu's "Discourse on Teachers" (Shishuo 師説). See *Han Changli wenji jiaozhu*, 42–44; *Xinyi Changli xiansheng wenji*, 75–79. Translated in *Sources of Chinese Tradition*, ed. Wm. Theodore de Bary et al. (New York: Columbia University Press, 1960), 374–75.

3 *Han Changli wenji jiaozhu*, 573–75; *Xinyi Changli xiansheng wenji*, 555–58. Translation by J. K. Rideout, in *Anthology of Chinese Literature*, ed. Cyril Birch (New York: Grove Press, 1965), 253–55. I have made minor modifications to Rideout's translation.

4 An allusion to *Mencius*, 5A:7. See Legge, *The Chinese Classics*, vol. 2, 363–64.

CHAPTER 23. ARDUOUS CULTIVATION

LEADS TO AN AWAKENING

1 *The Great Learning*, 3.2. Cf. Legge, *The Chinese Classics*, vol. 1, 362.

2 A play on elements of Han Xiangzi's name. The two characters of Zhuowei (卓韋) put together become the surname Han 韓. The combination of the two characters used to write Mumu (沐目) results in the character *xiang* 湘. Hence these names are a hidden reference to Han Xiang(zi) himself.

CHAPTER 24. RETURNING HOME

1 Wordplay: the Chinese term for "fisher drum" (*yugu* 漁鼓) is a homonym of *yugu* 愚鼓 (stupid drum, drum of stupidity).

2 Sanskrit: "wisdom."

3 The legend of the Immortal of the Rotten Axe-handle (Lanke Xianzi 爛柯仙子) tells of a certain Wang Zhi 王質 (4th cent.), who went to cut wood in the mountains. There he came across two immortals playing chess. Captivated by the game, he did not notice the passing of time. When he finally came out of his trance, many years had passed and the handle of his ax had rotted away. A sort of Rip van Winkle story.

4 The foregoing two sentences are quoted from a poem by the Song dynasty "Daoist of the Clear Brook," Qingxi Daoshi 清溪道士. See *Daojiao da cidian* 887.

CHAPTER 25. MASTER LÜ SENDS A DREAM

1 An allusion to a famous episode of the fourth century. A wife was about to murder her husband's new concubine, when she was so struck by her beauty that she said, "Dear child, even *I* feel affection for you as I look at you; how much more must that old ras-

cal!" She lowered her knife and befriended the concubine. See *Shih-shuo hsin-yü: A New Account of Tales of the World*, second ed., trans. Richard B. Mather (Ann Arbor: Center for Chinese Studies, University of Michigan, 2002), 377–78.

CHAPTER 26. MINISTER CUI PRETENDS
TO ACT IN THE PUBLIC INTEREST

1　This refers to an ancient belief that the sphex (a kind of wasp) catches earworms and carries them to its nest where they change into young sphexes. In fact, the worms serve as food for the wasp larvae.
2　A reference to the story of Dou E 竇娥, who is unjustly accused of a crime. Snow falling in summer is a sign from Heaven proclaiming her innocence, and condemning her accuser and her corrupt judge. Subject of a famous play by Guan Hanqing 關漢卿 (c. 1240–c. 1320) entitled "The Injustice to Dou E" (Dou E yuan 竇娥冤).
3　The whole poem is an assemblage of famous cases of injustices wrought by slander.
4　An allusion to the *Analects* of Confucius (9.5). See Legge, *The Chinese Classics*, vol. 1, 218.
5　Following the emendation proposed in the Shanghai Guji edition (p. 275).

CHAPTER 27. AT THE ZHUOWEI HERMITAGE

1　From *The Book of Odes*. See Legge, *The Chinese Classics*, vol. 4, 445. The fish and the kite are examples of naturalness, i.e., natural grace.

CHAPTER 28. ON CHEATING MOUNTAIN

1　These are all references to examples of misfortunes following one after another. The last line refers to a famous story of an impoverished scholar who wanted to make a rubbing of a famous stele at Jianfu Monastery, planning to sell it so he could afford to sit for the civil service examinations. However, before he could put his plan into action, the stele was destroyed by lightning. This story is also alluded to in chapter 2. See above page 37.
2　See "Jingming zongjiao lu," in *Daozang jiyao* 道藏輯要, vol. 5 (Chengdu: Bashu Shushe, 1995), 225. The text is also included in the collection *Zangwai daoshu* 藏外道書, vol. 7 (Chengdu: Bashu Shushe, 1992–1994), 826.
3　The Hemp Maiden (Magu 麻姑) is a famous immortal.
4　The Bird Nest Chan Master (Niaoke Chanshi 鳥窠禪師) was an eccentric but highly respected Buddhist monk named Daolin 道林 (741–824), who made his home in a pine tree.

CHAPTER 29. A BEAR-MAN CARRIES HAN QING

1   *Wuzhen pian, shang*, 6. Wang Mu, *Wuzhen pian qianjie*, 10–11. Trans. Crowe, "Annotated Translation," 43–44. Cf. Robinet, *Introduction à l'alchimie intérieure taoïste*, 210; Cleary, *Understanding Reality*, 38.

2   A quote from the morality book *Taishang ganying pian* 太上感應篇. Cf. translation by James Legge, "The Thaî-shang Tractate of Actions and Their Recompense," in *The Texts of Taoism* vol. 2 (reprint, New York: Dover Publications, 1962), 235.

3   *Wuzhen pian, shang*, 5. Wang Mu, *Wuzhen pian qianjie*, 8. Trans. Crowe, "Annotated Translation," 43; Robinet, *Introduction à l'alchimie intérieure taoïste*, 209; Cleary, *Understanding Reality*, 36.

4   A paraphrase of *Wuzhen pian, shang*, 7. Wang Mu, *Wuzhen pian qianjie*, 13. Trans. Crowe, "Annotated Translation," 45; Robinet, *Introduction à l'alchimie intérieure taoïste*, 211; Cleary, *Understanding Reality*, 40. Reading *tufu* 土釜 for *erfu* 二釜.

5   Trans. Lu-ch'iang Wu and Tenney L. Davis, "An Ancient Chinese Treatise on Alchemy Entitled Ts'an T'ung Ch'i," *Isis* 18(1932):251.

6   *Wuzhen pian, zhong*, 25. Wang Mu, *Wuzhen pian qianjie*, 13. Trans. Crowe, "Annotated Translation," 65–66; Robinet, *Introduction à l'alchimie intérieure taoïste*, 228; Cleary, *Understanding Reality*, 82.

7   The last two sentences are a quotation from Xue Shi's commentary to *Wuzhen pian*. See *Ziyang Zhenren Wuzhen pian san zhu* (*Daozang* #142). *Zhengtong Daozang*, vol. 4 (Taipei: Yiwen Yinshuguan, 1977), 2839.

8   A paraphrase of *Wuzhen pian, shang*, 4. Wang Mu, *Wuzhen pian qianjie*, 13. Trans. Crowe, "Annotated Translation," 41–42; Robinet, *Introduction à l'alchimie intérieure taoïste*, 228; Cleary, *Understanding Reality*, 82.

CHAPTER 30. THE MUSK DEER IS FREED

FROM HIS WATER PRISON

1   *Wuzhen pian, zhong*, 13. Wang Mu, *Wuzhen pian qianjie*, 49. Trans. Crowe, "Annotated Translation," 58; Robinet, *Introduction à l'alchimie intérieure taoïste*, 223; Cleary, *Understanding Reality*, 71.

2   *Wuzhen pian, shang*, 4. Wang Mu, *Wuzhen pian qianjie*, 5. Trans. Crowe, "Annotated Translation," 42. Cf. Robinet, *Introduction à l'alchimie intérieure taoïste*, 207. The novel's text has *yu* 于 instead of *fei* 非. This translation follows Crowe's rather than Robinet's interpretation of this passage.

3   *Wuzhen pian, shang*, 7. Wang Mu, *Wuzhen pian qianjie*, 13. Trans. Crowe, "Annotated Translation," 44. Cf. Robinet, *Introduction à l'alchimie intérieure taoïste*, 211; Cleary, *Understanding Reality*, 39–40.

4   *Daodejing* 4. Cf. Lau, *Lao Tzu: Tao te ching*, 60.

5   These are rearranged excerpts from a long poem by the Tang poet Bai Juyi 白居易 (772–846). The complete poem can be found in *Quan Tang shi, juan* 437, 4871. The translation follows (with some modifications) that of Howard S. Levy in his *Translations from Po Chü-i's Collected Works* (New York: Paragon Reprint Corp., 1971), 97.

www.ingramcontent.com/pod-product-compliance
Lightning Source LLC
Chambersburg PA
CBHW032006110726
47901CB00004B/987